ALSO BY KRISTEN BRITAIN:

Green Rider

KRISTEN BRITAIN

FIRST RIDER'S CALL

EARTHLIGHT

SIMON & SCHUSTER

London • New York • Sydney • Tokyo • Singapore • Toronto • Dublin

A VIACOM COMPANY

First published in United States by DAW Books, 2003
First published in Great Britain by Earthlight, 2003
An imprint of Simon & Schuster UK Ltd
A Viacom Company

1 3 5 7 9 10 8 6 4 2

Simon & Schuster UK Ltd
Africa House
64–78 Kingsway
London WC2B 6AH

www.simonsays.co.uk

Simon & Schuster Australia
Sydney

A CIP catalogue record for this book is available from the British Library

ISBN 0-7434-6113-4

Printed and bound in Great Britain by
Bath Press Ltd, Bath.

ACKNOWLEDGMENTS

Whew. What a long journey this has been. Many thanks to you readers out there for making my first book, *Green Rider,* such a success, and for your enduring patience, encouragement, and support since its publication. I hope you find this tome worthy.

I would not have survived the long haul without the support of my friends, notably Jill Shultz, John Marco, and Cheryl Dyer. I can't express my appreciation enough to you guys, the way you helped me through some terrifically difficult times. You have no idea, and I am indebted.

Thank you to: Betty Lyle for the use of her firepit, Julie E. Czerneda (AWA) for averting wardrobe panic attacks and advising me on writing and publishing stuff, Ruth Stuart, Jana Panacia, Jihane Billacois, and all the other sff.net newsgroupers for making me laugh pink, Tess Gerritsen who kindly listened and advised, Brooke Childrey for being Brooke, and belatedly Richard Grant and Joyce Varney, whose early encouragement years ago at the MWPA Tanglewood retreat made all this seem possible.

For the contributions of their expertise in various fields (from geology to the eating of . . . *things),* that helped me create a sense of verisimilitude when necessary, I would like to thank Peggy Doak (and her herd), Cheryl Dyer, Tim Bowie, and Kate Petrie.

Thank you to Saabrina Mosher for arranging a special meeting with Pat Smith, a reader whom I never got a chance to know, but felt privileged to meet. I'd like to remember her here. She loved the color green.

In the publishing department, Betsy Wollheim stuck with me during the creation of this book despite the seemingly endless and sometimes bumpy road this journey took. Thank you, Betsy, for your give-and-take and your eye for story (and your New York City tour guide expertise!). DAW Books is a rare and special publishing house in an era of large corporate multinational media giants, which possesses an author-friendly atmosphere that does not treat creative works as widgets. So I'd like to recognize the rest of the crew behind the DAW logo, too, who truly make the organization special: Debra Euler, Sheila Gilbert, Sean Fodera, Amy Fodera, and Peter Stampfel.

In addition, thank you to Anna Ghosh for thinking of the future, and for not holding against me that really hard-shelled lobster I tortured her with a few years ago, and to Danny Baror, international rights agent extraordinaire.

Keith Parkinson creates some of the most spectacular cover art I've ever seen, and I'm honored to have his art grace this book. Not just honored, but thrilled! It's beautiful, Keith!

During the creation of both *Green Rider* and its sequel, I worked a day career as a national park ranger. The National Park Service is a special organization of dedicated people working to preserve America's natural and cultural heritage, and I had the privilege of working with many fine and talented people. Like becoming a Green Rider, for many in the Park Service, the work is a calling. The uniform, the nature of the work, the shared experiences, the legends, and the traditions, conspire to create an *espirit de corps* that is relatively unknown in other organizations. Rangers certainly aren't in it for the money. (And the uniforms aren't all that comfortable.) I would like to thank all my colleagues for carrying on the work and for being a part of my Park Service experience, and especially Deb Wade for her patience and understanding while I was slaving away on the writing by night, and coming into work the next day a bit tired and off-kilter. Deb, you understood the importance of my dream, and you supported my efforts. For that, I cannot thank you enough.

For their career counseling and listening, and just for being there, I'd like to thank Laurie Hobbs-Olson, Meg Scheid, Wanda (Wand) Moran, and Pat Murrell.

No acknowledgment section would be complete without mentioning my furries, Batwing and Percy. When all else seemed to fall to pieces in my life, they helped me keep steady on a very curvy road. Gryphon? Maybe next book you'll get an acknowledgment of your very own. But in the meantime you'd better stop chewing on the manuscript.

Finally, rest in peace, T.O.S. You live on in the pages of this book.

In honor of my grandparents:
Leona Springer and Alan Britain, Sr.
Emma Momberger and George C. Momberger

FIRST
RIDER'S
CALL

Journal of Hadriax el Fex

We sail into the night. The winds finally favor us with a strength to move us more swiftly than oars. In this way we may conserve precious etherea, and allow the artisans time to effect repairs on the mechanicals.

At first it was disturbing not to hear the throb and thrum of the mechanicals, which have been so constant since our departure, but now I feel utterly at peace here in my cabin, with only the creak of timbers and the gentle sway of the ocean as backdrop. The darkness has settled in, and it is just me, my journal, and a prism to illuminate my writing.

The continent we seek is still far off, so says Captain Verano. Alessandros is extremely anxious, climbing to the crow's nest daily as though to espy the New Lands by sheer will. This is his expedition, after all, his quest to find the resources that will heal Arcosia, and to establish the Empire's authority in the New Lands.

A son, Alessandros is, to the Emperor, and the chosen one of God to succeed him. And so it is known to me that Alessandros organized this expedition for a reason beyond those already stated: with his success, he wishes to prove himself worthy to God and the people of Arcosia, and especially to the man he loves as a father.

This voyage has been good for him. His cheeks are ruddy and the sunshine sparkles in his eyes. He has become a youth again and I can feel his excitement. For both of us, this is a grand adventure. His excitement is so infectious, in fact, that tonight, my young squire, Renald, overhearing our talk, nearly spilled wine on us as he served us. Alessandros laughed in good nature. Renald is a fine boy mostly, like a little brother sometimes, and I am very fond of him. This journey will be the making of him.

As the countless days pass, I occupy myself by poring over the captain's sketchy charts of the continent. Accounts tell of a barbaric race who inhabit these lands, and of a wealth of resources. Such accounts cannot always be trusted, as they so often are exaggerated. Still, we are eager to see what these lands of mystery may reveal, and none more so than Alessandros del Mornhavon.

✥ THE RIDER CALL ✥

The apparition's soft, otherworldly glow fell across the sleeping form on the canopy bed.

Sultry night air tinged with sea brine flowed through the wide-open window, stirring the sheet that covered the girl. Her long brown hair was splayed across her pillow, and her chest rose and fell in slow, even breaths. She slept unaware of her ghostly visitor, an expression of utter tranquility on her face.

And that was the problem.

Displeasure flickered across the apparition's smoky features. *You can hear me, but you won't listen, hey?*

The apparition nudged at the girl's shoulder as if to awaken her, but her hand simply slid through it.

Cannot feel me. Cannot see me. WILL NOT listen.

The girl had become very disciplined at ignoring the call, and if there was one thing that annoyed Lil Ambriodhe most, it was being ignored.

Lil had, in her own opinion, exercised a great deal of patience, actually biding her time during the year the girl took to finish her schooling, thinking it couldn't hurt, and that afterward she would finally heed the call and return to Sacor City to take her oath before the king as a Green Rider.

She did not. She defied the call and went home to Corsa instead, and for what? To count bolts of wool on one of her father's wretched wagon trains? To balance ledgers? What was alluring about *that?* Why did she resist?

Lil paced until she realized her feet no longer touched the floor, but hovered above it. *By all the hells!* She tried to focus on the floor so she might at least achieve the illusion of standing on it, but the effort bled too much energy from her. She cursed in frustration at the limitations of her current form, and glowered at the sleeping girl who made all this necessary. If she could manage it, she would've hauled her right out of bed. Thankfully most Riders weren't this difficult.

And even while she thought this, she observed that the floor beneath her feet was covered by a rare Durnesian carpet, and that the carved beams overhead brought to mind the mastery of shipwrights. The furnishings were deeply burnished and inlaid with ivory wrought with intricate ornamentation. They had a foreign look, as though brought from across the sea. Even the mattress the girl slept on was stuffed with eiderdown, and the sheets were of a delicate weave.

As the daughter of a wealthy merchant, the girl lived at a level of luxury incomprehensible to most Sacoridians, and Lil could understand how trading this privileged and comfortable life for that of the rugged, dangerous duty of a Green Rider might prove difficult.

In another sense, she could not. The Riders did important work. There were enough merchants in the world and far too few Green Riders.

She was needed, this girl. This girl who over a year ago defeated a rogue Eletian and played an essential role in saving the king's throne. And there was more ahead for her.

A positive sign that all was not lost was the gold winged horse brooch resting on the table next to the bed. It was the most substantial thing about this realm in Lil's vision, more solid and brilliant than anything else. It seemed the girl could not part with it; the bond still held. Had it abandoned her, there would be no possibility of her becoming a Rider.

And our link would have been lost.

Lil touched her own brooch, which was clasped to the green-and-blue plaid she wore draped across her shoulder, and drew comfort and strength from it. It had helped her come this far between the layers of the world. Its resonance sang through her and the girl's brooch seemed to sparkle in response.

A Rider's true heart the brooch shall seek . . . Lil cocked a smile as she remembered the old tune. *Great heart, stout heart, strong and bold, the iron hearts of Riders glitter as gold . . .* How could she forget? Every self-proclaimed bard and halfwit of the lands had taken up the tune wherever she rode, whether she sat in a great clan lord's banquet hall or in a dilapidated tavern with goats chewing on the rushes strewn across the floor. She couldn't escape it! It was better, she supposed, than having stones thrown at her, though some of the singers had been painfully bad.

She glanced out the window at the moon and cast off the memories like an old cloak. There was work to do here and time was growing short. She leaned over the sleeping girl, and using every ounce of command she could summon, she said into her ear, *Karigan Galadheon, you must go to Sacor City. Hey? You are not a merchant—you are a Green Rider.*

Lil watched on in satisfaction as the girl murmured and shifted. Her satisfaction turned to dismay, however, when the girl wrapped her pillow around her head.

Ach. Lil shook her mane of unruly hair in disgust, and wondered if the girl's lineage had anything to do with her contrary nature.

She had but one last recourse to fall back on, and if this failed, she had no idea of how to rouse the girl. Lil drew to her lips a twisted horn she kept slung at her side. It had been a gift from a p'ehdrose named Maultin for a favor rendered. It was fashioned from the tusk of a komara beast, a woolly herd animal that roamed the arctic wastes. Maultin had imbued the horn with a special spell of use only to the captain of the Green Riders.

Lil inhaled and blew into the horn. The notes of the Rider call rang out sure and strong. She sensed it pulsing through the layers of the world, ringing with need and urgency. Would it reach far enough? Would the girl hear it? Most importantly, would it reach her heart?

Lil lowered the horn, listening still as its crisp notes faded away. And she watched. At first there was nothing and Lil's hopes plummeted, but then the pillow was flung aside and the girl—young woman, really—sprang upright into a sitting position, eyes wide open and bright. She hurled herself out of bed and in a flurry of sheets and nightgown sprawled across the floor in a tangled heap.

Unaware of all else save the call, she disentangled herself and scrambled to her feet. She swiped her brooch from the bedside table and threw open her wardrobe, withdrawing a saber sheathed in a battered black scabbard, and ran from the room as if all the demons of the five hells pursued her.

Lil listened in satisfaction as bare feet raced along the corridor then thunked down a series of stairs.

She convulsed with laughter, her feet rising a few inches more above the floor. She wondered just how far the girl would get before she realized she was riding to Sacor City in her nightgown.

⇴ DEEP IN THE
NORTHERN GREEN
CLOAK FOREST ⇴

*O*ne year later . . .
     Condor side-stepped nervously be-
neath Karigan.

"Easy," she murmured. She steadied him with the reins and caressed his neck to settle him. Condor's disquiet echoed her own, but as she peered intently through the sunshafts and shade of the forest, she detected nothing unusual. Birds fluttered from limb to limb twittering at one another, and a red squirrel sat on a nearby tree stump scaling a spruce cone.

All was as it should be—quite ordinary really, but for some reason she could not shake off her sense of disquiet.

Karigan glanced over at Ty who sat atop Flicker several paces away. His own expression was wary. Did he feel it, too, whatever *it* was? He gave no indication, but hand-signaled that they should proceed toward a clearing awash with sunlight a short distance ahead.

At first Condor balked and back-stepped at Karigan's command, but with an extra jab of her heels he walked on, swishing his tail defiantly.

Karigan tried to convince herself that while Green Rider horses might display an uncanny intelligence at times, they were still prey animals driven by instinct, prone to spooking at the silliest things like the odd glint of light. Sometimes they spooked at nothing at all.

7

She half-smiled and whispered, "You're just an over-sized meal for some hungry catamount, aren't you?"

Condor swished his tail again and stomped.

Karigan chuckled, but it was half-hearted at best. For all her rationalization, she had learned to trust Condor's instincts.

As they neared the clearing, her sense of unease heightened. She wanted to rein Condor away, but she held firm, for it was her duty to scout ahead and seek out the safest path for Lady-Governor Penburn's delegation. Duty often required Green Riders and their mounts to ride directly into situations they would much rather flee, or at least avoid—as in this situation—but she had no choice other than to forge ahead.

The hoof falls of the horses were oddly silent on the needle-packed ground. Abreast of her Ty and Flicker wove in and around the gray trunks of spruce trees, fading in and out of shadows, ghostlike.

Maybe, Karigan thought, her apprehension stemmed from the strange reputation of the far northern borderlands through which they now rode. Few inhabited the region, though long ago this had not been true. During their journey, the delegation had come across the ruins of old settlements, stone foundations, and well shafts nearly swallowed by field and forest. They had followed the remnants of an ancient roadbed for a time, passing stone waymarkers buried beneath mounds of moss. Ty had cleaned off one marker, finding it deeply inscribed with runes and pictographs no one could decipher.

Those who did live in the remote far north told tales rife with superstition and ghosts, of banshees that broke into homes on wild winter nights and stole children. They spoke of black wolves large enough to drag off a full-grown man, and of witches that danced on graves. At one time, they claimed, a great, terrible clan chief ruled the north, and his unrest spawned other evil things.

It did not help the reputation of the north that it bordered Eletia, a country cloaked in mystery. Until two short years ago, the reclusive folk of the Elt Wood had fallen into legend as mere fairy tale characters. No one had known if they truly existed anymore, or if they had died out.

Now it was the mission of the delegation to penetrate the cloak of mystery, to enter Eletia itself and contact whatever power held sway over that land, for its people had been spotted in Sacoridia in increasing numbers. King Zachary desired to know Eletia's intentions. Lady-Governor Penburn, who represented the king, had reason to hope for the best, and reason to fear for the worst.

A raven squawked from a branch above, jolting Karigan in her saddle. Condor bobbed his head as if to laugh at her and say, "Look who's nervous now."

Karigan licked her lips and focused on the clearing ahead. What might await them there? Groundmites? Eletians? Which would be worse? She thought she knew. Through the trees she glimpsed a shape in the clearing's center that did not look natural.

Ty signaled a halt. "Carefully," he mouthed.

Karigan nodded and wrapped her fingers about the hilt of her saber. A soft breeze made the tall spruce trees sway and creak.

Ty motioned forward and they rode into the clearing.

Sunlight dazzled Karigan's eyes and she blinked furiously, then an itchy sensation crawled across her skin.

"Wha—?" she began, and then just as quickly it passed.

"Did you feel *that?*" Ty said.

Karigan nodded. "It felt like a warding."

She took stock of the clearing. Dominating its center was a great rock cairn from which no tree, grass, or moss grew, though the edges of the rocks appeared blunted by weathering as though over a great span of time.

Along the clearing's perimeter stood obelisks like stern fingers admonishing them to turn back. There were no groundmites or Eletians lying in wait for them, but the loathing Karigan felt increased tenfold.

Ty edged Flicker over to one of the obelisks. "These must be ward stones." He pressed his hand against the pale stone but quickly snatched it away. Then, more tentatively, he placed his palm against it.

"Come tell me what you think of this."

Karigan reined Condor over to the obelisk, amazed that "Rider Perfect," as the others liked to call Ty, requested her opinion.

The obelisk was carved with runes and pictographs like those they had seen earlier on the waymarkers. Some were so worn or encrusted by green and blue lichens that they were difficult to make out. Karigan trailed her fingers across the cool stone and immediately felt a tingling swarm up her arm. A faint hum sputtered in her mind. She withdrew her hand.

"The ward is dying," she said.

Ty nodded in approval, still the mentor, though Karigan's days as a messenger-in-training were well past.

"Doesn't feel like it's going to hold up much longer," she added.

"I agree."

Just like anything else in the world, it seemed even magical spells had only a certain lifespan before they wore out. It made Karigan think that the wards set around Rider waystations were much newer than these, though it had been a hundred years or more since a Rider had possessed the ability to work with spells of warding. If this were the case, then the obelisks must indeed be ancient.

They explored the clearing further, stopping to examine

each obelisk, each of which looked much like the ones before. There were fourteen in total. Karigan gave the cairn a
wide berth while they looked about. The loathing never left
her, but she sensed no immediate peril.

"Do you suppose it's a burial cairn?" she asked Ty.

He gazed hard at it. "I can't think of what else it might
be. Long ago, important people used to be buried with all
their household goods beneath such cairns." He rode around
it, apparently unaffected, or at least unperturbed, by any
sense of dread that might arise from it. "Those had ornamental seals over the entrances. This has no entrance, and
it's like all the rocks were just dumped on top of it for good
measure."

"Not exactly a sign of respect," Karigan said. What it *was*
a sign of, she couldn't imagine. Maybe to discourage grave
robbers? Why else ward a burial cairn? And why wasn't
Westrion, god of the dead, pictured on any of the ward
stones? Even to this day, the Birdman's visage was a common funerary emblem.

No, not Westrion, but . . . She passed her fingers across
one of the faded inscriptions. A horse? Could it be Salvistar,
Westrion's messenger? Salvistar was the harbinger of strife
and battle. It was said that wherever he appeared, battle,
destruction, and death were certain to follow. She shook
her head. It was impossible to know, for the figure could
have meant anything to those who erected the obelisks. The
pictograph of the horse might simply represent, well, a
plain old horse.

Ty rejoined her, Flicker's hooves clopping on the granite
ledge. He glanced up at the high sun. "I'm afraid it's a mystery we'll never unravel. We should head back."

They left the cairn behind, much to Karigan's relief. The
magic itched across her skin again as she passed between
the ward stones, and a new thought occurred to her.

"Ty," she said, "how do we know the wards were set to keep things out?"

"What do you mean? What else could they be for?"

"What if the wards were meant to keep something *in?*"

Ty had no answer for her.

The soldiers who served as outriders for the delegation had come up with the motto: "There is no road to Eletia." And it was true. The North Road, which was the northernmost road that cut through the dense Green Cloak Forest, reached only so far, and after a certain point even the trails of foresters and trappers petered out.

The delegation had had to leave behind its carts and carriages in the village of North, loading all essential supplies onto a string of pack mules. Nobles, servants, soldiers, and Green Riders alike rode horseback, a pleasure for some, and a hardship for others unused to long days in the saddle.

The outriders had ended up being assigned the task of clearing the way for the delegation, though often enough the delegation moved freely through the woods thanks to the expertise of the bounder who guided them. At other times, however, deadfalls and underbrush had to be hacked out of the way.

Over the weeks of the journey, the soldiers had modified their motto to: "There is no road to Eletia, but there will be by the time we're through."

Upon their return, Karigan and Ty first encountered soldiers who stood guard over those who toiled over a massive tangle of deadfall. Ty called out so he and Karigan would not be mistaken for intruders.

The foremost guard "Hallooed" them in return. His black and silver tunic was askew over his mail, indicating he had already taken a turn with an ax.

"Anything new since this morning?" Ty asked.

"Sign of groundmites in the area," the soldier said.

"Lady Penburn has stopped the works to decide what to do, but I've heard nothing more than that."

With this news Karigan tensed. Upon reaching the relative safety of the delegation, she had just begun to relax a little. Scout duty was extremely nerve-racking: always having to be on high alert, especially with the constant threat of groundmites hanging over them, and the uncertainty of the Eletians' reception should they by chance have an encounter. She and Ty had spoken little since the clearing, trying to ride as quietly and inconspicuously as possible through the dense woods, maintaining that high level of watchfulness at all times.

They continued on, passing weary soldiers taking a break, and guided the horses through the narrow clearing in the snarl of deadfall the soldiers had hacked out.

Others stood guard here and there some distance into the forest. One knelt amid a patch of bracken fern, and another leaned against a boulder. They all watched outward, their crossbows held at ready.

Karigan and Ty passed the drovers who stood with the mules and horses. Servants gossiped in small groups, and a scattering of more soldiers waited close at hand for their next order. Standard bearers in bright livery bided their time, their standards furled and packed away to prevent them from becoming constantly entangled in low-hanging boughs.

A fine delegation we make, Karigan thought. Even the nobles had put away their finery in favor of rougher but more practical riding breeches and tunics. *The Eletians will wonder what kind of ragtag rabble we are.*

She straightened her own soiled shortcoat trying to remember the last time she had bathed in something other than an icy stream. Ty, she noted with a ripple of envy, looked as fresh and dapper as the day they had left Sacor City.

Rider Bard Martin detached himself from conversation with a drover and strode over to them. No one knew his real first name, but "Bard" suited him for he had a penchant for singing and the telling of tales, an ability the Riders found most welcome.

The gold embroidery of the winged horse emblem on his shortcoat was coming unraveled, Karigan saw, then noted a long rip in the sleeve itself.

"Are you all right?" she asked.

"What?" Bard stopped short looking up at her in surprise. Then he followed her gaze to his sleeve. "Oh. A soldier nearly took my arm off when he mistook me for a 'mite. Everyone's on edge and I should have announced myself better. I'm fine—I've good reflexes." He smiled in appreciation for her concern.

"I'll take Condor and Flicker off your hands," he said. "No doubt Lady Penburn will want your report immediately. Ereal has been right in the thick of it."

After Karigan and Ty dismounted, Rider-Lieutenant Ereal M'Farthon waved them over to a knot of people surrounding Lady Penburn. They were engaged in an intense discussion. Among them were select nobles: Captain Ansible, who oversaw the military aspect of the delegation; Master Banff, secretary to Lady Penburn; and the bounder Brogan, who, in his stained buckskin, was the most disreputable of the lot. Karigan crinkled her nose and moved to an upwind position.

"What have you to report?" Lady Penburn asked.

Ty stepped forward and bowed, and while he told them of their mostly uneventful scout duty, Lady Penburn listened avidly.

Karigan found she rather liked Lady Penburn. The lady was undoubtedly accustomed to every luxury accorded one of her station, but had taken the rugged nature of this expedition in stride. In fact, she threw herself into it with a girlish enthusiasm as if she were on holiday. Perhaps it was like a holiday to her, compared to her usual work of managing a province. Karigan thought she would've made a good Green Rider, at least in spirit.

Lady Penburn's enthusiasm was contagious enough that it kept the other members of the delegation moving forward without too much grumbling. She kept their minds on birdsong and wildflowers, or the latest court gossip, rather than oppressive heat or the occasional sudden downpour. Still, there was no mistaking who was in charge, for her leadership was straightforward, and her orders sometimes sharp.

When Ty described the clearing with its warding, Karigan saw some decision click in Lady Penburn's eyes.

"Thank you, Rider Newland," Lady Penburn said. "You are certain there was no sign of groundmites?"

"Yes, my lady."

She sighed. "Your lieutenant here saw a band of the creatures moving west of us, and Brogan found fresh sign of them to the east."

Karigan inhaled sharply. Thus far Lady Penburn's scouts had found the occasional old sign of 'mites, but nothing to suggest they were near enough to endanger the delegation. Lady Penburn's use of extreme caution, however, was well warranted, for long, long ago groundmites had been bred by Mornhavon the Black to be ferocious killers, and they had been harrying Sacoridia's borders very hard of late. Settlers were forced to flee the northern territory for more tame and populated lands, causing problems for provincial lords who suddenly had to contend with refugees.

"It's certainly not safe for us to set up camp here," Lady Penburn said. "Although I expected we'd eventually find ourselves in this situation, I wish we'd find signs of Eletians instead."

Karigan suspected that Eletians would leave signs of themselves only if they wished to.

"We daren't go west or east," Lady Penburn said. "And south would be backtracking. Therefore we shall continue due north, and try to reach Rider Newland's clearing by nightfall."

Dread washed over Karigan at the announcement. Brogan, who had seemed to be in his own world during much of Ty's report, shook himself to life.

"I wouldna do that, m'lady," he said.

"And why not?"

Brogan licked his lips and squinted at her from beneath heavy eyebrows. "Begging pardon, m'lady, but there are some places you just want to avoid in this territory. Places of evil."

"We've encountered numerous ruins and you've not had any complaints about those."

"This is different. I've heard of this place, and I know trustworthy bounders who'd swear on their mothers' graves it was ill-omened."

"What makes it so? Are demons going to rise out of the earth and murder us while we sleep? Or is this just another bit of northern superstition?"

"No, m'lady. Not superstition." Brogan groped for words. "It's just . . . it's just bad." He looked at his boots, knowing how ridiculous it sounded.

Lady Penburn turned on Ty and Karigan. "Did either of you feel there was anything wrong with this place?"

"No," Ty said.

When Karigan hesitated, Ty glanced at her, raising an eyebrow.

"Rider G'ladheon?" Lady Penburn's voice was tinged with impatience.

Heat rose up Karigan's neck and flooded her cheeks as everyone, from Captain Ansible to Lord Clayne, stared at her. So many eyes on her was a tangible, uncomfortable force that pressed on her from all sides.

And still she hesitated, fearing how very foolish she would sound if she told them of her feelings.

Lady Penburn's eyebrows narrowed. "We haven't all day, Rider."

Ereal placed her hand on Karigan's shoulder. "If you observed anything unusual in that clearing, we need to know about it."

Karigan licked her lips. The silence that engulfed the group grew more immense as seconds passed and they waited for her to speak. If Lady Penburn hadn't liked hearing of Brogan's "superstitions," then she certainly would find no merit in Karigan's feelings. Yet duty required her to answer, and it was not in her nature to lie. What if her instincts meant danger for the delegation and she had failed to warn them?

"It was a feeling I had," she said.

"A feeling?"

"Yes, my lady. A feeling of wrongness." There. She had said it.

"A feeling, but nothing more?"

What else could Karigan say? "That's correct, my lady."

"Is it—" Lady Penburn cleared her throat and shifted, looking immensely uncomfortable, "—something you detected with your special ability?"

Lady Penburn referred to Karigan's Rider magic, and while the lady had been briefed on the "special abilities" of each Rider attached to the delegation, Karigan knew that among the few who were aware of Rider magics, most failed to comprehend their limits. They only recalled the stories of the terrible mages who had wreaked havoc and destruction during the Long War; mages who possessed immeasurable powers. This was so ingrained in their minds that magic in any form was regarded with suspicion. They did not differentiate between the great destructive magics of the past, and the humble abilities Riders possessed.

"No, my lady," Karigan finally answered, "my ability does not run along those lines."

Lady Penburn looked pleased by the answer and she turned back to Ty. "And you *felt* nothing, Rider Newland?"

"Nothing unusual. The place was odd because of the tomb, but nothing more than that."

Lady Penburn nodded in satisfaction.

Karigan sighed. It was only natural, she supposed, that Lady Penburn should dismiss her words and support Ty's. Ty was a senior Rider, and Karigan was still perceived as the most inexperienced of the four who accompanied the delegation. She was even beginning to wonder if her feelings about the clearing had been just a bout of nerves.

Ereal squeezed her shoulder. "Well done," she whispered. "It was good of you to speak up."

"Brogan," Lady Penburn said, "I appreciate that you bounders have your hands full in this wilderness. It is true these lands have a long past. We've seen the relics of that history, and this clearing appears to have yielded yet another.

"However, I will not tolerate any member of this delegation falling prey to fear wrought by superstition." Her eyes seared those around her, and lingered on both Karigan and Brogan for what seemed like hours rather than seconds. "We have enough of what could be a truly dangerous situation to concern ourselves about. That clearing sounds defensible to me should we find ourselves attacked by groundmites, a rallying place where we could stand shoulder to shoulder in strong lines rather than being scattered throughout the forest. That is where we shall set up camp for the night."

"M'lady," Brogan said, "you brought me along as a guide, and I feel it my duty to warn you about such a place—"

"Enough! I have heard your warning and made my decision." Lady Penburn's expression brooked no argument.

"We've much to accomplish before nightfall. I will hear not another word of superstition or bad feelings. Captain Ansible, I want you to get this delegation moving. We've long hours ahead of us."

As the group dissolved, each to his or her own duty, Karigan grabbed Ty's arm. "Are you sure you didn't feel anything in that clearing?"

"I'm sure." He tugged his arm free of her grasp and straightened his sleeve. "Karigan, I honestly think you ought to heed Lady Penburn's words about superstition. People are worried enough by the threat of groundmites. Whatever lies beneath that cairn is dead and buried."

Karigan watched his back as he strode off, feeling somehow betrayed. Maybe he was right, and maybe she *was* suffering from nerves. But still . . .

Brogan sidled over to her, perhaps finding in her a kindred spirit. "I don't like this one bit." Worry lines furrowed across his weathered features. "If people were meant to be near that clearing, why place stones of warding around it?"

❧ A CAMPFIRE, A NIGHTGOWN, AND A SONG ❧

Karigan watched in dismay as Lady Penburn's tent went up beside the cairn, soon followed by those of the other nobles. The entire delegation could not fit within the clearing, so the rest set up nearby in the surrounding woods.

I am not superstitious, Karigan kept telling herself as she walked away. *I am not superstitious . . .* And she was not—far from it in fact, but the sensation of dread had come over her again when they arrived at the clearing, and she found it rather disturbing to be the only one bothered by it. *Not the only one,* she amended. Brogan the bounder stayed well away from the clearing, making the sign of the crescent moon before disappearing into the woods to find his own camping place.

She carried her gear as far from the clearing as she dared, while still remaining within the guarded perimeter. She chose a place considered undesirable by most near the horses and pack mules. It might be smelly, she thought, but it was far more comfortable than being next to the clearing.

She started a cheerful little fire for herself. Others sparked up around the encampment as dark settled in. One fortunate aspect of the whole undertaking was the availability of deadwood so that no one in the delegation was deprived of warmth and light during the night.

"Not a bad fire for a merchant."

Karigan looked up surprised and pleased to see Bard

with his bedroll slung over his shoulder, bearing two steaming bowls. "Mind if I join you? I bring food—if you can call it that."

"Yes, please," Karigan said, gratified by his show of support.

Bard passed her a bowl. She peered into it and sniffed dubiously. "Gruel. Again." And with a burnt wedge of pan bread sticking in it. She nibbled on the coarse bread, frowned in distaste, and set the bowl aside.

Bard dumped his bedroll on the ground and sat across the fire from her. "Lady Penburn's people talked about doing some hunting for fresh meat tomorrow morning, though as far as I can tell the nobles are eating well enough."

Karigan had been under the impression that on a well provisioned delegation the meals would prove far better fare than what she was accustomed to when on an ordinary message errand, but she'd been wrong. The Green Riders, the king's own special messengers, had been lumped together with common soldiers and servants, and were served accordingly.

The two Riders spoke quietly of inconsequential things while Bard ate his gruel. Karigan itched to ask him what he felt or did not feel about the clearing, but she gave him his peace while he ate. When he finished, he took out a sewing kit and attempted to thread a needle by firelight so he might fix the rip in his sleeve.

"You're going to burn off your eyebrows if you get any closer to the fire," Karigan warned him.

"Match the top of my head then, I expect." He patted the thinning spot at his crown and smiled.

"Bard," Karigan said, deciding to broach the subject that had been plaguing her, "what do *you* think of the clearing?"

It was some moments before he spoke, so focused was he on trying to find the eye of the needle with his thread, his tongue sticking out the corner of his mouth. Karigan waited in suspense, seeking some validation of her feelings.

"Can't say I much care for the idea of camping next to some old tomb, though I'm sure it would make for a good embellishment in our report."

Bard, Karigan knew, tried to make all his reports as entertaining as possible for Captain Mapstone. His philosophy was that since the captain rarely left the castle grounds these days, she ought to at least have the vicarious experience of being on a message errand. Karigan wondered if it had the intended effect, or made the captain miss the open road all the more.

Lines formed across Bard's forehead and he squinted at the needle. Suddenly he smiled in triumph. "I did it!" He showed her the threaded needle to prove it, then took up his shortcoat and jabbed the needle into the sleeve. "As for my sensing anything about the clearing as you seem to, I don't know. I don't like it, but I don't feel it as strongly as you do. That doesn't mean your feelings are wrong about this place.

"I'd guess," he continued, "that there are all manner of strange magical relics like the clearing throughout the lands, and maybe Lady Penburn was onto something when she brought up your ability. Maybe the wards resonated with your magic for some reason, the way the wards around Rider waystations dampen our magic."

"This is different," Karigan said.

Bard shrugged. "I'm not surprised. Likely the magic is different, but if it sets you at ease, look at it this way: that tomb has lain quietly for several hundreds of years at least. I doubt anything will change by the time the encampment has picked up and moved north by tomorrow morning."

Bard was right, Karigan thought. She was letting it all get to her far too much. It still did not explain, however, why *she* was more sensitive to it than the others.

"Ouch!" Bard sucked on his index finger. "I am far too clumsy to be using such a sharp object."

"That's what Arms Master Gresia keeps trying to tell you about your swordplay."

"Hah! A point for you, my dear, and no pun intended. Are you any good at this?" He thrust his sewing at her, and she saw his stitches were rather haphazard.

"Sorry," Karigan said. "My aunts tried to teach me to sew, but I'm afraid I was hopeless."

"What? You the daughter of a textile merchant and surrounded by all that cloth—and you can't sew?"

"I was much too busy getting under the cargo master's feet or playing down by the wharves in Corsa Harbor. My friends and I liked to look for crabs under rocks or sea stars on the pilings."

Bard snorted. "That's a good place for a child. Corsa Harbor is as rough as any waterfront I've ever seen."

"Oh, my father's people kept me out of trouble, but my unladylike behavior scandalized my aunts." Karigan sat tall and prim to take on the demeanor of one of her aunts. " 'Child, you are the heir of the premier merchant of Sacoridia, not some urchin to be running barefoot about the docks among sailors and other riffraff.' That's what my Aunt Brini would say."

"And what did Aunt Brini think of you becoming a Rider?"

"Not much." It was as though someone had lit a fire beneath a hornet's nest when all four aunts heard of her decision. "My aunts and father grew up dirt poor on Black Island, helping my grandfather haul fish. It was a rough life, so I've been reminded time and again. Now that they're living very well under my father's roof, they see me only as childish and ungrateful, spoiling their expectations that I should create a respectable marriage alliance with another powerful merchant clan."

She closed her eyes against the memory of the bitter arguments. For all her aunts' upset, facing her father had been the hardest.

"Your mother?" Bard asked.

"She died when I was very little."

He nodded. "Mine, too. In childbirth, actually. I think she would have been rather proud of me working in the king's service."

Karigan brushed back a strand of hair that had fallen into her face. She had so little recollection of her mother, Kariny, that she had no idea of what Kariny would think of her being a Green Rider. Karigan only knew that it was not at all what she had intended to do with her life, and for all her aunts' angst, their vision of her future had been more like her own from a very young age: to follow in her father's footsteps and carry on the name and work of Clan G'ladheon. She wasn't, however, too sure about the marriage alliance part of it.

"The calling to be a Rider can force upon you a path in life not of your own choosing," Bard mused, as if an echo of her thoughts. "After years of hard work as a cooper, I had finally hoarded away enough currency for a term's tuition for minstrel training at Selium . . . and then I heard the call." He chuckled and shook his head at the irony. "Even though the king has since promised me a place in Selium when my time with the Riders ends, it still has been a delay to achieving my dreams." He paused, falling into deep thought. Then quietly he added, "Despite it all, I do not regret this life."

Karigan had struggled against the call for a very long time so she might continue in the life she had chosen for herself, but the call had chipped away at her will, almost torturously, the hoofbeats always like a rhythm in the deep regions of her mind and heralding visions of the freedom of the ride. She would awaken some nights sweating and feeling as if she must saddle Condor immediately and heed the call to ride, as if her life depended upon it.

To fight the call, she had tried ridding herself of her brooch, knowing it somehow bound her to the messenger service, but whether she hid it deep in a drawer or tried burying it in the woods, she inevitably found herself wearing it by day's end without memory of having pinned it on. Magical objects, she had once been told, often had minds of their own.

As time wore on, her behavior grew more eccentric. The color green came to dominate her wardrobe by no intention of her own, and it led her father to the conclusion that she was inordinately fond of the color. The struggle also left her irritable. "What's eating at you?" her father had asked in exasperation after she lost patience with a servant one day. She never yelled at servants. Normally.

How could she explain to a man who, like so many other Sacoridians, held a deep aversion to magic, that magic was trying to rule her life?

Instead, she had said, "You never let me accompany the barges or wagon trains." She believed that getting out of Corsa and being on the road or a river beneath the open sky might ease the call gnawing at her soul. "It's always, 'Karigan, inventory storehouse five,' or 'Karigan, schedule next month's routes and deliveries.'" She had breathed hard with the unexpected fury that had built up in her chest. "You always leave the dullest chores for me."

Her father had looked at her in astonishment, as if some stranger stood before him. "I thought you wanted to learn more about the business. It isn't all traveling from town to town, or overseeing wares on fair days."

The portrait of Karigan's mother loomed large on the wall behind her father. She knew he would never forgive himself for Kariny's death, or for that of the unborn child she had been carrying at the time. It was he who had scheduled her to lead a wagon train to a fair that, unknown to him, was rife with fever.

No, no matter Stevic G'ladheon's innocence, he would never forgive himself.

"You're being overprotective," Karigan said. She had not shouted, but she might as well have.

Her father had followed her gaze to the portrait, then slowly turned his eyes back upon her. "You are my only child," he said, "and I love you."

Karigan swallowed hard, remembering the hurt and grief in his eyes, but as if thrusting a sword into his heart had not been enough, she had twisted the blade by telling him he didn't understand anything. Then she had stomped out of his office and slammed the door behind her for good measure. The memory of it still left an ache of guilt within her.

Did she regret the Rider life? Over the past year she had come to accept it to a degree, and she even liked it well enough in some ways, but she believed she would always resent how it had utterly wrenched her out of the life she knew. And she would never forgive the call for the gulf it had opened between her and her father.

"It's not a call," she murmured. "It's a command."

At her quiet words, a devilish smile played on Bard's lips.

"Oh, please," Karigan began, knowing exactly what he was thinking. "Please don't bring up—"

"Halfway to Sacor City in your nightgown!"

"I was not! I only got as far as Darden!"

"Two towns over. Gave the marketplace something to jabber about for weeks."

Karigan's face heated, and it wasn't because of the crackling fire before her. The night she had finally succumbed to the call, it had crashed over her like a storm wave that washed her away in a dreamlike undertow from which she was unable to awaken. She only snapped out of it the next morning when she reached Darden. In the middle of the market. In her nightgown. She groaned at the memory.

"I can only use my imagination." Bard shook with laughter. "My, but it makes an amusing picture—and tale."

"Don't you dare!" She wouldn't put it past Bard to make some outrageous ditty of it. His talent for fashioning absurd lyrics was going to drive the more conventional masters at Selium out of their minds.

"There once was a girl from Corsa," he began, "who rode a big red horsa—"

"Ugh!" Karigan scooped up handfuls of pine needles from the ground and tossed them at him. Most fell into the fire, giving off a sweet balsam scent as they burned.

The whole incident was funny now, she had to admit, but at the time it had been humiliating. The market had grown unnaturally quiet as everyone pointed and stared at her sitting on Condor, in nothing more than her light linen nightgown. Fortunately the matron of a prominent merchant clan had recognized her and supplied her with clothing for her return ride to Corsa.

The story of Stevic G'ladheon's daughter managed to spread outward as the merchants traveled on to other towns and villages. Karigan's aunts had been terrible to behold upon learning she had embarrassed her clan so extravagantly.

The incident had finally broken Karigan's resolve to fight the call, and upon her return to Corsa, she had informed her father of her intention to be a Green Rider. She just didn't have it in her to fight it anymore.

Bard couldn't contain his laughter. Karigan glowered at him which seemed to incapacitate him further.

At that moment, Ty and Ereal wandered over, burdened with their gear.

"What's so funny?" Ereal asked.

Bard wiped tears from his eyes. "Darden." It was all he had to say, for all the Riders had heard of Karigan's unusual and long overdue response to the call, and regarded it as a curiosity. Apparently everyone else had acceded to the call without a fight. Ereal chuckled and Ty smiled. Both Riders sat and made themselves comfortable by the fire.

Bard took up his sewing again. "I think Karigan's ride to Darden makes a good story. There is, after all, a dearth of Rider stories told by the minstrels."

"You would think your grandmother's chin hairs an interesting story," Ereal said.

"Hah!" Bard rose to his knees—and the challenge—and made up a clever rendition of "Grandmother's Whiskers" on the spot. It left the others clutching aching bellies, they were laughing so hard. Soldiers passing by eyed the Riders curiously.

"I do not think," Ty said, after things quieted, "that Karigan in her nightgown is the image of Green Riders we wish to project."

Not an appropriate image of a Green Rider, was she? Karigan held her tongue, but Bard, the big tease, winked at her. He was having too much fun.

"It's certainly not on the same level," Ty continued, "as the heroic tales of Lil Ambrioth, Gwyer Warhein, or any of the others."

Ereal leaned back against her saddlebags. "I don't know. Look at the stories we're missing precisely because of that reason. No one has ever written a history of the Riders and as a consequence we know so very little of our own heritage. The stories we do know are so embellished that the First Rider in particular is larger than life—hardly human— and there is scant mention of other Riders and their deeds in any of the histories."

"Exactly my point," Bard said. He drew his needle through the cloth as Ty watched very closely. "There are many generations of forgotten Riders and I think it very sad."

"Then I think," Karigan said, "our first tale should be about Ereal and Crane."

They all looked at her.

"Crane is the fastest horse in all the provinces." She gazed at Ereal. "When was the last time you lost a Day of Aeryon race?"

Ereal raised her eyebrows, her mouth open in surprise. "Never. We've never lost a race."

Bard was laughing again. "A good thought, Karigan. A story would put ever more pressure on our good lieutenant and her valiant steed—she'd never live it down if she lost!"

Ereal blinked. "I thought I was already under *that* pressure."

"An officer racing horses." Ty shook his head in disapproval, his eyes still following Bard's inexpertly guided needle.

"And *Captain* Mapstone hasn't lost one silver betting on them," Bard said with some acerbity. "In any case, certain stories take on lives of their own. Who knows what the citizens of Darden may be saying ten years from now about the girl who rode to town in her nightgown."

"They'd say nothing if you'd drop it," Karigan said. Then the terrible thought occurred to her that this accursed incident might be the one thing in her entire life that anyone remembered her for. Her life's legacy. Wouldn't her aunts be furious!

Ty, suddenly unable to contain himself, reached toward Bard. "Give me that." He snatched the sewing right out of Bard's hands. "Awful," he muttered, examining the handiwork. He drew his knife and ripped out the stitches.

Ereal and Bard traded knowing looks. "Rider Perfect" had struck again, and Karigan watched as Ty deftly sewed tiny, neat stitches in the sleeve.

Bard leaned back on his elbows, content to let Ty wrestle with his sewing.

"I believe this calls for a song," he said. "When I was last on an errand to Selium, Karigan's friend Estral dug up an old song for me about the First Rider. It's not one most remember. The title is 'Shadows of Kendroa Mor.' 'Mor' in the old tongue meant 'hill.' 'Kendroa' did not survive as a place name, so the mor of the song could be almost any-place in Sacoridia."

Bard cleared his throat, and in his baritone, began the fast paced tune:

> *Hee ya, hi ya, the Riders ride*
> *Gallop 'em down the mor*
> *Gallop 'em fast, Lil*
> *Slay them 'mites, Lil*
> *And ride down the clans of dark*
>
> *Their chiefs with branched crowns*
> *Burn black pale brows*
> *Ride 'em down, Lil*
> *Ride 'em down the mor*
> *Faster than an arrow, Lil*
> *Beware the dark chiefs, Lil*
> *Ride 'em down the mor . . .*

The song depicted a desperate nighttime ride—a charge or retreat?—led by Lil Ambrioth. Since the song relied mostly on its fast beat, the particulars of the story were vague at best. If the song depicted an actual event, then the particulars had been well known to the singers and audience at the time it had been written.

"It could have simply been inspired by the First Rider in general," Bard said afterward. "Maybe a conglomeration of events in her life. The actual theme of outrunning and slaying the enemy isn't too specific."

"What is meant by 'clans of dark'?" Karigan asked.

Bard shrugged. "Estral thinks it refers to Sacor Clans that took Mornhavon's side during the Long War."

The Riders fell silent. Ereal stirred the embers of the fire with a branch and threw on some more wood. Growing flames hissed and popped as they consumed the wood.

The idea of clans betraying their own people had quieted the Riders. Sacoridia had come a long way in its sense of unity since those days. But the thought of Sacoridians joining a monster like Mornhavon who committed atrocities against their own people was sickening.

"Hah!" Ty said, startling the others. He broke the thread with his teeth, and knotted it off. He then presented Bard with his expertly mended shortcoat. "This is the way it should be done."

Bard took the coat, smiling. "My humble thanks, Rider Newland. Next time I need some mending done, I'll know who to call on."

This brought more laughter, but despite the lightened mood, when Karigan finally kicked off her boots and wrapped herself in her bedroll, she still heard Bard's rhythmic song ghosting through her mind as she fell into sleep.

❧ BLACKVEIL ❧

Far beneath the canopy of dark, twisted trees and vaporous shroud; buried beneath layers of loam, moss, and decayed leaves—a thousand years' accumulation of growth and decay—a sentience stirred in deepest Blackveil Forest.

Even as it struggled to shudder off the captivity of sleep, voices called it back, lulling it, willing it to sleep. *Sleep in peace, ancient one,* they sang. *Disturb not the world, for it is not for you. Sleep in peace . . .*

The sentience tried to block the voices and their enchanting songs, but it was a terrible labor. The sentience moaned, which in the forest was a breeze that rattled tree limbs and sent drops of moisture plinking into still, black pools. Forest creatures paused their scavenging, yellow eyes aglow and alert.

The sentience wanted nothing more than to obey the voices, to slumber undisturbed. Yet it was too restless, and so it resisted, spreading tendrils of awareness, like vines, creeping outward through duff and leaf litter to try and feel itself out, to understand itself, to seek and comprehend its boundaries.

Though it was the barest ripple of resistance and awareness, the voices climbed an octave in alarm; increased the rhythm of their song; and pursued the sentience.

Panicked, the sentience surged through moss and scattered leaves. It flushed fowl from undergrowth and rushed through a hollow log shredding spider webs. It sent wavelets across a sludgy, slow moving stream and followed it to the sea.

The sea, it found, lapped a rocky shore. The sentience slid along the stems of rockweed, tasting brine and swaying with the undulation of the waves, but it could not travel beyond the shore, for a great submerged barrier sang it back.

It traveled inland, and was absorbed by tree roots and sucked upward through the very fibers of the tree's blackened heart. When it emerged as a droplet of dew at the tip of a pine needle, it found only heavy clouds of vapor.

The sentience raced northward, but found again a barrier, a massive wall of stone and magic. Here the songs intensified; interwoven songs of resistance, barriers, and containment.

The sentience backed off.

It was hemmed in, surrounded on all sides, *trapped.*

The voices lulled and cajoled, and as drowsiness bore down on the sentience, it perceived just the tiniest hint of weakness in the song, a fragility that was an off-key note that emanated from the wall.

Rebellion had bled most of the strength from the sentience. Unable to resist further, it began the inevitable slide into sleep.

But even as it was overcome, a name from ages long past came to the sentience, and childlike in its desperation, it called out for an old protector: *Varadgrim!*

This the voices could not repress, and even after the sentience drifted into heavy slumber, its cry penetrated a weak section of the barrier wall, and flowed into the land of Sacoridia, taking on a life of its own.

⇜ NIGHT INTRUSIONS ⇝

Perhaps it was Bard's song that caused Karigan to toss and turn in her blankets, its eerie images and heady rhythm coursing relentlessly through her mind, or maybe it was the ill feeling of the clearing all too nearby. Whatever it was, when exhaustion finally did claim her, she fell into a heavy slumber only to be plagued by troubling dreams.

She dreamed that the surrounding forest decayed and darkened. Seedlings sprouted and grew above her, unfurling branches that blotted out the moon and stars, and twined together in a net that trapped her.

Beneath her, tree roots roiled to life. They churned and snaked through the ground, breaking loose and showering her with soil. Karigan wanted desperately to arise and run, but she was held a captive of her own sleep, her body like stone.

The roots lashed around her limbs and coiled about her neck. The ground began to give way beneath her, the roots pulling her down.

No! she wanted to cry, but her nose and mouth became clogged with earth.

A root slithered along her side and plunged into her shoulder. It tunneled within muscle and sinew and wrapped about bones. Shoots spread throughout her body seeking to take it over; to take *her* over.

Karigan wanted to fight, but could not move, nor could

she breathe, suffocated as she was by the weight of the earth that buried her. A scream she could not loose threatened to explode in her lungs even as the roots inside her needled ever closer to her heart.

When all seemed lost, when it seemed the forest might claim her wholly, the clarion notes of a horn rang out, shattering the roots that bound her and thrusting her back up for air as one who has been drowning.

Karigan gagged on a sharp inhalation of air. When the fit passed and she realized she could breathe freely, her eyes fluttered open to stars winking between the limbs of tall, spindly spruce and fir. She could almost still hear the fading tones of the horn like an echo of the dream. It stirred some dormant memory, but she couldn't place it.

The dream left her exhausted as though the struggle had been a physical one. Tears shed in her sleep cooled on her cheeks, and she discovered she had wrangled her bedding into a tangled wad.

A sharp pain stabbed at her left shoulder and she rubbed it. There was an old wound there, a tiny pinprick of a scar where once she had been attacked by tainted wild magic. She hadn't thought about it in a very long time, and why now it should bother her when it was normally just a small point of numbness, she did not know. Just as quickly as she wondered about it, however, the sensation passed.

She rubbed her eyes and then rose on her elbow, now fully awake. The fire was but glowing embers. Ty and Ereal slept nearby, but Bard's bedroll was empty and Karigan recalled he had been assigned to second watch.

It'll be my turn soon enough.

She decided to stay up rather than attempt sleep again and risk more bad dreams. She shivered at the cool night against her clammy skin and drew on her shortcoat and boots. She stepped carefully by Ty.

"Everything all right?" The scratchy voice belonged to Ereal and she popped open a bleary eye to watch Karigan.

"Yes," Karigan said.

"Are you sure? I thought I heard someone cry out."

"I'm fine, it's nothing—just a dream," Karigan said. "I go on duty soon."

Ereal murmured something and rolled over. Karigan stepped quietly away, rather embarrassed she had awakened her superior officer because of a dream, as though she were nothing more than a child experiencing night terrors. She sensed Ereal had been keeping an eye on her ever since their departure from Sacor City. It brought Karigan mixed feelings of gladness that people cared about what happened to her, and resentment that they might think her incapable of taking care of herself or doing her job.

Now *that* sounded childish, she thought, yawning deeply. It was only natural for Ereal to watch out for those under her command, especially the most junior of the lot. Karigan shook her head thinking that a cup of tea and a hot steaming bath would do much to dispel her cranky mood.

She headed for the horses and was struck by how quiet the night was. A few small campfires and lanterns flickered like fairy lights here and there throughout the woods, and the hushed voices of those on duty drifted to her. She inhaled a mixture of woodsmoke, manure, and pine, and she did not find it unpleasant. As she walked, the peacefulness of the night lifted the darkness of the dream from her shoulders.

She greeted a sleepy guard on his rounds near the picket line and found Condor staked between Crane and a snoring mule. Condor welcomed her with a nicker, his eyes aglitter with starshine. She pressed her cheek against his warm neck and closed her eyes, receiving from him the solace only he could provide. It worked even better than tea or a hot bath ever could.

"Steadfast friend," she murmured to him. Through everything, from the torment of the call and sundering from her family, to her assimilation into Green Rider life, he had been there for her, an encouraging presence that provided comfort and unconditional love.

She did not know what she would do without him and was aware that other Riders shared similar bonds with their horses. It came of a close working partnership, of course, and the fact that horse and Rider must rely on one another not just to get the job done, but for companionship and even survival. And it went deeper.

Somehow, and Karigan was still unclear about this, messenger horses were able to pick out or sense the Rider with whom they'd be most compatible. Condor had never had a chance to "pick" her because of the dire circumstances that originally threw them together, but they certainly developed a deep fondness for one another that surpassed an ordinary relationship between horse and rider. It went a long way on a lonely road.

He was an unbeautiful horse, her Condor, gawky in proportion, with his chestnut hide scored by old scars, but she didn't care. She would not trade him for the most beautiful horse in the world, and she had had access to some truly fine steeds in her father's stable, but they weren't Condor. There was no other horse like him.

Even now he provided her comfort from bad dreams, and gave her a light *chuff* in her face with breath sweetened by grain. She smiled and pulled on his ear and he lipped at her sleeve, begging for a treat.

"Sorry, I don't have anything for you tonight."

They had played this game often since they had been with the delegation. She had needed to come to him for his familiar comfort. This whole delegation business had taken some getting used to. Compared to her usual duty, it was like a traveling circus. So many people moving at such a

slow pace. It was the same routine every day—riding from
sunup to sundown, stopping to pitch camp for the night,
breaking down camp in the dusky hours of morning, only
to begin the cycle anew. The repetitive nature of it chafed
at her.

On an ordinary message errand, she had the freedom to
set her own pace and stop where and when she desired.
Sometimes this meant sleeping in the open, and sometimes
it meant the camaraderie of an inn. With the delegation, she
had no choice over pacing or people.

While she missed the independence, she did enjoy getting to know the other Riders better. It was a rare occasion
when Riders rode in one another's company because, by
necessity, they must work alone to cover the far reaches of
the countryside, bearing King Zachary's messages. But then,
this was an unusual mission.

A mission for which Karigan had been hand-picked.

There were several other Riders better suited for a diplomatic mission, Captain Mapstone had informed her, than
Karigan who was not—and here she smiled—the most "diplomatic" among them. But it was she who had the most experience with Eletians.

"The most experience" did not amount to much, Karigan
thought. She combed her fingers through Condor's mane,
flipping it to the right side.

A couple years ago, an Eletian named Somial had saved
her life, mending her until the poison that raged in her
blood had dissipated. Her memories of that time were dim,
but she seemed to recall dancers amid moonbeams in an
emerald clearing, and Somial's gentle laughter and ageless
eyes.

Were most Eletians like Somial? Magical and healing?
Or were they more like Shawdell, who had wished to crush
the D'Yer Wall so he might claim whatever residue of dark
and powerful magic remained beyond the wall in Blackveil

Forest? It had not mattered to him how many lives he destroyed in the process, and in fact the more lives he took with his soul-stealing arrows, the stronger he became.

Karigan grunted as Condor's great weight settled against her. He had decided to use her as his leaning post. She heaved him off. "Hold your own self up, you great oaf." He yawned comically and shook his mane out of sorts again.

As Karigan stroked Condor's neck, she found herself unsettled by thoughts of Shawdell. He had come close to bringing about her undoing, and King Zachary's, too. The memory of Shawdell sighting the king down the shaft of a black arrow still made her shudder. It had been a close thing. Fortunately, Shawdell and his ambitions had been thwarted, but what was to say there weren't more Eletians like him? Even just one such as he could present untold danger.

And so here was the delegation, tramping through the northernmost wilds of the Green Cloak Forest. King Zachary needed to learn the Eletians' mindset regarding Sacoridia. He hoped they still honored an alliance made with the Sacor Clans a thousand years ago, but who knew with that strange folk?

Karigan suspected the Eletians wouldn't be particularly concerned with Sacoridia unless it suited their own needs. And did something now concern Eletia? It was like the sleeping legend had awakened. People had not seen Eletians simply slipping through a forest glade in the light of a silver moon, but on busy roads in full daylight. Passersby gawked at them, but no Eletian deigned to speak with any Sacoridian, and none sought out King Zachary.

Mysteries.

Despite the annoyance of riding with the delegation, despite the element of danger, Karigan felt a certain thrill at the possibility of being one of the few to enter the Elt Wood. One of the few in what must be centuries, if not ages.

She patted Condor's neck. "Well, boy, as long as I'm up, I ought to find Sergeant Blaydon and see where he wants me tonight."

Condor jerked his head up, ears alert and flickering, but it wasn't her he was listening to. Crane's head came up next, and he whinnied. Like a chain reaction down the length of the picket, the other horses and mules came awake, shifting and whickering.

"What is it?" Karigan peered anxiously into the dark, her hand trailing along Condor's shoulder, and she wondered what the horses sensed that she could not. She saw nothing, and perhaps nothing out there had roused Condor, but . . . Now he scraped his hoof on the ground and yanked at his tether as if to break free.

Had they caught a whiff of some wild predator prowling in the woods? Even if it was just a catamount or wolf, Karigan thought it best she inform the watch that something was bothering the horses. Trying to quell her own apprehension, she left Condor and searched for the soldier who was posted near the picket, but couldn't find him. It occurred to her that she hadn't seen him come by while she was with Condor.

Where was he? If he was off taking a nap or dicing with companions, she would make sure Sergeant Blaydon heard of it immediately.

When she made one last sweep down the length of the picket line, she found some mules at the very end churning up the earth with their hooves, their eyes rolling, and sweat foaming on their necks and flanks.

She peered into the darkness beyond the encampment made more immense by the thick canopy of the woods that blocked the glow of the moon. In the distance, something pale on the ground caught her eye. A sunbleached piece of deadwood? A rock or mushroom?

She wavered for a moment on the fringe of the emcampment, then, drawn forward by her own relentless curiosity—and a desire not to rouse the sergeant unnecessarily—she left behind the flickering lights of the encampment and plunged into the forest shadows ahead.

A branch promptly snapped beneath her heel and its splintering cracked through the woods. She stifled a yelp and put her hand over her racing heart.

Calm down, she told herself. If Bard heard of this idiocy, he'd be sure to make a ditty about the Green Rider who frightened herself to death.

She proceeded forward again, stepping more carefully this time. When she came upon the object, she gasped and stumbled backward.

It was not bleached deadwood or a rock, nor was it a mushroom. A hand, pale fingers open . . .

The rest of the soldier lay obscured behind a bush, face up, an arrow jutting from his chest. A tendril of moonlight gleamed in the whites of his eyes. The scent of his blood in the air must have disturbed the horses.

Catamounts, Karigan thought uneasily, did not use arrows. The arrow was crudely made, the type that groundmites used when they could not steal something better.

She glanced frantically into the dark and thought she discerned a glinting—a flash of yellow eyes?—then nothing. She backed a step with shaking legs—she could not seem to make them obey her need to run. She put her hand against a tree trunk to steady herself, her breathing harsh in her ears. She perceived movement and then—

Thwack!

Bark shattered into her face. Through stinging eyes she saw the arrow quiver in the tree trunk just above her hand.

Karigan backed away, and then swung around, racing toward the encampment.

She crashed through a cluster of saplings, batting away pine branches that wanted to cling to her clothes and limbs and hold her back. When she was clear, another arrow sang past her and impaled a tree just ahead of her. She zigzagged her course between the trees to elude any other arrows that might be aimed at her back.

She chanced a glance over her shoulder, but saw nothing beyond the wall of dark.

She stumbled over roots into the encampment's perimeter, and put on a new burst of speed.

"Groundmites!" she cried as she tore past the horse pickets.

She ran through the ashes of a dead campfire. Without shortening her stride she leaped a sleeping soldier who came underfoot.

"Groundmites!" she shouted at the top of her lungs.

Faces of those on duty turned toward her.

When she reached the heart of the encampment very near the clearing, she skidded to a halt, panting raggedly. Soldiers stared incredulously at her. Some peered at her with groggy eyes from their bedrolls.

What were they waiting for? She grabbed the nearest soldier by his tunic and started shaking him. *"Groundmites!"* Her scream, by now, was half hysterical.

The soldiers sprang to life, grabbing weapons and heading toward their posts. Others who had been asleep emerged from bedrolls as they were jostled to wakefulness by their comrades. Swiftly word passed among the ranks and Sergeant Blaydon appeared, barking orders.

The sergeant strode toward Karigan, arms swinging, a no-nonsense expression on his face. Undoubtedly he wanted a word with her to ensure this was no fancy on her part, that she was not overreacting to some little noise in the night. She feared that by having revealed her feelings about the clearing earlier in the day, she had probably done little to instill the confidence of others in her.

Just five steps from her, an arrow ripped into the sergeant's stomach.

When the sergeant fell, panic seized the soldiers who, without someone to shout orders at them, didn't seem to know in which direction to go. They scrambled, pushing into one another, shouting ineffectively into the night.

Inhuman howls filled the surrounding forest. They were banshee wails that crested over the encampment, railing in an intolerable crescendo of low tones to a high, piercing pitch that Karigan felt crawl along her flesh. More than one soldier near her blanched and covered his ears.

There were groundmites out there all right, and a very large band of them by the sound of it.

Abruptly the wails ended and arrows rained into a knot of soldiers. Many fell. Their anguished cries mobilized the others.

Buffeted and jostled by soldiers, and without orders, Karigan took off for her little sleeping place hoping against hope that Ereal and Ty had heard the warning in time. They were protected the least on the edge of the encampment.

She touched her brooch as she went, calling on its power, her very own special Rider ability, to help her vanish, to allow her to fade into her surroundings. As she faded, a haze of gray settled into her vision. She would have a whopping headache later, but the discomfort of using her ability was worth it if it meant being invisible to the enemy and its arrows.

Behind her she heard orders shouted out as someone thought to take charge of the panicked soldiers. She even heard Lady Penburn snapping out commands, but she ran on, thinking only of Ereal and Ty.

She shouldered by a soldier who paused to puzzle over what it was that brushed by him. Arrows hissed past Karigan, striking the soldier.

She cried out, but kept running. *Hold steady,* she told herself, *hold steady.*

More groundmite cries permeated the air. These were shorter cries, like the yips and barks of a pack of coyotes. Unlike coyotes, however, these were rhythmic and held a certain intelligence behind them.

The woods shattered with movement as dozens of the hulking creatures loped into the encampment's midst, howling and slashing with weapons, and trampling anything or anyone that came underfoot.

A couple veered toward the horses and mules, and Karigan knew the creatures would slaughter them just for the kill.

Condor! She slowed, suddenly torn between locating Ereal and Ty, and trying to rescue her horse.

In her distraction, she almost slammed broadside into a huge groundmite. It towered over her, half its bulk lost to the shadows of the night. Its limbs were covered by patchy fur. Agile catlike ears, tufted at the tips, flickered back and forth catching the screams and shouts, the clatter of steel as battle ensued, and the terrified whinnies of horses.

It wore a thick leather jerkin and carried a farmer's scythe for a weapon. Tied to its broad belt was a brightly painted child's spinning top, like some sort of good-luck charm or war prize. A sandy blond scalp also hung from its belt.

Karigan backed off in revulsion, but the groundmite followed her, grinning with sharp canines, its eyes flashing yellow as they caught some shred of light.

It then dawned on her that not only was her own vision clear of the haze that ordinarily obscured it when she used her ability, but the 'mite could see her very well, too.

It pointed a massive claw at her hair. "Want." It was a guttural sound it shaped into a word.

Karigan tried to fade again, but the brooch would not obey her command. Why did her ability fail, and why *now?*

She had no weapon—her saber, and even her knife, were with her other gear by her bedroll. No ability, no weapon. There was only one option.

She feinted to the left and dodged to the right, and ran around the groundmite. For all their size and power, groundmites just weren't very nimble, but this one decided to pursue anyway.

Someone appeared out of the darkness ahead, running toward Karigan. It was Ereal.

"Karigan!" Ereal cried. She carried not only her own sword, but Karigan's, too.

It was like some vast space opened between the two Riders that was impossible to cross, that they'd never meet, that their legs just could not carry them swiftly enough no matter how hard they ran. The groundmite gasped wet breaths behind Karigan.

Two arrows whined out of the dark on an inescapable course and Karigan could only watch in horror as they smacked into Ereal in rapid succession. The force of the double impact bowled her over hard onto the ground where she lay crumpled like a discarded rag doll.

"No!" Karigan cried.

She could do nothing but continue to run toward Ereal with the groundmite pounding hard after her, for her sword lay beside the fallen Rider.

Did Ereal's hand twitch? Did she still live? Incredibly, Karigan's saber levitated off the ground and floated erratically through the air toward her. Ereal's special ability was moving objects with her mind.

Renewed hope surged through Karigan, even as she perceived the groundmite catching up with her.

The saber floated swiftly toward her. She stretched her hand out to receive it. Just inches from her fingertips it faltered and plummeted to the ground. She dove after it and felt the *shoosh* of the scythe against the back of her neck as she barely missed losing her head.

She exclaimed in triumph as she grasped the hilt of her sword and shed its sheath. In the next breath she rolled as the scythe descended and cleaved into a tree root with a solid *ka-chunk* right where she had just lain.

The blade of the scythe caught on the root for a moment, but undismayed, the groundmite tugged it free and grinned showing yellowed, pointed teeth. Thinking its quarry well in hand, it swept the scythe at her once again.

Karigan, caught at a profound disadvantage—overpowered and on her knees—knew in a fleeting instant she would be unable to halt the momentum and strength behind the scythe that whistled toward her.

~ ATTACKING FROM THE SHADOWS ~

K arigan dropped flat on the ground as the scythe swept over her. She scrambled on knees and elbows beneath a dense stand of young trees with low hanging branches. The scythe crashed down after her, splintering branches and showering her with pine needles.

She squirmed deeper into the stand, blinded by the darkness, thrusting branches out of her face. Her hands sank into damp loam and she banged her knee on a rock, but she did not notice the pain.

Behind her the groundmite barreled through the trees, unstoppable. Karigan tightened her fingers about the hilt of her saber and turned in a crouch to face it.

It perceived her as cowering and emitted an alarming, growly laugh. It raised the scythe, but—just as she hoped—it got fouled in the stand's branches and it couldn't jiggle the scythe free. The groundmite's laughter ceased.

Karigan shot up in a flurry of branches and drove her sword into its belly. It looked down in surprise, still holding the scythe aloft. She yanked her sword from it and it crashed to the ground like a mighty tree felled, the scythe belatedly breaking loose from entangled limbs and tumbling on top of it.

Karigan stood over it for some moments, chest heaving, the air thick with the scents of blood and balsam.

It took several moments for it all to catch up with her

47

racing mind. When it did, she wanted to give in to panic and weep, to get sick, to curl up in a hiding place. But she could not. The din of battle raged on, and her sword was needed elsewhere.

She stepped over the dead groundmite, pushing her way through the stand and into the encampment proper. From what she could discern, except for a few smaller bouts here and there, the thrust of the groundmite attack centered on the clearing. In the nearby woods, there were only the dead.

Karigan set off across bloodied ground littered with weapons, utensils, and other articles. She paused by Ereal who lay curled in a pool of her own blood and, as she expected, she found no life there.

Just a few hours ago, four Riders had sat laughing around a campfire. How had everything turned upside down so quickly?

She swallowed back a sob and trotted on. She encountered an injured soldier overmatched by a groundmite. The soldier could barely stand, much less defend himself from the ax the groundmite wielded. As the ax rose for a blow that would surely slay the soldier, Karigan darted up from behind, and screaming something incoherent, hacked her saber into the groundmite's side.

After the groundmite fell, the injured soldier wobbled and collapsed. Karigan knelt beside him and determined he still lived despite his wounds, but there was nothing she could do for him at the moment.

She left him and found herself moving from one small clash to another, streaking out of the shadows to aid defenders, taking groundmites by surprise. Though her ability to fade out continued to elude her, she was still able to take advantage of stealth and darkness.

She became remote from herself and strangely calm, as though she watched from afar. It was, she knew, the only way she could do what she needed to do. Karigan G'ladheon was not a killer, but she must kill to survive, and she must keep moving forward.

She found herself near the pickets where drovers did their best to defend horses and mules. But they were horsemen, not swordsmen, and even as Karigan came upon them, a groundmite struck one down. As it raised its sword to kill another, Karigan drove her own into the space between its armpit and breastplate. The groundmite keeled over, howling, nearly wrenching the saber out of her hand. She jerked her blade free, feeling it scrape ribs.

Another drover fell, leaving one youth so frightened his face stood out pale in the night. The groundmite who threatened him noted Karigan and pummeled the boy aside as though he were of no consequence.

This groundmite wielded a hefty sword. Its first blow was crushing. Nerves jangled from Karigan's fingers to her elbow and she nearly lost her sword. She and the groundmite warily circled one another. Their blades flashed in a quick exchange of blows, and then they backed off, assessing. Karigan had fought opponents far more powerful than herself before, but never had she crossed swords with something so strong.

Without warning the groundmite bore into her again, slamming its blade against hers. It used its sword like a club, and the force of the stroke made Karigan's saber dip to the ground. Another caused her to stumble backward.

She thrusted and ducked, sidestepped and blocked. She used trees as shields and practically danced around the groundmite seeking advantage or safety. The fight lacked rhythm, for whatever fine techniques she knew were next to useless against her opponent's hack and slash methods.

Sweat streamed into Karigan's eyes and the muscles from her wrist to her shoulder burned. Her focus was such that the sounds of battle, even the cries of the dying, fell into the background of her awareness. The *clang* and *ding*

of her sword against the groundmite's, and her own panting, were sharp counterpoint.

The groundmite grunted, heaving the blade down on
her. Karigan darted to the side to evade the blow and stumbled over a root, nearly falling into the hooves of thrashing
horses and mules maddened by the stench of blood.

It gave her an idea.

Before the groundmite could bring down its blade another time, she darted between a pair of mules.

If the groundmite didn't get her, she reflected, the mules
probably would. Stepping between two maddened animals
with iron-shod hooves and a ton of weight between them
was a foolhardy move. If they didn't get her with their
hooves, they could crush her between them. Yet, it was this
very power she was relying on.

In the mere moments it took her to slip between the
mules, she was jostled, her foot stomped, her shin grazed,
but she came to their heads in one piece, relatively unhurt.

The groundmite, intent on its quarry, dove in heedlessly
after her, and this she had anticipated. Though she hated
to do it to the poor animals, she slapped them across their
sensitive noses.

The mules plunged and squealed anew. One of them
kicked the groundmite and its howl of pain only intensified
their rage. The mules came together, smashing it between
them. It writhed, eyes rolling, and lost its sword somewhere
beneath the deadly hooves.

Karigan left the groundmite to the mules. She ran from
the pickets and through the woods, once again on the fringe
of the encampment. She thought she heard Condor's
whinny somewhere behind her, and she closed her eyes.
There was no time to check on him. . . .

She trotted steadily onward and then paused, peering
through the dark. From what she could discern of the main
battle through the trees, the Sacoridians were outnum-

bered, but able to hold their own. They stood shoulder to shoulder and shield to shield in the clearing repelling the enemy, just as Lady Penburn said they would. Groundmite blows pounded on shields and defenders surged through to cut down the enemy. Among them she saw Bard, his saber rising and falling, his face lined in concentration.

As she stood pondering how she might go about aiding them, she became aware, belatedly, of some massive force crashing through the woods toward her. It burst from the undergrowth and hammered her into a tree.

Her sword arm and shoulder took the brunt of the impact and she scraped down the tree trunk, unable to breathe, her sword somewhere far away. Her vision crackled and blurred, and when finally she slid to her knees, she felt as though she had been shattered into pieces against an anvil.

A groundmite towered over her—the one she had left for the mules. Its trousers were shredded and bloodied. One of the mules had bitten a hunk of flesh out of its arm. It glared down at her with glinting yellow eyes, and she could only stare back up at it, too stunned to move.

"Greenie," it said, and followed it with some coarse, garbled speech she did not understand. It found her saber, and raised it for a death blow.

It all registered dully in Karigan's mind. She couldn't move and in but a moment her own sword would come bearing down on her.

Insanely she laughed. She laughed because of her thought earlier in the evening about how her ride to Darden in a nightgown would be the most notable thing anyone would ever remember about her.

Even as she laughed, tears rolled down her cheeks. There were too many things left undone. She had to make peace with her father, tell him she loved him. Yet, when she closed her eyes against her fate, the image that came to her was that of King Zachary. There was a questioning look in his brown eyes, and for him Karigan felt some sorrow, some great depth of loss. Not for him, necessarily, but for . . . for herself?

Light footfalls passed by her, accompanied by a strangely familiar rank smell. It had been taking a rather long time, she realized, for the groundmite to kill her. She popped one eye open, and then the other. Brogan the bounder bent over the still hulk of the groundmite lying on its back with a forester's knife lodged in its throat. Brogan yanked the knife out and wiped it on the groundmite's tunic.

He then gazed down at her. His expression was feral, that of a predator on the hunt. Without a word he crept stealthily away, vanishing through the dark woods.

Brogan, Karigan realized, was doing as she had done herself—attacking from the shadows. He had looked at her just as she had others, to ascertain if she lived.

Karigan herself found it hard to grasp that she was still alive. She grew aware of a wave, building power and momentum, and that it would swamp her if she allowed it. At all costs, she knew she must hold it at bay.

She drew in a raspy breath, and sat very still, trying to settle her mind and take stock of her condition. Her entire side ached. When she flexed her arm, a tearing sensation ripped through the muscles. Her arm was not broken, but she would be unable to handle her sword again this night.

She rose unsteadily to her feet, cradling her arm against her. She peered again to the clearing, wondering what she could do to help.

Then something curious happened. It was impossible that she *hear* something so faint over the clamor of battle. No, it was more that she *felt* it, as though it traveled through the tree roots beneath her feet, or that it was whispered from branch to branch above her in the forest canopy.

Varadgrim, Varadgrim, Varadgrim . . .

And onward it hastened toward the clearing. Had she really heard . . . felt it? Somehow it reminded her of her dream. It had that tang of darkness. Even as she thought about it, she was overwhelmed by an awful feeling of impending disaster. It was as though the air had grown taut, as though there was a great pressure on it and it was about to explode.

In the clearing, there grew the steady rumble of thunder. The ground trembled beneath her feet. The battle seemed to pause as combatants perceived the change as well. The rumbling grew and intensified into an unbearable roar until finally there was release—a rupturing within the clearing.

The lines of defenders broke apart and chaos took hold. Groundmites threw down their weapons and bolted. Shields fell and figures ran and darted, flickering in the glimmer of lanterns and campfires.

Searing white energy coalesced about the obelisks, crackling up and down as though the magic of the wards was building up power.

A dark figure appeared between a pair of obelisks. Groundmites and Sacoridians both fled before it, terror-stricken and screaming. Intricate spider webs of energy arced throughout the clearing, explosive and bright, lighting the sky above, scoring through anything and anyone in their path.

Tendrils of energy pounced on the figure like live things in attack, fusing onto it, causing it to stagger backward. Though buffeted by the force, the figure shrugged off the magic and forged ahead, passing between the obelisks.

The ward stones shattered.

The white bolts of energy sputtered out and evaporated, and the figure vanished like a shadow in the night.

And then there was nothing.

Nothing but a haze of smoke. Darkness descended over the forest quenching the afterlight of the magic. Small campfires and lanterns still glowed here and there, insignificant and incongruous with the events of the last several moments.

Nothing moved. Was everyone dead, or, like Karigan, too terrified to move?

After a period of silence, there were finally some cries of pain and fear, invocations to the gods, and coughing. Karigan's own throat was raw. Had she been screaming all along, or was it the result of simply holding back the screams she had been unable to loose?

The dread that once inhabited the clearing now advanced on her. It moved toward her like a great inescapable wall and surrounded her. Her screams came out as whimpers.

A figure emerged from shadow and paused before her. It was made of the night, and only the black dusty rags it had been buried in gave it a man's shape. The moon shone on the pale face of a corpse. An iron crown of twisted branches gleamed upon its brow.

It lifted its arm and pointed at Karigan with a bone-thin finger. The gesture was like a lance thrust into her chest and she stumbled backward.

"Galadheon." The figure's voice rasped out of nothing, clung to her, wrapped her throat in cold fingers. *"Betrayer."*

 BENEATH THE CAIRN ⟢

The wraith of rags and shadow dropped its arm to its side. It tilted its face up and, curiously, it snuffled the air. Then it averted its dead gaze to something behind Karigan.

She whirled. Before her eyes registered the Eletian with his bowstring released, before her hair had the chance to settle on her shoulders, or before she could even draw a single breath, an arrow grazed her cheek and ear before hurtling onward.

She spun, following the arrow's flight, but the wraith was gone, the arrow impaled in a tree. The dread that had cloaked the wraith was absent; the oppressive weight of its presence all but gone from the woods.

A current of night-cool air stung her face. With a trembling hand, she touched along her cheekbone and ear. When she withdrew her fingers, she found them smeared with blood.

"You should not have moved." The Eletian's voice was light and accented. It possessed the timbre of a cool, fast-flowing stream. "A hair's-breadth more, and I would have killed you."

Karigan glanced over her shoulder, trying to comprehend just the Eletian's presence, much less her close call with arrow and wraith.

The Eletian strode past her. Pearlescent armor glowed in the moonlight, and rippled with subtle tints of green, pink, and blue, changing continually as he moved. From his shoulder pauldrons bristled odd, deadly looking spines, and barbs jutted in rows along his forearms. She watched him thoroughly bespelled.

He stopped before the tree and tugged his white-shafted arrow out of the trunk. "My aim was true," he said, "but one cannot kill that which is the substance of death." On the arrow's shining tip was a snatch of black cloth. He rolled his eyes to gaze at her without turning, and she perceived a tight-lipped smile.

He spoke in his own language and she thought of water smoothing over rocks in a stream. Despite its beauty, she found no comfort in it, though she could not explain why. Finally, using the common tongue again, he said, "Remember well the precision of my aim, Galadheon." And before she could make sense of his words, he added, "Telagioth who leads us will speak to you in the clearing."

Karigan stumbled away, wondering what new dream she had entered.

She picked her way among the slain, groundmite and Sacoridian alike. It appeared that very few of the delegation had survived. The night hid details—faces—but the tang of gore clung in her throat. When she reached the clearing, it was alight with the crystalline shine of *muna'riel*, the moonstones of the Eletians. The dead came into sharp focus.

Between two shattered obelisks lay Bard. His eyes were closed and his expression peaceful. Silver light gleamed against the golden threads of the winged horse emblem on the sleeve so recently and meticulously mended by Ty. If not for the pool of blood beneath Bard's mouth and nose, and the gaping hole in his back, she'd have thought him merely asleep.

"Galadheon." The silver light intensified to a blinding white as an Eletian joined her. "Follow."

Karigan stepped over Bard with quavering legs and trailed behind the Eletian. The great wave threatened to overwhelm her, but for now she held it back, if one young woman can hold back the ocean.

The clearing was filled with others like Bard—defenders, servants, nobles, all dead, all with similar wounds as though some immense force had simply punched holes through their bodies. Some soldiers looked among the dead for survivors, but Karigan sensed they'd find none.

The Eletian led her to the clearing's center, to the cairn. Two soldiers supported Captain Ansible whose leg was deeply gashed and hastily bandaged. He seemed to be surveying the carnage, and Karigan thought her own expression must reflect his unfocused look of shock. Another Eletian stood next to him speaking quietly.

"It was the force of the magic which warded this place that killed them. It was loosed when the unspeakable one left its tomb."

Captain Ansible murmured inaudibly.

"We shall assist you as we can," the Eletian replied.

The captain nodded in acknowledgment. When his gaze fell upon Karigan, he said, "Rider, this Eletian wants to speak to you." Then his eyes darted away and he muttered to himself, "Must send word to the king." The two soldiers helped him limp away.

The Eletian turned to Karigan with appraising eyes. "I am called Telagioth. I am *ora-tien,* leader of these *tiendan.*"

The word shone through Karigan's foggy mind as a bright memory. She had met *tiendan* before—Somial had been one. They were hunters of the king. The Eletian king.

Telagioth, as well as other Eletians who moved about the clearing and encampment, were all clad in the odd, milky armor, though no others possessed spines that she could discern.

At Telagioth's side was a sword sheathed in the same material as the armor which, she was certain, wasn't steel. The sword was girded with a belt of embroidered cloth. Lengths of it dangled from the knot at his hip to his knee, the complicated patterns woven into it seeming to move and swim as though alive.

"How do you know me?" Karigan's cheek was stiff with drying blood, and as she spoke, fresh blood trickled along her jaw.

"We know you," Telagioth said. "You are touched by Laurelyn's favor . . . and other things."

He took her by the elbow, holding a *muna'riel* aloft in his other hand. He guided her around the cairn, taking special care to avoid the dead.

"Where are we going?" Karigan asked, wishing that the whole nightmare would just end and she'd wake up safe and sound beside the campfire and other Riders. Where was Ty? Had he been slain, too? Was she the only one among the Riders to have survived?

The Eletian paused and gestured toward the cairn. A portion of it had been blown outward. Rubble was strewn before a gaping hole. The light of the *muna'riel* revealed steps that descended into darkness. He guided her toward them.

"You—you're not taking me down there," Karigan said, backing away.

Telagioth turned to her, the crystalline light of the *muna-'riel* making his features smooth and well-angled, and alien. Cerulean eyes, with the transparent depth of blue glass, regarded her with interest.

"You would not enter an empty tomb when there is far more death beneath the open moon?" His demeanor was not hostile, nor was it kind. It was merely curious.

Karigan had no wish to enter that blackness from which the wraith had emerged. She hated tombs.

There were other things that required her attention besides, more pressing needs. "The injured need tending." And the dead, too, she did not add. She started to walk away, but Telagioth caught her elbow again.

"Come. The air is sound and nothing is below that can harm you. Others shall tend the injured. You must see what lies below, as a witness, so you may tell your king of it."

Karigan wanted to argue that she had witnessed more than enough already, but she was too weary for argument. And, in a way, his words appealed to her sense of duty, for she knew it was true that King Zachary would want to know the details. *She* wanted to know the details. Just what had been loosed into the world?

She followed Telagioth down the steps through what had been an entranceway, framed out by stone and now-rotted timbers, before the tomb builders had covered it with rocks. They had to clamber over the shattered remains of a stone door. Karigan's fingers trailed over glyphs as she worked her way around it.

Their descent took them down a rough shaft that had been cut right through the bedrock. The walls glinted with wet and slime. Currents of damp smelling air that had been trapped for too long beneath the earth lifted tendrils of hair out of her face. She slipped on a step and jolted her arm painfully as she fought to regain her balance.

"The black moss is slippery," Telagioth said belatedly as he helped her right herself.

"Thanks for the warning," Karigan muttered under her breath.

The *muna'riel* brightly lit the way. The black moss was like a disease that grew on the steps and walls.

"How did you happen upon us?" Karigan asked, perhaps to keep her mind off the tomb they descended into.

"We did not happen upon you," Telagioth said. "Our scouts were monitoring your scouts and the movements of the delegation. When we realized where your encampment was placed, we knew we must come and make ourselves plain to you."

Their timing could have been better, Karigan thought bitterly. "Why didn't you come to us sooner? Certainly you must have known our mission."

"We did know of your mission, but we are hunters, not emissaries. And once we knew of your danger, we came as swiftly as we could."

Before Telagioth could speak further, a chamber opened up before them and his feet splashed into water. "Hold," he warned her. He proceeded forward, testing the footing. "Ai, they delved too deep and the water has flooded in. There are two steps more."

He held out a hand to help her navigate the submerged steps. Ice-cold water seeped through her boots. It was above her ankles.

The chamber was low-ceilinged and dripped with moisture, sounding like rain as it plinked into the pool of water that covered the floor. In the dancing light of the *muna'riel,* she detected carvings on the walls slimed with more of the moss, and other glistening, moving things.

"This is but an antechamber," Telagioth said, his voice taking on a hollow sound. "Beware the unevenness of the floor."

He had to duck as he made his way through the chamber, the ceiling was so low. Karigan hurried after him, feeling the blackness of the subterranean world pressing at her back. She slipped and slid on the uneven floor in her haste and made herself more wet than she wished, but she was across the room in no time, ducking her head beneath a lintel into a tight corridor.

"All of the seals are broken," Telagioth said. "There should have been one as we entered the corridor."

The passage elbowed, but the *muna'riel* was bright enough that it offered her light even around the corner. Wet hanging things fell across her face and she wiped them away with a shiver of disgust. Pale spiders skittered into crevices as light found them. Karigan had been, she thought, in better tombs.

The burial chamber opened up before them, much vaster than the antechamber. The darkness of it swallowed the light of the *muna'riel.* Karigan caught glimpses of colorful walls and of a basin of black water with a rectangular stone platform in the center like an island.

Telagioth stepped down, the water now as high as his knees, and he turned to her offering his hand again. "It will not get deeper than this."

Karigan shuddered with revulsion as the cold water poured over the tops of her boots and soaked through her trousers. It may only reach Telagioth's knees, but for her, the water came to mid-thigh. Who knew what existed in water that stagnated in a tomb?

The *muna'riel* cast the water with silver light, causing liquid waves of that light to reflect onto wall murals. Though somewhat obscured by layers of moss and oozing slime, the murals depicted battle and death, and images of the gods. The gods, painted larger than life, averted their faces and held their hands palms out, either in warding or in denial. There were Aeryc, god of the moon, and Aeryon, goddess of the sun, Dernal the Flamekeeper, Vendane the Harvister, and others, except, Karigan noticed, Westrion, god of death.

While Westrion himself was missing, his steed Salvistar was most prominent of all the figures. Salvistar leaped across the wall, black neck arched and mane flowing like the tongues of a flame. His head was tossed back and his teeth bared. The wavering light seemed to lend him motion and life.

Karigan and Telagioth stood in wonderment, their own reflections on the mirrorlike water mingling with that of the gods, the light of the *muna'riel* somehow cleansing the darkness that had gripped this place for centuries.

Telagioth's cerulean eyes glittered as they followed the walls. Then with a shake of his head he continued across the room toward the stone slab at its center.

"Do you comprehend what has happened here?" he asked Karigan.

Karigan drew her eyebrows together as she trudged through the water after him, remembering all the dead up above. "I think I have a sense of it."

Telagioth halted before the slab. "Truly?" He gestured toward it.

It was not unlike other funerary slabs she had seen. It was inscribed with pictographs and incomprehensible runes, but unlike the others, it lacked Westrion's image. Broken, rusted chains lay in pieces across its surface. Manacles. She began to understand.

"This was not so much a tomb," she said, "but a prison."

"Yes."

"The wards . . ." she murmured. The wards above had been meant to keep "something" in, just as she had surmised when she and Ty found the clearing. Had it been only yesterday afternoon? It seemed like years ago. A prison would explain many things—the covered entrance, the seals Telagioth spoke of, the absence of Westrion's image, and the chains.

"The folly of your people," Telagioth said, "released a great evil back into the lands."

Karigan looked sharply at him. "What do you mean?"

"Your encampment diminished the wardings of the tomb."

"Those wards were already dying."

"Yes, but they might have held for at least a time longer, and the tragedy averted."

Karigan found it hard to believe the delegation alone could have brought such disaster upon itself. She closed her eyes remembering a sensation or force traveling through the forest just before the cairn ruptured: *Varadgrim, Varadgrim, Varadgrim . . .* Had this been the power that ignited the clearing and enabled the wraith's escape? She was uncertain for her sense of it was more that it had been a calling of some sort. Perhaps a calling that had awakened the wraith. If so, who—or what—had been doing the calling?

"The wards were not maintained, as the D'Yer Wall has not been," Telagioth said. "Your people believed they would be maintained in perpetuity, but strength, knowledge, and magic faded over the generations, and so did memory. The discontinuity of mortal lives endangers the world."

So many emotions entangled Karigan, though dulled by shock and exhaustion, and the Eletian had sparked another in her: anger. The wave hovered above her, threatening to crush her with its full fury lest she lose her grip.

"Certainly the Eletians would have done better," Karigan said. "Yet evidently they did not take responsibility."

Telagioth did not react to the anger in her voice. Instead his fair features drooped into sadness. "It is true, but we were a broken and defeated people after the Long War. We had not the strength, except to succor our own wounds. *I remember.* Even now as your kind prospers and spreads its influence, we work to recover."

Karigan hugged herself, not sure if it was against the chill or his words.

"The break in the D'Yer Wall has stirred powers on both sides of the wall, Galadheon. Our own time of tranquility and rest is over, and this you must tell your king. The warning is before us." He gestured at the abandoned funerary slab and broken chains. "This creature that escaped, it was once a man. A man given an unnatural, unending existence by his master in exchange for his allegiance and his soul. I faced one such as he in battle long ago. And now he has found his way back into the world, as will others. Dark powers are awakening."

Telagioth shifted his stance and a quizzical expression crossed his features. He bent over and plunged his arm into the water up to his shoulder. "My toe nudged something," he said. He pulled himself erect, holding at arm's length, a dripping object. "This is an evil thing."

Looking more closely, Karigan saw it was the rusted guard and shard of a sword blade, with a broken, moldy wooden hilt. The hilt had probably been wrapped in leather at one time.

"Your people did think to break it," Telagioth said. "It was a sword used to steal souls, one of this creature's cruelest weapons. Broken, it will serve him no more."

The wood of the hilt must have come from Blackveil Forest. Such a weapon would have given the creature the ability to command the dead. Now there was little question in her mind as to who the wraith's master had been.

Telagioth nodded as though he could detect her thoughts. "Yes, this creature was, long ago, a favored servant of Mornhavon the Black."

❧ CRANE ❧

When Karigan and Telagioth returned to the world above, gentle summer night air wrapped around them. The scents of fresh forest growth mingling with that of blood and viscera clung to the back of Karigan's throat, leaving an acrid taste she could not swallow away.

Soldiers called out to one another through the woods, and the chirruping of crickets rose and fell in erratic waves. The startling beauty of silvery moonstones alight in the clearing and among the trees revealed, once again, the carnage. It was too much of a sensory assault after the dank, cold silence of the tomb. It unbalanced her, and Telagioth placed his hands on her shoulders to steady her.

Just then, soldiers approached, carrying a body in a makeshift stretcher made of two pikes and a blanket. An arm swung lifelessly over the side with the motion. When they passed, Karigan saw it was Lady-Governor Penburn they bore.

I warned her . . . But the thought brought Karigan no solace. Nor was there anger. Not even for the woman whose decision it was to camp in the clearing against the advice of a seasoned bounder. The price had been paid, and Karigan was too tired to lash out at a dead woman.

"You may tell your king our passage through his lands is peaceful," Telagioth told Karigan. She had almost forgotten his presence. "We merely watch. Sacoridia lies in the immediate path of anything that should pass through the D'Yer Wall. Tell him he must turn his attention there, and not to seek out Eletia. Eletia shall parley with him when the time is deemed appropriate." He hesitated, then added, "We shall meet again, Karigan Galadheon."

"G'ladheon," she murmured, but Telagioth had already left her to join some of his fellows at work in the clearing. Karigan watched after him for a moment, then shook her head at Eletians and their enigmatic ways.

Enigmatic or not, it appeared the Eletians had done much to assist with the removal of bodies and the mending of the injured. She would help, but not until she sought out Condor and Ty and learned their fates. She strode from the clearing trying to steel herself against what she might find.

Along the horse pickets there was more carnage; many horses and mules that had been slaughtered by the ground-mites piled up against one another, as though they had fallen panicking and fighting to the last. Her steps quickened as she passed them. Those animals still alive whinnied and lunged, frenzied by the death that surrounded them. They received little attention, however, for that was being focused on the human faction of the delegation.

Among the dead horses Karigan found Bard's lightfooted gelding, Swift. She broke into a run, frantic to reach Condor, praying he had not met a similar fate. She grew disoriented, thinking she should have seen him by now. It was difficult to distinguish between horses in the dark. Shouldn't she have come to his picket by now? Where was he? Heart pounding, she paused, thinking to go back and take a closer look at the dead horses. No, she did not even dare contemplate it. . . .

Then, a little farther down the picket, one horse raised his nose above the others as if checking the wind, and whinnied. Condor!

She ran to him, wrapping her good arm about his neck

and pressing her face into his unruly mane. He lipped at her hair, and after a time, started rubbing his head on her hurt shoulder to get at an itch.

"Ow!" Karigan pulled away laughing and sniffing at the same time, her shoulder throbbing. "You oversized meal for a catamount." Condor gazed at her guilelessly.

She stepped back, sizing him up. He appeared fine, but when he shifted, he favored his left rear leg.

"Oh no." She felt down his leg, lifting his hoof and cradling it in her hand. It was difficult to make out in the dark, but it appeared he had a gash across the fetlock joint. Such a thing might appear minor, but if not treated well and swiftly, it could cripple him. Already it swelled. She would need to soak it in cold water and prepare a poultice. . . .

She and Condor were suddenly showered with the light of a *muna'riel,* and she saw the extent of the gash. It was ugly. She released his hoof and straightened, finding herself face to face with another Eletian, this one a woman with raven hair tied tightly back.

"Mending needs poor beast, mmm?" The woman's accent was much stronger than Telagioth's had been.

"Yes," Karigan said.

The Eletian then took Karigan's chin in her fingers and tilted her face, surveying the wound on her cheek. "Messenger, too." She set aside her *muna'riel* and dug into a satchel she wore over her shoulder. A small pot emerged in which she dipped her fingers. She brought her fingers, now covered by goo, up to Karigan's face.

Karigan pulled away. "What is that?" Too many times her aunts had insensitively slathered stinging potions onto scrapes and cuts when she was a child.

In the struggle to find the right words, the Eletian screwed up her perfect features. Under different circumstances, the effect would have been comical. It did, at least, seem to demystify the Eletians somewhat; put a more *human* face on them. Karigan sensed that this Eletian was much younger than the others she had met, but that still meant she could be hundreds of years old.

Ultimately the Eletian gave up trying to find a common name for the healing salve, and said, "We call it *evaleoren*. It's leaf. Healing it is." The woman made a crushing motion with her hand as if to illustrate the process of its making, but quickly gave up with a slight frown.

Karigan nodded and allowed the Eletian to dab the salve on her face. It did not sting at all, and in fact dulled the pain. It possessed a pleasant herby scent, and she felt her cares lightened, as though the salve mended more than the wound on her cheek, but her spirit, as well.

"Good for horse, too," the Eletian said.

Karigan lifted Condor's hoof so the salve could be smeared across his wound. He bent his neck around, trying to see what was going on.

When the Eletian finished, she smiled. "Heal he will. A poultice—I will make it."

"Thank you," Karigan said with genuine relief. It was the first moment of sanity she had felt all night.

The Eletian then glanced down the picket line, and her bright smile faded. "Other messenger . . ." She shook her head, again unable to express herself.

"Ty?" Without another word, Karigan sprinted down the picket line.

She found Ty soon enough. He squatted next to Flicker, who lay on her side weakly thrusting out her legs. Her mouth foamed with blood. There was a deep wound in her belly. Ty ran his hand along her neck, again and again.

An Eletian knelt next to Ty at Flicker's head, his hand beneath her forelock, rubbing between her eyes. He spoke to her softly in his own language, calming her. She stopped thrusting her legs, but her sides heaved, and labored breaths gurgled in her throat.

"She will stay quiet," the Eletian told Ty.

He nodded. With his back to Karigan, she could not see his expression, but Flicker's ears moved, listening to words he whispered. He stroked her neck once more, then clenched a knife in both hands and raised it above his head. He stabbed downward, throwing his whole body into the stroke.

Karigan reeled away with a sob. She squeezed her eyes shut and clapped her hands over her ears. She couldn't bear to hear Ty's grunt of effort, the knife thudding into Flicker's neck again and again. She could not bear to witness Flicker's crazed screams and thrashing. The mare would not understand why her Rider was hurting her, why he was using brute strength to saw through the thick layers of flesh and muscle of her strong neck. She would not understand he was doing her a mercy.

Karigan prayed he found and severed the crucial artery quickly.

Blind and deaf to Ty's plight, her mind carried her to other dark imaginings. What if it had been Condor? What if it was she kneeling there at his side, having to wield a knife into his neck? She bit her lip to force the images away and tasted blood.

It was a long time before she mastered herself and dared to open her senses to the scene she had turned away from. Ty stood over the still form of Flicker, his uniform blackened by blood. Some had splattered his face. Fleetingly she thought how unusual it was to see Ty disheveled, to see any stain on his uniform. It was surreal.

Light from distant *muna'riel* gleamed in Flicker's dulling eye. Her tongue lolled slack from her parted mouth. The blood still gushed from her neck, forming a river in the soil.

Ty did not weep. He merely stared down at her. Karigan stood beside him and put her hand on his shoulder.

"The Eletian knife," he said. "It was very sharp. Made it quick. The Eletian kept her calm, magic I think."

Karigan closed her eyes and released a slow breath. There had been mercy after all.

"She was in great pain and mortally wounded," he said. "I had to."

"I know." Karigan spoke comforting words that eventually trailed off into silence. There was, she realized, nothing she *could* say.

Karigan did not know how long she stood there with Ty when a soldier approached them.

"Captain Ansible asks that one of you ride to Sacor City to take the news to King Zachary," the soldier said.

"My horse is injured," Karigan said, and then she glanced significantly at Ty and Flicker.

"There're other horses."

At first Karigan bristled, then forced herself to cool off. There was no way the soldier could know the bond between Green Rider and messenger horse, and she could not blame him for the callousness of his words. He looked just as weary and strained as anyone else after the night's events, and had likely lost close companions. One dead horse would mean little to him by comparison.

"I'll do it." Ty's words were so quiet, Karigan wasn't sure she heard them. "I'll ride to Sacor City." This time they came more strongly.

"Ty—" Karigan began, but his look of pain and resolve silenced her.

"One of your messenger horses is over yonder," the soldier said, jabbing his thumb over his shoulder. "Won't let us near one of the corpses."

"Oh gods," Karigan murmured.

*　　*　　*

They found Crane standing over Ereal. He must have slipped his halter during the melee with the groundmites and come in search of her.

He nudged Ereal's shoulder with his nose, but of course she did not respond. He stood forlornly there with head lowered, until he detected their approach. He ran at them, ears locked down and teeth bared, and stopped before them, scraping his hoof on the ground.

"Oh, Crane," Karigan murmured.

Crane whirled on his haunches and returned to Ereal to stand guard over her. He clamped her sleeve between his teeth and shook her arm trying to awaken her. Ereal had once told Karigan that Crane was better than a rooster. When encamped during a message run, he would unfailingly awaken her this way every sunrise. Karigan remembered Ereal's laughter as she told of the time Crane had actually pulled off her blanket. "He loves to run," Ereal had said, "and he's eager to go every morning."

Ty's face blanched as Crane tugged at Ereal's sleeve. "I can't do this," he said, and he walked away.

Karigan sighed. There were several reasons why Ty needed Crane, not least was Crane's experience as a messenger horse. Messenger horses were trained for endurance and cross country travel in ways that ordinary horses were not, and of course, Crane was the fastest messenger horse. King Zachary needed to know what had happened here as soon as possible.

And there were the other reasons.

She started toward Crane, cautiously. He peered at her from beneath his forelock, watching closely, tensing his body. As she neared he snorted and the ears went down again. Karigan halted.

"You know me, Crane. Easy, boy."

She inched toward him, talking to him all the time, trying to explain to him how things were. Messenger horses were intelligent, but she had no idea how far that intelligence went. Was it asking too much for Crane to understand what she said? Or, was it simply the tone of her voice that calmed him, and allowed her to approach? When finally she was within reach, he gently breathed on her outstretched hand, took a tentative step forward, and rested his head on her shoulder.

"Poor boy," Karigan said. "I'll see to Ereal. I promise."

She caressed him for a time, then slipped the halter she had brought over his nose and ears, and led him away from his slain Rider.

Karigan watched Ty and Crane ride off and disappear into the night. She sank to the ground and huddled her knees to her chest, staring into the dark long after they were gone.

When she had returned to Sacor City to become a Green Rider, she had a better idea than most new Riders of what dangers messengers faced in the daily execution of their duties. The danger ranged from riding accidents to coming face to face with cutthroats seeking king's gold. And of course, there was battle.

Even so she had not been prepared for this. Trained for fighting, yes. Trained to deal with burying friends, no.

Karigan thought back to the murals of the gods down in the tomb, their faces averted, their hands up in denial. Maybe they had abandoned the delegation, for hadn't they allowed all this to happen?

I do not regret this life, Bard had said just hours ago, but he said it thinking ahead to the future when he'd finally pursue his dream of studying at Selium. Now he would never fulfill that dream. It had all been cut short. Cut short by his duty as a Green Rider.

Journal of Hadriax el Fex

Though we have been here two months, I still marvel over the magnificence of these New Lands. The coast is rugged with thick spires of evergreens that grow boundlessly beyond the horizon. We could make fleets upon fleets of ships from them for the Empire. Our own vessels rest at anchor in a large bay the inhabitants call Ull-um.

These lands have no lack of resources—abundant wildlife and amazing fisheries. Vast schools of fish swim in the bay, and it is almost impossible not to catch them. Captain Verano laughed that they were trying to flip right into his gig as he sailed about the bay.

This is a primitive place, wild and nearly untouched. The fresh water is cool and refreshing, and the air good to breathe, far better than the noxious vapors above our cities in Arcosia, and the dying lands that surround them. This is a vital place.

We have also found evidence of etherea. Mostly it is the heathen priests who possess the use of the art, and it is used in the most ridiculous "religious" ceremonies to prove they are touched by the favor of their numerous gods. Alessandros and I have been much amused by their displays. Alessandros has not yet shown them his own command of the art, and has likewise ordered the other mages to conceal their abilities for the time being.

The Sacor people are squalid, living in rough longhouses, their children crawling on dirt floors with vermin and dogs. They are warlike among one another, the chieftains waging war over petty differences. They are quite in awe of our fine dress and trinkets, and look upon our mechanicals with some curiosity and fear. Alessandros thinks these people should be easy to tame, and will welcome the embrace of the Empire.

≪ THE SUMMER THRONE ROOM ≫

*S*ix . . .
     Laren Mapstone, captain of His Majesty's Messenger Service, the Green Riders, silently counted off the hours as the distant notes of the bell tolled down in Sacor City.

Seven . . .

The bell had been installed in the Chapel of the Moon's tower on the occasion of the king's last birthday. It—and the rumbling of her stomach—reminded her all too well that the supper hour had come and gone quite some time ago.

Eight . . .

The final doleful tone hung in the air for a time before mercifully fading away. Laren grimaced and shifted her stance, eyeing the king's elderly castellan with envy. Sperren slept as peacefully as a baby in his chair. She, on the other hand, had been standing for hours at the king's side as he listened to petitioners. Her back was killing her.

Nothing unusual, she thought.

Lord-Governor D'Ivary now stood before King Zachary. He had ambled into the throne room just as the king was ready to pronounce the long day done, but with eminent patience, Zachary granted D'Ivary an audience and listened as the longwinded lord-governor blustered and complained of refugees from the north flooding into his provincial lands.

Colin Dovekey, one of the king's advisors, sat in his own

chair with his chin propped on his fist, stone-faced but attentive. All others, except for the statuelike black-clad Weapons standing in alcoves along the walls, had abandoned the throne room hours ago. The lingering gold-orange summer light cast hazy columns through the west side windows. Soon pages would enter to light lamps.

"I appreciate your concerns, Lord D'Ivary," King Zachary said.

Laren watched the king carefully as he gazed down at the lord-governor and his secretary standing at the base of the dais. Zachary's features appeared placid and unperturbed, his tone even and polite. But Laren, who had known him since he was a boy, noted the slight tightening of his jaw and the narrowing of his brow.

"Begging your indulgence, sire," D'Ivary said, "but I'm not sure you do appreciate the extent of my concerns." He was a pear-shaped fellow who had a tendency to thrust his belly about as though his recently acquired power and status were a physical thing. Laren failed to dismiss an image of an overfed rooster.

Hedric D'Ivary had arisen to his current position after the death of his elder cousin. The former lady-governor had left no surviving heirs, forcing the provincial clan elders to debate over who the most suitable successor was. They had chosen Hedric.

The process of choosing a new lord-governor was painstaking and prickly business, for should the current monarch's line fail, any lord-governor was eligible to assume the monarchy. In the past, this had led to grim and bloody civil war.

Other provinces had recently undergone this process, for many nobles had been murdered during Prince Amilton's coup attempt a little over two years ago. Several new lord-governors, or "new bloods" as their more established counterparts had taken to calling them, had never expected to rise to such a lofty position in life, and relished their new power. They lacked the tradition and statesmanship of their predecessors. The governing clans were in flux, and so were their loyalties. King Zachary had his hands full.

"These 'refugees' as you call them—outlaws and cut-throats I call them—wander the countryside and set up their shanties wherever they please," Lord D'Ivary said. "Never mind if it's a field under cultivation or pasture land. It's thrown the common folk who cultivate that land into disarray, and mark my words, there will be trouble come harvest time. Even our towns suffer. They beg in the streets, these refugees, and resort to thieving when no one hands over what they want."

Much of what D'Ivary said was true to a degree, Laren knew, without even having to touch her special ability to read him. The other lord-governor feeling the brunt of the northern exodus, Jaston Adolind, had issued a similar complaint. Groundmite attacks in the north had scared enough settlers that whole villages had packed up and moved south into more civilized and protected provincial lands. The towns and farmsteads were ill prepared to accommodate the influx. Adolind, poorest of all the provinces, suffered a good deal more than D'Ivary. While there might be a cut-throat element among some of the refugees, however, most were simply families seeking safety.

"Could it be," Colin Dovekey said in his gruff voice, "that this is an internal matter which you must resolve within your own province?"

D'Ivary turned to him, jutting his belly out and lifting his chin. *Chins, rather,* Laren thought. "I would not be here if it were an internal matter. I haven't the resources to cope with these people."

Colin raised a bushy gray eyebrow, searing through D'Ivary with hawk's eyes, an intensity borne of twenty-five years as a Weapon. "Your lands are counted among the most fertile and rich in all of Sacoridia, my lord. You haven't the resources?"

"Yes, I've fertile lands now being occupied by squatters who trample and ruin growing crops and steal livestock. The nobles who look to me have not the resources to patrol every acre of their holdings to remove these people before the harvest is destroyed."

"Ah," the king said with a soft intonation. "I now see what resources you are speaking of. You seek to forcibly remove these refugees, but you haven't the soldiers to do so."

D'Ivary brightened, thinking he had at last found a sympathetic ear. "Yes, sire. In D'Ivary, we are farmers, not soldiers. This is not something we could do ourselves."

"Tell me," the king said, steepling his fingers, "what would you do if you had the necessary troops?"

"I would have them patrol the countryside and weed out the squatters, and return them to the north. Then I would seal off the northern borders except to those who have legitimate business in the province. Armed soldiers would be just the thing. A display of force is the only tactic they'll understand. They have shown nothing but insolence to provincial and local authorities thus far."

"So, if I understand your request," the king said, with a slight smile, "you wish for me to provide you with the force necessary to remove these people. A force bearing the royal banner of Sacoridia."

D'Ivary grinned. "You understand my needs completely, sire. A king must show his strength to his people."

A silence hung in the air.

When the king finally replied, his voice was entirely reasonable. He did not shout, yet his rebuke resonated with kingly resolve. "You forget yourself, Lord D'Ivary. These people you seek to remove forcibly under the royal banner of Sacoridia *are* Sacoridians. They may look to no lord—not even to me, their king—to govern them in the northern wild-lands, but they still live within Sacoridia's borders.

"Do you fail to comprehend their importance to commerce? They provide the timber and pelts our merchants require. They have also been a buffer in the north, fighting off raiders. Fighting for survival is an everyday occurrence for them, making them independent-minded. Only now has the frequency and intensity of groundmite attacks forced them to seek safe harbor. And you would turn them out, refusing them help in their hour of need?"

Zachary shook his head in disbelief. "In time these folk may tame the north, further strengthening Sacoridia's commerce, and its borders. Until then, Lord D'Ivary, Sacoridia may be made up of twelve provinces and the free holdings of the borders, but it is all one land. Devastating battles were fought to unify this country, and I will not turn Sacoridian against Sacoridian.

"Think of some other way to *help* them. Your cousin, the late lady-governor, might have found some other solution in which the refugees were put to work assisting with farming in exchange for food and lodging."

D'Ivary's smile faded to a ghost of itself, and a hardness settled into his eyes. "My cousin was a kindly soul, but weak-minded. A flaw with her line."

Laren clenched her hands behind her back. His cousin had died because she courageously resisted Amilton's claim to rule. She had died in this very room, a torturous, painful death. Weak-minded, indeed.

"She allowed our provincial militia to dwindle to a house guard. My nobles would be hard pressed to call up an army of commoners more interested in farming, as they should be. These northern outlanders are of no use to my province."

"Not all strength is shown in force of arms," Zachary said.

D'Ivary rubbed his chin, a shrewd gleam lighting in his eyes. "Well said, sire. I could not agree more. For instance, there is the matter of an heir to ensure the strength of Sacoridia's rule. I would not be alone in expressing concern about the country's stability should no heir be produced within a reasonable amount of time."

The king froze at the abrupt change of topic—a veiled threat?—his knuckles whitening as he clenched the polished armrests of his throne. Laren could tell he struggled to contain himself. The *scritch-scratch* of a pen as D'Ivary's secretary made notes was counterpoint to silence.

It would not be the first time the matter of an heir had been brought up, nor would it be the last. It seemed every noble in the lands desired to parade a daughter or sister before Zachary in hopes of securing the favor and alliance of the high king. One eastern lord-governor in particular had been more persistent than the rest.

Had Zachary's father lived longer, no doubt this matter would have been resolved long ago. Left to his own devices, however, Zachary turned away all prospects, and this one issue he refused to discuss with Laren. His subjects called him, appropriately enough, the "Bachelor King," and the situation was a favored topic of speculation among aristocratic circles. Laren had even caught wind of actual wagering; nobles casting lots on who and when Zachary might marry.

To keep the confidence of the realm, to end this speculation, he must marry one of suitable rank and produce a royal heir. *Soon.*

Laren found his resistance confounding. There were no ongoing illicit romances, despite various rumors of a secret lover tucked away in some tiny hamlet on the coast somewhere, and though he had not always led the chaste life of a cleric, he hadn't even sired any bastards. She had checked.

Colin Dovekey broke the tense silence. "We were speaking of refugees."

"And so we were," D'Ivary murmured, his gaze intent on the king.

Zachary crossed his legs. He was not in good humor, but he refused to rise to D'Ivary's bait. "I do not condone the use of force," he said, ignoring the subject of an heir altogether. "Nor will I provide you with soldiers. Much of my force is patrolling the north anyway. If the refugees are such a drain on the province, find a way to make use of them so they help themselves. Lord Adolind has found a way to manage, and he possesses fewer resources than D'Ivary Province."

D'Ivary scowled, then forced a neutral expression on his face.

Zachary leaned forward. "Not so long ago you swore an oath of fealty to me when you took on the mantle of lord-governor. Will you give me your word on your honor that no harm will come to these refugees?"

D'Ivary puffed out his cheeks. "Of course, sire." He bowed. "I shall abide by your wishes. On my honor."

Laren fingered her winged horse brooch, reaching out to D'Ivary with her special ability to determine the honesty of his words. The answer came to her like a caress in her mind, and it surprised her.

After D'Ivary departed with his secretary in tow, the king turned his gaze upon her. No longer the stern king, he simply looked a very weary man.

"Well?" he said.

Laren smiled weakly. "He spoke truth. He will not harm those people."

Zachary raised his eyebrows. "You are certain?"

"It was a clear reading."

He removed the shiny silver fillet from his brow and passed his fingers through light, amber hair. "Of course. I shouldn't even have to ask. You've never been wrong before. It's just . . . It's just that he's difficult to trust."

"That goes for the whole cartload of 'em," Colin said. "The lord-governors."

The grumpy disgust in his voice made Laren and Zachary—both tired by the long day themselves—laugh.

"Truly," the king said, as the laughter died down, "as much as those border people disdain governance, they are within our borders. With no lord to speak for them, especially to the likes of Hedric D'Ivary, they've only me."

"And not the sense to appreciate it," Colin muttered.

Hear, hear, Laren thought. The border people had no notion of the champion they had in their king. They certainly wouldn't thank him for it even if they knew. Non-interference was what they desired in their lives—until they needed help, of course. While she agreed with Zachary's support of them, it would not endear him further to the lord-governors, or to the hardworking folk of the provinces who faithfully paid their taxes and obeyed king's law.

Before they could speak further, there was a commotion at the throne room entrance. A boy in the livery of the Green Foot burst through the doorway and hustled down the throne room runner. Laren and Zachary exchanged glances, wondering what else could possibly happen this day.

The boy slid to his knees before the king, and Laren grimaced at the clumsy obeisance, but she observed the hint of an amused smile lingering on Zachary's lips. Perhaps he remembered himself as a boy.

"Rise, lad," he said.

The boy did so, cheeks pink from running. He was no more than eleven years old with a mop of sandy hair falling over his eyes.

"You've a message for King Zachary, Josh?" Laren asked.

The boy looked startled to hear his name issue from her lips. The runners of the Green Foot regarded her as rather imposing, she knew, from discussions with Gerad, their leader.

"Ma'am . . . Captain," the boy faltered, with a slight tremble to his lower lip. "Yes'm. I've a message."

The Green Foot consisted of fleet youngsters—many of them offspring of the lesser nobility or favored servants—who ran messages about the castle. They were placed here to learn the ways of court, and to attend the castle's little school, definitely a boon to those with impoverished families. Melry, Laren's adopted daughter, had run messages for the Green Foot before going off to school in Selium.

Unlike Green Riders, they fulfilled no magical calling to do their work, nor were they gifted with any special abilities. Laren did not oversee their day to day operations, but Gerad reported to her as a formality.

Because the Green Foot did resemble the Riders—they wore messenger green with little winged feet embroidered in gold on their sleeves—and because they were, after all, messengers serving an important function, Laren made sure she knew each youngster's name, and that they understood their responsibilities and proper conduct in court. She would speak to Gerad later about Josh's rather graceless demeanor before the king.

Josh turned to the king but looked at his feet. "Word has been passed up from the main gate that Major Everson and Captain Ansible have ridden through the first wall and are on the Winding Way this very moment."

Laren immediately forgave the boy any impropriety whatsoever, even those as yet uncommitted. The delegation—at least its last remnant—had finally come home.

⋘ RETURNINGS ⋙

After Josh's announcement, the sleepy throne room came to life. Servants were beckoned and Josh was sent off to alert the mending wing to prepare for the arrival of the wounded. Word was sent to barracks and stables to prepare as well.

A table was brought out and set with food and drink, and pages came through lighting extra lamps as the last glint of daylight waned in the west side windows. Sperren continued to snooze in his chair, not at all disturbed from his dreams by the commotion. Laren, Zachary, and Colin waited, and for Laren, the waiting was intolerable.

When Ty had ridden ahead with news of the attack on the delegation, he told them all he knew at the time. That had been several weeks ago. Now that the others had made their way home, perhaps holes in his story could be filled in. The waiting would be over.

It would be over, too, for those wanting word of their loved ones. Laren could see in her mind's eye people gathered at the castle gate, straining to glimpse the return of a husband, sister, father . . . Some would end their evening rejoicing, others in heartbreak.

It had been hard enough, she thought, to see Ty riding onto the castle grounds on Ereal's Crane. She had known instantly what it meant. And then to hear of Bard, too . . .

She tried to shudder away the dark thoughts, but they

clung to her like her very own shadow. It was a shadow that grew darker and heavier with the passing of each Rider under her command, and she wondered if it had been the same for every other captain that had preceded her.

Successions of Green Foot runners brought news of the delegation's progress. The bulk of it was slowed down by carts carrying the wounded, but Major Everson and Captain Ansible rode ahead with an escort. And, oh yes, the runner told Laren, the Green Rider was with them, too.

At that, Laren took heart and loosed a sigh of relief, much more loudly than intended, and Colin glanced sharply at her. She didn't care. All her Riders were now accounted for. Karigan had come home.

Not long after the ringing of nine hour, Neff the herald hurried down the runner to inform them that they had at last arrived.

The three entered slowly, for Captain Ansible leaned heavily on a crutch that looked to be fashioned from a stout tree branch. Major Everson and Karigan kept pace with him out of deference. Ansible looked to have aged a hundred years—his skin had gone gray from sickness, and his chin and now-gaunt cheeks were covered by silvery beard bristles. His uniform, such as it was, hung from his shoulders. It was quite a change from the impeccable officer she knew him to be.

To Ansible's right walked Major Everson, who looked sharp and well fed as only an officer of the light horse could, all shiny buttons and high polished boots. Upon Ty's return, the king had ordered the cavalry to intercept, aid, and protect the survivors of the delegation. Everson was a grotesque contrast to his haunted companions, beaming from behind an ostentatious mustache as though he were entirely responsible for the deliverance of the delegation.

Karigan walked at Ansible's left. She wore her hair tightly bound back which made the hollows of her cheeks stand out all the more. Her swordbelt slipped down her hips and she hastily snatched it back up. Every movement of her body suggested exhaustion and she walked with a footsore gait. Her boots, Laren noted, looked worn as if she had done more walking than riding. What of Condor?

Karigan's entrance held faint resemblance to one she had made a year or so ago. Laren well-remembered *that* whole affair; she could still hear Neff's voice ringing through the throne room as he announced Karigan's name—and *title:* "Karigan G'ladheon, sub-chief of Clan G'ladheon!"

Zachary and Laren had exchanged surprised glances, surprised because they thought by this time never to see her here again.

Karigan had been accompanied by an entourage of a cargo master and guards, a secretary, and numerous servants; an entourage large enough to rival any noble's. Zachary stood—unconsciously, Laren had thought—as Karigan glided down the runner, the sun that slanted through the tall windows shining on long brown hair, worn loose across her shoulders. She was draped in elegant silks of purple and blue, the clan colors.

When finally she had come before the throne, she put her hand to her heart and bowed. Her entourage was two seconds behind in emulating her.

What followed was an unbelievable display of wares— servants bringing before Laren and Zachary bolts of high quality wools dyed a perfect forest green, five different grades of leather, from supple to hard, gold silk and thread for formal uniforms, furs to line winter greatcoats, and the finest linens Laren had ever seen. Servants presented hogsheads filled with buttons and buckles, and samples of silver and iron.

Stevic G'ladheon was following up on his agreement to supply the Green Riders, but previous shipments had gone straight to the quartermaster without much ado, and none had been of this magnitude. It made Laren wonder what lay behind this display. Had Karigan come to flaunt her status as sub-chief and her defiance of the Rider call? If so, such arrogance was not like the Karigan she remembered.

Laren glanced at Zachary and had to do a double take. He looked entranced, not so much by the wares brought before him, but by Karigan, who supervised her servants with gentle authority, using but a nod or a gesture of her hand to direct them. She held herself, well, aristocratically, a description she would not have appreciated. She had matured a good deal since last they had seen her. Zachary's expression was inscrutable.

When the display of wares finally ceased, Karigan had said, "Clan G'ladheon makes one final offering." She turned to the cargo master and started pulling rings off her fingers. "Sevano, these are my official seals and clan rings. Please see that they return home safely."

The old man's eyes grew large. "What are ye doing, lass? Those are important—"

She did not stop but removed a medallion from around her neck. "I do not need this either."

Laren thought the old man was going to faint. "Your authority from the guild as—as sub-chief. What are ye doing?"

Karigan ignored his question and turned to her secretary, who blanched. "Robert, I will leave all receipts, ledgers, and written authorities in your care."

Addressing all her people she said, "This decision was made over a month ago." She removed her cloak and handed it to a servant. When she faced Laren and the king again, Laren saw not only the glitter of tears in her eyes, but pinned to her blouse, the gold winged horse brooch which had lain concealed beneath her cloak.

This all had been a carefully executed statement after all, Laren thought. Not a flaunting of what Karigan had become, but a demonstration of what she was giving up.

Karigan then fell to her knee before Zachary, her deep blue skirts pooling on the floor around her. She bowed her head. "I offer my service to the king as a Green Rider."

Laren's heart sang with gladness and she saw a flash of triumph in Zachary's eyes. He stepped down the dais, took her hand, and raised her to her feet. "I accept."

In Karigan's face, she saw not only resignation, but relief. Relief of a deed finally done.

After Karigan's bewildered entourage had left, and before the Chief Rider could come collect Karigan to get her outfitted and situated at Rider barracks, Karigan had handed Laren an envelope with the G'ladheon seal on it.

"From my father," Karigan said.

When Laren unsealed it much later, she found the message simple and direct: *Take care of her.*

Laren was certain, as she looked upon Karigan now, almost an entire year later, that Stevic G'ladheon would be much displeased with her. As the trio neared, she caught more details—the pink healing cut across Karigan's cheekbone, and what might be mudstains on her shortcoat . . . or dried bloodstains. Was the blood Karigan's, or that of the enemy? She grimaced, imagining Stevic G'ladheon's ire.

Yet she could not coddle Karigan no matter her father's wishes. It was now Karigan's duty to serve, just as the other Riders must serve, even if it meant facing untold dangers. Even death.

Everson bent to his knee before the king with a flourish. Ansible managed a nod of his head. Karigan's own obeisance looked so exhausted as to be painful.

"Welcome home, friends," Zachary said. He had removed his king's mask, Laren noted, not concealing his concern and genuine joy at their return.

"Glad to be out of that tangle of woods," Everson said, his thumbs hooked in his belt. "Give me a good, clear field for a direct charge at full gallop any day."

Laren fought the urge to wind the curlicues of his mustache around her fingers and yank. Her own Riders never, or at least hardly ever, complained about hard travel through Sacoridia's thick forestlands. The light horse was just a bit too pampered to Laren's mind, but it was, after all, the territory of the privileged. Few commoners filled its ranks; it consisted mostly of the offspring of nobles with no land to inherit. They sought to make their name in the military, and gravitated to the elite light horse. It took a special appointment by an important sponsor to get in, something far easier for a noble to obtain than a commoner.

Many years ago, during the reign of the Sealenders, the captain of the Green Riders answered to superiors in the light horse, but that had ended with King Smidhe's reign, for which Laren was grateful. The king had reverted the Riders to an independent force, answerable only to him and his successors, just as the First Rider had originally intended when she founded the messenger service.

Rider tradition rejected the chain of command above and beyond the authority of captain—except for the king, of course, who was their ultimate authority—and they possessed more independence than members of the other branches of the military. Considering the covert nature of some of the work Zachary required of his messengers, it was a good thing.

"Please sit," Zachary said. "I know how weary you must be from your travels." He clapped and servants moved the table and chairs before the throne. Wine was poured and meat brought forth. Even Laren got to sit finally, but her appetite was considerably diminished by the appearance of Ansible and Karigan.

Karigan nibbled a little at her food, but the effort seemed too much for her. Everson speared a slab of roast for himself and ate with relish. Between mouthfuls, he spoke of how he and his troops intercepted the delegation several miles beyond the North Road.

"As sorry a group as you could expect," he said. "Two hundred diminished to forty-three. Half or more injured, and half again so injured they could not walk or ride. Ten more perished with the traveling. I find it remarkable they got so far on their own.

"We set up camp so our menders could look to the wounded. Rider G'ladheon here showed me and some scouts to the clearing where the battle had been fought." Everson shook his head. "Terrible. Our folk had been placed in a mass grave, but the area was alive with carrion birds feasting on groundmites and horses. Other beasts had been at them, too, and these snarled from the shadows of the forest at our intrusion."

Karigan pushed her food away, eyes downcast as Everson described the scene. It was the most unanimated Laren had ever seen her, as if she weren't even there at all. Little wonder after what she'd been through, and now Everson was bringing it all back to life as he described the scene of death.

"Eletians aided us with our dead," Captain Ansible said, speaking up for the first time. "They helped us with the burying, among other things in the aftermath of the battle. If not for their medicines, I would have lost my leg at the very least, and probably my life from wound fever. We'd have lost even more people, too, if not for their aid."

"I would like to hear more about the Eletians," Zachary said, "but perhaps we should start with the beginning."

"I may not be the one to tell you of the beginning," Ansible said, with a brief aside to Karigan. "You see, when the 'mites attacked, I was well asleep on my cot. It had been an evening like so many that had come before . . ."

He went on to describe being awakened by shouts and the clatter of battle, and how he had quickly thrown himself into the fray, fighting for order among the lines, trying to draw his soldiers shoulder to shoulder around the clearing's perimeter to defend themselves, with the nobles and servants within.

"It was working," he said. "Our lines held tight. Where one defender fell, another took his place. I never did see who took mine when the 'mite blade caught me in the leg." His hand went absently to his bandaged thigh and he shook his head. "That 'mite saved my life."

Laren leaned forward, anxious for him to explain the curious statement. The captain's eyes took on a faraway look, and then he shuddered.

"Many pardons," he murmured. "I was, at the time, in great pain and stunned. But even now, I have a difficult time believing it all."

"Take your time," Zachary said.

Ansible inclined his head in thanks, and took a long draught from a cup of wine before him. He licked his lips and began again.

"I had fallen from the line, practically beneath the feet of the 'mites. My whole body was pressed to the ground. I felt it tremble—the ground trembled with thunder, and when I looked up, it was . . . it was like all the lightning of the heavens was contained in that clearing. I can still feel the heat of it . . . the hairs raising on my arms, the sensation of that loosed power crawling across my skin." He shook his head. "I saw it sluice right through my soldiers—through anyone in its way. *Everyone* in the clearing. Magic, the Eletians said it was. Magical wards erupting." He made the sign of the crescent moon with his fingers. "And then . . . and then . . ."

"A wraith came through," Karigan supplied. "Its emergence from the tomb set off the wards."

Everyone looked at her, astonished to hear her voice as though she were a wraith herself.

"I saw nothing," Ansible said. "Just felt as though I wanted to hide myself under the nearest rock."

Ty had said something very like this, of a terrible *something* that had fought its way through the dying wards and emerged from the clearing. He had glimpsed only a shadow before it disappeared.

Captain Ansible would say nothing more of the wraith, but he went on to speak of the Eletians appearing in their "moon armor," as he called it, and of their aid.

"They were led by a fellow named Telagioth. Tall he was, with eyes of blue that . . ." He shook his head as words failed him. "An odd folk in any case. I have never seen their like. This Telagioth, he was intent to speak to Rider G'ladheon here, but how he knew of her, I am not certain."

Laren watched as the king's gaze swung over to Karigan and rested there, a thoughtful expression on his face. Karigan stared into her cup of tea as though sunk deeply into her own world. She clenched the porcelain teacup so hard Laren feared she would crush it.

"Rider G'ladheon," the king said, his voice soft, "perhaps you could tell us your version of events."

Karigan looked up, blinking. For an odd moment, Laren swore she saw a figure standing just beyond her, a shimmer like a wave of heat. She blinked her eyes to clear them, but it was still there—a tall figure, but without definition. It hovered there as if waiting or listening. Listening?

This time Laren rubbed at her eyes, and when she looked again, the figure was gone.

I haven't had enough to eat, she thought. *I'm seeing things.*

True, her ability told her, without her requesting feedback. She wondered which was true—that she hadn't had enough to eat, or that she was seeing things.

Both, she decided.

⋙ KARIGAN SPEAKS ⋘

"**I** could not sleep," Karigan began, "so I went to the pickets to check on Condor."

As Karigan spoke, Laren found herself drawn into the inky black of the forest night and the hush of the slumbering encampment, the embers of distant campfires glowing orange. Even as Karigan described it, she felt the jolt of discovering the soldier impaled in the chest by a groundmite arrow. Details about the actual battle were few. It was as if Karigan did not wish to relive the fighting, and so spoke very little of it.

"I found myself on the outskirts of the battle and witnessed the eruption of the wards just as Captain Ansible described." Karigan spoke carefully, sitting rigidly. She set her teacup aside. "I saw the wraith pass through the wardings. Moments later, it approached me through the woods."

This Ty had not told Laren. Perhaps in the aftermath of battle, and due to Ty's quick departure, there had been no opportunity for him to learn of it.

"The wraith—it knew my name," Karigan said.

The room grew ominously quiet. Everyone was intent on Karigan. Even the fresco painted figures on the ceiling, the likenesses of Zachary's ancestors, seemed to listen.

"Rather," Karigan corrected herself in reflection, "it called me *Galadheon,* as did the Eletians."

Disturbed, Zachary stood. Everyone rose with him as

protocol demanded, Ansible struggling. "No," the king said, "please remain seated." He rounded the table and placed one hand on Ansible's shoulder and the other on Karigan's, pressing them back into their chairs. Laren sank into her own. "Please continue," he told Karigan.

Karigan seemed to struggle with something before she spoke. Finally she said, "The wraith also called me 'Betrayer.'"

Everyone remained silent, Zachary standing behind Karigan and slightly to her left. It brought back to mind the—the *whatever* Laren had seen before. Maybe it had been a film in her eye.

Colin Dovekey broke the silence. "How in the name of five hells would this creature know you, Rider? And are you certain it spoke this word to you? Battle can disorient one's mind."

"Yes, sir, I am certain the wraith called me 'Betrayer.' I have no idea as to why, or how it might know me. I realize how strange this must sound . . . It has been strange for *me*. It was a terrible time, a nightmare. I—" and she struggled for words again. "I have thought about this long and hard, but still I have no answers."

Zachary started pacing, head bowed in thought. "The name . . . G'ladheon is no doubt a contraction from an older name. Perhaps an error in census records caused the change, and it was adopted as the true name of the line. Or maybe it changed as things do in the course of generations passing. No doubt this wraith has abilities—magical knowledges beyond our ken. We are dealing with a very different kind of threat. An unknown threat."

The feeble glow of the lamps seemed unable to fend off the weight of night. The windows were coated with black, and darkness had settled into the throne room's corners and rafters.

"How did you escape this wraith?" Colin asked Karigan.

"I did not escape it. The Eletians came. This seemed to frighten it off, though I'm not sure 'frighten' is the appropriate term." She paused, caught in some memory, her fingers touching the fading wound on her cheek. Then she went on to describe her meeting with Telagioth and how he led her beneath the cairn and into the tomb.

Zachary halted his pacing, a spasm of anger fluttering across his features. "To what purpose? Why would he take you into that creature's tomb? That was an unnecessary risk. Who knows what else could have been down there?"

Still caught up in her memories, Karigan didn't appear to note Zachary's anger on her behalf. "He wished to show me that this tomb was, in fact, more a prison. The wraith, he told me, was once a living man, a favorite of Mornhavon's, granted an unending existence in return for his servitude. Telagioth wanted to impress upon me that many things from the past are reawakening."

Karigan turned in her chair to more directly face Zachary. "Excellency, he asked me to tell you the following." And in what Laren liked to call "messenger voice," Karigan recited the message as close to the original as possible, just as she had been trained. "He said that the passage of Eletians through your lands is peaceful, that they merely watch. Sacoridia lies in the immediate path of anything that should pass through the D'Yer Wall. He said you must turn your attention there, and not to seek out Eletia. Eletia shall parley with you when the time is deemed appropriate."

"The D'Yers now watch the wall," Zachary said. Anger still lingered in his eyes. "The immediate threat has been to the north. I do not trust these Eletians."

"For good reason," Laren murmured, thinking of Shawdell who had sought to tear down the D'Yer Wall.

"They did help us, sire," Ansible reminded them. "If they had not come, who knows what that wraith might have wrought upon the survivors? The fact the evil thing fled the

Eletians ought to say something to the good of them, and I've already spoken of their aid to us in the aftermath of the battle."

"There are varying degrees of good," Colin said, "and their contempt in crossing our borders without seeking the king's leave says another thing about them. To say they will parley with the king when *they* deem appropriate is cavalier in the extreme."

"All of this could have been avoided," Major Everson said, slicing a wedge of cheese off a wheel, "if Lady Penburn had had the sense to listen to that bounder."

"This is not the time for judgments," Zachary said, "but mourning. She followed her best instincts."

"Which I supported," Ansible growled. "I supported her decision to use that clearing. It is easy to say aught else after the fact."

Everson put up his hands. "No offense intended, Captain."

The truth was that Lady Penburn's death was a blow to Zachary when so many supporters among the old bloods had perished at his brother's hands. Now Penburn Province, Laren's own home province, would have a new lord-governor, the lady's first-born son. Where would *his* loyalties lie?

"What became of the bounder?" Colin asked. "It may be useful to question him."

"Died of his wounds," Karigan said. The haunted look returned to her eyes. Then she gazed directly at Major Everson. "The decision to camp in the clearing was unfortunate for the delegation, but even if we had not, it wouldn't have prevented the wraith's escape."

A silence built up in the throne room again. Zachary stood at the end of the table gazing down at Ansible and Karigan. The anger left him and something like pity softened his features.

"We have detained you here long enough," he said. "There is time enough to answer questions later after you have had sufficient rest from your terrible journey."

Ansible started to protest, but Zachary cut him off. "You have done your duty this night, Captain."

As Karigan and Ansible slowly made their way out of the throne room, Laren watched the king watching after them. Another monarch might not prove so compassionate, instead retaining them to be questioned long into the night. She could read the concern etched into his features as he watched them. This compassion was one reason Laren was so fiercely loyal to him. She would fight to the death to ensure his reign continued.

She would also, in her role as advisor, see to it that this same compassion never jeopardized the peace of Sacoridia, or Zachary himself.

Laren wished to follow Karigan out. She wanted to question her further without the others present, but she couldn't leave yet, and of course the king had excused Karigan so she might find rest—not get interrogated by her curious captain. It was just that she sensed something had been left unsaid, and it nagged at her. She sighed. No doubt Mara would see that Karigan was comfortably settled into her room at barracks.

As if to contradict her thoughts, Karigan reappeared at the throne room entrance. She strode back toward them with purpose, now unhindered by having to keep in step with Captain Ansible.

"Forgive me, Excellency," she said, bowing her head. "I meant to leave some things in Captain Mapstone's care."

"There is no reason to ask forgiveness, Rider," he said.

"Thank you." Karigan rounded the table and stood before Laren. She rummaged in her message satchel and withdrew an object which she clasped tightly in her hand.

"Captain," she said, "this was Ereal's." She pressed cold

metal into Laren's palm. Ereal's brooch. The gold of it winked in the lamplight.

"She died trying to bring my sword to me," Karigan said. "She was always watching out for me during the journey. Two arrows took her. Even while she lay dying, she tried to 'carry' the sword to me."

The expressions of the others, except Zachary, were baffled. They could not see the brooch as a Rider could, nor would they know that Ereal's special ability had been moving things with her mind. Laren swallowed as she looked at the brooch cradled in her hand, her throat constricted. She saw also what it cost Karigan to do this. She had gone pale, fighting memories.

Karigan reached into her satchel again and there was a flicker of gold when her hand re-emerged. "This was Bard's." But when she handed it over, it was not a brooch perfectly shaped as a horse rising into air, wings outstretched for flight. No, it was a formless blob of melted gold.

"The eruption of the wards killed him," Karigan said. "The magic of the wards did this to his brooch."

Before Laren could reply, Karigan bowed again to Zachary and hastened from the throne room as fast as her sore feet could carry her.

Laren gazed down at the brooch and the melted gold in her hand. The brooches always found their way home when a Rider met his or her end. It was astonishing, really. The Rider might be gone, but the brooches always returned home to carry on the mission of the messenger service. It had been this way for a thousand years.

We are mortal and fleeting in our time on Earth, she thought, *but these endure.* She closed her fingers around them. The brooches may return, but there were too few who heard the Rider call these days. She had far more brooches than Riders. Would someone one day hear the call and wear

Ereal's, as had generations of Riders before her? Or, would it remain untouched in the coffer in Laren's quarters with the others as the messenger service dwindled out of existence?

And what of Bard's brooch? Could it be reforged? How could an ordinary blacksmith see it to reforge it? Even if it could be reforged, where was the mold that was used in the original making of the brooches? Would Bard's lump of gold even retain its magic?

Laren shook her head. In this Age, there were many questions, for the answers had been lost. Like the secrets of the D'Yer Wall . . . Things that must have been common knowledge at one time were unknown to the current generation.

If I had some of that old knowledge, she wondered, *would Bard and Ereal still be alive?*

It was impossible to say, and of no use to even consider, for it would change nothing. She would never hear Bard sing again, nor would she ever watch on in satisfaction as Ereal and Crane once again crossed the finish line of a Day of Aeryon race far ahead of every other competitor.

No, she had but her own experience and wisdom to rely upon, and often those seemed paltry enough. Her shadow was growing heavy, indeed.

"Laren?"

She started, not realizing the king had come to her. He touched her wrist.

"It is eleven hour and we're all tired."

Eleven hour? Only then did Laren register the dreadful bell clanging again down in the city. When had ten hour passed them by?

Old Sperren finally stirred. "What have I missed?" he demanded of Colin. "I see food here. What have I missed?"

"It is my wish," Zachary said quietly to her, "that you return to your quarters and rest. You've been standing by my side all day. We all shall retire, and perhaps when we are refreshed by a night's sleep, we can examine things anew."

Laren was so relieved to be dismissed, she could have kissed him on the cheek, but professional restraint held her back. It might have been all right when he was but a boy and she his "big sister," but not now, and not here.

As she started away, Major Everson rose from the table and called after her.

"Yes, Major?"

"That Rider of yours," he said, "young G'ladheon. Should you ever feel inclined to release her from the messenger service, I'd be more than happy to sponsor her into the light horse."

Laren was so taken aback she almost laughed in his face.

"What do you think?" he asked.

Never, was what she thought, but what she said was, "You may ask Rider G'ladheon herself, and I shall respect her decision should she choose such an opportunity." Laren felt safe knowing it unlikely the Rider call would release her.

"Perhaps I shall. She comported herself well and without complaint through the duration of our travels, helping with the wounded and camp duties. I had my doubts, her being the daughter of a merchant and all, but frankly I could use more like her."

Laren raised an eyebrow. If the Rider call did not prevent Karigan from joining the light horse, her distaste for the sort of elitism exhibited by its members would.

Laren walked away thinking she could not afford to lose another Rider, but feeling secure Karigan would not, could not, switch over to the light horse no matter the enticements and privileges that might accompany it.

So I hope.

* * *

"Look at these." Rider Mara Brennyn raised a pair of muddy boots to eye level. There were cracks in the soles and gaps where sewn seams had gone loose.

"Karigan's?" Laren asked.

Mara nodded vigorously. "She practically walked all the way home because of Condor's injury."

"Injury?" Laren groaned inwardly at her own dull responses, but it was late and she was very tired. After taking leave of the king, she had crossed the castle grounds to Rider barracks to ensure Karigan had been settled in. Mara, who now so often filled in as her second, had met her at the door, boots in hand.

Now they stood in the Rider common room, a comfortable place with a stone fireplace and a long table smoothed and notched from use by generations of Riders. It had probably been here since the days of Gwyer Warhein, the Green Rider commander who had ordered the barracks to be built two hundred years ago. There were worn, overstuffed chairs facing the fireplace, a rocking chair or two, and shelves stocked with a few books and games. A single lamp on the table splashed a yellow glow across Mara's face.

"Condor got cut across the fetlock joint," Mara was saying, "during the battle. It is healing quite well, thanks no doubt to his Rider who walked most of the way." She rolled her eyes.

Laren was incredulous. "There was nothing else for her to ride?"

"Remember Ty had said many of the beasts were slaughtered by groundmites?"

"Yes, yes, of course." How could she forget? She closed her eyes, and saw again Ty sitting on Ereal's Crane, not his Flicker.

"What I got from Karigan is that the surviving beasts were used to bear the injured. It wasn't until some of the injured died that she had a mule to ride."

"She is settled in, then?"

Mara nodded. "She about collapsed on her bed. It was all Dale and I could do to pull off her boots and shortcoat."

"Excellent. Let her rest as she will. I will speak to her when she is ready and able."

"Yes, Captain."

Laren left barracks, moving slowly toward officers quarters to savor the quiet of the dew-laden night. The scent of horses came to her as she passed Rider stables, and the lush smell of the pasture grasses beyond. A crescent moon shone sharply in the sky. She discerned guards standing high up on the wall that wrapped around the castle grounds. They were dark silhouettes against a field of stars.

Seemingly everything was normal and as it should be, but she knew this was not so. Talk of the battle and the loosing of the wraith had shaken her. If ancient, dark powers were awakening into her world, how could anything be normal?

Her only hope was that they would be prepared when the time of need was upon them.

Journal of Hadriax el Fex

Alessandros has devoted much time thinking about another people who inhabit these lands. The Clans of Sacor call them Elt, and seem to keep their distance. From what we understand, the Elt live in various kingdoms, the closest being the peninsula to the east of the bay Ull-um. Captain Verano took us for a sail around this peninsula in his gig, but could find no safe landing, for the reefs and currents are treacherous. I am drawing these into the charts I am drafting for the Empire.

Alessandros is keen to find the Elt, for the chief of Hill-lander Clan claims they have much command of etherea. Alessandros plans to mount an expedition into their lands.

⇝ BACK TO BARRACKS ⇝

 ara Brennyn, burdened with a platter of steaming food and a pot of tea, tapped lightly on Karigan's door with the toe of her boot. There had been no sign of life here all morning, and Mara was reluctant to awaken her. But now, as it neared early afternoon, she figured hunger pangs might have surpassed Karigan's exhaustion.

When there was no response to her initial tapping, she tried again, more soundly. When this elicited no response either, she nudged the door open with her foot and found, to her astonishment, the room empty.

Fresh air curled through the open window, and with it the sweet scent of grasses from the pasture. Mussed sheets on the bed indicated Karigan *had* slept here—her arrival last night hadn't been simply a dream of Mara's despite the late hour.

She lowered her burden to the table and blew a crinkled tendril of hair from between her eyes, feeling a bit put out after having carried the platter all the way from the castle kitchens to Rider barracks, only to find Karigan gone. If Mara had been in Karigan's place, she reflected, she'd still be in bed, sleeping for a week or more. And that's where Karigan should be—in bed, recovering from her horrendous journey.

Where is she?

Mara moved to the window, which looked out over the pasture, and then she knew.

Karigan waded through the tall grasses of the pasture to check on Condor, the dark dream that had aroused her earlier finally beginning to dissipate. In the dream, black tree limbs had crashed through her window, the moon gleaming cold and sharp on shattered glass strewn across the floor. Tree limbs had snaked into her room, seeking her, beckoning . . . When she tried to run away, glass shards splintered into bare feet.

She shuddered, though the sunlight fell warmly onto her shoulders. The dream had interrupted an otherwise lovely sleep on a *bed* with a real *pillow*. How long since she had last slept on a bed? All she could recall was rocks and roots. She had made up for some of the lost sleep this morning by wallowing in a blessedly hot bath for over an hour. The still fresh memory of it made her smile.

She came upon Condor grazing in the middle of the pasture, apparently enjoying the sunshine beating down on his back, which gleamed a rich chestnut from the attention Dale had lavished on him.

She checked his wound and was satisfied with how well it had healed. There was no sign of festering or swelling and it even appeared there would be little scarring. She sensed it had more to do with the *evaleoren* salve of the Eletians than anything else. The Eletian who had provided the initial treatment slipped her a pot of the salve, which she used up on the journey home.

She found nothing else to warrant concern. Condor huffed as though annoyed by her attention and moved away to crop at another patch of grass.

I guess I know when I've been dismissed.

Karigan watched after him as he ambled across the pasture, flicking his tail in lazy fashion at flies. There were a few other horses grazing as well. A butterfly flittered over the tops of the grasses, and the song of birds lilted to her from clumps of trees at the base of the wall that bordered the pasture and surrounded the castle grounds. She couldn't quite reconcile this peaceful scene with the darkness of her recent journey. It was as though she had been plucked right out of a nightmare and dropped into this pastoral, tranquil setting.

Nightmares . . . She figured she'd be having them for a while. Who wouldn't?

She turned to head back to barracks only to find Mara striding purposefully toward her.

"He looks good," Mara said, nodding in Condor's direction.

Karigan followed her gaze. "Considering his journey, I'd have to agree." When she turned back to Mara, she found herself under the Rider's critical gaze.

"You, on the other hand," Mara said, "look underfed. I've hauled food all the way from the kitchens to your room only to find you gone."

Karigan smiled sheepishly when her stomach betrayed her with a rumble at the mention of food. Her work tunic and trousers were baggy—she always lost a little weight on a hard run, but this delegation duty had been another thing entirely.

"I suppose I wouldn't mind a bite to eat," she said.

"You *suppose?*" Mara rolled her eyes. "All right then, you follow me."

"Yes, mistress."

Mara emitted a strangled noise as she headed up the slope toward barracks. Karigan grinned, thinking it was good to be back.

* * *

As they neared barracks, a bellow erupted from within that carried out into the sunshine through an open window. Mara hastened her steps, Karigan on her heels wondering what in the world was going on.

Inside, Mara paused in the doorway to the common room, hands on hips, taking in the scene before her. Karigan, stuck behind her in the mud room, peered over her shoulder.

Three Riders occupied the common room. Dale Littlepage sprawled limply in an armchair, helpless with laughter. Garth Bowen towered over Tegan Oldbrine, who struggled to maintain an expression of complete innocence.

Karigan smiled to herself, wondering what Tegan had done this time to rouse Garth's ire.

"I really don't know what you're going on about," Tegan said, "roaring at me like an angry old bear."

Karigan thought Tegan's description of Garth apt—he was large and bearlike, and gregarious, but he also possessed a hot temper when pressed.

"You don't know what I'm going on about?" he demanded.

Dale looked so weak from laughter, Karigan thought she might melt onto the floor.

"My uniform." He waggled his finger in Tegan's face. "You gave me that soap. That's what you did."

"I really don't know what you're talking about," Tegan said. "What could soap have to do with it?"

"As if—as if Clan Oldbrine isn't the pride of the dyers guild!"

"Ahem, Riders," Mara said.

Tegan and Garth turned at her quiet interruption, and it was then that sunshine pouring through the window revealed the basis of the matter. Garth was a big—*yellow*—Rider! His entire uniform was the yellow of sunflower petals. Karigan covered her mouth to muffle a snort, thinking that if they painted black stripes on him, he'd resemble an oversized honeybee.

As Garth had indicated, Tegan's clan was well known for its master dyers, and even Stevic G'ladheon did frequent business with them. Tegan had been, of course, a journeyman in the clan trade when she heard the Rider call.

Amazingly, Tegan maintained a straight face, though her eyes held a glint of merriment. Garth stared blankly, and Dale still sat helpless in her chair, wiping a tear from her cheek.

Mara sighed, and it carried overtones of tiredness and disappointment. "Tegan, you are hereby assigned laundry duty for the next month." The Rider's mouth dropped open, but before she could lodge a protest, Mara cut her off with a shake of her head. "I know you too well, so there is no use in denying your part in this." Tegan clamped her mouth shut.

"Those fine uniforms are supplied to us by the generosity of Stevic G'ladheon," Mara continued, "the materials are expensive. I will not see the uniform so degraded."

Tegan glanced at her feet, ashamed.

"Garth," Mara said, "you will change immediately."

Well, Karigan thought, Mara had certainly assumed an air of authority in her absence. At one time, Mara would have been as helpless as Dale from laughter. In fact, Mara would have joined in on whatever scheme Tegan had conjured.

Garth brightened upon hearing Tegan's punishment, but now he tried to see past Mara, to figure out who stood in the shadows behind her.

"Is that you, Karigan?"

Karigan squeezed past Mara. "Hello."

Garth barrelled over and wrapped his thick arms around her. Air *whooshed* from her lungs as he lifted her off her feet and planted a kiss on her cheek. When he set her down,

Tegan hugged her in turn. Dale finally collected herself and stood to pat Karigan on the shoulder.

"Good to see you looking lively. Compared to last night, anyway."

Karigan grinned, a bit breathless and genuinely happy to see them, too, but when they launched into a thousand questions about her journey, she found herself backing away, overwhelmed. It was Mara who came to her rescue.

"Leave off the poor woman—she hasn't even had breakfast yet." Turning to Dale, she said, "Don't you have someplace to go?"

Dale straightened. "Right!" She patted the message satchel slung over her shoulder. "We'll catch up later," she told Karigan, and she dashed off on whatever message errand had been assigned her.

Garth gave Karigan another, albeit less crushing, hug, before lumbering off to change his uniform.

"Good to see you, Karigan," Tegan said, and she slipped away down the corridor.

"Laundry!" Mara called after her.

"I know, I know . . ." her voice trailed back.

"That was quite a welcome," Karigan said, thinking she had never received one quite like it when returning from an ordinary message errand.

"They're very glad to see you in one piece," Mara said. "It's been rather gloomy here ever since we heard about Ereal and Bard. I'm fairly certain Tegan is up to her old tricks just to lighten things up."

They left the common room and walked the central corridor that ran the length of the narrow barracks building. To Karigan, the building had an abandoned air about it, but that was often the case with only a few Riders in residence at any one time.

Still, even if all the Riders were present, the majority of the rooms would go unused. Karigan wondered what the place had been like in the old days when every room was occupied. How busy this corridor must have been back then. Its plank flooring was worn from the boots of two centuries of Riders.

Mara was determined, Karigan found, that she eat every last crumb—which wasn't difficult considering the flatcakes were piled with freshly picked blueberries. She discovered she was famished and had to chew consciously before swallowing.

Two people were a crowd in her room—an over-glorified closet, really—but she was glad of the company. While she ate, Mara took the opportunity to fill her in on a few months' worth of Rider gossip.

She was about to launch into tales about Yates' latest conquests when Karigan interrupted. "How is Ty doing?"

"Dark and moody. So I sent him on an errand to Adolind and Mirwell. On Crane." She half smiled. "I think we have a match. Ereal would have been pleased."

Karigan was glad. Ty had never been known to be jovial, and he was hurting. He and Crane must have bonded enough on their ride here from the clearing to be still working together.

"How about you? How are you doing?"

"Me?" Mara tipped the teapot and poured herself another cup. "Helping the captain mainly, what with Connly off to the Cloud Islands bearing trade documents." Connly was Chief Rider, and ordinarily it was his duty to oversee the day to day operations of the Riders. The fact he had been sent on a far distant errand spoke of how short-staffed they were. "And of course, Ereal is gone now, too."

"So, not only have you been the acting Chief Rider, but you've been doing Ereal's job, as well?"

Mara blew on her tea and shrugged. "I was the most senior Rider left. When Connly comes home, I think the captain is of a mind to elevate him to lieutenant. I wish he'd hurry up!"

Then she heaved another tired sigh. "The king runs the captain ragged, but she won't confide in me the way she used to with Ereal. I think she doesn't want to overburden me."

That sounded just like the captain, Karigan thought. But it *was* her job to carry the heaviest of responsibilities, and Mara already had enough of her own to contend with in light of Connly's absence and Ereal's death. Captain Mapstone was doing what one should in her position, but it was not a load anyone could carry alone for too long.

"I expect you'll want to know Alton left some weeks ago for the wall," Mara said.

Alton! "The wall? Why?"

"He and his clan kept requesting it, and finally Captain Mapstone and the king relented—another reason we're short-staffed, by the way. The king believes it a good idea to have a Rider at the wall, keeping an eye on things for him."

Karigan tried to hide her disappointment, but she couldn't conceal her concern about the wall. Mara's news filled her with foreboding. "So the cracks are still spreading?"

Mara nodded and leaned forward conspiratorially. "Word is the D'Yers can't figure out how to stop the cracks. They can't even figure out how to access the towers, which are magically sealed or something. The clan thinks that because Alton has a special ability, he might be able to figure out things for them." She shrugged, obviously skeptical. "I suppose he's as close as anyone to understanding the magic."

A new layer of gloom settled on Karigan's shoulders. Telagioth had been right, it seemed, the wall needed watching. But watching didn't seem as if it was going to be enough. And now her friend, Alton D'Yer, was going to be in the middle of it.

"That's pretty," Mara said.

Startled from her thoughts, Karigan followed her gaze to a bowl of crystalline shards on her table. Sunlight flowed through the window in such a way that the crystal fragments sparkled and reflected a rainbow of color against the plain wall.

The shards were all that remained of an Eletian moonstone that had been given her, its moonbeam long gone. She wasn't sure why she kept the shards, except that they retained their own particular beauty, and even now their play of light and color soothed her. It also served to remind her of the kindness of two elderly ladies who lived in a stately manor in the forest. She kept their other two gifts, a bunchberry flower and a sprig of bayberry, pressed in her favorite book.

Mara started clearing dishes and piling them onto her tray. She was about to carry it out when she paused and patted her shortcoat.

"I nearly forgot. Two letters came in for you while you were away." She pulled them from an inner pocket and dropped them on the table. "Osric carried the one from Selium, and the other came in via the merchants guild."

Mara took the tray and paused again in the doorway. "One more thing. Captain says you are to speak with her when you are able."

⇜ KING JONAEUS' SPRING ⇝

Letters in hand, Karigan headed for the central courtyard gardens. The day was really too fine to stay indoors. She had sought out Captain Mapstone, but learned she was closeted with the king and his advisors. Left to her own devices, with no duties yet assigned her, the central courtyard gardens beckoned.

She stepped beneath a stone arch into the gardens. The courtyard was bordered on all four sides by the castle, yet still maintained a sense of spaciousness and tranquility. There were many nooks and wayside paths that offered seclusion, and Karigan followed one such, hopping across stepping stones strategically placed in a trout pond. Dark fish shapes darted into shadows at her passage.

She paused at the head of a path that led to a garden nook. Hidden by dense shrubbery and artfully situated boulders, it was a favored meeting spot of lovers. If no one was there, it would be a quiet place for her to read her letters, but as she approached, sure enough, she heard voices.

"There must be a better place for us to meet," a woman said. "This feels too exposed—we're taking too big a risk."

"I have keys," a man responded. "We can—"

Karigan retreated down the path, smiling at the thought of having nearly intruded upon an illicit romantic meeting. When she heard footsteps crunching on the gravel path behind her, she paused, pretending to take a deep whiff of a

112

rose. She shifted her eyes and watched a woman in a baker's smock hurry along the path toward her. When the woman saw Karigan, her eyes widened and she turned on her heel to head in a different direction.

Karigan laughed softly at the woman's expression. Obviously she hadn't wanted to be discovered with her paramour, and hadn't expected anyone to witness her departure. Who was her mysterious suitor? Some courtier afraid to meet openly with his common lover?

She held her pose by the roses hoping to find out, even as she concocted tragic love stories in her mind.

Moments later, a shaggy bearded man with muscular arms and soot smudged on his cheeks emerged from the nook and strode down the same path taken by the baker. No nobleman this, but one of the castle blacksmiths.

Karigan found herself disappointed he was not some exiled prince or impoverished noble. With a sigh, she straightened and walked toward the nook. Now that it was free, she could make use of it.

Her long strides carried her into a collision with a man who emerged unexpectedly from behind the shrubbery. His armload of papers erupted into the air and they both crashed to their buttocks.

Karigan shook her head feeling rather bruised. The man was already on his knees, grabbing at his papers even as they flurried down around him.

Karigan moved to help him. "I'm sorry."

"*Sorry?* Important papers, these are." He glared at her through specs that lay askew on his face. "Documents for the king, these are."

"I said I was sorry." She leaned forward to grab a paper just as he did, and the two cracked heads. "Ow!"

"Just stay out of my way." He snatched the papers she had collected right out of her hands, stood—keys at his belt jingling—and hastened down the path.

Slowly it dawned on Karigan, as she rubbed her throbbing head, that her hands were completely empty.

"Wait!" she called. She sprang to her feet and raced after him, grabbing at his sleeve.

He scowled at her. "Now what? You have delayed me enough."

Karigan sucked in a breath in an effort to remain civil. "I believe you picked up a couple of letters that belong to me."

The man made an exasperated noise and picked through his papers. When he found the letters and saw her name upon them, he glanced at her, something odd lighting in his eyes. Then he flung them at her and continued on his way.

Karigan stared incredulously after him. She was of half a mind to pursue him and give him a tongue lashing, but better sense prevailed. She told herself he was beneath her attention and nothing would be gained by confronting him.

"Rotten little man," she muttered.

She headed into the shady nook and found it empty. Sparrows splashed in a birdbath, but that was all the activity she found. The recently raked gravel path had been disturbed by the passage of several feet.

"I guess I was wrong about the illicit romance." Whatever had brought the blacksmith, baker, and clerk together, she guessed she'd rather not know.

She sat on a rustic stone bench and heaved a sigh, closing her eyes for a moment to listen to the spring that bubbled nearby. Water trickled over mossy rocks like a miniature waterfall, pooling into a basin before streaming away to the trout pond. The sound of it soothed her. It was said that the first high king of Sacoridia, Jonaeus, founded the castle on this hill because of the natural spring he found there. In his memory, it was called "King Jonaeus' Spring." To drink of it was said to gift one with wisdom worthy of a king.

Karigan had sipped of it, and found it cool on a hot day,

but otherwise unremarkable. She became no wiser than before. Only experience, she had learned somewhere along the way, led to wisdom.

Finally she broke the seal of one of the letters. It was from her father. In it he detailed preparations for the fall trading season. He described yardage of cloth, and tonnage of river cog, wagon train routes, and square foot of lumber. The entire letter went on in this vein until the very end, where he wrote:

I need you just as much as the King and Captain Mapstone do. You are a G'ladheon and a Merchant! But do know I am ever Proud of you. Your good service to the King can only bring Honor to the Clan.

Karigan reread the letter, much relieved by it. Her father was still hurting from her "decision" to become a Green Rider, but by the conciliatory tone of the last paragraph, he had finally accepted it to a degree.

Thank goodness, she thought, feeling some of the guilt lift from her shoulders.

She put his letter aside and took up the second. It was in the fine hand of her friend Estral Andovian, a journeyman minstrel at Selium. She described happenings at Selium in animated detail.

I've been busy teaching the summer term of mostly basic level and uninterested students. You may guess these are largely the children of nobles and that they are less intent upon their lessons than upon one another.

Karigan snorted, not envying Estral her task.

Estral then described some renovations being done to the archives, and Karigan chuckled at the images she wrought of master archivists scurrying about to protect ancient papers and tomes, wringing their hands and practically shedding the hair right off the tops of their heads from worry.

In the process of expanding the archives, workers knocked through a wall uncovering a remarkable treasure—an alcove that had been sealed over long ago. In it we found a manuscript from the days of the Long War in fine condition. Most of it is written in the Imperial tongue, and bits in Old Sacoridian. When we complete the translation, I shall send you a copy which you may share with your father. I think you will find it of interest.

There was no further explanation, just *Mel sends her love,* and Estral's signature. Karigan dropped the letter onto her lap and stared into the trees before her. Leave it to Estral to be so mysterious as to not explain why the manuscript might be of interest to her. Estral could be so confounding sometimes.

Karigan noted the letter was dated two months ago. There was no telling how long it would take this manuscript to be translated and then conveyed to Sacor City. In the meantime, curiosity would eat her like a moth in a closet of woolens.

A light crunch on gravel startled Karigan from her reverie. She thought maybe the rude clerk, or one of his friends, might be returning for some reason, but when she saw who it was, she immediately stood and bowed.

"Welcome home," said Lady Estora Coutre.

Estora was perhaps the most beautiful woman Karigan had ever seen. Her summer dress of dusty blue enhanced the light blue of her eyes, and her golden hair cascaded down her back in loose braids. The light, fresh scent of lavender wreathed about her. Unconsciously Karigan smoothed her hand along her tunic, all too aware of its baggy fit. She ran through a mental list of other deficiencies: her ragged fingernails, the skewed braid she had knotted without care that morning, and her old boots that were threatening to fall apart.

"Are you not going to say hello?" Estora asked.

"I—" Karigan smiled feebly. "Hello."

Estora took Karigan's hands into her own. "I am ever so pleased to see you well after your long journey. Shall we sit?"

When Karigan had returned to Sacor City a year ago, an unlikely friendship had evolved between them. Unlikely because Estora was heir to Coutre Province, and normally inaccessible to a common messenger. Yet over the past year they found themselves encountering one another in the gardens, where both came to think over whatever was on their minds.

Karigan found Estora a ready listener to the frustrations of Rider life. Estora, in turn, spoke of growing up in Coutre Province and life in court. Perhaps she found some connection with Karigan because she could speak of her lost secret lover, Rider F'ryan Coblebay. Karigan had been the last to see him alive, and at his dying, she had "inherited" his saber, horse, and brooch. Did Estora think of F'ryan when she looked upon Karigan?

"I am sorry for the loss of Lieutenant M'Farthon and Rider Martin."

The unexpected words, like a key turned in a lock, were all it took. Grief, otherwise all but suppressed by other more immediate needs, suddenly founted to the surface. They came from the depths of a soul exhausted by loss and a harsh journey. Karigan had not allowed herself to give in to the grief before, that great threatening wave, but somehow with a few simple words and the sympathy Estora all but radiated, the breakwater Karigan had so firmly formed in her mind was destroyed.

Estora rubbed Karigan's back and murmured soothing words until her racking sobs abated, and then handed her a handkerchief scented with lavender. Karigan blew lustily into it. In the wake of her tears, she felt tired to the bone, as if the last of her energy had been stored for this moment;

and a little embarrassed by having lost control in front of someone else.

She found herself telling Estora about the journey. It was not the same as the telling of the previous night, a factual line of events; now she colored the telling with her own fears and anguish.

Estora did not interrupt, but listened gravely, sadness clouding her features as Karigan related the grittier portion of her tale. When she finished, the catharsis left her feeling more tired than ever, yet eminently relieved by finally having let go.

"Thank you," she said, "for listening to all that."

"I am sorry you experienced it, but I am glad you could speak to me of it. You Riders undergo dangers I cannot even imagine, and you do it out of love for the king and Sacoridia. Yet many take your service for granted." She shook her head, her braids sweeping across her back. "I know if Alton were here, he'd be of great comfort to you."

Karigan looked sharply at her, wondering what she knew about Alton. He had, by Karigan's design, rarely entered their conversations.

Estora did not miss her reaction and laughed gently. "Now, don't give me that look, Karigan G'ladheon. You did mention his name just often enough for me to make some guesses, and even now in your expression, I see them confirmed."

Karigan frowned. Was she always so transparent?

"You see, life in court has taught me the art of observation," Estora explained. "Expression, voice, and even gestures can tell one much that is not revealed in words." Her eyes twinkled at Karigan's discomfiture. "Do not worry, I am much practiced, and you did not reveal yourself easily."

There was that, Karigan supposed. "What is it you think you know?"

"I know you are good friends, and it was once almost

more. It is not such a bad thing for those who would be lovers to find friendship instead. Sometimes it makes the binding closer.''

Binding? How close was that binding? Karigan wondered. The fact was, she and Alton rarely saw one another. This, as much as anything, had quelled any romantic feelings they might have entertained. It was awfully hard to carry on a relationship when both parties were constantly on the run, but such was the life of a Green Rider.

Karigan had taken some leave time with Alton to Woodhaven, the stronghold of Clan D'Yer, and it had been a special time. Yet it reinforced the fact that both of them had changed over the year she was away from Sacor City; time had opened a gulf between them.

Yet she intensely missed Alton and wished he were here for her to talk with. More so than even Estora, he would've understood all that she had gone through while on delegation duty. Estora was right about the binding of friendship— it allowed a freedom of openness between them, and dispensed with the awkwardness they had felt as almost-lovers.

Mostly she worried about him being near the wall. What could he do to stop its deterioration? He was but one man against an ancient bulwark built by his ancestors so long ago. At the wall he'd be at the threshold of Blackveil Forest and its legendary darkness.

Karigan had learned the importance of friendship time and again. Alton had once saved her life by putting himself between her and an arrow. Would she ever have a chance to show him the depth of her friendship when he was in need?

Currently he was too far away, and Estora was all too correct about the dangers Green Riders faced.

Journal of Hadriax el Fex

Alessandros has been in a state ever since the Elt rebuffed his overtures. I have never seen him so angry. They wish to have no part of us or the Empire, and have, in fact, told us to leave these shores and never return again. They will be dismayed to learn that additional ships bearing imperial troops and supplies are en route.

Still, as stubborn and high-minded as these Elt have proven to be, they are entrancingly beautiful, and gifted in the art. In fact, their land fairly reeks of etherea, which we detected though they did not permit us far beyond their border.

It is as though meeting them has awakened something in Alessandros that he cannot shake off—a longing. They are all he speaks of. He has commanded our patrols to capture any Elt they encounter.

⤷ WITHIN SHADOW'S REACH ⤷

 burst of wind plastered Alton D'Yer's hair back from his face and pelted him with dust and debris. He tore off his glove to rub grit from his eyes. All around him understory trees lunged and thrashed like wild beasts, and far above, the spires of great pines swayed against a backdrop of rapidly moving clouds.

Change of weather, he thought, undismayed. The wind kept the biters off, and he'd be at the wall encampment long before any storms rolled in.

He guided Night Hawk along at a leisurely walk, resting him after the driven pace they'd already traveled that day. Alton found it hard to settle in to the slower pace, what with a wide path recently carved into the woods before him and the wall drawing him like a spark to tinder.

The wall. Slowly he tugged his glove back on, looking ahead to see if he could glimpse it, but no, the thick forest still hid it. He would see it soon enough.

Or would he?

Alton had felt the unrelenting pull of the wall for some time now; as unrelenting as the Rider call. He heard voices calling out to him when his mind was quiet and subdued by sleep. Voices of grief and alarm, and they grew increasingly urgent as time passed.

Simple dreams?

Dreams that would not leave him then, if dreams they

were. The voices were many, male and female, and twined with song and a strong beat, as of a hammer on rock. There was also a discordance that went against the rhythm, part of the wrongness within the wall.

Maybe his ancestors of old once knew the voices, or maybe it was something yet buried in the minds of the other members of his bloodline, but not awakened. If it wasn't just some wishful thinking of his own, might he be able to tap into the powers of the wall and gain some understanding of it, and maybe even fix it?

He had a proven magical ability. This gave him more of a chance of succeeding where the rest of them failed, or so his father and uncle reasoned. Odd how his father, Lord-Governor Quentin D'Yer, felt his son's vocation as a Green Rider beneath him, yet wanted to use at the wall the very abilities that made him a Rider.

Alton's ancestors used magic to build the wall, but in the years following had shunned it as had much of the rest of Sacoridia. Many users of magic had died in the scourge of disease that followed the Long War, their secrets dying with them. At first the D'Yers had faithfully watched the wall; guarded against whatever menace lay behind it in Blackveil Forest, but at some point that watchfulness faded, until none of the clan even bothered visiting the wall.

Now Alton felt guilt, guilt that his clan had not maintained their watchfulness or kept the secrets of the wall. Now, their ignorance endangered all of Sacoridia, and it was their responsibility to restore their vigilence, and somehow repair the breach created by Shawdell the Eletian.

Alton shifted the reins in his hands. It didn't matter, he supposed, what his father or uncle thought. It wasn't just clan duty that brought him here. He would've come on his own, to answer the voices that haunted his dreams.

Wind blasted him again, stealing his breath, and Night Hawk side-stepped beneath him.

"A little wind tickling your belly?"

The black gelding snorted, and Alton grinned, clapping him on the neck. "It won't be long before you've got your nose in a grain sack, old boy."

The turning of the wind carried to him the sounds of a struggle ahead—outcries and thudding, the crushing of vegetation.

He took up the slack in Night Hawk's reins and squeezed him forward at a cautious jog, laying his hand on the hilt of his saber, unsure of what he might find. Around a bend he came upon two ponies munching happily on the lower branches of trees that lined the trail. One had already stepped on the reins of its very fine bridle and snapped them.

Just beyond the ponies, two little boys locked together in a fight rolled on the ground batting at one another.

"Did *not!*" one cried.

"Did *too!*" the other shouted back.

Alton's eyebrows shot up in surprise—and consternation.

"Did *not!*" That one, with the black hair, was his young cousin, Teral.

"Did *too!*" And that one, with the sandy hair, was Alton's younger brother, Marc.

Alton sighed and let his hand fall from his sword. He dismounted Night Hawk and strode over to the boys, towering over them. Too caught up in their struggle—Marc was now yanking on Teral's hair—they were oblivious to his presence.

He reached down and grabbed each boy by his collar and hauled him to his feet. Though he held them at arm's length, they still swung at one another, pummeling the air.

"Stop!" Alton jostled them a bit to get their attention. "What's this all about?"

The boys paused, and smiles curved on their faces when they realized who restrained them. Then they both began to giggle. Alton hoisted the boys under his arms and whirled them around in a dizzying ride.

"Fighting, eh? Why, I'll teach you to get into fights!" The faster he whirled, the harder they laughed and yelled in delight.

Alton realized belatedly that the boys had put on some serious weight since he had last played with them in this manner, and he thought his arms might stretch till his knuckles dragged on the ground. Rather unsteadily he set them down, and just as quickly his brother looped his arms about his waist. "Alton!"

In a shot Teral was at Night Hawk's side, trying to clamber up the stirrup leather to mount the gelding, tongue sticking out the corner of his mouth with the effort. And he was succeeding quite nicely, too. Night Hawk tolerated it, but he didn't look happy.

The boys' finery was ripped and covered with dirt. Both were scratched and bruised, but from what Alton could tell, neither seemed seriously hurt.

"Why were you fighting?" he demanded. "And more importantly, what are you two doing out here all alone?"

"Not alone!" Marc said.

"Yeah," Teral said, triumphant atop Night Hawk. "My brother's watching us."

"Oh? Where is he then?"

"He was kissing Lady Valia in the trees where he thought no one could see them," Marc cheerfully reported, "so we run away."

"Ran," Alton absently corrected. Had Uncle Landrew gone mad by allowing small boys and noblewomen within shadow's reach of the wall?

Teral puckered his lips and made loud smooching sounds, which Marc thought was just hilarious. Both boys became helpless with giggles and Alton found himself smiling. He wondered how Pendric, Teral's older brother, had convinced Lady Valia to kiss him. In any case, Pendric wasn't doing a very good job of keeping watch on the boys, and Alton couldn't blame them for taking the opportunity to escape him.

"Hey! I wanna ride Hawk, too," Marc said.

Alton lifted his brother onto the saddle behind Teral. Teral shook the reins and banged his legs against Night Hawk to make him go forward, his feet barely extending beyond the saddle flaps. Night Hawk's expression was decidedly glum.

"Go easy on him, Teral, and he'll walk for you."

The boy listened, and Alton whispered an encouragement to Night Hawk who lumbered forward at his command. Alton then collected the two ponies and led them beside his own horse.

"Hey, are you going to marry Lady Estora?" Marc asked.

The directness of the question so startled Alton he stumbled over a root. Yet it shouldn't surprise him too much—the matter of ending his bachelorhood was practically dinner conversation among the adults within his clan, and something the boys were apt to overhear. He was the heir to Quentin D'Yer, and next in line to govern D'Yer Province. Naturally, finding him a wife of suitable quality and station to be the future lady of D'Yer Province was of utmost importance.

"Pendric says he has a pig's chance," Teral piped up.

"Good! I hope he marries Karigan."

Alton's mouth dropped open. Where was *this* coming from?

"He can't marry *her*," Teral said.

"Why not?"

"'Cuz she's common."

"I don't care—I like her. She brought me candy—*loads* of it from Master Gruntler's Sugary in Sacor City."

"Did not!"

"Did so!"

Alton wasn't sure who poked whom first, but another full scale scuffle was threatening to erupt, this time on poor Night Hawk's back. The gelding lowered his head and heaved a mournful sigh.

"Now stop!" Alton cried. "Stop or you can both walk back."

This settled them down—a little.

"Did so," Marc said under his breath.

Teral turned in the saddle to stick out his tongue, but they banged foreheads, and ended up laughing uproariously. Alton rolled his eyes.

When he had brought Karigan to Woodhaven for the mid-winter holiday, Marc had taken to her like a long-lost sister. Karigan, with no siblings of her own, and little experienced around young ones, was a bit overwhelmed at first, but soon the two were fast friends. Marc showed her his favorite pony, a litter of pups in the stable, his collection of toy warriors, the decorative short sword he wore on state occasions, his secret place in the wine cellar he thought no one else knew about, and that was within the first half hour. He dragged her along by the hand, she laughing all the way. It was certainly a side of Karigan Alton hadn't seen before.

"So are you gonna marry Lady Estora?" Teral demanded.

"And have babies?" Marc chimed in.

Alton halted so abruptly one of the ponies bumped its nose into the small of his back.

"Why do you ask?"

"'Cuz Pendric told Lady Valia that Lady Estora wouldn't have some Greenie for a husband. It's beneath her."

"She wouldn't have *your* brother neither," Marc said.

Aaah, Alton thought. Pendric's offer to Lord Coutre had been rejected then. He licked his lips, relieved. Not that Lord Coutre hadn't received and rejected a hundred such proposals from other prospective suitors, but it would have been galling if, out of all of them, Pendric's had been accepted.

Alton walked on, tugging on the reins of the ponies, wondering what the status of his own proposal was. His father had sent it to Coutre Province with one of his most trusted retainers, about two months ago. Thought of it made his insides churn.

Lady Estora was desirable to many a suitor, not only for her near legendary beauty, but for her status as heir of Coutre Province. Marrying her would create a very beneficial alliance for whomever won her favor—not only with Coutre Province, but with all the other provinces east of the Wingsong Mountains, as well. Old Lord Coutre, it was said, kept his daughter at the castle in Sacor City to exhibit her like a prize, and those seeking alliance and power were undeterred in their pursuit of her.

Alton had had few interactions with her, but was impressed by her genuine warmth and kindness. He knew she had been F'ryan Coblebay's lover. All the Riders knew, and kept her secret, a secret that could cause her conservative father to disown her if he ever found out. Yet, he felt uncomfortable around her, like she was more of a masterwork of art than a real woman.

He shook his head. It was just as well he had left Sacor City where he was apt to encounter Estora, or Karigan for that matter. He had always known he'd marry for station and alliance, not love or friendship, but it didn't make things any easier.

Wind tousled his hair and flipped leaves, revealing their silvery undersides. Two riders approached and he immediately recognized Pendric's broad form and thick black hair.

He sat upon an impressive bay hunter, a finely bred animal to say the least. Pendric's countenance was angry, and he looked no happier to see Alton.

Beside him Lady Valia rode side-saddle upon her mare, her skirts draped decorously behind her. He had seen her a couple years ago when she was—what?—twelve? She had grown and blossomed into a pretty young lady.

Pendric swatted his horse with his riding crop to canter the short distance to Alton and the boys, then pulled sharply on the reins when he reached them.

"What do you think you were doing by running off?" Pendric demanded of the boys, ignoring Alton altogether.

The boys chattered their excuses in high-pitched voices until Pendric cut them off. "Enough." He pointed the crop at them, spooking his horse in the process. He yanked on the reins again. With such rough handling, it wouldn't be long before the hunter had a sour disposition. Not unlike its rider. No matter, Uncle Landrew would likely buy without hesitation another finely bred steed for Pendric to ruin.

"You will have Jayna and father to answer to when you get back," Pendric said.

"Then we'll tell Da you were kissing Lady Valia," Teral said.

Pendric glowered, and a pretty pink blush colored Valia's cheeks. "You will not." He whirled his mount around to ride away.

"What?" Alton called out after him. "No greeting for your cousin?"

Pendric halted and turned in his saddle. "Hello." The word came out cold and gruff.

Valia, in contrast, smiled warmly and bowed her head. "Hello, Lord Alton."

Alton inclined his head in return. "My lady."

This pleasant exchange set Pendric off. His pock-marked cheeks flared crimson. He grabbed the bridle of Valia's mare and swerved her about, almost dislodging her from her saddle. He slapped his own mount with the crop and sped off at a canter. Teral and Marc made smooching noises after them. Alton smiled, doubting Pendric heard, and thinking it was probably a good thing.

"Your brother is in a hot temper," he told Teral.

The boy shrugged. "Sometimes he's like that."

"Sometimes?"

Teral nodded. "Sometimes he's not angry at all but fun. He helped us build a tree fort, and gave me a practice sword."

Alton supposed it was possible. Maybe it was just that he brought out the worst in Pendric, though he couldn't imagine why.

Eventually the forest gave way to a tent village. Alton let out a low whistle—things had changed considerably since his last visit, when there had been but a solitary company of Sacoridian soldiers to keep watch. Now there were precise rows of tan tents belonging to the ranks of D'Yerian provincial militia. Their standards, bright with unit and company insignia, rippled and snapped in the gusty wind.

King Zachary had withdrawn all but a small detachment of Sacoridian soldiers, and they were set off by standards of black and silver bearing the country's emblem of the crescent moon and firebrand. They took up but a small space in the tent village.

The inevitable camp followers, in their own patched and colorful tents, made their place on the outskirts of the military perimeter. No doubt a goodly number of wives had followed with their children, "to do" for their husbands.

Where there were soldiers and camp followers, there was commerce. Peddlers had set up stalls, and hawked wares from atop well stocked wagons.

"Master Wiggins' cure-all for gout, foot itch, and other

more, ahem, personal ailments, gentlemen." A group had assembled around one such peddler's wagon and listened as he extolled the virtues of his "magic" elixir.

There were more than just soldiers, camp followers, and merchants, however. Rising above all other tents were those bearing the colors of D'Yer Province's noble houses, and even a few from out-province. Disconcerted, Alton walked right into a rope supporting the tent of House Lyle. In front of the tent, a minstrel strummed his lute for some elegant ladies.

The aroma from a food vendor's stall made Alton's stomach rumble. The boys were digging in their pockets to assess whether or not they had enough currency between them for a meat pie.

What was going on here? What had once been a stark outpost in the wilderness had become a—a *festival.* What insanity had lured these folk to come within throwing distance of the wall?

Alton's gaze was drawn above the tents. The great wall loomed over the gaiety, above the tallest trees, to the roof of the world, it seemed. Amid the noise and festival atmosphere, Alton stood there awed, as awed as the first time he had looked upon the magnificent working of his ancestors.

Suddenly he understood why all these people had come; they had come to see this wall of legend. The breach had brought it to the forefront of their minds. Impenetrable it stood there, this great ancient working, impenetrable to the mightiest of armies, impenetrable to all but the gods. And this was the great fallacy, for this wall had been breached. Breached by *one* Eletian.

He took a deep breath, trying to break the hold it had on him. It wasn't easy—the thing was overpowering. The crystalline quartz of the granite ashlars sparkled in the sunlight, and he was beguiled by it. His hand lifted from his side as though to reach for it, even beyond the many yards separating him from its granite facade.

"Ow!" Teral cried. "Alton, he punched me."

"Did not."

"Did too."

Alton tore his gaze from the wall and sighed, grateful for the respite. Uncle Landrew's tent was not difficult to find. It was the largest one, and centrally located. The blue, red, and gold standard of D'Yer Province with Landrew's sigil of an owl in the center field flapped above it.

Alton passed the boys a stern look and headed for Uncle Landrew's tent. Once there, he handed the reins of the ponies to a servant, and helped Teral and Marc slide off Night Hawk. The two tore off into the tent village before their nanny, Jayna, could even open her mouth for a scolding. With a determined expression, she hoisted her skirts and rushed after them.

Alton chuckled, silently wishing her luck, and passed Night Hawk's reins to another servant. "Make sure he gets the best grain. He's had a long ride today."

"Yes, my lord."

Alton pulled aside the tent flap and entered. His uncle, seated in a campaign chair before a pile of drawings, rose to greet him.

"Be welcome, nephew," he said.

"Thank you, my lord."

Landrew clasped Alton's hand. Like his own, his uncle's hands were large and callused, the wrists thick from working stone. From a young age the D'Yers were trained to wield hammer and drill. Marc and Teral had begun training about the same time they learned to walk. Building blocks, not of wood, but of stone were their first toys.

They were stoneworkers without compare, Clan D'Yer, the builders of Sacoridia. Among their great works were the academic buildings in Selium and the castle of the high king in Sacor City.

Landrew sent servants scurrying after food and refreshment, and uncle and nephew sat in chairs opposite one another.

"Do you bear me a message from the king," Landrew asked, "or have you come to provide help to your clan?"

"A little of both. King Zachary wishes me to look over the wall with the eyes of one of his messengers, and to encourage you in your work. I am also to provide help as needed."

Landrew nodded, appraising him, perhaps wondering if he were more a king's man than the clan's man. To Alton, the roles were one and the same.

"Seeing you in that green uniform, it is difficult to know, sometimes, who you serve."

"I serve Sacoridia and her people," Alton said evenly, "whether I wear the uniform of a king's messenger, or stand as the heir of Clan D'Yer." There, let that little reminder of his status quiet his uncle who would, one day, take an oath of loyalty to Alton when he became *the* Lord D'Yer and clan chief.

The words seemed to have worked, and Landrew relaxed. The two men exchanged pleasantries about Alton's journey and the weather as servants brought in cool barley water and sweet bread, cold meats, and pickled fiddleheads.

Alton eyed the papers on the table before him. They appeared to be structural drawings of the wall, and maps depicting its length, though showing only the Sacoridian side. Blackveil was a vast, blank space. There was also a broader scale map showing the locations and names of the wall's watch towers.

Tower of the Summits, Tower of the Rain, Tower of the Trees, Tower of the Sea . . .

There were only ten towers to cover the extent of the wall, which stretched from Ullem Bay in the west to the Eastern Sea, and each was named as though to invoke the powers and strengths of the elements and nature. The Tower of the Heavens was closest to the encampment, within a day's ride. *Haethen Toundrel,* it would have been called in the old Sacoridian tongue.

Alton sipped at his barley water and said, "I see you've been studying plans."

"Recent drawings, I'm afraid. I've archivists going into the mustiest, darkest corners of records rooms throughout the province to see if they can find a mere mention of the wall. So far, nothing useful has turned up. I wouldn't put it past our ancestors to have burned their records, blast them. If they intended to keep secrets, they've done it well."

It was rather odd, Alton thought, that the clan wouldn't have preserved such records, but then again, if they feared some enemy, they certainly would not have wanted the records to fall into the hands of one who might desire to unmake the wall. Unfortunately, it also meant their descendants had no idea of how to maintain the wall's magical aspects.

"I suppose you've heard it isn't going well with the repair work?" Landrew said.

"Yes."

"Want to take a look?"

"Yes, Uncle." Alton grabbed a hunk of sweet bread and followed his uncle out of the tent. Once again he was struck by the festive activity about the encampment that seemed so incongruous with the wall and all it represented. He noted beneath a pavilion his Aunt Milda chatting with some other ladies intent on fancy work.

"This way, my boy." Landrew put a hand on his shoulder and steered him away. "If Milda sees you, it will be hours before we can get to the business at hand."

It was the first glint of humor Alton had seen in his uncle's eyes, and he smiled. "What is it with—with all these people here? I came expecting to find only soldiers and some of your laborers."

Landrew sighed as they passed a billowing tent. "I couldn't stop them from coming. All of a sudden there's all this interest in the wall, as if it hasn't been around for a thousand years or so." He rolled his eyes. "I can't deny them if they want to see a piece of their heritage. It is a fantastic thing, after all, this wall."

Alton was thankful to find the soldiers had established a substantial perimeter line in front of the wall beyond which no one could pitch a tent. Of course, there was nothing stopping them from doing just that if they wanted to ride down the wall just a couple miles or so away from the encampment.

"You've been doing some clearing," Alton commented. Vegetation had been burned back in both directions along the wall.

"I am certain it was done so historically," Landrew said. "And there's been a bit of blight."

"Blight?"

"Yes. It was affecting the trees near the breach. Turning the leaves black, then the branches and trunks, so we've been burning to keep it from spreading. Just as soon as this wind dies down, we'll resume burning tonight."

Blight does not bode well, Alton thought, *especially if it originates from across the breach in Blackveil.*

The magnetism of the wall drew hard on him now. His gaze roved up its lofty heights. Some said it reached the heavens where the gods dwelled. Some said it touched the clouds as a mountain summit would.

It was illusion, and it wasn't. The actual stone wall reached about ten feet high, serving as the foundation for the magic, which surged above and beyond, seamlessly mimicking the texture, appearance, and durability of the real thing. It could repel whatever lurked in Blackveil as assuredly as the stone wall.

As the sun traveled on its course, shadow crept across the face of the wall and into the perimeter held by the soldiers.

A soldier uniformed in Sacoridian silver and black, with sergeant's chevrons on his sleeves, approached. He was heavily armed with long sword, dagger, and a cocked crossbow, a quiver of bolts swinging at his hip.

He passed a dismissive glance over Alton, but bowed to Landrew. "How may I serve you, my lord?"

"My nephew here would like a closer look at the wall, Sergeant Uxton. He will have the same authority as I do to approach it."

The sergeant's gaze flicked back to Alton, reassessing. "I had heard there was a nobleman among the Greenies."

"Green Riders," Alton corrected, bridling his annoyance.

"Of course, my lord. Many pardons. We of the Mountain Unit so rarely step near court, that we are lacking of its graces."

Another dig. Alton could not make out whether the sergeant chose to be impudent on purpose, or was simply naturally abrasive. Whatever the case, Uncle Landrew was either used to it, or chose not to notice.

"I will escort you to the wall if you wish," the sergeant announced.

"I don't need—"

Landrew raised his hand to quell Alton's protests. "Things have changed since you were last here. We've procedures to follow. It's just a precautionary measure that we're accompanied by an armed guard when we approach the wall."

Alton was not pleased. He'd be unable to move about the wall without eyes constantly following him, but it appeared he had little choice.

"If you will follow me." Uxton turned to lead them into the wall's shadow.

 ALTON AT THE BREACH ❧

The cold of the wall's shadow penetrated Alton's shortcoat, causing an unexpected shiver to course through his body. He stood before the breach, and instantly the presence of his uncle and Sergeant Uxton were shunted to the back of his mind. There was nothing else but him and the wall.

The breach was as wide as his arms outstretched. It had been filled in with granite cut from ancient quarries once used in the making of the original wall they had uncovered nearby. The stonecutters, Alton among them, had sized blocks of granite to match exactly those of the wall. Craftmasters examined the original mortar and came up with their best binding material ever, and the repairwork was put in place, painstakingly and precisely matched with the original wall and its materials.

It was some of Clan D'Yer's best work in a hundred years, maybe more; painstakingly crafted to the minutest detail. Yet it was not enough. One essential ingredient was missing: magic.

The illusory magic of the wall did not extend above the repairwork of the breach. As though a slice of stonework had been cut right out of the wall, Alton saw only sky.

Then the wind picked up again and sulfurous mist from Blackveil roiled and drifted over the repairwork. Alton remembered the mist well. As he had worked to repair the wall, it had clung to him, to his skin and clothes. He'd felt soiled by it, and though he washed vigorously every night, he was never quite able to cleanse himself of it.

He remembered glancing into Blackveil, as if to catch someone or *something* watching him, but observed nothing—just the shifting mist animating the black branches of trees into snakes or tentacles.

There were creatures that lived in Blackveil, one of the reasons the wall was so important a bulwark, and Alton fancied it was these twisted monstrosities that had watched him and the other laborers. And if they could not see the creatures, they were certainly able to hear their hoots and screams.

Then there was the night a big laborer named Egan slipped away from the campfire to relieve himself. He was never seen alive again. The only trace they found of him the next morning was blood staining some of the stonework he'd helped place in the breach the day before. No one dared venture into the forest to search for more evidence of Egan's demise. From then on, the night watch was augmented by additional troops sent by Landrew.

Alton frowned as he drew his gaze along the repairwork. The granite ashlars he helped cut, shape, and set a couple years ago looked duller, older, than the rock around them, which had been cut and set a thousand years ago. The old rockwork retained its pink hue as though freshly cut. Black lichen splotched the repairwork, but none marred the original wall—not even a fleck of lichen, as though it were impervious to the weathering of nature and time.

It was very strange, he thought, how the same granite, drawn from the same quarry, could look so different.

Yet the wall was not impervious to all damage. Cracks radiated outward from the breach. Alton trailed his fingers across the rough texture of the wall, tracing one of the spidery cracks. He walked for several yards, following it. From one crack was born dozens of others, and no amount of re-pointing fixed the problem. The mortar merely cracked, too.

His frown deepened as he saw the extent of the damage. It had nearly doubled since his last visit.

How were they ever going to fix it?

"What do you think, nephew?" Landrew asked.

Alton had forgotten about the presence of his uncle and Sergeant Uxton. To his dismay, he saw that Pendric had joined them.

Rubbing his chin, he said, "Doesn't look good."

Pendric snorted. "We knew *that.* I told you, father, that he'd be of no help."

"Perhaps if I had some time and less of an audience," Alton said, glowering at his cousin.

"Of course," Landrew said. "There will be time enough for you to examine the wall in detail during the days to come. We will leave you for now, though Sergeant Uxton must remain. Don't linger too long, however, for your aunt will wish to see you."

Alton waited until his uncle and cousin were well away before he turned to the sergeant. "Would you move off some paces, please, so I can think in peace?"

"A *few* paces, my lord, aye."

Alton wasn't sure why he was so self-conscious about having anyone witness him work. Maybe it was just more difficult to think and act when someone's eyes were trained on him. Or maybe, because the Riders were so careful to conceal their special abilities, he did not want to expose himself before others should any magic come into play.

Somehow, he sensed the exposure of magic wasn't going to be a problem just now. Despite the pull he had felt for so long, the wall remained as immutable as, well, stone, as though to mock him. No voices called to him, and the pull was inexplicably absent.

He laid his palms flat against the cold stone, his nose

but inches from the wall. What did he expect? The wall to whisper its eternal secrets to him?

Nothing.

Alton debated whether or not to give up and return to his uncle's tent when, like the shot of an arrow, silver lines streaked beneath his hands, forming glistening runes which swirled to life around the cracks, only to vanish in the blink of an eye.

Startled, he jumped backward, looking wildly about the wall for another sign, but finding nothing.

"Did you see that?" he demanded of Sergeant Uxton.

"See what, my lord?"

"The—" He stopped. The sergeant waited, watching intently. How could the sergeant have missed the flash of runes? Unless . . .

My imagination? I wished to see it?

He placed his hands against the wall again, cajoling, wishing, and even cursing, but the wall revealed nothing. After a half hour of this, Alton pulled away, disgusted with himself for thinking he alone would discover the secrets of the wall.

He turned his back to it and stalked toward the tent village with Sergeant Uxton in tow, the wall rearing up ominously behind them. Then someone cried out in fear and Alton whirled just in time to see a large dark shape winging toward him.

❧ BLACKVEIL ❧

The sentience awoke to silence. The voices that entrapped it were strangely absent, focused elsewhere.

Cautiously, it extended a thread of awareness, gently probing through the forest, remaining as tiny and inconspicuous as possible so as not to alarm its guardians.

It slipped along the slime trail of a glistening slug for a short distance. It hid beneath rocks, and tunneled in the damp underground as a blind mole.

Warm blood gushed through the mole's body, pumped by its heart in a rhythmic throb the sentience found oddly comforting and familiar. The mole burrowed deeper, using its powerful shoulders and spadelike front feet to shovel aside soil.

It stopped abruptly, and twitched its nose. The sentience felt its hunger, and with unthinking instinct, it gnashed at something soft, damp, and wriggly.

Repulsed, the sentience expelled itself from the mole and traced its way back through the tunnel.

What am I? What am I that I have no beating heart? No pulsing blood?

The mole had a body, but it was a dim, stupid creature that relied on instinct.

I am no such creature. Perhaps I am the air that fills the creature's lungs.

This did not seem correct either. The air could not be trapped this way, trapped behind walls and barriers.

The sentience resurfaced to the world above as moisture sucked from the ground by the roots of a limp, dark fern. It joined with an insect, which sped away on buzzing wings. Through multifaceted eyes, it spotted a young avian tearing into the carcass of some unfortunate prey animal, gulping down flesh to bulge out its sinuous, scaled neck.

The insect alighted on the avian to feed on its blood, giving the the sentience an opportunity to transfer itself to a new host. The avian flapped its wings in agitation at the intrusion, but the sentience stayed quiet, sensing the creature's hunger and lust for blood, feeling the warmth of its prey easing down its gullet and into its gnawing stomach.

The avian was merely base instinct, aware of nothing but its own needs, a vicious creature on all counts, its very heart dark. The sentience decided to seize control of it.

The avian struggled mightily, waving its head back and forth and squawking in protest, but it did not take long for the sentience to overcome its small mind.

Through the eyes of the avian, the world of the sentience's confinement sharpened—the contrast of dark tree shadows and gray mist, logs decaying into duff, insects hovering in the dim light, the fuzz of mosses carpeting the ground. Something slurped into a black pool, piquing the avian's interest, and registering "prey" in its mind.

The sentience stilled the avian's predatory excitement, and again sent out a pinpoint of awareness through the forest. The guardians had not yet noted its wakefulness. Something else had taken their attention; they strained to reach out to the other side of the wall.

Intrigued by their preoccupation, the sentience, too, wished to see the other side of the wall.

It released a measure of control over the avian so it could fly. The avian stretched its wings, flapped, and spiraled upward through the trees, deftly missing entwined branches, and surged above the canopy. Thick mist enclosed the forest below, except for the spires of tree tops poking through. Even above the forest, the mist was still thick, banishing the sun to a murky white disk.

The sentience forced the avian unwaveringly northward, toward the wall, seeking the place where it had once detected weakness.

It wasn't long before the layers of mist peeled away, revealing the wall directly ahead. The avian wheeled away, barely in time to avoid a collision. The sentience reined the creature into a glide, the wall swirling past its wingtip.

A brightness shone where there should have been wall, signaling the place of weakness. The sentience forced the avian to land on the broken wall, talons scrabbling on stone as it backwinged. The avian extended its serpentine neck, and with a blink, peered to the other side.

The sunlight, so unfamiliar to the creature, was too bright. It dropped nictitating membranes over its eyes to protect them.

A myriad of structures billowing in the wind filled the world below, and moving among them were many creatures.

Men, came the unbidden memory.

They were scattered everywhere, these men, milling, moving, thriving. There was a power here, too. A power reminiscent of that which entrapped the sentience. Somewhere among these men, there was one who could speak with the guardians, one who could fix the weakness in the wall. One who could seal off the sentience's prison forever.

Hunger roiled in the avian's belly, and its gaze settled on the back of one who walked away from the wall.

The guardians chose that moment to become alert to the sentience's wakefulness. Alarm buzzed through the wall and beneath the avian's talons. Startled, the avian flapped its wings and launched into the air.

Come back to us, ancient one, the voices called.

Overcome, the sentience lost control of the avian. The creature angled its wings for maximum speed and soared toward the man's back, talons extended.

Men pointed and shouted. The man turned, eyes wide as it took in the avian arrowing in on him. He dropped on the ground just in time to evade talons.

The guardians screamed at the sentience, or maybe it was the wind screaming past the ears of the avian. The sentience could make no sense of it. The billowing structures— *tents*—were but blurs below. Men scattered in all directions, yelling and running in confusion.

Fear radiating from so much available prey aroused the avian's predatory hunger to a new height. It turned on a wingtip, screaming for blood, bearing down again on the man, but this time he held a shiny object.

Sword.

The sentience wanted to avert the avian's mad flight, but the guardians distracted it with their songs of peace and contentment, and promises of tranquil slumbering. All it had to do was return; return to the other side of the wall and end the struggle. Just rest. Rest and sleep . . .

The avian circled above the man, flicking its forked tongue, before stooping into a dive.

The man did not cower but slashed with his blade, cutting the avian above its talon.

PAIN! RAGE! REVENGE!

Maddened, the creature surged upward with great wing-strokes to gain altitude for another diving attack. A projectile whizzed by its head.

Stupid creature, the sentience thought, fighting the grogginess brought on by the guardians. With a mighty effort, it again exerted its will into the avian's mind.

Survival, it urged the avian, fearing for its own survival should the avian be killed. *Seek safety.*

The avian tossed its head and screeched in angry resistance, and pursued prey.

This time it hunted for one without defense. Men scattered as it skimmed above their heads, and it lunged upon one who could not run fast enough. The man—*no, woman*—loosed a bloodcurdling scream as talons sank into her shoulders.

HUNGER!

The avian attempted to carry the woman away, but its wings had not the strength. It dropped her, and landed atop her back, spreading its wings over her to protect its prey from interlopers, screeching threats at the men who rushed toward it with shining, sharp weapons.

Survival! the sentience screamed in the avian's mind, but the scent of warm blood overcame all else. It reared its head back, ready to lunge its raptor's beak into the whimpering prey beneath it for the kill.

Fly! Survival! Panic allowed the sentience to exert the whole of its will upon the avian.

SURVIVAL—FOOD!

The men had projectile weapons among them, but the sentience comprehended their fear of using them lest they inadvertently kill the woman. They feared the avian, too. The sentience encouraged the avian in a fierce display to keep the men off.

The man the avian had attacked initially advanced with grim resolve. He wore green, and this sparked some memory of hatred.

The avian recognized him, too, saw its own black blood on his blade, and remembered pain. It launched from the woman.

Yes, survival, the sentience crooned. *Safety.*

The avian started winging toward the gap in the wall.

And now the guardians welcomed the sentience's return

in song, *Come back to us, ancient one, come sleep in peace . . .*

A volley of arrows hissed past the avian, arcing over the wall. The avian swung its head around to screech at the men below.

Safety, the sentience urged. *Seek safety.*

Just as the avian glided through the gap in the wall, there came another flight of arrows. A barbed head drove into the avian's side, tearing muscle and tendon, crushing bone, piercing lung.

The avian careened into the mist of the forest and plummeted, trees coming at it in a mad rush. It crashed through branches. Wing bones snapped. It hit one bough, and tumbled to another, until finally it fell into a heap on the ground.

There it lay with neck limp, and wings splayed and rumpled. Nictitating eyelids peeled back, and the avian drew one last rattling breath.

The sentience flowed from the avian in its blood, soaking into the moss beneath. Exhausted by its strivings with both the avian and the guardians, it let itself be drawn into sleep with one final lingering thought: *What am I?*

Journal of Hadriax el Fex

The clans have proven more difficult to subdue than we originally perceived. They will hear nothing of joining the Empire, and refuse conversion to the one God. They have even sneaked into our camps and stolen supplies, thinking it great fun to accomplish this beneath the noses of a superior race of people.

Alessandros' answer to their treachery was to lead a raid into one of the nearby villages to make an example. Their heathen altar was destroyed and the moon priest burned to death. We then set about torching their longhouses, where families remained huddled inside in fear. It was nasty work, but needful.

The village warriors were fierce, but we made quick work of them with our concussives. Alessandros is pleased with the day's events. Now, he believes, the other villages and clan chiefs will see their folly in opposing the Empire.

I, for one, am relieved our stockade is nearly completed.

⋙ SWORDPLAY ⋘

Captain Mapstone dipped her pen into the inkwell, but paused before signing off on the sheaf of papers before her.

"Is there anything else you wanted to add to the report?"

"I think that's all." Karigan hoped the captain didn't detect any hesitance in her voice.

"I know it hasn't been easy regurgitating those terrible events over and over, but the king appreciates your efforts to provide a detailed and accurate record."

Karigan nodded, glancing down at her hands folded across her lap. She had stood before the king and his inner circle three times to be grilled about the delegation's journey and its disastrous end. The king's advisors thrust question after question at her.

Why did you believe the clearing was unsafe?

Where were you when the fighting broke out?

Why do you think the Eletian wanted to speak to you?

Why didn't you join the main body of the fighting?

The king questioned her more quietly, more gently than his advisors, as if more sensitive to what she had endured. More than he spoke, even, he listened. He listened intently to her answers, or perhaps "intensely" was a better description. He sat there on his throne, his chin propped on steepled fingers, his eyes focused on her as though he could

148

discern more from watching her closely than by simply listening.

The questioning had gone on for hours each time, with no one any more satisfied than when they had begun.

Now Karigan sat in Captain Mapstone's quarters going over the whole thing once again. The captain hadn't exactly grilled her, after all she'd been present during the other questionings, but she wished to verify the events as described in Karigan's written report.

Every time Karigan had to revisit that night of terror by the cairn, images of carnage flashed back to her. So did images of broken shackles on a funerary slab, and the wraith pointing its bony finger at her, its voice rasping, "Betrayer."

She tried to answer the questions as thoroughly as possible, but one thing she did hold back, even from the captain, was the failure of her special ability during the battle. She didn't know why she didn't—*couldn't*—bring it up. Maybe it was shame, or maybe she felt the problem would rectify itself in time. Maybe she was too frightened to admit aloud her ability had failed her.

There had been a time when she wished her ability would go away forever so she could have the life she planned for herself, but now that it had, it unnerved her. Something had changed, and whether her lack of ability was a personal failing, or something else was going on the world, it couldn't mean anything good—could it?

For now she would keep it to herself. There was no use in getting anyone overly concerned in case it was nothing.

"Karigan?"

She shook herself from her reverie. "No, Captain, I really can't think of anything else to add." She hoped the captain interpreted her long silence as a pause to go over events in her mind, as if searching for something new.

The captain nodded in satisfaction and signed off on the

report. With a tinge of guilt, Karigan knew the captain would not call on her own ability to check the honesty of her words. She trusted her Riders.

The captain set her pen down and turned to gaze squarely at Karigan. "I want you to know how very proud the king and I are of your actions while you were with the delegation. Major Everson was so impressed with your comportment during the ride home, he has offered to sponsor you into the light cavalry."

The distaste must have been so evident on Karigan's face, that Captain Mapstone, absently fingering the ragged brown scar that slashed down her neck, said, "I take it you're not interested."

"If I had a choice of going anywhere, I'd return to my clan," Karigan replied, "but I don't think the call would let me go. Not even to join the light cavalry."

Captain Mapstone looked positively relieved—she'd actually been worried! Her hand fell away from her scar. "I would hate to lose you," she said in a quiet voice. "I think you have developed into a fine Green Rider."

Karigan tried to look anywhere but at the captain. She glanced down at her hands again, over at the map spread on the captain's worktable, its curling edges held down by a half-filled mug of cold tea and a crust of bread, and at the shelves on the far wall piled with books. Pleasure and guilt both warmed her cheeks. Pleasure at receiving a rare bit of praise from the captain whom she respected. Guilt of being unworthy because she had never truly embraced being a Green Rider.

The captain sighed. "The business of the kingdom does go on, and so does the king's correspondence. If you are feeling up to it, I'd like to ease you back into the work schedule. No strenuous or lengthy rides to begin with, just some simple, short-range message errands to help you catch your wind again. What do you think?"

"I'm ready." Karigan had been back a couple weeks now and was itching to return to work. Currently she had too much free time to think about things, those terrible things that had happened to the delegation. The loss of her colleagues who were also friends.

Captain Mapstone smiled. "Excellent. I'll let Mara know. You are dismissed."

Karigan decided to stroll about the castle grounds to stretch her legs after her long session with Captain Mapstone. The wind blew through her unbound hair. The afternoon sky was fair, but the clouds and a change in wind direction indicated the weather might take a new tack by daybreak.

She wandered by the barracks of the regular militia, and the outdoor riding arena where horses and riders alike were trained. Sometimes contests of fighting and riding skill were held here, where various divisions of the military competed against one another. The competitions were friendly, but serious. No division wished to experience the dishonor of losing.

Some members of the light cavalry were currently using the arena to exercise their horses. Karigan shook her head, unable to imagine herself in the deep navy uniform and wearing a helm with a ridiculous red plume. Even if the Rider call released her, she had no desire to serve with a bunch of aristocrats, who during their escort duty of the remnant delegation spent their evenings in their tents, sipping brandy and being attended to by servants, while the delegation's survivors—many exhausted and injured—slept fitfully on the bare ground.

No, she could not serve with a group for which she held so little respect.

She walked on, passing stables and more barracks, the parade field, and the quartermaster's storehouses. All the while, the castle stood tall and imperious to her left. The castle was huge, and its grounds vast, once garrisoning hundreds upon hundreds of troops and other inhabitants. Those days were long ago, in less peaceful times.

Though the grounds were fairly quiet, she did find two men in sword combat practice on a field set aside for such training.

They raised puffs of dirt about their ankles as they scuffed around one of the small, worn practice rings. To Karigan's surprise, they did not use simple wooden practice swords, but true edged steel blades. She paused to watch, transfixed.

One of the combatants was Arms Master Drent, unmistakable even from this distance. He was a huge hulking man who had something of the look of a groundmite about him, with thick features and hair cropped close to his skull. Mere mention of his name was enough to instill fear in the stoutest of trainees. Even after swordmasters finished training at the academy, they must face Drent if they wished to join the elite ranks of the Weapons. Drent oversaw one of their final cullings.

The arms master fought as fearsomely as he looked, and his size did nothing to slow him down. Blades blurred in a rapid *cling clang* of blows.

His opponent, dressed in black trousers and a white shirt that allowed free movement, did an admirable job of keeping up with Drent. His back was to her, but she could still admire his grace, and the shirt did nothing to conceal broad shoulders strong enough to block Drent's blows. His footwork was pretty good, too.

Then Drent feinted, and drove his blade so swiftly and at such an angle that the trainee's sword flew right out of his hand.

"Must I go back to basics with you?" Drent shouted. "How many times must I go over it?"

Karigan grimaced at Drent's tone. It was severe enough

to make anyone want to slink away into a dark corner and hide, yet his trainee didn't even flinch, not even during the demeaning upbraiding that followed.

"Fastion," Drent called, "I need your assistance for a moment."

Karigan was surprised to see the Weapon emerge from the shadow of a nearby maple. Weapons excelled at hiding in shadows. The trainee must be a swordmaster he was mentoring.

Fastion and Drent exchanged some words she couldn't quite make out, then Drent turned in Karigan's direction.

"You there, come over here."

It was like being struck by lightening, having Drent's attention on her like that. She wanted to shrivel into her boots. When the trainee turned to look, too, she nearly fainted. The man whose physical form she'd been admiring was none other than King Zachary.

"I—"

"Come here *now.*"

One did not dare disobey a direct order from Drent of all people, unless they wanted a verbal flaying. Karigan's legs trembled as she approached the practice ring and bowed to the king.

"Fastion's job is to guard the king," Drent explained, "and as he rightly pointed out, he can't put his full attention to that duty if he's practicing with the king. Therefore," and Drent's little eyes stabbed into her, "you shall help illustrate what is being done wrong, and how to correct it."

Karigan glanced helplessly at Fastion, but the usually stone-faced Weapon gave her a tight smile and a wink—a *wink!*—before melding back into the shadow of the maple tree. She groaned inwardly.

The king passed her his longsword, his eyes glittering. The sword was hefty, much more so than what she was accustomed to. She adjusted her hold higher up on the grip to make it balance better, but she knew, even though her arm had mended well since the battle at the clearing, it would tire quickly.

"Now here's what I want you to do," Drent told Karigan. He wrapped his massive hand around her wrist and directed it in the movement of the feint and angle he had used against the king. Karigan licked her lips in concentration, trying to memorize the feel and motion of the technique.

"Got it?" Drent asked.

"Yes, sir, I think so."

"You don't *think*. Yes or no?"

Karigan just wanted to crawl away. "Yes."

"Let's try it then. You will attack me using that technique, but we'll go slowly so the boy can see his mistake."

Karigan was surprised by Drent's disrespect, but it didn't seem to faze the king. She did as instructed and went through the sequence of moves, Drent all the while explaining why the king's block failed.

"You met the angle all wrong. Your sword was too high. Now let's see what it looks like done correctly."

Karigan and Drent went through the entire sequence, again slowly, but this time the arms master demonstrating the correct block.

"Got it?" he asked the king.

"Indeed," the king said with a wry smile.

"Good. Then you show me. Girl, you will—"

"Rider G'ladheon," the king corrected.

"Hunh?"

"She is Rider G'ladheon."

Drent hacked and spat. "*Rider G'ladheon,* you will attack the boy, full speed."

"What? I—! But he's the king!"

Drent rolled his eyes. "Gods have mercy. Of course he's the king." He passed his sword over to the king. "Girl, Rider, you will commence the attack."

The king smiled encouragingly at her. "Don't worry about me, so long as you are wary of the blade edges."

Karigan unsuccessfully tried to brush away her apprehension. She had never *practiced* with edged weapons before, and she feared that a single slip could seriously maim the king.

"Ready yourselves," Drent said.

Reluctantly Karigan faced the king, the sword feeling like lead in her hand.

"Begin."

Karigan brought up her sword in reflex, touching off with the king's. As they commenced the sequence Drent desired, Karigan's own timid moves were matched by hesitant ones from the king. All the strength and power she had observed in his earlier swordplay was now lacking. With some surprise, she realized he was concerned about hurting her, too.

Drent groaned. "Stop, stop, stop. Pitiful, absolutely pitiful. Girl, you are not doing your sovereign any good by being gentle with him. He won't learn to defend himself with this pitiful tapping." Then he turned to the king. "And you shall respond in kind. If you do not, then she will draw blood and I shall have to hang her from a tree. Now. Harder, faster."

Karigan swallowed, but as ordered, launched into her attack. A spasm of surprise rippled through the king's expression as he stepped up to catch the blow. If it was her speed or strength that surprised him, it quickly faded from his features, which became angled with concentration.

About halfway through the sequence, the weight of the sword and Karigan's previous injury took its toll. Her initial speed slackened, and her movements felt jerky. Pain stabbed through her arm from wrist to elbow to shoulder. Grimly she bumbled through the sequence, the king's swordplay flawless, and his control precise.

Karigan raised her sword to absorb the king's final blow, but pain like jagged edges of glass grinding in her elbow stole all strength from her arm.

Unable to block the final blow, the last thing she saw was the edge of King Zachary's blade hurtling at her face with unstoppable momentum.

KING, SWORDMASTER, MAN

Laren didn't know who to throttle first—Zachary or Drent.

Fastion stood outside the doorway of Karigan's room and, sensing her mood, stepped aside. Was it her imagination, or did the Weapon look just a bit sheepish? If she found out he had anything to do with this, she'd throttle him, too.

She turned to enter the room, and nearly collided with Master Mender Destarion, who was on his way out. Destarion held his hand up, indicating she should step back into the corridor.

"The room is a bit tight at the moment, Captain," he said.

She peered over his shoulder and saw Drent's bulk hogging up most of the space. Zachary was in there, too. The two men blocked her view of Karigan.

"If Drent would—"

"A few words please." Destarion's voice was always level and pleasant, his expression mild. He was well trained in the mending arts, and his manner calmed her. A little.

"Your Rider is fine. A little bump on the head. There shall be some bruising and a headache, but I suspect no serious head injury. Just in case, however, I'd like someone to look in on her periodically through the night."

"I'll do it."

So intent upon finding someone to throttle, Laren hadn't noted Mara shadowing her. Mara had been the one to bring her the news of the swordplay gone awry.

"Additionally," Destarion said, "she won't be able to use her sword arm for a time. Apparently she wrenched muscles and tendons already weakened by an injury received during her recent delegation duty."

Laren began to feel a headache of her own coming on. "She never told me she had been hurt." She would definitely add Karigan to her list of throttlings.

Destarion shrugged. "She tells me she felt it had mended on its own, and I suspect it mostly did. It was not healed enough, however, for the activity she engaged in today. Not an uncommon injury, I might add, among swordfighters. I recommend very light duty until I deem the arm sound."

Very light duty. That meant no message errands. Laren frowned and entered Karigan's room, leaving Mara to receive the mender's more detailed instructions.

She pushed between Zachary and Drent to stand over the bed. Karigan lay sprawled across it, boots still on. Her arm was slack across her stomach, and with her good hand, she held a wet compress to her temple.

"I would like an explanation," Laren said.

Karigan tried to sit up, winced, and laid back down. "I—"

"It was not her fault," Zachary interrupted. "I am—"

Laren turned to him, glowering. "You mean she isn't at fault for not informing me of a prior injury?"

A gleam lit in Drent's eye at the prospect of Karigan receiving all the blame, but he blinked when she transferred her glower to him. When she looked back at Zachary, she noticed he cradled his wrist in a compress.

"What did you do to yourself?"

"He sprained it trying to snap back the blow he landed on the girl," Drent said. "If he hadn't, your Rider would be ascending to the heavens with Westrion right now."

Zachary's cheeks were ashen, and no doubt the guilt of his part in Karigan's injury would eat away at him for weeks. *Good.*

"Practicing with edged blades, were you?"

"Yep." Drent again. "Teaches precision, adds to the reality of combat." His smile was gruesome. "Helps teach not to make mistakes. It's standard practice for swordmasters."

A little gasp from the bed told Laren that Karigan hadn't known that the king she served possessed this level of swordsmanship.

"Yes," Laren said, "standard for swordmasters such as yourselves, but Karigan is not a swordmaster."

Drent passed his hand over his spiky hair and cast a calculating look at Karigan. "Maybe with a little work . . ."

Oh yes, Drent was going to get throttled, with a black eye thrown into the bargain. This conversation wasn't going at all the way she intended.

True, her ability told her.

Who asked you? She retorted. Her ability had been passing judgment of its own volition just a bit too freely of late. And now she was talking back to it? She'd have to clamp down on it.

"Not only did you endanger *my* Rider," Laren said, "but now the messenger service is more short-handed than ever."

"I can ride," Karigan said weakly from her bed.

Laren forced herself not to laugh. The sword blow may have knocked out Karigan's common sense, but it did nothing to extinguish her spirit. It was spirit that made Karigan such a good Rider, but it was her lapses of common sense that tended to get her in trouble. Maybe it wasn't just lapses of common sense . . . The girl was a magnet for trouble. Whatever the case, for however long Karigan answered the Rider call, she sensed things would be quite interesting around here.

"Right," she said. "I can see I won't get any useful information with the three of you here together, so I shall speak with you individually. Excellency," she said, then turned on her heel to leave. "Drent, you're with me—to my office."

The captain's swift anger gave Karigan more of a headache than the sword blow. She winced as boots rapped down the corridor.

Drent rolled his eyes. "The five hells have no fury like Captain Laren Mapstone."

"Drent!" The captain's shout came like the crack of a whip.

The arms master groaned. "I hope she didn't hear that." He bowed stiffly to the king and started to leave. He paused in the doorway and peered back at them. "If no one hears from me in an hour or two, send reinforcements!"

"Drent!"

He grimaced, and like a dog with his tail tucked between his legs, headed down the corridor.

The king whistled softly. "I know she's really upset when she calls me 'excellency' in private," he said, "but I've never seen Drent intimidated before."

"I'm sorry," Karigan said.

"For what?"

"For getting you in trouble with the captain."

The king raised his eyebrows in disbelief, then hooked his foot around the leg of a chair and dragged it over to the bed so he could sit beside her. The room, Karigan thought, was feeling rather close. It was too much—the swordplay, the king helping her back to barracks with soft words of encouragement, and she found herself, despite the pain and embarrassment, finding pleasure in his attention.

I did *get whacked on the head, didn't I?*

The king leaned forward. "Karigan, Laren and I go back quite a few years. She's like an older sister to me." A smile flickered across his lips. "I've been in trouble with that formidable woman more times than I care to remember, and have managed to survive."

"But I—"

"Rider, your captain happens to be correct. Drent and I should not have involved you in such advanced swordplay. You were doing so well we didn't think much of it. As a result of our negligence, your captain is short one Rider for an undetermined time, and more importantly, you have been hurt."

"Your wrist—"

"Will be back to normal in a couple days." He grinned and she liked the effect it had on his eyes. "I've received far worse from bouts with Arms Master Drent."

He regarded her for many moments, his features now very solemn. "I want you to know that I'd never intend you harm."

She wanted to reassure him she knew this, but the words caught in her throat when he reached over and touched the back of her hand, just very lightly, with his fingertips. Heat radiated from his touch, and her own heat flooded her cheeks. She wanted to push the compress over her whole face to hide the blush.

She closed her eyes. *I am addled. The whack addled my brain.*

This was her sovereign, her king. The same man she'd seen as mysterious and commanding a couple years ago before they had entered the tombs of Heroes Avenue. She had seen him cold and terrible as he presided over the executions of traitors. By his own hand he had executed the former lord-governor of Mirwell. Mirwell, at the block; King Zachary tall and his features as stony as the castle walls surrounding him, in his hand a shining blade arcing down . . .

Her sovereign was also a man. She had witnessed his humanity. Tears over the fallen at the Battle of the Lost Lake. Expressing his passion for the land of Sacoridia and its people, even when forced to kneel and submit before his traitorous brother. A walk in the gardens and a chaste kiss on her hand, the glimmer of humor in brown eyes, the warmth of his touch . . .

The man frightened her more than the king.

When she opened her eyes, he was gone. Only Mara stood there in the doorway, peering at her, then glancing down the corridor with a bemused expression on her face.

⇜ FOOTPRINTS ⇝

"**P**ut this book on the top shelf."

"This book" was *Lint's Wordage,* a compilation of famous quotations. Karigan gazed at the thick tome with dismay, but gamely reached for it with both hands.

"No," Captain Mapstone said, not even looking up from her papers, "use only your right hand."

Karigan obeyed. If this was what it took to prove to the captain her arm was sound, so be it. Immediately the weight of the book pulled on tender joints and muscles. Swallowing back a curse, she walked across the room to the captain's bookshelves. She raised the book, her arm quivering, while what felt like daggers twisted in her elbow joint. She couldn't seem to lift the book any higher than her waist. She just hadn't the strength.

Still she tried, gritting her teeth against the pain. A rivulet of perspiration glided down the side of her face and tears overflowed the edges of her eyes.

Captain Mapstone left her papers and crossed over to Karigan. Gently she removed the volume from her shaking hand. Karigan sobbed with relief, and slipped her strained arm back into its despicable sling.

"When you can shelve this book," the captain told her, "I'll take you off light duty. With Master Destarion's approval, of course."

Karigan glared at the offending book.

"In the meantime, I've some documents for you to carry over to administration."

Karigan tucked the documents under her arm—her good arm—and set off from officers quarters across the castle grounds.

The welt and bruise had nearly faded from her temple, and Destarion's cold treatments were working wonders on her elbow. But not enough. She couldn't even help much at the stable because too much of what was needed to be done required lifting and carrying.

Karigan found light duty all too reminiscent of what her father had her doing before she gave in to the Rider call: going over inventories, ordering supplies, assisting Mara with scheduling, running errands . . .

The irony of the situation was not lost on her.

She glanced at the sky. The change in weather she'd been expecting had held off. The day was bright and lovely.

The records room was located in the bottom level of the administration wing. Karigan didn't know the area well, for she usually had little reason to venture there. It was usually the Chief Rider who handled administrative duties. The corridors were mazelike, a regular warren. The rough rockwork and the low, arched ceilings indicated she had entered an older part of the castle.

She strode along, worrying about when she'd be able to ride again. Was there some way she could convince Captain Mapstone that her arm didn't have to be perfect to ride? How would she ever get her arm in shape to lift that bloody book?

Caught up in her concerns, she rounded a corner and kept striding until, with surprise, she found herself in the dark.

An abandoned corridor. The castle had been added on to over the centuries. Originally it had been more of a fortress keep rather than the large, sprawling structure it now was, but as the castle population shrank in peacetime, inhabitants moved into newer, more spacious sections, abandoning the old corridors.

Karigan had been in some of these deserted corridors once before. The Weapon, Fastion, was her guide. The Weapons, he said, were the only ones who really knew their way through the old sections.

She sighed at the memory of walking through abandoned corridors in the dance of a single candleflame; of a sense of timelessness. It had been a frightening experience and she had no desire to blunder down those dark, ancient passageways again.

She turned around to head back, but a figure hovered on the edge of her vision in the dusky space where light spilled into the dark. Her brooch stirred.

She perceived a swirl of green cloth as the figure swept by her, retreating down the corridor into complete darkness. The ring of boots on stone sounded strange, as though separated from her by the distance of time.

"Wait!"

Wait, wait, wait . . .

Her cry carried into the dark, down countless unknown corridors where, perhaps, no living voice had been heard for a very long time. The footsteps faded out and there was no response. Though she did not like the thought of sending her voice into that darkness again, she tried anyway.

"Hello?"

Hello? Hello? Hello?

And then in answer, only silence.

Who would go running down a pitch black corridor? A ghost?

She swallowed, not really wanting to know, for she had dealt with ghosts before and hoped herself free of them. She hastened from the dark corridor with a shiver, but when she stepped blinking into the lit corridor, she paused. It all could have been her imagination.

Cursing her own curiosity, she stuffed her papers into her sling and grabbed a lamp from a nearby alcove. Shadows leaped when she returned to the abandoned corridor. Light glinted dully off an old suit of plate armor some distance away.

She examined the floor. A layer of dust coated the flagstones—not too thickly, as the air currents that flowed through the active sections of the castle must find their way here—but it was thick enough to pick out distinct footprints. Her own set went a short distance, serpentined by the tiny footprints of mice. A second set, much like her own, clear and new in the lamplight, ran off into the dark. And there was something more. Karigan knelt, and setting the lamp aside, touched the floor. Splotches of water.

A wet apparition?

Who had run by her? Why hadn't they acknowledged her?

Then, even as she gazed at the footprints, dust filled them in, erasing their existence. The drops of water evaporated. All this though nothing shifted or swirled, her own footsteps remaining unchanged and clear.

Heart pounding, she grabbed the lamp and exited the corridor, the dark rolling in behind her retreating lamplight.

Imagination. I imagined it all.

But a prickle of premonition on the back of her neck warred with that simple explanation.

The records room was a vaulted chamber of tables and shelves overflowing with books and scrolls and crates of paper. Lamps had trouble illuminating the vast space and shone like small, insignificant orbs. With no windows but arrow slits along one wall, it might as well have been night. A decorative frieze was lost to the shadows, and the torsos of carved figures soaring toward the ceiling were severed in half by light and dark.

A clerk sat at a writing desk. He was so absorbed in his penmanship he hadn't heard Karigan enter.

"Excuse me," she said.

The clerk squawked and bounced up from his stool, knocking it over, which in turn pushed over a pile of books on the table behind him. The cascading books toppled a barrel of rolled maps. He squawked again when he saw that the ink of his pen had splattered across his papers. Hastily he grabbed a container of sand to sprinkle on the wet blotches, but the container's lid fell off, and the entire contents of the container poured out into a little mound on his papers.

The clerk could only stare at the mess.

He was so expressively mortified that Karigan nearly laughed, but knowing it wouldn't be appreciated, she swallowed it back. She stepped forward and the little man jumped again, eyes wide through his thick specs, and his hand over his heart.

"I'm sorry," Karigan said, "I didn't mean to startle you."

"I thought you were a . . ." But he just trailed off, shaking his head and muttering.

Feeling somewhat responsible for the mess, Karigan set aside Captain Mapstone's papers on a nearby table and said, "Let me help you." She set to work righting the map barrel, and re-stacking the books.

The clerk watched her for a moment, then shook himself and tended to his sand-covered papers.

"You don't get many visitors here, do you?" Karigan said.

"Very few."

She wasn't surprised she had startled him, if he wasn't accustomed to people walking in very often. He'd also been concentrating on his work and was probably unaware of his surroundings. Still, it didn't account for the way he now darted his gaze about, as though he expected someone to leap out of the shadows at any moment.

Considering the dark ambiance of the place, and what appeared to be a solitary job, it would be easy for one's imagination to run wild. The ancient surroundings, the life a building could take on of its own—the moans of the structure, its wheezings and exhalations as air currents shifted, the flickering shadows . . .

Yes, all fodder for the imagination.

Had her own imagination been similarly triggered when she stood in the abandoned corridor?

When she placed the last book atop the pile—a dusty volume containing a ten-year-old inventory of castle livestock—she turned to the clerk. He seemed to have the sand situation in hand, but he'd have to copy over the memorandum he'd been writing. The splotches of ink rendered it illegible.

Hoping she wouldn't spook him again, she said, "I'm sorry you'll have to start over."

The clerk sighed and fiddled nervously with his black sleeve guards. "It wouldn't be the first time." He then gazed nearsightedly at her. "You're not Mara."

"No, I'm Karigan, and I'm helping out Mara and Captain Mapstone. I brought over some documents. And you are?"

"Dakrias Brown, recordskeeper."

"Tell me, Dakrias, did anyone else come by here shortly before I arrived?"

"No. No one has been here all day, except the chief administrator, and that was hours ago." He glanced anxiously about. "Why do you ask?"

"I thought I saw someone near here just a few moments ago."

Dakrias' gaze turned penetrating. "It happens sometimes."

"What? You said very few come here and—"

"Yes, I did. I did, indeed. Very few *people*."

"I don't understand."

"I am often here alone," Dakrias said, "filing records, copying correspondence, that sort of thing. The other clerks call this place the crypt." He frowned with distaste. "*They* are all on an upper level, in a more active section of the castle. *They* have windows. They just don't understand what it's like down here for me."

"Why are you down here away from the rest of administration?"

Dakrias shrugged. "Too much effort to move hundreds of years of census records, and all the birth, marriage, and death registers . . . No one wants to deal with moving it—*no one*. It's just easier to leave it be, because they know Dakrias Brown will take care of it, and they just forget about me. Hmph. *They* don't have to be stuck down here."

His eyes roved about the chamber. "This was once the library, before the castle expanded prior to the Clan Wars."

A library . . . A dark and gloomy one at that.

As if picking up on her thoughts, Dakrias jabbed his finger toward the ceiling shrouded in shadow. "Used to be domed with glass, but they built right over the top of it."

Karigan thought she'd like to travel back in time to see how things once were. It was the way of civilization, she supposed, to tear down and rebuild, or to change and expand so the original structure was unrecognizable.

"So, I am here alone," Dakrias said, "in this miserable place, except for the rats and the occasional visitor like you. And . . ." He trailed off as though not sure he should go on.

"And?" Karigan prompted.

He leaned forward and dropped his voice to a near whisper. "Sometimes—sometimes something catches the corner of my eye, as though a person were walking by the door, but when I look, no one is there. Sometimes I hear things, like distant whisperings or far off conversations, yet when I investigate, no one is there. Then, a time or two, I have felt something brush by me, *but no one was there*." Dakrias shivered.

So did Karigan.

"Brown!"

They both jumped and squawked. The two had been so drawn into Dakrias' tale, they hadn't noticed the entrance of the same unpleasant clerk Karigan had bumped into in the gardens. He strode imperiously over to Dakrias' writing desk.

"Brown, where is that memorandum I wanted?"

Dakrias swallowed. "I'm—I'm sorry, sir, I—"

The man followed Dakrias' gaze to the writing desk, saw the mess of splotches, and frowned. His specs flashed in the lamplight when he turned to glower at Dakrias.

"Your copy is abominable. What happened? Did one of your little ghosts come tweak you on your back end?"

"N-no, sir."

"I'm at fault," Karigan said, "for disturbing him while he was focused on his work." The man turned his withering glare on her, but she lifted her chin. She wasn't afraid of him.

"You again," he muttered. "What are you doing here?"

"Delivering documents on behalf of my captain."

She picked them up and passed them to him. He glanced at them dismissively and dropped them on Dakrias' desk. Karigan saw the flash of a black stain on his palm. Likely his penmanship was less neat than Dakrias'.

"I need that memorandum in three copies," he told Dakrias, "and I need it now."

"Yes, sir," Dakrias said, and the man strode out of the records room.

Karigan waited until she was sure the man was out of hearing range. "Who was that?"

A totally deflated Dakrias replied, "The chief administrator, Weldon Spurlock."

"Oh." She had now managed to get on the wrong side of
the head of administration, which did not bode well if she
was going to be handling more administrative duties. She
hoped her elbow mended *really* fast.

She took her leave of Dakrias so he could get back to
work. As she passed the abandoned corridor, she did not
dare to pause lest she see another apparition.

As Karigan approached officer quarters, she stopped in her
tracks when she saw Mara leading Reita Matts away from
Captain Mapstone's door. Reita had been a Rider for only a
few months longer than Karigan, and had proved to be perfect morale support during those early, difficult months.

Now Reita's face was ashen. Tears leaked from her eyes,
and she seemed unaware of her surroundings.

"What—?" Karigan began, but Mara curtly shook her head
to forestall questions. She wrapped her arm around Reita's
shoulders, guiding her in the direction of Rider barracks.

Reita must have received some terrible news. Perhaps
the captain could tell Karigan more, but when she entered
officers quarters, she found the captain slumped over her
worktable, head in her hands. A winged horse brooch glittered next to her elbow.

"Captain?" Karigan said, with growing alarm. "What's
wrong? I just saw Mara and Reita."

Without looking up, the captain said in a heavy voice,
"Reita's brooch abandoned her. She wasn't with us for even
a whole year and a half, and her brooch abandoned her."

Reita was no longer a Green Rider. No wonder she had
looked to be in a state of shock. She loved the messenger
service, and the other Riders were her only family. Not only
had she "lost" an occupation she loved, but she'd be unable
to be with her "family."

"It's the shortest term I've ever known a brooch to stay with a Rider." This from the captain who had spent most of her adult life as a Green Rider. She had seen many Riders come and go during her years of service, but Karigan could tell she was taking this one particularly hard.

"It just seems odd," the captain said. "The shortest term I have seen is three years. Five is more common, barring a Rider's death."

Not just odd, Karigan thought, *but wrong.*

Aye, wrong, a separate voice seemed to echo her.

She shuddered it away, thinking that Dakrias' notions about ghostly conversations were getting to her.

"Karigan—" the captain rubbed her face with both hands as though fatigued. "You're excused for the rest of the day, unless Mara needs some help with Reita."

Karigan nodded in acknowledgment and turned to leave.

"Just a moment." The captain reached down beside her and hauled out a large leather pouch. "This is for you, from Arms Master Drent. Careful, it's heavy."

Karigan took the strap of the pouch with her left hand and immediately the weight of it dragged down on her. When she set it down, she heard a metallic clinking within. She opened the flap and found inside iron balls of various sizes. Hand weights.

"You will report to Arms Master Drent at nine hour sharp tomorrow morning," the captain told her. "You are to bring the one pound weight with you."

Drent? Karigan opened her mouth to protest, but the captain cut her off with a crooked, mirthless smile.

"Penance."

THE MUSIC OF
THE NIGHT

In the starlit night, a horse jogged along the road with a perky clip-clop that had its rider humming a new tune to accompany the rhythm. The frogs chorusing in a bog he'd passed by and the chirruping of crickets filled out the harmony of his tune. Music was Herol Caron's life, and he tried to fill every moment he could with it. His mother claimed that when he was born he came into the world singing.

Herol was on the road because of Estral Andovian. Estral had a manuscript that needed delivering to a Green Rider friend of hers in Sacor City, but no one was available to take it. She was not unaware of the irony of the situation. Herol smiled as he remembered Estral standing in Selium's library, hands on hips, asking the gods in a tart voice, "Where's a Green Rider when you need one?" She then looked about as if expecting one to materialize out of the air.

Herol offered to change his plans to carry the manuscript to Sacor City, an offer Estral gladly accepted. He did not mind such diversions, not at all. Minstrels often conveyed messages, letters, and small parcels as they moved about the realm. And he'd be delivering it to the castle grounds. He hoped that while he was there, he might persuade someone to let him play and sing in court, and maybe even for King Zachary himself.

He'd have a better chance, he reflected, if he were a master minstrel rather than a junior journeyman. If he couldn't play for King Zachary's court, he was sure the castle servants would enjoy some entertainment, and see to it he was well fed and looked after.

He also knew of some Sacor City inns where he'd likely receive excellent tips.

He clucked at the horse to keep its rhythm, enjoying the jingle of harness that added to the music.

The road he traveled was a curving side road that wound north of the Kingway. There was an out-of-the-way inn that would be more than eager to show its hospitality to a Selium minstrel. Inns on the main roads were all-too-frequented by minstrels. Those innkeepers were less than delighted by the sight of yet another minstrel, and the food and ale was less free-flowing, the common room less attentive to his talents.

Herol adjusted the lute case he wore strapped across his back, and rode on, enjoying the pleasant summer night. He still had a few miles to go before he reached the inn, and there was nothing between here and there except the music of the night.

He hadn't traveled much farther when the horse, a reliable old plodder, shied and attempted to bolt. Herol held it in, cursing. The horse must have gotten a good whiff of some predator.

It flattened its ears and tossed its head, scraping at the road with its hoof. Herol peered about to see if he could discern what was disturbing the horse, but even with good night vision, he couldn't make anything out.

Then Herol realized the sounds of the night had faded to silence—the frogs, the crickets. Nothing stirred in the surrounding woods.

A shadow slithered across the road ahead. No, it was darker than shadow, if that were possible. Cold desperation washed over Herol and a claw of ice wrapped around his heart.

The horse went berserk. It bucked and reared, and wheeled on its haunches. Herol held on for all he was worth, but the girth broke away and he flailed off backward, falling hard on the road and smashing his lute case beneath him. Disharmonious notes twanged from the lute as it broke into pieces.

The crazed horse bucked the saddle and saddlebags right off, and galloped in the direction from which they had come.

Herol tried to roll over onto his hands and knees, but the lute case rendered him helpless like a turtle stuck on its back. The fear that penetrated his heart made it hard to move or think.

He stopped struggling when he realized that terrible something, that deep shadow, stood over him, staring down at him with eyes of flint, its face that of a corpse.

Crooked, bony hands emerged from tattered black sleeves and reached for him.

Herol Caron may have entered the world singing, but he left it screaming.

Journal of Hadriax el Fex

Alessandros finally allowed me to lead an expedition into the interior. He was loathe to part with me, for he likes me by his side at all times. He tells me he depends on my counsel, and that I am a good friend. I hope so! I told him General Spurloche will provide him with excellent advice in my absence. Alessandros frowned and said it would not be the same.

My men and I trekked deep into the lands of the Sacor Clans, to discover a place much revered by these people. It is a lake, a mirror lake, they say. Our indigenous guides appeared untroubled by us, despite their knowledge of our attacks on many villages. Our trinkets, it seems, bought their loyalty.

Finally we did come upon the lake, and a fine lake it is. Like everything else, it is ringed by rock and tree, and the water is astonishingly fresh. I stared into the water for a long time, and saw only my own reflection. A rogue, I look, after all my time in this wilderness! How the nobility back in Arcosia would view me I can only guess.

I did not detect any special powers within the lake, but the guides told me to wait till the full moon. More of their moon superstitions it sounded to me, but since the full moon was only two nights later, we bided our time by the lake, fishing and taking our leisure. The men made a joke of daring one another to swim. Renald, my squire, took them up on the dare and emerged from the lake unscathed, but pronounced it icy cold. Our guides looked at us askance that we should so misuse their sacred place. More trinkets placated them.

When the full moon came, it reflected beautifully on the still water, as did the stars. It was like looking into the heavens themselves. Again, the only vision I saw was my own roguish facade, and the guides laughed, saying that only those pure of heart would know the "magic" of the lake.

I tried again, and to my astonishment, I believe I did see something . . . a young woman's face staring back at me. Comely she was, with bright eyes and long brown hair that fell thickly about her shoulders. Curiously she wore a brooch, golden, fashioned into a winged horse. But the vision faded quickly. I have never seen her before, yet there is a familiarity to her visage I do not understand.

✥ THE STONE STAG ✥

Karigan arrived at the practice field just as the last note of nine hour pealed from the bell tower down in the city. Soldiers were already at work in the practice rings going through drills, their efforts punctuated by grunts and the clack of wooden practice swords. The morning was hot and humid, and many were already stripped down to tunics.

A couple arms masters prowled about evaluating their trainees, pausing to correct them, and setting them off on additional sets of drills. One was Arms Master Gresia, who trained the Riders. She was a reasonable woman by all accounts, and Karigan watched after her longingly, knowing Drent was an altogether different matter. What did he have in store for her?

"Girl."

Karigan resisted the impulse to cringe, and turned about knowing exactly to whom the voice belonged, and exactly what "girl" he addressed.

There Drent stood, in all his puffed up glory, fists planted on his hips and biceps bulging, his little eyes glaring. "While your right arm mends, we're gonna do a little work on you. I'm going to teach you how to fight with your left side."

If Captain Mapstone had been looking to punish Karigan, she had certainly succeeded. Karigan had one last straw of hope that just maybe she could get out of this.

"Shouldn't we check first with Master Destarion? I mean—"

"Don't Master Destarion *me*." Drent hacked and spat. "What we're doing is with his approval. We're not touching your bad arm. Yet. In the meantime, the rest of your body is mine." He gave her a harrowing grin. "Just because you have one bad arm doesn't mean the rest of your body should waste away. I want ten laps around the practice field."

"Laps?"

Drent's eyes narrowed. "You got legs, don't you?"

Karigan nodded.

"You will respond with *yes, sir.*"

"Yes, sir."

"RUN!"

Karigan dropped her hand weight to the ground and sprinted off—

"HALT!"

—and she skidded to a stop, glancing back at Drent with trepidation.

"That hand weight you've brought," he said, "you will carry it in your left hand. How are you going to fight with your left side if we do not build up the strength there? Now pick it up and RUN!"

Karigan did not hesitate one moment—she scooped up the weight, and she ran. By the third lap, sweat made her shirt and work tunic cling most unpleasantly to her skin, and the hand weight felt more like a hundred pounds instead of just one. Arms Master Gresia spotted her as she passed by, and fell in beside her with long, easy strides.

"I see Drent has taken you on," she said.

Karigan grunted an affirmative.

"That's quite an honor, you know," Gresia said. "He takes on only the most gifted students, and leaves the rest to Brextol and me."

How could the woman run and speak so effortlessly at the same time?

"Not honor," Karigan puffed, "*punishment.* From Captain Mapstone."

Gresia smiled at her. "Are you so sure?" Then she winked, and peeled off.

Karigan was sure. Absolutely sure. As she drove herself onward, she could only believe it was punishment.

The bright side was that the sooner Drent got her physically fit, the sooner she would be on a message errand riding away from him.

Laren smiled slightly as the city bell tolled nine hour.

Zachary glanced down at her from his throne chair. "You look like a cat who's caught a mouse."

Laren flashed him a quick grin, but did not explain. She wondered how Karigan would fare with Drent. Or maybe she should wonder how Drent would fare with Karigan. She and Mara had made a bet on how long Karigan would tolerate Drent's style of training before it wore thin enough for her G'ladheon ire to flare up.

She couldn't wonder for long, for moments later, Sperren pounded the floor with the butt of his castellan's staff to begin the king's public audience. The great oak doors of the firebrand and the crescent moon were drawn open, and a line of petitioners filed in. There were bored aristocrats, and awed countryfolk whose wide-eyed gazes took in the vast room with its tall windows, along with the Weapons who lined the walls in shadowy recesses, the banners, the soldiers, and most of all, their king.

Also standing in line were the frightened, the downtrodden, and the schemers. Every week it was the same, and every one of them wanted something from the king.

Zachary wore his king's mask, an expression that would not permit any of the petitioners to guess what he was thinking, and in this way, he held an advantage over those less adept at hiding their emotions. If the common folk believed their king cold and forbidding, then let them judge him by his justice and impartiality.

The first pair brought forth by Neff the herald were sheep farmers disputing grazing rights. Zachary listened to their arguments, asked a few questions, then sat in silence for a few moments, stroking his beard. If he wished Laren to use her ability to read a petitioner, he would look at her, and she would nod or shake her head to indicate truth or falsehood.

In this case, Zachary found the dispute rather straightforward, and worked out a compromise by which both farmers could use the pasturelands by cooperatively tending their flocks. The farmers were surprised, but not displeased.

As the morning dragged on, a craftsman accused a minor nobleman of shorting payment for a fine knife. The nobleman was quite arrogant, something, in Laren's experience, that was not uncommon. The more minor the nobleman, it seemed, the more arrogant he was.

Not once did Zachary turn to her. Over the few years he had been king, he had managed to hone his instincts and learn what questions to ask. He listened to his advisors, but had developed a sense of when to heed their advice, and when to dismiss it. From Laren's perspective, his decisions on each case proved to be just and appropriate.

The next man in line shambled forward with his eyes downcast, nervously twisting his cap. "My name is Vander Smith, Excellency. I come from the county of Aidree in Wayman Province."

"What do you wish to petition of the king?" Sperren asked.

Vander Smith's gaze flicked from the castellan to the

king before returning to his feet. "I've nothing to petition, sir. I've come to make a report."

That caught the king's attention, and Laren's, too.

"You see, I am a game warden for Count Gavin Aidree, cousin to Lord-Governor Wayman. He asked me to come speak." Vander Smith tugged a sealed letter from his pocket and passed it to Sperren.

Sperren cracked the seal and read the letter. "His lordship writes: *Please hear the tale my game warden, Vander Smith, has to tell. No matter how strange his statements, I swear on my honor he speaks the truth. By my own hand, Gavin, Count of Aidree.*"

Sperren passed the letter to Zachary, who glanced briefly at it before handing it over to Colin Dovekey.

"Please tell us your report, Warden Smith," Zachary said. "You've traveled a long way for this." Wayman Province was on the southwest border of Sacoridia, with Mirwell Province its neighbor to the north, and L'Petrie Province to the east. The country of Rhovanny sprawled on its western border.

Vander Smith bowed. "Aye, Your Highness. It's an odd thing to tell." He wrangled his hat some more and licked his lips. "The count and I were leading a hunting party through the west woods of his forest preserve. A stag was sighted and the count loosed an arrow." Here Vander Smith paused, his eyes darting from one to the other of them. "The arrow bounced off."

Colin chuckled. "Come, come, Master Warden. I've heard *that* tale often enough. It's right there with fish stories, and how the big one got away. The arrow bounces off the stag, and it runs off. The hunters return home without their prize, but of course it has nothing to do with their poor prowess as hunters and marksmen. No, it's because the deer has a tough hide!" Some within hearing range laughed.

Vander Smith's expression remained solemn. "No, sir,

the arrow bounced off the stag, and it didn't run away. There were eight of us in the party to verify this, including the count. You see, the stag was turned to stone."

"*Turned* to stone?" Laren recognized a hint of doubt in Zachary's voice. "You are saying this deer was not a statue of some kind?"

"That's correct, Your Highness."

"Are you sure about that?" Colin asked.

The warden licked his lips. "The count and I, well, we know every inch of those woods. A right good hunter is the count. There is no statuary in those woods—no reason for it. And if it was something carved by a sculptor, it is the most amazing thing. Accurate to every detail, capturing even the texture of its hide and antlers. What's more, it wasn't just the deer."

Even though Zachary did not request it of her, Laren touched her brooch to affirm the warden's words. Oddly, her ability did not answer. Before she could wonder about it, Vander Smith continued his story.

"You see, it was a whole grove of trees around the deer. And the birds in the trees. And the flowers and moss."

Now Zachary turned to her, but she could only shrug. He raised a questioning eyebrow, but returned his attention to the warden, who now held something in each hand. Sperren took the objects with wide eyes, and passed them to Zachary. One object was a pine cone, the other a butterfly, each made of granite. Zachary gazed at them in wonder, then glanced sharply at the warden.

"A whole grove, you say?"

"Aye, Your Highness."

Zachary passed Colin the pine cone, and handed Laren the butterfly. It was amazing. She held it up before her eyes. Its wings were paper thin—but stone. The delicate object was so lifelike to the smallest detail, she almost expected it to flutter its wings and lift from her fingers. But it did not. It was unnaturally heavy.

Zachary sat back in his chair and crossed his legs. "Thank you for your fascinating report, Warden Smith. I'd be most appreciative if you and the count maintained your vigil over your lands for any other . . . unusual happenings of this nature, and report them to us."

The warden, very obviously relieved, bowed. "Aye, Your Highness. It is my honor to serve."

"May we keep these?" Laren asked, enchanted yet disturbed by the butterfly.

"Certainly, ma'am."

Warden Smith bowed again, and dismissed, he stepped aside so the next petitioner in line could move forward to seek audience with the king.

Laren beckoned a Green Foot runner to her side and whispered, "Make sure this is put in my quarters." She passed him the butterfly, and the lad ran off on his errand.

A petitioner was in the middle of a tearful plea to release a son jailed for public drunkenness when an angry muttering broke out near the throne room entrance.

What now? Laren wondered.

Two men pushed their way through the crowd to reach the head of the line.

"King's business," one of the men told them. "Make way for the king's business."

"I've got my own business with the king!" shouted one man who had been in line for a very long time.

Much to Laren's surprise, the man pushing his way through the petitioners was one of her Riders. He was a tall rangy man with a thick black beard, his chin streaked with gray. Long hair was tied back into a ponytail. He went only by the name of Lynx—it was how he had signed his papers when he entered the messenger service.

A brooding, silent man who grew up in the northern

wilds, he would not set foot in any city or large town if he didn't have to. To Zachary's line of thinking, that was just fine, for he had other uses for Lynx, such as keeping a secret watch on the boundaries.

Lynx did not wear the green uniform of the Riders, but the buckskin of a woodsman, nor did he carry the traditional saber—he preferred his forester's knife and long bow. Laren had also heard he was handy with a throwing ax. The only thing about him that revealed his affiliation with the Riders was his brooch, but even that was invisible to all but other Riders.

So what sort of "king's business" had brought Lynx out of the woods? Another stone deer?

The man following him was thin and haggard, his face ashen. He pressed his hand to his ribs as though in pain.

Lynx finally emerged from the crowd and bowed before the king. "Excellency," he murmured, "the information I bring you is urgent."

Zachary did not waste time. He gestured to Sperren, who banged his staff on the floor. "The public audience is concluded until further notice."

There were glares and indignant protests, but no one resisted when guards in silver and black herded them out of the throne room. The great doors shut resoundingly after the last petitioner passed through.

"Greetings, Lynx," Zachary said. "What is this urgent news of yours?"

"Excellency." Lynx's voice was like sandpaper. "I have with me here Durgan Atkins of the northern border, and recently a refugee in D'Ivary Province."

The man glanced at Zachary, and Laren thought she caught a flash of anger and hatred in his eyes.

"Why have you come before me?" Zachary asked.

"Go ahead," Lynx said to Atkins. "Talk."

Atkins then raised his baleful gaze defiantly to Zachary.

"All right. I'll talk. My family and I fled to D'Ivary Province seeking safety. Groundmites repeatedly attacked our village on the border, and after losing kin and some of our best fighters, we saw no alternative except to seek safe haven within guarded borders. It was not an easy decision. We did not want to leave homesteads that we had carved from the forest with great hardship, and worked so long to defend.

"We tried to find some clearing or field where we might set up a household for a time. Some among us were injured, and most of us grieving. At every turn we were harassed and evicted. Even the common folk spat upon us and called us trespassers. We tried to offer work in exchange for refuge, but were refused.

"Thugs hired by the landowners forced us off the land, and so we were set to wandering. We were even attacked by bandits, but I suspect they were the hired cutthroats of the landowners. We were stripped of any belongings of value, and our young men beaten, and our daughters . . ." His expression nearly crumbled.

Zachary and the others said nothing, giving the man time to regain his composure. Although Zachary exuded quiet calm, Laren could almost feel the white hot fury building within him.

"Eventually we found others such as we," Atkins continued, "encamped on a field that was no more than mud. It was cramped—there were hundreds—but none permitted to go beyond a perimeter guarded by soldiers."

"Soldiers?" Zachary asked. "What soldiers do you speak of? D'Ivary has no militia."

Durgan Atkins did not conceal his hatred. "Soldiers like the ones I see around here. Soldiers in silver and black."

Sacoridian soldiers? Laren thought. *That's impossible . . .*

The throne room had gone silent, and it was as if the air had been sucked out of the place. Zachary let go his king's mask and no longer hid his fury.

Lynx nudged Atkins. "Tell them the rest."

Atkins grunted. "One day the landowner comes down, looks at us as though we're no more than cattle. Lord Nester, he was called. He picked some of the girls and women, and the soldiers took them away. They've not been returned to us . . . my nine-year-old girl was with them."

Laren's own hackles rose at this last. She had heard rumors about Nester and his appetites, but nothing had ever been proven. And no doubt he'd be well shielded by his brother-in-law, Lord-Governor D'Ivary.

"This Lord Nester," Atkins continued, "he stood up on a block and announced to us that by proclamation of King Zachary all refugees were to be returned to the northern border."

Zachary stood, hands clenched.

"They marched us." The man's voice had ground into a painful whisper. "They marched us hard to the border. Those too weak or sickly were killed outright so as not to slow the march. At night we were bunched together so there was hardly room to lay down. We were not given much food or water, just enough to keep us marching. Whatever girls or women Nester hadn't chosen, the soldiers made use of. My wife . . ." He pointed at the king. "You brought this upon us! They were *your* soldiers, *your* words!"

He sprang up the dais steps to attack Zachary, but in a blur of motion, two Weapons were on him and dragged him away. They pinned his arms behind him, his chest heaving. He spat at Zachary's feet.

How could this be? Laren wondered. Her ability had indicated D'Ivary spoke truth when he promised the refugees would come to no harm.

False, her ability said, without her request.

What?

Her attention was then drawn to Zachary slowly

descending the dais to stand before Atkins. His expression had turned from fury to sadness.

"Those were not my soldiers," he said softly, "nor did I issue a proclamation to have your people marched to the border. Regardless, I am very, very sorry."

Atkins was unconvinced. "Apologies won't bring back the dead, will they? Apologies won't bring back my daughter."

"Ellen," the king said, suddenly addressing one of the Weapons, "will you see to it that Master Atkins is made comfortable in one of the guest suites? Ask the steward to accommodate his wishes, and perhaps have a mender look in on him."

"I don't want your hospitality," Atkins growled.

Zachary simply said, "We will talk more later."

With that, the two Weapons escorted him from the throne room.

"It's true what he says," Lynx said in his harsh voice. "I've seen those soldiers, but I figured they were mercs dressed to look like ours. I tried to convince Durgan of it, but he wouldn't hear me. I've seen the trail of bodies left behind from the march, and talked to other borderers, so I guess I can't blame Durgan for his anger. He was the only one willing to come, and I think it's because he wanted to see the face of the king that brought so much misery upon his people."

Disbelief warred with anger in Zachary's face. He tore off his royal mantle of heather, tossed it on the throne chair, and started pacing. "I had thought D'Ivary understood my wishes in this matter."

He hadn't directed the comment at Laren, but she felt the thrust of it into her gut.

"I will need to speak with you further, Rider," Zachary said, "but go eat and rest. When Atkins is ready to talk again, we shall resume."

Clearly dismissed, Lynx hesitated.

"Is there something else, Rider?"

"Yes, sire. Not having to do with the refugees, but I thought I should mention it. The forest, it's restless. The wild creatures—well, they're spooked. They know of some darkness passing through the woods, but are vague on exactly what it is."

Zachary sighed. Lynx's ability was to communicate with animals—not so much as speak with them directly, but to feel the currents of mood and emotion, and understand their meaning.

Lynx departed and Zachary said, "First stone deer, and now spooked wildlife." He shook his head. "I'm afraid that'll have to wait. Our refugee situation is more urgent." He called a runner of the Green Foot to him. "Find General Harborough and tell him to attend me immediately."

"What are you going to do?" Colin asked.

"What needs to be done." He didn't pause before turning to Laren. "Captain, do you care to explain to me why you felt D'Ivary could be trusted?"

She grasped her brooch. *False,* her ability offered. Why was it doing this?

"I—"

True.

"Were you using your ability that day, or not?"

"Of course. I knew how important the truth was."

False.

Laren's fingers quavered at her neck scar. "I don't know what happened."

"Well, I do." Zachary pivoted away from her and resumed his pacing. Then he halted and turned back to her. "Lord D'Ivary lied to us that day. He hired mercenaries to harass and hurt refugees, but he had them impersonate our Sacoridian troops. Not only has D'Ivary given those border people more reason to hate me, but they were beaten and raped. A nine-year-old, Captain. A nine-year-old taken by Lord Nester. How could you have read D'Ivary as honest?''

Laren backed away, hurt and astonished, and fighting for control, unable to explain herself. The reading she had taken of D'Ivary couldn't have been more clear.

True.

She slammed her barriers down around the inner voice of her ability, but her control eluded her; slipped out of her hands like a wriggly fish.

Zachary walked away from her to speak with Sperren and Colin Dovekey, his body posture stiff as though he tried to contain intense rage.

Laren closed her eyes. She would never forget how he looked at her, and his words: *A nine-year-old, Captain. How could you have read D'Ivary as honest?*

It was her fault, the rapes, the beatings, the deaths. All of it on her shoulders.

True.

❧ INNER VOICES ❧

Alton surveyed the empty field that had once been a thriving, busy encampment. There were no longer colorful striped tents pitched here, no wandering minstrels plucking a tune, no merchants shouting out the virtues of their wares. Nor were there fine ladies gossiping beneath pavilions with servants scurrying about with refreshments.

The field was barren of life. Only the refuse that littered the ground, and the beaten paths made by feet and hooves, indicated there had once been tremendous activity here.

Beyond the field, precise rows of military tents remained, and among them, Landrew D'Yer's. He had shifted his base of operations as far from the wall as possible.

After the avian's attack on Lady Valia, all the nobles and common folk had hastily packed up and left—some that very day. Much to Alton's relief, his little brother and cousin had been immediately sent home, too.

The avian's attack had been a swift and brutal reminder of why it was dangerous to take the D'Yer Wall and Blackveil Forest lightly. This was no place for a summer holiday. It would be a long time before those who witnessed the attack would forget the image of that huge winged monster digging its talons into Valia's back. It would be even longer before they got over the sound of her screams, which through the night had weakened until they faded to nothing.

Valia's parents had brought a vibrant young woman to the wall for a summer holiday, and they had left with a corpse.

Alton sighed, thrusting his hands into his pockets. He let the sun beat down on his shoulders as if it could burn away the darkness of his thoughts. But he would never forget Valia's screams. They were etched into his soul.

Nothing had ventured over the wall since, but Alton couldn't help but think it was only a matter of time. He sensed something about Blackveil, an alertness or some kind of intelligence.

He shook his head. He couldn't explain it. Nor was he able to explain why he couldn't call upon the magic of the wall. It had responded to him only that once—if in fact it hadn't been his imagination. Why should he expect it to awaken again?

Because it has to, he thought. *Because if it doesn't, we may never learn the secret of repairing the wall, and more monsters will come from Blackveil to terrorize Sacoridia.*

If the wall completely failed, there would not be enough soldiers in the world to hold Blackveil back.

He could only keep trying, even if it meant he kept failing.

With new resolve, he turned toward the wall, but found Pendric standing in his path. Pendric had not spoken to him since the attack on Valia. In fact, he had hardly spoken to anyone. He ate little, and looked unkempt as if he had given up combing his hair and bathing. There were dark shadows beneath his eyes from too little sleep. Alton had begun to pity him.

"What is it, cousin?" Alton asked.

Pendric looked about for a moment as though confused, then a familiar contempt crept into his eyes.

"It's all your fault."

"What are you talking about? What's my fault?"

"Look at me." Pendric jammed his thumb into his chest. "Look at me. I have nothing—it's always you that has gotten everything."

Alton drew his eyebrows together, a little warning going off in his head. He knew he should just walk away, but maybe if Pendric unleashed whatever it was that gnawed at him, he'd feel better and stop being so nasty-tempered.

"What do you mean?" Alton asked quietly.

Pendric shook from whatever emotion had seized him.

"You are heir to the province, I'm not. You don't deserve it—you're never home to take care of the clan or our people. *I am.* I'm always there—I'm the one always there doing all the work, the things you should be doing. And what will my reward be? Scraping the ground before Lord-Governor Alton D'Yer."

So this was the basis of the matter. Pendric was jealous.

"I'd be home," Alton said, "but I've been called to the king's service."

Pendric clenched his hands into fists. "You could leave."

"No, I couldn't." There was no use in trying to explain the Rider call with his cousin in such a state.

Pendric laughed harshly. "No, you couldn't. You like being close to the king, don't you? You can win his favor. And you like being near Lady Estora, don't you?"

Alton shifted his stance. There was a wildness in his cousin's eyes he had not seen before. "Is there a point to this, Pendric?"

"You turned Lady Estora away from me. You told her, 'Don't marry Pendric, he's ugly, and he has nothing to show for himself.' Isn't that right?"

"No. That's an outright lie."

But Pendric ignored him. "All Valia could say was how handsome Lord Alton is, how kind Lord Alton is. You even turned *her* against me."

"Look, I—"

"Handsome Lord Alton, the heir, the honored son. He gets everything. He's the one who will save us from Black-veil. He's the one the king looks to, the one Lady Estora listens to." Saliva foamed at the edge of his mouth. "The only thing I ever got that you didn't was the fever." He dragged his fingers across his pock-marked cheeks. "Even my own mother can't stand the sight of me."

Alton had had no idea of the depth of Pendric's anger and self-loathing. For whatever reason, he had twisted the truth to feed his pain. He wasn't thinking rationally, and nothing Alton could say or do would sway him to the truth.

"You bastard," Pendric whispered. "You killed the one thing I loved."

Alton's mouth dropped open.

"It wasn't enough to turn her against me, was it. Your magic, your evil magic lured that monster over the wall and you let it kill her."

Before Alton could overcome his shock at this accusa-tion, Pendric landed his fist across his jaw. One moment Alton had been standing, the next he was on his back star-ing at the sky, wondering if his jaw was still attached to his face.

Pendric dove on him, pummeling him with his fists. Alton protected his face with his forearms, but was clouted in the ear. Pendric was as strong as any stoneworker.

Slam! A fist against his temple.

A knee in his gut.

Alton hazed out with pain, pretty sure he'd lose his dinner.

He rocked back and forth trying to dislodge Pendric, kicking, and blindly struck out. Once he thought he clipped Pendric's chin, another time he thought he hit his nose.

And then suddenly Pendric was off him. Some soldiers restrained Pendric, and there was shouting and running feet. Sergeant Uxton gazed down at him.

"You all right?"

Alton felt his jaw. It was intact, but he tasted blood. He probed his teeth with his tongue, but none were missing and he concluded he had bitten the inside of his mouth. He rolled to his side and spat blood, then took Sergeant Uxton's proffered hand and rose carefully to his feet. Despite the violence of Pendric's attack, it looked like Alton would escape with only some sore muscles and bruises.

Two soldiers restrained Pendric who gritted his teeth and issued a growl. Blood flowed from his nose. Landrew had come to see what the ruckus was about, and slipped his gaze from Alton to Pendric.

"Who started this?" he demanded.

"I did," Pendric said, "to purge ourselves of his evil."

"What nonsense is this?" Landrew glanced at Alton, who could only shrug.

"His magic brought that monster upon us," Pendric continued, "the monster that killed Valia."

"Son," Landrew said, his voice gruff, "you dishonor me and our clan with such hateful talk. I know you're grieving, but you've no call to make such accusations. Alton is your cousin, your blood."

Despite Landrew's words, Alton sensed doubt and suspicion emanating from the soldiers that surrounded them. The special abilities of Riders were not widely known, but the soldiers were aware of why Alton was here. Considering the distrust most Sacoridians held toward magic, Pendric was not helping the situation.

People cannot trust what they do not understand, Captain Mapstone had once told him. When he replied that no one would ever learn to understand magic when it was concealed, she told him that the tide was too strongly against magic, and it was too soon to expose their abilities. Too dangerous. Maybe, she said, one day magic would be accepted in everyone's hearts as part of the world's fabric of life.

Now Alton stood face to face with that distrust and fear. Except for Sergeant Uxton who looked unruffled by Pendric's accusations.

"My ability with magic is negligible," Alton said. "There is no way I could have called that creature."

"Evil calls to evil," Pendric said.

Landrew slapped him. "You forget, son, what our clan is founded on. You forget what your bloodline represents. Our craft is in stone, yes, but it was also based in the arcane. Now get out of my sight."

Pendric's gaze speared Alton with hatred. He shook loose of the soldiers and stomped off toward the woods without looking back.

"I have never known what to do with that lad," Landrew said, watching after him. "I could never please him, and he could never please himself." He walked away shaking his head.

That left Alton, Sergeant Uxton, and some uneasy soldiers staring awkwardly at one another. The latter returned to their posts. Sergeant Uxton remained, gazing at Alton as if waiting for something.

Alton sighed. "I'm going to the wall."

Sergeant Uxton grunted as if this was what he expected.

At the wall, Alton placed his palms against the stonework as he customarily did. This time, however, he let himself feel the stone—really feel it; the cool, individual grains that made up the wall's rough facade. He visualized the crystalline quartz, the feldspar that lent the rock its pink hue, and the black flecks of hornblende. And as he did so, he began to hear the voices within the wall, threads of song in harmony—and discord.

Beneath his hands, silver writing swirled, shimmering for a bright moment, then fading, and the song with it.

Alton tried to hold onto it, but it was of no use. His connection with the wall was gone, and would not come back.

"Damn it to all the hells." He kicked the wall, which did nothing but hurt his toes.

"Something wrong, my lord?" the sergeant asked beside him.

Alton faced him. "Are you going to tell me you didn't see it this time?"

"See what, my lord? You kicking the wall? Aye, I saw *that.*"

"Forget it," Alton grumbled, and he strode away.

Pendric trudged through the woods, pushing branches out of his way. He didn't care about the blood smeared across his face, or the welt swelling around his eye. No, those things did not concern him one bit.

Away from the encampment and the wall, he finally found a boulder upon which to sit. A beam of sunshine broke through the canopy of the woods and fell softly upon him, warming him. Alton had won again, as he always won. He had won the approval of Pendric's own father. His father was blind—he had to be! Maybe Alton had cast some evil spell on him; infected him.

Just as I've been infected.

Pendric shivered. Ever since Alton had arrived, voices swarmed in his mind like a mass of silvery eels. There were so many and they slithered so easily in his head; he could not understand the words, but they intensified every time he neared the breach in the wall.

Inexorably they pulled on him, hooking tentacles into his soul. He resisted. He would not let himself succumb to evil magic.

He whimpered in exhaustion and put his head in his hands. He just wanted to go home and get away from this place, but his father wouldn't let him. Landrew insisted he stay because of his duty to his clan.

Pendric did not know how much more of this he could take, how long before he was finally overcome by the taint of Alton's evil magic.

Deep in the heart of the dark tangled forest, the sentience slept. The guardians of the wall continued their ancient vigil, weaving songs of tranquility and peace. The discord continued to undermine the harmony, but they still retained enough power to lull the sentience into its deep slumber.

The guardians, however, had no control over its dreams.

Dreams of a land called Arcos, a land of many lands, many oceans away. A land of soaring architecture and culture. A land of diverse peoples all united into one. A land of powerful magic.

As the dream meandered on, the beauty, people, and especially the magic, faded into a gray, dismal landscape, with only crumbling towers and solitary columns amid bleak windswept grasses to mark the existence of a once-vast civilization, now extinct.

The sentience, still enwrapped in the dream, called out in sorrow. The forest trembled. Trees toppled over, beasts screamed, and rain poured down from the clouds that covered all of Blackveil.

The guardians of the wall shuddered in fear.

Journal of Hadriax el Fex

The clans have proven more resilient, more stubborn, than we believed they would. They lie in wait and ambush our patrols, and have had the upper hand in a few skirmishes. Their knowledge of the land aids them, and they can disappear into it at will.

Alessandros has taken more dire action, walking into villages, holding some of the folk as witnesses, leveling their homes, and destroying most of the population with the simple use of his powers. The etherea is strong in these lands, so he has no fear of diminishing it by such extreme use.

The example only mobilized the clans further, so Alessandros has taken yet another tack, by currying favor with certain clan chiefs who seem sympathetic to us, and with the enemies of certain other clans. Alessandros gives them many gifts and fine words, and even gives them concussives as an act of faith. He plans to turn the clans one against the other, to weaken them, and finally bring them into the embrace of the Empire. It is a worthy strategy.

 ➥ THE RAIN ⟫

Karigan walked to her daily arms training session beneath darkening clouds.
Finally, the long-awaited change in weather
had come, and she hoped Drent would cancel
the day's training.

Cancellation, however, didn't appear to be on the arms
master's agenda. As soon as she arrived, he barked orders
at her to run fifteen laps around the practice field, a two
pound weight in her left hand. She had to admit that these
sessions were making her more fit overall, but after training,
all she felt was achy and abused.

It started to sprinkle during her final lap. Drent called
her over to one of the small practice rings, and belted her
bad arm—sling and all—to her body. He'd begun doing this
when the jostling of swordplay, and her natural reaction to
use her right arm for balance, left her screaming in pain. It
was not unusual, he informed her, for him to belt down a
trainee's dominant arm anyway, when he was working the
non-dominant side.

He then handed her a wooden practice sword. When
they had begun the sword training, the bouts were pure
misery. Drent had worked her through the most basic of se-
quences, but every few seconds, it seemed, he slammed the
sword out of her hand, or jabbed her in the ribs, or slapped
his sword across her thigh. In a quarter of an hour, he
"killed" her nearly a hundred times over.

Disgusted with her poor showing, he dropped the sword-play for a few days, and repetitively ran her through basic sword exercises. The exercises not only improved the strength and precision of her left arm, but helped her foot-work and body control, too. These exercises were less gruel-ing because Drent wasn't constantly swatting or jabbing her.

When she improved sufficiently, he brought his practice sword back into use.

The sprinkles turned into a soft but steady rain, and still Drent did not terminate the training. He attacked her with the same basic moves, but this time Karigan found herself better able to meet his blows. She had grown quicker and stronger, and her mind and body had begun to adapt to her left side acting dominant.

Then he accelerated the speed of his blows and raised the level of difficulty. Once again, her practice sword went flying out of her hand. She clenched and unclenched her smarting fingers as she went to retrieve it. Usually onlook-ers watched Drent working with her for the entertainment value it presented, which Drent did nothing to discourage, as though embarrassment would force her to improve more quickly. Today, she and Drent were the only ones on the practice field, and now the rain was coming down in sheets.

When Drent overheard her grumble about her soggy tunic, he pointed his sword at her and demanded, "Do you think battle stops for a little rain? It slows troops down, it rusts steel, it makes soldiers miserable, but battle does not stop for rain."

And so the swordplay went on. When Karigan thought she could take no more of the cold rain and the pounding she received from Drent, he kicked her feet right out from under her. As she lay there in the mud, the rain pattering on her face, Drent took the opportunity to explain to her that in real battle, swordfighting was not polite.

"If you are going to survive a real battle," he said, "you will have to learn every aspect of it."

Karigan was having doubts about whether or not she was going to survive the *training*.

The bell down in the city tolled ten hour, and Drent finally released her. He collected the practice swords and strode toward the field house, leaving her lying in the mud.

"I hate this," she told the stormy sky. "I really hate this."

Rider barracks was deliciously warm and dry. Karigan paused in the mud room, thinking that the only way she was going to keep the mud from tracking would be to totally strip down and proceed in the nude. Male voices and laughter from the common room made her drop that notion immediately.

She slipped into the common room, which was a cozy scene. Yates Cardell and Justin Snow sat beside the fire playing a game of Intrigue. Yates had blue pieces, and Justin the green. It appeared the blue were currently routing the green.

Osric M'Grew sat on the other side of the fireplace reading a book, a pot and cup of tea at his elbow. Tegan gazed out into the bad weather, her back to everyone.

Yates flicked his gaze to Karigan. "You up for a game of Intrigue? We could use a Triad."

Already the mud was drying on Karigan's cheek. "No." She had certain negative associations with the game, and had vowed never to play it again. Besides, she inevitably lost.

"We're playing for Dragon Droppings," Yates said. He picked up a little paper bag and shook it, the aroma of chocolate wafting to her.

Justin clouted Yates' shoulder. "Look at her, stupid! She's been training with Drent."

That brought her sympathetic groans from the other two men. Osric closed his book and stood up to steer her to his chair by the fire. He poured her tea and handed her his cup.

"Drink up while I get a bath started for you."

Karigan smiled gratefully as she wrapped her hand around the warm cup.

"Let's get your boots off," Yates said.

"Careful," Justin warned her, "he won't want to stop with boots."

"I beg your pardon," Yates protested. "I have only the lady's best interests at heart."

"Yep, and I bet there are a few ladies who've heard that line a time or two."

Karigan chuckled. She had heard all about Yates' conquests. Whether or not the stories were true, he had acquired quite the reputation. And, she thought she knew why. He was most charming the way he bowed to her and knelt to the ground, easing one boot off with the utmost style and care.

The amount of muddy water that sloshed out of the boot appalled her.

By the expressions on Justin's and Yates' faces, they were appalled, too.

"Karigan," Justin said, "why are you wearing these wrecked old things with all the cracks in 'em?"

"I didn't want to ruin my new pair."

Justin rolled his eyes.

Yates pulled off her other boot with similar results. He glanced inside the boot. "Is that a trout I see swimming in there?"

Karigan laughed. "It's *really* rainy out." Was it her imagination, or did Tegan flinch at her words? Oddly the Rider remained quiet, not joining in with the good-natured banter as she normally would. She just kept staring out the window, her reflection pale.

Yates pointed at the leather strap binding her arm. "Would you like that removed?"

"Please."

He turned triumphantly to Justin. "She said 'please!'"

"Don't encourage him, Karigan."

As Yates worked the strap's buckle, he said, "I can only imagine what use this might have." He waggled his eyebrows provocatively.

Karigan laughed, and kicked him in the shin.

Yates made quite a show of it, hopping on one foot, shouting, "Ow-ow-ow! The lady is spirited—I've been wounded!" His face was twisted in mock agony.

"Aw, cut it out," Justin said, "or I'll wound you for real."

Yates did stop and put his hand over his heart. "I fear it is my heart that is wounded." He sniffed, his expression piteous.

By now Karigan was laughing hard enough that she forgot how damp and clammy she was. When the laughter died down, she explained exactly what the strap was for. This brought instantaneous—and gratifying—pity. Yates gallantly covered her with his shortcoat, and Justin poured her another cup of tea.

"Forget the tea," she said, "give me those Dragon Droppings."

Justin grabbed the bag off the table and handed it to her. Karigan rolled her eyes in ecstasy as she bit into the chocolate, its creamy filling melting on her tongue. Master Gruntler, the city's premier confectioner, was indeed the master of his craft.

When Yates tried to rub her feet warm, however, she almost spewed the chocolate all over him. She was terribly ticklish.

"Stop! Stop!" she cried, laughing again, with tears streaming down her cheeks.

Yates' grin was devilish. "I love to hear a woman beg." But he let her foot go, not wishing to torment her too much after her morning with Drent. They had, of course, heard all the same stories she had about Drent, but would never have imagined he'd work her so hard with her injured arm. Karigan didn't even have to show them her bruises.

Osric reappeared and announced with a flourish, "Your bath awaits you, my lady."

Justin elbowed Yates in the ribs. "He been taking lessons from you?"

They assisted her from her chair and moved with her toward the corridor.

"I can walk, you know," she told them.

"But we wish to escort you," Yates said.

And so, with a Rider on each side of her and Osric leading the way, the little procession set off for the bathing room, leaving Tegan behind to continue gazing out into the rain.

When they reached the bathing room, Karigan took one look at the steaming bath, stepped inside, and closed the door in the faces of her eager escorts.

"But, Karigan," Yates called, "don't you need our assistance?"

"Hah!" She drove the bolt home, and listened to their amusing protests as she peeled off her wet clothing. By the time she was in the tub, they left her in peace. As she sank into hot water, she was aware only of sore muscles loosening and relaxing, and the rain drumming on the roof.

A tapping interfered with her snoozing. She ignored it and returned to the dream where her bath water merged into a mirror-still lake, and falling stars etched whiskers into the night sky above.

"Mmm . . ." She sank deeper into the bath water, up to her chin. In the dream, she looked into the lake to see her reflection, but it was not her face she saw. It was a woman with leonine features and wild tawny hair . . .

"Karigan," the reflection said.

The knocking grew more insistent. Karigan cracked

open sleepy eyes. The reflection was still there in her bath water.

"Karigan!" it said with Mara's voice.

She yelped and slapped the bath water, sloshing it over the brim of the tub. Heart hammering, completely coherent now, she realized the reflection had been just a lingering image from her dream. It had to be.

"Karigan, am I going to have to get the men to break down the door?"

Definitely Mara.

"What is it?" Karigan asked.

"Captain wants you to run some errands for her."

Karigan groaned. That meant going out into the rain again. She sighed and glanced at the wet heaps of muddy clothes she had dropped onto the slate floor. She asked Mara to find her a dry set, and while she waited, she hauled herself out of the tub. She had been in long enough to wrinkle, but the bath did wonders for her muscles.

By the time she toweled dry, Mara arrived with a fresh uniform.

"Osric told me you got it pretty good from Drent this morning," she said.

"I always do."

On Karigan's way out, she paused in the common room. Justin and Yates still sat hunched over their game of Intrigue—Justin had lost half of his infantry already. Osric was gone, and Tegan now sat in his chair, gazing into the fire, her expression bleak.

Karigan wondered what was eating at her when Garth burst through the door, sopping wet. His hair was plastered down his face, and rainwater dribbled off his chin. He shook water from himself like a drenched bear.

He slicked his hair back and sloshed into the common room. When he espied Tegan, he pointed at her and roared, *"You!"*

Tegan's eyes went round and wide.

"Sunny and fair, eh?" Garth demanded. "Thanks very much, Rider. I have ridden hours in the rain without my greatcoat because you said sunny and fair."

Justin and Yates snickered, believing Tegan had pulled off yet another very fine—and funny—practical joke on her favorite target.

When Tegan was in residence, she was much sought after by other Riders because of her special ability to sense and predict weather. It allowed the Riders to head out on errands well prepared for the weather.

Her ability had emerged, as it so often did for Riders, in time to save her life. She had been on a midwinter errand when her ability warned her of a devastating blizzard that would soon descend. She was able to seek safety in a Rider waystation just as the first snowflakes swirled down from the heavens.

Though Garth might believe she had provided him with misinformation for the sake of a practical joke, Karigan wasn't so sure. Tegan had blanched at Garth's arrival, and all her ordinary buoyancy was lacking.

"If this is how you treat fellow Riders when they go out on the king's business," Garth said, "I will never trust you again."

Tegan put her hands over her face and ran from the room, sobbing. Garth, mired in wetness and anger, seemed not to notice or care. Justin and Yates simply shrugged and resumed their game, probably attributing her behavior to it being "that time of the month."

Karigan drew the hood of her greatcoat over her head and walked out into the rainstorm, believing that what she just witnessed was very wrong.

☙ A LIGHT IN THE DARK ☙

Lightning flashed across Captain Mapstone's face, highlighting her features in harsh planes. Rain drummed on the slate roof of officers quarters and a downdraft stirred the flames in the fireplace, scattering sparks and ashes onto the stone floor.

Karigan stuffed the documents into a message satchel to protect them from the weather, and pulled up her hood.

The captain sat slumped over her work table, her chin propped on her fists. She gazed down at some papers, a fresh cup of tea Karigan had brewed for her steaming forgotten at her elbow. Karigan wasn't sure what it was the captain read, if she even read at all.

A cascading roll of thunder heralded another flash of lightning.

"I'm off to the castle," Karigan said. "Anything you need from there?"

Captain Mapstone looked up, as though surprised to see her still standing there. "No, I don't need anything. Just those requisitions sealed, and the reports dropped off."

Karigan hastened from officers quarters into the deluge, which had turned the castle grounds into a sodden quagmire. She clutched the satchel close to her and splashed through flooded pathways.

Lately the captain seemed more distant than usual. Karigan had heard pieces of the stunning news out of D'Ivary

Province, and she wondered if this is what preoccupied the captain. Being in the king's inner circle, she was privy to any plans he might carry out against Lord-Governor D'Ivary. No doubt the captain was playing a role by advising him in the matter.

Lightning streaked across the sky, followed by an ear-splitting peal of thunder.

That was close! If Tegan had indeed predicted a sunny and fair day, she couldn't have been more wrong.

That gave Karigan pause. Could it be she wasn't the only one who had experienced difficulties with her special ability? She made a mental note to speak with Tegan as soon as she finished Captain Mapstone's errands.

Lightning ripped down from the heavens in a jagged blue-edged bolt that exploded on the tip of a castle turret that bore the Sacoridian banner. Karigan winced at the blast and squeezed her eyes shut, still seeing a crooked blue after-image of the bolt. Her hair fairly stood on end and a prickling sensation traveled all the way down to her toes. It stirred within her, awakened something, but the sensation passed quickly.

I hope that wasn't an omen of some kind.

She burst into a run, wanting to reach the castle entrance before the next flash of lightning.

Karigan's greatcoat dripped all the way down the corridor to the administrative wing. The dark and damp pervaded every corner of the castle. In the main passageways, all who she encountered were subdued in tone and mood, as though the weather dampened even their spirits.

On her way to the records room, she paused at the entrance of the abandoned corridor where she had seen the disappearing footprints. She peered into the darkness, but nothing stirred. She shivered, but whether from the damp or thoughts of apparitions, she wasn't sure.

She entered the records room clearing her throat so she wouldn't startle Dakrias Brown. She found him picking up papers scattered all over the floor, but he straightened and set them aside to come greet her.

"Hello," he said, his voice pitched just a notch too high. "What can I do for you, Rider?"

"Hello." Karigan may not have startled him this time around, but he plucked nervously at his sleeve and looked pale. His hair was mussed as though he'd been caught in a whirlwind. "I have papers—"

From somewhere deep within the chamber came the sound of copious amounts of paper falling to the floor. Dakrias closed his eyes and moaned.

"Is everything all right?" Karigan asked.

Dakrias absently set her bundle of reports aside on a table. "It's been—" Suddenly he cocked his head, listening.

Karigan discerned a grating, scuffing sound, as of something very heavy being shifted.

"N-no! Not again!" Dakrias tore off toward the back of the room, his robes fluttering behind him. "No!" he shouted from somewhere behind shelving. "Not that crate of—!"

There was a great crashing sound and Dakrias emitted a strangled cry.

Alarmed, Karigan dashed after him, pausing to peer down aisles of shelving to find him. She soon located him in the far back, standing amid flurrying papers. Next to him, files spilled out of a smashed wooden crate.

"What happened?" she asked. "How did that crate fall?"

"Didn't fall," he said with a quaver in his voice. "It was pushed."

"Pushed? By who?" There wasn't anyone else here.

"Not *who*," Dakrias said, "*what*."

"*What?*"

"What." He nodded emphatically. "The apparitions— something has stirred them up."

"Something has . . ." Karigan trailed off in disbelief. "You've seen them?"

"Not exactly, but this—" He gestured at the smashed crate. "It's been happening over the past few days. I—" He swallowed hard. "I don't know how much more I can take."

Karigan suddenly had the amusing notion of dozens of mischievous ghosts leering down at them from atop the shelving and laughing at their little joke. Dakrias was genuinely upset, however, and she couldn't offer him any other explanation as to how large crates kept falling from the shelves of their own volition. Considering her own past record with ghosts, she should be the last person to doubt him.

"Maybe you ought to take a break from here, get away for a while."

Dakrias sighed mournfully. "I've got to clean this up, or Spurlock will kill me. It'll take years to refile this mess."

It was curious, Karigan thought, that as much as the apparitions were driving Dakrias to breaking point, he was more rattled by fear of his superior. She offered to help him, but he waved her off.

"You'd be in my way," he said. "I know where everything goes."

Since he refused her help, Karigan could only wish him luck and leave, adding his haunted records room to her growing list of strange occurrences.

Thunder rumbled, muffled by thick castle walls, as she stepped out into the corridor. She hadn't gone far when she thought she heard the stirring of notes, like a horn being sounded in the distance. She paused and listened, and recognized the notes of the Rider call. Her brooch blossomed with warmth and hoofbeats pulsed in her blood.

"Hunh—?"

The call compelled her forward step by step, until she reached the entrance to the abandoned corridor.

Galadheon . . . It was a whisper close to her ear.

Standing in the entrance to the abandoned corridor was a figure in green. It was not quite . . . substantial. Its features swam in her eyes.

"Who are you?"

The figure threw back its head in silent laughter, and darted into the abandoned corridor. Karigan followed, halting just inside the dark passage.

Another figure in green stood there, where the light melted away to the dark, peering down the corridor. She was not as much of an apparition, but was more solid, her details discernible. She carried a bundle of papers, her arm in a sling. The Rider had brown hair and an intimately familiar stance and body shape.

Dear gods.

Karigan G'ladheon looked upon herself.

But she did not have even a moment to wonder about it. The corridor reeled. The other Karigan smeared in her vision and a glow of light appeared far down the corridor. Funny, she hadn't seen it last time she was here. *Then.*

Galadheon . . .

Hoofbeats thundered within her and she charged down the corridor after the light, leaving behind wet footprints and a trail of raindrops on the dusty floor.

It felt like she pursued the tiny bobbing light through a passage of the ages rather than through a corridor of stone. Her footsteps fell muted on the floor. No matter how fast she ran, the light stayed out of reach. She thought she ought to return the way she came, but the hoofbeats drove her on; the light drew her.

Then the light whisked out of existence. Karigan halted as complete darkness settled over the corridor. It was eerily quiet except for her own breaths.

Now what?

What became of the mote of light? What had the call drawn her into?

The light of the main corridor had vanished far behind her. Should she feel her way back? She had to admit, with some acerbity, that running down an abandoned corridor without a lamp hadn't been the brightest move she'd ever made. She reached out and felt for the wall. The stone was cold beneath her hand, but it was real, and it would help her find her way.

The sound of weeping stopped her. Someone else was back here with her, and not far away. The bearer of the light?

The empty corridors carried the weeping to her from several directions, but it appeared to originate from deeper within the abandoned corridors—opposite the direction she wished to go. She hesitated, wanting to return to the light and sanity, but what if the person who wept was hurt or sick?

Or just as lost as I am?

With a sigh of exasperation, she felt her way down the corridor in the direction of the weeping, deeper into darkness. A couple times her hand fell upon musty, tattered tapestries, which crumbled beneath her fingers.

The weeping grew louder, then faded. The corridors twisted the weeping into moans of a thousand tortured souls. Sometimes, it sounded like the whimper of a child.

She did not know how long she went on like this, groping in the dark, for there was no way to measure time in this fathomless place. She couldn't even see her hand in front of her face.

She wondered if enough time had passed for anyone to miss her, and if they'd come looking for her. Captain Mapstone would not be amused by this latest escapade of hers. Probably she'd be assigned extra training sessions with Drent as punishment.

Her hand fell into nothingness where the wall inter-
sected with another corridor. The air changed subtly upon
her face, and some distance away, a tiny light flickered. It
pierced her eyes after so long in the dark.

The weeping grew increasingly louder, but no longer
distorted by echoing corridors. As she approached, the light
did not retreat as it had before. She discovered it was a
sputtering candle on the floor, the flame on the verge of
drowning in its own melted wax. Beside it sat a young boy,
maybe seven or eight, with his knees drawn up to his chest.
The light fluttered against his tear streaked face. His
breeches were ripped at the knees and dirty.

"What's wrong?" Karigan asked, but he didn't respond
or even look up at her.

She knelt beside him. "What's wrong?" When he still
didn't answer, she placed her hand on his shoulder. It
passed through him. She jerked her hand away and drew a
sharp breath.

Was he the ghost, or she?

She patted herself. Solid and warm. Her greatcoat was
still damp from the rain, but it had taken on a silvery green
cast. She felt real enough. Perhaps ghosts felt real to themselves, too.

No, I'm alive. Was the boy?

The candleflame sputtered out and after a moment's af-
terglow, everything plunged into pitch black. The boy
whimpered and sobbed harder.

Poor boy, Karigan thought. *He's stuck here and I can't
help him. I'm as stuck in the dark as he is.*

Even as she finished the thought, another light appeared
at the end of the corridor and approached steadily. It was a
bright burning lamp that wrapped its bearer in a golden
sphere. A Green Rider.

Karigan smiled in relief. Leave it to a Rider to come to

the rescue. But as the Rider drew closer, she did not immediately recognize her. There was a strong familiarity, but . . .

I thought I knew everyone . . . Karigan started to run through names in her head, but then the Rider spoke.

"My prince?"

Prince?

The boy sniffed and looked up.

The Rider knelt beside him, carefully setting the lamp on the floor, and hugged him fiercely. Her expression was one of intense relief.

"I was so worried! Joss is tearing himself apart and your grandmother is beside herself. Thank the gods I found you." Now she grew stern. "I thought I warned you not to wander around back here. These old passages are like a maze and it might have been days before we found you. What possessed you?"

The boy sobbed against the Rider's shoulder. She caressed his light, almost blond hair. "Am—Am—" He hiccuped. "Amilton."

The name sent a shockwave through Karigan.

"Amilton?" Anger suffused the young woman's face, but her tone remained gentle. "Has he been bothering you again?"

"Y-yes."

Amilton was dead. How could he—? Then with startling clarity, Karigan realized who the young Rider was: Captain Mapstone.

Red hair, bound back in a characteristic braid, shimmered in the lamplight. A young Captain Mapstone of many years ago, maybe Karigan's own age or close to it. There was no gray sweep at her temple, no creases about her eyes, and most startling of all, no brown scar marring her neck. Her features looked more ready to smile and held a sense of lightness absent in the Captain Mapstone Karigan knew.

If this was Captain Mapstone of many years ago, then the young prince could only be—

"Zachary," the Rider said, "you musn't let your brother bully you. Or, at least, don't let him know you've been bullied."

"He was . . . he was teasing Snowball. More than . . . more than teasing." He looked ready to burst into tears again.

Captain Mapstone—she would have been *Rider* Mapstone back then—set her mouth into a straight line. "I know Snowball is your favorite, and Amilton knows it too, which is why he chose to tease her. Pyram promises he won't let Amilton near any of the dogs again."

"But Pyram's—he's just kennel master and Amilton is—"

"A prince? Amilton is a boy. Your grandmother agrees with Pyram, and if Amilton makes trouble, he will have her to answer to. And she's the queen! His cruelty has cost him the privilege of going anywhere near the dogs."

Zachary, *little* Zachary, sniffed. "Really?"

Captain Mapstone—Karigan couldn't think of her as otherwise—nodded. "Really."

The boy hugged her. "Thanks, Laren!"

A bright smile crossed her face, and it occurred to Karigan she had never seen the captain smile so naturally or easily.

"Now, why don't we find Joss before his nerves turn his hair gray?"

Zachary screwed up his face. "Why can't *you* be my Weapon?"

Captain Mapstone laughed. Again, it was astonishingly natural. "Because I'm a Rider, and the queen needs Riders, too. Joss is nice to you, isn't he?"

"He's an old statue."

Captain Mapstone snorted and tousled Zachary's hair.

"That's the way Weapons are. That's how they're trained to be. Can you see me like that?"

Zachary shook his head. "I want you to stay the way you are."

"Good. But don't forget how important Weapons are. Remember they need to keep a distance in order to protect you, and that they are very skilled at their jobs."

"I'll 'member," Zachary said.

"Excellent. Now, my little moonling, let's go before Joss gets in trouble for losing you again. Besides, don't you think it's a little spooky back here?" She looked in Karigan's direction, but her gaze went right through her.

"I bet there's lots of ghosts here." He sounded hopeful.

"I suppose," Captain Mapstone said, with markedly less enthusiasm than her young ward. They rose and started down the corridor hand in hand, the captain bearing the lamp. "Let me tell you a thing or two about dealing with brothers. I have four big brothers and two little brothers, so I do have some expertise in the area . . ."

Karigan watched after them. Was—was she really viewing something that had occurred in the distant past? Had she really just looked upon younger versions of King Zachary and Captain Mapstone?

I have known him since he was a boy, the captain had told her. The change time had wrought in them both was stunning. The easy-going young Laren Mapstone was now the captain who wore her cares as a mantle, and the boy who cared so deeply for a dog had grown into a confident man who cared passionately for Sacoridia and its people.

Before the light diminished, she trotted off after them, for she didn't wish to be stranded alone in the dark, no matter she could not communicate with them. But even as they walked away chatting gaily, a formal procession of Weapons approached. Karigan thought Zachary and Captain Mapstone would collide with the Weapons for they seemed unaware of one another's approach, but they merged, and the captain and Zachary faded out of existence.

The floor rocked beneath Karigan's feet. Hoofbeats surged in her mind. No, no, it was the marching feet of the Weapons. She steadied herself against the wall. This, at least, was real and remained constant. An anchor.

The Weapons were almost upon her. One in front wearing a formal black tabard bore a torch and a light blue standard with a seagull emblazoned on it, its wings outstretched in flight. Above the seagull was an embroidered gold crown.

Six Weapons marched briskly behind, their faces grim. They carried a bier laden with a body draped in a gauzy shroud. Upon the body's chest rested a gold crown embedded with glittering jewels. Torches hissed and roiled as the formation swept past Karigan, leaving behind a haze of oily smoke.

She started to follow them, but another light came from behind, and she paused.

Two men approached. One wore the long, flowing white robes of a high priest of the moon, and carried a lantern. Beside him hobbled a bent old man dressed in the robes of a castellan. He leaned on what appeared to be the very staff of office Sperren used during ceremonial occasions.

Their murmuring rose and fell as the marching feet of the Weapons faded away.

"We must see his soul safely into the hands of Westrion," the priest said, "no matter his deeds in life, or his legacy."

"Of course." The castellan's voice was a low rumble. "And Westrion shall have him. If we'd gone the normal route, the mobs would've desecrated his body and stolen the crown." He glanced fearfully over his shoulder, but no one followed.

Karigan fell in step beside them, but they were unaware of her.

"Dying without naming an heir," the castellan said with great distaste. "He's left us a legacy, by the gods. A legacy I hoped to never see."

The priest sniffed in indignation. "Beware of how you speak of the blessed ones."

"Even that Rider-mender could not make his seed bear fruit. And the king saw him executed for that and—"

"Yes, yes, yes. He disbanded the Riders. An ungodly, deceitful bunch of traitors, those. The talk is that the Rider-mender *prevented* the king's seed from bearing fruit."

Karigan's ears perked at that. She had never heard of the Riders being disbanded or considered traitorous. Never.

The castellan grunted and nodded. "He suspected goings-on behind his back. He was right, of course. Too shrewd not to be. Warhein sided with Hillander, and the time of chaos they sought is now upon us. There are none of the king's clan left true enough of his blood to rule."

"It seems to me," the priest said very delicately, "the king had something to do with that."

The castellan laughed. It was a creaky, rusty sound. "Your spies figure that out, Father?"

The priest sniffed in disapproval. "You would accuse me of—"

"I accuse you of nothing the king didn't know about."

The priest frowned.

The castellan laughed again, shaking his head. "Come, come, Father. It is not too difficult to figure out that the disappearances and sudden deaths of potential successors were in fact assassinations. The old man didn't wish his supremacy challenged while he lived."

The priest scowled. "I fear much precious blood will be spilled as a result of his—his misguided attempts to safeguard his throne."

"Much blood already has been."

The two men walked on in silence for a time before resuming their conversation.

"Who do you think will—?" the priest began.

"Who can say? But mark my words: whoever succeeds the king must conquer all the other clans to show he is strongest."

"War," the priest murmured.

"War," the castellan agreed. "Between the clans. That is the legacy the king leaves us."

The priest curved his fingers into the sign of the crescent moon. "May Aeryc watch over us."

The castellan shook his head. "I fear it is Salvistar who watches over us now."

His voice dropped low, and Karigan had to listen closely. "It's the old fool's fault. He could have named an heir, or found a way to produce some child and call it his. It is he who always played the clan chiefs against one another like it was some game, some game of Intrigue. He enjoyed it, the bloody bastard. He enjoyed it." The castellan paused and rubbed his chin. "I wouldn't be surprised if this was what he wanted, his final jest on the Sacor Clans."

"Whoever wins this war," the priest said, "may he unite all of Sacoridia once again. May he bring peace."

Karigan's mind spun. Was she dreaming, or had she just witnessed the roots of the Clan Wars? The seagull was the coat of arms for Clan Sealender, and upon the bier must have been King Agates Sealender, the last of his line, on his way to be prepared for the gods. The clan chief who waged war and won the right to succeed him was King Smidhe Hillander. As the castellan and priest had hoped, he united the clans and brought about the two hundred years of peace and prosperity that Sacoridia still enjoyed.

Two hundred years. What she had just seen was two hundred years ago . . .

And the hoofbeats came again. The floor slid beneath her feet and she was swept into a slipstream of light and dark, the flames of torches hurtling by her in ribbons of light, casting odd shapes of shadow across stone walls, only to pitch her into the dark again. And then into the light.

People emerged and vanished, leaving but brief impressions. Their speech lagged behind in slurred echoes, like ghost voices.

The traveling, or whatever it was, halted jarringly. Karigan sprawled across the floor from sheer momentum. She clambered to her feet shaking her head. As far as she could tell, this was the same corridor she had been in with the castellan and the priest. She hadn't moved—physically.

Torches crackled in sconces, smoke spiraling upward to the soot-stained ceiling. Brightly woven tapestries and shields hung on the walls, their proud devices glinting in the dancing light. Here Karigan saw the Sea Rose and the Black Bear, the Peregrine and the Evergreen. Devices not used in hundreds of years by companies that no longer existed.

How far have I come? she wondered. How far in time . . .

Soldiers, mostly in silver and black, milled about the corridor, but there were other uniforms with other devices making a colorful mix. Their conversations clamored in her ears. The light, the color, and the noise all buffeted her.

As before, no one was aware of her, but voices hushed and eyes glanced in her direction. The soldiers parted before her.

Two people brushed by. One was a tall woman in half armor with a green cloak thrown over her shoulder. She wore a cross sash of blue and green plaid, and a saber girded to her hip. A horn swung at her side. As she passed, Karigan caught the gleam of a winged horse brooch. Her own brooch hummed, filled her head. A thrill sang through her nerves.

Karigan had seen the plaid before, and the saber. The plaid had been draped across the remains of the First Rider, Lil Ambrioth, down in the tombs beneath the castle. The sword Karigan had held in her own hands.

The man who strode beside the First Rider had a striking mane of gray hair and a bristling beard. He, too, was armored and girded with a greatsword. He wore the jeweled gold crown Karigan had just seen resting on the body of Agates Sealender. The soldiers murmured and dropped to their knees as the man swept past them.

He could be none other than King Jonaeus, the first high king of Sacoridia. He had been crowned a thousand years ago near the end of the Long War.

Karigan had traveled far. Very far.

Journal of Hadriax el Fex

Alessandros' use of his art to destroy clan villages has drawn the Elt out of their stronghold. In the night, emissaries came to us, resplendent in a milky armor that seemed to absorb the moonlight. They demanded we leave these shores immediately, and not return.

I saw in Alessandros' eyes the reawakening of his longing as he gazed at them. He once told me he believed they embodied etherea, not just possessed the art to draw upon it. He ordered them detained, except for one he sent back as a messenger to their queen, to tell her that she must kneel to the Empire, or suffer war. General Spurloche and I were alarmed by this bold statement, but agreed later that it must be a bluff. Who knows what these Elt are capable of? The emissaries we hold as hostages.

Alessandros circles his prisoners like a lion examining prey, questioning them. These people refuse to answer his questions, so he had no choice but to force some answers, but the resistance of one ended his own life. Alessandros is upset, and so were the other two emissaries. One told Alessandros that his act was heinous to the Elt, because they hold life as so precious. Alessandros said it was the same for Arcosians.

"Do you Arcosians live eternal lives as we do?" one of the Elt asked, then realized he shouldn't have. His companion was very angry with him, and Alessandros more eager than ever to continue with his questioning.

⇜ SPURLOCK ⇝

eldon Spurlock stalked along the row
of writing desks, his clerks working fu-
riously to copy correspondence and documents. There was no other sound in the room
except for the *scritch-scratch* of pens and his own footsteps.

He paused at Fenning's desk. The young clerk was not
doing anything wrong. On the contrary, he was making
rapid progress on the letters he was copying, his hand neat
and clean, but it pleased Spurlock to no end to see his mere
presence intimidate the young man into working even more
feverishly. Blotches of red formed on his cheeks. He became
so nervous he spilled ink on his paper.

Spurlock rapped his wooden stick on Fenning's desk.
The clerk jumped, his eyes wide.

"Sloppy work, Fenning," Spurlock said. "Start over."

"Yes, sir."

As the young man fumbled for a fresh sheet of paper,
Spurlock continued along the row of desks with a self-
satisfied smirk on his face. He enjoyed keeping his clerks
and secretaries on their toes, of reminding them who oversaw them. If he made them nervous, all the better. Fear was
an excellent motivator.

Oh, he knew they talked about him behind his back, but
in his presence he kept them on edge, and punished them
with extra work if he caught wind of any talk. Often they
had no idea of what they were being punished for, and that

kept him unpredictable, and them even more on edge. They never knew what to expect next.

I am chief administrator, and this is my empire. It was a bitter thought, for didn't the nobles look down upon him as some petty bureaucrat? Wasn't he despised by his common subordinates? His immediate superior, Castellan Sperren, was a doddering old fool who left all the work to him, but berated him soundly if something was late or the slightest bit imperfect. Certainly the king took him for granted.

It was a paltry office for one destined for much greater things. One day he'd give these clerks something to truly fear. In fact, all of Sacoridia would be shaking at his feet, especially its king. He'd—

Irell was staring dreamily out the window, as if willing the noon hour bell to ring. Spurlock grinned maliciously and tapped his stick on the floor. Irell came to at the sound, and gulped when he noticed Spurlock's gaze upon him.

"Hungry, are you, Irell?" Spurlock asked very softly.

Flustered, the clerk shuffled his papers and blushed. "No, sir." As if to betray him, his generously sized gut rumbled. His blush deepened in humiliation. The other clerks snatched glances at Irell, and someone snickered.

"Dreaming of those pasties fresh out of the oven down in the dining hall, hmm?"

Irell stared at the surface of his desk.

On cue, the noon bell began tolling. His clerks looked eagerly to him for dismissal. Even after the twelfth note faded, he did not release them. He held them there, stretching their anticipation to the brink. But Spurlock couldn't waste his time here playing games—he had other things to attend to. Important things.

"You are dismissed for the midday meal," he said, "except for you, Irell. You shall remain here and continue your work."

Chairs scraped back and the clerks raced out of the room

to be relieved of his presence. All except Irell who contin-ued to gaze at his desk, his expression morose.

"If I do not see your work satisfactorily completed upon my return," Spurlock said, "I shall keep you here until after five hour. Clear?"

"Yes, sir."

"Good." Spurlock knew he'd remain here, working dili-gently. Irell could not risk permanent dismissal, for he had a burgeoning family to feed. How many brats did he have now? Ten? And with an eleventh on its way.

Spurlock left the chamber, seeking the spiral stairs that would take him to the lowest level of the administrative wing. His destination, however, was not the records room for a visit with that ridiculous recordskeeper, Dakrias Brown, the superstitious lout. No, he had a different sort of meeting to attend.

When he reached the lower level, he took a lamp from the wall, and ensuring no one was nearby to see him, he darted down an abandoned corridor.

These corridors were useful. His group ought to have used them to begin with, rather than taking chances in more well traversed areas, like the central courtyard gardens. He still couldn't believe how close they'd come to having that Galadheon girl stumble upon one of their meetings. What a disaster that could have been.

She was a problem. While he was pretty sure where he stood on the Galadheon issue, it was not a simple matter. No doubt the group would have to address it eventually. The greatest irony to Spurlock's mind was that she had be-come a Green Rider.

❧ THE FUTURE FROM
THE PAST ❧

Karigan followed Lil Ambrioth and King Jonaeus into a sunlit chamber. It was a startling contrast to the darkness she'd been immersed in, and the stormy day she had left somewhere far behind, ages into the future.

A guard closed the door behind them and Karigan took in a low-ceilinged and plain chamber. There was nothing to ornament it except more battle banners and shields. The thick leaded windows were thrown wide open, and sweet summer air lilted in, dissipating the gloom of her time spent in the corridors. Outside came the sounds of marching feet and the shouts of a drill sergeant.

A long, rough-hewn table mounded with scrolls and parchments dominated the center of the chamber. Karigan wondered what treasures of information these might hold, but a single glance assured her she would never know, for they were written in the old tongue.

Lil Ambrioth was pacing, and the king watched her with his arms folded across his chest. They were in a heated discussion, but about what, Karigan had a difficult time deciphering, for their dialect was archaic. Gradually, she began to pick up on words, and finally whole sentences.

"The intelligence is reliable," Lil insisted. "He's breaking with Mornhavon."

"Rumors," the king said. "You cannot believe rumors."

Lil made a frustrated sound in her throat. She was a

powerful presence as she swept back and forth across the room. Suddenly she halted and gazed out the window. "More than rumors. He wants to meet with me."

"No!" The king's response was ferocious, and Karigan saw fear in his eyes. "I won't have it."

Lil turned to him, and when she spoke, her voice was lower, more intense. "Eight Riders died to bring me this information. How many more lives will it take before we have another chance like this—a chance we may never get again? How many more children born in war will grow up never to know peace? How many children will never know their parents because they've been slain on the field of battle? The orphan camps are overwhelmed, but I suppose when the children grow, they'll be arrow fodder, able to carry a sword against Mornhavon. Like me."

"I want to see this war ended just as much as you," the king said gruffly.

"You want to see this war ended, hey? Well this may be how we do it. Hadriax el Fex has broken with Mornhavon, wants to see the atrocities ended. Think of the intelligence he'd give us that we could turn against Mornhavon. It will turn the tide of war. El Fex has been Mornhavon's most trusted confidant, his closest companion."

"Exactly my point," the king said. "I do not trust him. It's a trap—I know it is. Mornhavon hates you."

Lil bared her teeth into a feral smile. "With good reason. I hope bringing his friend to our side will only make him hate me more."

"I don't like it. I don't trust it."

Lil threw her arms into the air. "You stubborn fool. We could end this war."

"Or lose one of its greatest heroes for nothing." The king's expression was fierce, but softened. "I don't want to lose you, Liliedhe Ambriodhe."

"You will sooner or later, if this war goes on."

"Hush." The king drew her into his arms, pressing her cheek against his. "We will prevail."

Lil leaned into him, wrapping her arms about him. "You are still a stubborn fool."

"Am I now? Perhaps to love you."

Karigan's cheeks heated as the embrace grew steadily more intimate, and she bumped into the table, knocking over a pile of scrolls. Before she realized what she was doing, she caught one before it rolled off the table. The king and Lil broke their embrace and looked her way, though they could not see her.

"Who is there?" Lil demanded.

King Jonaeus' sword rang out of its sheath. "Reveal yourself, mage! Only a coward stays cloaked in invisibility."

The First Rider touched her brooch. Karigan's own brooch seemingly stabbed her and she cried out in pain. She fell back as though jerked from behind, and the traveling began all over again.

Lil Ambrioth and King Jonaeus bled into an oblivion of streaming lights. Voices screamed by at an incomprehensible velocity, only to fade into some void of distance. Through light and dark she traveled, yet she never moved.

The traveling lasted longer this time, and she began to wonder, with rising panic, if it would ever stop, and if it did, where—or when—she'd end up.

She closed her eyes as air currents blew across her face, fresh then musty, cold then warm, damp then dry and smoky.

When the sense of motion ceased, she opened her eyes to black. To emptiness. To silence. Silence except for the throbbing of her own heart.

Had she returned to where and when she had begun? How could she know? As she sat there wondering what to do, a heavy cold settled over her, like the mantle of winter.

It seeped into her flesh and she shivered uncontrollably, teeth chattering.

A dim light began to define the doorway of the chamber she was in, first softly, faintly, then growing steadily stronger. She forced her chattering to stop, and she heard light footfalls.

"Hello?" she called, but there was no reply.

The light grew bright enough that it leaked into the chamber itself. At its source was a lamp, and a face that peered in. Karigan gazed at herself. Startled, she could say nothing.

Her other self raised the lamp and squinted as if to see something.

A figure paused in the doorway just behind her. Dressed in black, he faded mostly into the corridor beyond, even though he carried a lamp of his own. Fastion!

"Reliving memories?" he asked.

Her other self did not answer. She seemed too far away in her thoughts, perhaps indeed, reliving memories.

Fastion left the doorway. "This way, Rider."

Her other self did not follow immediately, but licked her lips and glanced back into the room. "Hang on," she said into the darkness, a quaver in her voice.

Whom was she addressing? Herself? Was her other self aware of her presence?

"You've come too far forward—you must go back," she said, then turned from the doorway.

"What?" But her other self—her future self?—could not hear her, and hastened away, her lamplight fading with her retreating footsteps.

"Wait!" Karigan cried. She tried to stand so she might follow, but she hadn't the strength and the effort left her trembling. She was trapped again in complete dark and silence, the cold penetrating to her very bones.

I've come too far forward. Now I must go back . . . She mulled over the words of her other self, and wondered how she was supposed to "go back." How—?

She brushed her brooch with her fingers and the traveling took her hurtling away through time once again.

WHISPERERS

"For the glory of Arcosia," Weldon Spurlock said.

"For the glory of Arcosia," the others intoned.

One by one they lifted their hands, palms facing the center of the circle. Each palm was tattooed with a dead black tree.

They were the true bloods, his followers, direct descendants of those who, a thousand years ago, had come from the Arcosian Empire on the continent of Vangead to colonize and incorporate new lands into the empire, and to seize whatever resources the lands might yield. Particularly resources of a magical nature.

The true bloods now wore the smocks of bakers and blacksmiths, carpenters and wheelwrights. They might be tanners, coopers, laundresses, and yes, a chief administrator, but their ancestors had once been among the elite of Lord Mornhavon's forces. Despite the fact their ancestors had been stranded here in these new lands following the Long War, their pride of empire never faded, even with successive generations. The descendants called themselves Second Empire.

Over time, lineages were documented—records now entrusted to Spurlock, as they had been to his father, and his father before him. The names of all descendants were known, and Second Empire inculcated its children from

232

birth to the rightness of the empire, its customs, and the fragments of its language that had survived a thousand years. The true bloods married among themselves, not sullying their lines with those who had persecuted their ancestors after the Long War.

Second Empire retained a network of sects across the provinces, using trade guilds and business relationships to allow its members to congregate without arousing suspicion. They assimilated into Sacoridian culture only to protect themselves and their purpose; to remain invisible. Their heritage and artifacts from the imperial past—whatever fragments could be preserved—remained hidden, always hidden.

Of course, there had been many who broke with Second Empire over the generations and the group's numbers were not as great as they had been. Some who had abandoned the cause were non-believers, or just not interested in their heritage or events of hundreds of years ago, and faded into the fabric of Sacoridia and Rhovanny, marrying outside the true blood. Others, more vocal in their condemnation of Second Empire, were dealt with severely, and permanently.

Candlelight and Spurlock's lamp flickered across the faces of the faithful, leaving the shabby background of the chamber in shadow. This was an ancient room they had chosen for their meeting. Spurlock wondered what the first high king, Jonaeus, would think of the enemy meeting in his halls. No doubt he was writhing in his grave. For that matter, what would the current king, Zachary, think? Spurlock grinned at the thought of them meeting right under the king's nose.

"The signs are upon us," said Madrene the baker. "I've heard talk of some strange things afoot in the countryside."

"Like a stone deer in Wayman," Robbs the blacksmith said. "The city is full of such talk."

"Yes, perhaps they are signs," Spurlock said slowly. "I have believed all along that Blackveil is awakening."

Carter, the wheelwright, scratched his chin, "What word do you receive from the wall?"

"Nothing in a good while." Spurlock fingered the cool silver medallion he usually wore concealed beneath his robes. His ancestor had worn it a thousand years ago. His ancestor had been a celebrated general, and Lord Mornhavon gave him the medallion as a mark of favor. "A lack of a report means nothing. I am not concerned."

"If the forest is awakening," Madrene said, "and the D'Yers find a way of fixing the breach—"

"Yes, dear Madrene, I know." Spurlock used as placating a tone as possible. "But you think they can really relearn craft they lost hundreds of years ago?"

This spawned a whole new debate among the group. Spurlock let them have at it. He would interject as necessary to soothe ruffled feathers. It was a sign of his leadership that they all listened to him for his counsel and deferred to his wishes. Should the empire rise again—and Spurlock knew in his bones it would be soon, and in his own generation—he would be a favored leader.

As he only half-listened to the debate, it felt as if someone watched, impossible as that could be. He glanced over his shoulder, but saw nothing except the moving shadows of the group.

He shuddered and returned his attention to the debate. He was letting the superstitions of that fool Dakrias Brown get to him.

Voices rasped against the inside of Karigan's skull; agitated whispers that would not go away. Didn't they know she was resting? She was so very tired, on the brink of sleep. She needed to escape the pain in her head, and she was so cold, but the whisperers would not leave her in peace.

She cracked her eyes open, and through the haze, saw the whisperers. They were huddled together in a circle, the glow of light falling upon faces and etching the shapes of bodies out of the dark. Their shadows danced weirdly against stone walls. Their features wavered in her vision as though they were under water, and she seemed separated from them by a hundred miles, though they might be just a few yards from her.

Was this the future she was seeing, or the past? Was it simply a dream?

"We must ensure the destruction of the wall," one of the whisperers said.

No, Karigan wanted to say, but when she opened her mouth, nothing came out.

"The power is flowing from the breach. It has to be what's behind all the strange occurrences."

"Our time has come. It's the sign we've been looking for."

"—arising. The D'Yers will be dealt with if—"

"The Second Empire will—"

Karigan found herself unable to focus on the words, and the haze shadowed her vision further. There were others here, listeners who floated about the whisperers, veils of milky light that darted to and fro, above and around the group, which was quite unaware of them.

One of the listeners paused long enough to coalesce into a luminous man-shaped figure standing just outside the whisperer's circle. It wielded a translucent sword, and ran it through one of the whisperers, but the whisperer did not fall, and did not even appear to feel the phantom blade. The listener lost shape and darted upward to hover above the group.

A strange dream, Karigan thought. Pulling her knees to her chest, she closed her eyes and sank into herself. *So cold . . .*

Journal of Hadriax el Fex

I grow weary with the passage of yet another year in these lands. Our stockade has grown into a large town, garrisoning the thousands of soldiers who have arrived from the Empire. The forest retreats ever northward as it is hewn to be shipped back as raw lumber to the Empire. The shore of the bay of Ull-um has become muddy and filthy with civilization, and the wildlife scarce. Even the fish are not as plentiful. Alessandros, however, is very proud of the settlement and calls it Alessanton after himself.

Alessandros' plan to pit the Sacor Clans against one another has proven successful, averting their attention and weapons from us. And he has drawn four powerful clan chiefs to his side. They promise to be faithful servants, and Alessandros promises in return a magnificent gift: unending life. How he will accomplish this, I am uncertain, but at the moment, he and his mages are focusing on creating a device that will augment their powers tenfold, so we might invade the Elt land of Argenthyne with success.

Alessandros says that he will do this to find the answers on how to heal Arcosia; that surely the Elt know the secret of how he can bring etherea across the ocean. He has always been taken by these people who appear to me as earthly angels, God's chosen ones who stand to humble the rest of the lowly.

I am a soldier, but I fear this invasion. I fear battling what appear to me the earthly angels of God. Still, I promised Alessandros I would stand beside him no matter what comes. It brought tears to his eyes to hear it, and he told me he loves no one better.

☙ FOLLOWING FOOTSTEPS ☙

When the noon bell rang, Mara wondered idylly where Karigan had gotten to. After all, the captain's errands shouldn't have taken very long. Maybe she had stayed at the castle to take her midday meal in the dining hall, though it was unlike her not to report back immediately after the completion of an errand.

One hour soon came and went. When Yates and Justin returned from the midday meal and informed her they hadn't seen Karigan anywhere near the dining hall, she grew a little more concerned.

At two hour, she checked in with the captain, who agreed Karigan's absence was unusual, but probably nothing to worry about.

"How much trouble can she get into on castle grounds?" the captain asked. Then they looked at one another, suddenly taking into account just who it was they were discussing. "Right," said the captain. "Best begin looking for her."

Mara sent Yates and Justin to search the stable and castle grounds. They trudged unhappily into the rain.

Mara decided to search the castle, though she realized it was an almost impossible task considering the size of the place.

As she stood inside the entry hall of the castle mulling over how to best proceed, she spotted the Weapon Fastion on his way in. He drew back his hood and shook the rain off his cloak. Even wet, the Weapon made an elegant form, all in black, each movement one of grace and economy. Others in the hall skirted around him. Perhaps it was the sense of mystery surrounding Weapons that caused people not to step too closely, although more likely it was the aura of razor-sharp danger they exuded.

Green Rider history might be shrouded in mystery, and they might conceal their special abilities, but Weapons *lived* as enigmas. Mara was convinced they liked it that way, but of course none would deign to show how pleased with themselves they were.

Some regarded Weapons as cultish, with their devotion to duty and their own kind. They were more properly titled "Black Shields," but their skill in fighting was so deadly, so excellent and *earnest,* someone long ago had started calling them "Weapons," and the name stuck. They were well known for swordmastery, but they killed just as effectively without a sword.

Fastion draped his cloak over his arm, and strode toward Mara, slicing through the crowded hall like a blade. He possessed a gaze that did not waver, yet encompassed everything. Mara had observed this with other Weapons—they watched for trouble without seeming to. Somehow Fastion had picked her out of the crowd, noticed her watching him, and sensed she wished to speak with him.

"Good day, Rider," he said. "Is there something with which I can assist you?"

"I'm looking for Karigan."

He blinked. Was that a flicker of surprise? "Is something wrong?"

"No. I mean, I don't think so. Karigan came over to administration on an errand ages ago, but no one has seen her since. I'm looking for her. It isn't like her to not report back after an errand."

"Hmm." Fastion tapped his chin with his forefinger.

"She does have a tendency for trouble. Would you like some assistance? I think the watch sergeant would release me for a couple hours, especially if it has to do with Rider G'ladheon."

Mara was relieved, and surprised, although she gathered Weapons held Karigan in some sort of esteem. They greeted her when they'd ignore most others, and in general were friendly to her as though she was one of their own. Mara assumed it had to do with Karigan's efforts to save King Zachary's life during Prince Amilton's coup attempt.

"Yes," Fastion said, "let me speak with the sergeant, then we will retrace Rider G'ladheon's footsteps."

And retrace her footsteps they did. Back out into the rain to barracks they went, to begin at the beginning. From barracks they sloshed through puddles to officers quarters, and then followed the path back to the castle. They walked the corridors to the administration wing, asking servants and clerks, including the surly chief administrator, if they'd seen Karigan. None recalled seeing her.

They visited Dakrias Brown down in the records room.

"Yes, she was here."

Mara took in the room with wide eyes. It looked like it had been hit by a maelstrom, with papers strewn everywhere. She knew Dakrias to be meticulous and this was an uncharacteristic state of affairs for his work area. He himself appeared disheveled and quite out of sorts. She wondered what was going on.

"How long ago?" Fastion asked.

"I don't know," Dakrias said. "I've been . . . I've been busy. It was quite a while ago, I think."

They thanked him and left him to his work. "What now?" Mara asked as they strode down the corridor.

Fastion walked with his head bowed in thought. "We've visited all the places she was meant to go. I—" Suddenly

he halted by an adjoining unlit corridor. He stared a moment into the darkness. "Would you hand me a lamp,
please?"

Mara retrieved one from its alcove. He took it and began
to examine the floor. "Many feet have passed this way," he
said. "Most unusual." He stepped into the corridor, continuing to gaze at the floor. "You see all the footprints?"

She did. Much of the dusty floor was covered in a stream
of footprints. They were recent, for there wasn't a layer of
dust on them.

Fastion investigated closer to one of the walls. "May I
see the bottom of your boot?"

Mara joined him, and lifted her foot. "What do you—?"

"Just as I thought," he said. "This footprint here is very
close to the shape of your boot. A Green Rider's boot." He
pointed it out, a clear footprint not obscured by all the others. "What do you say we follow these and see where they
lead?"

Mara looked hard at the Weapon. Was it her imagination,
or could it be he was excited? "If you think we might find
Karigan . . ."

Fastion pointed at the footprint. "I believe we might."

He guided her deep into the nether regions of the castle.
Mara had known of the abandoned corridors, but had not
guessed their extent, and even now, could not. Walking into
darkness, having it roll in behind you, and staving it off
with only one small lamp distorted all sense of distance
and time.

Fastion assured her he knew every inch of the castle, but
was proven wrong when they followed the footprints into a
chamber.

"The footprints end here," Fastion said. "Fascinating,
isn't it? I've not been in this room before. I didn't know it
existed."

Mara crinkled her nose, not sharing in the Weapon's enthusiasm. It was a low-ceilinged room of rough-hewn ash-lars and crude support columns, clearly a part of the original fortress-keep that had eventually grown into the present castle. Either the artistic side of Clan D'Yer's stone-craft had not evolved when this room was built, or war-time did not permit the luxury of architectural embellishments.

Old furniture and shelving, much of it rotted beyond recognition, sat in jumbled heaps about the room, coated with dust and cobwebs. Tattered tapestries, their once in-tricate designs now a tangle of snarled threads of no distinguishable color, hung on the walls or had been incor-porated into ancient mouse nests on the floor. Windows were shuttered.

Fastion touched the frayed edge of a tapestry and the whole thing crumbled beneath his fingers. He frowned in dismay. The lamp he carried and his black uniform had the unsettling effect of dismembering his hands and face from his body. The lamp cast gold light on his face which seemed to float in space, moonlike.

Fastion was unaccountably delighted with the discovery of this new room, but they hadn't found Karigan. She gazed at the numerous footprints in the heavy dust. One set, the set that looked like her own footprints, simply ended at the edge of the lamplight. How could Karigan simply vanish?

Then it was like a whack in the head. How could Kari-gan vanish? Quite easily, as a matter of fact.

"Fastion," Mara said, "let's remove the shutters from the windows."

He blinked at her as though he had forgotten she was there. Mara made a noise of annoyance and strode across the room. She tore at the rotted wood and it easily fell apart. Fastion joined her, pulling out the upper portions. In the end, it did not help them, for the window was walled in.

Fastion stood in an attitude of deep thought. "They must

have added on, at the other side of the window. I'm trying to think of what's on the other side . . ."

"That's all very good and interesting," Mara said, "but we're here to find Karigan. Let's cover every bit of this room."

Understanding, and a certain amount of discomfort, dawned on Fastion's face. "You mean you think she has . . . ?"

"Faded out? Maybe. If we don't find her here, we'll retrace our steps and look in every nook and shadow until we do."

And if their lamp did not shed sufficient light, she had the means to call upon another source of illumination. Light would reveal Karigan if she had faded out. It would be, Mara reflected, like searching for a ghost.

"Wouldn't she let us know if she was here?" Fastion asked.

"Who knows?"

Strange things occurred around, and to, Karigan. Mara had seen her own share of danger since becoming a Green Rider—her hewn-off fingers proved the point. But she hadn't contended with ghosts or Wild Rides as Karigan had, and that was just fine with her. Mara had her hands full dealing with all the management necessities Ereal and Connly had once seen to, and she was more than happy with such mundane work. Let others ride with ghosts. She would see to it they were at least well provisioned.

Mara and Fastion slowly paced the chamber, their lamp starkly illuminating the space around them. It was in the deepest, darkest corner that Mara nearly stepped on Karigan. She squawked in surprise.

Karigan sat on the floor, knees huddled to her chest, so transparent Mara could see the texture of the rockwork through her. Like searching for a ghost, she had thought, and how true it was.

"Karigan?" Mara could not control the quaver in her voice. Fastion went still beside her.

Karigan stirred, looked upward, a dazed expression on her face. *"Light?"*

Her voice came across some vast expanse.

"Karigan—" Mara began.

"I am lost . . . lost. Can you hear me? Can you see me?" Even across that distance, the despair in her voice was unmistakable.

Mara reached out to shake Karigan's shoulder, but her hand passed right through her into a cold, cold space. Mara gasped and stepped back. This was *not* how Karigan's ability was supposed to work.

"Karigan," Mara said. "I can hear you, and I can see you. Come back to us—drop the fading. Drop it *now.*"

Her eyes finally flickered in recognition. *"Now? Is this the right time? I've traveled so far . . ."*

Her words were nonsense to Mara. "Yes," she said firmly, "this is the right time. Drop it *now.*"

Karigan sighed so unlike a ghost that Mara felt some relief. Karigan passed her hand over her brooch. It was a weary gesture. Her ghostly form solidified and immediately she dropped her face into her hand and groaned.

Mara and Fastion exchanged worried glances. "What is it?" Mara asked.

"My head—it hurts. The brooch." Her hand muffled her words.

"The use of magic has that effect on her," Mara explained to Fastion.

Karigan looked up at them. The lamp cast half moon shadows beneath her eyes. Her flesh was bone white.

"It's never hurt so much."

"How did you find this place?" Fastion asked.

"The light. I followed it." She pressed back a loose tendril of hair with a trembling hand. "I heard the call, and I followed the light. And I saw . . ."

"Saw what?" Mara was almost afraid to hear the answer.

"The captain, but she wasn't the captain yet. And King Agates, but he was dead. Then I saw the whisperers."

"*That* explains things," Mara muttered. She did not feel as cavalier as she sounded, however. She cleared her throat and squatted beside Karigan, scrunching her nose against the odor of her damp wool greatcoat. "Have you been hurt?"

Karigan shook her head and grimaced at what the motion did to her headache.

Mara touched Karigan's cheek, then drew away in shock. "You're cold!" She was stone cold, far colder than sitting damp in an old castle on a rainy day warranted.

"Cold. Yes."

Mara removed her own greatcoat and wrapped it around Karigan's shoulders. She passed her hand over her brooch. She did not experience the strange things Karigan did, but like every Green Rider, she possessed an ability with magic. She first discovered its form during a message errand when she fell through the thin ice of a pond. She pulled herself out, but would have frozen to death had it not been for her ability.

She summoned thoughts of warmth of flame, of campfires and hearths. Heat rushed through her body and enfolded her like a blanket. She focused it on her upraised palm. Blue flame rose flickering from her fingers as though they were on fire. They *were* on fire.

Yates had once suggested that this particular ability would best suit Captain Mapstone because of her red hair and temper. Captain Mapstone had overheard the remark and Yates earned a month's worth of stall mucking duty. Mara smiled at the memory; she smiled at the flames dancing on her palm.

She kept calling on her ability until those blue flames turned to a steady orange-gold. The heat radiated against her own face, and great joy flooded her heart at the manifestation of her ability; a joy she knew several Riders, like Karigan, never experienced.

The flames worked best on her right hand, as though the stubs of her missing fingers let them burn unhindered and more intensely.

With the warmth, the deathly pallor of Karigan's cheeks gave way to a faint pink blush. She watched the flames on Mara's hand in wonder, this uncommon display not lost on her.

"Thank you," she whispered.

Mara had never demonstrated her ability to the others. They knew about it, but there had never been a legitimate reason to simply call on the flames. It was too powerful a thing to use lightly. It *was* powerful, but even she could not imagine its depth. Sometimes she felt like some great well from which power could flow unquenchable.

"Fastion," Mara said, "we should get Karigan someplace warm."

"Of course."

Mara had to admire his discipline. It was not often one witnessed raw magic. She guessed it would take a visit by the gods to shake him from his rock-solid foundation, and even then she had her doubts.

"Does it hurt?" he asked her.

Mara chuckled that his curiosity overrode that discipline. "No, but if I started off a campfire, then reached into the flames of it, it would burn me as any fire would you."

"I see."

They assisted Karigan to her feet. She seemed all right, if a little unsteady, and her features were drawn with the pain of her headache. Mara felt fortunate that the worst aftereffect of using her own ability was a mild fever. She extinguished the flames with a thought, and they left the chamber at a slow walk.

✤ CASTLE TOP ✤

Karigan awoke in a strange bed. She was buried beneath a pile of blankets, with a bunch of hard, warm lumps settled against her side. Rocks? She felt around herself. Yes, rocks. Stove-warmed rocks to stave off a winter's chill. *Winter!* Had she somehow slept through the last of summer and autumn?

Impossible.

With a pang of fear, she realized it might not be, the memory of her journey to the past—and future—just returning. Maybe she'd been drawn too far into the future and had lost months of her life to the traveling. What if it really was winter?

And those thoughts brought a flurry of memories of the traveling, and of Fastion and Mara flaring like beings of light, drawing her out of the dark. She had been so very cold. She remembered Fastion leading the way through dark passages, or did this belong to some older memory? In any case, she recalled little else after they had found her.

Now here she was, in a strange bed. Drapes were drawn across a small window, leaving the chamber in a gray light that dimpled across the grainy texture of stone walls.

Stone walls—maybe she'd been trapped in time after all. What was this place?

She fought the layers of blankets, which shifted the rocks, making them clink together.

Her right arm stabbed with pain at her fussing. The left was oddly stiff and cold. She laid back, breathing hard.

Think.

If she had been in as bad shape as she felt when Mara and Fastion found her, it wasn't likely they'd have dragged her all the way back to Rider barracks. It would have been easier to leave her at the castle. She sniffed the air, and caught a whiff of the herby scent that usually pervaded the mending wing. It made sense.

She nestled down into the blankets, calmer now, grimacing at a rock that had wedged itself uncomfortably into the small of her back. She didn't feel too bad, though there was the lingering residue of a monster headache, and her gnawing stomach, not to mention a growing desire to use the chamber pot. The pull of sleep, however, proved stronger. She was so tired, drained to the core.

She began to drift off, her eyes drooping, when she saw a tiny flutter of light at the foot of her bed. She blinked, but saw nothing, and so began to sink into sleep again.

—hold them together.

"Hunh?" Karigan dreamed she opened her eyes and saw the ghostly figure of Lil Ambrioth standing at the foot of her bed. An otherworldly phosphorescence defined small details of her features—the curve of her lips, a tendril of tawny hair, the glow of a golden brooch, but the gray light of the chamber absorbed far more of her than was revealed.

Lil was speaking to her, but few of the words were able to pass whatever barrier existed between the living and the dead.

—always in bed, Lil said, with what sounded like a note of exasperation. Dreams were funny that way, causing the characters within the dream to do and say things that made little sense.

The door will close shortly, Lil continued. *—must be quick. The Riders are— You must hold them together.*

When Karigan did not respond, Lil began sweeping back and forth across the room in agitation, a luminous blur. She spoke rapidly, and Karigan could not understand any of it. Moments later, like a candleflame blown out, Lil faded away.

Some final words emerged from nothingness: *Hold them together, hey?*

The dream ended, and Karigan closed her eyes, falling asleep for real this time.

Sometime later, Karigan awoke again, overheated and sweating from all the blankets piled on her. Her need to use the chamber pot was overwhelming her. She kicked off the blankets and attended to her needs.

Afterward, she padded about the room checking out her surroundings. A more golden light suffused the drapes now. She threw them open, squinting her eyes at the day, wondering exactly what day it was. At least it wasn't winter! Whatever the answer, the rainstorm was long gone, and had left behind a brilliant blue sky.

The window looked out upon the north castle grounds. Down below were the kennels, more stables, and outbuildings. Guards moved upon the wall that surrounded the castle grounds, and beyond on the horizon, the Green Cloak Forest rose up on rounded hills and tucked into deep green folds of valleys.

Someone had dressed her in a short, rough gown, and she plucked at it with distaste. She felt fine, though hungry, and she wanted to get on with her day. Maybe it was the blue sky outside her window pulling at her.

She searched the tiny chamber for her uniform, but it was nowhere to be found. There was a stand with a pitcher, washbowl, and towel, and after splashing her face with water, she went to the door and flung it open.

Standing there in the doorway with his hand poised to

knock was a young man in the pale blue smock of a mender, a journeyman's knot on his shoulder. He goggled at her in bewilderment, clearly not expecting her to be up and about.

"Where are my clothes?" Karigan demanded. "It's time I got ready to leave."

Hand still upraised, the mender said, "Um, sorry. Wrong room, I think. Wrong patient."

He reached for the door to close it, but she grabbed his wrist. He glanced at her hand in surprise.

"I am *not* a patient," Karigan said, "and I want my clothes."

"I can't—I'm not allowed—"

"I don't care," Karigan said. "Just show me where my clothes are."

"Now, now, what have we here?" The voice belonged to Master Mender Destarion. He ambled up the corridor, appraising the scene with narrowed eyes. The young journeyman stepped away from the doorway with obvious relief.

"Rider G'ladheon, there is no reason for you to trounce on poor Ben here. He is only newly made a journeyman and on his first rounds today. Furthermore, you *are* a patient here, and you may not leave without my permission."

Karigan thought up an angry retort, but took a deep breath to suppress it. "When will you give me permission to leave?"

"That is not known until I have had a chance to examine you."

"But—" Destarion's stern look made her clamp her mouth shut.

"Now, Ben," the master mender said to the journeyman, "you need to hold your ground, hmm? You cannot let troublesome patients have the upper hand."

"Yes, sir," Ben said.

"Troublesome!" Karigan sputtered.

"Green Riders are notoriously troublesome," Destarion

continued, as though lecturing a class. "They come in injured and mangled, we put them back together, then they stand in *my* halls making demands. A thankless lot to be sure."

Karigan's cheeks heated with outrage. "But I'm not mangled!"

Destarion ignored her outburst. "And our most notorious patient is that captain of yours."

Karigan blinked in surprise, and nearly burst out laughing. Destarion, noting the change in her attitude, smiled warmly.

"Ben," he said, "see if you can find Rider G'ladheon here biscuits and broth, and a pot of tea."

"Yes, sir." The young man hastened off.

Destarion gestured for Karigan to return to her chamber and followed her in. "What I've asked Ben to do is an apprentice's duty—fetch and carry—but I don't suppose he'll mind just this once."

After giving Karigan a cursory exam, he said, "You certainly seem in fine fettle, considering yesterday. How does your arm feel?"

Karigan tried to flex her right arm. Threads of pain shot through her elbow, but it wasn't the dagger-grinding pain of before. "Getting better, I suppose."

"Actually, I was wondering about the other arm."

"My other—?"

Destarion nodded. "When you were brought in yesterday, you had the body temperature of one who had been caught in a blizzard. Your left arm showed signs of frostbite. I am not even going to hazard a guess as to how you got into such a condition in the midst of summer." He rolled his eyes. "I'll leave *that* to your captain."

"It—it feels fine."

Destarion looked her arm over critically. "So it is." He

pronounced her fit, but would not allow her to leave till she finished off the broth and biscuits Ben brought.

Karigan was pulling on a boot when Captain Mapstone appeared in the doorway.

"Glad to see you up and about."

"Thank you," Karigan said. "I was just about to come report to you."

"Do you feel up to a little walk?"

The question surprised Karigan, but it took her only a moment to respond. "Yes."

She draped her greatcoat over her arm and followed the captain into the corridor. They passed through the mending wing, Captain Mapstone asking her a few polite questions about how she felt. The mending wing had a subduing, sober atmosphere. It was very quiet, with thick carpets underfoot to muffle sound, and many hangings on the walls featuring pastoral scenes. They encountered a few menders in the corridor, and a soldier hobbling along on crutches.

To Karigan's surprise, the captain did not turn down the stairway that led to the main floor of the castle. Instead, she turned right as they exited the mending wing.

"Where are we going?" Karigan asked.

Again, the half-smile. "Since you have spent so much time in dark abandoned corridors, I thought you'd like to see the castle from a new perspective."

Intrigued, Karigan gave the captain a sideways look, but she seemed content to keep their destination to herself.

As they walked, the carpeting grew more plush, with intricate designs that could only be Durnesian. Large portraits hanging on the walls depicted fine noble ladies and gentlemen, some wearing armor and royal crowns. Along the walls were chairs with velvet cushions, and small tables with fresh-cut flowers arranged in vases. Lamp fixtures were golden and glittering. There were marble busts, too, of princes and princesses, kings and queens.

This was the west side of the castle they had entered, which contained meeting rooms and offices for the king's personal staff, all hidden behind ornate oak doors. Guards stood at attention at intervals along the corridor, their leather and metal gear at high polish.

Well-dressed persons passed them, some in earnest discussion over some matter, others hastening on to wherever they needed to go. A few military officers mixed in with the civilians, nodding to the captain as they passed by.

Karigan had never been in this section of the castle before, though she had heard enough about it from Mara, whose recently acquired duties had her here on occasion. Captain Mapstone appeared very familiar with it.

They came to a pair of grand doors. Carved in relief upon them was a crescent moon hanging above the spires of evergreens. Two Weapons guarded the doors.

"The king's apartments lie beyond," Captain Mapstone said.

To Karigan's disappointment, they weren't going through those doors, but past them. She found herself imagining what those halls must be like—they had to be far more luxurious than even this corridor they now walked. She wondered what it was like for the king having all that space to himself. Was he lonely? There must be a great hall for dining and gatherings, a nursery for children, parlors and dens, probably a personal library, not to mention sleeping chambers.

Perhaps much of his private apartments was like the abandoned corridors—left in darkness by lack of need. Karigan found herself feeling sorry for the king, that he hadn't any close family members with whom to share all that space.

Soon the king's doors fell well behind them, and Captain

Mapstone turned a corner into a stairwell and started climbing. They kept climbing, spiraling to the highest floor of the castle, of which there were five levels, if one didn't count the tombs far beneath.

They passed through a wrought iron door into a small chamber, and another flight of stone stairs appeared, leading upward to yet another door. Karigan glanced questioningly at the captain, but the captain merely jogged up the steps to the door. When Karigan joined her, she smiled and opened it. Sunlight and fresh air rushed in, and Karigan took in a deep breath, sighing.

"Welcome to the top of the castle," Captain Mapstone said.

They stepped out onto the battlements. A soldier on guard near the door greeted the captain when he saw who it was.

"They don't let just anyone up here," the captain informed Karigan with a smile.

Karigan, reveling in the freedom of the open air about her, whirled around and around. She took in the network of battlements and guard towers, busy with soldiers. It was almost like a whole other city up here in the sky. The castle sat atop a high hill, and being on top of the castle was like standing among the clouds.

Captain Mapstone followed along as Karigan explored, her curiosity leading her to look over the edge of the battlements to gaze down at the west castle grounds, and southward into Sacor City. The city's buildings sprawled out before her, edged by avenues that ran between them. The Winding Way curved away from the castle entrance through shops and homes and passed between the city walls.

As the city had expanded over the generations, new walls were built to protect the population, so now there were three walls, including the one that encircled the castle. Their gates were deliberately not aligned, for defensive purposes, just as the Winding Way traveled a circuitous route to confound an invading army.

Carts and carriages and people down on the Winding Way were very much toy-sized, and in the distance, ant-sized. Captain Mapstone had brought her up here for a different perspective, and it certainly was. Usually Karigan only got to look up at the castle, but here she got to look down on the world.

She saw features of the castle up close that she had only viewed from a distance, such as the waterspouts carved into shapes of fierce catamounts and bears, eagles and fish. Rainwater flowed along a miniature canal system of gutters on the battlements, and drained through the mouths of the stone animals. From there the water poured into catchbasins down below, where yet another drainage system of underground aqueducts allowed the water to empty into the moat. In times of siege, the flow could be diverted to the castle's cisterns if other sources of water dried up.

The drainage system was as ingenious as it was intricate, and with good reason. Alton had once told her that a stone structure's greatest enemy was water, especially when it froze and thawed. With a nod to Alton, she made sure she looked over the drainage system with admiring eyes.

The strangest structure atop the castle was an enclosed dome on a platform. "What's that?" Karigan asked, pointing.

"The king's observatory. It houses a large telescope so he may watch the stars."

Karigan glanced at the captain incredulously. "Have you ever looked through it?"

Captain Mapstone chuckled. "I've been invited, but I never liked the idea of coming eye to eye with Aeryc or one of the other gods peering back at me. The king often hosts star masters to watch the night sky and chart the movements of the heavens."

Invigorated by the fresh air and sunshine, and vastly impressed by this uppermost level of the castle, Karigan leaned contentedly against a crenel and looked down into the city and toward the green patchwork of farmland beyond.

Captain Mapstone turned her back to the vista, and leaned upon a crenel of her own, gazing at Karigan. Karigan gathered that the leisurely aspect of this little expedition was over, and that Captain Mapstone was ready to hear explanations.

Sure enough, she said, "Mara and Fastion told me they found you deep in the abandoned corridors yesterday afternoon, in a room Fastion had never seen before, and he claims he knows those corridors pretty well. Mara said you were faded out—beyond faded. And that you were incoherent. What were you doing back there?"

Karigan watched a gull glide by on the thermals. She took a deep breath, and launched into her story, beginning with the day she had witnessed the disappearing footprints in the abandoned corridor. She linked it to the realization she was seeing a future vision of herself.

She almost listened to her own story in disbelief, of how she followed a tiny light into the dark, only to witness visions of the past. Standing here now in the bright, open air, she could only feel she had been overcome by some temporary madness. However, when she told of seeing the young Laren Mapstone and Zachary, the captain's eyes widened. She stroked her neck scar.

"That . . . That actually happened. I remember that incident just the way you've described it. You speak truth."

Karigan was rattled by the captain's intensity.

"I've not called him a 'moonling' in years," the captain murmured.

Karigan thought there was more underlying the captain's reaction—unhappiness, distress.

Her gift is failing.

Karigan jerked her gaze about wondering who had spoken the words, but no one else was nearby.

She decided it must have been her own thought, but she wondered about the word "gift." Did it refer to the captain's special ability? If so, it was not a word she, or anyone she knew of, used to describe a magical ability.

Karigan shrugged and continued her tale. She described seeing the bier of King Agates Sealender and listening in on the conversation between the castellan and the priest. As she spoke, she felt strongly that someone else watched and listened, but none of the soldiers were near enough to hear a word, and none looked their way. Then she sensed a presence just beyond Captain Mapstone, and in a blink, it was gone.

"Something wrong?" the captain asked.

Karigan hadn't realized she'd let her story trail off. She shook her head. "N-no. I—I don't know."

Captain Mapstone raised an eyebrow.

Karigan began to wonder if one of Dakrias Brown's ghosts had followed her from the records room, but she shuddered it away, and began telling the captain the rest of her incredible story. The ending became a bit jumbled, as Karigan had been unable to distinguish past from present, or present from future at the time.

When she finished, Captain Mapstone turned toward the vista, folding her hands atop the crenel. She was silent for many moments.

Finally she spoke. "I'm not sure what to make of your tale, but every part of it rings true." Here she hesitated, and Karigan thought she was about to reveal something, but instead she simply continued. "It's extraordinary, Karigan, to see what you've seen, to see our history—the *First Rider* even." And here she smiled. "I'd have loved to be in your boots."

Karigan rocked back on her heels, stunned. She hadn't

looked upon the traveling as a privilege, but as an extremely strange and frightening experience.

"Tell me again," the captain said, "what did she look like? How did she act?"

Karigan thought hard, trying to recall all the details she could, amazed by the expression of delight on the captain's face.

After she finished, there was another long silence. The captain grew distant as she continued to gaze out to the horizon. She rubbed her chin with her forefinger.

"I cannot even begin to guess what brought this experience upon you. It has a tang of the Wild Ride."

The Wild Ride had allowed Karigan to travel a great distance in a very short time. "There were no ghosts this time, and I didn't really cover a distance."

"Not a physical distance," the captain said.

"The feeling was different. With the Wild Ride, I felt carried away by the ghosts. This time I felt pulled by . . . I don't know."

Captain Mapstone shrugged. "I guess we'll never truly understand any of it, but you seem to have an extra dimension to your ability, of being able to slip between the layers of the world."

Karigan didn't know what to say. Whatever caused the traveling, it wasn't something she had control over.

"Report to me," the captain said, "if anything remotely like this ever happens again." Then she grinned. "Perhaps you'll be able to fill in the missing gaps of our history. I don't ever recall hearing of Mornhavon's friend—"

"Hadriax," Karigan filled in. "Hadriax el Fex."

"Yes." The grin vanished. "I'm going to tell you that yours is not the only strange story I've heard recently. You may have heard some of the rumors."

"About D'Ivary Province?"

The captain frowned. "No, that's not what I was alluding

to, though it is a matter consuming much of the king's attention these days."

Karigan thought she detected some deep sadness within
the captain.

"No, I meant tales brought to us from folk in the countryside. One such was of an entire forest grove turned to stone
in Wayman."

Yes, Karigan had heard rumors of this, but when the captain told her of the game warden's report, she found the
rumors hadn't been too far off the mark.

"There is also talk of something haunting the western
fringes of the Green Cloak," the captain continued, "a dark
presence that freezes the souls of men and frightens the forest creatures into silence."

Karigan shuddered involuntarily. "The wraith from the
clearing?" She had avoided thinking about it, hoping the
nightmare creature would simply evaporate into the ether.

"Who's to say? I just want you to be aware that there are
unexplained things going on, and to be watchful. I've already discussed this with Mara. With the king's attention
focused on D'Ivary, someone has to be paying attention to
these oddities. Most people just see them as superstition, or
isolated occurrences. I don't."

"I don't think I do either," Karigan said.

The captain put her hand on her shoulder and sighed, as
if relieved by her support. "Maybe it only makes sense to
those of us who use magic."

Without another word, the captain strode away toward
the door that led back into the castle. Karigan hesitated before following, taking in one more grand view of the countryside, wondering what force was at work out there.

Journal of Hadriax el Fex

It is long since I last wrote in this journal. The taking of Argenthyne was over a year ago. Many died in this campaign, even among our mages. Alessandros' device, the Black Star, and our concussives overpowered the Elt.

Renald has grown into a fine young man, and saved several soldiers, including me, in the latest action, with much risk to himself. Alessandros awarded him a medal of valor, and I found a tear of pride in my eye for my young man. He has become like a son to me. There is talk he'll be inducted into the elite Lion regiment. It would be a tremendous honor.

Meanwhile, Alessandros occupies himself with many things these days, such as examining his captives. He has taken a scientific interest in them, he says. Many escaped during the battle, including the queen, we presume, but there are enough left for Alessandros to do with as he wishes. He has left it to General Spurloche and the clan chieftain Varadgrim to begin the assault on the clan territories to bring them to heel once and for all. Alessandros helps where he wishes. He drained the mirror lake the clans had so revered, and I find myself regretting its demise, for it was beautiful.

Our latest shipment of troops and supplies from the Empire is several months late. Perhaps they have run into foul weather.

FALLING OFF THE
SIDE OF THE WORLD

Alton swiped his hand through his lank hair and paced back and forth alongside the wall like an angry catamount. Why wouldn't the wall respond to him? Every time he tried to make contact, the magic was just out of reach, slipping through his fingers like a handful of water. For days now, he had spent most of his time at the wall, even the evening hours, trying to reach the voices that sang within rock, but he couldn't hear them.

Instead, the wall towered above him in stolid quiescence. He sensed a tension about it. He snorted, thinking it had be his own tension at not making any progress. Then there was a restlessness that rolled over the breach from Blackveil. An intelligence that chilled him from the inside out.

He paused, gazing at the breach and the heavy gray mist hanging over the repairwork. The wall, he supposed, could not communicate with him because it was focused on other things. Maybe the wall and Blackveil were having a stand-off.

But wasn't that what had been going on for centuries now? The wall had been built, after all, to hold back Blackveil, to prevent its spread into Sacoridia.

Something's different, he thought. *Blackveil is more . . . active.*

His reverie was broken by his uncle calling to him. He

260

turned to see his uncle wave and stride toward him with a servant bearing a picnic basket a step behind.

"It's well past supper, my boy," Landrew said, "and you missed the midday meal."

Alton scratched his head. He had? Trying to remember, he found only that one day merged into the next. He *was* hungry, now that he thought about it, and the sun was steadily descending to the west. The servant spread a blanket on the ground and started setting out biscuits, cold chicken, slices of watermelon, and a bottle of his uncle's wine, a Rhovan white.

"Sit and eat," his uncle ordered. "I won't have you collapsing from overwork."

Alton obeyed, noting with some amusement from the corner of his eye, how Sergeant Uxton licked his lips when the servant withdrew a slab of blueberry pie. Alton smiled—he did not intend to share.

His uncle sat on the blanket joining him for a cup of wine.

"No luck today, eh?"

Alton shook his head, not missing his uncle's flicker of disappointment. They remained silent as Alton polished off two plate-loads of chicken and biscuits, then dug into the pie. He almost laughed when Sergeant Uxton's hopeful expression wilted.

Landrew swallowed the last of his wine and wiped his mouth with the back of his hand.

"I suppose there is always tomorrow."

"I plan to work more this evening. I am close to a breakthrough, I know I am." Alton had said it with confidence he did not feel.

"You just take care of yourself," Landrew said. "I've got one boy who won't come near the wall, and one who won't leave it." He rolled his eyes.

The one blessing for Alton was that he'd hardly seen his cousin Pendric since their fight. Word was he went riding every morning to keep his distance from the encampment until sunset. From Alton's glimpses of him, Pendric was unkempt, his hair a mess, his face unshaven, and his clothes unclean.

Sort of like me. Alton scraped at the bristles on his chin.

Landrew stood up and patted Alton on his shoulder. "We may not have answers yet, but we will soon. Your diligence is making me proud."

Landrew lumbered off, and Alton stood, staring at the breach. He hoped he'd live up to his uncle's praise, but now he was assailed with doubt more than ever. Even if he was able to communicate with the wall, it didn't mean he'd be able to *fix* it.

The light breeze shifted, pushing the billowing mist back into Blackveil. Maybe Alton needed to look at the wall in an entirely different way. There was something he hadn't done yet . . .

A ladder the soldiers used to make periodic observations of the forest lay nearby, leaning against a boulder. It was not the most sought after duty, especially after the avian creature's attack, but Sergeant Uxton always managed to talk someone into "volunteering," and had made several observations himself.

Alton retrieved the ladder and hauled it over to the wall, Sergeant Uxton eyeing him with interest.

"Decided you're going to make an observation?" he asked.

"Yes. I just want to look at things differently. Maybe it will inspire something." Alton leaned the ladder against the repairwork of the breach.

"You aren't going up there without me," the sergeant said.

"I didn't figure," Alton muttered. Actually, the sergeant

hadn't turned out to be so bad after all, despite first impressions, even keeping a respectful distance while Alton mulled over the wall.

He climbed the ladder without hesitation, eager now to see if it would jog any ideas. He stepped off the ladder onto the top of the repairwork itself. The stone slabs they had used to fill in the breach were as wide as the wall, and comfortable enough to stand on.

On either end of the breach rose the magical barrier that mimicked the look, strength, and texture of the stone portion of the wall. Alton touched it, but even knowing the difference, he could not discern it.

He moved aside for Sergeant Uxton to join him. The sergeant held his crossbow level, a bolt locked into place.

Alton peered into the misty world of Blackveil, but he could not see far. Snaking black tree limbs wove together in a dense net, stringy lichen hanging from them. Some beast cackled in the distance. Growth, such as it was, did not approach the wall. The ground was sterile for a few yards between the wall and the forest, except at the breach. Moss crept up the base of the repairwork, and flakes of brown lichen gave the ashlars a sickly look.

As he surveyed the murk of the forest, he thought he felt its attention focus on him, its—its curiosity.

He shook his head. Surely it was simply his imagination, but the sensation did not dissipate. Was there really some intelligence within the forest? Did it have a soul?

He turned to his companion to ask what he thought, but the butt of Sergeant Uxton's crossbow hurtled toward his head, and he fell off the side of the world.

Westly Uxton stared down at the seemingly lifeless form of Alton D'Yer. He lay crumpled at the base of the wall.

With any luck, the young man had broken his neck in the fall and was now dead. How easily the young lord had brought about his own undoing by climbing atop the wall. It was just the sort of opportunity Uxton had been waiting for.

In one sense, he felt some regret, for D'Yer wasn't a bad sort, but in the greater scheme of things, he was a threat. Oh, yes. He had seen how D'Yer's touch had ignited the magic of the wall, and if anyone was going to effect a repair, it had to be this young man. Uxton could not permit any such thing.

As he stood there trying to think of what to do next, he heard a rustling on the forest floor, like a snake winding its way through fallen leaves and grasses. It turned out not to be a snake, but a black vine. It slithered toward Alton D'Yer, paused to assess its prey, then proceeded to coil around his ankle. Then with sickening ease, it dragged Alton D'Yer into the forest and out of sight.

Uxton swallowed back his revulsion even though he knew this made his situation much easier.

Luck, he thought, uneasily.

He supported the power that was Blackveil, but its seeming intelligence unnerved him.

He realized time was elapsing quickly and any moment someone was going to notice him standing alone for too long atop the wall.

"Help!" he shouted toward the encampment. "Come help! The forest has taken Lord Alton!"

The soldiers on guard duty mobilized at his cry. He would tell them that a vine had shot out from the forest and grabbed Lord Alton. The closer he kept his story to the truth, the easier it would be to make them believe him.

As the soldiers hastened for the breach, Uxton suddenly noticed the blood staining the butt of his crossbow. He cursed and wiped it off with his hand.

Hell.

Now it was smeared across the tattoo on his palm. He wiped his hand off on his trousers even as the first soldier mounted the ladder, hoping the blood would not be detected on the black fabric.

⋘ PENDRIC ⋙

No matter how far away Pendric rode from the encampment and the wall, no matter how hard he tried to bend his thoughts elsewhere, the voices followed. They called to him in song, pleaded with him, tried to command him . . . He didn't understand what was happening to him, or why they harassed him so, except that it was Alton's fault for awakening the evil magic of Blackveil.

It was evening when Pendric reluctantly started to lead his horse back through the woods, trudging alongside it as if to delay his return to the encampment. The voices might call to him no matter where he went, but it was always worse near the wall, as though it would draw him to it against his will.

He tried to focus on the forest sounds around him—the distant, repetitive knock of a woodpecker against a tree, the rustle of undergrowth as some small creature foraged nearby, the thud of his horse's hooves. Biters buzzed around his ears, and birds burbled and railed throughout the forest.

Pendric thought this might even be working, until the voices screamed in his head. They overpowered all the gentle forest sounds, they overpowered his own thoughts. They overpowered everything. He fell to the ground burying his head beneath his arms. When this did nothing to dampen the keening voices, he rose to his knees and smashed branches against a downed log and screamed out his own anguish, unable to distinguish his voice from the others.

Finally he stopped, panting with exertion. Something must have happened at the wall, and he needed to find out what. His horse was gone, he had spooked it into running off. He climbed unsteadily to his feet and trotted in the direction of the encampment.

Eventually he found his horse grazing on leaves alongside the trail. He approached it carefully, speaking softly so as not to spook it again, and collected the reins. Once mounted, he slapped the horse with his riding crop, sending it into a breakneck charge.

The sky was darkening when finally his exhausted horse stumbled into the clearing of the encampment. Bonfires burned everywhere, and many torches and lanterns were clustered at the breach. Pendric kicked his horse onward, until bloody foam dripped from its mouth, and its sides heaved. He'd kill it if he had to, to get him to the wall. The horse took up a tired trot. When he reached the breach, he swung out of the saddle and simply let go the reins of his horse, not caring if it fell over and died.

A couple of soldiers stood atop the breach, peering into the forest. Others crowded around his father, who spoke rapidly with officers. Pendric shoved aside several soldiers to reach him.

"Corporal, I want you to carry the news to Lord D'Yer with all haste," Landrew was saying to a soldier in D'Yerian blue and gold.

"Yes, my lord."

"Sergeant, as the only witness to this event, you are to ride straight to the king so he may know what has befallen here."

"Yes, my lord."

The sergeant was Uxton, if Pendric remembered rightly.

Both the corporal and sergeant left the group at a run to attend to Landrew's orders.

"What's happened?" Pendric demanded.

His father finally took notice of him, his regard withering. "Your cousin has been taken by Blackveil."

An involuntary, almost hysterical giggle erupted from Pendric's throat. "Evil takes evil."

His father's slap rocked him like a blast of white lightning, but it helped clear his head, made him feel better. He almost wished his father would do it again.

"Remember who you speak of," Landrew growled. "Your own flesh and blood." Around them, soldiers shifted uneasily. "He at least attempted to do something about the wall, and he was sacrificed for trying." With that, he totally dismissed his son.

"My lord," shouted one of the soldiers on the breach, "there's something going on down there, I don't—"

Human cries of terror rolled over the wall in waves, and all were shocked into silence.

"Someone's coming!" the soldier reported. He and his companion moved about the breach to help whoever it was over the wall.

Pendric watched in fascination. The man who descended the ladder was not his cousin, but another soldier.

"What happened, Mandry?" one of the officers demanded. "Where are the others?"

Tears streaked down the man's cheeks. "It opened up."

The officer knelt beside Mandry, who sat on the ground, his back to the wall. "What are you saying? What opened up? Where are the others?"

"The ground—it opened up and took them. It almost got me, but I ran. I could hear their screams . . . from beneath the ground. I looked back—there were only bumps on the ground where they'd been, like newly buried dead. Then Carris, I saw his face in the moss. 'Help me,' he says. 'It's—

it's swallowing me.' And then he was pulled under. I tried digging after him, but the ground, it started moving beneath my feet again, so I ran."

Murmuring and cries of dismay broke out among the soldiers.

"Silence!" Landrew shouted. Pendric watched as his father's face became as set as granite with determination. He then called to his servant. "Bring me my sword. I'm going in there myself."

The officers protested strenuously, but could not dissuade him. Even as Landrew climbed the ladder, giggles bubbled in Pendric's throat.

If neither his father or Alton returned, there was a very real possibility he might be next in line to be the lord-governor of D'Yer Province, and for some reason it struck him as very funny.

❧ BLACKVEIL ❧

The sentience undulated in the moss beneath the man's body, taking in its weight and contours. It absorbed blood that trickled from his head wound. The sentience penetrated the man's mind, but found only dark nothingness. Bewildered, it fled, back into the world of moss.

The man was not dead, that much the sentience gathered, but the guardians of the wall were keening in anguish. Not only were they alarmed by the sentience's wakefulness, but they were distraught by the man's presence in the forest. So distraught were they, their efforts to coax the sentience back to sleep proved weak and ineffective.

The sentience was intrigued. What could upset the guardians so about this one man? Why was he important to them? With him in his darkness, it was difficult for the sentience to learn much about him.

Red stinger ants filed out of the nearby mound of soil and forest debris that was their nest. Attracted by the man's scent, they formed a line leading in his direction, marching relentlessly forward over leaf and under twig. Bite by bite, they would return to their nest bearing tiny bits of human flesh. If the man's consciousness returned at some point during the process, the poison the ants injected with each bite would leave him paralyzed, and a helpless witness to the slow devouring of his own body.

The ants were not native to this land, but had adapted

well. They had unwittingly stowed away amid some cargo aboard a sailing ship from Arcosia.

Arcosia . . . The sentience savored the word like a fine wine. Arcosia was a land of many lands. Little fragments of memory had begun to emerge of late, memories of what could only be the sentience's own origins. Memories of sailing from a far land to this place.

I was once a man. Of this the sentience was certain. Not only that, it—*he*—had been a leader among men.

Suddenly, it wanted to understand being a man again, somehow connect with the one who lay here. Maybe he had answers.

The sentience turned its attention back to the thousands of ants tromping across the leaflets of moss it currently resided in. Eagerly it diverted the ants, sending them in the direction of some carrion rotting some way into the woods. It had this power, the sentience did, to command the forest, to *be* the forest. But it wanted to understand being a man.

It removed an ant out of line. The sentience became a part of the ant, directing it to climb the toe of the man's boot, to crawl along his leg and hip, stolidly following the folds of clothing, and march across his stomach and chest.

The sentience skittered, causing the ant to back away from something on the man's chest. *Something* that was *nothing.* The contradiction made no sense, but the sentience detected some minor power at work here, that the nothingness protected the something by hiding it.

A power. The art.

Perplexed, the ant crawled in circles around it, but learned no more. The sentience would leave it now as a curiosity to be mulled over later. It continued its exploration, stepping onto the flesh of the man's neck. It climbed the chin and wandered the man's face, following contours of lips and cheeks, dipping into depressions of eyes.

On the cheek, the sentience allowed the ant to do what

it instinctually was born to do: bite. Venom flowed beneath the man's skin. The sentience prevented the ant from carrying away the tiny piece of flesh to its nest, but made it consume it.

The ant did not possess a wide ranging palate, but it was more the essence of the man the sentience sought anyway, the consistency of flesh, the meaning of blood.

A disturbance near the wall distracted the sentience. It sent a part of its awareness hurtling through duff and moss to the area. The guardians had stopped screaming, but they were taut.

Boots tread across the ground.

Men.

The sentience surmised they sought the one who lay unconscious deeper within the forest. It didn't want them to find him, for it was curious about his possession of the art, and why the guardians were so worried about him.

It simply opened the ground beneath their boots, heaving back moss like a great maw. It whipped roots around their legs and torsos, and pulled them down. It felt the reverberations of their screams, but screams were harmless. The steel that armored their torsos could not protect them, for tree roots were stronger than steel.

It rolled a blanket of moss over the men, using roots to pull them ever deeper, squeezing them apart. Corpse beetles, and other earthly denizens of the forest, would take care of the rest.

All of this sudden contact with men evoked memories of men the sentience had once known. There was the frail, elderly man who sat high upon a golden throne. A fatherly figure, one who loved him well. *Arcos.*

There were others—Varadgrim, yes, faithful Varadgrim, and Lichant of the east, Mirdhwell of the west, and Terrandon of the south. All faithful, all friends. Unlike the red stinger ants, they were natives of this land. The sentience called out for them, and could feel Varadgrim somewhere out there, but he was far off. Of Lichant and Terrandon, there was no response at all, but Mirdhwell did stir . . .

Then there was the man who meant the most to the sentience, to the man he had been. Hadriax.

My dear friend, my best friend.

A surge of longing made the rain pour in the forest, pattering the man's face. On impulse, the sentience called out for Hadriax, and to its surprise, it felt something, a brief hum of life. The sentience pursued it, and once found, held onto it.

This was not Hadriax after all, but something of him was present. As the sentience probed, it found the imprint of a familiar aura of power, but the feeling was decidedly feminine. And far away, so far away.

Desperately the sentience called out to Varadgrim and Mirdhwell, revealing to them the aura of the female before it lost contact.

Find her!

❧ MIRROR
REFLECTION ❧

Karigan plucked bits of straw from her work tunic as she strode away from the stable in the dimming light of evening. She'd been helping Hep with feeding, as much as her bad arm allowed. He forked hay down from the loft, and she threw the appropriate amount into each stall. Scooping out grain wasn't too difficult either, and helping made her feel more useful.

In light of all her recent and strange experiences, it didn't hurt that the work was nothing but ordinary. It involved no "traveling," no hauntings, no magic. Being surrounded by all those horses was a tonic for her soul. They asked for nothing more than food, water, shelter, and a scratch behind the ear, and those were easy enough to provide. For those simple things, the horses returned love and affection in earnest, and unconditionally.

Karigan's sense of peace, however, did not last. As she approached Rider barracks, a tide of wooziness rushed over her, forcing her to an abrupt, unbalanced halt. The castle grounds darkened in her vision, and she forgot where she was going and why. She thought she heard a calling. Not the Rider call, but a lonely mournful calling tinged with desperation. Something touched her mind, like cold fingers leafing through her thoughts and memories.

Sorrow and loneliness turned to surprise and hope, and led to more probing.

She staggered when it finally released her. A residue of that touch clung to her like moist, black roots. A residue of dark intelligence.

Karigan tried to shudder it off, but could not. Her left arm prickled insistently.

She pushed on toward Rider barracks along the well worn path, caught in a fog. When she entered, she found Yates and Justin in the common room playing Intrigue. As she gazed at their pieces arrayed on the board, she suddenly saw patterns and strategies as she never had before. On impulse she pulled up a chair and started setting up the third set of pieces—the red—while Yates and Justin gaped at her in surprise.

"I thought—" Yates began. He and Justin passed a look between them, shrugged, and started repositioning their own pieces to start anew.

The game ran fairly swiftly in terms of Intrigue. Some matches were known to last for months and even years. Karigan dominated the entire game, first attacking Yates, the stronger player, and lulling Justin into thinking she had formed an alliance with him. With the two-pronged attack against Yates, he was quickly weakened, and though Karigan sacrificed some of her own pieces, she set up the attacks so Justin sacrificed more than she.

It was almost a miracle how she could formulate strategy, as though she'd suddenly been endowed with the ability. Instead of seeing disparate, individual pieces, she saw patterns drawn on the gameboard like the lines of a map she could follow. It was so clear to her now—why hadn't she seen it all before? How could she have missed it? How easy it was to annihilate Yates' knights, assassins, infantry, courtiers, and archers, and how easy it would be to do the same to Justin.

When Yates finally surrendered, she turned on Justin, pulling him into an intricate trap that killed off more than half his pieces. He gazed at her slack-jawed, even as she moved in to take his king.

Afterward, she slumped in her chair exhausted.

"You're the most merciless Triad I've ever played with," Yates told her in awe.

"She's not the Triad," Justin said, "she's an empress." He looked up at her. "I thought you didn't like this game."

Karigan gazed at the game board as if seeing it for the first time and could not believe the carnage. She had led a conquest, taking over all of Yates' and Justin's countries. She had done it with trickery and cunning, and excellent strategy. She had been cold and calculating.

A part of her congratulated herself on doing what was necessary to expand her holdings and win domination. There had been major casualties, but that was the price of power.

Another part of her was so appalled her stomach lurched.

Abruptly she pushed away from the table and sprinted from the common room, leaving behind two baffled Riders.

She ran into her room and slammed the door shut behind her. She felt so—so unclean—tainted even. That hadn't been her who played so ruthlessly, had it? She hated the game, and whenever she was coaxed into playing it, she always lost. Except this one time.

"Madness," she said.

She went to her table and grabbed her mirror to see if she had sprouted horns since the last time she looked.

The mirror had once belonged to her mother, a wedding gift from her father, part of a beautiful silver dressing set, etched with wildflowers. Karigan remembered, as a little girl, slipping out of bed and peering into her parents' room. There in the candlelight sat her mother on the corner of the bed in a white shift, looking into the mirror and giggling while her father tenderly brushed her long, brown hair.

Karigan had watched, enraptured, until one of her aunts found her and sent her back to bed with a pat on her bottom.

Karigan smiled at the memory. It lent her balance. But when she looked into the silvered glass of the mirror, it was not her own face she saw.

The power of Blackveil is rising, said the face in the mirror.

Karigan squawked and flung the mirror across the room. It stopped a hair's breadth from smashing against the wall. It hung there, floating in the air.

Madness, madness, madness, she thought.

It got worse. The mirror floated straight toward her as though carried by a phantom's hand. Karigan raced for the door, but the mirror flew there before her, and advanced on her again. She backed away, until she got wedged between her wardrobe and the wall.

The mirror "faced" her. Blue-green eyes peered out at her, from leonine features framed by tawny hair. A face Karigan had seen a thousand years in the past.

Time is short, Lil Ambrioth said, *before the door closes again, so listen to me for once, hey?*

Inanely Karigan wanted to know *what* door.

You've been touched by the influence of Blackveil—resist it! I will help as I can, but it is up to you to resist—

Lil's face vanished and the mirror plummeted toward the floor. Karigan snatched it from mid-air. She pressed it to her chest, and slid down the wall to sit dazed on the floor.

Barston Grough puffed on his pipe as he took in the dimming light of day over the rolling grasslands of Mirwell Province. The stem of his pipe fit comfortably between a gap in his teeth, and white smoke twisted up into the air.

Polly and Bill watched over the flock, tongues lolling, alert for wanderers or predators. Sheep bleated and
munched on the grass with great contentment. Their woolly
backs were sheeny against the lush grasses in the waning
light.

Barston was as content as a ram this fine summer evening. In a couple of days he and the collies would bring his
fat, woolly flock to market in Dorvale, and he'd get himself
a bulging purse in return.

Good feeding was the key. He didn't have to compete
with anyone else for these grasslands. The good feeding
helped the mommas make strong lambs in the spring, and
when the lambs weaned, they grew eating that same fine
grass. All the other grasslands were overgrazed and trodden
to death by other farmers' livestock. If Barston had chosen
to graze his sheep there, he'd have scrawny, sick lambs,
instead of the fine, strong beasties dotting the land before
him now.

As dusk deepened, mist crept along the rolling countryside. On a near hillock, the huge old cairn and the obelisks
that surrounded it turned into menacing silhouettes.

Barston grinned. *Mad Grough,* the other farmers called
him. *The crazy old man.*

"Crazy? Bah."

He'd have thought they'd figure it out when at every
market he got the best prices for sheep and wool. The rest
of them were a bunch of superstitious crybabies.

"All the better for me," he said with a scratchy laugh.
He didn't have to share with anyone.

The old legends claimed this was haunted ground, that
a demon spirit inhabited it, and that anyone who lingered
here was doomed.

Barston admitted the old cairn was forbidding enough,
the ground within the circle of obelisks barren of the grass
that grew so prolifically elsewhere. The obelisks were

carved with strange sigils, but he figured they did nothing more than tell the story of the one interred beneath the cairn. Probably a clan lord.

He was surprised grave robbers hadn't broken into it to plunder whatever treasures had been buried with the clan lord, but he supposed the legends kept off thieves as well as sheep farmers. Or, better yet, maybe the fact the tomb had no entrance had discouraged thieves.

The clan lord probably had been terrible in life, spawning the legends, but the fact remained he was dead. Dead for a good, long time, Barston guessed, and gone to dust. Not a threat to one sheep farmer, two collies, or a flock of sheep.

The legends only served to keep others away, much to Barston's profit. He'd been bringing his flocks here for a very long time, and no demon spirit had bothered him yet.

He turned back to his little campfire and stirred up the embers. He had made himself a little shepherd's hut here on the grasslands, lugging all the materials himself, piece by piece, except for the sod that covered the roof. He found that aplenty all around him.

Barston was just contemplating making himself a modest supper when the ground began to tremble beneath his feet.

"Wha—?" His pipe slipped from his mouth and landed in the fire.

A silent concussion slapped the air, followed by terrified bleating by the sheep. Polly and Bill started howling.

Barston whirled about, holding his shepherd's staff before him. What in the five hells was going on? Were wolves on the prowl? He hadn't heard any, nor seen sign of them. This was more than wolves, though; the ground had shaken.

When lightning exploded in spidery arcs between the obelisks, crowning the hillock of the cairn in white-blue light, Barston threw himself to the ground. His sheep stampeded. They stampeded right past the dogs, right past him.

Some even trampled over him. Polly and Bill ran off whining, tails tucked between their legs. They ignored Barston's calls and whistles.

Silence followed, and Barston did not move. He dared not. Immense, cold dread fell across him like a blanket. When he risked looking up, he saw a shadow form with the face of a gaunt cadaver staring back down at him with pale, dead eyes. A length of chain dangled from a manacle on its wrist.

Skeletal fingers twined around the hilt of an ancient sword, the blade etched with strange jagged runes that burned Barston's eyes and made tears stream down his cheeks.

All the others who had forsaken these grasslands had not been so foolish after all. They were right: a demon haunted these grounds.

The slit of the demon's mouth parted, and there was a subtle shoosh of breath that had not been released for a very long time. It moved its jaw as if to speak, but at first nothing came out. When it did, the voice was cracked and grating like rusty hinges.

"I seek the Galadheon."

With those words of death ringing in Barston's ears, his heart failed from pure terror.

Journal of Hadriax el Fex

The ships from the Empire stopped coming a long time ago, and we do not know why. We send courier ships back to the Empire, but they do not return.

I do not know what to do with Alessandros. He has always been high-tempered, but now he is given to bouts of grief and depression, declaring the Emperor, his father, has abandoned him, despite his successes here. These bouts turn into rage, which leads to broken objects and dead slaves. This then turns into long periods of silence and melancholy, where he locks himself in his chambers to work on "experiments."

Without resupplies from the Empire, our mechanicals are falling apart. Our artisans have been doing their best to fabricate new parts, but now the clans have targeted them for assassination, and we have lost many skilled men. We are also out of ammunition for the concussives, and we've found no source of saltpeter. The one thing that keeps the clans at bay is Alessandros' Black Star device.

Renald has made lieutenant in the Lion regiment. I attended the ceremony, as I am the closest thing to family he has in this wilderness. He is devoted to Alessandros, and shows only courage, loyalty, and honor. I miss him terribly, and not just as a squire, but as a friend and confidant. I even miss his boyish jokes, but he is a true man now, and I see him more often on the field of battle than elsewhere.

⋘ TRUE AND FALSE ⋙

Laren had to hurry to keep pace with Zachary. He swept through the castle corridors leading the way, his attendants and Weapons striding behind him. They were headed toward the throne room for the day's public audience. There was no urgency despite the haste, but she knew that expending physical energy was Zachary's way of coping with unpleasant problems, namely Lord-Governor D'Ivary. Hopefully he'd scheduled a bout with Drent for later in the day, to take off some more of the edge.

More reports had come in confirming D'Ivary's ill treatment of refugees. Laren could not believe the lord-governor's gall, going against the king's word and hiring mercenaries to impersonate Sacoridian troops. It was tantamount to treason. Zachary would have to deal with D'Ivary swiftly and decisively.

He'd also have to handle the situation with great care. He could not risk causing the rest of the lord-governors to align against him if they perceived him misusing his powers toward one of their own.

There had been very little grumbling at the punishment of the old lord-governor of Mirwell, because Mirwell had been the engineer of a plan that had killed many nobles and their children. Zachary, performing the execution himself, however, had stunned them. For better or worse, they witnessed a new side of their king, and Laren believed it unsettled them knowing how willingly he shed noble blood. Not just any noble blood, but that of a lord-governor.

In D'Ivary's case, the lord-governor had not acted aggressively toward the crown itself, unlike Mirwell, nor had he threatened the other lord-governors. No one, in fact, beyond his borders.

The only ones who had suffered were the refugees. Yes, the other lord-governors thought D'Ivary's behavior stupid and appalling, but the people he hurt, they believed, were leeches to Sacoridian society. They looked to no lord-governor, paid no taxes, yet lived within the borders of the kingdom, using its resources and demanding its protection.

For Zachary to forcefully bring D'Ivary to justice was to chance turning most of the lord-governors against him. Some would stand true to him no matter what, but there were too many new bloods; too new to know precisely where they stood, or how far they'd go to support their king, and a king was only as strong as the support of his vassals.

Yet Zachary could not let D'Ivary off unchallenged and unpunished. This would not only signal to the lord-governors they had free rein to do as they wished within the boundaries of their provinces, but it would seriously undermine the king's authority and credibility.

There were a few lord-governors, Laren knew, who would not mind a weaker monarch, or a completely different monarch altogether.

The parameters of the problem were enough to make Laren's head throb, and she knew it must gnaw at Zachary. When he had first heard the news of what had happened to the refugees, he'd called in General Harborough, ready to storm D'Ivary Province with the entire army at his back. Fortunately, Sperren, Colin Dovekey, and the general had been able to bring him around to consider less drastic measures.

Just what those measures might be preoccupied Zachary to the point it diverted his attention from other important matters. The politics of the situation frustrated him; throttled his ability to mete out justice as he wished.

The king and his party left the carpeted west wing, and entered more utilitarian corridors, their boots ringing on flagstones. Servants and other folk bowed out of the king's way.

"Rider Ty Newland has returned from Adolind and Mirwell," Laren told him.

"Yes?"

Their rapport had suffered ever since her misreading of D'Ivary. Zachary remained curt with her, and did not consult her at all during audiences or meetings, despite the fact her ability had been behaving of late. Mostly, anyway. It was as though he had lost all faith in *her,* not just her ability. Nothing could have saddened her more, for they had always been close.

"He says Lord-Governor Adolind is very pleased with the arrival of northern refugees. He says Adolind is experiencing what looks to be a bumper harvest this year, one like they've never seen, and they need all the help with it they can get."

The news brightened Zachary. "That is certainly good to hear. Adolind usually suffers through the winter for lack of stores. And it sounds like the refugees have found much more of a welcome there."

Laren nodded, pleased by Zachary's positive response. "In addition, Ty brought a message from Beryl Spencer."

Beryl Spencer was a Green Rider who, like Lynx, did not run message errands. Her special ability to assume a role, her ability to *deceive,* was much too useful to confine her to ordinary messenger duties. No, Zachary had other, more secret uses for her ability. Portraying a major of the Mirwel-

lian militia, she had played no small role in the demise of
the old lord-governor, and now kept watch on his son.

From an inner pocket of her shortcoat, Laren withdrew
an envelope sealed with the emblem of Mirwell Province, a
war hammer crushing a mountain.

The king actually halted to read it. His attendants and
Weapons came to a stop a split second behind him, the
Weapons arraying themselves all around him in a watchful
attitude.

"Hmm. It appears Adolind's good fortune has not
reached Mirwell. Crops are withering in the soil." He
looked up from the message to Laren. "How can that be?
They're in the same region."

Laren shrugged, just as surprised as he.

He read on, raising his eyebrows in disbelief. When he
finished, he passed the message back to her. As she read it,
she saw how peculiar the failure of crops was in Mirwell—
the weather had been superb for growing, and there was no
sign of widespread disease or pestilence. Mirwell should be
having a fine harvest to look forward to.

As she read on, she came across the section that had
raised the king's eyebrows:

> *I know this may seem odd, as though I've been spending too
> much time in the wine cellar, but I cannot discount what I saw,
> nor the words of several other eyewitnesses.*
>
> *I was out on the keep's grounds when I noticed a commotion
> at a nearby ornamental pond. The groundskeepers were wrangling
> with an ancient monster of a snapping turtle—it was huge—
> that had been feeding on the ducks that frequent the pond. A
> crowd had gathered to witness the creature, and the amusing
> antics of the men trying to capture it.*
>
> *Here is the part that is difficult to believe: the snapper sud-
> denly raised its beak as though to strike the nearest man, but
> instead, flames roared from its mouth and scorched him. I swear,*

by all that I am or ever will be, that this truly occurred. The man did not survive the burns, and an ax made quick work of the snapper. When Lord Mirwell heard of it, he was furious it had been dispatched, for he would have liked to study it.

Laren looked up incredulously. "A fire-breathing snapping turtle?" If this hadn't been Beryl—serious, pragmatic Beryl—she would've believed someone was pulling her leg.

"Read on," Zachary said.

Laren did. Apparently there were other odd goings on in Mirwell. Young apples, for instance, had turned to lead and snapped the limbs of trees they were growing on. Beryl, not an eyewitness to these other occurrences, could not verify the words of the folk who came to the lord-governor to tell their stories. Beryl did add that there was much apprehensive talk among the common folk about all the strange events. *Undoubtedly it gets exaggerated with each telling,* she wrote, *making it all the more incredible.*

When it was clear Laren had finished reading, Zachary strode off.

When she caught up with him again, he asked, "What do you think?"

"I think none of it is a coincidence. There is too much of it going on."

"Like a stone deer in Wayman."

"Yes." She considered telling him about Karigan's adventures in the abandoned corridors then and there, and confiding to him the extent of her own troubles with her ability, but they turned into a more crowded corridor and she hesitated. They'd be at the throne room within moments, and it wasn't the sort of story you told quickly. Plus, she didn't want anyone to overhear it. She decided she'd wait until after the public audience when she might get some time alone with him.

"I don't know what we can do about it," Zachary said. "We don't even know why it's happening."

"I—" she began hesitantly. "I believe something has gone awry with magic. The nature of magic."

Zachary cast her a questioning glance, but by now they had reached his "secret" side entrance to the throne room. He paused before passing through the door held open for him by a servant.

"We will talk more about this later," he said.

She nodded, more relieved than ever that finally he'd devote some thought to the problem, and maybe during the process, the rift between them would mend, too.

The audience proved to be as crowded as usual, with the typical kinds of supplicants. There was, however, an unusual buzz in the air, some layer of anxiety among the people, and it put Laren on edge. The scuffing of hundreds of feet on the floor, the whispers and murmurs among those waiting in line, and the heat and reek of all those bodies grated on her, began to make her head ache.

False, her ability told her.

She groaned inwardly. It was happening again.

False.

She tried to pull up her barriers, but they were so flimsy they would not stay in place. Her ability pronounced judgment on anyone and anything at random, often contradicting itself.

"I seek the king's blessing on the marriage of my daughter," a man was saying.

False.

Zachary smiled. "You do not need the king's blessing."

False.

"But it would mean so much to us—she is our only daughter, and it is a special event."

True. False.

Laren must have made some audible noise of irritation for Zachary glanced at her. "Captain?"

True.

She gritted her teeth, and waved him off, a rather disrespectful breach of etiquette, but she couldn't focus well enough to explain.

True.

Zachary flashed her a perplexed look, finished with the man, and turned to the next supplicant in line, a woman who fretted at her handkerchief.

"My husband," she began, "he has—he has lost his good sense."

"How so?" Zachary asked.

"It began with the rainbows," she said.

"Rainbows?" Colin Dovekey sputtered.

"Yes, sir. Twenty-five, at last count, crossing our land."

"I find that a bit incredible," Colin said.

"We counted them twice," the woman assured him. "They arched over one another. Some were triple-arched."

True, true, true.

Laren growled, and Zachary flicked another glance at her.

"It was the most amazing and beautiful sight," the woman said. "We just stood in wonder gazing at it. Our neighbors and the townsfolk came to see it. Some said it was a miracle of the gods. My husband took it to mean *he* was the chosen one of the gods."

Zachary appeared to be at a loss for words, but Colin was not. "Er, what is it you've come to ask of the king?"

False.

"Stop!" Much to Laren's embarrassment, her voice had rung out loud enough for anyone nearby to hear. "Sorry," she told the king. Her neck muscles were so taut her dull headache was turning into a maelstrom that made her ears ring.

The woman began to answer Colin's question, explaining how the rainbows appeared every day in different configurations, and how the folk who traveled from miles around came to pay her husband their respects.

"They leave currency, food, flowers—whatever little they own. My husband has become unbearable to live with. What I ask of my king is—is to stop the rainbows."

"Stop the—?" Zachary said in astonishment.

Laren would have liked to have heard his response, but shutting off her ability took all her concentration. The clamor of the throne room—the voices and shifting feet—grew more pronounced. The pain in her head enclosed her in an opaque haze, separating her from everyone else.

False, true, true, false—

The endless stream of her special ability's declarations burst her barriers and rushed into her mind like flood waters, and then all she knew was white noise and drowning.

In the days following the captain's collapse, Karigan found herself up to her elbows in paperwork. With the captain out of commission and Connly still absent, Mara had assumed the captain's duties, running off to one meeting after another, and attending the king.

Karigan ended up with Mara's old duties, with other Riders pitching in when they could. Fortunately, her time spent working with her father scheduling merchant trains, inventorying stores, handling payroll, and tallying the books served her well, though she had to work somewhat from scratch. All the most recent records were stored in Captain Mapstone's quarters, and the captain would admit no one, not even Master Mender Destarion.

Karigan did have to admit, one late night as she pored over sheets of paper spread out on the table in the common room of Rider barracks, that some things in the messenger service were more difficult to deal with than in the world of commerce. For instance, her father's wagon trains traveled fairly standard routes, depending on the season, and stopped at the same fairs annually. It was all very predictable.

The messenger service was not. There was no telling when the king might need to send a message, or where the message must be delivered. It could be the next town over, or over the Wingsong Mountains to the coast of the Eastern Sea. The challenge was scheduling available Riders in such a way so as to be prepared for either contingency.

Sometimes there just weren't enough Riders available, which meant Karigan must prevail upon the light cavalry to fill in. And they felt such work beneath them.

Karigan rubbed her bleary eyes, fighting off a yawn. It was getting to a point where the words on the papers were turning into squiggles she could make no sense of. Trying to figure out what needed to be done to keep the Riders functioning at least kept her mind off ghosts and floating mirrors. In fact, those things seemed far off, and far-fetched. Fairy tale-like. She had more immediate and *real* concerns to deal with.

The door to Rider barracks creaked open, admitting a rush of fresh, late summer air. The scent of dew on green growing things revived Karigan somewhat. She guessed it could only be Mara wandering in at so late an hour. What hour was it anyway? She had lost track of the time long ago.

Mara, as Karigan had guessed, entered the common room, looking as weary as Karigan felt. "Good thing there was a new shipment of whale oil today," she said, eyeing the two lamps Karigan used to illuminate her work. Mara stretched her hands high above her head and there was a distinct popping of joints. With a sigh of relief, she flopped into an armchair.

"Gods, I don't know how she does it."

"You mean the captain?" Karigan asked.

"Yep. Standing by the king day in and day out while he has his private and public audiences. And then having to attend all those hideous meetings. You would not believe the conniving and infighting."

"I believe it's called politics."

Mara rolled her eyes. "This was just a meeting of stable-hands and the chiefs of the mounted companies, bickering over who gets what shipment of grain and hay. Poor Hep had to do all the talking on our behalf. I don't know what to say—it's not the kind of work I'm good at." She pulled on a kink of hair. "It's enough to take out the curl."

"And when you're attending the king?"

"That's even worse. I think he wants me there just because he, and everyone else, is used to seeing Captain Mapstone at his side. You know, someone in green, out of habit."

Captain Mapstone a habit? Karigan stifled a smile, wondering how the captain would react to such a notion.

"I know the king depends on her as his advisor, but frankly, I don't have her experience or knowledge to play the part. I'm completely out of my element. So, I'm more or less an ornament."

The defeated way in which Mara described herself made Karigan laugh. Ornamental was the last word she'd use to describe Mara, who was one of the most capable Riders she knew. Mara, not knowing exactly what was so funny, smiled tentatively.

Karigan wiped her eyes. "Sorry, I think the lack of sleep is getting to me."

"I know what you mean. Have you heard anything about the captain?"

Karigan sobered immediately. "I was going to ask you the same question."

"All I know is that Destarion is furious with her for refusing him admittance to her quarters." Mara rolled her eyes. "That was another tirade I had to listen to today, and all I had said was 'good morning.'"

No one knew the cause of the captain's collapse. The king, and others who were present at the time, said she'd been acting erratically for a while. Ghost words came back to Karigan: *Her gift is failing.* Was the captain's collapse somehow tied to the failure of her ability? She regretted not telling the captain about her own ability's failure when she had had the chance.

After the captain collapsed, she'd been cognizant enough to declare herself unfit for duty, demand she be returned to her quarters, and informed the king Mara was in charge until Connly returned. Once in her quarters, she slammed the door and locked it. Food was left on her step three times daily. Sometimes it was drawn inside and consumed, more often not.

"So what did you tell Destarion?" Karigan asked.

Mara sighed. "I told him I'd try to talk to her when I had a few moments. I haven't had any time until now, and now it's well past midnight." She opened her mouth in a mighty yawn. "Whatever happened to the good old days?"

"What good old days?"

"The days when Ereal, and Patrici before her, did all this stuff and I was just an ordinary Rider whose only reason to stay up this late was to have a good, cold ale at the Cock and Hen. I've become much too serious and sensible of late."

"The Cock and Hen?" Karigan crinkled her nose in distaste. "You'd actually set foot in that place?" It was a seedy, rundown pub on the outskirts of the city, which catered to those of questionable reputation.

"Oh yes," Mara said dreamily. "They've the best, bitterest dark ale this side of the Grandgent—bitter enough to curl your hair."

Karigan snorted. "That explains yours."

Mara sighed long and mournfully. "Now I'm destined to wither away in meetings crowded with stablehands who haven't bathed in months, arguing over sacks of grain."

With that, Mara declared herself spent, and retired. Karigan finally set to clearing away her papers. Like Mara, she dreamed of all her cares drifting away, of sitting down in a pub—one much nicer than the Cock and Hen—downing cool, dark ale at her leisure. The only problem was that she couldn't rid herself of the image of Lil Ambrioth scowling down at her, and the feeling of guilt that scowl engendered.

She stumbled down the corridor to her room, yawning. Inside, she kicked off her boots and extinguished her lamp. Too tired to change into her nightshirt, she flopped onto her bed fully dressed.

Captain Mapstone would snap out of her difficulty, she had to. Maybe Connly would return soon, and take the brunt of responsibility she and Mara now bore. Maybe she had never really seen the image of Lil Ambrioth in her mirror, maybe . . .

Within seconds, she drifted off to sleep.

⇜ IN THE WATER BUCKET ⇝

Unfortunately, by the next day, none of Karigan's "maybes" came to pass. Captain Mapstone remained sequestered in her quarters, refusing to talk to anyone. Connly had not miraculously shown up, and she still had a schedule to untangle.

That morning, she actually looked forward to her session with Drent. She needed the outlet from all the sedentary paperwork she'd been doing, and to get her mind off Rider troubles. As usual, Drent whacked her pretty good in the practice ring, but at least the pain made her feel like she was doing "real" work.

Later on, she visited the quartermaster to ensure supplies were adequate for the Riders heading out on errands over the next week or so. She counted pieces of spare tack and uniforms, shelves of unused bedrolls, weaponry, tinder kits, and eating utensils. Next she visited the kitchens where the head cook patiently explained that the travel fare Riders required was available day and night—she had to but come and get it.

Karigan found she had taken for granted the role of the Chief Rider whose duty it was to see that message-bearing Riders were fully supplied and ready to go at a moment's notice. She had always taken on an errand with Condor already tacked and readied for her, the saddlebags bulging.

She never stopped to think about the fact the Chief Rider had seen to it all so she wouldn't have to.

If the Chief Rider forgot anything, it could compromise the Rider's errand. Karigan had never been on the road with any supplies missing, and the diligence of her Chief Rider was an example she intended to emulate. She would see to it the Riders were well taken care of.

Once everything returned to normal, she promised herself to be more conscientious about thanking Connly for his efforts.

As she crossed the castle grounds checking off errands on her list, she glimpsed Mara in the distance, doggedly trotting off to what was likely yet another meeting.

Karigan shook her head wondering if things would ever, in fact, return to normal. What was normal? She sighed and continued back to barracks, where the dreaded paperwork awaited her.

At four hour, Karigan had had enough. She couldn't take it anymore. She set her pen down and pushed her chair away from the table.

No more paperwork, she told herself.

She left Rider barracks and crossed over to the stable. It was time for the afternoon feeding, and as she entered the stable, she was greeted by whickering horses bobbing their heads above stall doors. Others circled impatiently in their stalls, kicking the wall in emphasis, to urge their human attendants to get a move on.

Hep had already tossed down hay, and was now descending the ladder from the loft. He gave her a big grin when he saw her.

"Why don't you start with the grain," he said.

Obediently she went into the small room in which the grain was stored, a whole great mound of it. She loved the

sweet smell of fresh grain, and in here it was almost overwhelming. She set to feeding, and soon the stable was filled
with contented munching.

There were actually twenty-six horses in the stable, including her Condor. Two served as spare mounts, which
were used in case a messenger horse came up lame. That
meant twenty-four Riders were in residence, an unusual
number.

One horse not typically seen was Lynx's black and white
piebald, Owl. Lynx rarely stayed in the city when checking
in with the king, but the trouble surrounding D'Ivary Province probably required that he keep close.

There was Mara's Firefly, and Crane who now served
with Ty. Garth's Chickadee munched away in a stall next to
Dale's Plover. When her gaze settled on Bluebird, Captain
Mapstone's gelding, she noticed immediately his forlorn
appearance and dull coat, and that he did not feed as enthu-
siastically as the other horses.

Hep joined her and followed her gaze. "Aye, that one's
off his feed. Longs for his mistress, he does." Shaking his
head, he hefted two water buckets and headed out to scrub
them down and fill them with fresh water.

Karigan walked over to Bluebird's stall and leaned
against the door. He gazed at her with liquid brown eyes.

"Poor thing," she said, stroking his neck. "The captain
will be back soon, I know she will."

Even as she murmured the words, she wondered if it
would be so. She and Mara couldn't keep up this charade
forever on their own. They needed the captain, for they
depended on her guidance and authority. They were used
to her taking all the responsibility and making all the
decisions.

Frankly, Karigan felt lost without her and was surprised
to learn how much she craved the captain's approval, even
that which often went unsaid. She wanted to prove to the

captain she was worthy of her trust and respect, and she suspected it was because of all the respect she held, in turn, for the captain.

She brushed flies away from Bluebird's eyes, wondering if he could sense whatever it was that afflicted the captain. Maybe he had a touch of colic or some other ill bothering him, but somehow she doubted it.

She resolved to provide him with extra attention and exercise when she could fit it into her schedule. Considering she'd neglected her own horse enough, thanks to her bad arm and new duties, she didn't hold out much hope for spending time with him.

Schedules. She frowned, remembering the work she had left on the table in barracks. Now that there were more Riders in than she thought, it would throw a kink into—

"Arg!" She shook herself to stop thinking about it. That's why she had come here, wasn't it? To free her mind?

With a final pat to Bluebird's neck, she went to Condor's stall. She stepped inside, but he ignored her, his nose deep into his grain bucket.

"Nice to see you, too," she said.

He didn't even bother to flick an ear.

She maneuvered around him, kicking at his bedding and finding it fresh. She checked his hooves, which were picked clean as well. There was only a light coating of dust on his back, and she was beginning to think Hep had been just a little too good at his job by not leaving her anything to do. But she knew he was aware of how busy she was.

Condor's water bucket caught her eye. *Ah ha! Maybe Hep hasn't cleaned* that *yet.*

She stepped around Condor's back end, and paused, startled by the sensation of someone's gaze on her. She caught the movement of a shadow along the wall just before it merged into a dark corner of the stall. A hasty glance revealed no one else had entered the stable. Was it a trick of the light? It was very possible, for the stable was dim with but a few dirty windows to let in the sun.

"Did you see anything?" she asked Condor.

He tugged at his pile of hay on the stall floor.

Karigan sighed, shaking her head at His Hindness, the High Lord of Fertilizer. "Didn't think so." She decided to forget about the shadow. Her recent dealings with the supernatural had her seeing apparitions where there were none. The stable couldn't have been more ordinary.

She peered into Condor's water bucket. It was low. Bits of straw and dead flies floated on the water's surface.

Good, she thought. She could clean the bucket and refill it, something she could do to care for her own horse for once.

But even as she gazed into the bucket, a smoky haze began to drift upward from the water.

"Wha—?"

It glowed green, illuminated by some inner light deep within it. Beneath the water, beneath the bits of hay and dead flies, a pair of blue-green eyes peered back up at her.

"N-not again!"

The eyes blinked, and with a liquidy shimmer, a face formed around them, the face of Lil Ambrioth. Her hair floated like seaweed beneath the water.

Karigan choked back a scream, but could not draw away, as if a pair of invisible hands held her head over the bucket. She became aware of Condor moving in the stall behind her, and looking over her shoulder. Warm breath sweetened with grain puffed against her cheek.

Lil Ambrioth blinked again. *Things are not well, yet you do nothing.*

"I—" Her breath sent ripples across the water that distorted the First Rider's face. "Nothing?"

Nothing.

Karigan tried to tug free of the power that forced her to

gaze into the bucket, but she could not. This was madness. "I've been—I've been busy." She did not know which was stranger: talking into a bucket, or seeing the face of the First Rider in it.

More is required of you than a mere meeting of basic duties.

"Basic—! Mere meeting—!" To Karigan's mind, it had been anything but, especially having to deal with unwelcome visitations by apparitions. She wanted to shake the water bucket to erase the image of the First Rider and rid herself of the madness, but the same power that made her gaze into the bucket also trapped her arms against her sides.

She shut her eyes. "I do not see you, I do not see you, I do not—"

But you can still hear me, hey?

Karigan's spirits sagged. Reluctantly she opened her eyes to meet the apparition's gaze.

You waste my time with such foolishness, and time is something of which I've too little.

Karigan ground her teeth wanting to make a tart reply about her own time, but she withheld it. Instead she asked, "What do you want of me?"

I have told you before, you must hold the Riders together. There is a change occurring in the world. The Riders do not understand what goes on with their gifts. They are without their captain. You must help them.

"Me? But how can—"

Lil cut her off with some ancient and exasperated invocation to the gods requesting patience. *To begin with, talk to them.*

"What am I supposed to tell them? I don't know any more than they do."

You do know more. If a submerged apparition in the bottom of a bucket could look annoyed and impatient, Lil had certainly achieved the effect.

You spoke with an Eletian, and you reported his words to your king. He spoke to you of the breach stirring powers on both sides of the wall, and that the warning was before you.

Karigan recalled a stone funerary slab in a flooded tomb. Only it wasn't a tomb, but a prison. A wraith had broken its chains and arisen to walk the world again. *Powers were stirring . . .* Powers, magic. And finally she made the connection.

"You're telling me that the breach is causing . . ." She dropped her voice into a whisper. ". . . my ability to fail?"

Yes, among other things that have gone awry. Magic is out of kilter.

"But how?"

My time is too brief to explain it all. The door will close at any moment. For now you must hold the Riders together.

"You put this on me, but you won't explain it to me?" Karigan licked her lips. "Why do you keep coming to me? Why do you think *I* can do as you ask?"

A bit of hay drifted over Lil's face. *You are a Rider, and that should be enough, but I see it is not. You are a Rider because you have intense loyalty to your country and your king, and an innate gift of magic. This is true of all Riders, but you've also the ability to bring them together, if only you would accept the responsibility.*

"I never even wanted to be a Rider."

Ta! Such a stubborn girl. You would not have answered the call if it wasn't in your spirit.

"That doesn't explain why you keep haunting me. Mara could do as you ask."

Lil's head turned, as though she were checking over her shoulder. *The door begins to close.*

"Explain it to me now!"

The First Rider sighed. *We share the brooch.*

Karigan blinked, startled. "You mean—?"

Lil nodded. *Made for me, it was.*

It was too incredible to believe, thought Karigan, that she should wear the same brooch the First Rider had once worn. The weight of history, the very idea of it, sent shivers down her spine.

This is why I come to you, hey? We are linked, you and I. And there is much struggle ahead. The Riders must be ready. There is something else important . . .

Karigan found herself lowering her face deeper into the bucket as if to ensure she didn't miss a word.

You are of interest to the darkness in Blackveil. Shield yourself well, keep your wits about you. Lil's voice and face began to fade. *The darkness seeks you . . .*

And she was gone.

Released by the power that had held her, Karigan grabbed the bucket and shook it vigorously. "What do you mean it seeks me?" she shouted. "Why is the darkness interested in me?"

But the green glow was gone, and there was no reply. She had only managed to churn up the water and cause the dead flies to whirl in circles.

Condor nosed her aside so he could get a drink, and a dazed Karigan looked up only to find Hep and Mara staring at her in astonishment from across the stall door.

"Are ya well?" Hep asked, his eyes wide.

"Um . . ."

Mara raised an eyebrow.

"Mara, we need to talk."

"I was going to suggest the very same thing."

The two Riders stepped outside and leaned against the paddock rails. The late afternoon sunshine felt good to Karigan— it seemed to chase away the shadows of apparitions and madness. All was tranquil, the late afternoon light glowing a bright yellow-green on the tips of grasses. There was a soft drone of bees visiting clover and lighting on the yellow and white asters that grew so prolifically in these waning days of summer.

Karigan told Mara everything, about how her ability had failed during the groundmite attack on Lady Penburn's delegation, the details of her "traveling" through the abandoned corridors, and even spoke of Lil Ambrioth's visitations.

She did not hold back as she had with Captain Mapstone. She now knew there was something much bigger going on than simply her own problems. She would not make the same mistake with Mara as she had with the captain: she would not hide the truth.

Mara took it all in calmly, interrupting only to ask for occasional clarification.

By the time Karigan finished, her throat was dry and the sun much lower, but she was glad to have it out. She no longer had to hide her madness; it was no longer her burden to bear alone.

Mara squinted as she gazed across the paddock. She twisted a curl of hair around her forefinger, and it was a while before she spoke.

"It's going to take time for me to absorb all this," she said. "I've heard bits and pieces from both you and the captain, but I had no idea of the extent of the situation. Some of our Riders haven't been themselves lately, and I guess I now know why."

She then glanced at Karigan and smiled. "The First Rider, eh? I guess there could be worse ghosts to meet."

"I wear her brooch." The smooth gold was cool beneath her fingers. "The very same one she once wore."

Mara nodded, seeming to be in less disbelief than Karigan. "All our brooches once belonged to a member of the original Green Riders. It only makes sense that the First Rider's would be one of them." Mara plucked a tall daisy and twirled it between her fingers. "I think your idea of a meeting is a good one. Maybe by sharing any problems we've experienced, instead of hiding them as personal failures, we might have a better chance of figuring out what to do."

⤜ A MEETING OF
RIDERS ⤛

The meeting was called for the following afternoon to take place in the common room of Rider barracks. With the king's approval, Mara withheld any new message errands from going out. Osric had arrived during the night, and Tegan that morning, bringing their numbers up to a whopping twenty-six Riders in residence. Fifteen others remained out in the field. They would be talked to individually as they returned from their errands.

Captain Mapstone did not appear despite Mara's coaxing. She refused even to open the door to speak with her face to face. In fact, she said nothing to Mara, except for a terse, "Go away." Karigan and Mara worried about her, but it made their meeting all the more urgent.

Karigan had never seen so much *green* jammed into one room before. The lucky few Riders who arrived first claimed all the comfy armchairs and rocking chairs. Most carried in chairs from their rooms.

The inscrutable Lynx chose to stand off by himself in a far corner, sucking on a long-stemmed pipe, his arms folded across his chest.

Karigan went around the room opening all the windows to let in fresh air, then took her place at the head of the table next to Mara. She grew uneasy with all the expectant faces looking their way.

Mara began with a smile. "I'm glad to see you all here.

It's not often we get together in such numbers, but Karigan and I felt it was necessary.

"Before Captain Mapstone's collapse, she told me she felt there was something amiss with the nature of magic, a concern she shared also with Karigan. She heard of too many strange occurrences happening throughout the provinces. Too many to be accounted an accident. Perhaps you've heard the rumors of a stone deer in Wayman, or about the rainbows over the village of Derry."

There was considerable nodding and murmured affirmatives from the assembled Riders.

"They're not rumors." Mara's pronouncement wasn't met with a great deal of surprise. After all, more than anyone else, the Riders had been out in the world and saw and heard much. "More reports of such things continue to trickle in during the king's public audiences.

"At the moment, I'm a little more concerned about what might be happening among *us,* though Karigan will have more to say about the larger scope of the problem. It is known only to Karigan and me, and to the king and his advisors, that Captain Mapstone's ability failed her during a very critical moment, while she evaluated Lord-Governor D'Ivary. If her ability hadn't failed, if she'd been able to detect D'Ivary's lies and true intent, tragedy in D'Ivary Province might have been averted."

Some Riders looked stricken, while others watched Mara raptly, waiting for more. Tegan stared at her hands folded on the tabletop, and Lynx stood calm as could be in his corner, blowing smoke rings toward the rafters.

"The outcome of the captain's ability failing is not what we're here to discuss," Mara continued, her voice rising above the general chatter. "The fact it failed is what brings us together today. The captain never shared with me whether her ability recovered after the incident, or if it continued to fail. From outward signs, I'd guess it's what led to her collapse." She gazed around the group, putting on a stern expression. "I want to know if anyone else here has experienced a lapse in their ability."

They had planned ahead that Karigan would come forward first if no one else did. Karigan's experiences, however, revolved around so many issues that Mara wanted to leave her last. As it turned out, Karigan didn't have to jump in. Tegan raised a trembling hand.

"Yes, Tegan?" Mara said.

"My ability," she said tentatively. "I've not been able to make an accurate foretelling of the weather for weeks."

Karigan, who wasn't surprised by her admission, watched Garth pale. He hung his head in abject guilt. "I'm sorry, Tegan. I had no idea. I thought you were playing a joke on me that day when I got caught in the rain. I shouldn't have yelled."

"How could you know?" she asked. "I was too ashamed to admit my failing to anyone."

Others chimed in. Osric M'Grew admitted he could no longer walk through solid objects, and had acquired several bruises attempting to do so. Though he made light of it, Karigan could see the fear in his eyes. Trace Burns said her ability, too, had failed, and this was why they had no idea of how Connly fared. Trace and Connly each possessed the ability to communicate with one another using thoughts, even over long distances.

"How do we know something hasn't happened to Connly?" Justin asked.

Trace shrugged. "We don't. But usually I can feel my ability in my mind, but that doesn't happen anymore when I try. I believe the problem is on my end, not his."

Other Riders said they had experienced no changes in their abilities, or hadn't needed to use them in months and were not aware of problems.

Ephram Neddick said, "I wouldn't call what's happened

to my ability a problem. It works better than ever." He screwed up his face. "Maybe too well, when I'm overnight-ing in an inn, if you know what I mean." His ability, when he chose to use it, was an extraordinary sense of hearing.

"I believe it's the same with my ability," Mara said. "Here is one more item for our list: some weeks ago, Reita's brooch abandoned her, prematurely it would seem."

Everyone began talking at once. Now that the problem had been aired, some were nervous, while others looked relieved they weren't the only ones afflicted.

"So," Lynx said, his gravelly voice quieting everyone, "some Riders' abilities have failed, at least two of you sense an enhancement, and the rest are not aware of any prob-lems. What does this add up to?"

Everyone turned their gazes back to Mara.

"I have no answers for you," she said, "but we now know there's a definite problem afflicting us, and the only way to begin addressing it is to acknowledge there *is* a prob-lem, to hear everything as a group. Why is Ephram's ability enhanced? Why can't Tegan properly sense the weather? What happened—is happening—to Captain Mapstone?

"Karigan has quite a tale to tell, which includes diffi-culty with her ability, and the broader problems. Karigan?"

She squirmed in her chair as everyone's attention shifted from Mara to her. Panic beat in her chest at the idea of hav-ing to reveal so much to so many others.

Mara nudged her foot under the table.

She licked her lips. It had to be done; she had to stop hiding things, but deep down, she feared they'd only con-firm her madness.

As she told her tale, just as she had told Mara the day be-fore, the common room quieted. The sounds from outdoors—birdsong, soldiers riding by in formation, the ringing of three hour—all seemed to be happening in some other realm.

The Riders listened to her with wonder and incredulity

registering on their faces. When she finished speaking of Lil Ambrioth, she was met with utter silence.

And then the babble erupted all at once, everyone demanding to have questions answered. Mara tried to answer, but she was drowned out by the commotion.

"Quiet!" Garth thundered.

Everyone did, and Mara passed him a smile of appreciation. "One question at a time, please," she said.

"What about the First Rider?" Ephram asked. "I find that far-fetched."

Karigan couldn't answer him. His words were like a pronouncement of her insanity.

"As I recall, Ephram," Dale said, "you were not yet with us two years ago during Prince Amilton's coup attempt. I was. I fought at the Battle of the Lost Lake. Karigan was there, too, struggling against the Eletian, with ghosts battling all around them. I think I even saw Lil Ambrioth there among them, though it could have been wishful thinking. I at least heard her horn." Others who had been there voiced their agreement.

"During Karigan's journey here that spring, she was aided by ghosts, including the spirit of F'ryan Coblebay, who in life had been a good friend of mine. If Karigan says she's been talking with the First Rider, then I believe her." Several Riders backed her with words of affirmation.

"Sorry if I'm a bit skeptical," Ephram said.

Karigan, grateful for Dale's words of confidence, said, "I hardly believe it myself, but the point of the matter is that something is going on with magic, and it's not just us. It's those other things, too; the stone deer and the rainbows.

"The words of the First Rider only confirm what the Eletian, Telagioth, told me. Powers are stirring, and there is trouble arising in Blackveil. No doubt this is the source of our problems, but exactly how or why it's affecting us on this side of the wall, I don't know. Magic has been kept hidden for so many years, who *would* know?"

The bright sunshine and birdsong flowing through the windows were counterpoint to her words.

"Has any message come from Alton?" Ty asked.

"No," Mara said. "None at all."

Karigan turned her thoughts to Alton, wondering how he fared, what he was doing . . . Had he made any progress with the wall? Just because they hadn't heard any news didn't mean anything bad. It just meant there was nothing to report. Still, it didn't sit well with her that he was there at the breach if Blackveil was, in truth, arising. He would be directly in the path of danger.

She missed several comments and questions being tossed about among the Riders as she considered Alton's well-being, until Yates spoke.

"What is King Zachary doing about this?"

"At present," Mara said, "nothing."

Some of the Riders cried out in dismay.

"Nothing?" Yates said.

When it appeared Mara was at a loss as to how to respond, Karigan said, "How can he do anything against magic? It's not something like—like a land dispute that can be easily solved. This is something completely new and unknown. He *did* send Alton to the wall, and Alton *is* trying to fix the breach, and that's something. The king, he—he is—" She stumbled to an ungainly stop when she realized how ardent her defense of him sounded.

She cleared her throat. "I guess it's, um, up to us to find the answers the king needs so he can do something about it." The room felt entirely too warm despite all the open windows. She clamped her mouth shut, hoping to keep it that way for the remainder of the meeting.

Mara flashed her a smile that was laden with a little too much smugness for Karigan's comfort.

"So, we are back at the beginning," Mara said, "without answers, but at least we're aware. I want everyone to be more careful than ever, especially when it comes to using your abilities. If they work, that is. Report back to me and the king anything strange—anything at all—you encounter while out on your errands."

An uneasy silence followed. It had been a meeting with no conclusions made, no problems solved. There was a threat that remained largely undefined; a threat on a personal level, and one that also encompassed the kingdom. It was a threat none of them could quantify. It had taken down their captain. Who was next? What would the arising of Blackveil portend?

Hold them together, Lil Ambrioth had told Karigan. The First Rider said she had the ability to bring the Riders together if only she would accept the responsibility. Karigan recognized that something more needed to be said, to give the Riders something to latch onto, to give them hope. She wasn't sure if she had the words, but she knew it was time to accept the responsibility and try to say what was needed.

"Um . . ." It wasn't an auspicious start, but it got their attention. She tried again. "Our job is filled with uncertainty every day. This is one more challenge, and who better to face it? We've got the use of magic, or at least had it, which means we're the best ones to figure out how to overcome the problem. That's our legacy. The Green Riders have preserved the use of magic since their creation, while it died out and disappeared among others.

"It may seem impossible, but we will figure this out. We have one another to rely on. We may not see each other often, but we are one in spirit. We will overcome this."

She finished, slightly breathless, and in wonderment she had gotten the words out. The mood in the common room was palpably lighter, and the Riders chatted together in encouraging tones. She watched Tegan and Garth hug.

Mara leaned toward Karigan. "Thank you!"

Karigan was much relieved herself, and grinned when Tegan announced that with so many Riders assembled at once, it was only proper that they have a party. Her pronouncement was met with cheers of approval—if anything would relieve their tension over the dire situation placed on their shoulders, this was it.

Lynx angled his way through the other Riders to reach Karigan and Mara, the bowl of his pipe cupped in his hand.

"Well done," he told them, and without waiting for a response, he turned about and wended his way out of the common room, the aromatic scent of tobacco trailing behind him.

"Well!" Mara said. "I get the feeling that's about as huge a compliment we could ever expect from him."

Karigan shrugged. The important thing was that the Riders had come together.

⇜ CROSSROADS ⇝

In the center of the crossroads stood a signpost of silvery weathered cedar. It gleamed against the backdrop of the night-dark forest. Hanging from each of its four arms, oriented north, south, east, and west, were shingles carved with the names of towns that would be found in the direction indicated.

The forest suffused the crossroads with its usual night clamor—a bard owl hooting, the grunts and clicks of frogs, the chirruping of crickets, but a wave of silence crept toward the crossroads and swept over it. One by one the forest voices faded and died until all that remained was the sound of the signpost's shingles creaking in the wind.

A horseman emerged from the shadows of the forest and reined a pale horse to a halt beside the signpost. A second horse was led on a tether. The two horses did not show signs of panic or attempt to flee. Their small minds had been mastered to bear who they were commanded.

An unmounted figure emerged from the forest to the west, an ancient sword girded at its side and the chain of a manacle dangling from its wrist. In the silence, the two did not speak. They did not gesture to one another or communicate. The unmounted figure simply took the second horse and climbed spiderlike into the saddle.

The two reined their horses onto the road that headed east, where the creaking shingle on the signpost indicated Sacor City lay.

Journal of Hadriax el Fex

Alessandros' grief and rage over the Empire's abandonment of us has caused him to declare the New Lands his Empire. The Empire of Morhavonia. Though we who are loyal to Arcosia find this blasphemous and even interpretable as treason, we have no option but to accept it. We are trapped here, and Alessandros leads us. Besides, he was to succeed Arcos V. Who better to be our new Emperor?

Slaves from Kmaern and Deyer Clan have nearly completed his new palace in the old Elt stronghold. Always fed by his grief and anger at Arcos' abandonment, he works on his experiments. I have recently witnessed the fruits of his labor. He used his transformative powers to change the laws of nature. He has transformed ordinary creatures into abominations. To a rat he gave snake skin, and he changed a gentle deer into a snarling, aggressive beast with fangs.

I told Alessandros that I feared this went against God, but he only chuckled and reassured me that, as Emperor, he was the earthly son of God, and therefore it was perfectly acceptable for him to use his God-given abilities thus. The priests who have spoken in outrage against these acts have been made examples of.

I try to spend time away from Alessandros and this madness when I can, but it is too treacherous to ride into the countryside, and he always wants me by his side. He tells me I am his only true friend. He fears others conspire against him, and regularly these "traitors" are rounded up by his personal guards and put to the stake.

I must be careful.

⋟ BLACKVEIL ⋞

Alton rolled the rotting log over, exposing all manner of beetles, worms, and grubs writhing in the moist soil. At the same time his stomach gurgled with hunger and heaved over in revulsion.

He had supped on these lowly creatures already, only to retch them up. He normally wouldn't even consider it, but his weakening condition, coupled with his desire to find his way out of the forest, drove him to do what he detested. He needed his strength to win his way out.

He grabbed the end of a worm before it had a chance to dart all the way into the earth. It wriggled in his palm, and he swallowed back bile.

Don't think about it. Just do it.

He dangled the worm above his mouth, closed his eyes, and dropped it in, swallowing before it could linger on his tongue, and fighting the impulse to hack it back up. He spat out the residue of dirt. On his very first try, he had learned to swallow whole after chewing left him with a mouthful of grit.

It was almost as if he could feel the worm crawling down his throat and winding through his innards. He gagged again, but miraculously the worm didn't come up this time.

The effort had cost him. He was exhausted, and one worm would not dispel his weakness. Water was easy enough to come by here due to frequent rain, and the forest was constantly clouded by a liquid haze that slimed his skin. He sipped water off leaves. It was acrid, but had failed to poison him thus far.

He didn't trust the murky pools and streams he had come across, nor did he chance eating any of the black berries growing on thorny stems. There were mushrooms growing everywhere in the decay of the forest floor, but he lacked the knowledge of how to tell the safe ones from the poisonous ones. He suspected few, if any, were without some taint in this forest.

Alton slicked his hair back, wincing at the tender bump on his head. He could not remember exactly what had happened, or when. He remembered standing atop the breach, then nothing. When he awakened to this nightmare, it took time for him to remember who and what he was, and he'd been very ill and disoriented from the head blow.

His body had other hurts as well. His cheek was swollen with an oozing, painful bite of some kind, and he ached all over. He hadn't broken any bones in his apparent fall from the breach, but his right side was pretty banged up, especially his hip.

Did his uncle send rescuers to search for him, or had they left him for dead?

I cannot depend on them to enter this hell and find me. I've got to find my own way out.

He was surprised nothing had attacked him while he was unconscious, or even when he dared to sleep fitfully in the overwhelming black of night that blanketed the forest. The undergrowth rustled all around him, and he heard the occasional pad of feet. Sometimes he caught the glint of baleful yellow eyes in the shadows.

At least once during the night, some creature had come right up to him and snuffled his elbow. After that experience, he never hesitated to draw on his ability to shield himself whenever he felt threatened. Doing so, however, exhausted him.

He sensed something else at work in the forest, as well. The intelligence he had sensed from the other side of the wall surrounded him here. He didn't doubt this very same intelligence was all that held back the predators that would otherwise tear apart an injured man. It chilled him to think that something without apparent form could possess such power.

He was grateful for the protection, but he suspected it was not provided out of a sense of charity. In fact, it frightened him to think it had so much power over him. What would happen when the intelligence grew bored with him and decided to drop its protection?

"Got to find the wall," he croaked.

It was his only chance of escape. But which way was it? The clouds and mist obscured the sun and moon, so he couldn't discern direction. If he actually located the wall, how would he know which way to turn to find the breach, without a point of reference?

One thing at a time, one thing at a time . . .

The first step was nourishment, for if the predators of the forest didn't take him, the constant wet and chill of the place, and starvation, would.

With this in mind, he scooped up a grub, feeling all the eyes of the forest watching him with great interest.

Occupying the body of a feline, the sentience crouched beneath the fronds of a fern and observed the man. It watched him constantly, watched him while he slept, watched him while he hunted, watched him while he voided. He was injured and weak, and this feline wanted badly to eat him, but the sentience suppressed the urge, and kept other predators at bay as well.

Somewhere, in some long ago time, the sentience had learned that observation was an essential tool for gaining knowledge about others. You watched the subject move about his daily life, and observed how he reacted to his environment. Sometimes you manipulated the situation to see how well the subject adapted.

In this case, the sentience observed the man was desperate, and not adapting at all well to the forest.

The man's presence also prompted the re-emergence of memories. At one time, the sentience considered the people this man belonged to as repugnant.

Barbarians, Hadriax had called them.

Hadriax—thoughts of him aroused even more memories. The sentience remembered him standing tall and proud as the ship he sailed upon departed home for far seas and lands unknown.

Oh, Hadriax, with your sandy hair and eyes of blue.

He had been a soldier, scholar, and gentleman in the court of Arcos V, and the sentience's fellow adventurer and best friend.

The sentience lingered in its memories of piers crowded with well-wishers who tossed flowers into the harbor waters as the ships made way. The fishing fleet and the flagship of the Arcosian navy escorting them out . . .

Terravossay, the capitol of Arcosia, and the imperial seat, rose above the harbor, and that was their last glimpse of home, of the great buildings of the city with their fluted columns and golden domes, their perfect symmetry and playful fountains, the carvings in bas relief and statuary adorning courtyards. A place of intellect and culture.

High above all the other great buildings were the turrets of the God House, and higher still, the palace of the emperor of Arcosia.

Sorrow washed over the sentience, and the feline it inhabited yowled in pain, and groomed itself to find comfort.

I am in this place, not Arcosia. Why?

The only answer it could summon was the idea of ad-venture, though this did not seem entirely correct. There was more to it.

As the sentience considered the man, it remembered bringing war to his people, many years of it. Yes, there had been conquest. Conquest for the glory of Arcosia.

But it had not all gone well, had it.

I was defeated.

The feline raised its hackles and extended its claws. Those such as the man who now fed on grubs had defeated the armies of the empire. The feline crouched, ready to leap on the man and disembowel him. The sentience hadn't felt such rage for an eternity. It would sink the feline's claws into his flesh and rip at muscle and sinew; feed on the soft underbelly of the enemy.

As the feline poised to strike, the entire forest tautened, a reflection of the sentience's emotions. Far-off, the guard-ians of the wall screamed.

Alton spat out the carapace of a beetle, sensing a dramatic change in the posture of the forest. The mist wafted down as usual, but the forest itself had gone stone cold and silent.

Somewhere off to his right came the threatening, low-rumbling growl of a large wildcat. Trembling, Alton rose to his feet and backed away. He could use his ability to shield himself from attack, but he felt the malevolence of the forest beneath his feet, quivering in every tree around him, in the very air he breathed. He could shield himself from the at-tack of a wildcat, yes, but from the entire forest?

Panic gripped him. He had to find the wall. He half ran, half loped in a random direction as though taken by sudden insanity. He slid on damp undergrowth and pushed branches out of his face, the running sending stabs of pain through his hip. Something pursued, the watchfulness rippling through the forest alongside him.

It occurred to him to simply give up, to lay down and surrender, but his D'Yer pride wouldn't permit it. He'd keep running until the end. Maybe he was running deeper into the forest, maybe he was running all the way to Ullem Bay, but he'd keep running no matter where his feet led him.

He sloshed through a black pool and creatures snapped at his heels. He fell to his knees, but rose painfully and set off again. Something screeched in the canopy above his head, but he kept on.

Over his own harsh breaths, he heard the miraculous voices of the wall calling to him, as they once used to. They were unclear, stuttered as though a barrier prevented them from fully reaching him, but all that mattered was that he heard them, and they gave him a sense of direction.

His lungs burned as he lunged through the forest, adjusting his direction toward the voices. He leaped a downed log and rushed through hip-high brambles. He howled as thorns ripped through his trousers and flesh.

He stumbled from the brambles and fell to the ground, air forced from his lungs. Slowly he looked up and found himself nose to nose with a huge feline, its glimmering gold eyes embodying intelligence and all the menace and evil the forest represented.

The feline was much like a catamount in shape and coloring, but it was at least twice as large as the average catamount male, and there were other not-so-subtle differences. Its whiskers were thick, barbed spines. Its extended claws, the color of blood, were like curved knives. Alton thought he saw venom sacs at the base of each claw.

The feline's back was arched, the hair along its spine standing on end. When it growled, Alton thought, *I'm going to die.*

They stared at one another, eyes locked, one assessing the other.

The very *human* regard of the feline fascinated Alton. It looked to be turning something over in its mind, struggling over baser instincts and emotions.

"What are you?" he murmured.

The creature cocked its ears forward in surprise. It paused, Alton was sure, to consider his words. It narrowed its eyes to slits, then turned tail and bounded silently off into the undergrowth and disappeared.

The malevolence still surrounded him, but the power of the forest held it at bay once again. He rose on shaking legs. His trousers were shredded and blotched with blood. He hoped the thorns weren't poisonous, but it might be too much to expect from Blackveil.

The feline was gone, and so were the voices. Still, Alton had his life, and he had a direction in which to travel. He picked through the forest, judiciously avoiding brambles.

After a long time of walking, it became clear he traveled upon an open path that was not an accident of nature. He bent down and ripped moss off the ground, and found sea-rounded cobbles beneath that must have once served as the paving of a road.

Long time ago, he thought.

He had never considered people once living here, but then again, Mornhavon had made this place his stronghold. He might have constructed the road, or perhaps the people who lived here before him had. Blackveil hadn't always been an evil place, but what it was before Mornhavon arrived, Alton could only guess.

As he walked, a human face peering out at him from the foliage along the road took several years off his life. Heart throbbing, he threw a rock at the figure. Rock clacked on rock.

Statue.

He drew closer, and saw better the texture of carved stone. Weathered eyes stared blankly back at him. The statue's arms were uplifted, but her hands were missing. Perhaps if he knelt in the duff and searched beneath moss and undergrowth, he might find them.

The figure was draped in intricately carved twining leaves. She must have been beautiful once, but now her edges and details were ravaged by weather and time, and blotched by lichens.

He continued along the road, some of the paving stones jutting out of the moss, making for a topsy-turvy walking surface. When he stumbled over an upheaved cobble, he could only hope he wouldn't break a limb, adding to his miseries.

The roadway rose ahead, and only as he mounted the rise did he realize he stood upon a bridge. From beneath came the sluggish gurgle of a stream. What civilization had this been before it was overcome by Blackveil? When something large and glistening slurped in the stream, he hastened on, leaving it far behind.

He saw more statues on alternating sides of the road. Some appeared whole, if marred by neglect, while others were missing arms or heads, or had tumbled from their pedestals altogether and lay shattered beneath the carpet of moss. A few held the fragments of curious amber orbs in their upraised hands.

He didn't pause long to examine the statues or anything else along the road, for the barely suppressed menace of the forest eyed him warily. As long as he was given the grace to retreat toward the wall, best he make good use of the time while he had it.

The road meandered now and again, but it generally traveled in the direction from which he remembered hearing the voices. Maybe the wall was only a mile or two away, maybe a hundred. It was impossible to tell with the interlocking branches of the forest overhead, and the opaque mist that shrouded all. So it was to his surprise when the wall appeared immediately before him. It had been constructed right across the road.

Alton pressed his body up against it, finding it as welcome as his mother's embrace. It was cold, and it was stone, but it was real. The wall did not react to his touch, nor did the voices sing out to him. With his hands still pressed against its stony façade, he looked over the surface and found a hairline crack.

He couldn't be far from the breach, but in which direction did it lay? East, or west? The crack provided no clue, for it wended off in both directions. All he could do was choose a direction and walk. If he didn't find the breach within a day or two, he could turn back and search in the other direction—providing he was still alive. The road would serve as a good marker.

He took a deep breath and headed east, the direction of the rising sun, wishing he could see it. The cloying fragrance of blooming roses in the damp-laden air washed over him.

"What are you?"

Taken by surprise that the man addressed it directly, the sentience paused the feline in its attack.

What am I? I am the forest. I can be the lowliest insect, or the mightiest feline. I can be a tree. I can make rain or drain a pond.

Yes, it was the forest, but once it had been a man. The better question was: *Who* am I? The sentience had some suspicions thanks to its re-emerging memories. As it gazed at the man laying there on the ground, it decided to try something, something that would get around the shield that protected him, and open his mind.

The sentience bounded off into the forest. It knew the guardians were trying to reach the man, to call out to him. The sentience itself barely felt the lull of the guardians anymore. They were losing their power to call it back, subdue it, make it sleep and remain ignorant.

Imprisoned.

The sentience had glimpsed the other side of the wall, and wanted to know more, to explore that which lay beyond. It wanted to crush the wall and bring to bear its full self. The man might be the key.

The feline loped through the forest ahead of the man. Near the wall, the sentience would set its trap.

Hidden in the underbrush, the sentience settled the feline down into a crouch, and set to spreading its influence to an area near the wall. It pushed away layers of mist so that a mere gleam of sunlight thrust its way to the moist ground, producing a tendril of steam.

The sentience then expanded its mind throughout the forest, seeking the agent that would subdue the man for its purposes.

Ah, just the thing.

Beneath the column of leaden light, beneath the duff and soil, the sentience germinated seeds that had long lain dormant for lack of sunshine. Spidery roots quickly spread through the soil and shoots probed upward, seeking that shred of sun. Fighting their way through leaf litter and decaying matter, the shoots snaked up from the ground sprouting thorns along stems. Buds, closed tight, led the way in their journey, until maturing within moments to blue-black roses in full bloom.

The sentience enhanced their aroma—not to attract pollinators, but to attract the man. It waited.

The feline was hungry, demanded release to hunt, and struggled against the sentience's hold, especially when the

man-scent drifted near, discernable despite the strong fragrance of the roses.

The man emerged into view. He blinked in dazed fashion at the bleak sunshine and roses, and he sank to his
knees and yawned. The sentience could tell he fought with
himself to stay awake, but the roses overpowered him, and
soon he wilted to the ground and slept. The man's shield
fell away.

The sentience retained enough control over the forest to
hold predators at bay, and seeped into the man's mind.

Unlike the last time the sentience had done this, when
the man lay unconscious, it found a mind filled with vibrant color and sparks of energy. It found language, vision,
and memory.

The sentience considered inhabiting the man's body,
using it to enter the world beyond, but it feared doing so. It
feared leaving behind the safety of the forest, which was so
much of what it was. It needed to know more about the
outside world before venturing there.

The sentience paused its probing just to feel what it was
like to be a man. It opened and closed a hand into a fist.
The hands were large and strong. It flexed an arm, and felt
gnawing hunger in the man's stomach. There was pain, too,
in his hip. Poison from the thorn scratches had begun to
work its way into his blood, and soon he'd be experiencing
the ill effects.

The lungs expanded with air, and the scent of roses was
strong in the nose, though lacking the layers of nuance possessed by the feline's olfactory organs. Eyes fluttered open
and it took some experimentation to focus them.

How very astounding!

It saw colors and shadings not even the sharp-eyed avian
could detect. The shifting gold light pouring through the
hole in the mist the sentience opened, the deep blue veins

in the dark rose petals, the diseased brown leaves of an overhanging tree . . .

Reluctantly the sentience withdrew from the external sensations, thinking this was most familiar, that once it, too, had possessed a physical body of its own.

Like Hadriax . . .

But the sentience couldn't allow thoughts of Hadriax to distract it. Instead, it followed bits of the man's memory—of suckling a mother's breast, and the comfort it provided. The excitement of riding his first pony. The man-child rode the pony around a courtyard waving a wooden sword about. *I shall slay the bad man,* the child declared. *I shall slay Mor'van!* His family watched him, faces aglow.

The sentience leaped from memory to memory, catching shards of the man-child's growth. Some included images of stoneworking, strengthening the sentience's suspicions . . .

Finally it caught hold of a name. *Deyer. This man is Deyer.*

It was like having double-vision as the sentience took in the memory of Deyer chipping away at a block of granite, while its own memories unfolded.

Deyer. Clan Deyer. Builders of fortresses and *walls,* expert stoneworkers who learned their craft from Kmaernians to whom rock was like a living thing.

Builders of walls. Builders of the *wall.*

Fury so took the sentience that it nearly brought the man's blood to a boil.

Calm, seek calm. There is more to learn.

It deflected its fury to the feline, which burned from the inside out and turned into a heap of smoldering cinders.

The sentience focused its attention again on the man, Deyer. It fought to remain calm as it comprehended the man's desire to repair the breach in the wall.

The sentience stumbled across a stray memory of the man looking at himself in a mirror, dressed in a green uniform.

Upon his breast was pinned a brooch of gold in the shape of a winged horse. This is what the sentience had sensed hidden and shielded upon the man's chest. But now it elicited a new surge of hate that toppled an entire thicket of trees south of their current location.

A Deyer and *a Green Rider.*

Only the utmost self-control prevented the sentience from killing the man. Instead, it formulated a new plan, a plan that would cause the wall to fall absolutely.

Before the sentience could carry out the next step of its plan, it stumbled upon a cluster of memories centered around a young woman. Her hair was brown and cascaded about her shoulders. She, too, was an accursed Green Rider.

They sat beneath a shade tree, overlooking a pleasant valley. They had eaten a picnic lunch, but the Deyer's stomach was all twisted with anxiety, his emotions a mix of hope, dismay, and desire. *The breach in the wall is a disgrace to my family,* he said.

A thrill surged through him as she took his hand into hers. He marveled at how slender and perfect her hands were, and how his dwarfed them. They locked eyes, smiling at one another, and he hoped they might kiss, but the young woman, whose name was Karigan, dropped his hand and said, *Stone walls crumble with time.*

The sentience sifted through the other memories of the young woman, but they were filled mostly with confusion and disappointment. Deyer's feelings for her were strong, but disordered.

There was something else about the young woman that brought to mind Hadriax, though the sentience couldn't quite touch precisely what the connection could be.

Her presence in Deyer's mind gave the sentience an idea that would help fulfill its plan. For now, however, it seeped

out of Deyer's mind, turning to its own memories of Hadriax dressed in full military glory, amid the splendor of
the imperial court. A fountain sprinkled merrily from the
snouts of whimsical sea creatures. Flowers were in full
bloom everywhere . . .

ILLUSION

Alton awakened stiff and sore, his body trembling with chills. He rubbed his eyes not knowing how long he had slept. A residue of dark and formless dreams lingered in his mind.

The waking nightmare that was Blackveil Forest still surrounded him, but held itself at bay. He sensed an eagerness about it, anticipation. He worried what it held in store for him, but he had the protection of his special ability and the wall at his back.

The wall. He allowed himself a grim smile. He would find his way out of Blackveil, and he'd make sure a message got through to King Zachary, warning him the forest was far more than it seemed. He'd give the king a first-hand account of it, of all he had seen and experienced. He had to, for he knew it was only a matter of time before the intelligence spread its power across the breach, and if they couldn't repair the breach, D'Yer Province would be the first land in the path of danger. What would happen to the fields, the forests, and the people?

No, I dare not think about it.

Alton had to help protect D'Yer Province and all of Sacoridia, no matter the cost.

He rose from the moist ground, body heat bleeding from him and gripping him in another bout of chills. Daggers ripped through his legs as he stood. The puckered thorn wounds oozed with a sickly yellow pus, and he knew it did not bode well for him. Nausea washed over him.

He supported himself against the wall, gagging, but bringing up nothing. It taxed his already weakened body, and he clung to the wall with all his strength.

I must find my way out.

Only sheer will propelled him forward, pain ripping through his legs with each step.

Behind him, the petals of blue-black roses shriveled and dropped to the ground, leaving behind only the thorny stems in a shaft of mist.

Someone lifted Alton's head and helped him sip water. As it passed over his cracked lips and down his parched throat, he swallowed rapidly like one who has spent days stranded in a desert. He blinked open crusty eyes to see his savior. At first she was a blur, but when his vision cleared, he knew her at once.

"Karigan?"

"Shhh, you are ill," she said. Her hair rested on her shoulders and was glossy with sunshine. Oddly, she wasn't dressed in green, but in an ivory dress that sheened in a brightness that made his eyes hurt. She looked to be a celestial being of the heavens—she was beautiful.

"What are you doing here? How did you find me?"

She set aside the bowl of water and stroked back his hair. Her touch was light and feathery, and it sent chills racking through his body. When he gazed up at her, she wavered in his sight.

He closed his eyes. "I'm not seeing very well."

"My poor Alton."

When he opened his eyes again, his vision was steadier. Karigan's features were serene and unperturbed. He could not remember her ever looking so peaceful, and it occurred to him that maybe he had died, and maybe she had, too. When he struggled to rise, she firmly pressed him back.

"Please, reserve your strength," she told him. "You've a fever. You must use your strength to fight it."

As if in response to her words, the chills left him and he burned. Perspiration beaded on his forehead.

"I feel terrible," he said. "I want to go home. I have to . . . I have to tell the king. I have to tell him about the forest."

She quieted him with shushing noises, all the while stroking his hair away from his face.

"I know, I know. You will be able to do this soon, but you've another task ahead of you."

Alton sighed and closed his eyes, listening to the soothing tones of her voice.

"I think . . ." he began. "Thirsty. I'm so thirsty."

She lifted the bowl to his lips, and when he finished drinking, he said, "I think I . . ."

He couldn't quite manage the words. Karigan always left him perplexed. One moment she was his confidant and friend, and the next she would say or do something that terribly confused him, causing his feelings for her to range from extreme frustration and anger that she would toy with him so, to hope and—and—

How could she do this to him? In his heart he knew it wasn't intentional, but the fire of his fever seemed to have stoked the fire in his heart, too, and here she was being so gentle, so caring.

"Karigan, I—"

"Shhh." She placed her finger across his lips. "Do not tire yourself."

"*But*—" He really wanted to tell her, to finally express himself.

She gave him a playful tap on the nose, and leaned over him so that her hair brushed his cheek.

"I will talk," she said, "and you will listen."

And she did talk. She spoke of the wall and how it was inhabited by the souls of those who had made it. They were the guardians whose magic made the wall so impenetrable. It was they who sang to keep the forest at peace, and now their voices were failing.

"They were singing the wrong words," she said, "and the wrong melody. This is causing the wall to fail. You must get them to sing the correct song, a counter-song to mend the wall."

Alton faded in and out, comforted by her voice, her soothing, light touches. This was the Karigan he loved. If he survived this, he would see about making her his wife, no matter his father's protests, no matter her common blood.

He came to after an unknown amount of sleep, her voice still murmuring comfortingly to him. She continued to sit beside him, her hand resting on his chest, over his heart. His heart throbbed faster, harder.

"I am going to teach you the song to sing," she was saying, "to mend the wall."

"Yes," he said, his voice weak. "Mend the wall."

She started to sing. He knew Karigan was rather tone deaf, but now she sang harmoniously. He did not understand the words, but she made him repeat them.

"*Mordech en trelish est,*" she said.

"*Mordech en trelish est.*"

"Yes, you do well."

It was a trial to concentrate on what he was doing, to overcome his fever to do as she asked, but he found he wanted to please her.

There were more and more words, and she gave him more water whenever his voice faltered. How many hours had passed? Had it been days? He did not know, but her voice was continuous in his mind, whether he dozed off or awakened.

At times he twisted and turned in feverish dreams, calling out her name. Sometimes behind her beauty he saw
some monstrous visage, but her words and gentle touch
would always ease him.

When he awakened once again, he discovered her hands
were on his legs.

"What are—?" he croaked.

She smiled at him. "I am taking the pain from your legs
so you may walk."

"Walk," he whispered. "I haven't the strength."

"I will help you."

He must be feather-light for Karigan helped him up
without difficulty. He nearly fainted away, but she propped
him against her.

"Think of the song I taught you," she said. "Sing it to
me, and it will help you overcome your weakness."

His awareness was vague at best. She put his arm over
her shoulders, and she put her arm around his waist. It all
seemed very distant.

"Sing," she said, "and walk."

He did, his awareness dimming still more, the walking a
dream. She must have been supporting most of his weight
because it felt like he walked on air. She had taken the pain
from his legs, though pus seeped from the wounds with
each step.

When his voice faltered, she spoke again in soothing, encouraging tones. "When you are in the tower, you must sing
the song to the stone with your mind. Do you understand?"

"Yes." He wasn't sure he did, but his answer pleased her.

He continued along in his dream, the forest not feeling
threatening in the least. His feet navigated the terrain without trouble so long as he leaned on Karigan. Yes, he was
safe with her. She took care of him.

*   *   *

He must have passed out, for he was lying on the ground again. When his eyes fluttered open, Karigan was right there next to him, as serene as ever.

"You have come far and reached your destination," she said, "but now you must eat a little to help you with your strength."

She dropped golden berries into his mouth, and when he protested, she assured him they were safe. They were sweet and refreshing, like ambrosia. Their juice moistened his dry mouth.

When she fed him the last berry, she said, "I am very proud of you. You have come far despite your illness, and you have learned the song. Now it is time for you to mend the wall."

"Now?"

"First you must enter the tower."

He rolled his head back and looked up. They were next to a tower that soared up into the clouds. It was doorless and windowless, and forbidding. It was one of the guard towers of the wall.

"I don't know how."

"First you must get up." Effortlessly she hoisted him to his feet once again, and supported him to the tower. "Put your hands upon it."

He did so. The granite of the tower seamlessly matched that of the wall that winged off from it in both directions. He liked the feel of the granite, so rough and so cool, so very solid.

"Now speak with the stone," she said. "Let it know who you are. It should let you in when it knows you are Deyer."

"I'm D'Yer," he said to granite.

The first hint of irritation crossed Karigan's face. "No, with your mind, as I instructed you."

"You're coming with me, aren't you?"

She hesitated, then smiled. "Of course." She kissed his

cheek. When he leaned into her for more, she pushed her palm against his chest. "If you love me, you will enter the tower and mend the wall."

"Yes. Mend the wall."

Just as she had taught him, he sent currents of thought right through his fingertips into the wall. With his mind, he announced to stone who he was.

Haethen Toundrel, Tower of the Heavens, absorbed Alton D'Yer through its granite.

Outside the tower, the glamour faded from the feral groundmite female the sentience had employed in its scheme. The ivory dress dissipated like smoke, revealing animal hide and the furry arms of a groundmite. She dropped to the ground, greedily popping "berries" into her mouth. The glamour faded from those, as well, revealing grubs.

Gone was the visage of a comely young woman. Deyer's fever had been most propitious, further enhancing the illusion. It had been exhausting to play the part of Karigan and control the groundmite at the same time. She had wanted to rip Deyer's head off.

In the end, it would all be worth it, the sentience thought. It allowed itself to be absorbed into the mossy ground. Deyer would sabotage the wall and bring it crashing down. Oh, the delicious irony of it, of a wall builder being its undoing.

There was more to look forward to. Varadgrim and Mirdhwell would find the one of Hadriax's blood and bring her here.

It all meant waiting, but the sentience would do so exploring its memories.

VISIONS OF AN EMPIRE

Karigan wobbled atop the beam. It was only a couple feet off the ground, but last night's indulgence of bitter ale, brought up from the Cock and Hen, and coupled with too little sleep, was more than enough to make her balance questionable at best.

She should have known better than to imbibe so much, but it had felt so good just to let her cares flow away amid the camaraderie of the other Riders . . . and the seemingly bottomless keg.

She wasn't the only one who had arisen with a miserable headache this morning, but she had to get up earlier than most to prepare horses and provisions for messages that needed to go out. She pitied the Riders who with heavy heads and nauseated stomachs would spend their day in the saddle, but at least they didn't have Drent screaming at them.

"What's wrong with you?" he demanded. "You're lurching around like a drunkard."

His voice ricocheted from one side of her skull to the other, and she scowled. Mara had insisted she keep up with these verbal and physical trouncings indefinitely.

She placed one boot in front of the other with utmost care as she made her way down the narrow beam. It didn't help there was a goodly lot of spectators; soldiers who decided to take breaks from their own training bouts to watch such fine entertainment.

One day, she'd make Mara pay. She wasn't sure how, but she would do it. She smiled grimly, thinking Tegan wouldn't be adverse to helping.

Back and forth Karigan moved along the beam, still wobbly, but managing to keep her perch. She thought it must be boring to watch, but the spectators did not leave. It made her suspicious.

Then, without warning, Drent whipped a practice sword at her legs. She side-stepped just in time, somehow maintaining her balance. The sword came again and she hopped down the beam to avoid it, arms flailing. Drent kept right with her, and this time, when he swept the sword at her, he struck her calves.

Karigan knew he wanted her to jump the blade, but it simply took her foggy mind too long to send the message to her feet. The leather of her boots shielded her calves pretty well from the impact of the blow, but it still hurt like the five hells.

To make matters worse, she lost her balance and landed face down on one of the straw pallets beneath the beam. The soldiers who had been watching laughed uproariously. This is what they had been waiting for.

"What's wrong with you?" Drent demanded again. "My granny could do jigs around you on that beam."

Then let her, Karigan thought sourly. She had had enough of these humiliating sessions. They were putting her into fine trim, but enough was enough. One of these days she was going to let Drent know just what she—

"On your feet," he ordered.

With a groan she obeyed. It felt like a chisel was hammering against her skull. Was he going to make her run now that he had abused her legs?

"This Green Foot runner is here for you," Drent said.

Her eyes registered the young girl in the green uniform who goggled at the arms master. Holly, she thought, was the girl's name.

"Yes?" Karigan asked.

Holly's eyes were just as big when they shifted to Karigan. "Ma'am, Rider Brennyn requests you to attend the king in his study, to receive message errands. She is just now tied up in a meeting."

Karigan nodded wearily. "Thank you."

The girl ran off, and Karigan made to follow.

"We will finish this tomorrow promptly at nine hour," Drent said.

Karigan was glad her back was to him so he couldn't see her expression of dismay.

She hurried to barracks for a quick wash-up and change of uniform. One didn't wear a work tunic to attend the king.

Karigan decided to cut through the courtyard gardens to reach the west wing. The king's study, once Queen Isen's solarium, was at ground level and looked out onto the gardens. Karigan had been there once before, but had not known what room it was at the time, for she had been seeking entrance to the castle—any entrance—in stealth and darkness, the night of Prince Amilton's coup attempt.

That far-off memory was another lifetime ago, and as she hopped across the stepping stones of the trout pond in the brightness of morning, she was amazed at how great the contrast from those dire circumstances two years ago to today's summons from the king.

It was quite a while since she had last seen King Zachary, and she found herself anticipating the meeting. She paused on the last stepping stone.

Ugh. For a very long time, she had refused to acknowledge certain . . . longings where the king was concerned, finding such feelings impossible at best. Who was she to think the king would ever . . . ?

No, no, it wasn't even worth bringing to the fore. It was all impossible. He was royalty, she was not even noble, and that was enough to create an unbridgeable gap between them. This was how she suppressed her feelings for him, but her heart did not always obey her head.

Bear up, she ordered herself. It was best she saw him as infrequently as she did. The distance made her feelings for him easier to contend with.

She lifted her foot to step onto the pond's embankment, when something jarred her, as if alien memories were being rammed into her mind.

. . . Crossing a court square blossoming with flowers in the sunshine that God poured from the heavens. The plash of fountains ornamented with fantastical creatures lent the square music. Framing the square were the buildings of the Empire's might—the exchequer, the protectionist, lords of the nation, the God House. The buildings were both all at once precise and forbidding in their architecture, and yet uplifting.

Peacocks strutted across the square with their tail feathers fanned. Persons of refined sensibilities lingered in the square chatting and walking slowly, followed by slaves bearing sun shades. Alessandros looked upon the scene with great contentment and would himself have liked to linger, but the Emperor had summoned him and—and—

"Karigan?" Someone jostled her.

"Hunh?"

"Are you all right?" Lady Estora asked.

"I—" Karigan gazed at her, stunned. "What? Where was I?"

Estora looked her up and down. "Far away I dare say, though you haven't moved an inch. I thought you had turned into a statue for a moment."

Karigan's arm, her left arm, was numb. She rubbed it, trying to bring life into it again.

"I just had a memory. No, that's not quite right. I don't remember it as *my* memory."

"How very strange. A daydream, perhaps?" Estora smiled kindly at her befuddledness.

"No. Yes. I guess that must be it. It has to be."

An awkward silence fell between them until Estora asked, "Have you time for a chat? It's a lovely day."

The bell down in the city rang out. That would make it eleven hour.

"The king!" Karigan said. "I've been summoned. I can't stay."

Lady Estora nodded in understanding. "No, you must not keep the king waiting."

Karigan was sorry she couldn't join Estora, for her additional duties had left her little time to visit with her. It had been ages since last they sat and chatted. But the lady was right—she couldn't keep the king waiting.

She sprinted down garden paths past courtiers who glared at her for disrupting their tranquil, leisurely walks, her footsteps bringing her to a skidding halt outside the king's study, where two Weapons stood on duty. She straightened her shortcoat and cleared her throat.

"The king wished to see me," she said.

"He's meeting with someone at the moment," said Erin, one of the Weapons, "but I don't think he'll object if you enter."

Erin opened the door for her. "Thank you," she murmured, and breathlessly entered the world of King Zachary.

The study was bright with golden light showering through the windows onto vibrant handwoven carpets and light oak furnishings. The walls were hung with scenes of mountains and the ocean. Others were hunting scenes.

The king sat behind a massive desk with a light marble

surface. A few books and documents cluttered it. Behind him, from floor to ceiling, were shelves of books interspersed with a curious collection of seashells, rounded cobblestones, and a mariner's spyglass.

The king's study, Karigan decided, differed little from her father's. Opulent, but not overbearing. Stately, but not uncomfortable, and definitely suggestive of a masculine presence.

The king sat back in his oversized armchair, his hands folded across his lap. His features lightened slightly when she entered. Was he pleased to see her? It was hard to say, for he was in the midst of a conversation with a visitor.

Karigan stood discreetly back, but when Old Brexley, an elderly white Hillander terrier, waddled over to her to sniff her boots, she knelt to scratch him behind his ear. Was that a fleeting smile of approval the king cast her way?

She started to rise, but Old Brexley plopped down on her foot and showed her his belly. Knowing a hint when she saw one, she rubbed his belly and was rewarded with his terrier grin. The old boy was named after a famous crusty general who had won many a battle for Clan Hillander during the Clan Wars. The terrier was often seen trailing the king around the castle grounds.

It took some moments for Karigan to register who the king's visitor was. She was a tall, imperious woman richly draped in dyed summer silks with fine pearl buttons, and ornamented with silvery thread details. Gems flashed on her fingers as she gestured. Her name was Celesta Suttley, chief of Clan Suttley, a merchanting clan that dealt primarily in tobacco.

Karigan frowned. Clan G'ladheon and Clan Suttley had clashed on more than a few occasions, to the point her father had acquitted himself of doing any business with them due to their underhanded dealings.

"It is an insignificant corner of Huradesh," Celesta Suttley said, "but the soil and climate there are favorable to tobacco growing. With your approval, and a promise of exclusive trading rights, we will establish a foothold in that territory that can only enhance commerce in Sacoridia."

"This remote corner of Huradesh," the king said, "what is it called?"

"Bioordi, Highness. The people there are mostly nomads."

Bells of alarm clanged in Karigan's head. Bioordi was not as insignificant as Celesta was making it out to be. That it was prime tobacco country, she had no doubt, but the people there also originated some of the finest dyes in the textile trade, and most of the more ordinary ones as well.

If Clan Suttley received exclusive trading rights there, it would effectively cut off other merchants, like her father, from that dye. They'd be forced to trade with Clan Suttley, at whatever price Suttley demanded, strangling textile and dye merchants financially. To some, it would be so disastrous they'd be put out of business, and send ripples of misfortune across other trades, ultimately hurting the common folk who purchased dyed goods.

Meanwhile, the powerful merchants guild would be up in arms, and none too happy with the king and likely withdrawing their support from him. No good would come of it, except for Clan Suttley, of course, which would be buried in unimaginable wealth.

Karigan rose, ignoring Old Brexley's whine.

"My clerks have drawn up some documents," Celesta continued, "outlining my proposed venture. Exclusive trade rights in Bioordi would not prevent other tobacco merchants from establishing themselves elsewhere in Huradesh." With a bow, she set the rolled documents on the king's desk.

Karigan emitted a strangled noise. Certainly Celesta's proposal was no threat to *tobacco* merchants. What about all the others who relied on those dyes?

"Karigan," the king said, "have you something to say?"

Celesta Suttley turned, and when she recognized Karigan, a mocking smile played on her lips. "Well, well, well.
So this is where Clan G'ladheon's wayward sub-chief ran
off to." The smile turned particularly cutting. "Oh, I nearly
forgot—you gave up all that, didn't you? I hear Stevic was
quite upset. From the talk, you'd think you had committed
the worst kind of betrayal."

A storm brewed within Karigan, and she thought up a
few choice words to spit in the clan chief's face, but conscious of the king's presence, and of her position and all it
represented, she restrained herself, but just barely.

Celesta's expression grew smug as she detected Karigan's fury, with a simultaneous understanding of why Karigan dare not respond in kind.

"Such a fine shade of green you're wearing," Celesta
continued. "I wonder where your father found the dye."

Karigan narrowed her eyes. Celesta knew full well where
it had come from: Bioordi. She was just trying to provoke
her in front of the king. No doubt she thought Karigan no
more than a flunky, just another servant without any standing in the king's eyes. Well, Celesta was in for a surprise.

At least, she hoped so.

She stepped past the merchant and bowed before the
king. "Excellency, may I have a private word with you?" It
was actually asking a lot, but she hoped he trusted her
enough, respected her enough, to grant her wish.

A little puzzled, he nodded. "Of course." When Celesta
did not move, he gestured at the door. "If you would, Chief,
please step out into the corridor."

Karigan could have jumped up and down and yelled in
victory at the darkening expression on Celesta's face. She
was fuming so much, Karigan envisioned black smoke roiling out her ears.

After Celesta exited and the door shut after her, King Zachary said, "I trust this is a merchanting issue you wish to bring up?"

"Yes, Excellency."

"Is there some feud between your clans? If so, you know I cannot show favoritism, and you must not use your access to me for your clan's profit."

Karigan was disappointed he thought she would misuse her position in such a way. "I admit there is little love between Suttley and G'ladheon. I also admit I am interested in the well being of my clan, and at this moment I am taking advantage of my access to you." When he did not comment, she took a deep breath and continued. "However, this proposal of Clan Suttley's would not only endanger my clan's ability to contribute to commerce in Sacoridia, but every textile merchant in the country. It would have widespread effects across the provinces, and here's why."

The king listened intently as she explained, and when she finished, he rubbed his chin. "Truth be told, I had never heard much of Bioordi before today, but you have quite enlightened me, and I will now pay closer attention to trade in Huradesh. I am wary of granting exclusive rights in any case, and your words have sealed it."

Suddenly he smiled and it was like the sun emerging from behind clouds. "I am very pleased with your intervention in the matter. Never hesitate to speak up if you have advice that may guide me."

Karigan's mind was awhirl from the trust implied by his words.

Old Brexley, tired of being ignored, let out a long whining yawn, and nudged her leg with his nose. She bent to pat him.

"Seems the old boy has taken a liking to you," the king said with a laugh. "He's a choosy bugger, but he's got good taste."

Karigan's hand froze atop Old Brexley's head. The king had caught her off guard and she dared not speak or move, or even breathe at all, lest she spill out something of her true feelings. Maybe his words meant nothing at all, then again . . .

The moment of danger passed as the king shifted in his chair. He seemed to sink into himself. "I appreciate your counsel, and it reminds me of why I miss Laren." He paused, and added almost as an afterthought, "She won't talk to me, plead as I might at her door."

Karigan hadn't known he'd done this, but it only served to elevate her regard of him even higher.

"Perhaps I'll call upon you more often," he said. His smile was genuine.

Karigan thought her own responsibilities heavy to bear with Captain Mapstone out of commission, but it was nothing compared to what the king must endure, and on his own. The captain had offered him support, as only a good friend could. The king's responsibility was one of a country and a people, and the thought of it humbled Karigan.

A light tapping came on the door.

"Come," the king said.

The chief administrator, Weldon Spurlock, entered. He bowed meekly. "I've some documents requiring your seal, Excellency."

"One moment, please." The king stood and picked up a handful of letters. He rounded the desk and handed them to Karigan. "Here are the messages I require to go out this afternoon. All but one are going to lord-governors. Urge your Riders to make all haste. The other is a less significant message to the mayor of Childrey."

Karigan bowed. Before she could leave, the king placed his hand on her shoulder.

"You did well today," he said, "and I look forward to hearing more of your input."

His smile was warm, and his words soft. Or was Karigan's mind wishfully playing it up? They gazed at one another for what must have been but mere seconds, yet seemed like much more. She didn't want his hand to leave her shoulder.

Weldon Spurlock coughed, and Karigan stepped away from the king. With another bow, she dashed from the study and out into the garden, confusion and fear knotting her heart more than ever.

Outside the stable, Karigan watched Harry ride off on a long journey to Arey Province. She had sent off all the king's messages, all but the letter to the mayor of Childrey, because there were no other Riders left to take it. The only Riders left in residence were her and Mara, and Ephram who had managed to break his ankle this morning on a loose floorboard in the stable.

This is not necessarily a bad thing. Here was her opportunity to escape the castle grounds, to flee all the responsibilities, the ghosts, and the problems that had been cropping up of late. She would carry on her duty as an ordinary Green Rider and return to the freedom of the road, with the wind in her hair and a fast horse beneath her. No doubt Condor would be just as eager as she to run.

She'd also escape proximity to the king, to ride away from the complex feelings he stirred in her.

"I don't see any other choice," Mara said glumly when Karigan caught up with her outside the castle entrance. "You're up to this?"

Karigan flexed her arm. Where once this would have caused intense pain, there was now only the slightest twinge. "I'm more than ready."

Mara sighed. "Rats. Wish you had said otherwise so *I* could take the message."

"What? And leave me to the wolves?"

Mara smiled. "Have a good ride, and think of me in that meeting with the stablehands again."

Humming, Karigan hurried back toward barracks to prepare for her message errand.

On her way off castle grounds, a ragged-looking sergeant of the regular militia urged his weary horse beneath the portcullis and toward the main castle entrance. With passing curiosity, she wondered what business drove him, but with the road and freedom of the ride ahead of her, she did not dwell on it.

⇨ SECOND EMPIRE ⇦

"**A**nd that is the last of it," Sergeant Westley Uxton said, lamplight flickering across his face. "I do not know if the young lord lives or is dead, but I *do* know the forest lives."

"Certainly that's not the same story you gave the king," Madrene said.

Uxton looked indignant. "Of course not. I told him that Lord Alton *fell,* but I otherwise did keep as close to the truth as possible."

Leave it to Madrene, so consumed with secrecy to protect her own hide, Weldon Spurlock thought, to overlook the two pieces of excellent news Uxton had brought them. Alton D'Yer was no longer a threat, and Blackveil was alive. The question was, what to do with the information. Bide their time till there was some more definite communication from the forest? For so long, the society of the Second Empire had been geared toward retaining its secrecy that now, faced with the actual awakening of the forest, they were a bit stymied as to how to proceed. Maybe there'd be some sign . . .

"Well done, Sergeant," Spurlock said.

Uxton nodded. "Wasn't easy to do," he murmured.

The group stood in silence in the musty, dark room. These abandoned rooms were useful for keeping out of sight of anyone curious enough to stick their nose where it did not belong, but as much as he didn't like to admit it, the place was distinctly creepy. Sometimes he thought he heard muttering, or caught sight of movement at the edge of his lamplight as he made his way through the abandoned corridors. Old structures were like that, he had to remind himself, full of odd noises like chatty old women.

No doubt water dripping somewhere, he thought. *Or the echo of my own footfalls down empty corridors.*

As for the movements? A trick of light and shadow, or maybe a rodent scurrying by.

The worst sensation, however, was a palpable touch on his skin, like cool fingers brushing him. Purely imagination, of course, wrought by primal fears of dark, abandoned places. It made him shudder all the same.

"I have one other item to address before we part," Spurlock said, finding comfort in his own voice, "and that is what to do about Galadheon."

"Nothing," Robbs the blacksmith said. "That line will bring us nothing but grief." The others echoed their agreement.

"I tend to see it your way," Spurlock said. "Through the records in my care, one can see this line has long forgotten its past, and indeed, there are even gaps in our own vigilance. For many a year, the line remained as quiet and ignorant fisherfolk on Black Island, until recently with the merchanting success and clanship of Stevic G'ladheon.

"Then, surprise of all surprises, his daughter comes here to the castle grounds as a Green Rider."

There was hissing and other noises of disparagement toward those who had helped defeat their ancestors.

"While our brothers and sisters in Corsa have determined the father as too rash and independent-minded for our group, they believed the daughter might prove otherwise. From my own observation, this hasn't been the case. She is much like the father and has shown herself very loyal to the king."

Spurlock recalled the scene in the king's study, the way the sun shone on Karigan G'ladheon's face, and the expression of the king when they locked gazes. More than just loyalty there, he thought, and perhaps something worth exploiting in the future. He tucked that bit of information to the back of his mind for later use.

"She is," he continued, "entirely unsuited for our society."

"I'm surprised we even considered her," Madrene said. "Hers is a line much cursed."

Uxton's booming laugh echoed down the corridor. "So cursed her father is one of the richest men in Sacoridia!"

Madrene scowled. "You know what I mean. Much cursed by us."

Uxton rolled his eyes. "Of course, Madrene. Galadheon is much cursed by us."

"I will continue my vigil on her," Spurlock said, "but I do not consider her a threat, or her father, but should things change, we and our sect in Corsa should be set to eliminate any threat. In the meantime, so long as Clan G'ladheon is ignorant of its heritage, no harm should come to them."

"Why not kill them now, like Lord Alton?" Robbs asked. "Why wait for something to happen?"

Spurlock nodded. "A good question, but we dare not act prematurely. What if we open ourselves to detection by a moment of carelessness? Wouldn't the murders of Stevic G'ladheon and his heir draw unwanted attention? I choose caution; to not make any moves unless warranted. Are there further objections?"

No one spoke. Spurlock felt cold hands around his neck and heard a muttering near his ear.

Five hells! His gut froze as the cold passed through it. He'd be glad to get out of here.

"Let us end then. Praise be to Mornhavon."

"Praise be to Mornhavon," they all chanted.

They raised their hands high, exposing the tattoos on

their palms to the light of their lamps, and Spurlock led the
closing in the Imperial tongue: *"Leo diam frante clios . . ."*

Mostly unaware of the ghostly presences that swept in
and around them in great agitation, Second Empire finished
its meeting in ancient ritual.

Journal of Hadriax el Fex

I have returned from a bloody campaign to the north. I am tired of the fighting. How many years has it been? I've nearly forgotten. We of Arcosia are a long-lived race, and this has allowed us to keep fighting as though in our prime, while a clansman might be born, live to old age, and die while we barely age.

We decimated many villages on our campaign. I can no longer differentiate one village from another, one herd of slaves taken from another, or the faces of those I've killed. Men, women, children. Children, Alessandros says, are the future breeders of our enemy, so usually they are slaughtered unless someone desires them for slaves.

In the small country of Kmaern, Alessandros used the Black Star to wipe out its people, and to topple most of their impressive stone towers. These folk were the stoneworkers who built defenses for the clans our forces could not penetrate. They will build nothing more.

Since our troops have not been replenished by Arcosia, we've begun to use our captives as arrow fodder, and we discovered a people deep in the Wanda Plains—more like cattle they are, for they are dim-witted and bestial, and live in dens of mud and dirt. Mornhavon has been capturing them and changing them with his powers. Once changed, they are cunning and ferocious fighters.

The Sons of Rhove have allied themselves with the clans, for they fear invasion of their own lands. And, there are indications that the Elt in the lands north of clan territories are interested in joining the fray against us. Alessandros is confident he will overcome them as he overcame Argenthyne.

I cannot help but think that all the unholy works of Alessandros have changed him. I cannot explain it, but he is ever darker in his thoughts, as though the more he uses etherea for his experiments and plots, the more it pollutes and poisons him. Many stay loyal out of fear, though there are others who revel in his change and feed off it.

I try not to think too heavily on it, but the perversion of etherea, which is the stuff of God, is madness. Perhaps that is the taint I sense.

❧ WATCH HILL ❧

The town of Childrey lay a half day's ride east of Sacor City. Because of Karigan's late start, she'd probably spend the night in Childrey, or beneath the stars somewhere along the road on her return trip.

As she had guessed, Condor was just as eager as she to take to the road, and as he stretched his legs in a soothing, rocking canter, her concerns flowed from her shoulders with the passing of each mile, leaving her in a state of contentment.

It was a truly fine day with a sky overhead the shade of a robin's egg. Woodlands alternated with blueberry barrens, and she waved to laborers raking in the last of the season's crop. They shouted back cheery greetings.

There were a couple of villages she and Condor passed through, with children watching from the side of the road to see the king's messenger. More merry greetings were exchanged, and she was asked to pass on good tidings to King Zachary.

Once outside the second village, she nudged Condor back into his pleasant canter, and with a switch of his tail, they were off.

Feeling cleansed and revitalized, Karigan laughed at the breeze against her face and the wide open freedom of the ride. It had been truly too long since she'd been off castle grounds. Now she drank in the deep greens of grasses and forest, and the wavering yellow and white flowers of late summer along the road. Some plants, spent by so much summer splendor, were already turned gold and red with the shortening days.

Later, when she slowed Condor to a walk to cool off, a rocky mount called Watch Hill rose above the trees. From a distance it often took on a bluish aspect, especially at sunset. Blueberry barrens left to grow wild long ago cloaked its slopes. Its summit was bald granite except for scraggly vegetation that clung tenaciously in protected crevices and pockets of gravelly soil.

The road skirted the base of Watch Hill, and then continued steadily eastward. As she passed into the hill's shadow, she felt a strange tug on her brooch, a resonance that called on her to climb the mount. Spooked, Karigan kicked Condor into a canter to put Watch Hill behind them. She wasn't about to let anything untoward spoil her pleasant ride.

The shadows had grown long by the time Condor's hooves pounded over the bridge that crossed the brook bounding Childrey.

Childrey was a prosperous little town, home to several gentlemen farmers and landowners. Some profited from the lumbering business that took place north and west, while others were merchants who specialized in crossing the Wingsong Mountains to do business with the eastern provinces.

Upon her arrival at the mayoral offices off the town green, she was treated courteously by the mayor's servants. This was her third errand to Childrey, and Lord-Mayor Gilbradney was an ardent supporter of King Zachary.

The mayor and his staff offered her every creature comfort possible, and she was not at all disappointed when he invited her to his table for a supper of wine-roasted grouse and bowls piled high with the mushrooms that were so plentiful this time of year. There were slabs of sharp cheese, and bread just pulled from the ovens. Her cup was never empty of apple wine, and dish after dish was passed her way.

It was over a heap of blueberry-rhubarb pie swimming in warm clotted cream that Lord-Mayor Gilbradney broached a subject that was not just simple table conversation.

"Rider," he said, "one hears all manner of strange tales emanating from across the country. As you know, we've a good deal of commerce here for an inland town." Here he smiled knowing her own family's business based on the shore of Corsa Harbor. "With our commerce, there are those who have traveled far and wide. Do you know the tales I speak of?"

The others at the table, the mayor's wife and some town officials, waited intently for Karigan's reply.

"I believe I do," she said. "As you may guess, those tales have also reached the king's ear."

Gilbradney shifted uncomfortably. "Is there truth in them?"

Karigan nodded slowly. "Of course, I'm not sure which ones you've heard, but yes, some have truth in them. But more likely than not, most are probably exaggerated beyond recognition."

"So I suspect, as well. Tell me, Rider, do you know the cause of these oddities?"

Karigan wasn't sure how much to reveal. This was one of the hardest aspects of representing the kingdom—everything coming from her mouth would be taken as the official word of the king.

"No decisive conclusions have yet been reached," she said carefully, "but the king is aware of the oddities, and we are being vigilant. Have you anything to report?"

The mayor and his colleagues seemed delighted to tell her of the tales they had heard. Some were familiar, some were not. She filed the latter away for retrieval later, when she reported back to Mara and the king.

The conversation turned cordial once again, the mayor apparently satisfied by her explanation.

The mayor's wife invited her to stay the night, but Karigan had an itch to be riding again. The moon was due to be full and she couldn't bear the thought of being stuck indoors. Also, she felt a twinge of guilt about having left Mara totally at the mercy of the "wolves." As much as she liked being away from Sacor City, the farther she got down the road tonight, the sooner she could get back to helping Mara.

After convincing Lady Gilbradney she must be on her way, and thanking her effusively for her hospitality, Karigan nearly had to roll herself out of the mayor's residence, she was so stuffed. Her head was a little light, too, from all the apple wine.

I suppose I'll have another headache in the morning.

She was yawning mightily by the time they reached the stretch of road that skirted Watch Hill. It was a domed silhouette against a tapestry of twinkling stars. The bright full moon reflected a glimmering crown of light on the summit.

Pretty, Karigan thought sleepily. *Magical.*

It was an ironic thought for what happened next.

At first the stirring of her brooch was a gentle hum, but insistent enough to awaken her completely. Condor halted as if knowing more was to come. A force tugged at her brooch, then yanked her right off Condor and into the streaming space of the traveling.

She screamed, but the sound was ripped from her throat and left in some other time. She traveled suspended through thousands of nights, the moon changing its size and visage faster than her eyes could blink, travelers on the road but brief impressions flaring past, and then there was no road at all. She passed through winters and rainstorms, forest fires, summers and autumns, and radiant springs.

When the traveling ended abruptly, she fell from space and hit the ground with an unceremonious grunt. She sat up groaning—unhurt, but very unhappy. Who knew when she had landed this time.

Physically she was in the very same spot as when she'd been atop Condor, but he was nowhere to be seen. Her perspective of Watch Hill hadn't changed an iota, and even the moon was full and a dazzling silver.

"Bloody hell," she muttered. She stood and slapped dirt off her trousers.

The air was crisp, like the lands north where a nip in the summer air reminded one of which season was the mightier and dominated the longest.

"Now what?"

It seemed a pitiful question when a powerful force had just carried her across the ages. *Why?* And with mounting fear, *would she be stranded here?*

She touched her brooch, but it felt no different than it ever had. Panic swelled in her breast and she hugged herself to contain it. She was alone here with no idea of how to get back.

To calm herself, she decided to build a campfire. By the time she remembered her tinder box was still packed in Condor's saddlebag, *elsewhen,* she had already accumulated an armload of wood. With a sigh, she supposed starting a fire without it would occupy her while she mulled over her situation.

She dumped the wood and went looking for more. As she walked, she caught sight of a movement beyond a thicket of trees. Startled, she halted, her heart skipping a few beats. It was a horse and rider, of that much she was certain.

She had to restrain herself from running to the rider for help. Instead, she moved forward cautiously, attempting to make as little noise as possible. Just because the people of the past had been unaware of her the last time she had traveled, she didn't want to take the chance the rules had changed.

She passed through the thicket, thinking the shadows of the spruce would help conceal her. She knelt behind a boulder and peered out beyond to a clearing.

The moon glinted on the rider's steel half-armor and the pommel of the greatsword strapped to her back. It was none other than the First Rider, Lil Ambrioth.

Karigan stepped out from behind the boulder and out of the shadows. "Hello," she said.

Lil didn't seem to hear or see her. She remained very still, sitting erect in her saddle, staring straight ahead.

Lil's horse was more draft horse than saddle horse. It was big and bony and underfed, and tired-looking. It was slightly sway-backed, and had the look of hard use. Its large head was ugly. Not exactly the image Karigan had of the warsteed that should be carrying a great hero.

Another rider entered the clearing from the opposite side, on a sleek black stallion that was a far finer beast than Lil Ambrioth's. The man riding it was no less impressive, in a crimson and black uniform, the like of which Karigan had never seen before. The velvet sleeves were full and slashed to reveal the crimson silk beneath. He wore a breastplate of enameled crimson, and a baldric of black that girded a longsword at his hip. He bore himself like an elite soldier.

Of his features, she could discern little. They blurred in her vision.

"Hadriax el Fex," Lil said.

The man nodded, his leathers creaking. "Liliedhe Ambriodhe." His accent was different from Lil's.

This was the meeting King Jonaeus had tried to talk Lil out of attending. This was her meeting with Mornhavon the Black's closest friend.

Lil did not answer the man, but nudged her horse a few steps forward. Then halted.

"I believe you requested safe haven."

"Yes, I did. Lord Mornhavon's atrocities have become more than I can bear, and I want to help bring them to an end."

"After all this time?" Lil asked. "You've only just discovered the various hells Mornhavon has created in these lands? You had your hand in enough of it, I daresay. Why shouldn't I just run my sword through you right now?"

"You won't do that."

"You sound rather sure of yourself. I wouldn't be if I were you."

"You won't kill me," the man said, "because you know I have valuable knowledge."

Lil laughed quietly. "So I imagine. Why should I trust anything you have to say?"

"I have given up much to come here. Risked everything I am, betrayed the man who was a brother to me."

To Karigan's ears, the words sounded flat. Too flat. He was lying.

The man sidled his stallion closer to Lil. She didn't move.

"You won't kill me," the man continued, "because without the information I possess, your people will have no hope of winning this war, and you know it. Mornhavon will defeat you."

Lil raised an eyebrow, a touch of amusement on her lips. "Will he now?"

"*Yes.*"

A throttled scream, a man's voice, erupted nearby in the woods: "Trap!"

Hadriax el Fex grabbed Lil and tried to drag her off her horse. The fog no longer clouded his features, which were sharp and hard. His hair was black and tied back into a ponytail. Upon his brow rested a crown of lead fashioned into intertwining branches. Karigan had seen the crown before, on the wraith in the clearing, the night of the attack on Lady Penburn's delegation.

Even as Lil struggled against the man, a hundred horsemen materialized out of nothing as though a curtain had been lifted. They all bore the black and crimson colors, the device of a black dead tree on their shields. They trotted their horses to encircle Lil and the man in their struggle.

Lil swung at him and landed a fist in his eye. He rocked back in his saddle. Like lightning the greatsword flashed into Lil's hands, but she'd be unable to fend off the archers who now bent their bows, arrows aimed directly at her.

The man laughed. "No, no. Lord Mornhavon wants her alive." Power crackled on his upraised palm. It crawled up and down his forearm. Lil paused as if to consider her predicament. Karigan yearned to help, but was unaware of what she could do. A distraction of some kind?

Last time, she could handle objects even if she couldn't make contact with people. Without hesitation, she hefted a large rock, and heaved it at the nearest horse. The horse whinnied and reared, dumping its rider. As she hoped, the soldiers' attention averted to their fallen companion. Even the man wearing the crown was distracted enough to look.

Lil didn't use the moment to escape. Instead, she raised her horn to her lips and blared out the notes of the Rider charge. No sooner did the last note ring out and she had dropped the horn to her side, was she slashing her sword at her would-be captor. Taken off-guard, his magic fizzled out. He concentrated on trying to reignite it and avoid Lil's blade, but Lil's big, ugly horse casually bit a chunk out of his leg, and swiftly whirled on its haunches to plant a well-placed kick on his high-tempered stallion's chest.

The man's scream, and the thrashing of his stallion, were lost to thunderous hoofbeats shaking the ground.

Green Riders boiled out of the woods and charged the enemy.

A counter trap, Karigan thought, practically jumping up and down with glee.

The Riders loosed their own arrows and many of the enemy fell. The Riders did not pause after their opening volley, but drove into the enemy, whooping and swinging their sabers above their heads. Green and white paint masked their faces, giving them a wild, frightening countenance. Green handprints decorated the necks and haunches of their mounts.

Karigan stumbled back into a thicket to avoid getting trampled.

The two groups merged into smaller melees, and the battle almost became quiet, with but the clattering of weaponry and thud of hooves, and the isolated shout or cry. It was almost businesslike, and perhaps for enemies who had been at war for so long, it was business.

At its center, Lil Ambrioth and the man who had masqueraded as Hadriax el Fex still strove against each other, but much of their combat was lost to sight behind others. It was hard to say which side was winning, but Karigan thought the Green Riders were outnumbered despite their initial volley.

She moved through the thicket, detecting the occasional flare of magic—a ball of flame thrown or objects flying through the air without hands to guide them. She sought a different vantage point, trying to determine how the Riders fared, silently rooting for them, apprehensive when one succumbed and fell. This battle may have occurred sometime in the far distant history of the lands, but anxiety hounded her that the Riders would be devastated.

She came upon three of the enemy in the woods. One was without a breastplate, and he leaned over his horse's neck as though wounded. His hands were bound behind him with black, writhing magic. Karigan remembered the pain of such magic all too well.

Sandy hair fell over the man's face. This could only be the one Lil had come to meet, Hadriax el Fex. He hadn't meant to ambush her, but was a prisoner himself, and undoubtedly the one who had warned her of the trap.

His two guards spoke to one another in a guttural, rolling language incomprehensible to Karigan.

Must be the imperial tongue, she thought.

One of the guards raised his sword and pricked el Fex in the arm, and burst out laughing. El Fex did nothing, his head hanging wretchedly. The guards exchanged several words, followed by more laughter.

Karigan approached closer, drawn as much by curiosity as anything. She wasn't intimate with the politics of the day as a scholar might be, nor had she heard of Hadriax el Fex until her previous travels. And she had no stake in the outcome of this battle. The past was the past, wasn't it?

Still, she knew Hadriax el Fex wouldn't have been held a prisoner if he hadn't intended to betray Mornhavon and provide the League with valuable information.

Should she intervene? Would doing so alter the course of history, for better or worse? Maybe there was a reason el Fex was not remembered. Maybe it was because he died this night before he could pass on intelligence to the League.

One of the guards stabbed el Fex's thigh. He jerked and gasped, and his guards taunted him.

Suddenly he whipped his boot from his stirrup and kicked out sideways at the guard on his left. The guard's horse swerved away. The other guard swung his sword at him, but he threw his leg over his horse's neck and slid to the ground. The wounded leg buckled, and he fell to his knee.

The first guard, having gained control of his horse, came

up behind el Fex and shouted orders at him. El Fex clambered to his feet with difficulty.

"Nast dritch ech, Galadheon!" the guard shouted.

Startled to hear her name, Karigan stood stock still, with eyes wide. Could they suddenly see her?

El Fex ran, but did not get far before he was run down by the mounted guards. One guard dismounted and raised his sword for a killing blow.

Without a second thought, Karigan drew her saber and stabbed it through the midsection of the guard. No blood spurted, the guard did not crumple, he didn't even flinch. Even her sword had no effect in this time. In desperation, she picked up a rock—it worked, although she couldn't analyze why until later—and pelted it into the face of the guard. He cried out and staggered back, dropping his sword to clutch at his bleeding face.

The second guard looked furtively about, seeking the source of the rock.

"Whuist das?" he asked. Then in a heavy accent, commanded, "Show yourself, mage."

Maybe, Karigan thought, her own sword didn't work because it hadn't yet been made. She scrunched her face at the logic, but wondered if, just maybe . . .

She grabbed the first guard's sword and swept it up in a defensive position. How must this look to the guards and el Fex? A quick glance revealed they were surprised, but not astonished. Maybe it was more common during this era to find invisible sword wielders.

Swiftly she stabbed the first guard. This time he bled. This time he crumpled.

The other guard watched the drifting blade, backing his horse away. She lunged, and he wheeled his horse around just in time to meet an arrow. He tumbled from his horse and did not move.

Lil and another Rider approached. "You lead the others

to the summit," she told him, "and I'll take care of this one." She pointed her bloodied greatsword at el Fex. "I'm going to sound the retreat." Her companion nodded and reined his horse back toward the main body of the fray.

Lil raised the horn to her lips and the call to retreat blared out, resounding in an echo as it bounced off Watch Hill. Karigan carefully set down the sword. Hadriax el Fex followed its motion with his eyes.

"Dreshna," he said. "Thank you."

"You're welcome," Karigan replied, though she knew he could not hear her.

She watched as the First Rider assisted Hadriax el Fex onto her horse before her, and kicked her steed toward Watch Hill.

⋙ SHADOWS OF KENDROA MOR ⋘

Andri's grip on Lil's hand slackened even as the life flowed out of him. His face was a ghastly hue beneath the cracking green paint.

"I—I am sorry I failed ye, Captain," he gasped.

Lil squeezed his hand. "You did well, Andri. Very well. Don't think otherwise, hey?"

She could only watch as life faded from him.

"Remember me," he pleaded with a whisper.

"I will."

By then he was gone. Lil gently closed his eyes. "Rest well," she whispered to him.

Before he was lifted away to the pyre, she unclasped his brooch from his plaid sash and placed it in her belt pouch with all the others she had removed from the dead. She nodded to Ludriane to ignite the fire.

If they hadn't had to ride up the mor, Andri might have survived with proper care, but the retreat was necessary. Had she left him behind, the empire's craven jackals would have hacked him to pieces. She carried away all wounded and dead whenever possible, to prevent such desecration.

Andri was the last of the mortally wounded to pass on to the Birdman's care. Some had to be helped along, humanely, with a sharp blade. They would now have a blazing pyre atop the mor for the dead, allowing their souls to lift easier to the heavens in the smoke, and the bright fire

365

consuming them would bring light amid the blackness of the empire's deeds. It was a good night for light.

Despite the deaths, the mission had been a success. Hadriax el Fex sat nearby, all alone, his wrists still bound behind his back by a tendril of wild magic. She knew it must cause him intense pain, but only a great mage could undo it, which meant he'd have to endure it until they reached the king's army. He looked to have been tortured, with open wounds bleeding, but he'd live. Eventually Merigo would dress the wounds, as soon as she finished with the more seriously injured. El Fex did not complain, nor did he ask for help. He bore his pain in silence.

As Andri was laid beside his brothers and sisters on the burgeoning pyre, she thought Hadriax el Fex had better be worth it.

Breckett, her lieutenant, appeared at her elbow. Blood streamed down his temple, but he paid it no heed. The wound would be just one more scar among many others.

"How long do you think we've got?" he asked.

"Not long enough. I stabbed him three times, but it will slow him down very little."

"Aye, he is an unnatural bastard, that Lord Varadgrim. He's got the magic of the Black One on him, he does."

"Next time I'll just take his head."

"He'd probably grow it back." Breckett made the gruff chortle that was his laugh. "Nay, that one won't die."

"Hollin and Dane will gain us some time with the wards," Lil mused. "But we dare not linger here."

"Agreed."

"I want you to lead everyone back toward the king's position. Alex will bear el Fex. This will be more a contest of stealth than speed, hey?"

"I understand. Where will you be?"

"Bringing up the rear."

Breckett gazed suspiciously at her with those dark piercing eyes of his. "And what would you be planning?"

Lil patted her horn, which always rode at her hip. "A slight diversion."

"I don't like it."

"I'm not asking you to. I'm asking you to obey your captain."

Breckett grumbled. "Then we best make good use of our time."

They gathered together all the Riders, wounded and unwounded, and linked hands in a circle beside the pyre. By the grace of the gods, the breeze carried the smoke and stench away from the summit of the mor.

Lil turned her face to the moon and began a litany all too familiar, one that was the Green Riders' own: "Aeryc, receive these souls into the heavens, may they walk beside you among the stars. They've fought the Dark One who would usurp your eminence with his one demon god, and murder all your children on this Earth. These souls fought bravely in your name, and were loyal.

"Even as you embrace these souls, please look down upon our circle and watch and protect us so we may fight on."

"Fight on," the Riders repeated in unison.

Lil turned her face from the moon and looked over each of her Riders in turn. Born in war, born for war. None of them cried, for there were no longer enough tears in the world to be shed for the fallen. Nearly a hundred years of war had devastated their people, destroyed their way of life. No one, not the smallest of children, was left untouched.

Children were quickly orphaned, as Lil had been herself, as both her parents marched off to war. Young orphans and children went to work at smithies and fletcher shops, to make the tools of war. Older children bore the tools they made to the battlefield. No, this was not a world for children.

Disease and starvation had wracked the Sacoridians, and Lil was convinced it was only by pure tenacity to survive that the clans had not given in to Mornhavon the Black. Of all the lands, besides Argenthyne, Sacoridia had been the most devastated.

She glanced at Hadriax el Fex. He had done much of the work himself as Mornhavon's right hand. She saw him lead the slaughter of thousands, his own blade dripping with blood. He spared not the young or the old, the infirm or the simple. He ordered prisoners to be tortured at will, even knowing they possessed no useful information. If he was not the key to turning the tide of the war, she'd take him apart layer by layer, piece by piece, rubbing salt crystals into his wounds as she went. Oddly, the fates had now made her his protector.

He didn't look so mighty just now, bent over and bleeding, sandy hair hanging in his eyes.

Turning back to her Riders, she said, "It is time for remembrance. I remember Andri."

"Andri," they responded.

As they went around the circle, each named a fallen Rider, and as a group they repeated his or her name. The lack of tears did not mean each death didn't hurt like a spear hurled into one's chest. Each Rider would handle each death in his or her own way.

"I remember Telan," Breckett said.

"Telan."

Breckett's back was to the pyre, and it seemed to Lil that someone walked behind him and into its light, and watched. It was a shadow figure, like an apparition, more night than substance. She kept her eye on it, warily, fearing it might be a trick of Varadgrim's.

The flames flared, and she had the impression of a woman's form.

Daron squeezed her hand. "Your turn," she whispered.

Lil blinked. She'd been so intent on the apparition, she hadn't realized they'd gone full circle with the remembrances.

She cleared her throat. "Riders, remember the names, for they are names of honor. Let us carry our fallen comrades in our hearts forever."

"Forever."

"Remember, Riders, so long as a few of us stand together, our circle shall never break."

"Never."

They raised their clasped hands above their heads.

"Aeryc, be our witness! We serve you, and so long as a few of us stand, our circle shall not break!"

They all whooped and yelled deprecations off the mor, all intended for the ears of Varadgrim and his warriors.

Even when the Riders went back to work preparing for their escape down the mor, Lil kept an eye on the apparition. No one else was aware of her.

The apparition watched all that went on around her, and when Lil strode toward her, a startled expression crossed her face.

Odd behavior for an apparition, she thought. *Not that I'd know . . .*

As Lil approached the figure, warmth rippled outward from her brooch. Surprised, she touched it, and it seemed to her the apparition grew sharper in her vision. She emanated a silver-green sheen, and wore her hair in a single braid down her back. Most astonishing of all, she wore a Rider brooch.

"Who are you?" Lil demanded. "Are you a demon spirit sent to haunt me?"

The apparition spoke, though Lil could not hear the words. If this one had been in life a Green Rider, Lil did not remember her, and that would be impossible. She remembered every Rider that served with her. It had to be some trick of the enemy, some illusion. The apparition licked her lips, then tried to communicate again.

A Rider galloped his horse onto the summit.

"It's Hollin," Breckett called to her.

The young man spotted her and rode right up to her, passing through the apparition. He did not see it. The apparition gazed at herself up and down, as if checking to see if she remained whole.

"Cap'n," Hollin said, gasping for breath, "Varadgrim is remounted. He's snuffing out our wards like candles."

Lil frowned. Time had just grown even more precious. She swept away from the apparition.

"Breckett! Get everyone mounted and ready to ride on my word."

He grunted in assent and did as she bade. Merigo was hurriedly staunching el Fex's wounds, a green glow of mending flowing from her hands.

"Merigo!" Lil snapped. "You are exhausted and the night is not yet done."

"But—"

"Bandage him if you must, and make it quick. Don't use your gift. He *is* our prize, but he won't be for long if you don't get a move on."

"Yes'm."

As Lil moved among her people, encouraging the wounded and yelling at the others to hurry, she was peripherally aware of the apparition walking with her, absorbing the scene. She had stopped trying to speak.

When finally everyone was mounted, Lil placed her fists on her hips and said to them, "You will go down the west ridge. Varadgrim will not expect it, for it is steep. Traverse it with stealth and care, but quickly. A few shall go at a time, hey? Follow Breckett. He knows the way."

"What of you, Cap?" Olin asked.

"I'm going to be leading a charge." And that's all she

would tell them. "Pensworth? I need an illusion. The rest of you will go. *Now.*"

"Aye," said Breckett, "this way then." He led the Riders toward the west ridge of Kendroa Mor. Lil prayed none of their horses would stumble. She prayed Varadgrim truly did not expect them to use so hazardous a route. She prayed he would fall for her ruse.

"What d'ya want, Cap?" Pensworth asked, reining his horse over to her.

"The appearance of Green Riders fortifying the summit, as though we intend to make a stand here."

Pensworth's brow crinkled in thought, and she knew he was considering whether or not his gift was strong enough. He scrubbed at his chin, eyed the moon, and brightened perceptibly.

"Silhouettes," he said. "Much less taxing than full-bodied."

She clapped his leg. "Good man! Do you think you can make them, eh, noisy?"

Pensworth smiled craftily. "I'll have 'em spouting every curse known at ol' Varadgrim. It'll make his face turn purple."

Lil laughed until she remembered the apparition. She wondered if it would flit off to Varadgrim to warn him of her plans. But no, the apparition stood there, hands clasped behind her back, watching curiously.

Lil turned back to Pensworth. "Set those illusions now, and as soon as you're done, you ride after the others, hey? No hesitation. You will be rear guard till I catch up."

"Aye, Cap."

Lil set off to unhitch her own horse, Brownie, who she had tied to a low growing, twisted pine. All her horses had been named Brownie. A long time ago she had lost track of how many Brownies she had gone through. She couldn't afford to get attached to the beasts, so they all got the same name regardless of their color. She did have to admit that her current gelding was one of her more sensible, if uglier, Brownies.

Before she mounted, the apparition picked up a rock and dropped it at her feet. The apparition wanted her attention, and got it.

"I can't hear a thing you are saying," Lil said, "and I've no time for the likes of you."

The apparition's eyebrows narrowed and she looked none-too-pleased. Then she extended her hand.

Lil regarded the outstretched hand warily. Obviously the apparition wanted her to take it, but what would happen if she did? If this was one of Varadgrim's ploys, might she be whisked away to Blackveil and imprisoned? No, she decided, for her brooch tingled, not in warning, but in encouragement.

Lil grunted, and reached for the hand. Their hands merged, and a shudder rippled down Lil's spine, for she felt as though she were reaching across the ages. The apparition grew more solid.

I'm Karigan, the apparition said. *Karigan G'ladheon.*

Lil almost jerked her hand away in shock at hearing the imperial word.

You don't know me?

"I do not," Lil said. "You wear a brooch, demon girl. A brooch you should not be wearing. You dishonor us. Are you a slave of Varadgrim's?"

No!

Cries and shouted insults erupted on the summit making Lil jump. She turned to find Pensworth's illusion at work. Flat, parchment-thin figures of black leaped about the summit waving swords and nocking arrows to bows. There were even a few horse silhouettes. One particularly large female silhouette, endowed with Lil's voice, screamed a phrase so foul about Varadgrim's mother that the real Lil's toes curled in her boots.

Pensworth grinned most proudly, saluted her, and trotted away toward the west ridge, and disappeared beyond the roiling flames of the pyre.

Turning back to the apparition, she said, "I don't have time for you."

Karigan was weary. She was weary from the traveling. Weary from her climb up Watch Hill. Weary at being forced to exist in a place and time neither here nor there. And she was weary of trying to communicate with Lil Ambrioth, and when finally they connected, the First Rider brushed her aside.

This had been a terrible night. Crossing the battlefield with its carnage left her gasping. Witnessing the pyre and inhaling its acrid stench of burning human flesh sickened her. She just wanted to sit down and weep.

How could Lil and her Riders stand it? Were they simply used to it? She thanked the heavens that she lived in the times she did, times of peace. Otherwise, this could be her life. Battle and the burning of dead comrades.

Now as she faced the First Rider on the summit of Watch Hill, she understood why the legends of her heroics endured. Here was a leader with the wit to meet a trap with a counter trap, and carry off Mornhavon the Black's closest friend. Here was one who could lead her Riders in mourning. And here was the leader who was about to divert the minions of Varadgrim so her Riders could escape in safety.

Lil glanced across the summit at the whooping and hollering silhouettes—another wonder among many—and nodded in satisfaction. She touched her brooch to fade out.

The force of it acted on Karigan. It absorbed her into the

body of Lil Ambrioth with such suddenness that she could do nothing to prevent it. Lil's rage at the intrusion crackled at her like bursts of lightning.

Within Lil, Karigan could feel the reins of the horse in her hands as though she held them herself. The beat of Lil's heart and the pulse of her blood became Karigan's too.

"Get out!"

Karigan heard it both through Lil's ears and in her mind.

I would if I could, Karigan informed her. *I think it's because our brooches are linked.*

"Linked?"

We wear the same brooch. It seemed idiotic to be telling her the same information she had once told Karigan.

"I've told you no such thing," Lil countered. "I have never seen you before. Now get out! I've got to go."

I can't! Do what you need to. I will not interfere.

"You've done that enough, I'll wager," Lil grumbled. "I don't trust you."

I am a Rider. I will not interfere.

Lil growled and mounted her horse, apparently accepting the inevitable, and kicked her horse between obscenity-shouting silhouettes. As Lil caught her thoughts, Karigan was privy to all the thoughts streaming through Lil's mind: Were her Riders all right? What if Varadgrim had the west ridge guarded? Where was Varadgrim? Had he become powerful enough to detect her even when she used her gift?

Lil's senses heightened as she guided her horse down the south ridge at a walk. No sense of flying down it when she was virtually invisible, and at a walk, her horse—also under the spell of fading—would be less likely to make a noise that would endanger her. She gazed into shadows and sniffed the air, seeking some tell-tale sign of Varadgrim and his troops.

Karigan was amazed at how effortlessly Lil wielded her ability. There was no headache, no veiling of gray over her sight. There *was* a wave of nausea, but it had nothing to do with the use of magic. Surprised, Karigan felt yet another life within Lil. She was pregnant.

Lil glanced over her shoulder at the summit as her horse ambled down the south ridge. The pyre continued to rage, and the silhouettes bounded about, hurling their mockery at the empire. They were thoroughly convincing. Lil grinned, and pulled her horn to her lips. Her lungs expanded, and she blew the Rider charge.

When she was done, Karigan became aware of movement down the slope. Orders were shouted and arrows *shooshed* into the air, but they flew wide, clattering into rocks far away from Lil. The moon glinted on a blade or two, and Lil attempted to discern the path of least resistance. It was too difficult to tell, really, and with a shrug, she kicked her horse into a headlong gallop, blowing the charge again as she went. Dropping her horn, she unsheathed the saber she wore at her hip.

The ride was terrifying. The big horse leaped down the slope, his hooves skidding down the solid granite ledge, almost convincing Karigan his legs would fly right out from beneath him. He jumped crevices in the rocky slope and almost stumbled to his knees a number of times on loose scree. Lil jolted sickeningly in the saddle, unfazed, while the headlong dash frayed Karigan's nerves.

Soon they came upon the enemy. Bewildered by the sounds of the charge and the silhouettes on the summit, they weren't sure of what to shoot. They heard Lil's horse upon them, but saw nothing. They died beneath her blade.

Leaning close to the horse's neck, they leaped a downed log and the two soldiers who'd been crouched behind it. A large hoof smashed a head, and they kept running.

Lil left more and more bodies behind her, clearing a swath through the troops, driving the enemy into confusion. They were unsure of where the attack was coming from, or where it would go next.

Sweat drenched her face, but her arm did not tire. She killed with a routineness that stunned Karigan. Lil was not bothered by the killing, but not triumphant either.

The enemy randomly fired arrows, trying to take out the unseen menace by chance. One arrow skittered across the horse's rump. He bucked and whinnied, but Lil dug her spurs into his sides so he'd keep galloping.

She spotted Varadgrim ahead, barking orders at his troops from behind. Lil laughed with glee. She veered the horse toward him, trampling and hacking down soldiers as she went. She readied her sword for his head.

Varadgrim knew she was coming, but was unable to discern her precisely. The blood drained from his features, and his cruel eyes widened in fear. He swept his sword before him, the jewels on his fingers flashing in the moonlight. He screamed at his soldiers.

"Here! She is here!"

Lil gritted her teeth, leaned over the horse's neck, and lowered her blade to the level of his throat.

Arrows rained all around them, impaling the saddle and skimming the horse's neck. Lil rode relentlessly toward her target, undaunted.

Pain! It exploded in her back. Her scream was Karigan's, too. The iron arrowhead tore through flesh, scraped rib, the wooden shaft sliding in after it.

Just short of Varadgrim, Lil's sword slipped from her fingers and clattered to the rocky ground.

The horse galloped on past him, Lil's back arched and mouth open in a soundless cry, blackness closing in on her. The arrow twisted inside with each lunge of the horse's stride, and she listed precariously in the saddle.

No-no-no! Karigan cried. Lil's insides ripped like they were her own. They then began to divide, the pain fading, Karigan becoming herself, and Lil a separate entity tottering in her saddle. She lost the fading, becoming visible to the enemy. Varadgrim took up pursuit.

No! Karigan couldn't let this happen. No one knew how or when the First Rider died, but Karigan couldn't let it happen now. She couldn't let Lil fall into the hands of Varadgrim, knowing what a prize she would be to the forces of the dark.

Even as Karigan felt herself sinking through the horse's haunches, she touched her brooch and reasserted her energy into it. At first nothing happened, but then Lil's brooch resonated, and she was drawn back in. The pain was unbearable, and Lil was just on this side of consciousness. Karigan withdrew enough so the pain did not overwhelm her or she didn't fall unconscious herself, but she remained merged with Lil enough so she could lend strength and support to keep her in the saddle.

Stay with me, Karigan pleaded her. *We've got to find your people.*

"Stay . . ." Lil murmured.

Karigan buoyed her arms so she might guide her horse. She gripped him with her legs to keep him galloping, to keep Lil in the saddle.

Tell me where to go, Karigan said.

Lil breathed raggedly, so close to incoherence.

Karigan shook her from inside and the pain of the arrow brought her a little more awareness.

Where do we go? Karigan shouted at her. *Where is King Jonaeus?*

At the king's name, Lil revived a little.

"West," she gasped. "West to Black Duck Lake."

Karigan knew the place, for the name had not changed over the ages.

She paced the horse so he wouldn't kill himself before they reached safety. From her observation of the other Riders, Lil had one of the "finer" steeds among them. Several had looked ready for the knacker's wagon.

Pursuit fell off behind them at the base of Watch Hill. Apparently she had been able to maintain invisibility. Now she just had to keep Lil in the saddle and alive long enough to find help, not an easy task considering the blood loss and rigors of the ride.

Karigan never did reach Black Duck Lake. They came upon a patrol of king's soldiers riding reconnaissance, which had also intercepted the fleeing Riders.

As they helped Lil from her horse, the Rider-mender Merigo came forward with a green glow clouding her hands.

It was the last Karigan knew, for the traveling swept her away through time once again.

⋘ INNER FIRE ⋙

Mara stumbled across the castle grounds in the thick night, rubbing her eyes, her head swimming. *Why* had Captain Mapstone left her in this position? Mara convinced herself she was well out of her league now that she saw what the captain was up against on a daily basis. Her day had started calmly enough, with a cup of tea at her elbow as she perused Rider reports. From there, all the various hells had broken loose.

Ephram broke his ankle on a loose floorboard in the stable. It wasn't too difficult to get him settled into his room with a mender looking in on him, but then Karigan had come to tell her the king had posted several long distance messages, and they were a messenger short. So now Karigan was gone, and Mara realized just how much she'd been relying on her to handle the nitty-gritty of the daily operation.

While Mara was on her way to another pointless meeting, the two back-up horses and her own Firefly, full of high spirits, decided to knock down the fence of their enclosure and run across the castle grounds, wreaking havoc with the castle guards' drill practice.

Mara ran after them—she was the only Rider around—and with some disgruntled assistance from the guard, captured the happy escapees and returned them to their stalls. Somehow, Robin, one of the horses, had gotten into the courtyard gardens and was found munching on the leaves of an ornamental shrub. Courtiers regarded the manure left on the pathway with disdain. Mara rolled her eyes, trying to imagine Robin trotting through the castle breezeway to reach the gardens.

She lost more precious time trying to locate someone to fix the fence. Hep the stablehand had gone into the city to tend to his wife, Flora, who had gone into labor with their first baby. In the end, she rigged a temporary fix herself.

As she put the final finishes on the fence, a breathless boy of the Green Foot ran up to her with a message from Captain Carlton admonishing her to join him and the captains of the other branches for their weekly meeting.

"He's a bit annoyed, ma'am," the boy warned her, "that you're late."

Sweaty and dirty, but with no time to spare for cleaning up, she ran full tilt to the castle and through the corridors to the meeting chamber. She charged into the room, and all the captains: guard, navy, cavalry, army, and Weapons, along with their aides, looked up at her. All Mara wanted to do, in her dirty and disheveled uniform, was turn and run back the way she had come.

Captain Carlton abruptly ordered her to sit, criticized her dress and lack of punctuality, and from there things deteriorated. Mara groaned, remembering how each captain angled and petitioned for their part of the treasury, and how every point she brought up in favor of the Green Riders was summarily cast down with, "You've got supplies freely given."

She tried to explain that Stevic G'ladheon's gift of supplies only covered uniforms and gear—not Rider pay, food, horses, or feed. She did not get a chance to add that having supplies freely given by Stevic G'ladheon left more of the treasury for the other branches to argue over.

This was a preliminary skirmish. The captains were to put their needs in writing and submit them to their superiors, who would hash it out from there. From that point, the captains pointedly ignored Mara. They discussed the crush of soldiers in their barracks, drill schedules, repairs needed, and so forth. Whenever she attempted to speak up, she was summarily cut off.

"Greenies don't drill," she was told, "so don't waste our time with your suggestions." Or, "You've got your own half-empty barracks. How could you understand how our soldiers must live?"

With growing frustration and alarm, Mara realized the other officers had the idea that Green Riders were somehow privileged and a useless holdover from the old days. "We carry half your messages these days," said Captain Hogan of the light cavalry. "What are you complaining about?"

All too clearly she saw how their disrespect for the Green Riders filtered down all the way to the lowest ranks. How could Captain Mapstone manage such open hostility on a daily basis? She was sure the captain had honed her skills in dealing with her colleagues, but it put her in a difficult spot. How could she explain to them there were so few Riders because the brooches were not calling out for enough to work in the messenger service? How could she explain the magic? The mere mention of it might put her on even worse footing with the officers.

Mara gnashed her teeth as she rehashed the events of the day through her mind. And her stomach grumbled. She had eaten a hearty breakfast, thank the gods, but had had no time for other meals, and it was far too late to pester the cooks in the dining hall. No wonder Captain Mapstone had begun showing signs of strain. A day like this one, day after day, was bound to wear anyone down. Mara was certain the meeting had been enough to straighten her springy hair. At least the captain had had an aide of some sort to depend on for many things. Mara had only herself. If she wasn't so exhausted, she'd cry.

Barracks loomed ahead unlit and quiet. Everyone was gone on an errand, except for Ephram. No light winked in the injured man's window, so he must have turned in for the night.

It struck Mara just how still and silent it was, like a brooding shadow. The crickets had left off their chirruping. No guards patrolled this way. Not even a breeze shifted on the dewy grasses. It seemed clouds had been drawn over the stars like a shroud.

I am tired. Mara tried to shake off her feeling of unease. *Barracks is empty, but for one Rider. Of course it's dark and quiet.*

Her sense of unease only intensified as she mounted the steps and paused on the threshold. An unlit lamp sat on a table by the entrance. She touched the wick, and with a mere thought, light sprang to life.

The light twisted and stirred, as if doing battle with the night, flickering ungainly at the walls. Floorboards moaned beneath her feet all too loudly in the dense, dark silence. She squinted into the shadows, but discerned nothing amiss.

She paused by Ephram's door. No light filtered from beneath. Carefully she opened the door to check on him. He writhed on his bed, muttering. Concerned, Mara entered and stood beside his bed. His eyes were wide open but unseeing. Was he dreaming with his eyes open?

"They seek . . ." he muttered.

"Ephram?" Mara said, alarmed. She nudged his shoulder. "Ephram, wake up!" But he did not. He stared at nothing and gabbled unintelligibly like a man with a fever.

With a prickling, Mara turned suddenly as though she were being spied upon from behind. The lamplight swirled across the walls. When it stilled, nothing seemed amiss, but a sense of extreme danger washed over her.

A door groaned open somewhere down the corridor.

Mara licked her lips, tasting the salt of perspiration. Her ability burned within her like the core of a blacksmith's forge. She must radiate the heat.

With a last apprehensive glance at Ephram, she stepped out into the corridor. It was a nightmare corridor of dancing, darting shadows and palpable dread.

The opened door led into Karigan's room.

What were the chances that it was Karigan who was within?

None.

By now, the lamplight would have announced Mara's presence to whoever was there. Should she turn and flee from the unknown terror? Get help? She could not. She was drawn forward.

Each shaky step drew her inexorably closer to the open door, which stood like the black entrance to a tomb.

Sweat slid down her temple, her internal fire burning ever hotter.

She stepped into the doorway. Her lamp failed to illuminate each corner of the little room. She had visited the room so often when Karigan was in residence that there should be nothing sinister about it. Her bed was neatly made with a blanket folded at its foot. An old pair of boots, bent at the ankles and scuffed from much wear, stood against the wall. Yet, now, the room became an unfamiliar landscape of stark, angular shadows and invisible terrors. The room was cold, terribly cold, and threatened to quench Mara's fire.

As she swung the lamp around, a brilliance flared on Karigan's table. Strangely attracted, Mara stepped over the threshold and into the room. The crystal fragments of Karigan's moonstone dazzled, reflecting and refracting the lamplight. They sparkled more than the dim lamplight warranted.

A hiss.

Mara whirled around.

A shadow detached itself from the wall, clutching Kari-gan's greatcoat in one bone white hand, and a bit of blue hair ribbon in the other. The chain of a manacle dangled from its wrist.

Mara's feeble lamplight gleamed on a lead crown.

Her mouth went dry. The summer evening had become bleak winter, a steely cold. Down in the city, the bell rang out the late hour in heavy, sonorous tones as though echo-ing the dread of this moment.

"We seek," the shadow said, its voice a frosty almost-whisper, "the Galadheon."

So stricken was Mara that she could not have spoken even if she willed it. Her hand fluttered at her hip where her saber would have hung had she been anywhere but on the castle grounds. She possessed no weapon, and she was certain it would have had little effect anyway.

The shadow creature stepped closer to her light. She made out flinty, impassive eyes; skin the shade of a corpse's.

"We seek," it repeated, "the Galadheon. You will tell us."

The lamp slipped from Mara's fingers and smashed to the floor, spreading oil across the old, wooden boards. Fire whooshed up between them, and the wraith brought up its arms to protect its face.

Laren gazed up at the clear sky. The Hunter's Belt was mi-grating into the eastern horizon, and as the nights grew longer and the days shorter, it would reign dominant over the summer stars. The moon was brilliant, but did not di-minish the brightness of the stars.

"Gods please help me through this," she prayed, as she did every night.

Only after the castle grounds settled for the night did Laren dare step outside her quarters. She had learned that in the quiescence of night, her ability assailed her less, as though all the mental activity of others during the day somehow contributed to her problem.

By day she lay in bed, a pillow wrapped around her head to stifle the voice of her ability. It did not work of course. Only sleep brought her some measure of peace, though sometimes she could hear her ability intrude even on her dreams.

It commented on anything and everything, including her own thoughts and emotions. Slowly, she knew, it would push her to the brink when she just couldn't stand the assault anymore. What she would do when that happened, she wasn't sure.

Overlying everything was the guilt, the guilt that she had abandoned her Riders, leaving the entire operation in Mara's hands.

True.

Whenever her feelings of guilt welled up, her ability unswervingly told her "true" like a finger of condemnation.

False.

A quiet cry of hopelessness escaped her lips and she continued prowling the grounds, trying to blank her mind.

The grounds near Rider barracks were quiet and the darkness held the weight of a cloak. A few tiny lights twinkled about the castle, but the grounds were soaked in shadow, only the moon outlining rooflines and walls.

The bell down in the city clanged out the hour, and she broke out in a sudden cold sweat. A sensation of terror overrode all other feelings of guilt and hopelessness. The source of the terror emanated from Rider barracks.

She ran toward barracks, though she desperately wanted to run in the opposite direction. The building was a shadow within shadow.

She ran toward what could be her very grave, and what compelled her forward in the face of such fear, she never knew. Did her fear for her Riders overcome her own sense of safety? Was it some inner strength? Or had she already been driven into madness?

A figure emerged from the shadow of the building. Loathing washed over her.

The figure crept toward her, paused, and crept closer.

Laren wanted to run, but she was held in place, as if ice had formed over her skin and solidified.

"We seek," the wraith said, "the Galadheon."

Lady Estora Coutre walked dim corridors, the lamps at low burn for the night. Her cousin would not be pleased if he ever learned she wandered the corridors unescorted at so late an hour, but she could not sleep, her heart filled with unease. Unease about the ultimatum her cousin planned to present to the king, from her father. She sensed she was but a game piece on an Intrigue board that others moved in some desired direction for their own benefit; powerless to move in her own direction. Her future was not her own.

She supposed her relationship with F'ryan Coblebay had been a secret retaliation against those who used her in their plots. A secret retaliation, yes, but one in which she held power—not over F'ryan certainly, for he had been as unpredictable as the winds, and not over her own emotions—but in the secret itself.

The castle corridors went for miles if one followed them through all their various wings, and up and down the various floors. She passed servants' quarters, her shawl pulled up to cover her hair and shadow her face so none would take special note of her. The quarters were subdued, though some folk were about: a cook with flour smudged on his cheek retiring for the night, a laundress who set down her burden of dirty linens and rubbed her sore back.

She avoided the administrative wing, its corridors dark, cold, and cheerless. Even during the day, those older corridors did not invite her in. They stirred within her a sense of age and ghostly presence, and things best left undisturbed.

She walked past guards and old suits of armor and tapestries telling stories few remembered. She mounted the curving stairs to an upper level and bypassed the rooms of sleeping courtiers and officials from other lands. More guards, more tapestries, more armor.

The west wing belonged to the monarch and his Weapons. This, too, she avoided, with statuelike Weapons standing guard, and the décor taking on a more regal demeanor. Portraits of past monarchs lined the walls, she knew. She had been down the corridor once before, for an awkward meeting arranged by her cousin with King Zachary. That had been long ago. Over a year.

He was showing me off as a merchant would his wares.

The thought did not make her angry. Much she had accepted in life as part of her position as the heir of Clan Coutre. Her father had always treated her this way, as an object of admiration and future alliances. A ware to be sold.

Her mother had taught her grace and composure. She had learned, though not consciously taught by her mother, a certain aloofness, as well. A detachment.

She turned away from the west wing, though it was possible one day she would have to live there among all the portraits of Sacoridia's monarchs, and with the present king. Zachary was a good man, and this she kept telling herself.

And she kept asking, *F'ryan, why did you have to leave me?* But the dead could not answer.

She shifted her shawl on her shoulders, head bowed, as she walked away from the west wing. The core of the castle was like a great rectangle, with the gardens at its center, and various wings added on over time, making it a labyrinthine puzzle to the uninitiated. There were places where one had to follow corridors to an upper level in order to get to a lower level. Only the gardens hinted at the castle's original configuration.

She turned a corner and headed for the south wing. She paused in mid-stride, her skirts brushing her ankles. Coming from the opposite direction, tailed by a Weapon and an elderly terrier, was King Zachary. His hands were clasped behind his back and his gaze to the floor as though he was in deep thought. He did not wear his fillet, the symbol of his power.

Estora thought he might pass without even noticing her, but when he approached, he looked right up at her. His eyes registered recognition and surprise. She curtsied.

"My lord."

"My lady," he said, with a half bow. The Weapon insinuated herself against the wall, as still as one of the suits of armor. The dog sat beside his master's feet, panting. "You are about rather late this evening."

"As are you, Excellency."

He smiled, chagrined, almost shy. "I suppose I am. To tell the truth, I've had a little difficulty sleeping. I thought perhaps a stroll would unknot my thoughts."

"As did I." They exchanged fleeting smiles.

The king stroked his beard, his expression suddenly distant and a little troubled, as though he strove within himself to decide something. Finally he said, "Perhaps we could stroll together."

Estora could decline, but it was like putting off the inevitable. Both he and she had avoided one another for long enough. If her father's plan should succeed, she decided she might as well get to know the king a little better before they must be forced into intimate circumstances.

"Of course, my lord."

Out of courtesy he turned to walk in the direction she

had been heading. She stepped alongside him and they set off with the terrier waddling behind them, his tail wagging gamely. The Weapon fell in behind as well.

Weapons swore an oath of discretion along with the other oaths that bound them to the king's service. Still, she couldn't imagine the Weapons not wanting to gossip now and then, and here she was presenting a perfect opportunity. She glanced over her shoulder, but the woman who followed remained expressionless, watchful, and seemingly disinterested in the concept of King Zachary and Lady Estora walking together.

An awkward silence settled upon them. Estora's mother had been instructive about such moments as well.

"Tell me," Estora said, to draw Zachary out, "what do you hear of Hillander Province these days?"

It was as though a mask crumbled away from his face at the mention of his home. His delight and grateful expression told her she had asked the right question. *Your function,* she remembered her mother saying, *is to put the man at ease. To do this, you must ask him questions that he can answer readily, and happily.*

The king stroked his beard and his eyes grew distant. "I expect the fisherfolk are hauling flatfish in by the basketfuls. The folk there lead the quiet lives they always have."

Estora could tell he wished to be among them. Had things turned out differently, he would be there now as lord-governor of Hillander Province, not in the castle of Sacor City as the reigning monarch. But things turned out the way they turned out, and a steward oversaw the workings of Zachary's province until he had a child of an age to look after it. Estora blushed at the prospect that the child could very well be one of her own.

As he spoke on about the sea breezes against his face, and climbing the rounded mounts that rose from the sea, it was as though he had been transported there, and she with him, his descriptions were so vivid. She realized Hillander was not so different from Coutre.

"I, for one, have always liked the occasional raw, foggy day," he said. "It is an excuse to stay by the fire and read a book, or to attend to some other quiet task."

"Yes, I am of that mind, too," she said.

As he went on, Estora noted they were making at least their fourth round of this particular set of corridors, but King Zachary did not appear to notice or care. The terrier followed merrily behind, tongue lolling. The Weapon maintained her discreet, silent distance.

King Zachary paused and chuckled. "Listen to me. I sound like a homesick schoolboy."

"You sound like someone who loves his home very much," she said.

"I thank you in any case for listening to all of that. My mind has been so tied up with other matters of late."

He must, Estora thought, think of the situation in D'Ivary Province.

She found some pleasure in that he had spoken so of his home to her. She wondered if he would tell more of what troubled him. *You will one day marry a man of rank and influence,* her mother once told her, *a leader of others. He will need someone who he can talk to. You must learn to listen, and to listen earnestly.* And Estora had watched her mother do just that over the years, ever-so-gently guiding her father into conversation and revealing exactly what weighed on his soul.

The king did not speak further of what troubled him, and she chose not to follow her mother's advice or pry. After all, she did not know him as a wife knew a husband, at least not yet, and she dared not attempt such a role.

For all her father's wishes, Estora wondered if the king would accede to the proposal of marriage. He had held off this long, and though an alliance with Coutre Province made all the political sense in the world, he was also known for being unpredictable.

It strengthened her suspicion that someone else had caught the king's fancy—no, not the rumors going around about a mistress in Hillander, but someone closer by, or at least close enough to retain his interest. It was either a well guarded secret affair, or totally unrequited. Otherwise, court gossip would have revealed the source of his interest long ago.

The notion intrigued her, and though she was an excellent observer, she couldn't pinpoint exactly who it was that had captured his heart.

She decided she liked King Zachary very much if he was the sort of man who chose not to marry immediately out of political expediency, and despite the consequences, chose to listen to his heart. Estora decided she envied whoever that other woman was, and wondered if the king himself realized his heart was stolen.

She smiled.

Just then, dimly, faintly, the bell down in Sacor City struck out the hour.

Mara's pounding heart stoked the fire within her and pressed it outward. She wore fire like her own skin, and its burning brought joy amid her fear. She delved deep inside for that vast, untouched reservoir of power, and drew it forth.

She molded a ball of flame in her hands. It pulsed like a heart bloated with blood. It pulsed in sync with her own heart.

She threw the ball of fire. It exploded on the wraith's chest. To Mara's dismay, the wraith absorbed the fire into itself, extinguishing it. The fire within her dampened, a great cold seeping through her veins.

The wraith drew his sword. The blade gleamed a sickly green.

"We have taken from those such as you before." The wraith's voice slithered through every crack and fissure of the old wooden building. "See it."

The blade glimmered with images. It had taken many lives. It had been forged with the screaming souls of thousands; thousands who fled from their villages before the dark ones and their minions, only to be struck down, innocents and warriors alike.

One was singled out from thousands, a man—a Green Rider in ancient garb—his fire bled from him by wraiths who placed their hands on him. The Rider screamed.

Mara's scream echoed his. Her brooch cried out in an agonized wail within her. *Memory.*

Only the fire blazing between them kept the wraith from advancing on her. It crackled as it fingered Karigan's bed. The straw mattress exploded into flame.

Mara perspired not from her own inner fire, but from the heat of the ordinary fire. Her limbs had gone cold.

"We have taken many such as you." The wraith's voice was not boastful or angry. It was dead, toneless.

Mara backed away from the fire trying to recall her own inner fire. Moonstone crystals blazed on the table beside her.

"We seek," the wraith said, "the Galadheon."

Ancient enemy. The thought came unbidden to Mara. These creatures had destroyed too many lives. Not just lives, but *souls.* Anger heated her blood once again.

She coughed on the suffocating smoke that filled Karigan's room.

"You will tell us," the wraith said.

The flare of the moonstone crystals gave Mara hope. She scooped them into her hand. In her other hand, the one with the missing fingers, a new ball of fire formed. She flung it not at the wraith, but behind it.

White-gold flame splashed against the doorframe. The fire fed hungrily on the old wood. She threw a second orb through the doorway into the corridor beyond, cutting off the wraith's escape. She might not be able to harm it directly with her powers, but the fire that burned around it appeared to be another thing. She heard its hiss above the hiss of flame.

The wraith tried to advance, but was stopped by the fire between them. It turned this way and that, seeking escape, its cloak swirling.

Mara threw more orbs of fire at the walls. It consumed Karigan's books; sped across the rafters. The old barracks building groaned as though mortally wounded.

The wraith stuck its hands through flame reaching for Mara. In one last desperate measure, she flung the moonstone crystals at it. They cascaded through the flame, glittering and beautiful, a shower of light and color. Then they vanished behind the veil of flame.

The wraith wailed; a wail like the shrieking of a thousand souls. It was echoed by another outside.

The wraith's hands withdrew into flame and burned.

Mara choked on smoke so dense she could no longer make out her surroundings. She smelled burning hair, burning flesh, and realized it was her own. Her inner fire could not protect her from the outer.

The fire surrounded her, but behind her she knew was the window that looked out over the pasture; the view Karigan so favored.

The wraith crept closer. "We seek the Galadheon."

Laren stood stricken, unable to react. Icy cold. A spell? She tried to shout for help, but where once her voice was strong and sure, it now failed her.

She smelled smoke, and tore her eyes from the wraith. An orange glow flooded the pasture side of barracks.

Fire!

A howl sounded from within. The dark one stopped its advance and threw its head back and loosed a scream in answer. Laren scrunched her eyes closed and covered her ears, trying to block the sound.

When the cry died, she opened her eyes. The wraith was gone.

Flames poked through the roof of barracks, smoke pouring out black and thick.

She had stood frozen in place with her fear of the wraith, but now she shook it off—barracks was burning.

Glass smashed on the pasture side of the building. Laren ran toward the sound and found a figure on the ground, trying to get up, and falling back down. It was on fire.

Laren tore off her cloak as she ran to aid the—it was a woman. A Green Rider? Karigan?

A Rider, yes, Laren saw. Mara, not Karigan.

Mara crawled atop glass shards that shimmered in a golden, fractured reflection of the fire. The Rider was on fire, and it was spreading.

Laren threw her cloak on Mara to smother the flames.

A Weapon appeared, running down the corridor. He spoke rapidly with the woman presently guarding the king.

"What is it?" the king asked.

At once the Weapons started hustling him down the corridor. "Trouble on the castle grounds, sire."

"Come, Lady Estora," the first Weapon commanded.

Another Weapon appeared from nowhere, as they were apt to do, and shepherded Estora down the corridor after King Zachary.

Before long she found herself in the west wing, in the private apartments of the king, being escorted past all the portraits of Sacoridia's monarchs; the very place she had wished to avoid.

"I want to know what is happening," King Zachary informed the third Weapon as he strode toward his apartments.

"Yes, sire. We shall tell you when we know more."

As Estora followed the king into his inner sanctum, Weapons appeared from the very cracks and corners of the corridor, falling in behind to provide a rear guard. She peered over her shoulder and counted twelve, then thirteen, and fourteen. Thick pile carpet silenced their purposeful strides.

"Come, my lady," the Weapon who escorted her said in a firm but courteous tone. She cupped her elbow in her hand to hurry her along.

Soon they spilled into the king's parlor. Four Weapons remained inside with them, quickly taking places along opposite walls. The others withdrew, closing the thick doors as they did so. The king helped her into a comfortable armchair. Finally she allowed herself to take a couple of deep breaths.

The king sat opposite her, crossing his long legs. He tapped his fingers on his armrest. The terrier laid down obediently at his feet.

"I've felt uneasy all evening," he murmured, "as though something were about to happen."

A sleepy-eyed servant brought them some steaming tea. Estora sipped hers gratefully, feeling weary. It had turned into a long night and the energy that had sent her strolling around the castle in the first place was thoroughly drained.

It was quiet in the king's parlor, except for the occasional panting of the terrier. The thick stone walls and heavy doors muted all else. Caught up in his own thoughts, the king stared into his teacup as if he could divine what was occurring outside.

Estora's mother would be appalled she didn't initiate some form of polite conversation to distract the king from his worry. *It is an art form,* her mother had explained. Estora's father in turn would be furious she didn't use this opportunity to cultivate the king's interest with her charm. King Zachary, however, did not strike her as the sort of man to put up with such inane chatter.

And certainly not now.

No, not the way he sat engrossed in his own thoughts. He would not take kindly to an intrusion just now.

Instead, she kept her peace, taking in her surroundings. The last time she had been in the west wing with her cousin, they had visited the king in a different, more formal parlor.

This one was remarkable for its lack of armament as decor. Over the hearth hung a maritime scene—not a battle, but a fully rigged ship with sails bent in a rigorous sea. Another painting depicted a scene of Hillander terriers at hunt. She always imagined men of power displaying warlike ornament throughout their private quarters as well.

Battle tapestries sewn by the nimble and graceful hands of ladies. Her own needlework was very fine and precise.

She liked the king's private parlor, with its heavy leather chairs and the dark colors and hunting scenes, but it still seemed odd that it lacked weaponry or any hint of Zachary's position as king.

Then she recalled her own father's manor house. All the public areas frequented by visitors did exhibit the usual display of power. Yet he allowed her mother to govern the family quarters. There was only a hint of battle in the decor when some ancestor figured in a prominent way.

King Zachary smiled as he noticed her wandering gaze. "Has something caught your eye?"

"No. Well, actually, yes. You've no shields or swords hanging about."

He patted his leg and the terrier leaped onto his lap. He scratched the dog's belly, much to its evident delight. "You should have seen it during my grandmother's reign." He rolled his eyes. "The place looked like an armory."

Estora had been too young to remember much about Queen Isen, but she had heard stories about the strong-willed woman.

"I prefer things that do not remind me of war." He fell silent, rubbing the dog more thoughtfully. "I guess I surround myself with things that remind me of why I continue in my role as king."

She looked more closely at the room. Fine glass vases from Oldbury Province adorned the mantel. One was filled with seashells from the coast. A wall hanging depicted the hills that gave Hillander Province its name. As she looked more closely, she found examples of artistry from numerous provinces, or expressions of those provinces in one form or another. This was a man who truly took pride in his homeland.

Estora had known this about the king, of course. She had seen him ready to sacrifice his own life to preserve Sacoridia. She simply had not expected to see it manifest in such an artful way.

A knock preceded the entrance of a Weapon, who knelt before the king.

"Report," Zachary said.

"Excellency, an intruder—some say two—slipped onto the castle grounds, slaying three soldiers to get in. The guard is mobilized here and in the city, searching. We're also searching the castle."

"This is terrible," the king murmured. "You will give me word when the intruders are captured?"

"Yes, Excellency." The Weapon hesitated before adding, "There's more."

King Zachary raised an eyebrow. "More?"

"Yes. Rider barracks is burning."

The terrier jumped to the floor as Zachary stood, his expression incredulous. Estora stayed her seat as though turned to stone.

"It cannot be saved," the Weapon said, "and at least one Rider burns within."

⋙ SPURLOCK ⋘

Weldon Spurlock had worked very late this night, though not as long as some of his clerks to whom he gave extra files as he left. They were not permitted to retire for the night until they completed the tasks he had set for them.

When he stepped onto the castle grounds, instead of finding the usual sleepy, quiet atmosphere he was accustomed to, he found soldiers running this way and that shouting into the night, bearing torches or lanterns and weaponry. It was like watching hundreds of crazed, oversized fireflies darting about. Had invaders marched on the castle?

He heard words of a fire, and smelled smoke upon the air. Dodging soldiers, he drifted in the direction of the most frenzied shouting, and the smoke thickened noticeably. Before he was even upon Rider barracks, he could see the flames shooting out the windows and quickly consuming the aged wood.

He was surprised the thing hadn't burned down years ago. After all, it would have taken only a careless moment with a candle, and there you were. He snorted in contempt. *Let the Green Riders burn.*

Before he was coerced into joining the bucket brigade, he scuttled out of the way of all the activity, cursing that his clothing would be replete with the stench of smoke. He'd have to air it out best he could in his cramped room down in the city. More soldiers loaded down with buckets ran past as he grumbled about the inconvenience of smoky garments.

Then death stepped from shadow. It dropped the stabbed corpse of a guard. Its dead eyes seized on Spurlock, and advanced on him.

"I seek the Galadheon."

Spurlock's insides liquefied. His tongue became too big for his mouth. He thought he was probably going to faint, hopefully before the thing killed him.

"I seek the Galadheon."

Spurlock's scrambled mind processed the statement, but barely. It was looking for that Rider?

"M-m-message errand," he said. "G-gone. Pl-please don't kill me."

The creature's expression did not alter. It simply raised its knife for the death blow.

"No!" Spurlock cried. He raised his hands and averted his face from the blade. Where were all those soldiers when he needed them?

When the blow didn't come, Spurlock peered back at the creature. It was gazing at the palm of his hand.

My tattoo?

"Lord Mornhavon's sigil," the creature said in its flat voice.

Spurlock looked at his tattoo as if seeing it for the first time. The wraith was looking for the *Galadheon,* not the G'ladheon. It occurred to him that this creature might have actually come from Blackveil.

Gathering his courage, he licked his lips and said in the imperial tongue, *"Urn oren veritate?"* Where do you come from?

"The north," it replied.

Spurlock shook at its icy tone, but it had understood

him. On impulse, he withdrew his ancestral medallion from beneath his collar.

"I—I support the empire. My ancestor—he was a general and—"

To his astonishment, the creature had gone to its knee with head bowed.

"Command me," it grated.

Just like that? He thought of a few junior clerks he'd like to introduce to this creature, and— Then he recognized the crown on its head. He had seen sketches of it in the records he protected for Second Empire.

"You are, er, were, Varadgrim," he said, "Lord of the North."

"Command me."

How extraordinary. This creature had been one of Emperor Mornhavon's own lieutenants, one among the four Sacor Clan lords he had recruited to his side. And now it was bowing to him?

Spurlock's head raised a little higher, and he smiled. It was as it should be. Yes, he was meant to be a leader, he was meant to usher in a new era where the empire reigned again.

"You must tell me," he said, "how my people and I can bring about the arising of the glory of the empire."

The answer was not what he expected. "Bring the Galadheon. To Blackveil. To our master."

Journal of Hadriax el Fex

Just when we think we have the upper hand in this endless war, we lose a battle. The clans have learned how to use their own mages in battle, and even bring their women to fight because we have decimated so many of their men. At first we laughed, but these women are fierce, fierce with a sharpness that frequently exceeds even that of the men. I am reminded of how wild creatures will defend their young, holding back nothing, all fangs and claws. We have taken so much from them, everything but their will, and they fight as though they've naught to lose.

Alessandros cannot abide one of these women in particular. She goes by the name of Lil Ambriodhe, and she leads a band of riders who have been essential messengers to the clans. She even leads them into battle. They have minor art, but it has been enough to foul Alessandros' plans more than once.

Now there is also word that the clans have found a king among them. They fashion him a high king, to lead the clans in unity. It was the efforts of Santanara, the lord of the Elt in the lands north, who coaxed the clans to begin working together, so they may fight in concert.

⋙ COBWEBS ⋘

Karigan lay face down on the scrubby ground, gasping and shivering. Remembering the last time she had been caught in the traveling and left in a faded-out state, she touched her brooch to ensure she was solid and real. She was.

But so *cold.* And there was the killer headache.

She pushed herself onto her knees, grimacing as each movement made her headache pound with new ferocity. Warmth. She needed to get warm.

She guessed the traveling had left her off in her own time, in the same location where she had separated from Lil. At least, she hoped it was her own time. Even so, it meant her tinder box was with Condor, many miles away at Watch Hill.

She needed a fire, even if it meant rubbing sticks together for the remainder of the night. She forced herself to her feet and staggered about, searching in the light of the moon for dead wood.

Was it her imagination, or did her breath fog the air? Her left arm was so numb as to be useless. By the time she had accumulated a pile, she was nearly senseless. She slumped next to the pile of wood, and closed her eyes.

No, came a tiny cry from within. To sleep would be her death.

But she was already submerging into darkness.

403

*   *   *

Her body rocked back and forth with violence, and unwillingly she was thrust from the embrace of blissful sleep into the world. She cried out and flung her hand as if to catch herself from falling.

Warm breath blew in her face.

Her eyes fluttered open to horse nostrils just inches from her own nose, making her cross-eyed.

"Condor," she murmured, and she closed her eyes to go back to sleep.

He clamped his teeth on the collar of her shortcoat and started shaking her.

Karigan finally came to enough to realize what was happening. "Stop, boy! Stop!"

He released her collar, and turned his head so he could watch her with one big brown eye. She reached with a quavering hand to stroke his nose.

Somehow he had found her. Somehow he had, of his own volition, left Watch Hill to come after her. And somehow he had the sense to arouse her out of a sleep from which she otherwise would not have awakened.

Later, she would take time to marvel over all that, and the traveling, too, but in the meantime, she was still freezing. She grasped the stirrup hanging down from Condor's saddle and hauled herself to her feet, then searched through the saddlebags and found her tinder box.

Once she had a roaring fire going, she wrapped herself in her bedroll, and sat before the fire, shivering uncontrollably as though she were caught in a raging blizzard, rather than sitting beneath the moon on a pleasant summer evening.

She kept feeding the fire until inevitably her eyes drooped and she dozed off. This time it was not a sleep of death.

*   *   *

Condor's soft whicker woke Karigan. Sibilant whispers hissed from the darkness beyond the dying embers of her campfire. She sat up with a start and the whispers hushed like a sharp intake of breath. Blinking blearily, trying to shake off sleep, she felt the ground around her for her sword, groping vainly at grass and twigs.

She peered into the darkness. Nothing. Nothing, but the grayish hulk that was Condor, the orange liquidy reflection of the fire shining in his eyes. His ears twitched attentively.

Crickets chorused, their song rising and falling like a quickened pulse, then silencing, only to begin again in a rush.

She gazed into the woods, discerning nothing, but before her groggy mind thought to stoke up the fire, she found herself ringed by tall figures of shadow, the spade-shaped tips of their arrows glancing in the moonlight.

Karigan's heart thundered. Each arrow was aimed at her.

A voice threaded from the dark, soft and musical, in a language she did not understand, but one she thought she knew.

She licked dry lips. Trying to hold her voice steady, she asked, "Are you *tiendan?*"

The other stopped speaking. Silence.

Moments passed. Did the archers tauten their bow strings? They seemed not to move.

Then one silver arrowtip streaked downward like a falling star, and one of the figures advanced.

A tall, slender woman stood over her. Karigan couldn't quite make out her features, but the moon gleamed on ghostly, flaxen hair pulled back into numerous tightly woven braids. Snowy feathers bound into the braids rustled with the subtle movement of air. She wore the unusual milky armor Karigan had seen on Telagioth.

She climbed to her feet, all too conscious of the

surrounding arrowtips following her movement. The woman was stillness itself, but finally she spoke.

Her voice was songlike, though it did not speak in friendly greeting. It spoke in quiet command, but Karigan did not understand the words.

"I'm Karigan G'ladheon," she said, interrupting the Eletian. "King's messenger, Green Rider."

Silence.

She wondered if they understood her.

The woman spoke to those who ringed them. Arrowtips lowered to a less threatening position.

Glittering eyes surveyed Karigan, and she was aware of her blanket fluttering against her leg, of the cold that still numbed her limbs.

"Your name is known in the Alluvium," the woman said. Her voice was not quite cold, but neither was it welcoming.

Karigan and the woman regarded each other at length.

Another of the Eletians spoke and the woman responded quietly to him, her eyes never straying from Karigan. She released the tension of her bowstring, and to Karigan she said, "You will come with us."

"I—"

The Eletian raised her palm to her lips. Moonlight pooled there, and she blew. A cloud of silvery sparkling motes of dust billowed into Karigan's face, and after that, she was unsure of what happened next.

When Karigan came back to herself, she was sitting cross-legged in a clearing of emerald grasses, the dawn raising a golden mist from stark white birches that ringed the clearing, their branches knit together like a net. Glimmerings of crystalline light winked among the birches, some close, some far off, deep in the woods. They were like a galaxy of stars, silvery amid gleaming leaves.

Moonstones.

Karigan shook her head for her mind was layered with a complex interweaving of cobwebs she could not seem to break through.

Moonstones and Eletians . . .

The Eletians had brought her to the clearing. It was an assumption, not a memory.

Why?

Were they just going to leave her here? Was she a captive, and if so, why? The one who had spoken to her—last night?—had said her name was known. What did that mean?

Eletians emerged from the woods as though the slender birches had come to life, arrows once again nocked. They did not step into the clearing, but rather stood in the fringes of the woods. She tried to discern them, but the color of their attire shifted with their stance, blending them in with their surroundings.

One did step into the clearing—the woman. Her armor, too, changed color subtly in the light with the iridescence of a hummingbird. Her flaxen braids gleamed brightly in the daylight, the snowy feathers drifting behind her as she walked. Her eyes were as emerald as grass newly grown in the spring. She was beautiful, but exotically so. And she possessed an edge, cold and dangerous.

She carried her longbow with a full quiver of arrows strapped over her shoulder. Girded at her side was a long, narrow blade.

The Eletian simply looked down at Karigan, her expression hard to read. Was it haughty? Searching? Disinterested?

"Yes, we are *tiendan*," the Eletian said, as if no time had elapsed since Karigan's query.

Angry at having been dragged from her campsite, horse, and her own concerns without explanation, Karigan tried to stand, but the cobwebs that clouded her mind confused her, and she could not rise.

"Why have you brought me here?" she asked.

The Eletian did not answer. She circled Karigan looking her over, evaluating her, making her feel like a beast in a zoo.

The wrath built so within her that her face flushed with heat. "I am a king's messenger, and your interference will find only ill will with my king. Laws protect Green Riders—"

"Your laws hold no power over us, and the regard of your king no meaning."

A rush of angry retorts surged into Karigan's mind, but before she could open her mouth to speak them, the Eletian drew her blade and knelt before Karigan.

Karigan's angry words scattered like ashes before a wind. The blade was of the same gleaming steel as the arrowheads, perfect and radiating cold light in the dawn's golden glow. Would the Eletian slit her throat or stab her in the heart before she could take another breath?

The Eletian slashed, ripping through her left sleeve, but not her flesh.

Karigan looked at her unhurt, exposed shoulder in disbelief. The slash revealed a tiny scar, like a cold white puncture wound.

The Eletian, hesitantly, touched it with her fingertip. Warmth, brief and fleeting, flowed inward from her touch. Something twitched within Karigan, and she shifted uncomfortably.

A vertical line appeared between the Eletian's eyebrows. She glanced sideways at Karigan. Concern? Fear? Surprise?

"Please," Karigan said. "I—"

The Eletian drew her palm to her lips and blew. Karigan faded into a haze of sparkling dust motes gone golden with the sun.

⇜ MIRROR OF THE
MOON ⇝

Karigan sat cross-legged in the night. As far as she could tell, she hadn't moved since—since her last awareness. But now a cloak draped her shoulders and kept her warm. It was of a soft weave, almost more a membrane of skin than cloth, with veins of green like a leaf.

Moonstones still shone among the trees, casting light into the clearing. No Eletians stood within sight, but they had left her food, laid out on platters like a feast amid the stars. She sniffed the contents of a flask and sipped. A warming fluid, like a fine liquor, spread throughout her body, chasing away the last chill of the traveling. It invigorated her and lifted her spirits.

She unfolded her legs, surprised they were not cramped from sitting this way for—for however long it had been. Minutes? Hours? Days? She ate of the wild roots, berries, and honey cakes. She had not realized how famished she was. She drank deeply of the flask, which never seemed to empty.

Her stomach content, she strode to the edge of the clearing. Her prison? She shook and rattled the interwoven limbs of birch trees, but they would not part.

Wish I had an ax.

She tried to crawl beneath tree limbs, but the tangle of brush stopped her, and so it was with the entire circumference of the clearing. She doubted an ax would be of much use, after all.

She placed her hands on her hips, wanting to know what the Eletians intended, but she supposed there was nothing she could do about it but wait and see how it would all play out, at their whim. There was no telling why they deemed it necessary to confine her.

As if I'm a threat!

If they wanted to talk to her, they needn't have imprisoned her in this clearing, a pretty prison though it was.

Too much had happened already. The traveling rushed back to her and she pressed her hand across her midsection, but felt no remnant of an arrow wound, only the memory of it, which remained powerful.

She paced around the clearing, going over the events of Watch Hill in her mind. By some strange fate, she had witnessed Lil Ambrioth's rescue of Hadriax el Fex. She had ridden with the First Rider.

Karigan had a strong sense of a story left incomplete and wondered if she would ever know the true outcome. Had Lil survived her arrow wound? Did she get to see her king again? Had Hadriax el Fex's information played a part in the actual demise of Mornhavon the Black?

Tree limbs parted before her and the Eletian woman emerged from the woods. Gone were her weapons and armor. She now wore a long dress that wrapped her with the hues of the ocean, all foamy greens and blues. Her hair, freed of the confining braids, flowed down her back in fluid waves.

Karigan stiffened under her appraising gaze.

"You are well?" the Eletian asked.

"When will I—?"

The Eletian raised her hand to silence her. "I know there is much you must wonder at. You will find answers soon enough."

"Where's my horse?" Karigan demanded, not willing to give in so easily.

"He is content." The reply was delivered with an ironic cant of an eyebrow.

"That's hardly an answer."

"Will it not satisfy you to know he is well?"

"Very little satisfies me at the moment."

The two stared at one another in a silent challenge, neither flinching.

Finally, without conceding, the Eletian said, "Come," and turned to leave the clearing, expecting Karigan to follow without question.

Karigan folded her arms and did not budge.

The Eletian paused, and truly mystified, asked, "Why do you not come?"

"Where are you taking me?"

The Eletian's features remained placid, but Karigan thought she detected a slight narrowing of eyebrows. *Good.*

"I am taking you to the king's son."

Karigan didn't bother to conceal her surprise.

"Yes, you shall see one whom no mortals have ever looked upon, Galadheon, for the prince, my brother, was born after the Cataclysm your kind calls the Long War, and the upheaval that followed."

"Why am I to see him?"

"Because there are things that must be spoken of."

Karigan frowned at the vague answer.

"You must follow." The Eletian turned back toward the woods, but still Karigan refused to obey.

This time, when the Eletian paused to see what was the matter, Karigan said, "I am not accustomed to accepting orders from anyone but my captain or my king."

The woman's eyes blazed with anger. "You are a guest among us." Then realizing how much it sounded like an accusation, she added, "Forgive my presumption, but it is not wise to keep the prince waiting."

If confinement was their idea of how to treat a guest, Karigan thought she'd hate to see how they treated a prisoner. "First," she said, "tell me your name."

The request startled the Eletian. "There is a reason you ask this?"

"It is a courtesy one extends to a *guest.* It seems you know who I am. It would only be courteous for you to tell me who you are."

Again, the eyes appraised her. "Very well. You may call me Grae."

Karigan nodded, satisfied by this one small victory.

The imprisoning trees lifted limbs to allow them passage. Karigan attempted no conversation with Grae, figuring there was no point. Eletians were more mystery than anything else, and Grae appeared more intent on obstructing her than helping her understand what this was all about.

Throughout the depths of the woods, moonstones glittered, turning white birches silver, their interwoven branches like stark spiderwebs. The effect was beautiful, and precisely the sort of thing she'd imagined when thinking of Eletians. Above, stars pierced the canopy of night with a painful clarity and closeness she had never known before. The constellations were familiar, yet at the same time foreign, as if slightly askew. She could not say if she was still within the bounds of Sacoridia, or if the Eletians had spirited her away to some netherworld of dream.

They emerged into another clearing, lit by the ever-present moonstones. Fair folk moved amid the clearing drinking and feasting, or so it seemed one moment, then the next they vanished away leaving no hint of their merrymaking, but for a goblet the prince held, as he sat upon a chair of woven tree boughs. His head was bowed as he listened to a woman singing at his feet.

Her voice was clear and pure, and the melody rent Karigan's heart with great sorrow, though she could not understand the words. When the song trailed off and the last notes hung in the night, the prince cupped the singer's chin in his hand. She rose and left him then, walking away with the light steps of a dancer.

The prince's hair was the same pale flax as his sister's, but his eyes were very different. While Grae's were the emerald of the forest, the prince's were the blue of a brilliant summer sky, and quite suddenly Karigan was shaken by images of another Eletian whose eyes had been strikingly similar.

The prince regarded her steadily, while Karigan stood paralyzed by the eyes of Shawdell.

"Ari-matiel Jametari," Grae introduced, "prince of Eletia."

The prince rose. No crown did he wear, no jewels, nor did he carry a scepter—nothing to indicate station or power. It was all in his bearing. He wore only a simple silvery-blue tunic tied with a cord about his waist, and loose trousers. He seemed to pull starlight to him and reflect it, so that it almost hurt Karigan's eyes to look upon him.

His contempt, however, was plain to see, his scrutiny worse than Grae's, for now Karigan felt herself not only an object to be viewed, but an object of disdain.

"If there is a reason you have brought me here," Karigan said, "I'd like to hear it." As a representative of Sacoridia, her disrespect was inexcusable, but so was their haughty treatment of her, and the passing of each second drew her patience closer to its limit. Whether or not they called her a guest, she felt more like a criminal.

Those blue eyes met hers, proud and chilling. "I would see you for myself." His voice was a melodious echo of Shawdell's.

"Why?"

"You sent my son to his death."

"Shawdell."

"Yes." The prince stood there, his eyes holding her captive. Accusing her? Assessing her? Eletians were too unknown a quantity, their minds too alien for her to guess what went on there. Had she been brought before the prince for some form of judgment or retaliation?

The prince broke eye contact, returned to his chair, and sat. Then the blue eyes captured her again.

"Can you comprehend an eternal life, Galadheon?"

"No."

The prince nodded. "A wise response. Death is a rare occurrence among my kind, though once many died during the Cataclysm."

Karigan waited for the prince to accuse her of murdering his son, for ending an eternal life, but the words of accusation did not come. His eyes merely became great wells of grief, and this was accusation enough.

"What do you know of times past; of the times beyond what you call the First Age?" he asked.

His question took her off guard. "Very little."

"Your folk have not the long memories of mine," Prince Jametari said. "Yours is fragmented and faded by the discontinuity of mortal lives. Our folk have seen the building of mountains and the encroachment of ice, and its melting into the sea. We've seen the birth of stars and the gathering of moons. We've watched forests grow and spread."

Karigan realized she listened to a voice of the ages.

"The *tiendan* brought you to me not simply because you ended my son's life. That is of little matter at the moment. No, they brought you because there are things that must be said. Things of the past, things of the future." He tilted his head and the moonstones turned his eyes into tiny silver mirrors, and he smiled, mystery sealed behind his lips.

"You are not unknown to us, and not only for your vanquishing my son."

Telagioth emerged from the shadows of the clearing, and Karigan realized there were others of the *tiendan* standing along its perimeter in their milky armor. Spines protruded from the shoulders of one figure, and she shuddered.

Telagioth brought forward a translucent and delicate bowl. He held it reverently and said, "Greetings, Galadheon. So we do meet again."

"How did you know we would?"

Telagioth smiled. "The prince is most wise."

Prince Jametari left his chair and took the bowl from Telagioth. He sat cross-legged on the ground and placed it before him in the grass. He indicated with a gesture that Karigan should join him. Grae and Telagioth drifted away to the fringes of the clearing.

Karigan dropped to the ground beside the prince, the starlight that gathered around him hurting her eyes in such close proximity. She blinked and looked away, wishing he'd just get on with whatever he wanted to discuss, but she gathered that with Eletians, everything was a dance. A mystery.

"Our people are diminishing," the prince said. "The flames of our lives are on the brink of disappearing from *Everanen,* the Earth, for all time. We are in danger of becoming but echoes of memory in tales and song, among the mortals, who have spawned in great numbers across the lands. Our decline began long ago.

"First we shall speak of the past, so you might understand our plight." His expression fell distant as though he traveled in a daydream. "In the time before your counted ages, preceding even the Black Ages, Eletians were the power of *Everanen.* It was our age, for the element of magic, which flows from all living things, was plentiful. We understood it, and harnessed it for good.

"Mortalkind, the bestial beings they were in those days, revered and feared us for it, though they, too, possessed rudimentary skills with magic, but did not recognize it as such. Abilities to heal or foretell the weather were seen as the works of their gods, not as something that came from within. Never did we expect your kind to grow in strength and knowledge—and cunning. We underestimated your ambition.

"And thus came the Black Ages, with war upon the Eletians, and the wars the mortal tribes committed upon one another. Truly we wished mortalkind would exterminate itself, but we also underestimated the tenacity of your kind, your will to survive and exist.

"Amid the turmoil of those years, Mornhavon came from across the sea."

Grae and Telagioth approached again, bearing a tall fluted vessel with twin handles fashioned into vines, made of the same translucent material as the bowl. They passed the vessel to the prince.

He unstoppered it and said, "Herein lies what remains of what your folk called *Indura Luin* of old, the Mirror of the Moon."

"The Lost Lake," Karigan murmured, wonder overcoming some of her apprehension. "It truly existed?"

"Yes. Before Mornhavon drained the lake, Fraleach the Long-bough was able to preserve a little of it in this very vessel. One of our great poet-warriors was he, of a time when words were more than mere language."

The prince tilted the vessel and water streamed into the bowl with the crystalline, cutting essence of starlight. Karigan was not sure, but she thought she could see a separate shimmer of movement within the flowing water, half-formed images striving to emerge and take on lives of their own. Even as the water flowed, a thin mist began to veil the perimeter of the clearing, turning the *tiendan* who stood there into formless shadows.

Prince Jametari was precise and careful not to let the water dribble or splash. When the last precious drop plunked into the bowl, sending out rings on the surface, he set the vessel aside.

"According to legend," Karigan said, "if one pure of heart gazed into *Indura Luin* during a full moon, he or she could speak with the gods.

"Your gods are not ours, and I cannot speak for the authenticity of your legends. The lake, however, did possess properties as ancient as anything of this Earth. Eletians held great reverence for it, as did your folk long ago, which is why Mornhavon drained it. We still mourn its demise.

"Perhaps your folk construed its powers as the works of gods. It was Laurelyn-touched, thus blessed in its own way. We Eletians need not a full moon to find our reflection in the water. And now I place it before you, Galadheon, the last remnant of *Indura Luin,* for within its waters lies your reflection."

The water lay still and concave, its surface silvery, reflecting bright points of moonstone light.

"Our forests were broken by the surge of mortalkind and their destructions," the prince continued. His hands moved gracefully as he spoke. "Our own kind splintered alliances and scattered. Because of this, there is no love of our people for yours. We became what we are now, dwellers of an Earth dominated by mortals, a quaint mystery for your historians to ponder."

As he spoke, the mist wafted about the clearing and trees, moonstone light dimming and brightening with its passing. Karigan fancied she could make out shapes forming in the mist.

"Our numbers diminish," the prince said. "Children are a rare joy among a long-lived race, and many of those who were eldest were slain in the Cataclysm or sleep the great sleep. Whether or not they shall awaken, no one can tell."

He spoke of Eletians, weary of their eternal lives, who lay upon the ground and fell into a sleep of unknown depth. Those who awakened returned to the world. Those who did not became part of *Everanen,* part of the living soul of the Earth.

"The souls of those who choose never to awaken become the hearts of great trees, and they reach for the heavens."

A vision of saplings sprouting from the water's surface took hold. They grew into tall, magnificent trees, their boughs swaying in a breeze. Karigan blinked rapidly, and in a single swift moment the vision was gone.

"Since the Cataclysm," the prince said, "the magic of *Everanen* has diminished to almost nothing, further endangering Eletians. This element that you call magic is essential to our existence. As a tree is the expression of sun and rain, so are the Eletians an expression of magic. Without it, we shall die. We are a fragment of what our race once was, and there is little hope of our recovering unless magic is restored in great strength."

"I don't understand why you are telling me this," Karigan said. It was all quite interesting, and she felt bad for the Eletians, but what did it have to do with her?

"Because you are an influence upon the future of Eletians."

"What? That's impossible." Karigan looked to Grae and Telagioth for confirmation, but they offered none. Grave and silent, they stood at the edge of the clearing, like statues carved of starlight and mist.

"Allow me to continue the tale," the prince said, "so you may understand. Beyond the D'Yer Wall remains a vast reservoir of wild magic."

Yes. Karigan thought back. *That is what Shawdell was after when he breached the wall.*

"Wild magic is the base essence of all magic. It is that from which all other magics arise. Why this reservoir of magic should remain in *Kanmorhan Vane,* the Blackveil Forest, while magic has not recovered otherwise, is little understood. Perhaps the wall has contained and thus preserved that magic, while after the Long War, magic died off on this side of the wall. Perhaps a remnant of Argenthyne preserves it."

"Argenthyne," Karigan murmured. "It truly existed?"

"You who have been touched by the favor of Laurelyn doubt it?" The prince raised his eyebrows, surprised. "Argenthyne was our people's greatest enclave, and Laurelyn its queen and guardian."

As he spoke, a city of slender spires amid a forest grew from the water in the bowl. Karigan leaned forward marveling at the city, at fountains glistening in gardens and an eagle riding the winds above. An almost-transparent palace, made of the substance of light, soared above the rest of the city, and she knew with certainty that this would have been Laurelyn's moonbeam castle of legend. A cluster of stars and a silver moon hung above it all, leaving the spires aglow in the night. It was a place of living beauty.

Movement caught her peripheral vision, and when she looked up, she gasped. Like an echo of the images in the water, the mist around the clearing uncoiled and undulated, creating phantom figures and buildings, and even a courtyard fountain. The images were without definition or sharp edges, and wavered and billowed as natural breezes carried the mist away. She heard distant chiming voices and she had the sense of being within the courtyard, of being caught in another place and time, or maybe in a dream.

"Argenthyne," Prince Jametari whispered, shaking his head. "Lost Argenthyne. Mornhavon and his legions took it, a blow from which we shall never recover."

The eagle above the water wheeled away and dissipated into the night. The bright city muted and tarnished. Vegetation choked the fountains, which became foul and sludgy. Thorny vines grew over and entangled the gardens, and spires crumbled and toppled. Laurelyn's castle faded from sight.

The mist around them turned leaden, and the fair figures and images melted away, replaced by crooked branches that rattled like old knucklebones. Karigan shrank away as they loomed above her as blackened skeleton hands, ready to grasp her. At the last moment, they lost form and drifted away.

The vision of the city floating above the Mirror of the Moon vanished completely, leaving only the placid bowl of water.

At the loss of such beauty, a tear ran down Karigan's cheek and hung from the end of her chin. The prince reached over and caught it in his palm before it could sully the Mirror of the Moon. The teardrop looked like a pearl in his hand.

"A great sorrow the loss of Argenthyne has been to us," he said. "One among many. There is hope, however, that there is some goodness left there, even in the heart of *Kanmorhan Vane.* Maybe some of that goodness leavens the dark that taints the wild magic now leaking through the wall."

"The wild magic is leaking through the wall . . ."

"Yes. You are aware of unusual events happening in the lands?"

She nodded.

"It is wild magic. I believe the awakening of dark powers on the other side of the wall has stirred the wild magic. You cannot expect an influx of pent-up magic not to have an effect in a world that has found its balance over a thousand years with very little."

It explained much, about what was happening to the abilities of the Riders, and everything else.

"War has ravaged us," the prince said, "and the loss of magic may finish us. And then there is you, Galadheon."

He reached over and touched the scar on her shoulder where Grae had slashed her sleeve. She jerked away, startled by the sudden contact, startled by the energy, the *power,* that coursed through her. Something recoiled inside her.

"Do you know what this scar resulted from?" he asked.

"I was attacked by—" She swallowed. "I was attacked by your son. With wild magic."

Prince Jametari nodded. "Tainted wild magic, which now resides within you."

"How do you know?" Karigan demanded. "I'm no different than I ever was. It didn't stay in me."

Prince Jametari tilted his head and it was plain he believed otherwise. "How is it, then, that you have surpassed the layers of the world to visit the past?" He searched her with his gaze, seeking the very depths of her soul. "You are one who journeys far, following roads that are impassable to all but a few."

"I don't know how it happens. The wild magic—not in me, but . . ." She felt feverish, wanting to disbelieve she'd been carrying tainted magic within herself for all this time. It made her feel unclean, like a poisonous serpent was hiding within her.

The prince watched her struggle with the concept before continuing. "The wild magic augments the slight ability you embody, in a way your brooch never could by itself. Alone, your brooch helps you to fade to the gray barriers of this world. Augmented by wild magic, it allows you to transcend the gray barriers into other layers."

Karigan clenched her hands. "I don't want this! I—" She looked about helplessly, knowing the prince must speak the truth, but not wanting to believe it. He gazed back at her unsympathetically. "How do I get rid of it? Can you help me?"

"It cannot be done."

Karigan's heart plummeted. The wild magic had mostly lain dormant, hadn't it? Was it only now becoming apparent because of the stirring on the other side of the wall? Had the same impulse that affected the other Riders awakened the wild magic within her?

"There is still more to be spoken of," the prince said, "and time grows short." He paused to see if she was ready, and then proceeded. "My people wonder what would happen should the D'Yer Wall fail completely, releasing all that power. Some hold it would bring ruin to all that lives; that the darkness of *Kanmorhan Vane* will rule this side of the world as well. Already it has aroused those who should never walk beneath the moon."

"The wraith—Varadgrim." Karigan shuddered with memory.

"Yes. And others. It is believed by those who envision this outcome that the Eletian people have not the strength to withstand an onslaught of tainted wild magic, and shall perish.

"There are others who hold that the wall's failure shall bring magic back into the world and restore the greatness of the Eletian people. They do not believe all the magic is tainted, and if the wall fails, the onrush of magic will cleanse *Everanen,* as a flood will cleanse a river valley and make it rich again. The Eletians will once again dominate a world now in the hands of mortalkind."

Karigan shifted her position, not at all liking the direction this was going. "You mean they hope an influx of wild magic will cleanse the lands of mortals."

The prince nodded. "They are of the mindset of my son. If a few mortals perish in the path of this flood, all the better."

His words chilled Karigan, and she wondered of which mindset *he* was: afraid the fall of the D'Yer Wall would mean destruction of all that was good, or hopeful it would bring about the restoration of the Eletian people.

"Bitterly this has been debated in the Alluvium," Prince Jametari said. "I fear that even the Eletian people can find no harmony on so important an issue. Our people fought hard to defeat Mornhavon the Black and his hordes, but there are those who are blinded by the needs of the present and future, who will not see the past. I am of a mind that both arguments are flawed, but only the future knows the truth. A future, Galadheon, in which you shall play a role."

Karigan definitely did not like the turn in conversation.

"Like my father, King Santanara, I've the gift of pre-science. This is not the first I've seen of you."

The sense of being caught in a dreamer's web threatened to overwhelm her.

"I have seen you interfere in the mending of the D'Yer Wall. Your actions may result in disaster across the lands, or hold off destruction for a time."

"N-no! You can't put this on me."

"I do not." The prince's voice was stern. "But the tainted wild magic has created a duality within you. I see the strands of life and time that weave fate, Galadheon, and you waver between the light and the dark."

Karigan jumped to her feet in a surge of anger. "How can you dare suggest I'd do ill?" She shook with emotion. "How dare you. I would never knowingly do anything to endanger the lands. Never!"

Grae and Telagioth were suddenly beside her. The *tien-dan* moved in closer. Light glanced off arrowheads, and it only incensed her more. When she stepped toward the prince to make another point, Grae and Telagioth grabbed her arms. She struggled wildly, spitting out words that would make even a cargo master blanch.

And then she was sitting calmly on the ground, and all was as it had been before.

What happened? Silver dust sparkled in the air around her. She shook her head to clear it. They may have controlled her outburst, but the fury still burned inside her.

"Would you hear more?" Prince Jametari asked.

Karigan narrowed her eyebrows but refused to answer.

"Very well. I have shared my vision in the Alluvium, and you should know it has placed you in some peril. There are those who feel your death would settle any question of how you might interfere with the mending of the wall."

Karigan's eyes darted to the fringes of the clearing searching for an arrow aimed at her heart, or a dagger glinting in the light of the moonstones, but the *tiendan* had withdrawn into the mist and she saw no weapons. Doubtless she was safe in the clearing with Prince Jametari, but when she left?

"There are others," the prince said, "who feel you have the potential to do much good, for you are touched with Laurelyn's favor.

"I cannot divine the future in absolutes. Visions do not work that way, nor does the future, which is always in motion, always affected by the influences of the moment."

"I don't want this," Karigan said, desperation creeping into her voice. "I don't want this wild magic. I don't want anything to do with Eletians. I never even wanted to be a Green Rider."

"So it is for those caught up in great events against their wills. It would not be the first time. For all this news, I have no remedy, just an offer—an offer for you to look in the Mirror of the Moon."

"Why?"

Prince Jametari blinked slowly, his long hands settling onto his thighs. "You would refuse a rare gift?"

"What would I see?"

"Perhaps the threads I have seen, or nothing. Perhaps you shall see loved ones, or yourself. I do not know. You have shown yourself wise in some of your words, and it is for you to determine whether or not to accept a gift freely given."

Karigan sighed wearily, both afraid and intrigued. If the mirror could show her something that might enlighten her to her own situation, it could prove helpful. But if the future was as fluid as the prince claimed, could she trust anything she saw in it?

After a few hesitant moments, she said, "All right, I'll try."

"You need but gaze in."

Karigan leaned over the bowl and looked into the silver water, and blinked back at herself. Enough time passed by in which nothing happened, that she nearly decided to pull away and give up, but then darkness spread in the bowl like a cloud of black ink. A man rippled into existence, staring back at her, a backdrop of night behind him. His hair was sandy, and he wore a pointed beard. They locked gazes.

She inhaled sharply in recognition. *Hadriax el Fex!* He looked far healthier, far stronger and unmarred, than when she had seen him on Watch Hill.

The prince hastily passed his hand above the bowl, dissolving the image. The water resumed its placid silver glow, a dash of stars sparkling over it.

"It is not good to call upon such images," he said. "Sometimes the mirror goes both ways. You may look again now."

She did, and immediately images came to life in the water. Her father sat at his office desk, writing in a ledger. He looked tired, but well. Quickly it flashed by, followed by another. Alton slept beside a wall—most certainly the D'Yer Wall. She was aware of the mist changing and taking on shapes along the clearing's edge, but she dared not take her eyes from the mirror, for Alton looked terribly ill. Circles had darkened beneath his eyes, and he perspired profusely, murmuring restlessly in his sleep. His cheeks were gaunt and pallid, and she was overcome by a sharp pang of concern.

The scene changed abruptly to a castle corridor where King Zachary walked with Old Brexley trailing behind. Lady Estora strolled beside him, conversing. She could almost hear their words, and the tolling of a bell . . . Then she saw Captain Mapstone standing in the night, the light of a fire dancing against her face.

A new scene unfolded, a scene of snow swirling against the night, and she sensed the mist around her mimicking it, setting the clearing in the middle of a maelstrom like a fine lady's snowglobe violently shaken. The storm's wind roared through tossing branches and flying snow—she thought she could feel the bite of it against her face. A figure trudged through the snow, hunched over as though badly wounded, on the brink of death.

The wind blew hair away from the figure's face revealing her identity. Karigan looked upon herself. She opened her mouth, but no words would form.

The figure in the vision glanced over her shoulder, and then pushed on with renewed determination as if she were being hunted.

Then the vision faded and the water turned to silver again. Karigan glanced up at the prince. What did the scene portend? How was she wounded? Would she die of it? When would this happen?

But the prince told her no secrets. Instead, he said, "It is not done. Look again into the mirror."

She did, but once again found only her reflection.

"No, look truly."

She drew closer, seeing herself peering back. Brown hair framed her face. Her features, an echo of her mother's, sagged a little in exhaustion. Otherwise, she looked much the same as she always had. The water simply reflected a Green Rider, the daughter of a merchant.

But as she gazed ever more deeply, she saw someone unable to admit how afraid and overwhelmed she was by the events flowing about her. She saw a young person caught up in grand things, shouldering weighty responsibilities. Perhaps too weighty.

Bright eyes reflected and counter-reflected. Those eyes had seen violence, and much that was strange and hurtful. With a heaviness of spirit, she realized a simple life as a merchant was truly lost to her.

She saw also her thin veneer of confidence that masked fear and fragility. There was so much on her small shoulders . . . Helping the Riders while leaderless, enduring supernatural visits by the First Rider, and travels to the past. And now there was all that the Eletian prince had told her. How could she carry such a burden? She had not the strength.

A current of self-doubt shook her. Her fears went deep, clutching at her heart. She feared losing her father, her one remaining parent and the foundation of her character. If anything happened to him, she would be alone in the world.

Alone . . .

She feared meeting terrors in the night, cloaked in shadows, that spoke her name. She feared for Alton, having seen his condition, and for all the Riders. She feared losing any one of them.

And she feared love. Love that would pass, unfulfilled.

Finally, she feared changes wrought across her homeland should the darkness of Blackveil persevere.

Fear, she realized, propelled her forward, not courage, and certainly not just duty to king and country. Fear.

The mirror had peeled away all her self-perceptions,

laid them raw and bare. She did not see the portrait of a confident and duty-bound Green Rider, but someone she did not like to acknowledge, someone with much to fear.

It was all there in the mirror, cradled in a fragile bowl, the essence of what drove Karigan G'ladheon, a young, frightened woman caught up in events greater than herself.

She passed her hand over her eyes. Only a patchwork of threads held her together.

"Galadheon," Prince Jametari said in a prophetic voice, "You shall hear Westrion's wings brush the air. To live, you must first die."

Birds chattered away and whistled in the branches above Karigan's head. The morning sun glistened on dew-laden leaves. She found herself sitting cross-legged next to a long-cold campfire, her hands on her knees. Had she been dreaming sitting up? Dreaming of a fanciful visit with Eletians?

The strange membranous leaf cloak, dappled with gems of dew, remained draped over her shoulders.

Not a dream, then.

She shook her head and cobwebs fell from her mind. Condor watched her from the fringe of the woods, grass sticking out the corners of his mouth.

Karigan stood and stretched, the membranous cloak dissipating like a mist from her shoulders. Just another oddity to add to her growing list.

"So, where've you been all this time?" she asked her horse.

He dropped his nose back to the grass to graze.

Eletians may have their mysteries, she thought, but at least some things never changed.

~ ILL NEWS ~

Karigan rode Condor at a slow jog, he tossing his head and anxious for a run, but she was too preoccupied by all that had happened. She judged she had been away for two nights, but caught in the web of the Eletians, it could have been twenty. No matter how many nights it had been, Mara would be worried, and with good reason, for Karigan's ordinary message errand had turned out to be anything but.

She darted glances up and down the road, and peered into the woods that bordered it. She expected any moment to see an Eletian emerge from between the tree trunks with bow bent, a shiny arrowhead aimed for her heart.

How dare they? she fumed again and again. *How dare they threaten me just because they think I might interfere with the wall?*

Everything she stood for, everything she would ever endanger herself for, was for the safety of her homeland and life as she knew it. The Mirror of the Moon had shown her this much. She did not want the wall to fail. How dare the Eletians suggest otherwise?

I am not the enemy.

One niggling doubt chewed at the corners of her confidence. She wouldn't purposely do anything wrong, but what if—? What if she made some mistake, or accidentally—

Condor bucked, not hard enough to dislodge her, but enough to gain her attention.

"What?" she demanded.

He snorted and champed his bit.

"Oh." He still wanted to run, and maybe he had picked up on her anxiety. She clapped him on the neck. "You're right, my friend. Let's forget this nonsense and get home." She had much to tell King Zachary and Mara.

She nudged his sides and gave him rein, and he stretched into an easy lope that helped dispel her worries.

Feeling she needed to communicate her experiences to the king before anything else, she went directly to the castle, letting a servant lead Condor away to the stables. Her plan was thwarted, however, for the throne room was packed. It was public audience day.

The crowd spilled out of the throne room entrance and down the corridor. She had to push to enter, getting jostled and shoved, with curses spat at her.

Above the heads of others, she could just make out the king on the dais, his chin on his fist, eyes hooded. From all outward appearances he was calm, but Karigan wondered how he could be with all these people thronging the chamber.

She elbowed two men out of her way, and slipped ahead of them.

"Hey," one of the men protested, "wait yer turn." He made to grab her, but she jammed the heel of her boot into the meaty part of his foot, and worked her way forward, leaving behind his sharp cry of pain.

Another look toward the dais showed Sperren banging the butt of his castellan's staff on the floor, but it proved ineffectual in gaining anyone's attention for it could not be heard. Colin stood before the king, more in a protective stance than one to quiet people, his training as a Weapon taking precedence over his role of advisor. Quickly she surveyed the Weapons and guards on duty, and to a one, they watched the crowd with wary eyes, their stance taut.

Anxiety was thick in the air, and plain on the faces of several petitioners. A woman fainted away from the heat of so many bodies pressed together, and was carried away by her companion. Others quickly filled their space.

The words "uncanny," "strange," and "evil magic" muttered through the crowd. Even those who had come to the king seeking his wisdom on ordinary topics were picking up on the currents of anxiety.

Karigan saw the herald, Neff, trapped in an alcove not far from her. He wasn't exactly shrinking away from the crowd hemming him in but he certainly wasn't choosing to get into the thick of it either.

She changed course to reach him. If some measure of mastery over the crowd wasn't achieved, the petitioners would never be heard, and they'd grow more hot and frustrated until something set them off, and then there'd be danger—danger to the king, herself, and just about anyone else caught in the crush. In her estimation, the first thing needed was to quiet the crowd so the king and his advisors could get their attention.

She worked her way to Neff's side, perspiration beading on her forehead from the heat. Neff warily watched her approach.

She pointed at the horn he held protectively at his side. "Sound that thing!" She had to shout to be heard.

Neff's eyes widened. "Wha—?"

"Do it! Sound a flourish, or better yet, a cavalry charge."

"I can't just—"

She grabbed a handful of tabard and drew him close. "Do it, or things could get much worse in here."

"But the king—"

Karigan growled and tore the long horn out of his hands.

She drew it to her lips and blew. The sound it issued was akin to a dying cow.

Some in the crowd looked about in surprise and those around the alcove moved away, but it hadn't been enough to quiet all the people. The king peered in her direction, and when he caught sight of her, he nodded his approval.

Karigan drew the horn to her lips again, but Neff snatched it back. He gave her a long look of disgust that let her know exactly how appalled he was, then raised it to his lips and blared the cavalry charge in high-pitched blasts. Karigan had to cover her ears.

That had the desired effect—the crowd hushed in surprise.

"Order!" Sperren called out in a reedy voice that had already done too much shouting. "Order!"

The king rose from his throne chair and looked gravely upon the people. Before the babble could resume, he spoke.

"Citizens of Sacoridia—" His voice carried strong and sure through the throne room. He looked every bit the monarch, from his tall, square stance, to the sunlight shining on his fillet. "I am here today to listen to your petitions. In order to do so, your cooperation is required. A line will reform, no more than two wide."

Angry voices broke out, but the king raised his hand and they quieted. "I swear to you, I shall hear every last one of you. However, those who do not cooperate will be summarily dismissed." He nodded at the sergeant of the guard, and soldiers moved in to help organize the crowd into an orderly line. Some tempers flared, and those people were removed.

Karigan hesitated. She knew what she had to tell the king was important, but if she interrupted the public audience, she risked angering all those people again to a dangerous level. It took her but a moment to decide, and she strode toward the dais in the clearing space. She bowed before the king. While the petitioners were being organized into their line, she could at least have a quick word with him.

"Greetings, Rider," he said. "Your intervention is most appreciated. Perhaps Neff can give you some pointers on the playing of his horn." There was humor in his eyes, and she felt a blush creeping up her neck.

She cleared her throat, and said hastily, "I wanted to advise you, Your Majesty, that I had a most eventful message errand. Can we speak at the end of your public audience?"

"Of course, but you can see it will be hours." When she nodded, he said, "In the meantime, I should like you here at my side." He indicated the space where Captain Mapstone usually stood.

Karigan glanced up at him in astonishment. *"Me?"*

"I need you," he said, "especially the way today's audience has gone so far. You have proven yourself . . . creative." He smiled kindly. "I would appreciate your input as necessary."

Karigan did not have a chance to protest or plead her lack of wisdom for so important a role, for the king began hearing petitions. She stepped into Captain Mapstone's space to the right of the king's dais, hoping she did not look as small and foolish as she felt.

Soon her self-consciousness melted into interest. She found herself enjoying watching the king at work. His outward facade was unswerving and authoritative, his questioning of petitioners deft and pointed. His decisions were fair and efficient, a good thing considering the length of the line.

She especially liked watching the way he moved his hands when he spoke, and how he leaned forward to focus on whomever stood before the dais. She liked the way the sun lancing through the windows lightened his eyelashes . . .

He happened to glance at her just then and she caught

her breath. It was fleeting, but enough for her to see he was startled by her regard. Karigan shook herself and straightened her shoulders, and decided she ought to pay more attention to the proceedings.

To her vast relief, he seemed not to need her at all. That is, until the petitioners brought forth complaints of a stream flowing backward, a neighbor's hoe turning to gold, and a husband vanishing from plain sight. "What will you do?" they all implored the king. Karigan saw he was a little at a loss, and he beckoned her close to his side.

"Do you have any suggestions of what I might say about these magical happenings without panicking everyone?"

She supposed he asked her since she was a user of magic, but she had no magical answers, with the exception of the first.

"The stream the man is talking about is tidal, and when the tide goes out, it seems to reverse itself." She was glad of her coastal upbringing, and that she knew of such a stream, and had even played in one as a child.

The king questioned the man further, learning he was new to the coast and unfamiliar with the workings of the tides. It became evident that the talk of other strange events in the countryside led him to believe the stream out of the ordinary.

The other questions Karigan had to mull over for a few moments. From her recent conversation with Prince Jametari, she knew the disruptions of magic would continue until either the world found balance with the influx from Blackveil, or the D'Yer Wall was mended, effectively shutting it off. There was no easy way to explain this to these folk without causing the very mayhem the king wished to avoid.

"I would handle them as you would any other petition, in terms they understand," Karigan said, "since there isn't much we can do about the magic, except reassure them that we're looking into it."

When the king waited for further explanation, she added, "The fellow whose neighbor's hoe turned to gold? He's jealous. The woman whose husband vanished, well, she's now got eight children to provide for on her own. She is, in effect, a widow."

The king's features lightened. "I see what you're getting at."

And so, following her inspiration, he questioned the fellow further about the golden hoe. True to the word, he was jealous of his neighbor as much as he was upset by the magic. When drawn out further, he admitted his neighbor was known for his generosity, and had planned to share his wealth with the village. Placated and reassured the king was aware of the situation, the fellow departed satisfied.

The king ordered a widow's dispensation for the woman whose husband had vanished, payable until such time as he reappeared. Though grieving openly for her missing husband, the "widow" left knowing her children would not go hungry.

While the king handled other cases with similar success, there was little he could do to assuage the general anxiety among people that something magical might happen without warning, and with disastrous effect.

Throughout it all, Colin took notes on each and every case, at once reaffirming to the petitioners their concerns were being heard, and ensuring the king and his advisors had a record of each magical incident so it might be examined later for patterns.

As the day wore on, the king asked her once or twice for her assessment on the character of certain petitioners. Her merchant background served her well. She was able to inform him a tradesman was "hiding something," and a horse merchant was exaggerating the quality of her stock, and thus was not so injured by the plaintiff as she claimed.

The king agreed with her appraisals, and she had the sense of being tested, for the king was much too practiced in hearing petitions to really need her intervention. Nevertheless, he seemed pleased with her responses, and she found herself basking in his approval.

Karigan provided her opinion when requested, with pride in herself as a Green Rider blossoming and growing as she did so. It was odd how earlier in the day she had doubted herself and feared that the duality within her might lead her into doing something that would cause the downfall of all that was good in the world. She had dissolved her doubts standing at the king's side today. Had she not done well?

I am still the person I've always been, and the words of an Eletian can't change that.

It was then that Lil Ambrioth appeared, a faint glimmering standing slightly behind an oblivious petitioner. There was enough of Lil to see her smile, a smile of affirmation of Karigan's place as a Green Rider.

That was all Lil's brief appearance allowed. A smile.

The king, true to his word, saw every last petitioner in line. The bell in the city tolling the evening hour, and the darkening sky outside startled Karigan. It was only when she knew the time that she realized how weary and hungry she was.

When the great oak doors shut behind the last petitioner, the king sighed and stood, stretching his arms above his head and stomping his feet to awaken them. For some reason, Karigan found it surprising, and she had to remind herself that her king wasn't a statue, but flesh and blood like everyone else.

He glanced at her and she straightened. "Relax, Rider, you've been standing like that all afternoon."

She did as he suggested, and found herself stiff and aching.

Sperren, looking more frail than ever, excused himself, pleading exhaustion. The king did not hesitate to give him leave.

"Long day," Colin said. "I feared it was going to turn nasty there for a while. Good thing Rider G'ladheon found our errant herald."

"Truly," the king said.

"Do you wish to discuss the day's audience, sire?" Colin asked.

"No. I shall reserve it for tomorrow. Get some food and rest, my friend."

Colin looked relieved and departed with a bow.

The king turned back to Karigan, his hands clasped behind his back. "You wished to speak to me about your message errand."

"Yes, Excellency. It will take some explaining. I—"

"What happened to you?" he asked suddenly, drawing his eyebrows together. "Have you been injured all this time and I didn't realize it?"

"Injured?"

Before she could even guess at what he was talking about, he was down the dais and next to her, examining the slash of her sleeve.

"Nothing I can see . . ." he said. "Just a torn sleeve?"

Karigan recovered enough to answer, "Um, yes. In a manner of speaking."

"In a manner of speaking? Would this be a part of your tale?"

Karigan nodded.

The king sighed. "We need supper before one of us perishes from hunger. While we're eating, you may tell me of your eventful errand to Childrey."

With but a flick of his hand, he was surrounded by servants who relieved him of his royal mantle and fillet, handed him a goblet of wine, helped him slip into a dusky blue longcoat, and generally fussed around him. A contingent of Weapons arrived to relieve those who had guarded the king all day in the throne room.

Before Karigan knew it, they were off, exiting the throne room through the side door hidden behind a tapestry. The king set the pace in long strides, as if finally finding some release for all his pent-up energy.

He was leading them to his study. As if anticipating the king's arrival, the elderly kennel master appeared in the corridor ahead, with three terriers. Upon seeing the king, they barked joyously and strained at their tethers. The kennel master laughed and loosed them. All three dogs bounded to the king, leaping up against his legs, snuffling his feet and sneezing, their short white tails whipping back and forth.

The king laughed, too, shedding his more serious demeanor in exchange for one of pure happiness as he patted heads and scratched behind ears. The sudden transformation took Karigan by surprise, but on reflection, he frequently surprised her.

The Weapons and servants stood by, unruffled by the king's display and the antics of the terriers. Once the pandemonium died down, they set off again, the terriers trotting at the king's heels, toenails clicking on the stone floor.

Before arriving at the king's study, a servant whisked Karigan off into a side chamber where she was provided with a wash basin and towels, and the opportunity to take care of other necessities before she sat to supper.

Her expression must have been dazed, for the servant said, "Don't worry, dearie, the king will treat you kindly. Why, he often supped with your captain after a day's work."

Karigan smiled weakly, and set to washing up.

* * *

A simple supper of cold goose, boiled eggs, fresh greens, and bread was laid out on a small table in the study. Weapons remained outside guarding the entrances from the castle corridor and the courtyard gardens.

A couple of servants remained in the study to refill their cups, to carve the goose, and to see to their needs. The three terriers sat on their haunches, watching the proceedings with tongues lolling. One in particular eyed Karigan's every move, obviously hoping she would drop some morsel on the floor. His interest was unmistakable.

The king chuckled. "It seems Finder the Second has high hopes for you. Don't give in, for Pyram spoils them atrociously in the kennels." He then spoke at length about the foibles of his various terriers, much at ease.

Karigan was not.

"Is there something wrong?" he asked.

She jerked her gaze to him, startled to find she had been only half listening to his words.

"You're picking at your food," he said.

"I'm fine," she said. She had been hungry, but now she found she was too nervous to eat.

Nervous? Well, it wasn't every day one shared a private meal with one's king.

He set his fork down and leaned back into his chair, gauging her. "Is it the tale you've to tell me that's bothering you?"

"Yes," she lied.

"You must forgive my insensitivity for making you wait all this time, but I dared not delay the audience. It was a difficult position I imposed on you, and I hoped a respite would—"

One should not interrupt a king, but Karigan did. "Please, it's all right. A little wait will not change my tale."

"I would like to hear it now, then."

Karigan took a sip of wine. This was not going to be easy.

"First I need to tell you I've—I've visited with the First Rider."

The king raised both eyebrows in surprise, but said nothing so she might continue and explain.

And she did, just as she had with Mara, starting from the beginning.

"Extraordinary," the king murmured when she paused, his eyes wide.

Karigan continued with her experiences at Watch Hill. When she finished that part of the tale, the king slumped in his chair with his chin on his hand, his expression incredulous.

"When you told me you had an 'eventful' message errand, I wasn't expecting it to be quite this eventful. Tell me, do you know what is precipitating your travels into the past?"

"That brings me to the next part of the tale," she said.

"There's more?"

Karigan nodded. "The Eletians—"

"Eletians?"

"Yes, Excellency."

He held up his hand to forestall her further and ordered his manservant to bring out an aged stash of brandy.

"I think we both need some before you continue," the king said. "At least *I* do."

Karigan watched him rub his temples as the brandy was served. She well understood his incredulity, for she barely had time to digest the events herself.

He swirled the amber liquid in his glass. "You are a wonder, Rider." He gave her a lopsided smile. "Coming from anyone else, I might not believe it at all."

Karigan found herself blushing, and hurriedly—too hurriedly—swallowed a mouthful of brandy, only to gag as it burned down her throat. The manservant quickly provided her with water and clapped her on her back. Doubly embarrassed, Karigan thought her face must also be doubly red. At least it could be passed off as the brandy.

There was nothing left for her to do but tell the king of the Eletian aspect of her tale. She told of Prince Jametari's explanation of magic leaking through the breach in the D'Yer Wall and upsetting the balance of magic in the lands. Reluctantly she revealed the wild magic that still resided within her to explain the traveling, but she did not mention the "duality," not wanting to give the king a reason to doubt her. She also downplayed any threat the Eletians might pose to her.

When she finished, the king sat deep in thought, running his forefinger across the carved armrest of his chair. All three dogs lay at his feet. Finder was snoring.

Presently he said, "This Prince Jametari was Shawdell's father?" At her nod, he continued, "Then I'm not so sure we can believe all he says."

"I do."

King Zachary did not gainsay her. "I must admit his words make sense. But Argenthyne?" He shook his head. "It is like the stories my nursemaid used to tell me when I was a lad." His shoulders sagged. "If only we knew more of magic. How can I defend my people against it? I can't have citizens vanishing and forest groves turning to stone at random. As more and more of this occurs, the populace will grow more disturbed, and then what? How am I to protect them?"

An awkward silence followed, and feeling a need to say something useful, Karigan said, "If Alton can fix the breach, then balance should return to—" The king's expression crumbled, and suddenly he looked very, very haggard. "What is it? Is something wrong?"

King Zachary stood, his eyes ineffably sad.

Alarmed, Karigan stood, too. "Please, please tell me—is it Alton? Has something happened?"

The king stepped closer. "I fear it is so. I'm sorry, Rider—Karigan, but Alton is with the gods now. He perished in Blackveil."

It was like the floor had collapsed from beneath her feet. It couldn't be true! She had just seen Alton in the Mirror of the Moon. He had looked so ill . . . She shook her head, denying the king's words.

His hand was on her arm, but she could not feel it—everything had gone numb.

"N-no," she said. "It can't be true. I'll ask Mara and she'll—"

The king cursed. "I thought you knew. I thought you'd have heard when you returned from your errand and saw Rider barracks."

Barracks? What was he talking about? She had to go see Mara. Alton couldn't be dead. He—

"Rider Barracks burned," the king said. "There were intruders on the castle grounds, and all I can guess is that Mara used her ability to defend herself. She is badly burned. Ephram, alas, perished in the blaze."

"No!"

The king drew closer to comfort her in his embrace. "Karigan—"

She pulled herself away and ran from the study.

☙ ASHES ☙

The young mender, Ben, splayed his body protectively across Mara's door in the mending wing. He licked his lips anxiously, his eyes fairly bugging out of his head.

"You can't enter!" he told Karigan. "She's too hurt. Please, Rider, burns are tricky things. Only Master Destarion and myself—"

The saber quavered in Karigan's hand. All she knew was rage.

Master Destarion hurried down the corridor accompanied by soldiers. Other menders huddled down at the far end, not desiring to venture any closer.

"Rider!" It was the first time Karigan had ever heard him raise his voice. "Put that sword down immediately!"

Sword? She gazed at her hand, at her fingers wrapped around the worn leather hilt of her saber. It was as if her hand belonged to someone else entirely, someone she didn't know. What in the name of all the gods was she doing?

She opened her fingers and the sword fell to the floor. She stared stupidly at it there on the carpet. Its nicked and scratched blade showed hard use, but it was sharp enough to split a hair. What had it been doing in her hand? Swords were for killing . . . Hadn't there been enough loss of life already?

In the next moment, the soldiers were on her, pinning

443

her arms behind her back. She did not struggle, but they weren't gentle.

Master Destarion glowered at her as if she was some sort of monster. "What in five hells were you doing?" he demanded. "This is a place of healing."

Karigan could only stare at the sword at her feet, grief stuck in her throat.

"Rider Brennyn is alive, but barely. Your intrusion could have brought her further harm."

Pain. It was shredding Karigan's guts. A teardrop fell to the carpet, making a dark splotch.

Destarion kept talking, but Karigan didn't hear him. She wasn't really even inside herself. She was somewhere else, isolated from all others, hearing but not listening, her eyes too clouded to see anything more than shapes and light. Until she heard King Zachary's voice.

"I believe I can explain, Destarion," he said, striding down the corridor with a pair of Weapons at his side, and his faithful terriers following behind. To the soldiers he said, "Release her immediately."

When they obeyed, Karigan discovered she had no legs. Destarion caught her, and Ben darted from Mara's doorway to help.

"I brought a shock upon her rather suddenly," the king said, a tone of apology in his voice. "This after, an 'eventful' message errand she endured. I handled things poorly." He was very near, but as he spoke, she only caught snatches of the conversation. She heard Alton's name, and Ephram's, and about barracks burning, and Mara. "Perhaps a draught would help."

"Yes," Destarion said. "A very good idea. See to it, will you, Ben?"

When the mender left her side, King Zachary stepped in to catch her elbow.

"How is Rider Brennyn?" he asked softly.

Destarion sighed. "Clinging to life. If there is one trait these Riders of yours share, sire, it's their fighting spirit. Sheer obstinance if you ask me. If her burns don't fester, and if she doesn't give up hope, she may recover, at least physically."

"And Laren?"

Destarion snorted. "Difficult woman! I dressed the burns on her hands and then she forced me out of her quarters and slammed the door shut."

"Captain Mapstone?"

Karigan hadn't realized she had spoken aloud until the king explained. "She extinguished the flames burning Mara, no doubt saving her life. I do wish she would talk to us, for she's really the only witness besides Mara who might be able to explain what happened."

Ben returned, bearing a cup. "Drink up," Destarion told Karigan. "It will make you easier."

As if someone else guided her actions, she took the cup and sniffed its contents. It was wine laced with something overly sweet. Something, no doubt, to make her sleep.

"No," she said.

"No?"

"No." She dropped the cup onto the floor, red wine splattering across her sword blade like blood. "No." The word wrenched up from within. She tore away from the king and Destarion. She ran. Behind her, she heard the king commanding the soldiers not to follow.

She flung herself out of the mending wing and down stairways to the main floor. She pelted down corridors, tears streaming down her cheeks, and she didn't care who saw.

Once she left the castle entrance, she kept running; she ran till she came to the still smoldering remains of Rider barracks, dark and ghastly against the night sky.

Little stood. The fire had greedily consumed the two-hundred-year-old building, leaving behind a few charred beams, chimneys, and ashes. The reek of smoke saturated the air.

"No," she whispered. Had she somehow brought this upon the Riders? Was it somehow her fault? Was Prince Jametari right about her? "No." But this time she didn't believe herself.

Alton was gone. So was Ephram. Mara barely clung to life.

She stood forlornly there, in front of Rider barracks, stray tears tracking down her cheeks. She needed answers. The king thought the captain might have answers—the captain who should be bearing this, not Karigan. How could the captain desert her in her time of need?

She wanted answers, and she wanted them now.

At officer quarters, she pummeled Captain Mapstone's door. A light flickered within, so she knew the captain was there.

Karigan wasn't sure how long she yelled and beat on the door, but when it creaked open, she stumbled back in surprise. The captain stood there in the doorway, backlit by a lamp that filled the hollows of her cheeks with shadows. Her usually neat braid was a mess of crazed strands. She wore an old, very rumpled shirt. She looked ravaged by illness.

At first Karigan could not speak, but when she found her voice, all she could say was, "Alton." It was like a recrimination.

The captain's silence stoked Karigan's anger. "What about Mara? What about Ephram? Why? How could you let this happen?"

She carried on, unleashing her rage. The captain swayed in the doorway, as if being physically battered.

"Why?" Karigan demanded. "Why did you let it happen? Why did you leave this all for me?"

The captain brought her bandaged hands to her face as if to fend off blows. By then, the fire in Karigan was quenched, and she felt as burned out as Rider barracks. She sank to her knees on the captain's step.

The captain receded into her quarters and closed the door.

Karigan did the only thing she could do: she went to the stables. But even Condor could not soothe her. She climbed up to the loft and curled up on a pile of hay, holding herself; too numb, too shocked to do anything more than stare into the dark, with only the shifting and scraping of horse hooves down below to disturb her.

Someone entered the stable with a lantern.

"Karigan?" King Zachary called.

She buried her head in her arms, angered by the intrusion. Why couldn't he just let her be?

Another part of her craved him to lend her comfort.

The light flickered and moved down below as the king searched for her. She should be flattered, she thought, that the king of Sacoridia thought enough of his Green Rider to seek her out.

He paused at the bottom of the ladder. She prayed he would go away, and she prayed he would climb up and find her.

The ladder creaked as he stepped on the bottom rung, the light rising and growing brighter as he climbed. When he stood upon the loft, she covered her eyes.

"Karigan," he said, "I am terribly sorry. For everything, and more than I can ever express. I know you and Alton were close."

He sat down beside her, and she willed the grief away, but his presence only seemed to incite it.

"I am sorry," he said again.

Before Karigan could entertain another thought, the grief engulfed her, racking her body with sobs that came from deep down. She didn't know when it happened, but the king had given her his shoulder in which to bury her face. He held her as the sobs took over.

"I can't believe he's gone."

"Shhh . . ." the king soothed.

When she ran out of tears, she leaned into him, her cheek against his throbbing heart.

The king held her until she exhausted herself into oblivion. Dimly she remembered him settling her into a deep nest of hay, and covering her with a blanket, and after that, she'd fallen asleep. She did not know how long he had lingered there by her side. Perhaps it had been a dream.

She smoothed her hand over the blanket. It was soft velveteen. She cracked open swollen eyes that ached from all the crying, and discovered it wasn't a blanket at all that covered her, but King Zachary's longcoat of dusky blue. She pulled it up to her chin, inhaling his pleasant scent. It brought her some peace as though he were embracing her again.

Gray light filtered through chinks in the stable's siding into the gloom of the loft. Down below the horses shifted, and she recognized Condor's distinct snore. Soon Hep would arrive for the morning feeding, and the castle grounds would bustle with the new day, as if Alton was not gone.

More tears wanted to come, some trickled down her cheeks, but she was so wrung out, she had little left inside her.

It's an old story, said Lil Ambrioth.

Her voice and presence ceased to startle Karigan. The apparition sat a short way away on a pile of hay, the hazy morning light lending some substance to her features.

Oh, yes, an old story oft repeated. How many Riders did I lead to their deaths over the course of the war? Some were dear friends, comrades all. Yet we forged on, even though more were struck down with each campaign. Do you know why we kept on?

"Because you had to," Karigan said.

Lil nodded. *Because we had to. We had to work to defeat Mornhavon, otherwise something worse than death awaited all who remained: loss of free will. To give up would have been to dishonor those who had perished fighting for the good of all the lands. In their deaths we found the spirit and courage to go on. It gave us new purpose.*

On a rational level, Karigan understood Lil's words, but the wound upon her heart was too raw.

I expect other Riders will return only to find shock and sorrow as you have, Lil said. *They will need comfort and guidance, just as you did through the night. Who will be here for them? Who will lend them strength?*

"I have no strength left to give."

No? I suppose your king shall have to do it then. Lil's tone was tinged with sarcasm. *Or, would he do it for only one special Rider?*

Karigan closed her eyes, remembering the king's embrace and soothing words. *One special Rider.* He had done it for *her,* Karigan G'ladheon, not just for one of his Riders. The concept took her aback.

How about your captain? Lil asked. *Do you suppose she's in any condition to support her Riders?*

The image of her suffering captain came back to her all too vividly, and she wilted in shame as she recalled how she had railed at her.

There was no one else.

Lil began to fade, leaving but the faint pigment of a cheek and the twinkle of eyes.

What had become of Lil's Riders when *she* passed on?

Did they continue to fight, or did they stagger without her leadership? Karigan was again struck by the feeling of a story left unfinished.

"Tell me," she said, "did you die of the arrow?"

There was spectral blurring as Lil stood. She strode across the loft in agitation, then looked down upon Karigan, and as she faded away, she spoke. *How did* you *die?*

Karigan sank back into the hay stunned, and found comfort only in the king's longcoat.

Karigan moved with great care atop the foundation of Rider barracks, side-stepping heaps of rubble. Laborers had knocked down the hazardous chimneys only this morning, and sawed down charred beams that had still been standing or hanging precariously.

All had been lost. She found only hints of the lives that had inhabited barracks: a boot heel, the charred pages of a book—when she touched it, the pages turned to ash and drifted into the breeze. She found deformed buckles and cutlery, and broken crockery protruding from the soot like fragments of bone.

Two hundred years of Rider history was gone, the corridors Gwyer Warhein once strode, the rooms in which Bard Martin and Ereal M'Farthon had slept, and the common room where generations of Riders had raised their voices in laughter and song.

She paused where her own room had once stood. The damage here was even more severe than other parts of barracks. Hep told her the fire had started in this vicinity. Gone were her few books and spare uniforms, and whatever other trinkets she had kept.

A sparkle in the rubble caught her eye. Stepping carefully on weakened floorboards, she squatted down and looked closely. More sparkles rippled in rainbow hues across the ruins in front of her. Moonstone fragments.

She took one into her hand. Sharp and clear, it refracted the sunlight in different intensities as she turned it over on her palm. She closed her fingers around it. It had been unblemished by the fire, and it was almost as if it had captured the light of the fire within itself. She dared not collect other fragments for fear of falling through the floorboards. In an odd way, it gladdened her that things of such beauty drew the sun to a place of such devastation. She dropped the fragment into the ashes.

Before she stood, she caught sight of something else, a pattern of black against black, an irregular circlet. Unable to reach it with her hand, she drew her longknife and retrieved it on the blade's tip. It was a lead crown of twined branches. A crown like the wraith Varadgrim had worn. But how could a crown made of lead have withstood the heat of the fire? Before she could even contemplate its significance, it lost shape and writhed on the end of her blade. She cried out and dropped it onto the foundation, where it oozed and boiled like a live thing, blue-black and oily.

Wild magic. Tainted.

It slithered off the foundation to the ground, and burrowed beneath charred earth and vanished.

Karigan shuddered. What had the wraith been doing here, *here* at Rider barracks? In her own room? What had it been after? Had Mara or Ephram had the misfortune of encountering it? There were so many questions, and only Mara had the answers, if she lived long enough to give them.

Covered in soot and ashes, Karigan turned to jump from the foundation when her toe nudged a piece of metal. She picked it up. Blackened and contorted, she nevertheless knew exactly what it was: her mother's mirror. Yet another piece of her own history destroyed. Never again would she gaze into the mirror as her mother once had, never would she see in it again the reflection her father said so resembled Kariny's.

The first Rider to return from an errand arrived that afternoon. Karigan found Garth kneeling in front of barracks, his face stricken with a shock she knew only too well. She stood beside him, her hand on his massive shoulder. His mare, Chickadee, stood on his other side, head low and ears flicking back and forth.

"Wh-what happened?" Garth asked.

She told him best as she could, about the fire, Ephram, Mara. And the news about Alton, a quaver in her voice. She had never seen the big man cry before. There had been no gentle way to break the news to him, and maybe in retrospect, he'd appreciate her forthrightness.

Chickadee lipped at her partner's shoulder, knowing something was greatly amiss. With Hep's help, Karigan walked Garth to the mending wing, where he accepted a sleeping draught without argument. Once he was safely abed and snoring, Karigan sought out the mender, Ben.

She found him in a workroom aromatic with herbs, jars filled with powders for remedies lining shelves. At a table he crushed dried leaves with a pestle. When he noticed her entrance, he dropped the pestle and backed away.

Karigan frowned, and raised her hands to show him she was unarmed. He relaxed, but remained at a safe distance.

"I came to apologize," Karigan said, "for my behavior last night."

"Thank you. I understand you were under great duress."

"I still am," she said softly, "but it's no excuse. I don't know why I drew the sword. It was wrong."

A period of awkwardness followed. "Rider Brennyn's condition is unchanged," Ben offered.

"I see."

Her disappointment was so plain, he added, "It's better than you think. She hasn't declined."

She smiled briefly. "Thank you. Will you continue to update me?"

"Of course, Rider."

"Please, call me Karigan."

This time Ben smiled.

Later, Karigan returned to the stable loft to sleep. She spread out her bedroll on the hay and laid down. She covered herself with the king's longcoat. She knew she should have returned it, but she guessed he wouldn't miss it for just one more night. Right now, it was the only comfort she had.

Early the next morning, she was summoned by a runner of the Green Foot to attend the king. Reluctantly she draped his longcoat over her arm and hastened after the runner.

To her surprise, the lad did not lead her to the throne room or the king's study, but to a normally abandoned corridor that was currently anything but. Lamps lit the work of an army of servants scrubbing down walls and the floor. The king stood with his manservant directing the work, using a sword, *her* saber, as a pointer. A pair of Weapons stood opposite one another against the walls.

"Good morning, Rider G'ladheon," the king said.

She bowed. "Good morning, Excellency."

"What do you think?" He brandished her saber down the corridor.

"What do I think? I—um, about what, precisely?"

The king reached over and plucked a piece of hay from her hair. Her cheeks flamed. "Don't plan to live in the hayloft, do you?" His voice was quiet, but there was a playfulness in his demeanor. He was like the month of Janure, always changing, always unpredictable.

Then she took his meaning and glanced again down the corridor, a corridor lined with doorways to small chambers.

"Yes, Rider," he said. "It is time the Green Riders came home." He took her arm and they strolled down the corridor, he pointing out the efforts of the servants to ready it for occupation. Karigan was dubious—the mold and dust were thick, and the rooms in decrepit condition.

"Before Agates Sealender came to mistrust his Riders," the king explained, "this is where they lived—right here, in this corridor. And this is where they shall live again."

The windows in the rooms, those not boarded over, were mere arrow slits, leaving the rooms dark and gloomy. How would they be furnished? How would they be heated in the winter? A hundred such questions paraded through Karigan's mind, but she didn't voice them because the king was so obviously pleased with himself.

"I know it won't be the same as the fine old barracks to which you've grown accustomed," he said, "but I think once it's cleaned up and made habitable again, Riders will bring new life to this section of the castle. I promise you it will soon be far more inviting than it may now appear.

"In the meantime, you and the other Riders shall be quartered in the east wing." He winked at her. "Quarters fit for visiting royalty—very nicely appointed. Sperren shall see to it."

Karigan swallowed that.

"I suppose you would like this back." He handed her the saber, hilt first.

She took it, and passed him his longcoat. "Thank you," she said, "for *everything*."

"You are very welcome." There was a hint of a smile on his lips meant just for her. He turned to leave, but paused and faced her once again. "I expect you to attend me during this afternoon's slate of meetings," he said. "Cummings will fill you in."

With that, he and his Weapons departed. Karigan stood in the corridor, the servants working around her. Who was Cummings, and where would she find him? What meetings?

She shook her head and started down the corridor. And came to a startled halt as a sensation of being watched crawled across her skin. She glanced back at the servants, but they were intent on their work. None even looked her way.

The light touch of an air current stroked her cheek, and there was a murmur in her ear. Drafts whirled around her legs, then dissipated.

She shuddered and strode rapidly out of the corridor, her future home.

≈ TIDINGS FROM
THE WALL ≈

Cummings, Karigan learned, was the king's personal secretary, a very efficient man who worked not out of the administrative wing, but in the royal offices of the west wing. Each morning he sent a Green Foot runner to Karigan's luxurious new quarters in the east wing with a list of meetings and audiences at which the king required her presence. The king also wished her to continue her training sessions with Arms Master Drent, and none of the meetings on Cummings' lists ever conflicted with these.

Karigan now better understood the running-around Captain Mapstone and Mara had engaged in.

When Tegan rode in, Karigan asked her to handle the daily needs of the Riders. Garth busied himself in overseeing the refurbishing of the "new" Rider quarters, including seeking out bits of furniture locked up in storage here and there. Some of the pieces he found were fancy and ostentatious, and some truly bizarre, often from another era and discarded as out of fashion or lacking taste. Most pieces were of a simpler, utilitarian nature, but the combination lent an air of eccentricity to the Rider wing. The important thing was that they were sound.

He found an especially ornate wardrobe of cherry carved with fancy scrollwork and some unknown coat of arms. The details were inlaid with yellowing ivory. Inside were drawer compartments with knobs of pearl, as well as space

456

to hang clothes. It had belonged to some wealthy but forgotten clan, Karigan supposed. Garth declared the wardrobe hers.

"You, um, didn't take this from the king's apartments, did you?"

Garth put his hands on his hips and gave her his most offended look. "Of course not. It was thrown in with the rest, where they store all the unwanted stuff. It had a broken leg, and *I* fixed it."

Chagrined, Karigan properly admired his handiwork, and helped him move it into her new room. Fortunately these rooms were larger than those of the old Rider barracks, for the wardrobe was a behemoth.

She helped Garth when she could, moving furniture or sweeping out rooms, scaring cobwebs from dark corners, and arranging for glaziers to fix windows. As more Riders arrived, they pitched in where they could, as if the work in some way helped them deal with their losses.

The king's meetings and audiences felt far less productive to Karigan. She stood mutely at his side as he and his other advisors met with dignitaries, courtiers, or anyone whose business was important enough to be brought before the king.

It was, on a level, interesting to be privy to such meetings, but like Mara, she felt no more than an ornament in green. The king did not need her. Rarely did he even seek her input.

There were some instances in which he did, but she was more of the mind of a teacher leading a pupil into solving a problem. He knew the answers before he even asked. She didn't take it as patronizing; he wasn't like that. It was his way of assessing her skill.

The king often took his meetings and private audiences not in the throne room, but in a smaller chamber in the west wing. It was richly appointed with velvet hangings and thick carpeting. A broad hearth was situated behind a smaller rendition of the throne. A long table and chairs could be moved into place if there was to be a large meeting.

It happened that a visitor arrived one midday, a young man in well made traveler's garb, accompanied by retainers. This was the newly confirmed Lord-Governor Hendry Penburn, son of the late lady-governor.

The king stood to greet him, taking both the young man's hands into his own, and murmuring condolences for the loss of his mother.

"She died serving her people," the young lord said, "and I think that's how she'd like to be remembered."

As the king and Hendry spoke more of Lady Penburn, Karigan found herself impressed by the young man's composure. Despite his innocent, unmarred features, he came across as competent and confident, no small tribute to his mother's upbringing.

"I am, of course, answering your summons, Majesty," Hendry said, "as well as seeking your blessing on my governorship."

"You are the first to arrive," the king said. "And you already have my blessings, but I shall formally recognize your office when all the others are present."

Hendry half-smiled. "An interesting event it shall be, then. More likely it will be remembered by whatever judgment is passed on Lord D'Ivary."

Karigan raised an eyebrow. She had known the Riders had been sent off on errands to each of the lord-governors, but she hadn't known the precise nature of the messages. Now she did. The king had summoned the lord-governors to Sacor City to debate the fate of Lord D'Ivary.

It was possible the king already had something in mind, but politically, it was best if he involved the other lord-governors so his decision would not appear arbitrary, but a consensus. He would have to work hard for their backing.

To Karigan's surprise, Hendry gazed directly at her. "Odd, but I always heard that Captain Mapstone had red hair." A slight blush colored his cheeks and Karigan liked him all the more for it.

She bowed. "I am not the captain, my lord, but a simple Rider."

King Zachary smiled. "Laren Mapstone has been my faithful captain and advisor for years, but I fear she has been unwell."

"A pity," Hendry said. "My mother spoke well of her, and was always pleased that one of Penburn Province had such access to the king."

"She used her access well." The king winked at Karigan. "During her absence, I've called upon the assistance of Rider G'ladheon here."

"G'ladheon?" Hendry said. "Of the merchant clan?"

Karigan nodded. "Yes, my lord."

Hendry brightened, looking suddenly very roguish. "I heard the most extraordinary story about a member of that clan, who rode astride a big chestnut to the town of Darden on market day, clad in nothing but her own skin."

Karigan strangled a groan before it could pass her lips. *Wearing nothing but her own skin?*

"Is it true?" Hendry asked.

A wave of heat washed through Karigan as she noted King Zachary looking from Hendry to her with a bemused expression.

"No. Yes. But I was wearing—I was wearing . . ." Words failed her.

There was a subtle upward shift of the king's eyebrows. Hendry waited, most intensely interested.

"I wasn't—" She was going to melt there on the spot. "I had on—"

The king cleared his throat, and she jumped. "A nightgown, if I've heard the story correctly."

Forget the melting. She was going to faint from embarrassment.

Hendry grinned. "I had always wondered about the young lady who possessed such gumption. I am very pleased to meet the inspiration of the story."

The king's peculiar smile did not aid her discomfiture. "I heard the story from Bard Martin."

Karigan didn't know whether to laugh or cry. Bard had told the king the dratted tale? *Oh, Bard, you are a tease even beyond the grave.* At least he hadn't concocted the idea of her riding without even a nightgown to cover her. Or had he? Sadly, she would never know.

The king said, "Rider G'ladheon served in your mother's delegation."

Hendry sobered immediately, his eyes wide. "You did? Would it—would it be too much of an imposition for you to tell me of her final days?"

"I would do it gladly." Contrary to her words, her heart sank, for she did not relish recalling those days when she was currently so full of her own sorrow. She did, however, understand the young man's need to know, and perhaps her words would bring him some peace. "Lady Penburn led us bravely."

His expression was so earnest, so grateful, Karigan forgave him for bringing up that story about her ride to Darden.

The king asked Sperren to see to Hendry's accommodations, and after the young lord left, he sat back upon his chair.

"What do you think of the new Lord-Governor Penburn?"

Karigan assumed the king did not seek an off-hand opinion, but rather the measured assessment of an advisor.

"He is genuinely grieved by his mother's passing." The words brought her own emotions painfully close to the surface. "He is inexperienced, but not unfamiliar with what his new role requires. And I think . . . I think he'll do well."

The king brushed his fingers over his chin. "I agree. He shall be an asset to his province."

And to his king. Karigan thought she could almost hear the words from him.

Then, not quite as an afterthought, the king added, "He is yet young and untried, and his new position will be the making of him. His ethics will be forged by his new power, and it remains to be seen what results from that forging."

He spoke as a man who well knew what it was to be forged, and tempered, by leadership. He had been through the process himself, and emerged true and sound, but he had also seen what power could do to others, like his brother. Others who became twisted by greed, and a hundred other ills, and they then turned against the very people they were sworn to protect.

"Hedric D'Ivary was thought well of, as a kind and generous man," the king said, "until he succeeded his cousin to be chief of his clan and lord of the province."

The chamber door creaked open and Sperren poked his head in. "A messenger from the D'Yer Wall to see you, sire."

The king glanced at Karigan. "Are you up to this?" he asked her quietly. "He may have news about Alton."

She felt suspended in air, hoping against hope that maybe the messenger actually brought good news, that maybe Alton was all right after all. But she knew it could never be good news. Her hope was false. Alton was *gone.* Still, she had to hear it, she had to hear what the messenger had to say.

"I'll stay," she said.

The king looked at her in concern, but nodded to Sperren to let the messenger in. He was dressed in the blue and gold livery of D'Yer Province, and looked haggard, as one who has ridden hard. He knelt before the king.

"Rise," King Zachary said. When the messenger did so, he asked, "You bear me tidings from the wall?"

"Yes, sire. Lord-Governor D'Yer urged me on to you, with his wish to inform you of the passing of Lord Landrew D'Yer, his brother."

The king sat back in his chair, stunned. "So close upon the death of Lord Alton?"

The messenger nodded, his features troubled. "Yes, sire. Lord Landrew went over the wall to search for his nephew. He, and most of the soldiers that accompanied him, were slain. We were able to retrieve what—what was left of Lord Landrew."

"Gods have mercy," the king said.

He questioned the messenger further, asking how many soldiers had perished, and the circumstances. Karigan did not hear the answers, for her thoughts went to Alton. If his uncle had died so quickly, surely his had been the same fate. Whatever evil lurked in Blackveil, it had taken Alton as assuredly as the sun rose in the morning.

"And they found no sign of Lord Alton?" the king asked the messenger. He flicked his gaze to Karigan to see how she was taking it.

"No, sire, but there's the most astonishing thing . . ."

"Yes?"

The messenger shook himself as if lost in thought for a moment. "Lord Alton's horse, sire. I've never seen anything like it. He stands at the breach, and won't leave it, not for anything. We've tried to drive him off, but he comes back. We stake him with the other horses, but he breaks his tether and heads back to the breach.

"So, we've just taken to humoring him, you see, and we

bring him his fodder there. Not that he'll eat much. It's like he's on guard, waiting for his master to return."

That was enough. Remembering Crane guarding Ereal's body, Karigan dashed from the chamber, tears sliding down her cheeks once again.

Journal of Hadriax el Fex

This morning I awoke from an uneasy sleep, soaked with sweat and my head pounding. I had had a terrible dream in which the whole of the world fell into decay—vast forests rotting tree by tree, and clear lakes turning black and turbid; the sky above brown and acrid. The sun, though, shone brightly on a single bush of raspberries. The berries were large and perfectly formed, unmarred by the decay so prevalent elsewhere. I started eating of the berries and they were so sweet. Red juice dribbled down my chin and stained my hands. I looked up and saw Alessandros watching me with an enormous grin on his face. He gestured for me to continue eating as if it gave him great pleasure to see it, but when I glanced down at my hands, I realized I held not berries, but a half-eaten human heart. I had not juice staining my hands, but blood . . .

I still shudder as I think of this dream, even in the waning hours of the evening. The headache has stayed with me all day long, and I've not been able to hold down any of my meals.

As I reflect on the dream, I see the truth in it. I have so much blood on my hands and this war seems never close to ending. Alessandros does not mind; he keeps thinking up new perverse ways to use his powers, and continues to develop abominations to use against the enemy.

He still professes his love for me, and has made me his second, but this only makes me party to his evil acts. It taints me, even more so than the atrocities I've committed against the people of these lands.

Yet, I still see in Alessandros the boy who adopted me, a low-born nobody living off garbage in the streets, to be his best friend, an affiliation that allowed me to live in luxury as a gentleman, attend the best schools, and enter the military at an officer's rank. I never wanted for anything, and all Alessandros asked for in return was for my affection and support. I believe that's all he still wants.

As we grew up, we were inseparable, our lives irrevocably entwined. They still are, and so I am tainted. The boy who I used to play ball with, or go hunting with, has just shown me a harp made by a famous craftsman and presented to Varadgrim. It is a beautiful thing, the most beautiful such instrument I have ever seen or heard. Yet, it was not good enough for Varadgrim. So Alessandros "improved" it by stealing the voices of Eletians, and binding them to the strings. Now the harp is unearthly, filling the chamber with the voices of God's angels.

The Eletians who lost their voices are dying. For them, losing the ability to sing is like losing their spirit.

I no longer know Alessandros. He is not the same man I once loved as my closest friend and confidant.

⇜ TOWER OF THE HEAVENS ⇝

**A**lton moved in dreams. Dreams of dark, tangled branches and burning, of vast empty spaces. Karigan came to him during his moments of deepest despair, ethereal in her ivory gown, whispering to him in loving words, only to melt away into something hideous and terrifying. He writhed in fever, sometimes awakening to nothingness, and total dark.

During one such awareness, he felt around him with hands shaking from illness. He was on a stone floor, not the damp mossy earth of his dreams. It was cool and seemed to moderate his fever. He pressed his cheek to the stone, thinking he remembered something of a tower, of entering it. If it was so, he was safe. He was out of the forest and safe.

This time when he slept, the nightmares did not return, but the dreams were still strange. They were of talking to stone, and of a beat that swelled up from the floor and pulsed through his body.

Sometime later, awareness came again. He lay on his back, gazing up at the starlit heavens. He frowned in consternation, thinking he was supposed to be in a tower of stone. The floor was still beneath him, and he did not hear the usual sounds of night or feel a breeze, or the damp of dew. His fevered mind must have affected his senses.

He groped about himself and found a column of stone to sit against. The new position made him dizzy and nau-

466

seous, and he gasped and retched. When the illness passed, he used the column to haul himself to his feet. Sharp pains shot through his hip and legs, but he managed to remain upright.

The column, it turned out, was a waist-high pedestal. He groped the top of it, his hands gliding across a smooth stone embedded into its surface. Green lightning crackled within it, then softened to a steady glow, tinting Alton's skin a pale green. It did little to illuminate his surroundings.

"It is about time, Orla," a voice said out of the darkness.

Startled, Alton steadied himself against the pedestal, fear darting to the ends of his nerves.

"Did you take all this time to plot your next move, or have you been cheating again?" The voice, impossible to pinpoint, reverberated around him in what felt like a vast chamber.

Alton peered into the dark, trying to discern this new threat.

"Why are we sitting in the dark, Orla?"

"Hello?" Alton ventured.

A long moment passed before the voice, rather peeved, spoke again. "You're not Orla."

"Um, no. I'm Alton."

Miraculously, and with startling intensity, golden sunshine showered down on him, and he blinked rapidly to allow his eyes to adjust. He discovered he stood on a plain of rolling hills and grasses.

"What?"

Had he been transported to someplace else, or was this more of his feverish dreaming? Beneath his feet were blocks of stone patterned into concentric circles that looped outward before vanishing into the grasses. To either side of him were stone arches that led nowhere, but rather framed the horizon. Fluted columns encircled the area, supporting nothing on their scrolled capitals but the sky.

Nearby, an old man with long, drooping white whiskers, sipping at a cup of tea, sat at a table regarding Alton with some curiosity. At his elbow was a game of Intrigue draped in cobwebs.

Alton took in his surroundings, the feathery clouds stretched across the sky, and the sun warming his face. The silvery-green grasses of the plain rustled and bent in the light wind.

"Where am I?"

"*Haethen Toundrel,* boy, where else?"

A familiar name among much that was unfamiliar. "Tower of the Heavens . . ."

"Indeed."

It was unlike any tower Alton had ever been in. "I—I don't understand . . ."

The old man made an impatient noise. "What better way to view the heavens, boy, than from a wide open plain?"

"Then I'm not *in* the tower?"

"This is Tower of the *Heavens.*"

The old man said no more as if this were explanation enough. Alton supposed logic existed in his words somewhere—the odd sort of disconnected logic one found only in dreams.

"And you," Alton said to the old man, "who are you? Some kind of ghost?"

The old man snorted in derision. "I am no such thing. I am Merdigen, great mage and guardian. Er, a magical projection of Merdigen, anyway. Far more sophisticated and useful than a mere specter."

"You're not . . . real?"

Merdigen sputtered on his tea. "Not real? I am a real projection of the great mage Merdigen."

"Oh." Alton's vision dimmed and he swayed, hanging onto the pedestal before him so he wouldn't fall over.

"You awakened me when you touched the tempes stone," Merdigen said.

"Tempes stone?"

"Beneath your hands, boy."

The green stone atop the pedestal was polished into a sparkling oval. "The tourmaline?"

"Yes, yes, yes. I am a guardian. I assist the wallkeepers in assessing the wall's condition when summoned. Are you not a wallkeeper, boy?"

"No. Well, yes, in a manner of speaking. And a Green Rider."

Meridgen's eyes brightened with interest and he eagerly leaned forward. "How goes the war?"

"War . . . ?" Alton was having trouble making sense of it all.

"Yes. Has old Smidhe beat back the Mirwells yet? Last Orla heard was that the Riders had thrown in their lot with Hillander."

"Clan Wars." Alton shook his muzzy head. "Two hundred years ago."

"What?" Merdigen hopped to his feet, spry for an old man, or a projection of an old man. "Two hundred years have gone by and no one has checked with me since? What madness is this?"

If Alton had been able to, he would have explained how the wallkeepers were drawn into the war one by one until none remained, and how the wall, seemingly indestructible, was left to stand on its own, its corps of keepers never to return. Before he could say a word, however, he collapsed.

Alton rolled his head and groaned.

"The wall is in a terrible state, boy. What are you going to do about it?"

Alton blinked open his eyes to find Merdigen standing over him. "Water . . ." he whispered.

"I am a guardian, not a water bearer! Besides, I cannot carry anything material. It would slip right through my fingers. Only illusion." A large sea turtle suddenly appeared in his hands, looking every bit like the real thing, even propelling its flippers through the air. Then with a *poof,* it was gone.

Alton rubbed his eyes. He was having delusions again—serious delusions. "I need water."

"Very well then. Follow me."

The guardian strode away from him, his robes stirred by the breeze that flowed across the grasslands. He paused expectantly between a pair of columns.

"This way," Merdigen said.

Alton crawled painstakingly after him, across stone. Curiously, the stone was dusty, as though unexposed to the open sky. His fingers felt broken bits of clay pipes, a button or two, and even a large belt buckle, all fragments, he supposed, of the lives of the wallkeepers who had once served in this most unusual tower.

He followed Merdigen between the two columns and his world altered yet again—the light dampened and was no longer sunshine, but a glowing orb that floated overhead. Stone walls surrounded him, the grasslands banished. Banished to where?

He gazed over his shoulder. The columns encircled the middle of a chamber and supported the ceiling above. The two arches remained across the chamber from one another and were embedded in walls, leading not to the horizon, but into darkness only.

Merdigen's table, with its unfinished game of Intrigue on top, stood snug against one wall. In the very center of the chamber sat the tempes stone on its pedestal, and above it floated a glowing cloud of green and blue that captured all the essence of the grasslands and sky.

Alton rubbed sweat out of his eyes, uncertain of what was real and what was not, and thinking how extremely ill he must be to have fallen prey to such dreams.

Merdigen stood beside a stone basin in the wall, his hands clasped behind his back. Alton crawled to him and rested his face against the cool floor. After his brief respite, he hauled himself to his feet, using the basin to support himself. At his touch, water spouted from the mouth of a copper fish and filled the basin.

He glanced in wonder at Merdigen. "This is real?"

"Try it."

Alton dipped his hands into the streaming water. It was clear, cold, and wet, and very real, unless his fever had sent him into total delusion. The water did not smell foul, so he let it fill his cupped hands and he drank of it. He kept drinking till his thirst was slaked, splashing his face and chest in the process. He paused, leaning against the basin, water dripping from his chin. It cooled his fever and cleared his mind.

"Magic?" he asked Merdigen.

"An elemental conjuring, performed by Winthorpe. He did it in each tower for the convenience of the keepers."

"Thank the gods," Alton said. He rummaged through a nearby cabinet and found some crockery, including a cup. He filled it from the basin, and slid to the floor, his back against the wall.

Merdigen conjured himself a stool, and a teacup and saucer. Perched atop his stool, he looked down at Alton and asked, "Who won?"

"Won what?"

"The war, boy, the war! I have been waiting in suspense for you to regain your senses so I could find out."

"Oh. Smidhe Hillander became king."

Merdigen let out a whoop, spilling illusory tea on his robes. "Orla said he'd make a fine king, and that the D'Yers would join forces with him."

"We did."

"And he was a good king, this Smidhe?"

Alton shrugged. "Guess so. His reign was considered bloody, but he had to bring the renegade clans to heel in order to unify the country."

Merdigen's teacup clinked onto its saucer. "And this was two hundred years ago . . ."

Alton nodded.

"Dear, dear. Do the Hillanders still rule?"

"Yes. Since Smidhe's time, Sacoridia has had peace. King Zachary now sits in the high throne in Sacor City."

"King Zachary," Merdigen said, as if testing the name for himself. "Such a shame that Agates Sealender fellow never named an heir, starting the war in the first place." He tsked, tsked, and sipped at his tea.

Alton reflected it was surely odd to be discussing history with a magical projection—whatever precisely that was. An illusion? "How long have you been here, Merdigen?"

"Since they built the *Haethen Toundrel.* Since the closure of the Long War."

If his mind were less fuzzy, if he had felt well, Alton might have marveled at Merdigen's words, and at Merdigen himself. He'd have asked endless questions about the past, and about the building of the wall. As it was, he had a hard enough time keeping his eyes open.

He surveyed his legs, to take in the extent of the poison within him. The thorn scratches were still an angry red, swollen, and weeping pus.

"I don't suppose there's a way to make this water hot," he said.

Merdigen gestured at a kitchen hearth nearby. "A wood fire should do it."

Alton frowned. There was no wood to burn, unless he broke the furniture. He did not think he had the strength.

"Making the water hot would have required transformative power, and Winthorpe was no good at it, y'see. He was only good at elemental. Though," he added on reflection, "he could've started a roaring fire."

Alton let Merdigen rattle on, and set to bathing his wounds best as he could with cold water. His body shivered with more chills, and when he was done, exhaustion took hold and he slept where he sat.

He dreamed of Karigan coming to him, singing to him a song he remembered. Yes, he must remember it. She sat in a sunlit glade, her legs tucked beneath the skirt of her dress. White flowers were woven into her hair.

Remember, dearest, she told him.

Alton would do anything for her. "I'll remember," he promised.

He came to with a groan. Sleeping in a sitting position had produced an ache in his back, adding to his misery.

Merdigen remained perched on his stool, paging through some old tome. Alton wondered if such activity actually engaged the magical projection in some way, or if Merdigen did it to simulate life and bring an added sense of comfort to the keepers. For an illusion, if that's what a magical projection was, Merdigen certainly retained a good amount of personality, memory, and intelligence.

"Well?" Merdigen asked, noting Alton's wakefulness. His book popped out of existence.

"Well, what?"

"There is a breach in the wall. What are you going to do about it?"

"Fix it."

"Very good." Merdigen applauded. "When you are finished, we can pick up the game where Orla left off."

When Alton didn't move, Merdigen shifted impatiently on his stool. *"Well?"*

"I don't know quite where to begin," Alton said.

"Look here, boy, it is not my job to provide instruction. What are your clan elders thinking by sending me a novice, eh?"

"They didn't send me. Not exactly, anyway."

Merdigen sat back in surprise. "And what precisely does *that* mean?"

It was taking quite a bit of energy to converse with the cantankerous Merdigen, energy Alton could not spare.

"I am a D'Yer," he said, "and I came to fix the wall. Will you help me or not?"

Merdigen squinted and tapped a finger on his knee. "Hmm. Two hundred years since last there was a keeper. There ought to be a good explanation for *that*."

There isn't, Alton thought, but he did not comment aloud for fear of sending the chatty magical projection off on another tangent.

"So, after two hundred years everyone has forgotten how to join with the wall. Am I correct?"

"Yes," Alton said.

Merdigen puffed out his mustaches. "Very well, follow me." He hopped off his stool—which promptly disappeared—and headed for the center of the chamber where the tempes stone sparkled on its pedestal, dark night and stars now clouding above it.

Alton followed as best he could, lightheaded and with pain stabbing his legs with each step. He stepped between the columns and into night, the columns and arches delicate and bone-white against the black, the grasslands empty and infinite around him. The change was so abrupt, so drastic, he found himself off kilter and fought to restore balance before he fell over.

"First let me show you the schema," Merdigen said. He

fluttered his hands in mid-air, and silvery dots glittered into being right before Alton's eyes. The dots flew apart, slicing through the air, leaving behind spidery lines etched into the night. The lines changed direction and angle, creating depth and dimension, continuously growing and branching until they formed a floating, shining image of the wall, much like an architect's rendering. The length of it spanned the area encircled by the columns.

Merdigen pointed to a tower located near the center of the wall. "We are here," he said. "This is *Haethen Toundrel.*" He then pointed to his right along the wall, where swirling runes blinked in alarm. A chunk of wall was missing there. "The guardians have been screaming for a very long time, but no one has heeded their call." Merdigen tsked, tsked, again. "This is where the wall has been breached, to our west."

"I know," Alton said.

"You *know?* Then why am I going to all this trouble?"

Before Alton could stop him, Merdigen wiped away the schema with a sweeping gesture of his hand. "I suppose I'll go through the whole procedure and then you'll tell me you know how to do it."

"I know something of it, of talking with stone. The song."

"You don't need me then, hmm?" Merdigen grumped. He pointed at the arched doorway to their right. "The breach is to the west, so use the west portal."

"Just—just like that?"

"Yes. Now leave me, I'm busy. I must feed the cat."

Alton shook his head as Merdigen walked away and vanished. "And I thought Karigan had all the strangest experiences . . ."

Karigan. She had taught him a song.

He turned and the arched entry of the west portal stood before him, beckoning, mysterious, and imposing. The fascia framing the arch appeared plain, except when he shifted his stance and runes embedded in the stone suddenly shimmered to life. What material could do that? he wondered. So much stonecraft lost. Enchanted, he traced a rune with his forefinger. It was as smooth as marble, but made of some other unknown mineral or ore. They required no light to come to life.

He vowed to one day discover the process and replicate it. It was his dream to restore the old craft to Clan D'Yer.

His eyes roved to the center of the arch, to the keystone, and there, carved in relief, were the tools of the stoneworker's trade—hammer, drill, wedges, chisel. This more than anything called to him; it was his birthright to be here now, his destiny as a D'Yer, a worker of stone. He would fix the wall.

He limped through the arched entry of the portal into darkness greater than night. He put his hands out before him, groping in the air, but within a few paces he came to a wall of stone. *The* wall? It could be none other.

He settled his hands on it and opened his mind to it, just as he had been instructed. Silvery runes lit up around his hands.

Greetings, cousin, the guardians seemed to whisper.

Alton closed his eyes, and sank into the wall.

❧ SPURLOCK ❧

Spurlock fumed as he stomped through the abandoned corridor, a pool of lamplight shivering around him. Never was the girl alone, never! How could he carry out the will of Blackveil if he couldn't get near her?

Constantly she was in attendance to the king, which meant she was constantly surrounded by guards, Weapons, and witnesses. At other times she was training with that monster, Drent. Spurlock didn't dare venture near the training yard, knowing how suspicious it would look for him, of all people, to be there. On top of everything, she was currently housed in the diplomatic wing, which was also heavily guarded.

He entered a chamber and was welcomed by the glow of Sergeant Uxton's lamp. They chose a new room to meet in every time now, after nearly running into a Weapon in their old place. This room was located above the records room, so Spurlock planned the meeting for early in the morning before Dakrias Brown reported to duty, for the old glass domed roof was still in place above it, despite the construction of more castle overhead. Their lights would shine right through it.

As if responding to his thoughts, their lamps rippled across the glass in swirling colors. Spurlock had an impression of figures dancing to life and horses stretched out in full gallop, swords being swung, and pennants snapping in a breeze. He didn't know what events the stained glass depicted, and he didn't care. It was, no doubt, the usual heroic nonsense.

Uxton regarded him curiously. Spurlock hadn't invited the other members of the sect, deeming them unlikely to be as helpful as Uxton. The others were outsiders, for all they had business on the castle grounds, and he feared their too frequent visits would draw unwanted attention, especially after the "intrusion" of Lord Varadgrim. Security on the grounds had tightened perceptibly. Uxton, in contrast, was an insider, with a valid reason to be within the castle. He wore the king's own insignia, and the black and silver of Sacoridia.

"We have had, as you know, a call to action," Spurlock said, without even the pretense of a greeting. He dispensed with the ritual used to open meetings, as well. He was too irritated with Karigan G'ladheon, and he perceived there was too little time. After a thousand years, the time was *now*. He would honor his ancestors and the empire in actions, if not rituals.

Uxton waited expectantly.

"Our lack of progress is a disgrace to our ancestors. Karigan G'ladheon is too well protected."

"Not much we can do about it," Uxton said with an indifferent shrug, "unless we can get her alone."

That was not a helpful reply, but what could Spurlock expect from an uneducated man? He had brawn, but lacked intellect. One day Spurlock would surround himself with only the best minds. "Blackveil is arising. Here is a chance to further our glorious mission of resurrecting the Arcosian Empire, a chance we have not had in a thousand years, and all you can say is that there isn't much we can do about it?"

Uxton hooked his thumb into his belt. "You have an idea of how to move things along?"

Spurlock frowned. Why was it he had to find all the answers? Why was he surrounded by simpletons? "We must lure her away from the king and his protectors, and out of the diplomatic wing, to someplace where we can trap her."

"You just need the lure," Uxton said. "I think I know a way. It will require a little planning, and the help of our brothers and sisters."

Spurlock relaxed. Finally, something would get done. He would avenge those of Arcosia who had spilled their blood in these lands, and in so doing, prove his worthiness to the power in Blackveil. One day he would be accounted among the great of Second Empire, and his descendants would hold him in highest honor.

It was much too early to be up and about, to trudge up the Winding Way to the castle gate while the sun had not yet peeked over the rim of the world. Lanterns still ablaze, the guards at the gate had looked down at the bleary-eyed recordskeeper and chuckled.

"Ol' Spurlock drivin' ya hard again, lad?" one called down.

"Yes," said Dakrias Brown, even though it wasn't entirely true, but he would *never* tell these hard-bitten soldiers the real reason he needed to catch up on his work: that it had been upended by the spirits of the dead.

The guards made sympathetic noises and let him through the "small" gate, a normal-sized door in the big gate. Ever since the intrusion on castle grounds, and the burning of Rider barracks, they'd been shutting the big gate at sunset, and not reopening it till sunrise.

Dakrias had been slaving away in the records room, because of Spurlock, since the night of the intrusion. He had emerged from the castle only to witness the chaos outside, and the blaze of Rider barracks. Someone had died in the fire, and another was seriously wounded, both Riders. He hadn't known Ephram Neddick, but he did know Mara Brennyn, and the thought of her grave wounds hurt him.

He yawned hugely as he made his way toward the castle. He would much rather hide in his room at Mistress Charon's. Small as it was, it was blessedly unhaunted. What will the ghosts have left for him this morning? he wondered. More smashed crates? An overturned table or shelves? Papers he had labored to file in an organized manner now spilled across the floor?

These days Dakrias spent more time on hands and knees picking up than attending to his other duties. Good thing Spurlock had been so preoccupied with other matters of late. He rarely checked on the records room, and when he did, he seemed not to notice his surroundings.

He reluctantly mounted the steps to the main castle entrance. For days now he had been making this early morning walk to reclaim order from disorder. He'd also done some reading, surreptitiously, in the castle library. It contained too few books on ghosts, and most of the writings seemed too fanciful to be as true as the authors claimed.

One book, however, proved more useful and dealt with ghosts in a serious way, by examining and classifying their traits. It was called *Phantoms in My Attic,* by Lord Eldred Faintly. As Dakrias read, he thought, perhaps, he might be haunted by poltergeists, ". . . a type of ghost that leaves an unseemly mess in its wake," Lord Faintly had written. But poltergeists were also prone to "violent manifestations and unbearable wailings." Dakrias' ghosts were not otherwise violent, nor did they wail.

Of the more mainstream ghosts, there were "the curious ghost, the friendly ghost, the sorrowful ghost, and the mischievous ghost." Dakrias was not sure exactly what demeanor his ghosts displayed, though the havoc they wreaked in the records room might be construed as mischievous. He rolled his eyes.

Most ghosts feel they have left something undone, Lord Faintly wrote, *and so they forever walk the Earth trying to right a wrong, or to see some activity to fruition. Until those goals are achieved, the ghost will not rest.*

There are still other ghosts who are merely disturbed and seek attention. They can be a housekeeper's nightmare.

Dakrias had hit on his ghosts. They weren't only a housekeeper's nightmare, but a recordskeeper's, too. Just why they sought attention, or just why they were disturbed, was probably something he would never learn. Unfortunately, according to Lord Faintly, the resolution of their problem was the only way to get rid of them. And how was he going to figure *that* out?

He sighed as he scuffed down the corridor toward the administrative wing. The only one who hadn't laughed at his claim of ghosts haunting the records room was Karigan G'ladheon. Not only had she refrained from laughing, but the look in her eyes told him she believed.

If Dakrias hadn't profoundly felt his duty to the king and people of Sacoridia, he would run from the castle all the way to his uncle's farm in D'Ivary Province without looking back.

The hauntings had made a mess of his life. Where once he kept an impeccable and orderly records room, it now fringed on chaos, just like his personal life. He jumped at the slightest sound, and he felt like a cat afraid of its own shadow. The other clerks dropped books behind him just to see how high he'd jump.

He didn't know how much more he could take, how many whispers in his ears, or the cool touches on the back of his neck . . . He wasn't sure his heart could handle any new antics on their behalf.

Ghosts rarely alter their behavior, Lord Faintly reassured. *They are cursed to repeat the same motions time*

*after time unless, by good fortune, there is closure to what-
ever it is that anchors them to the Earth, and only then, at
last, may they rest in peace.*

Dakrias paused at the entry to the records room to ignite
a candle with which he could light the lamps within, and
unlocked the door. It swung inward with a screech. All else
was silence.

He took a deep breath and stepped inside, and immediately a chaos of strewn books and papers fell into the circle
of his candlelight. He groaned.

Then voices, distant whispery voices, raised the hair on
the nape of his neck. Slowly he gazed upward. There, high
above, were two spirits that manifested as colorful spheres
of light.

Dakrias Brown's ghosts had not read Lord Eldred Faintly's book. No, indeed. They had gone and done something
new and unexpected.

Dakrias' eyes rolled to the back of his head, his candle
extinguishing as he hit the floor in a dead faint.

Journal of Hadriax el Fex

The face of the young woman I saw in the mirror lake so long ago haunts my dreams. Why did she appear to me? Was she a messenger from God? If so, I did not hear her message; I do not know what it portends. All I know is that she appeared out of the etherea as though to look upon me, and that she wore a winged horse brooch, just as Lil Ambriodhe and her riders do.

KARIGAN RIDING

"**N**o," Karigan said.

"No?" Drent's eyes creased as he stared her down. He loomed over her, gigantic and bristling.

"No." Her outward calm did not reflect the anger roiling inside her. Her emotions were far too raw to tolerate Drent and his abuse anymore.

"On the beam," he growled. *"Now."*

Drent had raised the beam, and greased it, to test her "sure-footedness." All she saw was a new opportunity for him to batter her senseless with his practice sword, and to create a spectacle for onlookers. Well, she'd give him a spectacle, all right.

"I'm done here," Karigan said.

"Insubordination." Drent smiled in anticipation. "You know what—"

"I won't be cowed by your threats."

A heavy silence blanketed the practice field. Even the crows seemed to settle on treetops to watch.

Drent raised his practice sword to strike her. She ducked beneath it and rotated her own in a graceful arc, and smashed his knuckles. He dropped his sword with a howl of pain, a howl that brought her a gratifying amount of satisfaction. Had any of his other students ever heard him utter such a sound?

He watched her wordlessly, clutching at his hand.

"I learned that move from an arms master named Rendle, a good man who never beat me to teach me a lesson."

She pivoted and slammed the flat of her practice sword against the beam. The wooden blade broke and she dropped the hilt to the ground. Wiping her hands, again perversely satisfied, she strode away from Drent, the onlookers, and the practice field, never looking back.

They could, and probably would, lock her up for both insubordination and the purposeful injury she inflicted upon a superior, but it no longer mattered. Compared to her losses, it was insignificant.

By the time she reached the stable, she was shaking from all the anger she'd held inside. She went to Condor and started currying him with hard, circular strokes. He leaned into them with a grunt of pleasure, as the tension seeped out of her arms and shoulders.

She would go for a ride. A ride would calm her, help bring some balance to her frayed nerves. She remembered her promise to Bluebird, and decided she'd take him along for some exercise.

When she rode Condor out onto the castle grounds, Bluebird followed on a lead rope. The gelding pricked his ears forward, and there was a new spring in his gait. He looked about himself as if seeing his surroundings for the first time. His spark of interest in life gladdened Karigan, and it brought her closer to healing.

She rode to the west castle grounds, which were wide and open, an ideal place for exercising horses, and as about as far away from Drent as she could get and remain on castle grounds. A couple other soldiers sat astride their horses, sharing a conversation at the north end, otherwise the area was all hers.

The walk there had warmed up both horses, and she squeezed Condor into a trot. After making a couple of very large circles, she let him run, Bluebird nosing alongside them. All cares melted away from her, and she knew only the wind against her face and the rhythm of hoofbeats.

He watched her riding down below, how her hair streamed behind her like a wild horse's mane. He could not see her face clearly, but he imagined her lips turned up in a smile, those dimples of hers dinting her cheeks, and the sun shining in her eyes. She rode fluidly as though one with her horse, as if it were the most natural thing in the world for her.

Gone was her usual shortcoat, the sun blazing on her white shirt. She was unfettered and free, a wild spirit he could not capture, tame, or confine, but one he wished would come to him, as a deer is tempted by a handful of oats. Would she shy away and run?

Wild spirit that she was, she was not invulnerable, and he yearned to comfort and protect her, but she would only run, he knew.

No, she could not be captured, but he was. Inextricably.

"My lord?"

Zachary Hillander bowed his head before turning away from the window to face Lord Richmont Spane and the nobles of Coutre Province. Laid out on the table before him was a heavily inked document.

"My lord," Spane said, "I believe Lord Coutre's terms are exceedingly generous. The dowry alone represents considerable wealth."

Everyone wanted something from the high king of Sacoridia, whether it was a pardon, status by association, or his agreement to a marriage proposal so a daughter might become a queen, bringing a clan much prestige and power. Few wanted him for himself. Laren had always been his close friend and confidant, but the relationship was overshadowed by her sense of duty. His position seemed to put some sort of taint on all his relationships.

"You do realize you have much to gain," Spane said, with a look in his eye that reminded Zachary of a rodent. "Or, much to lose. As you know, Lord Coutre's influence over the eastern clan lords is critical to your power. For instance, there is the D'Ivary matter to consider . . ."

Zachary pretended to be unaffected by Spane's inherent threat. Everyone wanted something from him, everyone except Karigan.

Yet, even his own wish, a simple one at heart, was denied him. She rode free like the wind, while he remained hopelessly encaged.

⊰ BLACKVEIL ⊱

The sentience prowled back and forth across its domain, upturning rocks and tunneling beneath the ground. It pushed through underbrush like an unnatural whirlwind. Creatures scurried up trees or otherwise fled its approach, aware of its fury.

Mirdhwell had been destroyed. Varadgrim had failed in his mission of securing the one of Hadriax's blood. Neither Lichant nor Terrandon responded to its calls.

And there was more that agitated the sentience. Had its plan with the Deyer been a colossal mistake? Would the influence it had entrenched within the man's mind help bring down the wall? Or had it failed?

The waiting frustrated the sentience and it wanted results *now,* but there was nothing it could do except wait. It was impossible to know what the Deyer was up to inside the tower, for it could not penetrate the wall. Only time would reveal the success or failure of its efforts.

The sentience slumped to a rest, settling into a muddy pool to stew over its situation. It found itself recalling memories of Hadriax. Hadriax hunting wild boar in the imperial forest. Handsome Hadriax whom all the ladies admired. They had shared many good times together, running and darting about the court square as boys, and wading in the fountains . . .

I miss him. Oh, Hadriax, I wish you were here. I loved you well.

⋘ ARMOR ⋙

After Karigan's ride, Bluebird looked better than she had seen him in a long time. He even took to his feed with exuberance afterwards. The ride had done all three of them good.

As she untacked Condor and brushed him down, she expected soldiers to arrive at any moment to take her before General Harborough for judgment on her act of insubordination. When none came, she returned to her quarters in the east wing of the castle to wait.

She swung her legs over the edge of her high canopied bed. The suite was huge, with an attached private bathing room. She had spent many blissful hours soaking in the deep tub.

Hangings draped the walls, and the furnishings were of the highest quality. The merchant in her prompted her to inspect the makers' marks on several of the pieces, and she was impressed to find them made by some of the best mastercraftsmen the kingdom had to offer. She was afraid the Riders, herself included, would be so spoiled by the luxury that they'd refuse to move to the new Rider wing, with its comparatively spartan chambers.

She waited for hours, and still no one came to arrest her. Even Cummings hadn't sent his usual schedule of meetings for her to attend. She laid back on the cushy feather mattress with her hands clasped behind her head, and stared at the flowery pattern of the canopy above.

Her mind wandered back to Bluebird and how he had declined after the captain's collapse. She knew animals got depressed when missing their masters. Her very own cat, Dragon, had always sensed when she was sick or unhappy, and would curl up beside her, purring his heart out to comfort her.

Yet, the messenger horses went beyond that, or so it seemed to her. If he were an ordinary horse, Bluebird would have eventually gotten over the captain's absence, but he hadn't. This thought led her to Crane, who had guarded Ereal's body. Even Condor had found her after her traveling at Watch Hill. No ordinary horse would have done that.

And now, Night Hawk would not leave the breach in the D'Yer Wall, as if on a vigil, hopelessly waiting for Alton's return.

She closed her eyes against the pain the thoughts brought back to her, but she only saw images of Night Hawk at the wall, pining away as he waited for something that would never happen. She remembered how Alton had looked in the Mirror of the Moon. He had been sick, yes, but not dead. He had been near the wall.

She drifted into sleep thinking maybe Night Hawk had the right of it, that maybe there was a reason to wait.

In a dream, she played about the fountains of a court square with a boy, much to the vexation of the adults around them, but they were indulgent enough not to reprimand them. Even the soldiers on guard tolerated the children running about their legs. Of course, the soldiers had no choice, for they must stand at attention no matter what, until their commander ordered otherwise.

And, most certainly, no one would interfere with the emperor's favored one.

She—Alessandros—and Hadriax played with toy sailing boats in the fountains, getting sopping wet in the process. Their nurse scolded them, but she had little success in diminishing their boyish exuberance.

Alessandros pushed his sailboat into the fountain. It was a marvel of detail down to the rigging and the mermaid figurehead, the winter's work of the finest shipwright in all the empire.

"I'm going to sail around the whole world," he declared.

"Me, too," said Hadriax.

"'Course you are. We shall rule the whole world."

Hadriax beamed at him, his best friend. In fact, the only friend he was allowed to play with. A foundling he was, but tolerated because Alessandros had taken a fancy to him. The emperor humored his heir, but regarded Hadriax as little more than a "pet," a playmate for a lonely little boy surrounded by adults. Hadriax had been taken into the household, and was fed, clothed, and tutored, all for the service he provided in keeping Alessandros company.

Alessandros' sailboat, caught in a gust, surged toward the powerful spray of the fountain. Fearing it would be swamped and ruined, he stepped into the fountain after it. The bottom of the fountain was slippery, and he lost his footing. Down he went, cracking his head on the fountain's edge, surging beneath the water, unable to see or breathe, thrashing; the dark, the dark . . .

Then sunshine, and Hadriax's face above his, helping to get the water out of his stomach.

For saving him, the emperor presented Hadriax with a medal, and the county of Fextaigne. Before the imperial court, garbed more richly than ever before, Hadriax swore himself forever loyal to the future emperor of Arcosia, to forever be his friend and protector. From a foundling, he had arisen to an aristocrat just like that. Throughout the years, his loyalty and friendship remained undiminished.

Oh, Hadriax, I wish you were here. I loved you well.

She awoke from her nap with a start, the words lingering in her mind. Dream, or memory? She was confused. Sharp pain rippled through her left arm, and she rubbed it till it subsided.

She arose, drowsy, but feeling she must go to the wall. Why? She shook her head. *For Alton, of course.* That was it. If there was a chance he was still alive . . .

She threw on her shortcoat and put a comb through her hair. She would ask the king to give her leave to go to the wall. Surely he wouldn't deny her.

She stepped out of her fine room into an empty corridor, empty save for the ever-present suits of armor that lined the walls and brooded over all who passed. Where were all the flesh and blood guards that usually patrolled these halls? In between shifts, maybe . . .

The suits of armor made her feel edgy, watched. Empty and hollow of life they might be, there was yet something menacing about them. Maybe it was their simulated human shape and the shadowed regard of eye slits.

Karigan never failed to think of them as a strange form of decoration, but she knew they served to remind all who saw them of the kingdom's martial strength. Some suits had been the battle armor of great knights, and others gifts to Sacoridia's rulers from other nations. Those standing in the diplomatic wing tended to be more ornate, of blued steel, gilded with scrolling patterns and mythical creatures. They were parade armor, once donned to impress other courtiers, not to serve as a defense on the field of battle.

The suit standing guard beside Karigan's door was enameled with a shiny black veneer, with minimal gold trim ornamenting it. A halberd etched with armorial devices had been posed in its gauntlets.

Karigan had grown accustomed to its presence, and spared it nary a glance, instead thinking ahead on precisely how she would phrase her request to King Zachary to convince him he must send her to the wall.

Declaring, *I think Night Hawk knows Alton is alive!* would at best sink her credibility in the king's eyes, the last thing she wanted.

As she lingered there outside her door, she heard metal grind against metal. She glanced up and down the corridor. Nothing moved, nothing was out of place. Silence reigned.

She was hearing things, she decided, but as she prepared to step away, she heard it again. She darted her gaze to the black armor beside her. Was its helm tilted at a slightly different angle?

Impossible.

She shook her head to dismiss it, but on the trailing edge of her vision, she saw a gauntlet rotate in its armored cuff.

Karigan wheeled to gaze full upon the suit of armor. To her astonishment, it straightened with a clatter from its somewhat slumped posture.

If Tegan was having one on her—

Before she could lift the visor of its helm to find out, the suit jerked its arms above its helm, raising its halberd high, and then cleaved downward.

Only quick reflexes saved Karigan. She hopped away as the halberd skimmed the air where she had stood. The ax blade sliced into the thick carpet.

As she backed away, her heart threatening to hammer right through her rib cage, an ominous clamor arose behind her. To her horror, helms on other suits of armor swiveled as though to look upon her. Hinges creaked as elbows bent. Swords shifted in gauntlets, maces and war hammers were raised, and polearms hoisted. Knee plates pivoted as the armor took its first shuddering steps. Mail skirts jingled like rain against leg armor.

The magic in the air was almost palpable. It tingled about her brooch, and the wild magic writhed restlessly in her arm, twining down to her wrist like a serpent.

The black armor rattled as it advanced on her with halberd poised to strike. She skittered away, but now she had to avoid all the other suits that had come to life. They seemed bent on closing in on her and she knew she must escape or be slain.

She dashed for a gap between two suits before it could be closed, praying that speed would serve her. With only a few steps to spare she slipped between the two suits of armor, and was past them.

A glance over her shoulder revealed one of the suits responding to her passage with agonizing slowness. It turned, battering its companion with its mace, knocking it over with a resounding crash.

Karigan hesitated no longer, and hurtled down the stairs to the main floor where she might get help to deal with the armor come to life, but when she reached the landing, she was greeted by utter pandemonium.

Servants and nobles alike fled in every direction, screaming and shouting, some weeping. Soldiers jogged by, bearing away a bleeding comrade.

A suit of armor, helm missing, creaked, clanked, and rattled down the corridor after them, swinging its poleax indiscriminately. It smashed a side table to pieces, and nearly beheaded a terrified servant.

"Five hells," Karigan whispered, thinking she should have prolonged her nap.

Jointed steel plates screeched as other suits of armor awakened and staggered from their places along the walls. One knocked down a soldier with a mace. Guards rushed over to assist their companion.

Not knowing what else to do, Karigan struck out for the throne room. If nothing else, the king would be organizing defenses against this bizarre attack, and she could lend her help where needed.

She charged down the corridor, dodging others fleeing from armor. Soldiers did what they could to stop the errant armor, using their swords as cudgels. The din was deafening. The suits of armor mindlessly lurched forward, impervious to the battering.

She came dangerously close to one suit of armor, which thrust its long sword at her. She scuttled out of its reach, so close to being disemboweled that the sword slashed her shortcoat.

She pressed herself flat into an alcove to avoid another swinging polearm and to catch her breath. The armor targeted anything and everything, even the very walls. One suit clunked into a wall, stepped back, clunked into the wall again, and stepped back, never averting its path. Another found her in the alcove. She ducked under its arm as its war hammer shattered a statue on a pedestal beside her.

She continued her race toward the throne room, leaping a suit of armor the soldiers had successfully dismantled. It was a nightmarish journey, running through a gauntlet of rushing steel, and a mindless but powerful enemy.

The throne room doors were wide open and several melees were in progress when she entered, both soldiers and Weapons engaged in combat. The king stood upon the dais, defending himself and his advisors with Sperren's staff of office from a mace-wielding suit of armor. Sperren quailed behind the throne, and Colin lay sprawled motionless across the dais steps.

The mace cracked on the staff. The king, relieved of his heavy mantle, moved with the grace and skill he had displayed during their swordplay. He beat the armor with powerful strokes that would have felled any living, breathing opponent.

With a jab of the staff's haft, the armor's helm went flying, but the rest of it kept coming, undeterred. The mace flashed at the king, and he blocked it with the staff, which splintered to pieces in his hands. The king staggered back, now weaponless.

Without a single clear thought in her head, Karigan sprinted the length of the throne room, gathering speed and momentum, and leaped on the armor, grappling her arms around it and sending it off balance. It crashed to the floor, fell apart in her arms, and the life went out of it, except for one steel gauntlet that scraped toward her like an inchworm. The king kicked it away.

"Karigan!" he cried, lifting plates of armor off her and tossing them aside. "Are you all right?"

She groaned. Her whole body throbbed, and she knew the worst of the aches and pains were yet to come. She definitely should have prolonged her nap.

The king knelt beside her. "Karigan?" His voice was urgent with concern.

She stared back at him, stupefied. "I—" she began.

"Yes?"

She swallowed. "I'm going to have," she said, her voice wry, "some interesting bruises."

He laughed suddenly, clearly relieved. Then just as suddenly, he sobered. "That was a very brave thing you did. Thank you."

Others might have told her she had been foolish for endangering herself, but he did not. Others might have trivialized her act by claiming they had the situation in hand all along, but he did not.

When Karigan looked inward, she realized she acted out of fear for the king, not bravery. Fear, pure and simple. She couldn't have just stood by while he was weaponless against the enemy. While fear might have paralyzed others, it made her act, confirming what the Mirror of the Moon had revealed to her about herself.

"Will you be all right for a moment?" the king asked. "I must see to Colin—"

His face and presence had so filled her vision and mind, the clamor of the fighting had fallen into the distant background. When he shifted, she caught the glint of steel over his shoulder.

"No!" she cried.

She wrapped her arms around him, and rolled him onto his back. She sheltered him with her own body, clenching her eyes shut in anticipation of the battle ax that would cleave through her spine. She waited an eternity.

"Karigan—" the king's voice rumbled beneath her. "Karigan, as much as I'm enjoying this, I can't breathe."

She cracked her eyes open and realized she held him in a death grip. Hastily she rolled off him.

Helping hands lifted her to her feet. Weapons surrounded them and assisted the king to rise as well. The throne room was significantly quieter. Suits of armor stood in various positions, frozen in time, weapons caught in mid-swing. The armor that had come upon her and the king stood with its ax at its apex. Thinking about the old but sharp blade hacking into her spine made her lightheaded.

The Weapons caught her and supported her.

"The messenger service is wasted on this one," said Donal. "She has the mettle to join the Black Shields."

Other Weapons chimed in with their approval, and though light-hearted banter ensued, it held an earnest ring to it.

"I rather like her in green," the king said, and he winked at her.

He took complete charge of the throne room. Colin was borne off to the mending wing by Weapons, and he ordered every suit of armor in the castle to be disarmed, dismantled, and locked up in the armory.

It was time, he told Karigan as an aside, for a change of decor anyway.

Runners and soldiers came in and out of the throne room updating him on conditions elsewhere. There had been some smashed furniture, but surprisingly few injuries, and thankfully no deaths.

Karigan thought he looked splendid directing the work, with his shoulders erect, and his fine waistcoat and cravat all in place, none the worse for the day's events. She, on the other hand, felt battered and disheveled, and somehow inadequate.

When the soldiers carried out the last piece of armor, the king sat wearily on the top step of his dais, and patted the space next to him for her to sit. When she did so, he loosed a long, heartfelt sigh.

"It seems," he said slowly, "that the magic that has afflicted other regions has finally found its way here. Would you agree?"

"Yes, sire."

He shook his head. "I don't know how to counteract it. It is beyond me—I am a king, but not a great mage who would know what to do."

Karigan realized he was revealing to her what he would have admitted only to Captain Mapstone.

"Somebody could have been killed," he continued, "and I couldn't have done anything to prevent it."

Karigan licked her lips, hoping what she planned to say would come out well. "I know you take the responsibility upon your shoulders for this. But the truth of the matter is, you're right, you haven't the tools necessary to deal with the wild magic. The answer is . . . It's the same as it has always been: to fix the D'Yer Wall, to stop the influx of tainted wild magic."

He shook his head. "We've little hope of it now, with the passing of Alton and his uncle."

Karigan swallowed hard, but did not falter. "Excellency, I wish to have your permission to—to go to the wall. I have a feeling about this—that Alton may yet live."

He glanced at her, startled. "Karigan, please, I know how difficult it is to accept—"

"No. I mean, I think it's reasonable, that Alton may still be alive, and that we should try to find him. I suspect he is our best chance of mending the wall."

"I see." The king's demeanor hardened a little, as if he were faced with something he had no wish to hear. "What has you convinced Alton still lives?"

"I'm not convinced he is alive." She tried to tread safe ground, trying to sound as rational as possible to better her chances of him believing her. "But I have also made some observations about messenger horses. I think they know, that they can somehow sense, what condition their Rider is in."

The king raised an eyebrow. "Go on, I'm listening."

She told him about Crane and Bluebird, and Condor, too.

"You think Alton's horse is waiting for him, because it knows he's still alive?"

Karigan nodded emphatically. "Yes. And there's one more thing." She explained to him about the images of Alton she had seen in the Mirror of the Moon. The king was clearly skeptical. "Please," she nearly begged him. "If there is the slightest chance I'm right, shouldn't we try to find out if he lives?"

The king's shoulders sagged, and a sorrowful expression crept into his features. "Even if Alton is alive, I forbid any-one to cross the breach and search for him. It's just too dangerous to sacrifice anyone else." Before Karigan could respond, he added, "*However,* I see no harm in sending a Rider down to keep an eye on the situation."

Karigan stood. "I'll leave immediately. I'll—"

The king took her arm and pulled her back down on the step. "I'll send *a* Rider, but not you."

Karigan's mouth dropped open. "But—"

"I need you here," he said, "while Captain Mapstone is unavailable."

An response died on her tongue when she saw his resolve. She would win no arguments with him this day. She saw also his concern, and wondered fleetingly if it were more than his need of her in Captain Mapstone's absence.

"You may be dismissed," he said.

Karigan rose to leave, but he called after her. "You broke three of Drent's fingers."

With all the excitement, she had forgotten all about Drent and her outburst this morning.

"I'm sorry," she said, head bowed. "I'll report to General Harborough immediately."

"Don't bother. Drent says you are ready to move to the next level of training, now that you've tired yourself of being beaten on. His words, not mine." The humor was creeping into his eyes again. "Besides, your acts here today override any demonstrations of insubordination. No discipline is necessary—this time. By my order."

Karigan left the throne room less than satisfied with the king's response to her request to ride to the wall. Sending someone else was not good enough for her. She felt certain *she* must go. It had to be her.

She walked through the castle corridors wondering if there was some way she could change his mind. The king wanted her by his side while Captain Mapstone was unavailable. What if the captain became available? The king would have little reason to hold her back. Perhaps if Karigan could convince her of the urgency of her task, the captain would pull herself together and be able to stand by the king again.

Encouraged by her plan, she left the castle for officers quarters.

"Please, Captain," Karigan called through the door, "we need you back." *No lie there.* "If you come back, the king will let me go to the wall and seek out Alton."

The door groaned open, and Karigan jumped back, thinking her plan must have worked, but when she looked upon Captain Mapstone, she realized her mistake.

The captain stood in the doorway, gaunt and hard. She practically emanated ice. Even her hair had lost its vibrant sheen and seemed frosted over.

She pointed a shaky finger at Karigan. "Leave my doorstep." Her voice was weak, but harsh. *"Leave."*

And she slammed the door shut.

Abashed, Karigan headed back for the castle. Not only had she lost Alton, but now the captain as well.

Guilt washed over Laren, adding to her torment. She slid down the door to the floor, her head in her hands, her ability commenting on each and every thought and emotion as she experienced it.

She no longer lived, but merely existed, with the mental battering in her mind. It would be better to die.

True.

Not even when she had been so ill after the knife wound that had left the brown scar down her neck and all the way to her belly, not even when she had lost the man who had meant the most to her in her life, had she so seriously considered ending her own.

Her eyes roved over her saber and longknife hanging from her swordbelt on a hook on the far wall. The leather scabbards were shiny black, but she knew precisely the bright, sharp steel they concealed.

She loosed a trembling sigh, knowing she hadn't the reserves to actually stand and cross the room to draw her knife. Instead, she reached into her pocket and withdrew the stone butterfly she kept close by at all times. Each feature, each pattern and texture, was perfectly preserved. Life literally captured in stone. It only reminded her of how trapped she was as well.

"I have never been so low," she sobbed.

True.

She was a terrible captain—she had let down so many of her Riders—Ereal and Bard, Ephram and Alton . . .

True.

Let someone else make all the difficult choices and carry the weight of it. She was hopelessly incapable of it herself.

True.

She just wanted to bang her head against the wall, bang it bloody.

Laren.

Or, there was the honed edge of her longknife.

Laren.

"What?" She looked up, blinking rapidly.

Her quarters were dim. She didn't care to see the squalor she lived in. It seemed somehow fitting, for her mind moved in dark places. She had no covering, however, across the narrow arrow slit window, and dusty sunlight glared in her eyes when she looked in that direction.

I want to help you, he said.

She shielded her eyes and barely made out a figure.

"Who—who are you? How did you enter?"

He stepped closer, but his outline was fluid. *The one who was first of us all sent me here from my long rest.*

His words did not send an assault upon her mind. In fact, there was an easing, a sense of peace that overcame her. The voice of her ability was slowly closed off. Tears of joy ran down her cheeks.

"Who are you?" she whispered.

He came closer, but remained translucent. He was garbed in green, and there was the glitter of a golden winged horse brooch upon his chest. She barely made out ritual tattoos tracked across his cheeks. A gleaming mane of black hair fell down his back.

He was the half-breed Rider captain who helped deliver King Smidhe Hillander to his throne. "Gwyer Warhein," she murmured.

He nodded. *We share a brooch, you and I. It augments a singular gift, a rare one. It is something to rejoice in, not despair.*

"The pain—" The words wrenched from her gut.

I know.

All of Karigan's dealings with ghosts had not prepared Laren for this moment, but having the shade of one of Sacoridia's hero Riders in her quarters did not frighten her or make her question her sanity. No, it awakened her sense of wonder, and uplifted her spirits from the blackness of despair in which she had wallowed for so long. She stood, her legs trembling.

I have left my rest to help you, he said. He reached out with a translucent hand to her. *Will you let me show you how you may control your gift?*

"Yes, oh *yes*."

She felt a fluttering against her palm. Miraculously, a butterfly lifted from it, and into the air, free of stone.

Journal of Hadriax el Fex

Alessandros has turned his back on God. He has decided there is no God. If there were a God, he explains, his father would not have abandoned him here in these lands. If there were a God, he'd have conquered the barbarians by now. If there were a God, Alessandros would have brought a cure to ailing Arcosia and become the blessed ruler of the Empire.

So, he has declared *himself* the god. "Look at my powers," he tells me. "Are they not the powers of a god?"

Indeed, he uses his powers to alter the world to his own designs—the creatures he has made, the lives he has taken. All I see is ruin. When first we came to the New Lands, they were so full of potential, unspoiled and primeval, so unlike Arcosia, which was wasting away from the drain on etherea and the wear of a populous and long-lived civilization. Now Alessandros destroys everything he touches—the people, the creatures, and the land itself, which has turned brown and bleak as though wilting in despair. He misuses etherea in great quantities. The land is all toppled forests and battlefields. He has wrought more damage in the New Lands in less time than ever occurred in Arcosia with its large population of mages.

Tonight Alessandros proclaimed himself the one god before the assembled troops. The priests among us were tortured and flung into the fires. He said the sacrifice was essential to cleanse us of their blasphemous teachings. Anyone caught worshipping the former god would endure a similar fate.

I have never seen morale bleaker among the troops. Desertion is at its highest level ever. Inevitably these men are hunted down and slain, their bodies displayed for all to see, as an example of the wrath of Alessandros the god.

There are men I know of who still devote themselves, in secret, to the one true God, but I will not report them, because I am one of them.

Even Renald and his fellow Lions are uneasy, but they are far too loyal to speak out. They live to serve Alessandros, and are the bravest of all soldiers. None have deserted their ranks.

Tonight I will pray to God that Alessandros returns to the right path, and remembers our purpose, and that the madness leaves him.

⋘ BLACKVEIL ⋙

With little else to occupy the sentience while it waited, it drifted in dreams, daydreams and night dreams, dreams of remembrance, and in this way it came to know its name.

I was Alessandros. Alessandros del Mornhavon.

The son of Emperor Arcos, the heir to the empire.

The revelation elicited little excitement as though it had been remembered all along, deep within its consciousness.

Knowing the name, however, unlocked avenues to its history, its childhood, and to memories of growing into manhood with Hadriax at its . . . *his* side. Together they had gone hawking and battered down uprisings among the empire's holdings. There were parties and balls, dinners and festivals. Hadriax had snuck wine and women into their rooms when the devil got into him. Alessandros had enjoyed these diversions, but he cared less about them than he did about Hadriax.

Always Hadriax had been there beside him, the dashing soldier-courtier, his best friend, and his best champion.

Then there had been the time of exploration across the sea into the New Lands. Here had been the opportunity for Alessandros to prove himself to the emperor, and to clinch his favor with the people. Here has been his moment to achieve true manhood and, in the eyes of God, prove his suitability to represent Him on Earth.

Glory was to be had, and riches, and the greatest expansion of the empire's boundaries since the time of Arcos I. He would return home triumphant, bearing gifts to the emperor of gold, spices, slaves, and knowledge. Most importantly, he would bring back a new source of etherea that would heal lands throughout the empire left barren and drained by its overuse. It would make the emperor more powerful than ever.

No emperor would be as renowned as Alessandros del Mornhavon, Arcos VI. With Hadriax at his side, he could not fail.

But Alessandros had never returned home, had he? He had become something other than a man. Something greater?

Something trapped.

And where was Hadriax now?

They had come to these lands and things turned out much different than he ever imagined they would. The barbarians proved more and more resistant as time passed, initiating a war that never seemed to end.

Alessandros had been confident it was just a matter of time before they wore the barbarians down. The empire kept sending ships filled with supplies and soldiers. Then, inexplicably, the ships stopped coming.

He had sent messenger after messenger back home seeking assistance from his father, the emperor, but no word ever came back, the ships never returned. He thought the first few had been lost at sea, but as he depleted his fleet, another answer came to him: his father had abandoned him.

His father must have disapproved of the long war, and perceived his son as a failure.

Abandoned.

The forest trembled.

How could his father have done this to him? In anger,

Alessandros had indiscriminately killed slaves and prisoners, and flattened villages. He had declared himself Emperor of Mornhavonia, and pledged to return to Arcosia to wrest power from his father. Once he conquered the barbarians here.

Hadriax had pleaded with him to reconsider. Perhaps some ill had befallen the empire, he said. Surely there was some explanation.

Alessandros had not been able to believe something so disastrous could happen to the empire that it would cause his father to cease contact with him. Arcosia was vast, strong. So he had continued his campaigns here in the New Lands.

As years passed, Hadriax had grown aloof and spent more time on the field of battle. Their few meetings turned into arguments, and Hadriax expressed his revulsion for Alessandros' work with the Eletians.

"The experiments are necessary," Alessandros had said, "for understanding the species and the nature of etherea."

Hadriax had walked away with a disgusted expression on his face, and Alessandros killed a few Eletian prisoners to spite him.

What had happened to Hadriax? Why had he become so withdrawn? Alessandros had missed him during his absences, but filled his time in his workroom, creating a device to enhance his powers a hundredfold, and allow him to end the war once and for all.

The Black Star. It was his greatest work, a thing of entrancing beauty, a star of five points fashioned from obsidian. The points were as sharp as swordtips, but as a weapon, its true power lay in its ability to augment etherea, specifically, his ability to work the art, the way glass can intensify the rays of the sun. Eventually even that great power could be augmented . . . with a few sacrifices.

Amid his triumph of the Black Star, at a moment when

Hadriax should have been most proud of him, he had learned instead of Hadriax's plan to meet secretly with Lili-edhe Ambriodhe.

Blackveil Forest quaked so fiercely that branches fell from trees and creatures scuttled into their dens to hide.

Even more powerful than the abandonment by his father had been Hadriax's betrayal.

Black clouds roiled above treetops, a breeze whipped into a frenzy shredding leaves off branches.

Hadriax's betrayal had provided the League with intelligence that strengthened them. They had waylaid Alessandros' army in final battle across the Wanda Plains. He had watched as the League forced its way through his legions, somehow neutralizing his Great Mages.

He had watched them beat back his lieutenants—Lichant, Terrandon, and Varadgrim. Mirdhwell had been slain by his own son.

Alessandros had let his powers build within the Black Star. He had planned to sweep the battlefield clean, even if it meant decimating his own legions. For once and for all, he had planned to use his powers in a way a god should.

After all, was he not God himself, with the power of life and death in his hands?

But again, victory had been stolen from him. Somehow, that demon bitch, Ambriodhe, had gotten King Santanara of Eletia near him unawares. Santanara had wrested the Black Star from him, and turned it against him—not using the art, but by using it as a common weapon.

Down, down, down had come the falling star, a thing of entrancing beauty, Alessandros' finest achievement. Down it came, a sharp point, and stabbed into his chest.

Sharp pain, then darkness and slumber.

The forest stilled, lay calm and silent. From stillness came an explosion.

*   *   *

A tidal wave of rage funneled through the breach, knocking out the repaired section and sending more cracks through the wall. Trees shattered into splinters, killing several soldiers within the encampment.

The rage, like an extraordinary storm wind unleashed, raced through the Sacoridian forest, and all vegetation touched by it withered and decayed.

Elsewhere, an entire village vanished and the Broken-branch River reversed its flow. Vessels of all tonnages, from the smallest fishing skiffs to heavy merchant ships, foundered at sea.

In Sacor City, people going about their business along the Winding Way turned to stone.

In the castle, it began to snow.

THE MEMORY
OF STONE

Disembodied, Alton felt no pain or illness, no hunger or thirst. He had no need of sustenance here.

His soul and consciousness soaked through the pores of granite. At first he panicked that he was trapped, as inert as stone, caught in gray nothingness unable to move or float free. He had turned to stone, unmovable and dead. The sensation was akin to being buried alive, knowing there was no escape, even as the earth is being shoveled over one's coffin.

Then Karigan's soothing voice came to him, reminding him to relax and open his mind so he could go deeper, of how to enter another level of existence within stone. He did as she bid, and as he calmed, he found himself adrift among shining crystalline structures. Complex and perfect, they were the stuff of stars, like the homes of the gods in the heavens.

As he flowed and oozed through the stone, he grew aware of its memory. Each block knew of molten magma and ice sheets. Of the first touch of the dawning sun chasing away the chill of night. The granite remembered the cool shade of the forest and the crash of the raging sea. It remembered the painful bite of ice freezing and thawing, creating cracks and joints.

The stone recalled creatures scuttling atop it, and being quarried by man. It had many inconsequential stories to tell

511

of its enormous lifetime, stories of weathering and the cold of interminable winters. The memories elicited no emotions, they were simply there like the words in a book, but engraved within the stone.

The stories resonated through Alton, but he had to shake himself loose, feeling a million years could pass without his knowing it. He had work to do here.

He plunged into a yet another level of awareness within the wall, and this time he found energies inconsistent with the inert character of stone. There were other souls here with him.

A choir of voices sang in harmony, and he knew these voices, for they had haunted his dreams. Their tones vibrated through his being, through the wall. They were songs of strength and weathering, of peace and restfulness.

Underlying the choir, however, was crackling, the destruction of the wall. The voices held uncertainty, the rhythm of their song irregular.

The wall shuddered suddenly, like a house battered by a gale. The voices cried out and screamed as the wall strained against a surge of power. Alton was almost thrust out of the wall, but he wrapped his consciousness around a crystalline structure and held fast.

He knew his task was more urgent than ever. He must bring order to the rhythm of the wall. He must sing the song Karigan taught him.

WESTRION'S
WINGS

Disheartened and weary, Karigan mounted the steps back into the main entrance of the castle. She wondered if Captain Mapstone would get better. She needed her now more than ever.

How was she ever going to convince the king to let her ride to the wall? The captain wasn't going to be of any help . . . Maybe, just maybe, she would have to disobey the king and go anyway. Her heart pounded hard at the thought.

Inside the castle, the atmosphere had calmed considerably. Soldiers and servants were carrying away pieces of armor bit by bit, a helm under one arm and a leg thrown over a shoulder. The corridors looked strange and empty without the old sentinels standing watch along the walls.

"Rider!"

Karigan turned to find a runner of the Green Foot trotting toward her.

"Yes?"

"Down in the new Rider wing," the girl gasped, trying to catch her breath, "Rider Bowen has been hurt."

Garth!

Karigan dashed off without a second thought, fretting over what could have happened. Had he been hurt by the armor? Maybe he had pulled his back moving furniture.

She departed the populated corridors of the main castle

for the one that led into the Rider wing. She should have asked the runner to go fetch Tegan, but then again it was probably Tegan who had summoned her.

The Rider wing was quiet, eerily so, and she had the feeling of ghostly presences around her, murmuring into her ears. Unseen fingers plucked at her sleeve, and wall lamps flickered.

"Garth?" she called. Her voice rang hollow through the corridor. She received no answer.

She shuddered and broke into a clammy sweat as a shadow rustled by her. This didn't feel right, and she was about to head back to the main castle to get help, when she heard a very human groan.

Casting all caution aside, she ran to the one chamber with a lamp lit within. It was the room they had chosen for Mara, since it was the largest. They had cleaned out two hundred years of filth, making it cleaner than it probably had ever been in its entire existence. Garth was saving the best pieces of furniture for it, and had even used his own currency to purchase a fine carpet. All of this in hopes their positive thoughts and actions would help Mara heal. They dared not consider the alternative.

Karigan entered the chamber and gasped. Garth lay sprawled on the floor, a nasty bump rising on his temple.

"Garth!" She rushed to his side, placing her hand on his arm. "Garth?"

His eyes fluttered open and he groaned again. "Behind . . ." he whispered.

"What?" Karigan shook his arm, but he had fallen unconscious.

There were footsteps behind her, and before she could turn, a coarse sack smelling of potatoes was thrown over her head. All of Arms Master Drent's training came into play—she screamed and tussled like a wild thing, kicking, clawing, and elbowing her assailants. They elicited grunts and curses, and she managed to prevent the sack from being drawn over her shoulders.

In the one moment when all their hands were off her, she whipped the sack from her head.

There were three of them: a soldier, a woman whose nose was bleeding, and a big man who must be a blacksmith, for the soot engraved into the lines of his face. The blacksmith and woman looked vaguely familiar, but just now she didn't have the time to think about it. She stood in a defensive crouch and balled her fists.

"Look," said the soldier, who wore sergeant's chevrons on his sleeve, "we don't wish to harm you. If you'd just come along quietly—"

Just like they didn't wish to harm Garth? "Come along *where?*"

"Lord Varadgrim came looking for you." The sergeant had an easy grin despite the incredible words. "Seems you are wanted in Blackveil."

Karigan was so stunned, she nearly failed to duck in time when the woman swung a club at her head. She grabbed a broom leaning against the wall and used it to deflect other blows. The woman had no training as a fighter, and Karigan had little trouble dancing around her. A good jab with the broom handle into the woman's gut made her drop the club and retch.

The blacksmith and sergeant were another matter. They were both armed with swords and eyed her confidently.

They waited for her to make the next move, so she did. She broke the broom handle over the blacksmith's head. His eyes lost focus, and he wobbled unsteadily.

"I heard you were training with Drent," the sergeant murmured.

Karigan was pretty sure they didn't intend to kill her, so it perhaps made her more bold. She jabbed at the sergeant with her piece of splintered broom handle, but he easily pushed it aside, and knocked her arm backward with the flat of his blade.

The blow reawakened Karigan's old elbow injury and sent pain ringing all the way to the roots of her teeth. Her broom handle clattered to the floor.

"I also heard," the sergeant said, "about your arm injury."

Karigan rubbed her elbow. "Who are you, and why are you doing this?"

"My name is Westly Uxton, and despite this uniform I wear, I am loyal to the Second Empire. Did you not know the empire will arise again? No? Well this time it shall persevere over the people of these lands."

It took a moment for the words to register. Wasn't Uxton one of the "people" of these lands? It didn't make sense to her. She would have liked to question him further, but the blacksmith's eyes were regaining focus, and a determined glare was forming on the woman's face. She began to reach for her club.

Karigan sighed and sagged her shoulders as if beaten. Uxton relaxed subtly in response, thinking the day won. It was not.

Karigan kicked the woman out of her way and pelted into the corridor—where she went sliding across the floor and crashed into the opposite wall with an *oomf.* She scrambled to maintain her footing on the . . . *icy* floor? The corridor was freezing. What were these cold wet drops alighting on her cheeks?

"What in the world?"

Snow was falling in the corridor and had already left a thin layer on the floor that glistened gold and silver in the lamplight.

Uxton and his cohorts slipped and slid into the corridor after her and paused, just as astounded as she.

"You see?" Uxton said. "This is the empire's power! Lord Mornhavon is awakening!"

Varadgrim, Blackveil, empire, Mornhavon. Karigan didn't like the sound of this, not at all.

They blocked her passage into the main castle, so she had no alternative but to run in the opposite direction. Snowflakes filled in her footsteps as she went, and her breaths emerged in frosty puffs. Her assailants charged after her, trying just as hard as she not to lose their footing on the slippery floor.

She careened around a corner into an unlit corridor. She kept going until she ran out of light and stood in complete darkness. Now, she thought, was a perfect opportunity to find out if her ability was functioning yet.

She touched her brooch, but her ability did not respond. She supposed Uxton and the others only would have had to follow her footprints to find her anyway even if it worked.

Her assailants, bearing a lamp, rounded the corner. She ran blindly into the dark ahead, thinking her only weapon at hand was a snowball—not a very useful weapon.

Some strides into the dark, she collided with a suit of armor standing in the middle of the corridor, and went down in a tangle of steel arms and legs. It seemed the clean-up crews hadn't bothered to pass this way.

Uxton and the others were on her, grabbing her from the embrace of the armor. She fought like a cat, trying to keep their hands off her at all costs. Using a well-placed elbow here, a heel there, and a few fist blows helped. The club grazed her hip and a fist to her temple sent her crashing down into the snow and armor.

She scrabbled through the snow and her hand fell upon a weapon, a mace entangled in the armor. She whipped it up and crushed the woman's hand holding the club, and jammed the haft behind Uxton's knee. He fell onto his back.

The blacksmith held the lamp aloft and glared down at her. "You will regret your resistance." He raised his sword.

A maelstrom of wind and flying shapes suddenly appeared in the corridor. Snow swirled in great gusts and pelted
them, the lamplight leaping and sputtering. A dreadful
moaning coursed through the very stone of the corridor itself.

Cold, invisible hands helped raise Karigan to her feet,
and there was muttering in her ears. The blacksmith's eyes
widened in fear and Uxton darted glances in every direction, his hand clamped around the hilt of his sword. The
woman curled into a fetal position.

Translucent shapes lunged around the assailants, their
moaning increasing in intensity. Karigan began to discern
words: *Death to the empire, death to the Black One, death
to the empire . . .* And the ones who touched her, and urged
her on, whispered her name: *Galadheon, Galadheon,
Galadheon . . .*

She let the ghosts bear her away into the dark. The
darker it grew, the more their shapes defined. She glimpsed
among them all the races of the lands, from the Sacor Clans
to the folk of the Under Kingdoms, and some she did not
recognize. Briefly a Green Rider appeared before merging
into the mass of formless shapes.

*Death to the empire, death to the Black One, do not let
the empire rise again, Galadheon . . .*

They ushered her into a room, and in the unreliable
spectral glow, she stood there, chest heaving from her exer-
tions, and brushed snow off her shoulders. It had not
snowed in this chamber.

Now what? she wondered.

She supposed, on reflection, she should have guessed,
but the traveling took her off guard yet again. It latched onto
her brooch and dragged her through time. She wailed with
surprise and wondered if some residue of her cry, trailing
across the ages, came to the inhabitants of those times as
the wailing of a ghost.

What were ghosts, after all? Were they beings like her,

simply passing through time, or truly the spirits of the dead?

When the traveling ceased, she fell to the floor as if a carpet had been yanked out from beneath her feet. She arose to her knees to find a somber scene, her nose itching at the suffocating smoke of incense and candles. Every reflective surface in the chamber had been shrouded with dark cloth.

A figure lay in a bed, blankets drawn to her chest, her hair splayed across a pillow. There was a deathly pallor upon her flesh, and her breathing was barely perceptible. With some shock, Karigan realized it was Lil Ambrioth.

Two men hovered over Lil, one of whom was Rider Breckett.

"Aye, all that can be done has been done," the other man said, "magically and with herbs." He was, Karigan decided, a mender.

"I'd best get the king then," Breckett said.

The mender gazed down at Lil as if in an attitude of prayer while he waited. Karigan rose and moved closer, and discerned the tang of blood and illness beneath the incense.

King Jonaeus entered abruptly, paused to take in the scene, and rushed to Lil's side. He fell to his knees beside the bed and took her hand into his, and held it against his cheek.

"Tell me," the king said after many moments had passed, "the truth of it. Do not hold anything back."

The mender and Rider exchanged glances, and eventually the mender said, "The babe could not be saved. The women are . . . they're readying him for his rites."

The king closed his eyes and squeezed Lil's hand. "Rites," he murmured. "Birth and death rites for my boy child." Then he glanced sharply at the mender. "What else?"

"We—we have exhausted all our gifted menders and

used all our skills to help save her. She is very weak, my lord, very close to death. The miscarriage, and the arrow wound . . . Well, she has lost considerable blood, and I fear the wound is festering. I have prepared . . ." The mender licked his lips, and had considerable trouble bringing himself to utter his next words. "I have prepared a draught to ease her on her journey to Aeryc's embrace should you command it. It would relieve her of pain and suffering."

The king shuddered.

No! Karigan cried.

Lil murmured and rolled her head. Her eyes fluttered open.

Karigan could not reconcile this sickly, fevered woman with the Lil Ambrioth she had come to know. This creature in the bed was but a pale wraith of her. Karigan did not recognize her, the hero of the Long War, the powerful leader.

Lil's gaze took in Jonaeus, who shook as he wept at her side.

"Dearest . . ." she murmured. Taxed by speaking, she squeezed her eyes shut. When she opened them again, her gaze fell upon Karigan. "Are you here to take me to the gods?"

The others in the room exchanged glances, murmuring about delirium.

Thunderous, pulsating wingbeats descended into the chamber, a sound no living mortal should ever hear, the wingbeats of Westrion, the Birdman, god of the dead. Only Karigan and Lil heard it.

No!

Lil blinked at her.

No, Karigan said. *I thought* . . . She had never imagined seeing the First Rider die this way; maybe in the glory of battle, but not in a sickroom, not from birthing . . .

Breckett beckoned a moon priest into the chamber, who began murmuring scripture at the foot of the bed.

"No child," Lil gasped. "No legacy . . ."

The king tried to hush her so she might spare her energy.

"Delirious," the mender said.

Karigan knew Lil wasn't delirious. She was grieving. She touched her brooch and felt weak resonance within it.

You have a legacy, a great one, Karigan told her. *I am your legacy, and so is every Green Rider through every generation a thousand years into the future.*

Karigan told her of how the Riders were integral to the League's victory during the Long War. She spoke of how Lil Ambrioth was a celebrated hero in her own time, and continued to inspire Riders and non-Riders alike. She spoke of other courageous Riders who followed in her footsteps, helping to fend off tyranny.

As Westrion's wingbeats threatened to drown her out, she shouted to be heard.

We exist a thousand years from now because of you!

Lil's face grew peaceful at Karigan's words. "It is good then . . ."

Her luminous spirit began to separate and lift from her body. Karigan became frantic, overwhelmed with a sense that if Lil slipped away now, all those things she had described would not come to pass.

The shadow of Westrion's wings engulfed the chamber.

No! Karigan cried. *Please! The Riders still need you— without you, all is lost!*

Lil's spirit hovered in place, as if undecided. The priest droned on the rites of death. The king spoke quietly to Lil, but Karigan could not hear his words over the wingbeats. The mender began to pour his concoction into a goblet.

Karigan couldn't let them poison her. She launched herself around the bed and tried to knock the goblet out of the mender's hands, but her hands passed through his wrists.

This can't happen!

Remembering the last time she had traveled to the past, remembering how she had been able to handle a sword from that time, she grabbed Breckett's longknife from its sheath and rapped the mender's knuckles hard. The poison toppled from his hands, splattering across the floor.

The mender was too stunned to move and could only stare at the puddle on the floor. Breckett patted his empty knife sheath, and the priest's eyes nearly bugged out of his head.

"The gods—" he sputtered.

Lil's spirit wavered above her body, and Westrion's wings pounded the air.

❦ A WINTER'S DREAM ❦

U xton jabbed Karigan in the ribs with the toe of his boot. She groaned, for every part of her body hurt and she was freezing. He kicked her again, and she raised her head with a grunt.

Uxton's eyes were wild in the light of the lamp he carried. Ghosts whirled around and through him, tugging on his hair, moaning in his ears.

Death to the empire, death to the Black One, death to the empire . . .

The ghosts gained energy in their frenzy, and grew more obvious in shape and form. Uxton was pale and trembling, and even slashed his sword through them, which, of course, accomplished nothing.

The ghosts, as if sensing the effect they were having on him, made their chant more gruesome: *Find the one, the empire's spawn, strip his flesh and clean the bones, grind to dust and feed to dogs . . .*

"Get up," Uxton commanded, his voice strained. He lowered his sword blade and nicked Karigan's neck with its tip. Blood, warm against her freezing flesh, burned along the contour of her throat.

Find his heart and eat it whole . . .

A tick spasmed in Uxton's cheek.

"Where are your friends?" Karigan asked.

"Doesn't matter." He grimaced as a ghost reached into

his ear up to its elbow, and twisted. His eyes rolled back and he shook his head violently.

Karigan guessed Uxton's compatriots could not bear the ghosts, that they had abandoned him, the corridors, and their mission.

"Get up," Uxton ordered, teeth gritted.

"Or what?" Karigan was so weary, not so far from darkness. The traveling always seemed to drain her life's energy.

"Or I will batter you and drag you out."

Karigan shifted and realized with surprise there was an object in her hand.

Uxton raised his sword to land a blow on her. She rolled, evaded his blade, and drove the object into his foot, through boot leather, through stocking, through flesh and bone. He howled and the lamp careened into the air, its light flickering out before it crashed to the floor.

As Karigan sank into nothingness, she heard Uxton whimpering some distance away, and ghostly laughter tickled her ear.

The snow waned to a gentle flurry. Of all the things Laren had witnessed during her life, this was, well, one of the most "magical." Outside she had left a sunny late summer day, only to find winter within. Snow drifted against the corridor walls, and statues wore fresh mantles of white.

Servants shoveled paths through the corridors, and she saw more than one snowball arcing through the air. In fact, one almost hit her in the head. There was much laughter and merriment in the castle, the like of which she ordinarily associated with holidays.

The merriment, she thought, was preferable to the fear such a strange occurrence could have as easily inspired.

She permitted herself a smile, an unaccustomed use of

her facial muscles. For her own part, she had not felt happier, more free, in what seemed like a hundred years. The spirit of Gwyer Warhein had taught her how to block out the insanity that had been feeding on her mind. The block worked so well she sensed nothing wrong with her ability at all.

If she wished to call upon it, it would work for her unimpaired. She didn't think she would, however, not for a long while. She had had enough input from her ability of late to last a lifetime.

She turned a corner just in time to get *whomped* with a snowball. Some Green Foot runners had built snow forts and were engaged in battle.

Their laughter died promptly when they saw *who* they hit. She strode by them, brushing snow off her shortcoat.

"Carry on," she told them.

She left behind stunned silence, which moments later erupted into high-spirited shouts. She was feeling too good to be a killjoy, and now had a different perspective on the small pleasures of life.

Let the children enjoy what they have before they become too burdened with the cares of adults.

When Laren had finally emerged from her quarters, Tegan had practically launched into somersaults of joy, and then did her best to fill her in on all that had transpired during her absence. Laren had known bits and pieces, but now many of the gaps were filled in.

The Laren Mapstone of old would have felt guilt for all her Riders had borne without her, and brooded over it till the end of her days. The reborn Laren Mapstone did feel guilt, but it was not as dark or heavy as it once might have been. No, she felt instead immense pride in her Riders, for continuing on with their duties despite adversity.

For those they had lost, there was sorrow and grief, but

she knew that even if she had been well, there was little she could have done to prevent their deaths.

She halted before the door that led to the king's study. Guards and a pair of Weapons stood at attention along the walls. So did a snowman.

"You have a friend," Laren told Fastion.

The Weapon arched an eyebrow.

Laren glanced from Fastion to the snowman, and back. It was all she could do to keep from laughing.

"The king is expecting you," Fastion said.

She took a deep breath, squared her shoulders, and tapped on the door.

"Enter," came the king's voice from the other side.

To Laren's astonishment, Fastion winked at her as he held the door open for her, and murmured, "Welcome back, Captain. You've been missed."

She left winter and entered summer once again. Sunshine flowed into the study, and birds twittered in the shrubbery just outside the windows. Snow crumbled off her boots and melted on the floor.

Behind his big desk, Zachary toyed with a knife, but when she entered, he immediately set it aside and rushed across the room to enclose her in an embrace.

"Thank the gods you are well," he said. "You don't know how I've missed you."

This was a better greeting than she could have ever hoped for. He scrutinized her from arm's length and she was reminded of the little boy he had once been, his emotions unveiled and open, his cheeks slightly flushed.

She knew he saw her gaunt cheeks and the lines around her eyes, and the pallor of her flesh. His expression was at once gentle and worried.

"I don't think you know—" his voice quavered "—how much Sacoridia depends on you."

She gave him a wry smile. "Oh, I don't know. It seems my Riders have held the place together rather well without me."

Zachary laughed. "And so they have. But I never want you to forget how much I value you as a counselor and friend; how much I depend on *you*. It has always been so. I also wish to ask forgiveness—"

"No."

"Please." His face was set and serious. "I wish to ask forgiveness for my execrable behavior, and for any harsh words I may have uttered."

He did not set forth any excuses when it would have been easy to do so. *I didn't have any idea,* he could have said, *that your ability was failing you.* For this she found his request all the more admirable. He waited for her response and, she could tell from his eyes, hoped.

"I forgive you, Moonling."

Zachary laughed in genuine relief, and hugged her again. He led her to a chair in front of his desk, and took his own place behind it.

"I have been to the mending wing just now," Laren said, "to check on one Rider who received a nasty knock on the head, and on another who was found unconscious in an abandoned section of the castle. There was also a soldier under restraint yelling like a madman about ghosts. No one, not even Destarion, could tell me exactly what happened. Can you?"

The king sighed. "We haven't quite pieced it together yet, but here is what I know. The madman, Sergeant Uxton of the Mountain Unit, or one of his accomplices, attacked Garth, then used a Green Foot runner to lure Karigan to the new Rider wing by informing her Garth had been hurt. Once there, she was attacked as well. For what purpose, we haven't yet determined. Karigan put up a fight, and was found only after a servant discovered Garth and informed the guard.

"Uxton was found crawling through snow in the corridor, leaving a trail of blood behind him from a stab wound to his foot." He picked up the knife from his desktop. "Here, tell me what you think of this."

Laren took it into her hands. It was of an archaic style, with a wider, flaring blade. It was heavy, and not as fine as the blades she was accustomed to using, but killing sharp. The hilt was made of horn or bone, and inscribed in Old Sacoridian. She glanced up at Zachary.

"This looks like a piece from the Sacor City War Museum."

"Yes, it does, doesn't it."

"But it looks newly made, not worn as it should be for its age." She weighed it in her hand.

"Look at the inscription on the other side of the hilt."

She turned over the blade and found more Old Sacoridian, which she wished she could read, and a crude etching of a horse with wings. A shiver traveled up her spine and she looked at Zachary with wide eyes.

"It was found," he said, "clenched in Karigan's hand."

"She traveled," Laren murmured, "and brought it back."

"That's what I believe."

Laren heaved a sigh of relief that Karigan had had the wisdom to explain to him about the traveling. "Destarion didn't say much about her condition. He was . . . harried at the time. He did say her body temperature was low. I assumed it was due to the snow and her lying unconscious."

"She was in an old chamber where there was no snow."

"Then she traveled. She became ill with the cold the last time it happened. Of course, I've no idea why it happens at all."

Zachary filled her in on Karigan's experiences at Watch Hill and with the Eletians, giving Laren Prince Jametari's explanation for the traveling. His words were overwhelming.

"Why do I have the sudden urge to run back to my quarters and lock myself in?"

"Don't you dare!" Zachary was so emphatic he half-rose from his chair.

Laren chuckled. "Don't worry, I'm not going to. Not for anything."

They talked more, exchanging information about all that had gone on. She spoke of Gwyer Warhein and of the help he offered.

Zachary shook his head in disbelief. "I am thankful to him, apparition or not, but it seems all I once knew as true and normal has been upended."

There was a knock and the door cracked open. A soldier poked his head in. "Your Majesty? We've caught one of Uxton's accomplices."

"Sergeant Uxton has been giving us names," Corporal Hill said as they approached the blockhouse. "I know the sergeant, or thought I did, and it's like something broke in his mind." The corporal shook his head. "He keeps going on about some empire."

Laren and Zachary exchanged glances. The corporal opened the door and they entered the blockhouse. Within was an office and a few cells. Long ago, prisoners were locked away in dungeons beneath the castle, a horrible dark place Laren had been led to by Zachary on one of his expeditions as a boy. King Amaris II had discontinued the use of dungeons and had the blockhouse constructed. It was meant to hold those who committed acts specifically against the kingdom, but was more frequently inhabited by wayward soldiers who had gotten into drunken brawls.

The enforcement of other laws was carried out by constables and justices in various towns, cities, and provinces. It removed the king from the business of keeping a prison.

Seated within, and watched over by two strapping

guards, was the most unlikely of prisoners. He sat slumped in his chair, specs sliding down his nose. He was thin, and certainly no match for either of his guards.

"Is this some mistake?" Zachary demanded of Hill.

"No, sire. Leastways, he was named by Sergeant Uxton."

Laren was as surprised as Zachary to see the chief administrator, Weldon Spurlock. He bowed his head morosely.

"Please, Your Majesty, this *is* a mistake."

Laren had dealt with Spurlock from time to time. She thought him petty and mean-spirited, but had no reason to suspect he would harm any of her Riders.

"No mistake!" Uxton hopped on one foot to the bars of his cell, his other foot wrapped in thick bandages. His eyes were wild, his hair standing straight up. He'd been stripped of his uniform and made to wear the gray tunic and trousers of a prisoner. "He's the one who told me to get that Rider. He's the one who told me to take her."

"You're mad," Spurlock spat at Uxton.

"He's the one who told me to take care of any problems at the wall. By any means. So I pushed Lord Alton into the forest."

Laren stiffened. "*You* killed him?"

"I tried," Uxton said. "Pushed him off the wall. Don't know if he was dead or not when he hit the ground." He giggled insanely. "Spurlock made me do it, and the forest took Lord Alton."

"Murdering liar," Spurlock said. Looking up at Zachary, he asked, "You can't believe a murderer, can you?"

"I don't lie!" Uxton pressed his face against the bars. "You're our leader, aren't you. You're the head of the Sacor City sect."

"The what?" Zachary demanded.

"The Second Empire," Uxton whispered.

Spurlock's face blanched.

Zachary crossed his arms almost casually. "Why don't you tell me about the Second Empire, Sergeant."

Uxton launched into a tale right out of a novel, about a secret society made up of descendants of the soldiers and others stranded in the "new lands" by the Arcosian Empire. They called themselves Second Empire, for they waited over the generations for the proper time and opportunity to revive the ways and powers of the Arcosian Empire, and to subjugate all who did not bend knee to them. Spurlock, Uxton told them, believed the time was now, because of the breach in the wall, and the reawakening of Blackveil.

"Lord Mornhavon is coming back," Uxton said, eyes wide and his knuckles whitened from gripping the bars of his cell. "Spurlock spoke with his emissary."

"Nonsense!" Spurlock said.

"A wraith from beyond the dead." There was a tick in Uxton's cheek at the word "dead." "Varadgrim, lord of the north. He was . . . is . . . Lord Mornhavon's lieutenant."

"The night barracks burned," Laren murmured.

Uxton nodded vigorously.

"He lies," Spurlock insisted, a note of desperation creeping into his voice. "A madman's ravings; fantasies."

Laren looked sharply at him. "A wraith was here. I encountered it."

At the king's encouragement, Uxton continued his tale of the Second Empire, of how they secreted themselves into Sacoridian life by participating in all trades and levels of society. Yet, they remained separate, marrying only within the society, revering texts and artifacts from their ancestors almost as holy relics.

If true, a grave threat to the kingdom had gone unknown and unseen for a thousand years, ready and willing to reignite the Long War if necessary, to reclaim what they believed was rightfully theirs.

Or had the threat been entirely unknown? A glance to

Zachary showed he was disturbed, but not surprised by Uxton's words.

"Madman," Spurlock muttered.

Uxton stuck his hand through the bars and revealed a tattoo on his palm, a tattoo of a dead tree. "Members of the inner circles of each sect bear this mark."

Corporal Hill grabbed Spurlock's wrist and pried open his fingers. On his palm was an identical tattoo.

"It proves nothing." Spurlock snatched his hand away. "It's just a tattoo. I know nothing about this man's ravings."

Laren believed Uxton. She could read the truth in his maddened eyes, but to be sure, she did what she had no desire to do, for she feared unleashing her gift. She feared touching it would be like uncorking disaster, and she herself would fall into madness again, that dark place to which she had no desire to return.

She passed her hand over her brooch and her ability passed its judgment on Weldon Spurlock's words.

"Spurlock speaks false," she said.

Zachary nodded, not hesitating, not questioning. To Corporal Hill, he said, "Hold this man for further questioning."

Spurlock curled into himself like a wounded animal, his eyes turning to steel, his hands like bared claws. "You haven't a chance. We're in every province. There are thousands of us loyal to the cause. Unlike him." He glared at Uxton with palpable rage.

"I'm sure you have much to tell us," Zachary said. "Arms Master Drent has many years of experience as an inquisitor."

Spurlock turned even whiter, if it was possible.

Uxton chortled as the two guards dragged Spurlock into a cell, slammed it shut, and turned the key in the lock.

Sperren entered the blockhouse accompanied by anxious courtiers. "Sire, it's mayhem down in the city. We've been receiving reports of . . . of all manner. It would be helpful if—"

"Of course," Zachary said. "I'll come right away."

Laren started to follow him out, but then paused, and walked back to the cells. Uxton gazed at her with eager madness, and Spurlock sat on his cot, arms folded, his expression acid.

"Tell me," she said, "what it was you wanted with my Rider."

"It's not me that wanted her," Spurlock said.

"Then who?"

"Blackveil."

Laren crossed her arms, disturbed. "So you were just going to push her into the forest like you did Alton D'Yer?"

"I have nothing to say to you," Spurlock said. "I don't have to answer your questions." He stubbornly faced the wall.

"I expect Arms Master Drent will get what I need from you."

As she left, Uxton called out, "Don't trust her, that Rider of yours—she's Galadheon," and he returned to his own cot, giggling hysterically.

Karigan dreamed of a white world, a freezing place where snow flurries fluttered down. She wrapped her arms around herself. Trees in shades of gray could be discerned, their spindly dead branches dangling down like spider legs.

A figure hurried through the snow ahead of her and she pursued, trying to run through drifts, trying to see through the driving snow. The trees became denser, the branches snagging in her hair. She brushed them aside. Coated with ice, they tinkled like wind chimes.

The figure turned. A man with beautiful dark eyes and bronze skin. The snow grayed his jet hair. In her memory-dream, he had been a boy, his name Alessandros. Even as a man, his features were unmistakable.

His eyes swallowed her, and robbed her of all cover. She stood naked before him, shivering uncontrollably. She tried to hide her nakedness with her arms, wanted to run, but his eyes held her captive, and violated her by delving into her deepest desires and hates, and her secrets. When he learned her name, his lips curved into a smile of knowing.

"You will come," he said, and he walked off into the snow, and vanished. "I know where the Deyer is."

Something in Karigan's left arm writhed and bulged. Through the translucence of her skin, she could see a black snake wriggle and slither.

She screamed.

But then she heard a distant sounding of a horn, and hoofbeats. Green—she became submerged in green like a soft cloak . . .

◁≈ SPURLOCK ≈▷

Spurlock glared at the wall, one hand clenching the medallion at his throat. The medallion of his brave ancestor, a man stranded in a strange land and forced to live among barbarians. Throughout his life, Spurlock had felt much the same, stranded among barbarians who were unequal in intelligence and ingenuity. He had never fit in among the Sacoridians.

He gazed at the medallion. A depiction of the emperor's palace was engraved on one side and a stately cypress tree on the other. The medallion represented a very high honor. After the empire's abandonment, Lord Mornhavon had taken the sigil of the dead tree to represent his disconnection with Arcosia and the new regime he planned to build.

They were children of the empire, and no matter Lord Mornhavon's desire to build a new empire here, something stirred in their blood as though they caught a scent or flavor of a far distant land. One day, they would return to the land of their origin, to Arcosia. *He* would return. In his mind's eye, he could see the fine art and architecture of a highly cultured people, the lemon trees heavy with fruit, the furrowed fields of the rolling countryside. He would ask why the empire stranded them in these alien lands.

The upstart king of Sacoridia would be no match for the power Spurlock imagined must be awakening in Blackveil.

That awakening would bring about the deliverance of the children of the empire.

The door to the blockhouse creaked open.

"I've brought supper for the prisoners."

Spurlock straightened when he recognized the voice. *Madrene!* Had she come with some plan of escape?

"Mmm, looks good," the guard said.

There was a slap of a hand, followed by, "Those are for the prisoners. When your shift changes, you'll get yours."

The guard made a disappointed noise, clomped over to the cells and opened Uxton's first. Madrene slid a tray into the cell, and Uxton sprang upon it like an animal.

The cell door clattered shut and the keys jingled as the guard locked it. Spurlock was next, and Madrene took the tray from the boy that accompanied her. Was it her son? Spurlock couldn't keep track of everyone's brats.

She slid the tray into his cell and backed out with a curt nod to him, and a knowing wink. And left.

Spurlock wondered at her nonverbal message. Was it an acknowledgment the sect knew of his imprisonment and would work on a way to get him out?

He left his cot and retrieved the tray. She had brought a succulent stew of beef and vegetables, with bread. He ate absently, wondering how she passed herself off as a kitchen worker, shrugged it off, and daydreamed of Arcosia.

Eventually his spoon scraped the bottom of the bowl, and as he raised his spoon for his last bite, Uxton suddenly dropped his tray and clutched his throat, making a terrible wheezing sound. His face began to turn blue.

Spurlock dropped his spoon. "Uxton! Are you choking?"

But Uxton could not answer. His eyes rolled back into his head and he keeled over.

Even as the guard strode over to investigate, Spurlock knew the awful truth: Uxton was dead. Madrene had poisoned them before they could do too much harm to Second Empire.

As his chest tightened and he could not get a breath in or out, he realized it was a decision he would have made had it been someone other than himself in this cell. He wouldn't have hesitated to poison that person for the good of the whole, for the good of Second Empire. They had survived this long out of secrecy, by similar acts done in the past.

His lungs felt as though they would explode, and he clawed at his throat with one hand, the other gripping his ancient medallion. As awareness dimmed, a tear leaked from the corner of his eye because he would never see the attainment of his dreams, nor the shore of his forebear's homeland.

 ARGUING WITH
HORSES

Karigan left the castle feeling like one freed from a prison. She had spent far too much time in the mending wing this summer.

Once she stepped clear of the castle's shadow, gentle sunshine enveloped her. She paused on the pathway, closed her eyes, and turned her face skyward to absorb the sun. It helped warm the last of the chill from her veins, just as the snow in the castle corridors had finally melted away.

Her memory of the previous two days and nights were vague. She did recall the attack of armor clearly, the bruises and aching muscles a painful reminder. She also recalled being pursued into the corridors through the snow, and returning to the past to Lil's time. To Lil's . . . death?

Had Lil survived to fight on, or had Karigan shared the last moments of her life with her?

She ambled along, not sure of where she was going and not caring. She just needed to be out in the sun. Dimly she recalled a nightmare. About spiders? Ben had heard her scream, but the images from the dream were gone.

Her feet led her to the pasture where several messenger horses cropped at the grasses. Standing among them in the center of the field was a Rider. Karigan shielded her eyes to see better who it was.

"It can't be . . ."

The Rider shifted her stance, and with the way the

sun slanted onto her red hair, there was no mistaking her identity.

"Captain." She wanted to shout, but it came out as a whisper.

She stepped between the rails of the fence and into the pasture. She took a few strides, and stopped, hesitant. The captain would be angry with her, she thought, for all those accusations she had made. She felt a blush of shame creep up her neck.

Captain Mapstone just stood there watching the horses, or maybe gazing at nothing, as the tips of grasses glimmered at her knees and insects hovered in little clouds around her. In the distance, Karigan could hear the horses pulling at grass and munching. Bluebird grazed close to the captain, his coat glossy in the sunshine.

Karigan thought to retreat from the tranquil scene, to not intrude on the captain's peace. She feared her reception and didn't think she could face the captain's anger. The shame would be too much to bear.

Before she could leave, however, the captain glanced over her shoulder and saw her. The two gazed at one another for an endless moment, until the captain smiled. She *smiled!*

Karigan thought she might swoon in relief, especially when the captain started walking toward her.

"So Destarion released you," she said.

There was color in the captain's cheeks, gaunt though they were. She was too thin and there were hollows beneath her eyes. But the eyes were bright and snapping, full of life. The last time Karigan had seen her, those very same eyes had been dull and pain-filled.

"Yes."

"How are you feeling?" the captain asked.

"Captain, I'm—I'm sorry."

"Sorry? For what?"

Karigan thrust a strand of hair behind her ear. "The things I accused you of. I shouted at you, and you weren't well. I don't know what got into me. I—"

"That's true enough." The captain gazed off into the distance for a moment, stroking the scar on her neck, as if recalling the unpleasantness. "However, I left you and Mara in a very difficult situation. In fact, more difficult than usual, and I would have to say you've done very well under the circumstances." Her eyes twinkled. "I've never seen the Rider accounts look so good."

Karigan glanced down at her feet, glad of the captain's approval.

"In fact," the captain mused, "I don't see why handling Rider accounts shouldn't be one of your permanent duties."

Karigan stifled a groan.

"Were I you," the captain continued, "I'm not sure I'd have done so well with all you had to contend with, especially at your level of experience. Yes, I was ill, but you were correct to seek help from me."

"But the accusations, the shouting—"

"I wish they had shaken me from the despair, but that took a different kind of intervention." The captain smiled slightly. "I also know the kind of strain you were under at the time. Think no more of it."

"But—"

"*Rider.*"

"Yes, Captain." Karigan peered back up and couldn't help grinning. She wanted to jump up and down in happiness—the captain was back!—but managed to retain decorum.

"So," the captain said, "let me tell you what happened to me, then you can catch me up on your doings."

They strolled through the pasture as the captain explained her illness and the visit by Gwyer Warhein. Karigan found herself perversely relieved she wasn't the only one being visited by ghosts.

A monarch butterfly crawled onto the captain's hand from a cone flower as she spoke, and stayed there for some moments before fluttering its wings and flying away. There was a serenity about the captain Karigan had not seen before, and she was glad.

When it was Karigan's turn to talk, she found the captain knew most of what had been going on, but was missing some pieces.

"I don't remember much after being pursued into the abandoned corridors, and especially after the traveling. I don't know why that sergeant was after me. He said something about the empire, and that the wraith had come looking for me."

"Uxton was captured," the captain said. "He was part of a group called Second Empire." She described the group's origin and purpose. "Uxton gave us names of some of the members, including their leader, the leader of the Sacor City sect, anyway: Weldon Spurlock."

"The chief administrator?" He was unpleasant, but she never expected this from him.

The captain nodded. "But a few names is all we got. You see, Uxton and Spurlock are dead, murdered, we think, by one of their own. Poisoned."

Karigan shook her head in disbelief.

"While we don't know exactly why, we do know they wanted to take you to Blackveil."

Images of dark, spindly tree limbs reaching for her came back to her, of someone talking to her in the snow . . .

The captain stopped abruptly and placed her hand on Karigan's shoulder, her eyes searching.

"Uxton," she said quietly, "admitted pushing Alton off the wall and into the forest."

The news, Karigan thought, ought to upset her, but it was more like being jerked awake.

"He's alive." She babbled it before she could stop herself.

The captain's eyes widened. "You know this for certain?"

Karigan told the captain her theory about messenger horses and how they knew of their Rider's welfare. She told her of the image she had seen of Alton in the Mirror of the Moon.

"We have to find him. Now that you're well, the king will let me go." Karigan spotted Condor in a far corner of the pasture, and started away from the captain as though to catch him and ride straight away for the wall.

The captain grabbed her wrist. "Hold on. There's a catch to your plan."

"What?"

"*Me.*"

Karigan bit her lip in embarrassment. What had gotten into her? All she knew was that she needed to find Alton, and she *knew* he was alive somewhere near the wall.

"Not to mention," the captain continued, "you are the last person who should go there, considering that's where Uxton planned to take you."

Karigan felt constricted, thwarted, as though she would never get to take action. Her mind raced, trying to think of ways she could convince the captain to let her go. Maybe she would have to go against orders after all . . .

And then a curious thing began to happen, at first unnoticed by either Rider. Bluebird plodded over to them, shaking his mane with a snort. He bumped the captain's shoulder with his nose, and she patted him absently. The other messenger horses moved in as well, casually cropping grass as they came, and flicking their tails at flies.

In short order, Karigan and the captain were surrounded.

"What do you suppose they're up to?" the captain asked under her breath, glancing wide-eyed at the horse faces around them.

"I—I have no idea."

Condor lipped Karigan's sleeve, then clamped his teeth on it. He started to drag her away.

"Condor!"

Even if she ripped her sleeve from his teeth, the other horses were butting her from behind with their noses. Captain Mapstone was being similarly prodded.

Condor led Karigan across the pasture to the wall that skirted the castle grounds. Guards watched curiously from above. The captain joined her a moment later with an emphatic shove from Bluebird.

"I do believe we've been herded," she said, tugging her shortcoat back into place. "But to what purpose?"

They gazed at the horses without a clue to their strange behavior, and the horses gazed guilelessly back.

"Well?" Captain Mapstone demanded of them.

Some ears flickered, a few tails switched. Robin yawned, and Sparrow rubbed the side of his head on Condor's rump.

"Enough," the captain said, rolling her eyes. She started to stride away, but Bluebird swiftly blocked her. She grunted as she walked into his shoulder.

Karigan decided to try and walk away, too, but Condor nudged her right back to the wall until she was flat against it.

"Are you telling me what I think you're telling me?" she asked him.

Condor, of course, didn't say a thing.

"So," the captain said, "what is it you think he's trying to tell you?"

Karigan's fingers brushed across the rough texture of the

granite wall, a wall also built by Clan D'Yer. "The wall," she said. "They want me—us—to go to the D'Yer Wall."

There were a few satisfied snorts among the horses as they turned around and dispersed at a leisurely plod.

The captain rubbed at her neck scar. "Zachary isn't going to like this."

"Are you well?" the king asked Karigan.

"Yes, sire."

"I'm very glad." His voice was soft, and his gaze lingered on her for a few moments as if to make sure with his own eyes. Then abruptly he started pacing the room. He was attired in riding breeches and shiny black boots, with a shortcoat of midnight blue. To Karigan he looked stormy, but strong and unbending.

"I have been out riding through the city and countryside," he said, "to see for myself what the breach in the D'Yer Wall has wrought."

He told them of people frozen in time—turned to stone—down on the Winding Way, while grieving mothers, husbands, sisters, and children left flowers at the feet of these all-too-lifelike statues. He told of the village of Merdith, which no longer existed. The buildings, the people, everything had vanished.

"The work of the wild magic," he said, "was far more widespread than just the armor coming to life in our corridors, or the falling of snow. That's why," he continued, pausing to stand before the captain, "I would like you to take your Riders to the wall. I need information. I have heard nothing from the wall in too long."

Karigan and the captain exchanged incredulous glances. Here they had been expecting a fight. They had put their heads together conspiring a way to convince the king to let them go to the wall, and now he was handing them the opportunity.

"Your Riders," he said, "are trained observers, and know how to prepare a report that would be useful to me. They have experience as scouts, and in the use of magic. I had planned to send but one Rider. However, in light of recent occurrences, I think several should go. Take all who are available. This way you can send me messengers with reports should conditions warrant."

"Very good," the captain said, as though she had expected such an assignment from him all along. "I will assemble what Riders are here, and leave on the morrow."

The king nodded. "I am . . . reluctant to send either of you."

"We both need to go," the captain said.

"I know."

"Will that be all, sire?"

"Yes." Before they could leave, he stepped forward and touched Karigan's sleeve, softly, with only his fingertips. "Take care. Come home safely."

Although he addressed them both, his fingertips lingered on Karigan's sleeve, and she thought he gazed at her longer and harder, but the moment was quickly over, and she did not know what to think. As she hurried after the captain down the corridor, she was aware of him watching after them, and she absently caressed her arm where he had touched her.

A Green Foot runner hurried past them on his way to see the king. Karigan glanced back in time to see him bow before the king. "Lord Coutre has arrived with the other eastern lords, Your Majesty."

The expression on the king's face seemed to fall, but then Karigan turned a corner and saw no more.

In the darkness of the stable, the greenish glow of the apparition reflected in the eyes of messenger horses.

I certainly hope you know what you're about, Lil Ambri-odhe chided them.

Most of the horses were half-asleep, unimpressed by the presence of the First Rider.

I won't deny that a Rider must face danger in the course of her duty, Lil continued, *but you are delivering them right into the hands of the enemy. The enemy that is blocking me from communicating with the Galadheon.* She paced, her feet hovering just above the hay-strewn floor.

A few of the horses began to wake up. Condor scraped his hoof against the floor.

It's not my fault, Lil retorted. *It's a power at work greater than mine. I'm dead, after all.*

Condor whickered.

I'll keep trying to reach your Rider, but it may be too late. I fear Mornhavon, or what was Mornhavon, already has his hooks in her.

Condor began to circle in agitation in his stall.

Sorry, Red, Lil said. *You shouldn't have put the notion in their heads to begin with, hey? But it's done and now we have to make do.*

The apparition's glow dimmed and the horses fell into shadow.

Whatever happened to old-fashioned stupid horses? Lil wondered. As she faded away into the netherworld of spirits, she reflected that her various Brownies had never argued with her.

RIDING TO
THE WALL

 aren quickly understood what had so dis-
turbed Zachary. People along the Winding
Way had been caught, unsuspecting, turned to
stone as they went about simple, everyday activities, activities that would never be completed. A man
gazed perpetually into a fishmonger's window, his fingers
cupped around his chin as if he still deliberated the choice
of fish displayed on hooks and the prices posted for them.
Two women leaned toward one another as if sharing a secret, the laugh of one frozen in time. Their lines and details
were as true to life as Laren's butterfly had been, but their
edges were hard and sharp, their visages cold and gray.

A carter bore a sack over his shoulder, his stride seemingly purposeful, but going nowhere. A boy gazed into the
street holding a ball over his head that would never be
thrown . . .

The Riders left the city in relief, but in the countryside
they found other disturbing evidence of magic gone awry.
Once-healthy crops lay blackened and withered in the
fields, and there were empty places where houses had once
stood.

Laren rode at the head of a dozen Riders, her sword slap-
ping at her side. Through every village they rode, terrified
folk came up to her asking what the king was going to do to
make things right.

Laren had no answers, but reassured them as she could.

The farther they traveled from Sacor City, the quieter Karigan grew. She participated very little in campfire banter, as though preoccupied, and during the night she babbled nonsense in her sleep, or perhaps spoke in a tongue Laren did not understand. Although her behavior wasn't outlandish, it was different enough for Laren to take note of and watch her carefully.

More of an immediate concern was the discovery that they were being followed. Laren glimpsed a mounted figure on the edge of her vision, like a brief flash of white, but when she turned in her saddle to look full on, he was gone, vanished into the woods. Since the horseman did nothing to threaten them directly, she did not bring up his presence to her Riders, not wishing to alarm them unnecessarily. He seemed content to follow and watch them. For now.

Their fourth day out, they came to some ancient ruins, crumbling stone walls overgrown with vegetation. They decided to take a midday break there. Most of the Riders fanned out to sit in the shade and have a bite to eat.

Karigan, however, stood and gazed at the ruins. Laren took a swig from her waterskin and watched her, noting the glassy look in her eyes as if her mind traveled someplace very far away. Her expression was difficult to interpret, as though a thousand emotions moved within her.

Presently Laren joined her. "What do you see?" she asked.

"Battle. Here the forces of Alessandros del Mornhavon triumphed over insurrectionists who would not bend their knees to the empire. Burning, children screaming, arrows, magical fire . . ."

Laren drew her eyebrows together in concern. "Karigan?"

Karigan shook herself, blinked, and turned to Laren with a small smile on her face. "Yes, Captain?"

The transformation was startling. "Are you all right? If you are feeling poorly, I could send you back—"

Karigan registered surprise. "I'm fine, Captain, really. I don't need to go back. Is that all?"

Laren nodded, and Karigan strolled over to a shade tree and dropped down next to Dale, the two starting up an animated conversation. It was as if nothing unusual had happened.

She returned to Bluebird where he grazed nearby, and ran her hand along his neck.

"I hope you knew what you were doing when you convinced us to go to the wall."

Bluebird paused his grazing and raised his head to gaze at her. Was it her imagination, or was his expression sheepish? It certainly wasn't reassuring.

That evening, Laren sat off by herself next to a lantern, poring over maps of D'Yer Province and the wall. It had been some time since she last traveled the region, and she wanted to refamiliarize herself with it, especially the area near the breach.

Tomorrow morning she was sending Tegan off to Woodhaven, the seat of Lord-Governor D'Yer, to let him know what the Riders were up to, and the state of affairs elsewhere. Depending on how Tegan's meeting with him went, she would either return to Sacor City to report to the king, or catch up with the Riders at the wall.

Laren looked up at the sound of approaching footsteps, to find Ty heading over with a steaming mug in each hand. "Tea," he said.

Laren carefully took a mug. "Thank you."

"Checking our route?" he asked, gazing down at the map.

"It's fairly straightforward, and I understand a horse track has been cut all the way to the wall."

"I've never been to the wall," Ty said. "Seems we're

usually bound for Woodhaven when there's a message to deliver in D'Yer Province." He then hesitated. "Captain, would you mind if I sit?"

"Not at all." Laren gestured at the ground beside her. In the yellow lantern light, she discerned an apprehensive expression on the Rider's face. "Something wrong?"

Ty set his mug aside as he made himself comfortable on the ground. He glanced over his shoulder at the other Riders, then said in a quiet voice, "It's Karigan. She's been acting a little strange ever since we left the city, and I'm not the only one to have noticed."

"Oh?" Laren did not want to pass on her own thoughts about Karigan, lest she add fuel to the flames of any speculation on behalf of her Riders. She needed them to trust one another. Somehow she was not surprised it was Ty who came forward. He had been Karigan's mentor, and likely still felt responsible for her. His personality was also such that anything out of place required being defined, and if possible, put back into place. It made him a trifle unbending and strict, and for that reason alone, she had never promoted him to Chief Rider or lieutenant, positions that required flexibility.

"Just now," Ty continued, "she was murmuring about being abandoned. I could swear I saw a tear in her eye, and when I asked her who abandoned us, she acted confused and didn't seem to understand what I was talking about."

"I shouldn't worry about it," Laren said, despite the fact that was precisely what she was doing.

"But—"

"We've all been under enormous strain of late. We've lost Ephram and Alton, and barracks has burned. My mind wanders, too." Laren tried to sound reassuring, even as her own concern escalated. "If you notice anything else that warrants my attention, do bring it to me."

"Yes, Captain."

"Now, let's take a look at tomorrow's route."

The sky clouded over and it showered the following morning. They rode off, spirits dampened as much as bedrolls, and the usual conversation was stilled to silence. When Laren tired of listening to the pitter-patter on her hood, she drew it back and let the rain fall on her head. Doing so returned her side vision, and she glimpsed the horseman.

A gray cloak had been thrown over white armor, and he blended in well with the gloom and forest backdrop. When he perceived her gaze, he vanished again into the woods.

Laren veered Bluebird around, and much to the astonishment of her Riders, kicked him after the horseman. She looked for any sign of him, and when she found nothing, she began to wonder if he were an illusion. Then she saw the slight depression of a hoofprint.

She sat there in the rain, staring into the woods. He must be an Eletian. From what she knew, or thought she knew, only Eletians could move so swiftly, and with so little trace.

If so, why would an Eletian be tailing them?

Karigan rode through the mist and rain, fogged by shadow like a dark hand in her mind—someone peering in, violating all that should remain private. It was like living in a dream, her attention drawn inward, reliving memories that were hers . . . and were not. Terrible battles raged through her sleeping dreams, and sometimes she awakened with such feelings of power, she thought she could dash away the world with the sweep of her arm—all living creatures, any structure created by the hands of humanity, all traces of civilization.

And always, *he* was there in the falling snow, goading her to come.

Yes, I am coming. Her reply, involuntary.

As she rode, she thought she heard the muffled sound of a horn trying to break through the clouds and murk, but it was never enough.

Please help! she cried out, but all she heard in return was, *You will come.*

Journal of Hadriax el Fex

Today, Alessandros called me into his work chamber. I never enter it because I've no wish to view his experiments, but this time I had no choice. He was very excited, babbling about some finding or other.

I entered the chamber seeing nothing but that which lay on a table in its center, fully illuminated by the glow of prisms. It had been an Elt—male. Alessandros had surgically sliced out the Eletian's various organs, which now float in jars of syrupy preservative. His chest cavity lay open, the ribs drawn wide. Alessandros had made a circular cut of the brain case, like a cap cut off the skull.

I reeled out of the chamber retching, I who have slain countless others, in countless ways; I who have picked my way through battle-fields strewn with the dead, and tortured the living. Alessandros followed me out, laughing as I heaved, and that was even worse.

"What?" he said. "My staunch soldier cannot stand the sight of blood?"

I leaned against the wall, fighting to restore control of my guts and to stop weeping, while Alessandros nattered on about his finding—something to do with etherea and eternal life. I did not care.

Alessandros did more than kill one of God's angels—he had taken it apart piece by piece as if it were no more than the clockworks of a mechanical. And I know this can't have been the first time. Beneath the physical beauty and pure etherea they exude, are only flesh, bones, fluids . . .

I can no longer abide this long war, or Alessandros' madness. He is no longer the man I knew of old, but something twisted like the monsters he creates. Truly he is Mornhavon the Black, as the clans call him. For me, Alessandros del Mornhavon, the friend I loved so well, is dead.

It is clear that I must end the madness, and I now know what I must do. The vision of the young woman with her brooch in the mirror lake was truly a sign—a sign that I must contact Lil Ambriodhe.

≼ BLACKVEIL ≽

E xhilarated.
      That was the only way he could think of to describe how he felt. *She* was coming. She with the long brown hair and ready smile. She who was of Hadriax's blood.

He had pried into the mind of this young innocent, a mind curiously unblocked and unprotected. He learned her loves and loathings, followed her memories. He saw much of Hadriax in her, his courage and sense of loyalty.

Betrayer.

Mornhavon fought to contain himself, to remind himself that Hadriax was long gone. This young woman, this Karigan, he could mold her and twist her mind, make her his, as Varadgrim was his. He could bind her to him, and end his loneliness. He would have her at his side when the wall failed.

The wild magic was within her, and all he'd have to do is control it. She would shed all notions of being a Green Rider. She would be his.

Wouldn't this be his ultimate revenge against Hadriax? To pervert one of his own blood?

You will come, he whispered to her.

There was no sense of time within the wall. A day might have passed, or a million. The granite tried to coax Alton away from his work with its memories.

He barely remembered what it was like to live within a body of flesh, blood, sinew. He hardly remembered his name.

He did know that he must sing, that he must make the others sing with him. His voice resonated among the crystalline structures and carried through the entirety of the wall. He modulated his voice so it might overcome the others.

Sometimes when he paused, he heard their whispers around him: anxiety, suspicion, hatred. Why should they feel such for him when he was only trying to help?

Sometimes he pondered over the incongruity, but then an image of Karigan would come to him, and he knew he must continue his work for her. He could not disappoint her.

⋞⋟ THROUGH THE
BREACH ⋞⋟

L aren couldn't believe the devastation as
they rode into the encampment at the
D'Yer wall. Entire stands of forest had been
toppled as if a giant's hand had swept through
it. Whole trees had been uprooted, some splintered to the
size of tinder. Boulders, unmoved since the days of the
great ice, had been rolled aside leaving gaping craters
where they once rested.

When the wind turned toward them, they gagged on the
stench of carrion. Even the wildlife had been unable to escape the catastrophe. Vultures circled overhead.

The downed forest opened up views of the wall, and her
Riders were silent as they took it in. Laren hadn't looked
upon it in many a year, and even then, only at a distance.
The sun glowed warmly on it, making it at once innocuous
and magnificent.

Spoiling the effect was the breach, an imperfection that
looked as if a god had reached down and ripped out a
chunk of wall. Gray mist billowed through the wound over
smashed rock and debris. The repaired section had not held
during the destruction.

From the look of things, the power must have funneled
right through it. She dared not think what would have happened if the rest of the wall hadn't been standing to shield
the countryside.

At the encampment itself, they were greeted by a fresh

row of graves. Too many graves. Laren nudged Bluebird toward the wall, where soldiers stood guard. One broke off a conversation and started toward her. She met him halfway.

The soldier saluted. "Captain."

"Corporal."

"Corporal Hanson, ma'am."

Laren nodded her acknowledgment.

"We are glad to see you," Hanson said, "but we were hoping for a larger force. The soldiers here, they need relief."

"We are here on reconnaissance, Corporal. We've had no word from the wall in quite a while."

"Oh." The corporal looked disappointed. "We sent a man up some time ago, first to Lord D'Yer, then to the king." He did not speculate over what might have become of the messenger.

Laren swung off Bluebird, her Riders following her lead. "Tell me, Corporal, what is your situation? Who's in command?"

"Captain Reems, ma'am. He was injured. I'll see that he's awakened and—"

"No, no. Don't wake him. Surely you can brief me?"

"Yes, ma'am."

Hanson spoke of great whirlwinds crashing through the breach, slashing through the encampment and forest. It was miraculous, he said, that anyone survived. Those who stood directly in the path of the fury had been stripped of their flesh.

They had spent most of their time since then trying to take account of the living and dead. One soldier emerged alive from beneath the rubble of the wall's repaired section, while others had been impaled by splinters that had once been trees.

"We've also doubled our watch on the breach," the corporal explained. "The creatures within, they want out. We killed some half a dozen 'mites. They know the wall has weakened, and that we have, too."

"My Riders and I will help as we can," Laren said, "and I'll send one directly to the king with the news."

Laren was about to pass on the assignment to Dale when a shout went up near the breach. The guards stood with crossbows cocked and aimed at a figure that stepped through it and over the rubble. Mist curled around him, veiling his features at first, then ebbing away. She froze, startled to the bone.

"Lord Alton!" Corporal Hanson cried. "It's Lord Alton!"

Karigan experienced few moments of clarity. She had ridden much of the day in the dimness of his touch and call. Though she rode beside her fellow Riders, they could have been a million miles away. She was an island amid an expansive ocean. Isolated, except for *him.*

He must have been distracted by other things during those rare moments of clarity. She knew his mind was churning with plans. Plans to carry out when the wall was felled. Plans to make the world his. Churning, churning, churning like a wagon wheel, he made plans, and discarded them, or stored them away for later use. He planned that she be one of his tools, but she never figured out why he chose *her.*

When he was in her mind, he pried into her memories, feelings, attitudes, and layers of knowledge. The violation sickened her, made her feel more vulnerable. He went where he had no right to, into her innermost mind, laying it all naked—the loss of her mother, small moments of childhood, a birthday celebration for her father, her confusion over King Zachary . . .

All she could do was issue a mental whimper when he

probed her. She possessed no skill or weapon to stave off such an attack.

On occasion, he chose to be cruel for no other reason than it amused him. He planted images in her mind, of those she knew and loved, the dearest people in her life. One by one he decapitated them, or flayed their flesh off their bodies. Mara was shown to be roasting on a spit over a fire. The captain was slashed from her neck to her belly, her intestines squirming out of the cut. Her father was thrown overboard a merchant ship into waters boiling with sharks, the sea turning foamy red around him as he screamed and thrashed.

To the image of King Zachary, he included her participation. He made her wield a sword and cut off his limbs. His dogs attacked him, feeding in a frenzy that turned their white coats scarlet.

Her mind screamed, but she could not force the scream to become a physical act, could not make it cross her lips. The images were so intense as to be real while she saw them.

He was controlling her, he was testing her, he was breaking her.

In a brief clear moment, she wondered what had happened to the little boy who played with toy sailboats in a fountain, the young adventurer who set off on dozens of quests. Her wondering was met with quizzical silence. And a clearing of the mist. He departed again to carry out plans.

Through the evaporating mist, she became aware of her physical surroundings. She saw the wall for the first time in her life. The wall that contained Blackveil Forest; the wall that was supposed to contain *him*.

"Help me," she whispered, but no one heard her. There was some excitement occurring near the wall. "Help . . ." Why couldn't her friends hear? Why wouldn't they help her?

I hear you.

It was the voice of Lil Ambrioth.

The world reeled as Karigan looked around, and she stumbled against Condor's shoulder. He nickered at her. Her mind had been so caught up in webs and images that she could not find equilibrium. She could see nothing of Lil but a pale pair of eyes gazing at her.

You must block him out, Lil said.

"I—I can't. He's too powerful."

I feared it was so.

"Please help me."

I want to, but I'm not sure what to do.

Lil's words angered Karigan. "You're the First Rider— you have to know!"

Ghost eyes blinked. *The First Rider I may be, all-knowing I am not. That power is reserved for the gods alone.*

"Help me . . ." Karigan's anger dissipated into desperation. "He'll return."

I'll do what I can to buffer your mind, but it hasn't worked so far.

Wild magic roiled in Karigan's arm. She imagined it to be some hungry, insatiable beast that would feed on her life and energy till nothing was left. It allowed him to control her. If only she could flee and hide, but where could she hide?

The fog that clouded her mind continued to break, letting in sunshine. She felt lighter than she had in a while. Lighter, more aware, and more able to think.

Wild magic had done more than allowed Mornhavon to control her. Maybe, she thought, it wasn't a matter of hiding *where,* but *when.*

Because of the wild magic, she had traveled into the past, and forward into the future. And, if she were to have a "future," she would have to take a stand now.

She absently stroked Condor's neck as she considered

the madness of her thoughts. Abruptly she gazed into Lil Ambrioth's eyes.

"There is something we can try, but I'll need your help."

Karigan told Lil her plan. When she finished, Lil's eyes blurred from side to side as though she were shaking her head.

During my day, she said, *I was called insane by many for my actions. This is easily more insane than anything I ever did.*

"It won't work without you," Karigan said. Part of her hoped Lil would refuse, but she knew it must be done. *Something* had to be done.

Pray my energy holds.

"Our brooch should hold us together."

"Karigan," Dale called, "what are you standing over there for? Come see Alton!"

"Alton?" Karigan turned away from Lil in surprise. When she saw him, she didn't know whether to jump for joy, or to run and give him a hug.

She trotted toward where he stood at the breach, then stumbled to a halt. She took in his familiar form, the brown head of hair, the beard that had started to grow on his strong chin. He was woefully thin. When he saw her coming, he smiled.

Maybe it was tears of joy blurring her vision, but she couldn't quite make out his features clearly. And his smile . . . There was something wrong with it. It lacked his easy-going humor. It was dead.

Past, present, future. *Memory.* Memory of Lil facing Hadriax el Fex at the base of Watch Hill, only it hadn't been el Fex. Memory of illusion.

Her saber rang as it cleared its sheath, and she ran screaming at the illusion of Alton D'Yer. The Riders around her reacted slowly at first, shocked by her drawn saber, shocked by her scream. Then real time resumed.

"She means to kill him!" Dale.

She charged past Dale and Captain Mapstone, raising her sword as she went. Even the illusion appeared surprised. She ran until a giant in green knocked her sprawling to the ground, her breath whooshing from her lungs. Ty snatched her sword from her hand and the giant lifted her to her feet, and wrapped his arms around her so she could hardly move.

"Let me go, Garth!" She squirmed violently, but he held her firmly against himself.

"What are you doing?" he demanded. "That's Alton, your friend—remember?"

Oh yes, she remembered.

"Not my friend," she said, "illusion!"

"—been acting odd of late," Ty said of her, and there was general agreement among the Riders.

"*Not* Alton—the wraith!"

"I don't know what she's talking about." The voice was Alton's, but the intelligence behind it was not. "I thought she cared for me."

Karigan recognized the taint of Mornhavon in the illusion, and now she knew why he had left her, so he could attend to this illusion. It was he who had given Varadgrim the appearance of Hadriax el Fex a thousand years ago, it was he who gave him Alton's form now.

Captain Mapstone stood before her, full of concern. "Karigan?"

"It's a trap—the wraith—not Alton!"

Garth was strong, but Karigan had trained with Arms Master Drent and learned how to bring a strong man down. An elbow to the gut, a heel to his instep. She twisted her leg behind his and shoved him off balance. Down he went like a massive tree.

Karigan ripped her saber from Ty's grasp and held it before her to stave off her fellow Riders, her friends. They put their hands to the hilts of their own swords, and she could only guess what was going through their minds. *Yes,* they would be thinking, *Karigan has finally gone mad.* She wasn't sure they were far off the mark.

It wasn't her friends she wanted to engage, however. Her focus was the mind behind the illusion, and the only way to get him to do what she needed him to do was to goad him. Goad him as he had goaded her. She tried to push back her fear.

"A paltry illusion," she shouted at Varadgrim. "The captain knows the truth of my words."

From the corner of her eye, she saw the captain quickly assess her. Then the captain ordered the Riders to arm themselves. The swords, however, were held toward Varadgrim, not Karigan.

Her relief was minor, considering the magnitude of what she was attempting to do. "You are not as powerful as you think," she told Mornhavon.

"Girl, I could pick up a boulder and drop it upon you." It was revolting to hear the words spoken with Alton's voice. "I have seen in your mind your revulsion at the things that could be done to those you hold dear. Those things I could make reality."

Bile rose up in her throat, but she must not let the fear overtake her. "I don't think so. You are so weak you must use others to do your bidding."

He laughed. The illusion around Varadgrim dissolved, and Karigan prepared herself for what she thought would happen next, but it didn't.

Garth was suddenly after her, swinging his sword. By the bewildered look in his eyes, Karigan knew Mornhavon had seized control of him. Karigan blocked his blows.

"You'll have to do better!" she cried, and she ran away from Garth; she ran for the breach, away from the Riders, and right past Varadgrim.

Yes, run to me. Mornhavon's voice was low and breathy in her mind.

THE VESSEL OF
MORNHAVON

Laren watched in bewilderment as Garth fell limp to the ground and Karigan charged toward the breach and vanished through it. Then an Eletian emerged on the edge of the encampment and fluidly took an archer's stance, spines bristling on his shoulders and forearms. His bow was drawn taut, a white arrow nocked to the bowstring. The steel tip shone in the sun like a star.

His eyes narrowed as he focused his line of sight, and loosed the bowstring. The arrow sang, a beautiful sound as it sped by them and into the breach.

Laren cried out, and thought to go to Karigan, but an enormous winged creature rose above the breach and flicked out its tongue as it surveyed them. The wraith bared steel. Not a sword of ages ago, but new steel, and from the look of it, forged by the king's own smiths. Undoubtedly it had been taken from a dead soldier.

The Riders and soldiers were caught between two horrors— the winged monstrosity above, and the wraith.

The shadow of its wings moved over Laren and she flinched as the creature screeched at them. It lunged down and she watched helplessly as it clenched Dale in its talons. The Rider screamed and kicked as she was lifted from the ground several feet, the avian flapping its wings and creating a fetid wind. Dale's shoulder and chest blossomed with blood.

Riders and soldiers ran to aid her, but the creature threatened them with its sharp beak, its head swiveling on a long, snakelike neck.

Ty evaded the avian's beak and hacked at the talons that held Dale, partially severing the avian's leg. It jerked up, and Dale cried again. With another strike from Ty's sword, the leg was severed and Dale dropped to the ground, talons still hooked in her shoulder.

The avian rose into the sky with blood showering from the stump of its leg. Singing arrows, harmonious and deadly, streaked through the air and thudded into the avian's breast and beneath its wing. It screamed and plummeted earthward, and all beneath scattered. When it hit the ground, dust rose up around it. Its neck convulsed, then it moved no more. Smoke curled up from its wounds.

Laren ran to Dale's side, and was joined by Yates. "We need to . . ." But he was already prying the talons out of Dale's shoulder. Justin hovered nearby. "Bandages!" she told him.

Justin nodded and whistled to his horse. Several horses had scattered at the sight of the avian, but Justin's mare trotted over immediately and he set to foraging through his saddlebags.

Laren was both impressed and jealous—Bluebird had never answered to her whistle.

As they worked on Dale, the rest of her Riders, along with the soldiers, hemmed in the wraith. The wraith seemed unconcerned, but continued to stand there, neither engaging in a fight or acquiescing. Waiting.

Waiting for what?

Laren glanced where she had last seen the Eletian, but he was gone. She wondered where he went, why he didn't provide them counsel regarding the wraith. Why would he shoot an arrow at Karigan, then shoot down the avian to save the rest of them?

All was silence, except for Dale's weak moaning. Yates was working as swiftly as he could on her wounds, but she had lost a good deal of blood.

The silence was then shattered by cries issued from the other side of the breach. Not human cries, not quite animal, but ululating cries that stopped Laren's heart.

Groundmites.

They leaped through the breach like a pack of feral dogs, snarling and howling. They bore thick branches as clubs, and wore no armor. They were more primitive, more feral, than the others she'd seen. Some wore hide coverings, but many wore nothing at all, except for their shaggy, mud-colored fur.

As they poured through the breach and swarmed past the wraith, Laren did the only reasonable thing she could do when faced with overwhelming odds: she called, "Retreat!"

Karigan clambered over the rubble in the breach and ran. She ran as she never had before, knowing she needed to reach the forest before Mornhavon overcame her entirely, and before he learned her true intent.

"Coward!" she cried at Mornhavon. She could feel the heat of his anger burning within her, then nothing. He left as though distracted. Distracted by other things he must attend to.

"Damnation," she muttered. This wasn't going exactly as she planned.

Her brooch stirred, so she knew at least Lil was still with her. The wild magic twisted violently in her arm, as if roused by its return to Blackveil.

Paying no attention to the spindly trees above or the muck underfoot, she continued to run, intent only on what she needed to accomplish.

Down! Lil commanded.

Karigan fell to the moist earth. An arrow sang overhead, and when she looked up, it had embedded itself into a tree trunk. White against black, it absorbed all the light in this gloomy place, and it glowed. Tree bark peeled off around it as though it had struck a mortal wound.

It was an Eletian arrow, from an Eletian who wanted her dead.

Seems to me the Eletians have gotten a bit wrong-headed of late, Lil said.

Karigan couldn't agree more. "I think maybe it's time for you to go. You'll be listening for me?"

Truly, Lil said, and she left.

Karigan lay there, suddenly feeling very alone in the threatening environs of the forest.

And now there was something new to worry about.

Shapes emerged in the mist, and feet pounded the ground. Great hulking shapes that howled and screamed. Karigan threw her arms over her head and lay as flat as she could, hoping the groundmites would overlook her.

They're going for the breach, she thought in dismay. *They're going to attack the Riders.*

And quite suddenly, he was there again, in her mind. *Yes, they're going to annihilate your Riders.*

"Lil!" Karigan cried, and she clasped her hand around her brooch, and there was nothing but the overwhelming blackness that was *him,* amid the squalling snow.

Distantly she heard the notes of the Rider call, and she felt herself carried away.

Lil didn't think the gods would be pleased with her for bending the rules this way, but she had never been one to follow rules anyway. If she had, Mornhavon the Black and his forces would have overcome the League long ago.

And her reward? she thought with grim humor. *This.* Tangling with Mornhavon again. Mornhavon who should have been shattered and altogether dead, crawling tormented through all five hells for all eternity, or at least through the equivalent wrought by his empire's own religion.

Instead, he had somehow survived through time, defying the gods. His body was gone, yes, but his conscious mind remained. He was as dangerous and warped as ever.

Lil walked through Blackveil, but in some distant time in the future. She had no way of telling how far she had come, really, but she hoped it would be far enough to win Sacoridia and its neighboring countries time to prepare to bring an end to Mornhavon the Black, once and for all.

The forest was still, the mist much lighter. In fact, she could discern healthy green growth poking through the black wilt and decay. It seemed that with time, the forest had begun to heal, and this gave her hope that what Karigan planned would actually succeed. Or had succeeded. Or . . . Time was too confusing.

Even as a spirit, Lil was not permitted to see beyond the veil of time, to know what the future would bring, unless like now, she defied the gods and visited.

Here she was, but still there was the unknowing. What would become of Karigan? Even if the plan was a success, there was a good chance the young woman's life would be forfeited.

An acceptable risk. Lil had taken many risks herself, many for which she would have gladly laid down her life if it meant success. Yet, she had grown fond of the young woman, and knew what risks she had taken on her own behalf.

Defying the gods brought about a different kind of risk. Should she arouse Aeryc's wrath, she might find herself dwelling in the hells as punishment. The dead just weren't supposed to dally in the lives of the living. At least, not to this extent.

So she waited, fingering her brooch, waiting for an indication from Karigan to pull her through time. It was an audacious plan: Karigan would become the vessel that would carry Mornhavon to the future, and leave him there. That was how the Sacoridians would gain the time to prepare to deal with the menace. It was an imperfect plan. It might not work at all. She might be a hundred years in the future, or one, which would be of no use at all.

Lil!

The cry was faint. It barely pulsed through her brooch, but she had heard. Still clasping her brooch, she raised her horn to her lips and sounded the Rider call. She pulled on Karigan, on her brooch, the brooch that made them one. Wild magic might allow Karigan to travel, but now it had to be Lil's influence that determined to *when.*

She strained to pull Karigan through time, like a fisherman with a huge swordfish hooked on his line. It was hard drawing her forward. When she had been in the past, Lil's own corporeal form had been an anchor. But not now, since her corporeal form did not exist in the future.

She strained till she thought she must consume all her essence. Would there be nothing left of her with which to aid Karigan?

Before she saw them, she felt their presence, Karigan and Mornhavon both. Karigan's was a tiny particle of life, surrounded by the murk that was Mornhavon. Her body appeared, curled into a fetal position on the forest floor.

The forest subtly responded to Mornhavon's presence. The trees and plants seemed to thrum and bend toward Karigan.

The plan had worked, this far at least. Karigan had instructed Lil to abandon her in the future if Mornhavon would not leave her mind. Lil believed she deserved better.

I've nothing to lose, Lil thought, *except the niceties of the heavens should I be made to dwell in the hells.* There was also the possibility that Aeryc would banish her from existence altogether.

She used the brooch, used it as Karigan once had in the past upon Kendroa Mor, so they could merge.

When she did so, she found Karigan's presence diminished by Mornhavon's seething hatred. And what was with all the snow?

She blinked through the flurries, and saw him, a dark silouhette. He saw her, too.

YOU.

The world that was Karigan's mind quavered at the force of his voice.

Be gone, Lil replied. *You are not fit to occupy this space.*

I do as I wish.

How like a spoiled child he sounded. Lil glanced about through the snow, but saw no sign of Karigan, nor any spark of awareness. This did not bode well, and she supposed it called for drastic action. She didn't waste time.

She clasped her brooch and willed herself to occupy Karigan, to merge totally, mind, soul, and body. From Karigan's memories, Lil knew that the previous bearer of her brooch, F'ryan Coblebay, had done this to help Karigan overcome an opponent during a swordfight.

Her essence flowed through Karigan's body, through her limbs and to the tips of her fingers and toes. She expanded in Karigan's mind, shielding it to restrict Mornhavon's influence. For Lil, it was like drawing on a warm cloak, though Karigan's body was cooler than it ought to be.

She smelled loam and felt it beneath her cheek. A fern tickled her neck, and there was the warmth of sunlight gently blanketing her. For one who had walked in the spirit world for so long, this sensory awakening was ecstasy.

Mornhavon attacked her shield, chipping away at it, and

Lil knew she couldn't hold it indefinitely. She made Karigan sit up, open her eyes, and draw her longknife. *That* gave Mornhavon pause.

She turned the knife so the bladetip was touching Karigan's ribs, below her breast. She gripped the hilt with both hands.

You wouldn't, Mornhavon said.

"How do you know?"

You bluffed often enough in the past.

"But I wasn't always bluffing, was I?"

Mornhavon did not answer, he was thinking it over. She couldn't give him the time.

Adjusting her grip on the knife hilt, she hoped Karigan would forgive her, and she jerked the knife into her flesh.

Pain! Lil had forgotten about pain, of how it felt when cold sharp steel tore through flesh and muscle. She gasped in disbelief, and wished urgently to flee Karigan's body, but she could not. Not yet.

The forest around her raged with a sudden maelstrom. Trees were shorn of their limbs, and one was uprooted and fell over behind her.

Lil's ploy had been a success. Mornhavon had left Karigan's body, fearing to lose his own hold on life should Karigan die. Lil withdrew the knife, blood spreading across Karigan's shirt.

Mornhavon had been deposited in the future, and now it was time to return to the present.

As she traveled, Mornhavon called after her, *You cannot stop the wall from falling!*

❧ AVENUE OF LIGHT ❧

The groundmites tore Tierny from her horse and she vanished beneath flailing clubs that fell with sickening thuds. Soldiers who were without horses stood their ground in formation, back to back, hacking at their wild attackers. Yates was helping Dale to stay in the saddle with him, using his legs to guide his horse, and slashing at groundmites beside him.

Garth couldn't seem to get mounted, for the groundmites swarmed around him, as though attracted by his size. Instead, he faced the enemy and fought, his sword in one hand and his longknife in the other. Chickadee guarded his back, a hoof cracking a groundmite skull.

Laren whirled Bluebird around, blood streaming from her saber. Since the groundmites did not wear armor, they were, in a sense, not difficult to kill. It was just their sheer numbers that posed the problem.

So much for a retreat, she thought. They just couldn't break free.

The wraith watched from its place near the breach. It did not engage in battle, but stood there as an ominous presence, a silent general over barbaric soldiers.

Laren carved into the wrist of a groundmite, its howl echoing against the wall. Its club tumbled against Bluebird's hocks, and he bucked, scattering others from around him.

More soldiers fell. Justin was hauled off his horse, and

he fell victim to bloodied clubs. Yates screamed, torn between getting Dale out of harm's way, and hacking his way to his friend's side.

How long before the groundmites wore them all down?

Then, with a suddenness Laren could not comprehend, their ferocious assault began to fall apart. She was not one to believe in miracles, and couldn't even remember the last time she had attended chapel. She did make oaths in the names of the gods on a regular basis, but she just wasn't religious. But when the groundmites stopped their attack altogether, she decided she was overdue to light a candle at chapel.

The groundmites began to whine and howl. Some of her Riders pressed the advantage and started killing them where they stood. But when the wraith turned and ran through the breach into the forest, the groundmites fled after it, leaving Laren, her Riders, and the soldiers in stunned disbelief.

There would be time to wonder about it later, for she must first tend to her wounded. And the dead. She took one more glance toward the breach, and wondered if she should count Karigan among them.

Karigan's body had grown colder than ever, a result Lil knew, of the traveling. Why it happened, she did not know. Perhaps because flesh and blood were not meant to endure the strain of passing through the ages.

She brought them back to Karigan's present and now pressed her hand—Karigan's hand—against the knife wound to help staunch the bleeding. Lil hadn't stabbed mortally deep to accomplish what she needed, but it still bled profusely and hurt like the five hells.

She supposed she ought to return Karigan through the

breach to her captain. With Mornhavon removed from this time, everything ought to be calming down.

That's what she thought until she heard a stampede—a stampede of groundmites crashing heedlessly through the forest. She stood in the lee of a stout tree so she wouldn't get trampled.

Striding through the churning mist behind them came Varadgrim. Her hand went immediately to the hilt of her saber. An old foe he was, a foe that had taken the lives of many of her Riders. He might be little more than a walking corpse, and she beyond the grave herself, but still the old hatred kindled within her.

Sensing her, Varadgrim halted and turned to her, the shreds of his ancient cloak whirling at his knees. He possessed a sword of his own, bright and shining, but thankfully it was not a soul-stealer.

Her saber hissed from its sheath.

Not her saber, she remembered belatedly, and not her body to do with as she wished. Yet she itched to fight. The sword felt right in her hand. Her lust to take Varadgrim fought with her desire to be a good steward of the body with which she had been entrusted.

In the end, Varadgrim made the decision for her. "I will kill the Galadheon."

"I think not," Lil said. "Do you know who it is you truly face?"

"Liliedhe Ambriodhe is dead. The Galadheon must die."

Lil was a little disappointed that her presence failed to impress him more.

He strode over to her and initiated the fight without preamble. It was unlike the Varadgrim of old who had been prone to elaborate flourishes and dramatic declarations, but she supposed a thousand years chained in a tomb might have created a lasting stoical effect.

She eased the saber into place to block his blows. Karigan was of slighter build than she had been, and not as tall, so it took some adjustment on her part, but she was pleased to find Karigan in fighting trim.

The ring of blades filled the forest like a hammer hailing on an anvil. Mist swirled about them as they fought. Varadgrim's movements were unadorned, but not without purpose.

Likewise, Lil did not allow herself any superfluous movements. She had to preserve both her own energy and Karigan's. Out of necessity, Lil had always fought to kill, not to show off fancy footwork or some complicated move. No, for her, killing was a utilitarian skill she had put to constant use during the Long War. There was no time for embellishment or showmanship back then, and she wasn't going to start now.

Varadgrim moved rigidly, and it dulled his swiftness. In some ways, he turned out to be a disappointing opponent. Maybe Mornhavon's absence sapped him of his energy. He was a fearful presence, but it held no power over her, and gave him no advantage.

It was possible he would outlast her. Karigan's body was weakening from blood loss, and the swordfight had only increased the flow. And Lil had her own limitations as a spirit. The swordfight had to end, and it had to end soon.

She kept a tree to her back, and allowed Varadgrim to close in. She ducked under a blow that hacked into the trunk. In the moment it took him to free his blade, she came up and behind him, and severed his head from his body.

He crumpled stiffly to the ground. The flesh on his body puckered and decomposed as she watched, leaving behind a pile of rags and a leering skull. His crown melted into itself and oozed into the forest floor. Wild magic had bound him to Mornhavon, and now, in a sense, he was free. The pile of rags heaved a final sigh, collapsing as his bones turned to dust.

Long overdue, Lil thought.

She sheathed the saber. There was no sense of triumph, just as there never had been in her own day when she took another's life. Maybe in her early years making her first kills she had felt triumph. It was later on, with maturity, that she realized the ordinary legions of the empire were only doing the same as she: fighting for their ideals, fighting for survival, fighting out of desperation. It took the triumph out of killing.

Lil, at great expense to her own energy and Karigan's, wandered the forest disoriented by the heavy mist and the sameness of trees. She wished to walk the spirit path again, for Karigan's cold body was a weight now, a heaviness that she must drag around. But she couldn't abandon Karigan. She would not recover on her own, and no one would find her in the forest. Lil tried calling into her mind, but there was no answer, and she worried that Mornhavon had damaged her irreparably.

Karigan's body kept moving because Lil forced it to, one step after another. She had ripped off the sleeves of Karigan's shirt and wadded the knife wound with them. Finally she was able to slow the bleeding.

Karigan! she sent with her mind. She heard nothing in response, and perceived only the damnable snow.

Karigan plowed through the snow, hugging her arms around herself in an effort to keep warm. It piled up on her shoulders and head, and dripped an icy finger beneath her collar. She could not remember why she was here, or how she had gotten into this wintry wilderness in the first place. Blood oozed from a wound to her midsection, freezing in red crystals. She had lost feeling in her fingers and toes. All she knew was that she wanted to lay down and sleep.

No, she thought. *Must not do it.* But she couldn't figure out why.

She thought she heard her name shouted in the distance, but decided it was only the wind rushing through the forest.

Dusk was settling in when Lil stumbled upon the ancient road, a road built and once used by Eletians before the coming of Mornhavon. She had never seen Argenthyne in its full glory, for it had fallen before her birth, but like all children, she had heard tales. Yes, even in the war-ravaged orphan camps, there was the magic of stories, and the most magical were those about lost Argenthyne.

A gruff veteran named Ansel visited the children and told them the tales. He was missing an arm, and a patch covered one of his eyes, but he never failed to mesmerize them with his descriptions of Laurelyn's shining castle of moonbeams. The children, famished in mind and body, had hung on to his words as if they were physical sustenance.

She stumbled over a loose cobble, painfully jarring the knife wound, but at least managed to prevent Karigan from falling. She paused to rest, her eyes drawn to the side of the road. A statue stood there gazing back, arms upraised. A mage who had worked on the building of the wall claimed these statues had once held globes that collected the rays of sun, moon, and stars, and showed the way through the night. *Lumeni,* he called them. This statue no longer possessed a globe, nor did she have hands with which to hold one.

Lil had not known Argenthyne, but she was not unfamiliar with this road. The old mage had called it the Avenue of Light. She was unsure of the Eletian name for it. She had traveled upon it before, and it only looked more decrepit, more overcome than ever. Perhaps in the old days, some vestige of the goodness of the Eletians had lingered before Mornhavon had perverted the forest wholly.

She now knew where she was, and where the road would lead her. She would seek the tower, and even if there was no help for Karigan there, she could reach the other side of the wall through it.

She forced the body forward, realizing with alarm her fingers and toes had gone numb. She shoved her hands beneath her armpits.

"C'mon, Karigan, lass," she murmured. "Stay with me."

She decided to sing. Whether it was the novelty of using a real voice, or a way to amuse herself, she wasn't sure. She did hope a bit of the song found Karigan.

> *Great heart, stout heart*
> *Strong and bold,*
> *Molten and fiery*
> *Cast in a mold*
>
> *The winged horse emerges*
> *Iron and cold,*
> *The mage smith bids it*
> *To choose and hold*

Lil paused singing and considered the racket she was making. Karigan was completely tone deaf! It should, she thought, scare off any of Mornhavon's beasts that might be lurking about.

Inspired, and warmed by the singing, she took a deep breath and continued the song.

> *A Rider's true heart*
> *It shall seek,*
> *Great heart, stout heart*
> *Strong and bold . . .*

Karigan wasn't sure what inspired her to sing the inane song. She could barely move her frozen lips to form the words, and the cold air stole her breath away. Was it a song Estral had taught her? She hardly remembered who Estral was. A musician?

She sagged against a tree trunk and took up the words once again. They were more croaked than sung, the effort pulling painfully at her wound.

> *Worn with honor*
> *Worn with pride,*
> *Worn by Riders*
> *Of the Sacor Tribes*
>
> *Humble brooch*
> *Iron brooch,*
> *Strength it provides*
> *Against the evil tide*

> *"Too humble is this iron brooch,"*
> *The great Isbemic said,*
> *"for the hearts of Riders bold*
> *shine as pure as burnished gold."*
>
> *From cold iron he made gold*
> *Molten and fiery,*
> *Cast in a mold*
> *The mage smith Isbemic made it so*
>
> *Great heart, stout heart*
> *Strong and bold,*
> *The iron hearts of Riders*
> *Glitter as gold*
>
> *The iron hearts of Riders*
> *Glitter as gold . . .*

Lil liked shouting the song into the forest, hearing her voice—Karigan's really—echo, even though it was off key. She hoped all of Mornhavon's creatures were cowering at the sound. Truly, she was trying to send a message: A bold Rider walks here. Beware.

Perhaps she was taking an unnecessary risk by drawing attention to Karigan, but she couldn't help herself. There was nothing so empowering as walking nonchalantly through the enemy camp. Besides, Karigan's body was warming a little with the singing. She launched into it again.

> *Great heart, stout heart*
> *Strong and bold . . .*

By the time Lil reached the wall and had begun walking in the direction of the tower, she had sung Karigan's voice hoarse. It had helped pass the time at least, and helped her keep a steady pace. She had come this far even before the forest turned an inky black with nightfall.

When she finally came upon *Haethen Toundrel,* she wondered belatedly whether or not it would admit her, as it always had during her life.

I suppose there is only one way to find out.

She grasped the brooch, and pressed her other hand against the stone. The brooch tingled beneath her fingers, and the stone absorbed her.

She emerged into the central chamber of the tower, a place she had not laid eyes on for three ages. She gathered the keepers hadn't maintained their vigil from the towers in many a year, so it was with a little surprise that she found the chamber brightly lit, and a figure pacing back and forth across it, his long beard bristling. He halted when he noticed her.

"Well, well, well," he said, "as I live and breathe. I can see you, Liliedhe Ambriodhe."

"You do not live, nor do you breathe," she said.

"Hmph! Neither do you, for that matter."

"At least I'm accepting it."

Merdigen grumbled to himself. "Then what, may I ask, are you doing possessing the body of this young woman, hmm?"

"I'm not *possessing* it, I'm just borrowing it—to help save this Rider's life."

"Hmph." Merdigen tugged on his beard and drew his bushy brows together. "Well, don't bother."

"Hey? I don't believe I heard you correctly."

"I said, don't bother. The wall is going to fall and all will be lost."

At Lil's incredulous silence, he added, "One of those Riders of yours claimed he intended to mend the wall. Instead, he's undermining it."

Lil wanted to speak, wanted to say it couldn't possibly be so, but just then, her energy began to falter and fluctuate, straining her bond with Karigan. As she felt Karigan slipping away, across the chamber a hand grew out of the stone wall, followed by another. Then there was a face molded into stone, molded around a figure. Finally a person emerged into the chamber, an Eletian in white armor.

⇜ PENDRIC ⇝

At first, after Pendric's father was killed in Blackveil, the soldiers tried to watch over him. Captain Reems offered him an escort if he wished to accompany his father's remains back to Woodhaven.

He'd have liked nothing better than to leave, but traveling away from the wall, he knew, would only shred his mind. The voices were ever more persistent, ever more desperate as they clawed away inside his head.

So Pendric stayed. Initially the soldiers deferred to him because of his rank, but he had nothing to offer them, no leadership, no wisdom, nothing. He had nothing but the voices in his mind.

He entered the encampment only for food and wine, and the soldiers began to look upon him as something strange, a feral beast, and they kept their distance.

The voices screamed at him for help, pleaded him to come.

"I am mad, I am mad!" He banged the heels of his hands against his head trying to dislodge the voices.

It was all Alton's doing—he knew it. Alton had always hated him, and now Alton was making him go mad. It wasn't good enough he had killed Lady Valia and Landrew. Now he had to destroy Pendric's mind, too.

Suddenly there was a voice he recognized twining

through his mind. A calm, rhythmic voice from which all the others recoiled.

Alton!

If the other voices recoiled from Alton, then surely they were not the evil ones. And they were calling for help. Yes, all they had wanted all along was his help.

He allowed the voices to lead him along. He walked until he came to a tower embedded in the great stone wall. He blinked in surprise to find Alton's horse standing beside it, its dark coat dull and tail snarled with burdocks. Its ribs were sharp against its sides.

Alton, Pendric determined, was somehow in the tower wreaking his evil. He had no choice but to enter and stop him.

✑ AN ELETIAN
ARROW ✑

K^{arigan!}

arigan!
She heard her name called from afar, threading through the snowy forest. She kneeled in the snow, arms wrapped around herself, one shoulder leaning against a tree trunk. She closed her eyes. She was beyond freezing.

The call was too far away, and she too drowsy to respond. She wanted to rest and sleep. She sank deeply into darkness and peace.

A horn bellowed, and clumps of snow fell from branches above and plopped on her head. She fluttered her eyes open. The horn blared again, and she recognized the call, the Rider call.

Why wouldn't it leave her alone? First it had made her join the Green Riders, now it was forcing her to leave this place of tranquility. She decided to ignore it and close her eyes. She had ignored it before, and she could again.

But it wasn't to be so. It was as if somebody grabbed her by her shortcoat and slapped each cheek. Her cheeks stung and light assaulted her eyes. She found herself kneeling not in snow, but in a chamber of stone, and leaning not against a tree, but against a fluted column.

She gasped, trying to make sense of everything.

Columns ringed the whole of the chamber, and a green oval of stone glistened on a pedestal at its center. Above the pedestal a dark cloud floated glistening with . . . stars? An old man paced beside it. He was twisting his fingers in his long whiskers, and for some reason she had a sort of secondary vision of him pacing back and forth on a vast plain cloaked by night.

"Terrible, oh, most terrible," he was muttering to himself.

Beyond both the old man and the pedestal, on the far side of the chamber, stood an Eletian. Karigan did not know where she was, or why she was there. She had no idea of what was going on or why, but she *did* recognize the Eletian, with the tines protruding from the forearms and shoulders of his armor. He held an arrow nocked to a bow. The tip of the arrowhead glinted, and she could feel his line of sight searing into her heart.

She could not move, could not speak.

"The time of watching is over," the Eletian said. "And despite the warning, you came to the wall anyway."

"Let us be reasonable here," the old man said. "There is a crisis at the moment and—"

"I will not hear an illusion," the Eletian snapped. "I have my duty to fulfill."

"This is an outrage," the old man sputtered. "The wall is—"

"The outrage is that this Galadheon is tainted, tainted by dark wild magic."

"Indeed?" The old man turned to Karigan and crooked a bushy eyebrow.

"One," the Eletian continued, "whose presence could bring about the destruction of the wall."

Karigan's temper rose, and her anger warmed her. She rose unsteadily to her feet, sucking in a breath at the wound that stretched beneath her ribs.

"Endangers the wall?" the old man asked. "Like the Rider who calls himself a Deyer?"

Both Karigan and the Eletian looked at the old man and stared.

"Alton?" It was the first word Karigan managed to utter, her voice strangely hoarse.

"Yes," the old man said. "He called himself that. Claimed he was going to fix the wall. He's merged with it now, destroying it instead." He tugged on his whiskers, his face full of despair.

"Where?" Karigan croaked.

"I can't tell you," the old man said. "It seems you Riders have grown deceitful. So many lives were sacrificed to build this wall, and now you would undo it."

"No!" she cried. "Mornhavon is—we—"

"His taint is within you," the Eletian said, and he drew the bowstring taut.

"You don't understand!"

As the words left her mouth, the Eletian loosed the arrow. It barreled at her and she could not move. Then a familiar tug on her brooch carried her through time, briefly enough that she had been pushed ahead a mere moment. When the traveling ceased, Karigan stood in the same spot, but the Eletian's arrow clattered against the wall behind her as though it had passed right through her. It all had happened in the span of a heartbeat.

You are on your own now, said the distant voice of Lil Ambrioth. *I have nothing left to give.*

The Eletian scowled and was reaching for another arrow when behind him the wall came to life with silver runes.

A man emerged through the wall. He was wild and unkempt, his eyes haunted. His clothes looked as though they had once been the fine attire of a lord, but now they hung from him, soiled and torn. With some surprise, Karigan recognized Alton's unpleasant cousin, Pendric.

The runes pooled on the stone beneath his feet, and he seemed oblivious to all else. When the runes streaked across the chamber and veered under an arch and into its dark passage, he followed, and Karigan darted after him.

The runes illuminated the short passage that ended at a stone wall. Sprawled on the floor was Alton.

"Alton!" she cried. She pushed past Pendric and knelt beside him, and placed her hand on his chest. Its rise and fall was barely perceptible. Otherwise, she would have taken him for dead.

Pendric hovered over them, fists cocked, a face devoured by rage and madness. "He should die."

"No!" Karigan sprang up at him, but he punched his fist into her wound. She staggered back against the passage's wall. The pain stole her breath away, turned her sight red. She sank inward, inward into the darkness and snow again. The last image of her fading sight was of the Eletian and the old man peering in from the end of the passage, before she collapsed across Alton's legs.

⋞ HUNTED ⋟

Alton perceived the crackling around him. The fissures that spread through the wall were like vast, black crevasses he could not cross. The harder he worked trying to fix the wall, the more it seemed to fracture.

The guardians of the wall panicked around him, trying to resist his song. He perceived anger and enmity directed toward him. Why this should be so, he did not understand. At least, not at first.

As the stone continued to crack, slowly undermining the strength of the great wall, it dawned on him that maybe he was doing something wrong, that maybe he had the song wrong and he was somehow responsible.

But he sang the song Karigan had so carefully taught him, and she wouldn't lie to him, would she? She loved him, she . . .

He was confused, and in his confusion, he stopped singing, but he could still discern the crackling.

No reassuring words came to him, or urged him on. Karigan's voice did not guide him, and the intensity of his purpose faded away. It had been, he realized, someone else's purpose. It was as though a veil was now lifted from his mind. Shadows fled and the fabric of lies unraveled. He had been overcome, overcome and duped.

He looked anew at the chasms and cracks throughout the wall, and knew they were strung out for a great length. He had been working hard to accomplish what he believed was the mending of the wall, but it had only worsened.

What have I done?

Hastily he tried to pick up the true rhythm of the song within the wall, the true song of the guardians, but it was difficult to find the harmony. So many of the voices had lost the key, sang to a different measure.

He despaired of what to do, lamenting his weakness that he should fall prey to the darkness of Blackveil and bring all this upon his people. He was filled with self-loathing. It was too far gone for him to fix, too big a problem for him to overcome.

Idiot.

The word vibrated along the crystalline structures. The one who uttered it was different from all the guardians, and Alton thought he knew the texture of it, the venom behind it.

Pendric?

You have destabilized the wall.

I thought I was fixing it . . .

You are wrong, cousin, very wrong. You have wrought enough evil here, and I will be the one to fix it—I will be the one to save our people, and the glory will be all mine this time. May the king judge you guilty for your crimes, and hang you from the castle's highest turret.

The voices of the guardians clustered around Pendric, and it was like the build-up of a storm bearing down on him. They radiated all of Pendric's molten hatred and would tolerate him no more.

Alton was knocked out of the wall, back into the world, back into his battered and ill body. He was conscious long enough to feel a hot tear slide down his cheek.

It was the horses again. They herded Laren, Garth, and Ty to the tower. Garth barely had time to grab a lantern so they could actually see where they were going.

Condor had clamped his teeth on Laren's sleeve and practically dragged her all the way. When she saw the forlorn Night Hawk keeping vigil outside, she knew Alton or Karigan, or both, were within. They had to rein in their impatience and excitement as they puzzled over how to enter a tower with no obvious door.

It was Garth who happened to lean against the tower and brush his brooch with his hand. He fell into the tower—it *swallowed* him was the only way she could think of to describe what she saw. When he re-emerged, grinning broadly, they had their answer about how to enter the tower.

Among the wonders of the tower was an old man who claimed to be a "projection" of a great mage called Merdigen.

"An illusion," Ty explained, his equanimity unshaken.

Merdigen *hrrrumphed.* "I am much more than a mere illusion."

Ultimately, he led them to the passage where her Riders lay. Alton was unconscious, hot and feverish. Wounds on his legs festered, and there were old bruises on his face. He looked as though he had been through a great deal of torture and pain. Karigan lay across his legs, and in contrast, was freezing cold; so cold that ice crystals had formed on her eyelashes. Blood stained her midsection and Laren thought her dead until Ty knelt beside her and perceived her breathing.

A third body lying beside them showed no signs of life.

Laren gazed apprehensively at her Riders, one burning up, the other icy cold. How could they be alive? Maybe one had moderated the condition of the other . . . She knew they both must have incredible tales to tell, of their passing through Blackveil. But first she'd have to ensure they lived long enough to tell those stories later.

They decided to keep Karigan and Alton in the tower, wishing to move them as little as possible, and taking advantage of the shelter the tower offered. They were made comfortable near the hearth, and their wounds washed. They tried to bring down Alton's temperature, and raise Karigan's.

A soldier from the encampment with mending skills made poultices to draw out the poison lingering in Alton's veins. She made one also for Karigan's wound so it would not fester.

Periodically Alton came to, mumbling, whispering Karigan's name. They gave him water and broth as they could, and watched over him as he slept.

Karigan proved to be more of a puzzle. The stab wound was not life-threatening since the flow of blood had been stemmed, yet she remained in some deep level of unconsciousness. No matter how many blankets they piled on her, she continued to emanate cold. Eventually they set ablaze wood that Garth had collected, in the great hearth.

"Not all battles are fought with swords," Merdigen said.

Laren glanced at him, trying to fathom some hidden meaning, and then had to remind herself he was but an illusion, projection, or . . . whatever.

Eventually Alton's lucid moments grew longer, and with nourishment, he was able to speak of his nightmare in the forest.

Karigan's part of the tale, however, remained a mystery.

Karigan had never before been caught in so violent a blizzard. She blew into her cupped hands to warm them, but the wind sucked away her breath. There was no horn to call her back this time, only the wind assaulting her ears.

And she was being hunted. Hunted by some amorphous, shadowed creature that slipped through the forest. She heard its chuffing breaths as it loped after her, then paused to snuffle through the snow.

Her arm pressed against her painful wound, she ran through the blizzard as best she could, falling and forcing herself back to her feet. The creature cried out in triumph when it found her trail again, and pursued. Karigan swallowed back sobs, tears freezing in the corners of her eyes. She could not outrun this thing, it was catching up too swiftly.

I could give up.

It would be so easy just to lay down in the snow, to let her fate be what it would be. Just give in.

She plowed to a stop, and glanced over her shoulder at the creature closing in. She could run herself to death, or give up. Or she could face the creature.

Her stubborn streak refused to let her give in. She cracked a limb off a tree and waited.

The creature rumbled toward her, gathering speed, taking down trees as it came. The ground trembled, or maybe it was Karigan who trembled, thinking her branch a pitiful defense against something that could uproot trees. It was like waiting for an avalanche to roll over her.

Snow swirled up into a stinging fog as the beast slid to a halt in front of her. She could only make out the dense shadow that formed it. It snorted and pawed at the snow, and she could imagine large nostrils flaring as it took in her scent.

It plodded forward a couple more steps, and still she could discern no details. It seemed to ooze through the dark as if it were part of the night itself. Did it carry itself on hooves, or sharp claws? Or did it slither through the forest as a snake would?

What are you? Karigan wondered, shaking from cold and fear.

The thing reared up before her, reared up higher than the tops of trees, its forelegs with clawed feet stretching up against the backdrop of falling snow. It howled into the night.

Horrified, Karigan screamed, too, and plunged her branch into its underside. The creature bellowed, but her makeshift weapon did it no harm—it was absorbed into its body.

That's what's going to happen to me. It was going to absorb her and consume her. She had no doubt of it.

She spun and ran, calling on reserves of strength that really weren't there. She ran heedlessly, certain the end was near.

The beast charged after her. She could almost feel its breath on the back of her neck, and she knew she must be in range of snapping jaws or the swipe of a claw.

She did not want to die. She did not want it to end this way.

She stumbled down an embankment and her feet flew out from beneath her. She sprawled onto a hard surface, a pond sealed in glittering black ice. The wind had swept it clean of snow.

Her momentum sent her gliding and spinning away. She gazed into the ice as she went and it was like looking into the heavens whirling beneath glazed glass, for there were bright pinpoints of stars there. Spinning she went, spinning across the heavens.

Fractures marred the ice—she feared her weight would send her crashing through into the freezing water, but she glided safely over them.

The creature paused its pursuit by the pond's edge, at first hesitant. But with its prey so close by, it tossed caution aside and dashed onto the ice, at first scrambling for purchase, then unsheathing its claws to grip the slippery surface.

Karigan tried to regain her feet in the face of the creature's onrush, but she just kept slipping. Ice chips flew as the creature bounded toward her, its claws scoring the black ice.

This is it, then. Karigan closed her eyes, finally finding her end.

Yet it wasn't to be so. The splintering of ice cracked through the forest and roused her. The creature had reached the fractured patch, which gave way beneath its feet. It screamed and thrashed, fought to pull itself back onto solid ice, but only broke more ice. The creature sank beneath the pond's surface, and did not re-emerge.

The broken ice released the heavens that had been locked beneath it. Clear, dark night, unpowdered by snow squalls, spread upward from the hole, carrying with it a galaxy of stars.

Beyond exhaustion, Karigan laid her head on her forearm and sighed deeply.

They rushed to Karigan's side when she screamed.

"What's happening?" Garth demanded.

Ty shrugged.

Karigan had partially thrown one of the blankets off herself. Was she dreaming? Was it a nightmare? Laren had no way of telling, but thought it a hopeful sign, better than total lack of consciousness.

Karigan thrashed some more, then fell limp, breathing heavily.

"Look." Garth pointed at her left arm.

At first Laren thought Karigan was bleeding, but what oozed from her arm was a black, oily substance. She had seen its like before, in the castle's throne room two years ago. It pooled onto the floor, then slithered to and fro in the cracks between the stone flagging, as if to find an avenue of escape. It could not. Then quite suddenly it evaporated with a hiss of steam.

"Gods!" Garth exclaimed. "What was it?"

The illusion, Merdigen, had come up behind them and watched over their shoulders. "Tainted wild magic. She's better off for having expelled it."

As if to confirm his words, Karigan sighed deeply and sank into what appeared to be a peaceful, normal sleep.

Journal of Hadriax el Fex

Alessandros has betrayed us. He has betrayed everything. His madness is destroying the ideals upon which the Empire was founded, this world, and even those who have proven themselves loyal time and again. I can barely write—my hand shakes so from outrage and grief. Tears blur the ink.

Alessandros has committed a terrible act. He made a sacrifice today—not of prisoners or slaves, not even of Elt.

I had just returned this afternoon from a campaign to the west, and my men and I had barely dismounted when we found ourselves, along with others of the town and palace, being ushered inside to the great hall by Alessandros' guards. We were all confused and did not know what to expect.

Alessandros stood upon a raised platform—a stage, now that I think of it—before drawn curtains. He had news, he said, news of great import that would finally secure our victory in the war. A great cheer went up in the hall and the people chanted his name. He grinned and raised his hands to silence them.

When all was quiet once again, Alessandros explained he had made the Black Star immeasurably stronger, and that it was the greatest weapon the world had ever known. To do so, he had had to make sacrifices, but we shouldn't be sad, he said. The sacrifices would save so many more lives. The assembled shifted uneasily and I wondered what he had done this time.

Then he made the curtain vanish.

Seated in perfect rows upon the stage were the revered warriors of the Lion regiment. Our best and bravest soldiers, the pride of the

597

Empire. They wore tunics of purest white trimmed with gold. Lions embroidered in red and gold thread roared upon their chests. Beneath the tunics they wore their golden parade armor, glittering in the light of the prisms. Their golden helms were placed at their feet, and bared swords across their knees.

Renald sat in the front row with the other officers, his tunic adorned with glistening medals of valor, medals of service, and medals of merit. About his waist was the gold-embossed belt I had had crafted for him when he made captain. The belt buckle was a lion's head.

My squire, my young man, the brave warrior.

They were dead. All of them.

Crude stitches lashed together the gashes of flesh at their throats. They'd been drained of blood, and their skin was as white as their tunics. Mouths gaped open grotesquely, lips curled back, and their eyes had rolled to the backs of their heads showing only the whites. Corpses dressed up and propped up like macabre dolls; parodies of what these men had once been.

It took several moments for the enormity of it all to sink in. At first everyone was too stunned, then wailing exploded in the chamber as the assembled recognized loved ones and friends among Arcosia's Lions. Brothers, fathers, sons, and husbands.

I have never known better men, especially Renald. Merciful in battle, loyal to the core. They had sworn their hearts and lives to Arcosia. Not to this.

Even as the whole of my body numbed in shock, Alessandros walked among the corpses, gazing fondly at them, putting his hand on a shoulder here, gripping an arm there. He made the sacrifice, he explained, for the good of Mornhavonia. It had been the choice of the soldiers to willingly give up their lives thus, to strengthen the Black Star. They were now renowned martyrs, he said, and should be praised.

The hall smelled of bitter sickness and there was much weeping, but many seemed to want to believe Alessandros, as though it would soothe their pain. I did not believe him. I could not.

Later on, he called me to his apartments and confided that the

Lions never knew what was coming, that they'd been brought before him one at a time, and he slaughtered them systematically like a line of cattle. The words tumbled shakily from his mouth, and his foot twitched in nervous fashion.

He was confessing to me, as though I were a priest, to alleviate the burden of his sins. I think more that he wanted to justify his actions.

"I am god, after all," he said, "and it is my right to give or take life."

All I had seen was the taking, but I said nothing. He watched me carefully for my reaction.

After some moments I ventured, "You sent me away on that campaign so I wouldn't know."

"My dear, dear Hadriax, you comprehend me all too well. I couldn't take the chance you'd talk me out of it. I know how much you loved Renald, and the esteem you held for him. I am sorry for your loss, for he was a good young man, but it was necessary."

I could only swallow hard and will my tears to stay back.

"Think of it!" Alessandros said. "With the sacrifice of the Lions, the Black Star is stronger than ever. It now embodies their strength of heart, fighting spirit, and strategic skill. All of them live on in the Star. With it we will conquer the New Lands, and then take our war to the Empire itself. The Emperor will pay for abandoning us."

I wanted to kill him right there. I wanted to wrap my fingers about his throat and choke the life out of him. My fingers opened and closed even as the rage fired up in my heart. But I knew I could not do it. He had been using so much etherea and he was protected by the Black Star. He could not die by such ordinary means.

I could bear no more and so left. I now know, after this latest atrocity, that my alliance with the Green Riders is inevitable; that my pact with Lil Ambriodhe is sealed. Alessandros' betrayal has brought me to this.

May it bring him to his death.

✒ THE KING'S
DECISION ✒

T hey were doomed.
     Three of Laren's Riders would never
return to Sacor City, and others were badly injured. Dale, with her grave wounds, remained
in Woodhaven where she could receive care without being
moved more than necessary.

Alton stayed in Woodhaven, too, to discuss matters with
his father, and then he'd return to the wall to see what more
he could learn from it, and to investigate the unusual properties of *Haethen Toundrel.* His wounds appeared more
psychic than physical. He would not talk to Karigan, would
not even look at her. Some breach greater than the one in
the wall divided them, and both Laren and Karigan were at
a loss to explain the cause.

And now, after all their trials and losses, their sacrifices
in service to their king and country, that same king was
about to doom the country by splitting it asunder, by alien-
ating the one lord-governor he needed most on his side.

All the lord-governors, except Lord D'Yer, ringed the
long table in the council chamber. Most were attended by
an aide of some sort. Lord D'Ivary, though not technically a
prisoner, was closely watched by guards.

The lords Adolind, Mirwell, Penburn, and Wayman
were there, as well as L'Petrie, Oldbury, and Steward-
Governor Leonar Hillander, Zachary's cousin. Representing
Lord D'Yer was his own steward, Aldeon Mize. One side of

the table was occupied by the eastern lords as a block, as if to separate themselves from all others, just as they were geographically separated from the rest of Sacoridia.

They were proud and independent in spirit, attributes that lent them an air of superiority, and allowed them to survive isolation and the harsh conditions of sea and mountain.

In their isolation, they had almost become a law unto themselves, but through the strong leadership of Lord Coutre, they managed to retain loyalty to the crown. Singly, they were formidable. As a group, their support or lack thereof could make or break a monarch's rule.

Arey, Bairdly, Coutre.

All three watched Zachary expectantly. Lord Coutre, bent and elderly, his face beaten by sun and sea, was nevertheless a commanding figure with his heavy white brows and unsettling scowl.

Laren knew about Lord Coutre's ultimatum. Zachary must agree to marry his daughter, Lady Estora, or lose the support of the east. Though it made all the sense in the world that Zachary marry Estora, the coercion infuriated him, and he refused to give Lord Coutre the satisfaction of an answer.

They were doomed.

There was always the chance, Laren supposed, that the support of the other lord-governors would weigh in Zachary's favor, but it was only a chance. The lord-governors were a fractious and self-interested lot at best.

Zachary obviously hoped D'Ivary's appalling behavior would be enough to sway the others, but as appalling as his acts had been, it was hard to say whether or not the lord-governors would support or go against one of their own. They might try to force Zachary's hand so that he'd have to make an unpopular decision without their backing.

How could Zachary afford to offend Lord Coutre at this time?

Laren thought she knew the answer. Someone else had his heart and he couldn't bring himself to do what was best for his country and commit to marrying Lady Estora. This, despite the fact he had known all his life he would one day marry for political expediency, not for love.

Laren had her suspicions about who captivated him, and that was the most unsettling part of all.

She shifted her stance in the shadow of his chair. Sperren and Colin winged him at the head of the table. They looked just as unhappy as she felt.

"I have called you to this council meeting in regards to actions taken by Lord-Governor Hedric D'Ivary," Zachary said. "You have been briefed on his breaches of king's law and the charges I place against him. He used the power of his office against his very own people, subjects of Sacoridia."

"Those border scum aren't 'subjects'," Lord Oldbury retorted. "They refuse to acknowledge our laws and sovereignty."

Zachary's demeanor remained pleasant and calm. "They live within Sacoridia's borders, and therefore they fall under my protection." He paused, waiting for more disagreement, but amazingly, none came. "I wish to present to you the actions committed by Lord D'Ivary, personally or by his command, and you may judge him as you will."

He then gazed pointedly at Lord Coutre. "I should hope you would judge Lord D'Ivary without bias, and not condemn him or free him of charges because of some personal ambition or favor you seek of me. This is too important a matter to trivialize with political schemes and goals."

Lord Coutre's scowl deepened.

"I shall not present the case on my own," Zachary said.

Laren raised an eyebrow. Now what was he up to?

"My words," he continued, "are inadequate to convey the suffering of border folk in D'Ivary Province. Therefore, I have brought some witnesses to speak before you."

Sperren and Colin were clearly as surprised as she. When had Zachary arranged this? How? Why hadn't he informed them?

On the king's word, witnesses were ushered into the council chamber one at a time. Lynx came in and told of all he witnessed, swearing an oath it was true. Next, a captain of the Sacoridian militia spoke of finding mass graves filled with border folk. Two of his men dragged in a mercenary commander.

"It's true," the mercenary said. "Lord D'Ivary paid us to impersonate Sacoridian troops. Wanted to make it look bad for your king."

Even some of D'Ivary's own subjects came to speak. "Don't like squatters on my land," said a taciturn farmer, "but them squatters didn't deserve what they got."

Lord D'Ivary grew paler and paler as witness after witness filed in. The other lords questioned them as they wished.

Then border people themselves came in, telling all they had endured, of their flight from groundmite raids, of seeking refuge in D'Ivary Province where the former lady-governor would have provided them succor, only to find things had changed.

Several spoke of loved ones dead or missing, of women raped. One mother spoke of her twin daughters being borne away by mercenaries for their amusement. The girls were only eight.

Zachary's expression did not change. He merely gazed upon his lord-governors, watching them with interest. Lord Coutre's scowl crumbled. He was the father of three daughters, the youngest of whom was eight years old. He rose from his chair to comfort the weeping mother.

Laren, who had known about some of the atrocities, was rocked by these personal accounts, and now knew Zachary had been right not to bend to any of Coutre's demands just to gain his support. The case deserved to be heard on its own terms, and to speak to the hearts of each provincial lord sitting in the chamber.

Zachary had surprised her, and everyone else, once again. He was as formidable and brilliant as his grandmother, Queen Isen, had been, and Laren should have known better than to doubt him.

The testimony of the witnesses was not only damning, but emotionally draining, and when the last left the chamber, a heavy pall fell over them all.

Presently Zachary said, "I welcome your debate."

No one offered any. D'Ivary searched the faces of his peers for any sign of reprieve.

"Those—those people lied!"

"All of them?" Lord Adolind asked quietly. "The king's soldiers, the mercenary, your own subjects?"

"You betrayed your trust to the subjects of Sacoridia," Lady Bairdly said, "and to all of us."

D'Ivary's face drained of all color. "But I didn't do all those things! I—"

"You caused or allowed them to happen," young Lord Penburn said, disgust plain in his voice. "You allowed those things to happen, and *you participated*."

"A terrible misuse of power and trust," Lady Bairdly added.

D'Ivary's voice quavered. "B-but . . . I can fix things. I'll help them."

"Too late for that," Lord Adolind said.

He had welcomed the refugees into his lands, Laren knew, and well understood the hardships they faced on the borders. She had watched the disbelief on his face as he listened to the horrors the witnesses had fled from.

"Is there anyone here," Zachary asked, "who doubts Lord D'Ivary's guilt?"

Lord Oldbury seemed to struggle within himself, but did not voice dissent.

"Very well," Zachary said.

"Please," D'Ivary said, "please have mercy. I've a family."

"Having a family did not prevent what you did to the refugees," Lord Coutre said.

D'Ivary, his color ghastly, stared at the tabletop.

Zachary folded his hands before him. "Usually it is my decision as to how justice should be meted out. This time, however, I wish to defer that decision."

Upon his word, one of the border folk was brought in. Laren recognized him. Lynx had brought him in that day to report the atrocities in D'Ivary Province.

"This is Durgan Atkins," Zachary said. "He lost much due to Lord D'Ivary's actions. I have asked him to confer with his people and come up with an appropriate punishment."

D'Ivary suddenly lost control and sobbed. No one offered him their pity. No doubt he had thought his worst punishment would be some sort of comfortable confinement suited to his station, but instead he would face the enmity and revenge of the very people he had hurt.

Laren had to applaud Zachary. Certainly his lords would see the justice in the border folk deciding the punishment. By removing the burden from himself, Zachary did not have to make a decision the lord-governors could use against him at some later time.

"Your decision?" Zachary asked Atkins.

"We've talked long and hard. We'd like D'Ivary stripped of his lands, wealth, rank, and title. And we want him exiled."

D'Ivary loosed a sigh of relief. There would be no execution, and banishment wasn't always so bad.

"To where would you have him exiled?" Zachary asked.

Atkins turned and glared at D'Ivary. "To the northern border, with only the clothes on his back and a day's rations. We'll see to it he doesn't sneak back south."

"Done," Zachary said.

D'Ivary let out a heart-rending cry, but soldiers entered to haul him away. Laren wanted to wilt in relief that the whole affair was over. Zachary had done well. Better than well, in her estimation. The lord-governors looked relieved themselves.

No major plays for power, she thought. But it didn't mean there wasn't more to come.

"Shall we continue with business?" Zachary asked.

The resurgence of magic was discussed at length, Zachary alluding now and then to a conversation he and Laren had had with Karigan about events that took place down at the wall. Laren recalled how they met with her only after Destarion had given his leave. Karigan, though weak and easily fatigued, insisted they meet someplace other than the mending wing, of which she was heartily weary. The king recommended his sunshine-filled study, and Karigan made her painstaking way through castle corridors, batting away poor Ben's assistance.

The account she gave them of conveying Mornhavon to the future naturally astonished them, and when she revealed she had no way of knowing how *far* he'd been taken, they set to planning immediately. Laren and Zachary did, anyway. Overcome by fatigue, Karigan had fallen asleep in her chair. When Laren rose to send for Ben, Zachary urged her to let the slumbering Rider be, and produced a throw to drape on Karigan's lap. They then resumed their strategizing session with Karigan's light snoring in the background.

In discussing with the lord-governors how the power of

Blackveil had been thwarted, Zachary skirted the issue of the Green Riders' use of magic. It would not do to release too much information about the special abilities of his Riders. Doing so would undermine his ability to seek information, and possibly endanger them. Few would trust them.

Instead of focusing on what had happened, he turned to preparations for the threat to come.

The meeting went on for some time, with no clear course of action in the offing. Zachary ended the meeting on a positive note, with the confirmation ceremony of young Hendry Penburn to the rank of lord-governor. The pomp and ritual seemed to quell any ill residue left over from the D'Ivary proceedings.

Finally, Zachary dismissed the lord-governors for a well-deserved feast. As they filed out, he asked Lord Coutre to hold back.

He said, "I thank you for judging D'Ivary on the merits of his case, and not basing your decision on whether or not I had agreed to some contract."

The scowl emerged on Coutre's face again. "Let us just say D'Ivary's guilt spoke for itself. The ingrate deserves what he got. And don't think I was doing *you* any favor."

"Of course not," Zachary said, his tone cool but respectful. "I am glad you are frank with me, my lord, for I shall always know where you stand."

"Are you so sure?"

"Indeed."

What was Zachary playing at now? Laren wondered in alarm. Angering Lord Coutre wasn't going to prove anything.

Zachary removed some rolled documents from beneath his mantle of state. "I have here a contract of marriage to which I am tentatively agreeing, with some amendments, of course."

Coutre was stunned, Laren was stunned, Sperren and

Colin were stunned, and even the Weapons standing guard were stunned.

Coutre stared from Zachary to the documents, and back again, as if he couldn't quite believe his eyes or ears. "You're agreeing?"

"Tentatively." Zachary tossed the documents onto the tabletop. "I require Lady Estora's consent in the matter."

"Oh, she'll consent all right. We're all—"

Zachary slapped the flat of his hand on the table and Coutre fell silent. "I know what you want, Lord Coutre, and I know that you think you know what Lady Estora wants. I'd like to find out for myself."

Coutre blinked. "She'll be willing. No doubt about it."

"We shall see." And to everyone in the room, Zachary said, "This matter is not to be spoken of beyond this moment, or beyond these walls, until the contract is finalized and sealed."

Coutre and his aide left exultant and triumphant. Laren thought the old lord might do cartwheels of joy down the corridor. The image brought a smile to her face.

Zachary, by contrast, brooded. He did not look a man ready to rejoice over his future betrothal.

"There are, I suspect," he said quietly, "dark and difficult times ahead. I must do what I can to strengthen my position, and lend my people a sense of stability, even if it does mean marrying."

ARTIFACTS

Karigan paused her sweeping to scratch at her wound. Ben said it was healing nicely, though it was still sore. She still couldn't recall how she received the wound, but like many things, she was probably better off not knowing. At least she was alive, unlike those who hadn't returned with them from the wall. And now even poor Mara had taken a turn for the worse.

She wiped tears away from her face and swept up a fury of swirling dust. She worked in a chamber that might never be occupied by any Rider. The size of the Rider wing mocked their losses and declining numbers. Soon, she had no doubt, the Green Riders would be extinct, a memory to some, forgotten by most.

In a sense, she had lost Alton, too, a loss she could not explain. Why had he looked upon her with hatred when they parted in Woodhaven? Why wouldn't he speak to her? She couldn't think of what she had done to so anger him that he turned his back on their friendship.

There was so much she could not remember—could she have done something hurtful to Alton during one of these blank moments?

She jabbed the broom at cobwebs in the chamber's corners. How could she make amends without knowing for what? She guessed she would never know, unless he chose to talk to her. She wanted to reach out to him and try to settle the matter, but it was difficult right now with them so far apart. While she was convalescing, she had written and rewritten a letter that would be delivered by the next Rider to head down to the wall. It was terrible to have lost friends in battle, and worse to lose one of her best friends for a reason that was a mystery to her.

For now, he had his own grief to work through. Grief over the loss of three Riders, his uncle, and his cousin.

"Not dead," Merdigen had said of Pendric. "He has given his soul wholly to the wall, and it lives on with all the other guardians. Only his body is gone. It's no longer of use to him."

It sure sounded like death to Karigan.

Ironically, to the Eletian who had come hunting her, she was dead. Merdigen explained, after she regained her senses, that she had had enough blood on her to easily create an illusion of death. It proved convincing enough to send the Eletian on his way.

It wouldn't take long for the Eletians to realize she was still alive, but now that the wild magic had fled her, and as long as she kept her distance from the wall, she supposed they would leave her alone.

She sighed and tossed the broom aside, then noticed Garth filling the doorway. He held a package in his arms.

"Hello," she said.

"You aren't overdoing it in here, are you?" His no-nonsense expression indicated she'd better not be, or else.

"What are you going to do to me if I say yes?"

"Hang you by your thumbs and tickle you with a feather."

Karigan snorted.

Garth glowered at her with mock-sternness. "I happen to know where to find some really fine feathers. Brutal they are."

"Oh?"

He smiled smugly. "Lady Morane's hat collection."

Lady Morane, the elderly matriarch of a minor noble clan from Oldbury, had taken a shine to Garth, and never failed to ply him with tea and sweet dainties when he delivered a message. Her hat collection was renowned, and it was surprising to find birds with any feathers left on them in that province.

"How do you know the quality of the lady's feathers for, um, tickling?"

Garth reddened and sputtered, catching on immediately to her innuendo and realizing the trap he'd set up for himself.

"Here!" he said, pushing the package into her arms. "This came in for you—Connly brought it from Selium."

She weighed the package in her hands with interest. It felt like a manuscript. "Connly's back?"

"Yep. All nice and tanned, too. Said his ship was blasted off course by some amazing gale, and they grounded on a deserted island. Quite beautiful, he said. Took a while for the crew to make repairs. He's reporting to the cap'n right now."

The relief that a Rider had made it home safely almost broke her down to tears again. Garth clapped her on the shoulder and headed out.

"Give Lady Morane my best," she called after him.

All she heard in return was unintelligible grumbling.

She took her package into her own room, turning up the flame on her lamp. There was a covering letter from Estral with it.

Dear Karigan,

I had hoped you would receive this sooner, but the minstrel I asked to convey it perished unexpectedly on the road. It was brought back to me by an honest traveler who found it.

This is a copy of the manuscript we discovered in the archives. As I mentioned to you in my last letter, I think you and your father should find it of great interest. It has immense historical value, providing insight into the Long War and the occupation of our lands by the Arcosian Empire. The chief archivist is

*beside himself with excitement, and he and my father consider it
authentic.*

> *Very fondly,*
> *Estral Andovian, in my own hand*

Karigan looked under the letter and read the manuscript's title page: *Journal of Hadriax el Fex*. It was the last
thing she expected to see. She just stared at the manuscript
on her lap, not daring to look beyond the title page. Why,
she wondered, should it be of such interest to her and her
father?

She was about to read on when someone tapped on her
door.

"Come," she called.

The door creaked open to reveal a Weapon standing
there. "Fastion? Is there something I can do for you?"

"Not precisely," he said with a small smile. "I thought
perhaps there was something you might like to see."

"Such as?"

"Rider things," he said.

"Rider things?" As much as Karigan hated to set the
manuscript aside, he had piqued her interest.

"Some artifacts I've long meant to show Captain Mapstone, but she always puts me off, and something else I had
forgotten about that pertains to you Riders."

Now thoroughly intrigued, she joined him at the doorway. "Lead on."

He took her through rambling abandoned corridors.
Each of them bore a lamp to help chase away the dark.

"While we were rooting out the Second Empire," Fastion said, "I came upon a certain room I had not visited in
some time."

As Karigan recalled, Fastion prided himself on knowing
all the abandoned corridors, and he led her with sure steps.
There was also an eagerness about him a Weapon would

rarely deign to exhibit. She supposed that beneath the black cloth and leather of their uniforms, that Weapons were human, too. She smiled to herself.

The room Fastion took her to was full of rotted and jumbled pieces of discarded furniture that cast jagged shadows against the walls.

"Old Rider furniture?" Karigan queried, disappointed if this is what he had brought her to see. She raised her lamp and found an impressive spiderweb strung between the legs of some oddment of furniture, inhabited by an even more impressive spider. She frowned in revulsion and side-stepped to put a little distance between herself and the fat arachnid.

To her question, Fastion scratched his head. "I don't know."

She swallowed back laughter at his perplexed expression, as if he thought he ought to know to whom the furniture belonged. At least the rotted tables, chairs, and whatnot weren't the artifacts he had brought her to see.

"Over here," he said.

Nestled against a wall was a chest. It was not ornate, but its brass hinges and clasp shone in the lamplight as if newly made. Karigan was surprised it wasn't in the same condition as the furniture. There weren't even chew marks or droppings on it from rodents. That didn't mean there wasn't a rat's nest inside, or some really gruesome spider . . .

Fastion clearly expected her to lift the lid, and not wanting to reveal her trepidation to the Weapon, she set aside her lamp and did so. To her vast relief, no rats jumped out at her, nor was there any sign of big spiders.

"Are you sure these are *artifacts?*" Karigan asked, gazing into the chest. It smelled of pine wood freshly planed, and its contents looked almost new.

"Look closely."

Karigan lowered herself to her knees. She removed two mugs from the chest. Simply fashioned, they bore the sigil of the gray eagle.

"King Jonaeus' clan crest," Fastion said. "He was our first high king."

"Yes," Karigan said absently. "I know."

Next she lifted out the pieces of a mold, such as a smith would use to make buckles and other small articles. This mold had been used to make brooches. Winged horse brooches. She explored its depressions and edges with her finger, knowing them intimately in relief, just as she knew the details of her own brooch. Her hands trembled, and Fastion helped her set it aside.

There were some everyday articles also in the chest, like eating utensils and a comb made of bone. There was a length of folded cloth. It was soft and slippery cloth, not unlike silk, but stronger and more vibrant. Her merchant's instincts wondered what kind of cloth it was, and where it had come from. It was more finely woven than anything she had ever seen, even among the textiles her father traded in.

She unfurled the cloth—a banner—and caught her breath. A golden horse shimmered to life on a field of green, its great wings sweeping up and down by some trick of light and fabric, as if to fly away. In the golden border were stitched runes. Though she could not read them, they looked Eletian in character.

"It's beautiful," she whispered.

"Yes," Fastion said. "I believe it to have been a gift from the Eletian people to the Green Riders, but a scholar would have to translate the runes."

"But . . ." She glanced at Fastion. "If it's so old, how could it survive in perfect condition for so long?"

Fastion shrugged. "You are a user of magic. Perhaps there is some spell upon the chest."

"I suppose." Reverently she folded the banner. The last article was an oblong coffer with the sigil of the winged horse upon it. "And this?" she asked.

"I've never been able to open it. It is a mystery to me."

Karigan explored it with her hands, and her heart hammered with the echo of hoofbeats in her mind. Something special resided within. She touched the winged horse on the lid, and the locking mechanism snicked open.

"Huh," Fastion said. "It never did that for me."

Karigan opened the lid and found within, cushioned by green velvet, a twisted horn, one she recognized immediately. She ran her fingers across carved runes and the figure of the mythical p'ehdrose, a half man, half moose, that was said to once roam the lands.

"This was *hers*," Karigan said.

Fastion, awed, seemed to know to whom she referred. "We always wondered what had become of it," he said. "We wondered why it wasn't down below."

The "we" he referred to was the Weapons, and "down below" the tombs where the remains of Lil Ambrioth rested.

On impulse, Karigan drew the horn to her lips and blew. It issued no sound except her frustrated wheezing.

"I guess it doesn't work after all this time," she said in disappointment.

Gentle laughter filled her ear. *It will work, Karigan lass, but only for the captain of the Green Riders, hey?*

Lil! Karigan searched the chamber with her eyes, but the First Rider did not appear, nor did she speak again.

Fastion, unaware of anything unusual, eyed the coffer with interest. "What else is in there?"

Karigan held the horn to her breast, and handed the coffer to him. He drew out a length of cloth that, like the banner, was amazingly well preserved. It was patterned with the blue and green plaid of Lil Ambrioth. It was one of her cross sashes.

Karigan, who had spoken with the spirit of the First Rider, and had met her through time, nevertheless felt the immensity of these finds, the awe they inspired.

"I need to show these to Captain Mapstone," Karigan said.

"Of course, but let's leave them here for a moment. I have one more thing to show you."

When Karigan hesitated, Fastion added, "They've been here for nearly a thousand years. I should think they will be fine for a few minutes more."

Reluctantly she closed the horn away in its coffer and carefully put the artifacts back in the chest.

Fastion led her through another series of corridors. Karigan had lost all sense of direction, though where they walked now felt somehow familiar.

"Do you recognize this area?" Fastion asked.

"I—I don't know."

"Mara and I found you in the next room there, on the right, the time when you were substantially, er, faded out."

Karigan strode ahead of him to investigate. When she peered into the room, she remembered the place, at least vaguely. Her brooch hummed, and there was a prickly sensation on the back of her neck. Yes, of course she remembered. She had been caught in the traveling. She had come forward in time. She had looked toward the door, toward light, and seen herself.

This moment! The realization startled Karigan. She raised her lamp, but its light could not illuminate that far dark corner.

She thought to enter the room, but Fastion halted beside her and peered over her shoulder.

"Reliving memories?" he inquired.

She remembered him asking the question—the memory had a dreamlike quality, only she had seen him from a different angle, heard his voice from across the chamber, and across time.

Fastion walked on. "This way, Rider."

Karigan licked her lips and glanced into the room again. "Hang on," she told whatever shadow form of herself might be in there. "You've come too far forward—you must go back."

The words came unbidden, and just as she remembered hearing them that day. Amply spooked, she rushed after Fastion.

He took her up a stairwell of narrow, steep steps, and stopped at a landing with a door partially ajar. It led to a chamber with a low ceiling.

"I warned Dakrias Brown we'd be up here," Fastion said.

Warned Dakrias Brown? What for?

Glittering shiny panels of colored glass rippled in their light, and as they moved about, Karigan realized there was an entire dome of stained glass in the center of the floor, and now she understood. Dakrias had told her of the dome of glass that had once allowed sunshine to filter into the records room, until a ceiling was built over it some long ago time.

They circled the entire dome, Karigan's mouth dropping at the scenes that unfolded before her eyes. Scenes she knew must be shared with the other Riders.

The next morning, Karigan caught Captain Mapstone before she reported to the king for another long day of council meetings. Fastion and the Weapon Willis carried the chest into the captain's quarters, and then quietly withdrew.

"What's this?" the captain asked.

As Fastion had done with her, she did with the captain: allowed her to explore the contents and find out for herself.

Wonder crossed the captain's face with each new item,

but when she opened the coffer bearing the First Rider's horn, she wept.

"Only the captain of the Green Riders may make it sound," Karigan said quietly.

The captain snuffled, and cradled it to herself like a new baby. "How do you know?"

Karigan didn't have to answer for the captain to figure it out.

"Oh." Then after a few moments, she asked, "Should I?"

"It hasn't been heard in a long time," Karigan said with a smile. "Someone has to end the silence."

The captain gave her a slanted smile, wiped her tears away with her sleeve, and blew on the horn of the First Rider. The notes rang sharp and shrill. They blasted out of the captain's quarters onto castle grounds, resounding against the highest battlements and turrets.

Even after the captain finished, the notes echoed on, and Karigan imagined them coursing through the countryside and beyond. She felt them stir within her, felt her Rider spirit wanting to respond.

The captain raised her eyebrows and looked at the horn anew. "It works."

Karigan couldn't help but laugh at the understatement. The captain grinned in return.

Within moments, Riders rushed to the captain's quarters.

"We heard," they said, "and we had to come."

Garth peered through the arrow slit window. "We were called," he added.

The captain stepped outside to share with them the finding of the horn. They all wanted to touch it, to hear it ring out again. The captain laughed and said, "I'm sure you'll hear it soon enough."

She encouraged them to return to their duties, and told them she'd have more to show them at a later time.

"This didn't seem like the right moment," she said, stepping back inside, "to show them everything in the chest."

"I think I have an idea about what to do," Karigan replied, and she explained it to the captain who agreed fully.

"Yes, it is time we remembered our fallen."

A knock came upon the captain's door. This time it wasn't a Rider, but the mender, Ben. Karigan's spirits plummeted, thinking he had come to deliver bad news about Mara. Karigan could tell from the captain's demeanor that she had had the very same thought.

Ben just stood there on the step, looking bewildered. "Hoof—hoofbeats," he said. He stuck a finger in his ear as if to unplug it. "I hear hoofbeats."

The captain's face miraculously brightened with delight. "Come in, Ben."

The mender stepped in, oblivious to his surroundings. The captain went to her shelves and pulled down a coffer that looked much like the one containing the First Rider's horn. She set it on her work table and opened it.

Within were what had to be well over a hundred gold brooches, fashioned into winged horses. Karigan, who had acquired hers from a dying Rider far from Sacor City, had never seen it before.

Ben stood over the open coffer, fingering through various brooches. He nearly dug to the very bottom until he chose one of which he seemed to approve.

It rested in his palm and he just gazed at it.

The captain took the brooch and pinned it to Ben's smock.

"Welcome, Rider," she said.

The words stirred some memory in Karigan, like a feather brushing against her mind.

Ben blinked as if just awakening. "What am I—?" He glanced at the brooch now affixed to his smock. "What?" Then he looked at Karigan and Captain Mapstone. "What?"

"You've answered the call, Rider," the captain said gently.

"What?" His voice cracked in disbelief. "I can't—I can't—" He swallowed hard. "I'm—" He put his palm to his temple as if checking for a fever. "I can't!" he sputtered. "I—I'm afraid of—"

Karigan and the captain leaned forward, waiting in suspense for him to finish his sentence.

"I'm—I'm afraid of horses!"

They exchanged incredulous glances.

"I've got to go," Ben said. "Mara!" And he darted out of officers quarters and across castle grounds.

"Is that," Karigan asked, "a normal reaction for a new Rider acquiring his brooch?"

"No," the captain said. "Usually the Rider sits with me and has a cup of tea while we discuss his or her new vocation." She shook herself then, as if to break out of some reverie. "I guess I had better go explain things to Destarion. He'll be none too happy about this." She paused on the threshold and smiled suddenly. "But I am!"

Journal of Hadriax el Fex

Alessandros has been vanquished, they say, and Blackveil will be forever closed off until it heals. It was my words, Captain Ambriodhe tells me, my offering of intelligence that helped turn the tide of war. My betrayal.

For that service, I am offered sanctuary and the freedom to go and do as I wish. There is little in these war-torn lands that entice me, and no matter the offerings of the king, I am still to be reviled as Hadriax el Fex of Arcosia, the Hand of Mornhavon the Black.

I believe I shall seek a quiet, peaceable life on one of the outer islands where few know me and the ravages of war are not so evident. Maybe I will turn my hand to fishing, an honest livelihood. Ironically, the island I am considering is called Black Island. It somehow seems fitting.

I pray the inhabitants will accept me as I am, a hardworking man with good hands. And perhaps with time, I shall vanish away from my enemies and history, to live an ordinary life, and to die quietly in obscurity. I shall rename myself "Galadheon." Have not the forces of the Empire already named me as such? *He who betrays. Betrayer.* And so shall I be known.

Alessandros may be vanquished, but "forever" is a very long time. And I wonder . . . could so great a power be so simply overcome? If Alessandros should arise again, I would weep for happiness for my old friend lives on, the indomitable spirit. Yet, the man who was my friend is long "dead." I should, rather, fear for my children, and their children's children, for Alessandros does not forget, and he will never forgive my betrayal.

I am, as witnessed by God, no longer Hadriax el Fex, but Hadriax Galadheon.

≈ A HERITAGE OF RIDERS ≈

Karigan leaned back into her pillow, laid the manuscript on her lap, and closed her eyes. The enormity of it . . . She had read the journal from beginning to end three times now, her horror mounting with each reading, as Hadriax gave his account of the atrocities of the empire. Atrocities he participated in.

And this murderer was the founder of the G'ladheon line? She still could not grasp it. It did not matter that he redeemed himself in the end. It *did* matter that he allowed the atrocities to go on for so long while he struggled with his conscience.

Who am I? she wondered. Wild magic might no longer taint her blood, but her very own heritage did. *And my name means "betrayer."* She shook her head, feeling sick.

You are who you are.

Karigan looked about with wide eyes. "Lil?" A greenish glow drifted up from her washbasin. She got up from her bed and walked over to gaze into the water. Lil Ambrioth looked back up at her.

You have seen yourself in the Mirror of the Moon, Lil continued. *Would someone who overcame her fears— tremendous fears—to dispel a terrible danger to her country and those she loves, be even a shadow of a betrayer? I think not. Galadheon is but a name, which Hadriax took in defiance of the empire and in acknowledgment of his own ac-*

tions. He lived on for many a year with the knowledge of his crimes always torturing his mind. It was, he said, his curse.

"But—" Karigan began.

I have forgiven Hadriax his deeds of the past, Lil said. *He gave up everything to help us, and saved more lives than he ever killed. A monster he had been, a man he became.*

"I cannot reconcile—"

You have not known war, hey? Your perspective would be different.

"I don't want to know war."

And I don't want you to. I committed my own share of bloody acts, and for those I was called a hero, just as he had been by his own people until the time of his betrayal. But it is now time for you to live in the present and not be a judge of the past.

Karigan was stunned. She didn't know what to say.

Lil blinked, her features blurred beneath the water. *Do know you have surpassed my expectations, and continue to do so.*

Karigan couldn't help but blush at the First Rider's praise.

Continue to help the Riders, Karigan lass, they need you, and you need them. Lil sighed, and the surface of the water rippled. *I must leave you now. A higher power calls on me to answer for my transgressions.*

"What? No!" But Lil faded away, leaving Karigan to stare at her own reflection in the wash basin. "I didn't even have a chance to say good-bye," she murmured. "Wherever you've gone, Lil, I pray you are well, and in the good hands of the gods."

Karigan wandered through the breezeway into the central courtyard gardens, preoccupied by the journal of her apparent ancestor, Hadriax el Fex, and the words of Lil Ambrioth. Lil's words eased her mind, but it was still a monumental revelation for her to work through, that her blood was of the Arcosian Empire, the scourge of evil that had almost destroyed Sacoridia so long ago.

She hopped across the stepping stones of the trout pond. By the calculations of the calendar, it was still summer, yet golden birch leaves, shaped like spearheads, floated on the pond's surface. In not so many months, the pond would freeze over and the garden would turn brown and barren till the first snowfall transformed it yet again.

Karigan marked the chill in the air and the lower angle of the sun, and wondered what the oncoming season held for her. She prayed it would be more peaceful than her summer, and that she had truly sent Mornhavon the Black far enough into the future so Sacoridia might have time to prepare for his eventual return.

She continued along the garden pathway, not really paying attention to where she was going, until she rounded a bend and saw Lady Estora seated upon a granite bench in a patch of sunshine, her golden hair radiant. A cream-colored cloak cascaded down her shoulders to drape in luxurious folds across the bench. Tall spikes of dark purple flowers with drooping blossoms, and yet taller flowers of mauve, surrounded her like a frame; and at her slippered feet, pale blue asters clustered. The scene was breathtaking, almost unreal.

At first Estora did not see her, and looked to be as deep in thought as Karigan had been, and perhaps a little pale. Concerned, Karigan strode over to her, and she looked up with a sudden smile.

"Karigan! Hello."

Karigan bowed. "Do you wish for privacy, or would you mind a little company?"

"Please sit." She shifted her cloak to make room for Karigan on the bench.

They exchanged quiet pleasantries, both a little distracted. Karigan was not ready to speak of her heritage or Alton just yet, nor of her recent adventures. Not even to Estora.

And Estora, who was often keenly interested in the doings of Green Riders, did not ask for the latest news. They fell into a companionable silence, each wandering in their individual thoughts as leaves rustled on trees and ravens circled the castle heights. The roses of the garden were long past, and only their fruits littered the ground. The breeze that riffled Karigan's hair held an air of change about it.

A movement of shadow beside a shapely cedar startled Karigan, and she discerned a Weapon there, standing in a watchful posture. It meant the king must be nearby, and eagerly she searched the garden with her gaze, only to be disappointed.

"I wonder what—" she began.

Estora, who had also started to speak at the same time, said, "I've had—"

They glanced at one another and laughed.

When the laughter subsided, Estora indicated that Karigan should speak first. Karigan nodded toward the Weapon and said, "I was just wondering what he was guarding. I don't see the king nearby."

Estora's buoyancy faltered. "He is not assigned to the king."

"A tomb guard then? What would he be doing *here?*"

Estora turned in her seat to face Karigan directly. "He is not a tomb guard. He has been assigned to—to watch me." Her words flowed now in a freshet. "The king has agreed to my father's contract of marriage. I'm to be King Zachary's queen."

Karigan could only stare at her. Her world narrowed to just the two of them and the patch of garden they sat in. Everything else vanished, failed to exist.

Already burdened by other revelations, Karigan had to

turn Estora's words over in her mind until she comprehended their meaning. When she did so, everything she thought she understood about herself in relationship to the king tilted off balance like a foundering ship in a gale, and she had to grab hold of the edge of the bench lest she slide off.

Estora was to be King Zachary's queen.

A cargo hold of dreams and possibilities tore loose of their anchorings and rammed into her, and she found herself incredulous—not so much over Estora's announcement, though it in itself was stunning—but by the dawning realization that her feelings for King Zachary had sometime, somehow, surpassed mere admiration and attraction.

I . . . Am I in love with him? She had hidden it from even herself, made it a secret, a secret she had not wished to admit, for she knew it was an impossible situation to love one like him, one who was a king and so far out of reach for a mere commoner. How could she not have seen it?

And how could she not have seen how it made perfect sense that Estora would become Zachary's wife? It was like a piece of a puzzle fitting neatly into its space. Lord Coutre wanted to marry off his daughter as advantageously as possible. At the same time, the nobles were exerting pressure on King Zachary to marry and provide the realm with a heir. Politically? It was the perfect situation, the proper fit. Only Karigan's heart did not work in such political or logical ways.

Somewhere in that secret place in the back of her mind, she had hoped, despite it all, there would be a way that her commoner status could be overlooked, that the breach of rank wouldn't divide her and King Zachary after all. She almost laughed at herself, a cruel laugh, at how childish it all now seemed. How did she even know the king was interested in her in that way?

"King Zachary is a good man," Estora said. "He is a good

man, but it shall not be a marriage made of love." She shook her head and looked down, the liquid gold that was her hair flowing down her shoulders. "I've loved only F'ryan, and having known love . . . it is hard. This marriage, it is to fulfill a contract only."

Not a marriage made of love . . .

Unreasonably, hope surged anew in Karigan's breast, that there might still be a chance for her. She fought with it, wrestled it down. Emotions of every kind pummeled her and she felt as if she might drown in stormy seas.

The lilting call of a chickadee, absurdly cheerful under the circumstances, brought Karigan back to herself in time to hear what Estora had to say next.

"I envy you."

Karigan almost laughed out loud. What was there to envy? Her evil heritage? The battles and deaths of companions? Wounds that scarred her flesh and mind? Who was Estora to speak of envy? She led the life of a lady with servants to see to her every comfort. Her life was genteel, and lacked hard labor and danger, while Karigan's meant blood, sweat, and calluses.

And Lady Estora was going to marry King Zachary.

"I envy you," Estora continued, "because you are free— free to choose what you will do with your life; free to marry whom you will. But I must live a narrow life only to further the honor of my clan. I must obey the will of my father. It's what I was born to do."

Free? Karigan wanted to scream at Estora, tell her how she'd been forced into the life of a Green Rider, that because she was bound by magic, she wasn't free at all.

"How can you . . ." Karigan began, but her throat was so constricted it came out as a croak. "How can you have known F'ryan and say that to a Green Rider?"

But Estora's sad eyes pleaded for understanding. She had once loved a Green Rider, an affair forbidden because she was a noblewoman and he was a commoner. Had they been discovered, Estora would have been cast out by her clan and forced to fend for herself in the wide world, something her upbringing had not equipped her to do.

Yet in the end, there had been a far greater sacrifice, the death of F'ryan Coblebay, her one great love taken from her by two black arrows in his back. Because of Karigan's connection to F'ryan it seemed Estora tried to reach him through her, seeking comfort, and maybe forgiveness.

Estora gazed off into the distance, a tear in the corner of her eye. "He was more free of spirit than anyone I knew. He embraced the bonds placed on him, then broke them."

Karigan did not hear this last, because she was struck all at once at how eerily opposite, yet alike, their situations were. Estora was constrained by her status as a noble, destined—in servitude to her clan and country—to a noble marriage she did not desire. Karigan served her clan and country as well, but was bound to do so as a messenger, and a commoner.

Estora's love of F'ryan, a commoner, was forbidden, and any aspirations Karigan might hold for one who was of the lineage of the high kings of Sacoridia, was likewise forbidden.

They were both trapped, neither free.

Karigan could not scream at Estora, nor could she find words of comfort. She stammered an excuse and hurried away, the gardens blurring in her vision. None of it mattered. She had known all along King Zachary could not be for the likes of her.

I am so stupid.

And in her disappointment, more disappointment than she could have ever imagined, she grew angry and turned it inside.

* * *

Emotions stormed within her as she strode down castle corridors, but she allowed none to surface. Lil Ambrioth had shared her love with King Jonaeus, but he had not been royalty when he started out in life, just a brave clansman whose decisions in war earned him the trust of people, enough so that they made him their first high king and united behind his banner. And had Lil truly shared a life as his partner, or did she die prematurely?

Karigan let go a rattling sigh as she turned a corner toward the Rider wing. This was all for the best, wasn't it? Not just the political reasons, but for Karigan herself. It cut short any girlish notions she might entertain. This was the real world, and now she'd just have to throw herself into her work and drive King Zachary out of her mind.

Only, it wasn't going to be that easy.

She threw open the door to her chamber, halting just inside. She stood there, unsure of what to do. She wanted to be alone, to work this all out in private, but she'd go mad in the tiny room. She needed to *do* something, to work it out actively.

"Riding," she said. She'd go riding into the countryside where she could be both alone, and be doing something physical. It would make Condor happy, too.

"At least *someone* should be happy," she murmured.

She was about to leave when she spotted something different in her room, the sun slanting through the narrow window and shining on objects on her washstand. Cradled in an open coffer in deep, luxurious purple velvet, lay a silver comb, brush, and mirror.

She crossed the room and carefully took the mirror into her hands. Reflected light glared into her eyes until she tilted it away from the sunshine. It was a dainty thing, light to hold. A hummingbird poised at a flower ornamented the mirror's back, and so did her initials, just as her mother's mirror had been engraved.

She traced the hummingbird with trembling fingers, feeling as she had not in a very long time, like a young woman who had no need of swords or uniforms, or any special duty. Just free to be herself, to be as she should have been, without worldly cares. And she felt . . . she felt feminine. How long had it been since she had worn a dress, or even jewelry?

She couldn't take her eyes off the mirror and its fine workmanship, wondering where it had come from, and who would have known of the loss of her mother's mirror. She searched for the maker's mark and found it easily enough. Her cheeks flamed. The mirror nearly slipped from her fingers.

The royal silversmith.

Stamped above the maker's mark was a Hillander terrier.

She found him on the castle roof. The dome of his observatory had been opened like a clam shell, one half of which moved on hinges and ran on some mechanism of tiny wheels and tracks.

King Zachary straightened from the eyepiece of his telescope at her approach, his features registering surprise. Her step faltered upon seeing him.

"Karigan? How did you know where to find me?"

"Fastion."

"Of course." He stepped around the telescope toward her, his gaze roving to the coffer tucked beneath her arm, his eyes full of questions.

She wondered if she had made a colossal mistake by coming to confront him in person, for her resolve melted beneath his gaze. She knew that the extraordinary gift he had given her was not a simple one, but an expression of . . . his feelings. To what depth those feelings went, she was unsure. A part of her wanted to know, another part did not.

The gift, in fact, had proved more upsetting than even

Estora's announcement earlier in the day. If this was indeed a true expression of his feelings, what was she supposed to do about it? How was she supposed to respond? Even after a hard ride in the country, she had found no answers, only a swirl of emotions that grew more and more intense till it hardened into anger. How dare he, she had wondered, bestow upon her such an intimate gift even as he planned his betrothal to Lady Estora?

"They're exquisite, but I cannot accept this gift."

"I wanted you to have them," he said, his disappointment obvious.

"They're too great a gift."

"I heard your own very special set had been destroyed in the fire."

Karigan wondered from whom he had heard about it. Several Riders had lost special things, and yet the king singled her out, only reinforcing what she thought the gift meant.

"There is someone else more fitting to receive these." She held out the coffer, and he gazed at it for some moments before reluctantly reaching for it.

"It's a queen's gift," Karigan said. "Not a gift fit for a common messenger."

"Karigan G'ladheon, I gave this gift to *you*." His voice was firm. "And you are anything but common. You are special to me."

She trembled.

"Please take it," he said, offering the coffer back.

She backed away. "What is it you expect of me?"

He stepped closer and took her hand into his.

She wanted to run. She wanted to feel his touch . . . He was so close that the heat of him scorched her. She *needed* to run. To run was to find safety. She jerked her hand from his, and he drew his eyebrows together, surprised and hurt.

Good, she thought.

He stood there for some moments, the stars glittering in a backdrop of midnight blue behind him and a wisp of moonlight stroking his cheek. Across the roof, guards made their rounds carrying lanterns that glowed like large fireflies, bobbing, hovering, swinging along. While Karigan was aware of them in the background, it was almost as if she and the king were alone in the vast pool of night, if not the whole of the world.

She knew she should run, leave the roof. What she waited for, she did not know.

"Do you remember," King Zachary began, "a certain game of Intrigue we once played a couple years ago? You played terribly, and after I won, I told you so. I criticized your strategy, and you in turn told me a few things as well. You stood up to me and told me, among other things, that I should leave behind my stone walls and go among those I rule." A smile ghosted across his lips at the memory. "Excellent advice."

His words threw Karigan. Why was he bringing this up now? She swayed where she stood, confused.

"I think it was then," he continued, "that I was irretrievably caught. Caught off guard, caught by you. Here you were, this beautiful, clever, and courageous young woman, who had just ridden across the country through so much danger to deliver a message, and who had the utter temerity to instruct her monarch on how to rule his country." He laughed softly. "Yes, you, with your passion and fire, took my heart captive then, and I soon realized that I loved you, and have all this time. How could I not?"

Karigan could not breathe. Why? Why hadn't he ever told her? Why hadn't he acted on his feelings before? Why had he waited till *now?* Now when he was going to marry Estora. Now when there was no chance for them . . .

There never was a chance, she bitterly reminded herself. For all the political reasons, and she ticked them off in her mind. His pursuit of a commoner would diminish the esteem and support the mercurial lord-governors extended to him, and threaten his hold on power. The lord-governors might instead lend their favor to some other nobleman more to their liking and pliant to their collective will. Or worse, an ambitious nobleman, sensing the crown's weakness, might take advantage of the situation and force his ascension to power. Sacoridia could find itself at the mercy of a tyrant the likes of Hedric D'Ivary or Prince Amilton, instead of the benevolent ruler it now enjoyed. In the worst scenario, a struggle for power could embroil the country in all-encompassing strife and civil war, like that of two hundred years ago. None of these scenarios must be allowed to play out. They must not distract from the future threat that Blackveil Forest posed.

So much more was at stake than the hopes and desires of one insignificant Green Rider.

Maybe he decided to tell her of his feelings for her now because he had something else entirely in mind, and the revelation rekindled the anger in the pit of her stomach.

"Did you know," she said, her voice laced with that anger, "that my mother's mirror and brush set were a wedding gift from my father? Not just some pretty baubles he passed along because he fancied her."

"Karigan, I—"

"It was before he made his fortune. My aunts tell me he worked unbelievably hard at demeaning jobs, like gutting fish down on the wharves, just to afford such a gift. He did this because he adored my mother; loved her absolutely. And they both made sacrifices to be together, forsaking their homes and families.

"And now you want me to accept this gift, you who are to marry Lady Estora? What am I to make of it? Certainly there cannot be the bond my father shared with my mother. What then? To be your—your paramour? To slip into your bedchamber when your wife is away?" A blush raged across her cheeks.

"No! I did not mean for that, though—" and perhaps thinking better of it, he did not complete the sentence. "I meant this gift as an honest expression of how I felt about you. I would never purposely hurt you in any way. This gift . . ." he glanced down at the coffer. "It's a token of my feelings. Nothing more, no expectations."

Karigan warred within herself. She wanted to scream, throw herself over the edge of the roof. Why was he doing this to her? *No expectations,* he had said, but there had been that undercurrent in his words . . . Desire gnawed at her, tempted her, but she smothered it knowing that giving in would only worsen matters and prove more painful in the end. While others might not think twice about it, she respected herself too much to get caught up in such entanglements. No, she would not . . . give in. And while it was within his authority as king to command anything of her, he did not, and he being the sort of man he was, she didn't think he would. It made the loss of him all the more crushing.

"Do you know," the king said, staring up toward the endless sky, "there is no better way to gain perspective on one's life than by gazing upon the heavens. My days are filled with the needs of the country, the petty feuds, the politics. But when I come up here, I ponder great questions about the gods, the world, and the dark side of the moon. And when my eyes return to Earth, my daily problems seem minor in comparison.

"I am the king of Sacoridia, yet so much is beyond my grasp—I'm powerless in so many ways to affect things, just as I cannot touch the workings of the heavens. And yet, I am ever hopeful."

"What is it," Karigan said, her voice quavering, "that you hope for?"

"I hope there is a place for faith and dreams." He paused for a moment, gazing intently at her. "And I need you to know how I feel about you, Karigan, no matter what may come. If you will not accept the gift as it is, a queen's gift given by a king, then I shall respect your wishes. Do know that it will always be here waiting for you."

She turned and ran, never seeing the sorrow in his eyes.

It was with an odd combination of happiness and grief that on the last evening of the summer, Karigan watched her fellow Riders file into the records room. There was curiosity on their faces, and some were making nervous jokes, but she detected they sensed something larger afoot.

Ben, still preferring his mender's smock over Rider green, wore a perpetual expression of bewilderment these days. His special ability had manifested almost immediately—it was an ability that augmented the mending skills he already possessed. He could pour his own energies into a patient to help them heal.

The first patient to benefit from his gift was Mara. He had pulled her back from death and given her the strength she needed to fight the festering of her burns and the lung illness. She would forever bear terrible scars, but she would be well.

Ben told Karigan that Mara was already making the captain pay up on some bet they'd made about her and Drent. Karigan planned to get to the bottom of it as soon as she could.

In the meantime, the captain continued to negotiate with Destarion over just how Ben would serve as a Rider, while continuing with his mending duties. The poor fellow, Karigan thought, was going to be busy, but at least it might save him from dealing with horses for a little longer.

Dakrias Brown buzzed around the chamber in excitement. It wasn't often so many came to his domain. He was a decidedly happy host, greeting each Rider as she or he entered. In the absence of Weldon Spurlock, King Zachary had promoted Dakrias to chief administrator. Surprisingly, he chose to continue working out of the records room. When Karigan had entered, he told her conspiratorially, "They've become very friendly."

"Who?" Karigan asked.

"You know who."

"I do?"

"*Them.*" Dakrias gestured vaguely around the room, and lowered his voice to a whisper. "The ghosts, of course."

"Oh. Of . . . course."

"They've been very helpful with the filing, you know."

Well, Karigan had to admit, she had known a ghost or two to be rather helpful herself.

Then Dakrias drew closer. "Actually," he confided, "I think they were trying to be helpful all along."

Karigan raised an eyebrow, remembering the chaos the ghosts had left the records room in, and poor Dakrias' frayed nerves. How did he figure they were being helpful?

As if hearing her thought, he continued, "I think they wanted my attention. I think they were trying to tell me something was terribly wrong in these old corridors."

"Second Empire," Karigan murmured, remembering how the ghosts had come to her aid when Uxton tried to abduct her.

Dakrias nodded vigorously. "Spurlock and his cronies met in the old section. Good thing our ghosts are anti-empire."

Truly, Karigan thought, bemused.

Dakrias left her to greet other Riders trickling into the chamber. There was almost a full complement of Riders in attendance, which wasn't saying much considering their diminished numbers. Dale was still recovering from her wounds in Woodhaven, and Alton had so far chosen not to return. Destarion would not permit Mara to leave her chamber. And there were others who should have been standing among them this night, but they were forever gone.

"Let us make a circle," the captain said.

The idea might have been Karigan's, but it was the captain's place to carry it out. The Riders needed to look to their captain for solace and guidance, purpose and courage.

Karigan had enlisted aid from her friends among the Weapons. They carried in the chest of Rider artifacts with due respect. Item by item, the captain revealed pieces of Rider history.

Meanwhile, the Weapon Donal lit a lamp in a darkened space that illuminated the silky banner of the Green Riders. There was a collective intake of breath as the Riders took in its beauty and the shining gold winged horse moving as with life.

When the cross sash of Lil Ambrioth was revealed, the Weapon Allis passed out bits of plaid much like the original to each of the Riders. Karigan's father had hurriedly acquired the cloth and shipped it to her. How he managed such a feat in so short a time, she had yet to find out.

"In memory of the First Rider," the captain said, "you may pin these beneath your brooches so they make a fitting backdrop. From now on Lil Ambrioth's plaid will be incorporated into your uniforms."

That part was a surprise to even Karigan. She *did* suspect there had been some correspondence going on between the captain and her father, and this is what it must have been about.

By the time the captain revealed Lil's horn again, there were few dry eyes in the records room.

"There is much that has been forgotten over the years by and about Green Riders," the captain explained. "It is time to remember. Time to remember our history and the heroic

acts of the past. Time to remember our fallen. Would everyone please hold hands?"

The Riders did so, some looking at one another with
questions in their eyes. Yates stood on Karigan's right, and
Tegan stood on her left.

"Karigan learned of an old tradition practiced by Lil
Ambrioth and her Riders," the captain said. "A way to re-
member lost comrades." She then explained what to do.
"And so I shall begin by remembering Ereal M'Farthon,
Rider-lieutenant."

"Ereal," the group chorused.

Constance was next. "I remember Tierney Caldwell."

"Tierney."

"I also remember Ereal M'Farthon," said Ty, with head
bowed.

"Ereal."

He must, Karigan thought, remember her every time he
mounted Crane.

"Joy Overway," Connly said. "I remember Joy."

"Joy."

As the Riders named the fallen, Karigan kept an eye
toward the ceiling. Slowly, almost imperceptibly, the Weapons dimmed the lamps in the records room. They were perfect for this duty, for they could be like shadows that
vanished into the background.

Beyond the halo of dimming light, Karigan also perceived the others, the ghosts, watching and listening. She
wondered if there were a few Rider ghosts among them
looking upon the scene with pride.

Yates sniffled beside her. "Justin." It was all he could
choke out.

"Justin."

"I remember Bard Martin," Karigan said.

"Bard."

The Riders continued with more names—Ephram, F'ryan, and even Lil.

A light blinked to life above the ceiling, and another, and another. As Weapons worked in the chamber above to light lamps, images captured in glass emerged in a riot of color, unblemished, unfaded, and unfractured by time.

It took a few moments for the Riders to even notice, but when they did, they craned their necks and whispered in wonderment as the tableau unfolded, revealing their long darkened heritage.

Lil Ambrioth, her horn at her hip, stood tall in the stirrups of her fiery steed, her arm outstretched behind her toward Riders who rode prancing and rearing horses. One Rider unfurled the standard of the winged horse, and another the black and silver of Sacoridia. Many of the Riders flourished weapons in the face of a cowering foe.

The enemy retreated, threw itself down before Lil for mercy, or lay dead on the field of battle. They were rendered in black, gray, and crimson.

The backdrop was the deep evergreen forest representing burgeoning life, and blue-purple mountains, a symbol of strength. A storm receded over the mountains representing the retreat of the enemy and war.

The lamps revealed another scene worked into the domed glass, that of Lil draped in a cloak of green and kneeling before a moon priest. He held his hands up in benediction, while King Jonaeus looked on, his crown a bright glowing gold.

In yet another scene, the Eletian king, Santanara, handed Lil the winged horse banner, while both Riders and Eletians stood in attendance.

In the center of the dome, in a sky of midnight blue and silvery constellations, the god Aeryc, with crescent moon balanced on his palm, looked upon the Riders with beneficence and approval.